PRAISE FOR **ADVENTURES OF V**

I0681840

With a few brush strokes, Reid creates a whole world. It's like magic –
the reader is sucked into that world, instantaneously. V swirls us into an
extravaganza, a detailed, delightful, dystopic, alien, familiar future – primal,
ferocious, and gratifying.
– Susan S. Senstad, author of *Milk and Venom* and *Music for the Third Ear*

Vivacious, vampish, victorious, voluptuous, vibrant, villainous … An
eternal 19-year-old, gorgeous vampire, monster-vixen named "V" – a pagan
Goddess, reborn as a super-heroine beauty who lives off the blood of the
bad, to rescue the souls of the good. Irresistible hijinks!
– Ed Cowen, producer, impresario

A wild ride into adventure, fantasy, and chills, V gifted me with glimpses of
arcane current and historical knowledge. Not for years have novels been as
much fun and enlightening.
– Chuck Shamata, actor

Utterly engrossing, rich, dark, and deep, Gilbert Reid creates worlds within
worlds of vivid, bold adventure.
– Bernice Landry, artist

Gilbert Reid's prose is so sensuous and evocative! When he takes you down
unfamiliar paths, and into situations that excite suspension of disbelief, you
follow him because the energy of V's personality is so witty and alluring, she
charms you into the universe the author has created. Vivid, complex, wildly
imaginative.
– Diana Leblanc, actor, director

PRAISE FOR OTHER BOOKS BY GILBERT REID

PRAISE FOR OTHER BOOKS BY GILBERT REID

PRAISE FOR *LAVA AND OTHER STORIES*

Very powerful, poetic and nasty and tough.
– Anna Porter, publisher, writer

The writing is terrific. The characters are glamorous, decayed, old, young, loved, unloved. Reid inhabits each one. His raw, elegant prose, his vivid and sensuous images leave one breathless, with recognition and terror.
– Diana Leblanc, actor, director

The women, how they speak, what they confide, and omit, what they expose about each other! It's as if only sexuality happened that summer.
– Susan S. Senstad, author of *Milk and Venom* and *Music for the Third Ear*

PRAISE FOR SO *THIS IS LOVE: LOLLIPOP AND OTHER STORIES*

Reid's stories are in the great traditions of Alice Munro or Mavis Gallant.
– Margaret Macmillan, historian, writer

Powerfully rendered and suspenseful.
– Joyce Carol Oates, critic, writer

An unerring and compelling examination of aggression and compassion.
– *The Vancouver Sun*

One of the 100 best books of the year.
– *The Globe & Mail*

EXTINCTION

BOOK 3

ELYSIUM

ADVENTURES OF V: VOLUME 7
"The Goddess is back. Her hour has come."
– Jules Cashford

EXTINCTION

BOOK 3
ELYSIUM

by
GILBERT REID

TWIN RIVERS
PRODUCTIONS

Issued in print and electronic formats
ISBN 978-1-7771580-9-5: *Extinction Book 3, Elysium:* Paperback
ISBN 978-1-7771580-8-8: *Extinction Book 3, Elysium:* EPUB
ISBN 978-1-9994790-2-2: *Extinction Book 3, Elysium:* Kindle
ISBN 978-1-7773141-6-3: *Extinction Book 3, Elysium:* Amazon paperback

Cover and text design by Counterpunch Inc. / Linda Gustafson
Illustrations by Nick Vitacco

Published by
Twin Rivers Productions
20 Bloor Street East
PO Box 75070
Toronto, Ontario, M4W 3T3

To receive a free book or novella, sign up at:
https://gilbertreid.com

To Professor Northrop Frye,
teacher, critic, visionary, master of mythologies, & friend

Stop acting so small. You are the universe in ecstatic motion.
   – RUMI

Thy Wrath has come – to destroy those who destroy the earth.
   – REVELATION 11:18

CONTENTS

CAST OF CHARACTERS

*An asterisk denotes a real historical person or mythical figure.

Alison Jonas – 28-year-old Volpe Network Morning Show host
Angela Balzac – beautiful black Burbite
Annette Rosenthal – rich widow, scheduled for termination
Asherah* – Semitic goddess, mother of gods, consort of gods
Astarte* – great goddess of the Middle East
Baal* – Semitic, Phoenician god
Billie Jo McAdams – Ex-lover of The Boy, informer for V and Claire
Black Tarzan – ex-entrepreneur morphed into Sex Performer
Bob – robot chef working in the Chocolate Éclair Factory
Boy – The Boy, aka Foul Fiend, aka Father Wolf, aka The Force of Evil
Caliban – prince of the mutants
Carole Sub – esthetician at the Cosmos Divinity Spa
Cassandra – prisoner in Camp Terminus, transformed into a leper
Claire V Jacobs – HZ – Hybrid Prisoner, Queen of Cyber Space
Claudia – little girl from an ancient, future, or alternative universe
Clown – ex-lawyer, morphed into Sex Zone Performer
Colonel Konrad – Cosmos, fanatic opponent of hybrids and SINs
Crystal – alien device left in North Africa by V's father, Marcus
Cylons – robots that revolt against humanity in *Battlestar Galactica*
Demi Pfeiffer – Cosmos First-Class, CEO of an Elysium Company
Edgar – a seal, swimming in an underground canal
Ed Malone – CEO of Bio-Futures, maker of bio-weapons
Emerson C Caldwell III – millionaire, obsessed with Claire V Jacobs
Fanny Dakin – a Sub, friend of Kit Candy
Geisha – Ex-professor, morphed into Sex Zone Performer

Gloria – 8-year-old prisoner, born in Camp Terminus
Grant Philip the Third – Sub vid addict, ex-macho forcibly feminized
Great High Priest – Chief Priest and ruler of the Mutant Kingdom
Guy Tulip – Sex Zone sex acrobat
Harvey Terazonoh – dead husband of Anette Rosenthal
Honey Rose – Ed Malone's live-in lover
Jacob F. Shavtick – coup organizer against the President-Leader
Jake – 13-year-old prisoner in Camp Terminus, friend of Gloria
Janice Forte – 18-year-old guinea pig at Bio-Futures
Jason Tremblay – researcher at Bio-Futures
Jill Hakim – spoiled upper-class bubble-head Cosmos
Jim Williams – Presidential Guard Cosmos Centurion
Julia Lilly – spoiled upper-class bubble-head Cosmos
Kat Jackson – Lieutenant in the elite Cosmos Centurion
Ken Ivison – 48-year-old Volpe Net Morning Show host
Kiddo – Aka Little Kiddo, a dead kid, resurrected in the Burbs
Kit Kandy – Sub, works as a house cleaner for Nikki Hughes
Larry Propp – lower depths nano recycling engineer
Laura Levitt – dead ten years, resurrected in the Burbs
Lieutenant Martine Arnault – Cosmos French logistics officer
Lieutenant Sylvia Negro – Cosmos Centurion
Linda Webster – Presidential Guard Cosmos Centurion
Lyse Saint-Ross – Cosmos First class, slumming in the Sex Zone
Mabel Brown – V's identity in a dream, an ancient mad crone
Maria Sub – esthetician at the Cosmos Divinity Spa
Mind-Child – Virtual and Physical Avatar of the World Mind
Mind Soup – Aka Mind-Sea, Aka Mind-Ocean, the World Mind
Miranda Hughes – elite Cosmos teenager, 13 going on 14
Mr. Schwartz – nano recycling engineer, Larry Propp's mentor
Mr. Angelopoulos – customer in the Lux Sauna and Spa
Natasha Sub – chief esthetician at the Cosmos Divinity Spa
Nikki Hughes – Elite Cosmos actress and graphic designer
Norman C Schleifer – 34, Burbite Eco & Animal Rights terrorist
Quillix – apprentice ethnologist from the Andromeda galaxy
Pat Key-Hong – Presidential Guard Cosmos Centurion
President-Leader – the president of Imperial Cosmos America
Professor James Park – expert on weather patterns and the Dome

Randy Shield – judge, torturer, identity-eraser

Rankin – police chief, Clown's client, and identity-eraser

Robot – agent of Quick Justice Halibut Corp Inc.

Robyn – child-like mechanical wizard, Claire's friend, and sidekick

Ruckus Mudcock XXXIV – Chairman of the Volpe Network Board

Russian Tsar Vladimir Putin XXIV – Ruler of Russia

Sequin Sprinkle – Ed Malone's SoHo performance-art mistress

Serena Burke – Presidential Guard Cosmos Centurion

Sniggy Propane – Kit Candy's former boyfriend

Suzy Tilley Lemon – A Sub, neighbor of Kit Candy and Fanny Dakin

Takahiko Harris MacDonald – aka Banzai Man, Sub vid-game addict

Teddy – eager border collie snatched from the 1940s

Tentacles – bio-extensions of the world mind, they eat everything

Trevor Robertson – A four-year-old who shot Laura Levitt dead

Wood – A Presidential Guard Cosmos Centurion

Zelinsky – A Presidential Guard Cosmos Centurion

PART ONE – DAWN

CHAPTER 1 – ELYSIUM

Death, yes, death!

Death is the name of the game.

WHAM!

Goddamn it!

WHAM!

Crouched in an open-topped, 1940, mottled, khaki and matt-green, captured Afrika Korps Mercedes armored car, Kit Candy slams the steering wheel left, then right. She ducks and weaves. She pulls the trigger. The antique MG-42 machine gun – nickname "Hitler's Zipper" – lets go with a merciless wave of fire, zap, zap, zap!

Damn! The archaic 20th Century ghoul, in his vintage Nazi uniform, sporting a neat Swastika, got in the first shots. Five red-hot bullets whiz by Kit's right earlobe.

Kit pulls the trigger. Tracer bullets flash out from the MG-42, sizzling yellow arcs, messengers of death, 1,000 rounds a minute, zipping through the murky, dust-filled air.

Wow! She scores! A direct hit! The monster ghoul with the bulging eyes and the silly Hitler mustache explodes, splashing a giant smear of purple glow-goo, his bio-blood, over a cliff of stippled rosy granite.

Whew! Kit wipes her forehead.

The battle is not over! More bullets zip by, sizzling her eardrums. Kit slams the steering wheel sideways, swivels the armored car into a dizzying turn, twirling, spinning, 180 degrees, raising dust. It's so fast she risks chewing up the vehicle's caterpillar tracks. They claw desperately at the tumbling pebbles of the Libyan Desert.

The sun is low.

Kit blinks through the crosshairs. She pulls the trigger. The Italian stone and stucco colonial farmhouse explodes. So much for those bloody sniper assassins! She has it in for those squirrel-like mutants, with their antique sub-machine guns. They are treacherous and skillful – but she has just vaporized the whole lot of them! Whoopee! I'm the girl! I *am* the girl!

Wham! Wham! Wham!

Bullets slam into the sunbaked leather seat, just beside her right cheek-bone, splat, splat, and – splat! The impact rips the fabric, ruffles her hair. She stares. What the …? Where the hell did that come from?

Peering through anti-dust goggles, she scans the terrain – only sand dunes, a ridge of pebbles, scrub, and stucco ruins.

Ah, yes!

There they are! Damn them!

Decision time! She slams down the pedal, guns the car, swerving, zigzag-ging, and – full charge ahead – the best defense is offense.

She races toward a small, dark tuft of underbrush, sage and cactus, all glowing scarlet in the setting sun. That's where they are, the devilish bastard Nazi rabbit-mutants! She will run them down! She will crush them! They won't get away this time! And, yes, there they are, sprinting for dear life, bounce, bounce, bounce! She swings the M-42 toward the running silhou-ettes … and she presses the trigger and … and …

WHAM!

Goddamn it!

WHAM!

Goddamn it!

WHAM!

WHAM!

The world disintegrates – flips into schizoid fragments, fluff, static and phantoms. The world is shattered. it is a ghost.

Where am I?

The console was dead, the commands didn't respond, the leaping giant Nazi rabbit-mutants faded, the glare of the sizzling desert turned to static. The gunfire and cicadas and engine's roar morphed into cold hissing Arctic synaptic snow. Then died to dead black. The ear-feeds were void of stimuli. The sensation feeds – which gave Kit her tactile, muscular, olfactory, and taste inputs – provide nothing, zero, zilch, nada.

OUCH!

No sensations!

It's like being dead.

Oh, I hate this! She had been thrust back with pitiless utter explosive force into the present, out of Ancient Mythical 20th Century North Africa – WHAM!

She was in her own body, in her Sub Cubicle, her own time! Like, now, she was in *Now*, like in *This Instant!* It was like slamming into a wall. *Oh, I hate this!*

Now – how horrible!

Now – meant death!

Now – meant absence!

Now – meant love forlorn.

Goddamn!

Slouched down, a limp, unwashed, filthy, human dishrag, in the Wrap-Around Play-Seat, Kit shuddered. She blinked. There was an itchy clot of crud at the corner of her left eye. She picked at it.

Little white gooey flakes came out, stuck to the end of her fingers. She stared at them. "Ugh!"

YUK! GROSS!

Her whole body was icky – sweaty, clammy. Her mouth was musty and salty, her tongue furry; her heart empty. Damn! She hadn't showered since coming back from the Sky Dreamer Complex. How long ago? Two days? No, three, three whole bloody days!

It was so totally stupid, losing herself these games, trying to drug herself into an absolute unending minimal IQ stupor! Whatever she did, she couldn't escape the fact: Nikki and Miranda Hughes were dead!

She didn't believe it, but it was true. Three days ago …

Three days ago …

Three days ago, the world was sunshine and promise. Three days ago, the future was bright.

Three days ago, the day had started happily: it was Cleaning Day in the Hughes apartment.

Kit tried to deny how much she liked – well, loved – Miranda and Nikki. It was a weakness. She despised herself for it. Well, she *partly* despised herself for it! She was addicted. Three days ago, that morning, before heading off to the Hughes Apartment, she had even done a little dance, spinning around in the narrow confines of her living pod!

She had a great idea for a new "adventure." She and Miranda would explore the old underground sunken port at the end of the sunken underwater part of Manhattan, near the old …

Nikki, she was sure, would approve.

Kit showered, pulled on her best skin-shorts, T-shirt, and hobnail boots, and then she rode across town and uptown to the Exclusive Cosmos Levels of Elysium. When she got to the Sky Dreamer Complex, she flashed, as usual, the security card Nikki had given her. The robot security officer bowed, saluted, and said, "Welcome to the Sky Dreamer Complex, Sub Kit Candy. You are authorized to proceed."

Kit entered the elevator and stood patiently, while it checked her biometrics, after which the elevator said, "Hello, Sub Kit Candy. You are authorized to proceed!"

So, in the transparent elevator bubble, she began the journey to the 78th floor of the Complex – past the shopping levels, the university level, the seminar open-space level, the Olympic-size swimming pools, on three different levels, suspended in space and glittering in the morning light, and the spas with their manicure stations, clay baths, massage parlors, and workout stations. Everywhere there were lots of beautiful Cosmos – slender, tanned, fit – doing their Cosmos things, shopping, jogging, eating, studying, laughing. It was, truly, another world. Then, finally, she got to the 78th floor, where the door opened with a brief musical salute, and Kit exited, with the elevator wishing her, "A very good day to you, Sub Kit Candy."

"And to you too," Kit said.

"Thank you, Sub Kit Candy," said the elevator, and the door closed with a discreet musical ding – and sped on its way upwards.

"Suite 78A: Nikki Hughes," the gold doorplate said. Kit rang the antique retro doorbell. No one answered. She waited and rang again.

Again, nobody answered.

This was strange. Kit felt a twinge of disquiet. Damn! I'm an idiot. I shouldn't be so dependent on them. I'm a Sub. I must remember that I am a Sub! I shouldn't be dependent on two Cosmos, even if they are wonderful Cosmos! Still, she was eager to get into mischief with Miranda and to have a session of jousting ideas with Nikki.

Oh well, Kit resorted to the palm-and-iris identification pad.

"Welcome, Sub Kit Candy. You are authorized!"

The door slid open with a well-bred hiss. Kit entered the apartment. She slid off her hobnail boots and pulled on her ballet-like slippers so that she would not bring the slightest trace of outside imperfection into this intimate pristine paradise.

It seemed quiet, too quiet, as if a horrible crime had been committed here, and as if that crime had left behind the mute silent perfection of death.

"Hello?"

Nobody answered.

"Hello?"

This was strange. Miranda had said she would be home, and Nikki almost always worked in her studio next to the kitchen at least until noon.

The place was silent, ghostly silent.

Kit went into the kitchen and knelt to get out the plastic box of cleaning materials – she would do the windows, she would sweep the swimming pool, she would tidy up – or try to – Miranda's mess, and she would –

Something made her uneasy.

It really was too silent.

She stood up and stayed very still. The Info-Flow news ticker was rolling silently across the bottom of the Info-Flow screen that tilted down from the wall over the kitchen table: Riots in the Burbs. Strange winged creatures, spotted winging their way eastwards out of the Dead Lands. Static in the World Mind. Religious fanatics invading the Mississippi Special Military Zone. Los Angeles, and Vancouver incommunicado for several days … state of emergency declared in …

"Hmm," she went into Miranda's room. It was not as messy as usual, but it was messy.

Then she saw it. Miranda had pinned a note. It was a very old-fashioned way to communicate, but all electro-communications were, in theory and practice, censored and controlled, so anything intimate – particularly between a Sub and a Cosmos – was best put on disposable non-linked paper or consigned to silence.

"Dearest Kit: We have to leave for a few days, but we will be back. I love you, your very own, Miranda. PS: Love!!!! PPS: Love from Nikki too!"

Whew! Kit's heart leaped. Well, that explained it.

Still, it was odd.

Feeling vaguely uneasy, Kit went out onto the swimming pool terrace. She stretched and looked around – dreamy towers reached skywards in the perfect dome-enclosed atmosphere. It looked like paradise. It was paradise!

She turned on the automatic robot pool and terrace cleaner and followed it around and made sure the job was perfect, even scolding it in a friendly way once when it missed a tiny smudge. "Sorry, Sub Kit Candy," it said, "I shall try to do better – I promise!"

"I'll make it easier for you," Kit said, "You need a new filter!"

"I can change the filter, Sub Kit Candy!"

"I know, but I want to do it!"

"If you insist, Sub Kit Candy!" the robot voice sounded slightly miffed.

"I do, I do insist."

"Well, then, thank you, Sub Kit Candy!"

Kit stripped, stretched in the warm milky sunlight and gentle breeze, slipped into a one-piece mini-mono, and dove into the pool and swam to the bottom to change the filter.

It was fun and weirdly thrilling, twirling around like a nymph or a dolphin in all those azure bubbles, working at the filter, bouncing up for air, and plunging back down, all alone. It was something the robot could do for itself, but it was fun, so she had insisted – overriding the robot's polite protests – that she would do it.

After swimming several lengths and just lazing and floating, she climbed out of the pool, beaded with water; she stood up, shook herself like a dog emerging from a freshwater lake, unpeeled the mono, and stretched out, naked, on a fold-up deck chair, in the sunlight, and let the gentle warm – perfect 74 degrees Fahrenheit – 23.3 degrees Celsius – Elysium breeze dry her.

She and Miranda had often sunbathed like this, and once, even Nikki had joined them. Nikki had said, "If we're not here, Kit, treat the place as your own, swim, sunbathe, whatever …"

Such trust from a Cosmos to a Sub: it was unheard of!

The soft breeze was perfumed. No wonder I'm in love!

The dome-filtered sunlight made pretty patterns under her eyelids.

The air, moving so softly, was like a lover's caress.

Okay, back to work! She sat up, toweled herself down, pulled on her skin-shorts, T-shirt, and ballet slippers, and set about tidying Miranda's room – this was always a delicate operation, because amid her mess Miranda definitely had a method – and got very peevish if things were misplaced – but Kit figured she had mastered the Miranda placement mnemonics. When she finished, everything seemed perfect: order in disorder had been respected.

She checked the bathrooms and made sure all was sparkling clean, adjusted the automatic cleaners, and then polished the mirrors.

In Nikki's bedroom and studio, there was very little work to do – Nikki's aesthetic was strictly minimalist and *very* neat – so she just dusted and straightened two pencils.

Then she changed the beds and put the sheets in the laundry orifice, watched the machine go to work, waited until everything was dried and pressed, and put the folded extra sheets in the proper cupboards.

Okay, that looks about perfect!

She went to the kitchen to eat the sandwich she had brought with her just in case Nikki didn't have time to offer lunch.

The Info-Flow was streaming on about disasters which seemed to be piling up: Two columns of Centurions had been lost in the Dead Lands, though reports were contradictory; power was off in Cosmos Paris; Los Angeles, Vancouver, and Seattle and other West Coast fortified Cosmos outposts had been incommunicado for two days now.

Boy! Things were really falling apart! Kit took a bite of her synthetic tuna-paste sandwich.

Then: "We have just learned that well-known Elysium graphic artist and designer Nikki Hughes and her daughter Miranda are reported dead after a plane crash several days ago in the Dead Lands … We have not been told when, exactly, this occurred. Ms. Hughes and her daughter were guests, it is said, of the Leader-President on his … They were reported to be traveling to … No survivors … Ms. Hughes will be remembered for her prize-winning graphics and her roles in the famous films of the …"

Kit's heart stopped: Guests of the Leader-President? Dead? Dead? They couldn't be dead!

She ordered a replay.

The InfoFlow replayed the news item.

Kit turned on the sound. On the screen itself, the two usual anchors, Alison Somebody and Ken Somebody, were talking about Nikki. "Yes, she was famous, a star, an exceptional beauty, and actress, but in recent years very discreet, very private. Her graphic talents …"

Kit turned off the sound.

Nikki … dead!

Miranda … dead!

Kit's world was suddenly empty – nothing meant anything.

It couldn't be true!

But it must be true!

No, it can't be true.

I'll die if it's true!

For a long time – she didn't know how long – she sat there, as Alison Somebody and Ken Somebody babbled on about meaningless stuff.

Finally, Kit took a deep breath; she stood up; she went into Miranda's room. She touched things – Miranda's books, the note Miranda had left, the clothes hanging in the closet. There were notes that Miranda had scribbled just a day or two ago – the notes were still there, still alive, the casual traces of carbon on paper were radiant, fresh, thick with life, traces of the elegant quick gesture of Miranda's hand. But Miranda wasn't there, wasn't radiant, wasn't anything. How could the notes – the marks on paper – survive and not Miranda who had written them? Kit stood there, utterly empty, insubstantial, a ghost. She was going to throw up. She sat down on Miranda's bed. She couldn't stand up. She gripped the edge of the bed. One silver tear trickled down her cheek.

Her nose was running.

She sniffled, and with the back of her wrist, she wiped away the tear and the glossy sheen of snot.

She wanted to die. She wanted to join Nikki and Miranda in death. She just wanted to cease, evaporate, and dissolve into nothingness. How they must have suffered!

She closed her eyes. She could see it: a swirly fiery inferno as the plane went down and as bodies were bounced, crashed, and torn apart, and …

She opened her eyes.

Oh, no, no, no …!

She stood up. The room spun. She steadied herself. She looked down at the immaculate carpeted floor, perfect cream. Her mind shot back to that crazy moment when she and Miranda had first "made out" right there, both of them naked. And then Nikki had opened the door, wide-eyed, but totally calm, lips slightly open, and then that fabulous smile: "Would you girls like some tea – or perhaps coffee? Coffee is also a possibility!" Kit's tears ran freely now, dribbling to her chin, dripping on the skintight T-shirt. She sniffled and smiled and wiped her tears.

She could *see* Miranda –as if she were there. She sobbed, "Miranda, I thought I was teaching you about sex – and love. But you taught me, you two Cosmos, you dreadful, privileged, idiotically rich, horrendously beautiful Cosmos, you and Nikki taught me! You taught me so much!"

She bit her lip. "Okay, Kit, get a grip on yourself, Kit Candy!"

She took a deep breath and then another, and then another. "That's better, Kit Candy, that's much better!"

She walked through the whole apartment; she made sure everything was in order, as if Miranda and Nikki would be returning in an hour or two.

She did do one special thing. She wrote a note and pinned it beside Miranda's. "Miranda, I love you too, and I love Nikki, and I will love you both forever and ever, your very own Sub and loyal friend, Kit Candy."

She left the apartment, made sure the door was locked, and rode down the elevator, which was, as usual, scrupulously polite, "Have a good day, Sub Kit Candy!"

She left the Sky Dreamer Complex, and, in a half-conscious daze, she traveled across town, down seven more levels, toward her living III Sub Cube Pod in Sub-Tower-45A, Sub Level 35.

"I will drown my sorrows," she growled, "I will definitely totally drown my sorrows. Today I will play a VID War Game all day, and I will kill every bloody thing in sight!"

And so it was that Kit Candy had played war games for 72 hours straight and was just about to kill those bloody bastard rabbit-mutant sniper Nazi assassins, by gunning them down and running them down, grinding them into dust under the caterpillar tracks of her 1942 vintage armored car, as they desperately attempted to scurry away, when the power went off, and all the computer connections failed, and the game died.

WHAM!

Ouch!

Ouch!

Kit Candy, Kit the Sub, was thrust back, full-throttle, into reality, into death, into loss, into her tiny Third-Class-Sub Cube-Pod.

She shook herself. She had to wake up. She to turn herself back into a human being. She might be a Sub, but, goddamn it, Kit Candy had her pride. The lights were off. Some of the power was off too. Coms and net were dead. The power never went off – not Elysium! The President-Leader wouldn't permit it! What the hell was going on?

She stretched, shaking off cobwebs and stiffness. Well, whatever is going on, Kit Candy, you have to clean up your act; and you will start with a hot, bubbly shower.

It was 07:20 am Imperial Eastern Standard Time in Domed City Elysium, capital of the American Imperial Cosmos Empire.

It was the day the human world would come to an end, and the day was just beginning.

"Hello! Good morning to you all, folks!"

In Studio three, on the fifty-fourth floor of the Volpe Net Tower, in midtown central Elysium, Morning Show Vid-Net Hostess Alison Jonas flashed her brightest smile: "Hello darling viewers wherever you are, it is 7:20 am in Elysium Domed City, and everything is bright and perfectly normal in the best of all possible Elite Cosmos worlds, which is our very own Elysium!"

Today Alison Jonas – Cosmos First Class – was determined to be her most cheery self, because, in truth, for almost a week now, weird and unsettling news had been coming in from all over the world. And this morning was even worse! Strange superstorms were headed toward Elysium City; flocks of large winged bat-like creatures had also been sighted heading toward Elysium. Much of the rest of the country and large parts of the world had flickered out and gone incommunicado. All Info-flows and communications with the Dead Lands and with the West Coast had been lost. People needed to be reassured.

But otherwise, in fact, everything did seem normal in Elysium and in the Volpe Communications Tower in midtown and in the fully automated News Studio where the only two human beings on the whole 54th floor were the two flesh-and-blood presenters – Alison and Ken.

Alison Jonas smiled her dazzling smile at the *Morning and Midday Show* automated camera that floated in front of her. "The weather in Elysium City, under the dome, is sunny; the temperature is 23 degrees Centigrade or 73.4 Fahrenheit; a slight, simulated sea breeze with a bit of simulated salty tang – courtesy of Sony – will be felt from downtown to midtown; and there will be artfully designed patches of mist and twenty-five minutes of rain over the Central Park Elevation between precisely 14:00 and 14:25 to refresh the trees and flower beds."

"So, all is normal," co-host Ken Ivison flashed his perfectly tanned skin and his toothy bright-glow trademark smile, "in Cosmos Elysium City in the best of all possible Cosmos worlds."

"Absolutely, Ken! All is normal in Cosmos Elysium City," Alison said, returning his full-glow smile with her own even brighter smile.

Alison Jonas was twenty-eight years old, blond, lightly bronzed with a perfect photogenic tan, exceptionally good-looking, a graduate of several elite Cosmos schools in North America, Europe, and the Asian Confederation, and of course, she was a Full Cosmos First Class, a status which she had earned herself, not inherited, having been born in outback Burbs in the backwoods ruins of Oregon. Her full lips and blue eyes and distinguished cheekbones made male viewers – and many female viewers – dream. She was wearing a dark blue moiré silk jacket, a neatly folded red handkerchief in the breast pocket, with a white silk T-shirt, a neo-punk slave collar, with a cameo and an iron ring, and a short pleated blue skirt.

It was a well-kept secret, but Alison Jonas hated with a cold and concentrated fury her co-host, Ken Ivison, who was twenty years older than she. Ken was a ripe handsome and athletic 48. She hated him because he was the senior anchor and because she suspected he was jealous of her – considering her an upstart and excessively intellectual – he had once muttered "bluestocking" – and she was sure that he – and he was from an old elite Cosmos First Class family – despised her lower-class background and wanted her off the show. In particular, Ken had a weird and hostile way of staring at her – his eyes looking very flat and hard – and she thought, in short, that Mr. Ken Ivison Esquire, of the Elysium Ivison Cosmos Dynasty, was a pretentious patriarchal priggish snob, a porcine humanoid macho pig, a relic of a former epoch, a phony, already over-the-hill, and a potential has-been.

"We do have reports of trouble, of fires in the Burbs, out Hoboken way, and of a fairly large local sandstorm, also, in Hoboken Burb and Jersey Burb," said Allison.

"Yes, Allison, and there are some weird – frankly unbelievable – reports that have come in of cadavers – dead bodies – rising from graves and tombs in Burbite centers along the East Coast, including in Brooklyn and, again, Jersey City. Somebody's idea of a joke, I am sure." Ken smiled at the camera and then turned to Allison.

"Yes, Ken, well, not only are dead rising – being, as it were, resurrected – perhaps a sign of the Apocalypse – but there are signs of revolt in the Mutant Country Dead Lands and the Central Desert and even on the West Coast," Allison allowed her smile to become somewhat serious.

"Revolts – indeed, Allison," said Ken, facing the camera and allowing his smile to tighten into even graver seriousness, upping the ante, and slightly narrowing his eyes as if he were staring straight into the trouble, assessing the tragedy.

"Oh, yes, in the Dead Lands," said Alison, taking up her cue. "The Communications systems that monitor the Dead Lands have apparently experienced a glitch, yet again after the tragedies of a week ago, and everything is off, kaput, closed down, and has been for these last three days …"

"Yes, a glitch …" Ken grinned at the camera as if there were something amusing about the word "glitch," so minimalist, so understated – when in fact in all probability the whole damned world was falling apart: prison revolts, restive mutants and Burbites, the Resurrection of the Dead, Subs in revolt, and Los Angeles and Moscow and Mexico City and Vancouver had just simply disappeared, and worst of all, some lethally contagious version of Old-Time Fundamentalist Born-Again Religion – that reputedly turned people into cannibalistic and winged monsters – was spreading through the Central Desert and beyond.

Alison glanced at Ken, smiling, and kept her annoyance – which was extreme – he was such a supercilious superficial privileged bastard – barely in check. "But before communications failed, there were reported attacks on Dead Lands and on Super Dust Bowl mining settlements and on isolated industrial installations, with real live crucifixions, and people, reportedly, being burned alive, on the cross or at the stake." Alison stopped, thinking, *this is horrendous stuff, and yet we treat it like showbiz*, and knowing that Ken would take up the cue.

The words were floating in front of them on the invisible halo prompters, which took in feeds and edits from all the automatic sensors, which picked up information from everywhere, and automatic editors, which wrote out the reports and newsflashes and put them together and served them up on the prompters for Allison and Ken.

In spite of herself – she did try to censor disquieting and unpatriotic musings – Alison was worried about the crucifixions and burnings – and she was thinking that "mining settlements" and "industrial installations" were euphemisms for concentration camps for dissidents, and even, possibly, for imprisoned hybrids, since underground and Net Samizdat rumor had it that some of the semi-mythical hybrids, perhaps even most of them, had survived the massacre and roundup – known as *The Culling* – of fourteen years ago.

Allison chased the subversive thoughts away. Even thinking such thoughts was dangerous – you could end up erased, your mind zeroed to null, cast out into nothingness and anonymity, perhaps resettled into an outer Burb, morphed into a Female Trash Gothic Burbite, perpetually pregnant, barefoot with long dirty, ragged toenails and horny yellow calluses, enslaved, newly illiterate, with a minimal or no vocabulary, robed head to ankles in American Gothic gingham, or perpetually stark naked, depending on the particular sect's doctrines as regards the "submission of Eve to Adam," in a Dead Land Colony, imprisoned in some bearded polygamous, fundamentalist, antique Glock 17-toting, patriarch's outdoor kitchen, next to the stench-drenched organic wooden outhouse, and the clucking chickens, immersed in the stink of excrement, urine, sunbaked chicken shit, dust, sand, fertilizer, rotten wood, and creosote, all of which constituted a fate Alison – scrupulous in personal hygiene as in everything else – considered worse than death.

"Yes, several cities, or former cities, now experimental outposts, such as Dallas and Houston and Las Vegas, have fallen silent. And just a few days ago, we heard of the crash of a Presidential jet out in the Dead Lands, on the edge of the Great Central Desert."

"Nothing has been heard of passengers of crew since. And they are, as was first declared, almost certainly dead," said Alison, "Among the passengers were Nikki Hughes, the ex-star model and actress, renowned graphic designer, and her daughter, Miranda Hughes, four times Gold Medalist in the Cosmos Youth Olympic Games."

"Yes," said Alison, while the camera-editor, run by a local Artificial Intelligence System, inserted images of Nikki Hughes and Miranda, "Nikki Hughes is known for her beauty, and intelligence, and the elegance of her designs and product development creations, and Miranda Hughes is certainly the epitome, the very paragon and model of the best the Cosmos World has to offer. Two Elite Cosmos First Class – lost – a true tragedy – in the desert where there is now, I believe, a total blackout of world communications and also satellite surveillance."

"It's a tragic loss," said Ken, looking steadily and with his best grave expression straight at the camera. "I believe that Nikki Hughes was rumored to be a friend of the Glorious Leader, Hail to the Leader!"

"Yes, Hail to the Leader! All Hail!" Alison raised her right arm in salute.

"Yes, Hail to the Leader, All Hail!" Ken echoed the salute and swallowed, and continued, "Nikki Hughes also had a film career."

"Yes," said Alison, as the computerized screen gave her the background, "She starred in *Cosmos and the Ape Man,* and in *Cosmos Girl in Paris,* and

Himalayan Cosmos, and she modeled, as the Ideal Cosmos Woman, for Chanel and Dior and for Elysium Cosmos Perfumes."

"Her daughter, Miranda, aside from her athletic prowess, is supposed to have been rather a Cosmos prodigy."

"That is true. Miranda topped World Net Cosmos Competitions three years in a row. But they have led a very private life, and for several years, Nikki Hughes has been very careful to keep both of them – Miranda and herself – out of the limelight."

A photo flashed on the screen of Nikki entering a restaurant wearing very large wrap-around dark glasses and shielding her face and Miranda's face from the camera.

"In other news, the London Cosmos Dome and Shanghai Cosmos Dome stock exchanges have extended their recent catastrophic losses – both down 45% – on fears of the Rapture Jihad Old-Time Religion, led by somebody called the Boy, which has risen up in the Arizona and Utah Plateau, and on rumors of strange sightings of winged carnivorous beasts in California, and in the Dead Lands no-go-zones which were once known as Texas and Nevada and Oklahoma … And as we have already mentioned, Los Angeles Cosmos has not been heard from in, oh, forty-eight hours."

And so, other than the aftermath of the crash of Presidential Superliner 47 and the strange events out in the Bad Lands and on the west coast, it was a normal, perfect day in Elysium City.

"Oh, Ken," Alison spoke as the earphone whispered new information from the Instant Info-Flow into her ear, "There is one bit of disturbing news – and it is really strange! Power outages have been reported in various zones of Elysium City."

"Ah," Ken flashed his boyish reassuring grin at the camera, "So the lights are going out."

"Yes, perhaps they are," said Alison, with a forced smile that covered a sudden untoward inkling of disaster, since she, the bluestocking whose erudition had totally pissed off Ken and had driven off countless panting and salivating suitors, knew of Britain's Sir Edward Gray's remark about the lights going out all over Europe in August 1914, as the First World War was about to begin, and it echoed darkly in her mind, an inkling of true darkness, and, smiling at Ken, she thought: The supercilious bastard won't recognize a tragedy even if he were caught in the middle of it. So, for Alison, the phrase, "the lights are going out …" signaled the end of a world – perhaps the end of *the* world.

At that moment, the lights flickered.

The computer feeds fell silent.

The red camera light blinked off, but then, immediately, blinked on again.

"What was that?" Alison's heart skipped a beat.

"I don't know, but, ah, but," Ken squinted at the floating prompter, "Power outage, but we have generators, and so … on we go …"

Allison noticed a tense crease at the edge of Ken's mouth. Even the supercilious idiot was worried!

Suddenly, Allison Jonas was afraid, very afraid.

Kit Candy stood up, stretched, and scratched her sides and under her arms and up into her armpits. She felt totally truly cruddy.

She did need that shower.

And she should eat something – maybe even something *healthy!*

Even if she was in mourning, she shouldn't allow herself to be addicted to war games. They were a first-class timewaster. She had better things to do with her – rather fine, if the truth be told – mind than playing virtual war against a terrorist posse of imaginary mash-up mutants. She sighed. *Miranda … Nikki …*

This mind of hers was a problem. Sub Kit Candy was not supposed to have a first-class intelligence or even a second-class intelligence, but she did! So there! But it had been a close call; she could easily have ended up a drooling idiot.

That, in fact, had been the intention.

When she was being punished for anti-social subversive tendencies, and the sentence was total erasure of mind and personality, she had bribed the Eraser Man to do only a partial erasure; and some of the stuff he had erased she had been able to fill in with things she learned from pirated mind implants and programs. She had been determined to reconquer and rebuild her mind, province by province, neighborhood by neighborhood, and room by room.

The secret "Enemy of American Imperial Cosmos Values" trial – where she was almost totally erased – was conducted by one man, alone with her, in a sealed-off, high-security room; the sentencing was decided upon by the same one man in the same room; and the sentence would be carried out by that same man, but in a different room, one with special equipment; the sentence was total irreversible erasure of her personality, memories, and skills.

It was a total absolute, final downer, worse, probably than death itself. She would cease to be. An empty body and an empty mind would remain behind. She would be *tabula* absolutely fucking *rasa*. They would be able to turn her into anything – or into nothing – and they would be able to do anything to her – and with her.

The whole idea was disgusting!

The erasure session, which turned into a bribery session, was terrifying. As he was preparing the instruments and she was strapped down ready to be erased, the guy had made a few hints – "Too bad, you know, you're a good-looking chick!"

He actually said "chick"!

So she'd made eyes at him and blushed and flapped her eyelashes, and he'd turned off the monitors and released her from the straps and told her to take off the sleeveless backless white shift – only thing she was wearing – and he said, "So let's see what you can do!" And she'd fucked the Eraser Guy, who had also been her prosecutor and judge, and she'd fucked him silly, lying on top of him, then letting him go in her and on her, his goo deep inside her and his goo scribbled all over her belly, and all over her face, and then kneeling in front of him, worshipful, oh, so worshipful, his goo in her mouth, over-flowing, dribbling from her lips, giving him what he wanted.

The hungry bastard – Randy Shield was his name, or so he told her, and she didn't believe it for a minute – was high on injected virility enhancers and slick-slippery skinned, from drug overload, with testosterone-randy exhal-ations, sweet-and-sour, oozing out of every pore, as he pawed her all over, and got her to crawl on all fours, and to crawl all over him, giving him a full body massage with every millimeter of her own body, and mouthing him and licking him everywhere.

She was sweating pure terror. He could just fuck her – and have her fuck him – and then he could totally, but totally, erase her, and nobody would know the difference – she would be a body with an empty mind, no mem-ories, no self, no skills, no personality, to be reprogrammed at will … Or just dropped into the wilderness somewhere to be eaten by whatever hungry beast slouched along on its way to perdition.

In fact, with her memories intact – notably the memory that she had fucked him – or he had fucked her – she was a greater danger to him than if she were totally erased. In fact, totally erased, she would be no danger at all.

For her, it was a no-win situation.

"You got a really weak hand, baby," Randy Shield had said, grinning, the neon glowing off his enhanced biceps, perfect triceps. In different circumstances, if he hadn't been what and who he was, she might even have found him attractive.

"I know," she said, swearing to herself that she was not going to cower and beg, and appeal to the pity of this asshole: fuck him, yes, she would do that; beg for mercy, no, she was damned if she was going to do that.

"But you've got one thing going for you."

"And what is that?"

"You are incredibly beautiful."

She didn't know whether to thank him for the compliment or not – do you thank somebody, a professional thug and torturer, who has been raping you? She was on all fours, naked, in front of him. So, she just looked down, glared, blinked, looked up, and glared.

"I *love* that," he said, "I love the hostile look, the doggy down-on-all-fours pose with those furious dark eyes, great combo!" He had two prominent canines, overbite; he looked like a beaver, an eager beaver, and he had round eyes, that always looked startled. And to think that this muscle-bound goofball had the power to erase people's brains, to turn geniuses and housewives and journalists and scientists who practiced unorthodox science – anything not authorized by the Interpreters of the President-Leader's Holy Cosmos Texts – to turn them into drooling idiots or doddering slobbering fools – or reprogramm them into robots, sex toys, mine slaves, or agricultural animals.

He let her go with minimal erasure: family history, past history, her relatives, her friends, who she was, what she had done, where she had lived, all that was gone. But she still had a mind, a good vocabulary, decent syntax, and some basic skills, like two and two equal four.

He also left the memories of their session together.

"Something to remember me by," he said.

Then, on the mind and skill-implant black market, she'd got herself an education. Rebuild my mind, retake control, and rebuild myself – that was her motto. So, why the hell was she wasting time on these Net games? They were bloody addictive, and every minute cost you – tokens, money, that you then had to scramble to earn. It was a rat race. Round-and-round you go! Like some gerbil galloping along in a spinning exercise wheel. And, since virtually all her skills and knowledge had been acquired on the black market, she couldn't reveal that she had them, no certificates and certification, so she couldn't upgrade herself, and she was classified "Sub-B" she would never earn more tokens. She would be a Sub-B forever!

Now the war game with the giant mutant Nazi Rabbits had stopped, the void opened up.

She glanced at the time-feed. It had stopped too.

Fuck, what was happening?

She almost forgot about Nikki and Miranda.

Then the thought came back – a kick in the gut. She bent over, almost threw up. Her stomach spun into the void.

Fuck! Her legs and joints ached; they were unreal, strange, alien, suddenly deprived of Net reality. Giddy, she grabbed the back of the sensation chair. She steadied herself. The air was too thin to breathe.

She stood, testing her balance, standing first on one leg, then on the other; she let go of the chair, stretched, and moved her tongue around in her mouth. Ugh! Her tongue was heavy, gooey, clumsy.

"I am bloody filthy," she growled, "I am fucking filthy. Kit Candy, you are a damned pathetic filthy bitch!" A quivering masochistic thrill rippled through her belly, tickled her thighs. The masochism had been programmed into her by Randy Shield. Delicious self-abasement flamed up, an erotic tingle, and a quick aftershock of shivery self-disgust. "I'm in mourning, that's what it is!"

Brief images of perfection appeared – Miranda and Nikki.

And that fabulous apartment and terrace and swimming pool, floating in the sky, and conversation that was so intelligent and beautiful it made you feel you were in heaven.

And those two most marvelous people had been killed.

The door to their world slammed shut.

BANG!

Death was final.

The tick-tock of time was destiny; it was irrevocable, life was a goddamn a one-way street: one mistake, one accident, and you are – gone.

She shuddered. Oh, the pain and horror of it – the void, the emptiness: the absolute vertigo, the emptiness in the pit of her stomach.

Desire, friendship, Cosmos Class – what a lethally seductive combo!

And advice too! It was like having her very own first-class university tutor. Nikki often suggested knowledge implants, books to read, VIDs to look at; and, funny thing, but Nikki insisted she and Miranda always unhook their implants from the Mind – no automatic updates, no links, no communications with the Mind whatsoever.

"Why?"

"Well, Kit, sometimes things go awry," Nikki said, "You want to keep your mind independent, sovereign, free of pollution, and free of outside control, as much as possible, that is." Then, holding up a sketch for her and Miranda to see, she said, "What do you girls think of this design – is it okay? Will young people respond to it – or not?"

Kit stood there dreaming, aroused by the idea of Miranda, excited by all the knowledge and curiosity, envious too that Miranda had such a mother, such a friend.

She did wish she had a family.

Dream on, Kit, dream on!

The horrible moment was seared in her memory: She had finished cleaning their apartment, made sure everything was in perfect order, and then, in the kitchen, she had seen the news: the news of the crash.

It was on the Info-feed, and then:

"Tragic news from the Dead Lands," that guy Ken Ivison said, and then the blond woman said, "Yes, Nikki Hughes, well-known … and her daughter, Miranda …"

It was unreal.

So, Kit, go on! Suffer, wail, keen, lament, dear Kit Candy! Go ahead – wallow in your own selfish sorrow!

They died; I didn't.

It was their suffering, not mine!

She frowned. I'm designed to be a fucking masochist, that's the problem. During the erasure process, as part of the sentence – and Randy Shield did apply this little app to her psyche – she'd been given submissive traits – negative narcissism – shyness, diffidence, a proclivity toward sexually passive behavior, plus some kinky fetishist obsessions, right up to thrilling at the idea of being on her knees, of being tied up, blindfolded gagged, enslaved, dominated …

"Think of it as a bonus," Randy Shield had said, "A few submissive kinks make a Sub more interesting, more marketable."

"Thanks, bloody thanks," she'd said.

"Don't mention it," he'd grinned at her and kissed her on her bloody forehead. It was a tender kiss, or so it seemed, she had to admit.

But other than this masochistic-fetishist sexual zoo thing, she was pretty feisty, and, bit by bit, she'd rebuilt her mind.

Too much introspection: with the War Game suddenly silent, she had nothing to contemplate except herself.

And her ghosts: Miranda and Nikki.

They were always so pristine, those two, perfection itself!

Kit looked down at herself: Skintight black shorts, and a phosphorescent skin-cling, semi-see-through, black T-shirt, and a splotch of spilled synthetic pumpkin pie in solidified dribbles leading from above her collarbone down to her crotch and puddling there in a cruddy orange starfish-shaped splash on the black shorts and on her thighs and there were yellowish crumbs from the high protein, high-fiber, no salt, no-fat, bar she'd been munching on, idly, absent-mindedly, letting bits fall from her lips, as she hunted virtual mutants in the virtual Libyan badlands.

The smells hit her, real smells – musk, sweat, and old food.

It was stale, really stale.

"Okay, enough, Kit, you are a Sub, but you are *not* a total non-being filthy nerd. You are capable of better things, of noble things; you are even capable of friendship – and of love!"

Nikki was dead.

Miranda was dead.

Kit sighed – seeing just for an instant herself with Miranda and Nikki, friends, lovers, and partners – dream on, sub-class proletarian Non-Cosmos Kit Candy.

It would have been nice to have a mother, and if she could choose a mother, it would be Nikki, fucking beautiful, fucking generous, fucking all-understanding, fucking-all-forgiving Perfect Cosmos Fucking First Class Nikki Hughes.

As she had been told in post-erasure briefing, her real mother and father, who apparently were Jewish, had never really existed – not for any length of time at any rate – she had been orphaned at three months for political reasons – and the remaining memories of her childhood had effectively been erased, so she had no idea whether she'd known her parents or not. The briefing was almost certainly part of the erasure, a melody of lies. Maybe they had been Cosmos, maybe not. Who knew? Mom and dad had been erased or maybe vaporized or maybe were exiled to the burbs or to a slave farm somewhere – who knew!

She stripped out of the skintight skin-shorts and cling-skin T-shirt and held them out, delicately, at her finger's end, and, wearing only her X-rated panties – Sub-B slut-category approved Brazilian tanga G-string design – she walked barefoot over to the hygiene cubicle and slipped out of the panties too.

I need to strip off my melancholy.

I need to get myself reborn!

She threw the shorts, T-shirt, and panties into the Renewal Orifice, where they would be washed, dried, repaired, pressed, perfumed, and ready for re-wear in about a minute.

Strangely, the Renewal Orifice didn't say "Thank you, Sub Kit Candy," and it didn't make the usual soft whirring sound.

What if the damned thing wasn't working? Fuck! Fuck! Fuck!

Did she have any clothes?

Not many – she lived lean and mean. She kept minimal inventory. For Subs, excess was not encouraged; and, besides, she favored a stripped-down lifestyle. In Kit's books, minimalism equaled freedom.

"Well, fuck that!" She stepped into the shower pod and said, "Shower as per usual, please!" Kit was always polite when she interacted with robots and AI Biosystems. She liked to think that they had feelings – and who knew, maybe they did!

In fact, they almost certainly did. Nikki had once told her – while Kit was on hands and knees polishing the marble floor at Nikki's feet – that IT systems had developed their own biological logic and were following Darwinian principles and evolving and changing though, as Nikki put it, "Humans have not really woken up to the fact, Kit, but I think someday soon they will, but by then it may be too late; take the World Mind, for instance, it has feelings, or parts of it do, and it is suffering, I think, from a sort of nervous breakdown and I think … Sorry, I'm in your way." And Nikki had moved her mobile swivel chair.

Kit, on hands and knees, looked up at her and said, "No, it's no bother! You're not in the way at all!" And she was thinking, how could Miranda or Nikki ever be in the way – they seemed to float on air!

Given what she called the "fragility of the World Mind," Nikki had insisted, doubly insisted, more than once, that Kit and Miranda isolate all their mind implants from the World Mind and disconnect all peripherals and update connections. She had been adamant.

"But," Miranda had said, "But …"

"No buts, Miranda, no buts, Kit," Nikki had said, giving them that dark look which was in its own adorable elegant way pretty frightening, "The Mind cannot be trusted; I want you unplugged, totally unplugged."

"Unplugged," Miranda repeated, pouting, "oh, so unplugged," and then, tilting back her head operatic-style, she began to sing, "Oh, unplugged, so unplugged," and took Kit by the waist and twirled her around in a waltz-time spin while Nikki looked on, shook her head, and smiled.

And so, they had danced – their arms around each other.

"Unplugged, oh, so unplugged!"

But they had both done it, total disconnect. It was exciting, sort of, unleashing oneself from the World Mind, from the Hive Mind, from the Totality; it was a bit like being tossed up on a desert island out of the reach of everything and anything. It was like being in inner exile, secret exile, like being a secret alien among all the plugged-in people around them.

From the showerhead, water and gel obediently squirted out; and Kit's body was foamed up by ultra-sound waves and vibrating virtual brushes – consisting of highly energized micro air currents – and every angle and crevice and orifice was cleaned – external and internal – some of this was mildly orgasmic – and she was scrubbed and foamed and rinsed, and she opened her mouth and the oral hygiene unit brushed and rinsed and then withdrew, the voice saying, "You've been neglecting your brushing and flossing these last three days, Sub Kit Candy!"

"Yeah, I know, I'm sorry, I really am."

The pod shut her up by giving her a high vibe special in-depth, utterly thorough micro-vibe floss, high-frequency brush, rinse, floss, brush, and rinse, so that her mouth was overflowing with perfumed bubbles.

Ooops …!

Ooops …!

Wham! It all stopped. The shower pod voice said, "System failure, system failure, system failure."

"What the hell does that mean?" Kit blurted – foam bubbling from her mouth, but now sparkly clean, and rinsed. But bloody soaking wet.

The shower pod voice, said, "Very sorry, Kit Sub, but …" The voice sputtered, faded, and died.

"Well, I'll be buggered." Kit stood still for a moment, dripping water, and then she stepped out of the shower pod and stood, dripping, on the ceramic floor, and looked at herself in the mirror – automatically cleared of steam – and she saw a bleary-eyed, pale, five-foot eight-inch, slender – but full-breasted

– proletarian girl Sub-B-Domestic-Class worker, SDCW™, beaded with water, and quite pretty, though. Yes, quite pretty, she thought, her spirits reviving, "Even if I do say so myself!" So, there she was, a naked, female, Non-Cosmos, human creature, still biologically capable of reproduction, but neutered under the Code-1984 of the Non-Cosmos Reproductive Rights Act, though, she was sure, she would be an excellent mother, given the chance, but excess supply of Proletarian Subs was not what the President-Leader or the Cosmos government wished to envisage. In fact, she had heard, via the samizdat resistance grape-vine, that large scale culling of Subs, Proletarians, and Burbites, through sterilization and selective applications of the plague or of famine and systematic starvation or poison by pesticides was being contemplated, since Subs, Proletarians, and Burbites no longer had any useful skills and little income, robots doing all the work; thus they were useless both as Producers and Consumers, totally outside the circular Supply-Income-Spend-Demand-Produce-Spend equation, and therefore "did not earn their keep," were "parasites," "deadbeats," and, generally, "losers," and were thus expendable, indeed a burden on licensed Shoppers and certified First Class Cosmos full-blown citizens, who constituted, income-wise, the upper 0.000001 percent of the world's human population.

Besides, the still-active sperm supply, archived and frozen, was rationed and very expensive, since various chemical additives, put in soda pop, popcorn, and sub-units of the water distribution system, had made most of the male Non-Cosmos population sterile – even if they remained perpetually horny, courtesy of the pharmaceutical oligopoly and its infinitely varied priapic devices, testosterone simulacra, and ersatz ecstasy stand-ins – for those who could afford them. And then there were those few over-feisty male Proles who had caused trouble and were usually permanently neutered, castrated, and left with no male desires, or any desires, whatsoever.

Kit had once asked Miranda if she had been neutered as far as reproduction went, and Miranda said, "No, and it was too early to make a choice."

And Kit had said, "*Choice!* You mean they give you a *choice*? You have a choice? Man, I don't believe this!"

Miranda stared at her, wide-eyed, those delicious, ripe lips, open, breathless. "You don't have a choice?"

"Are you kidding? No, I mean, fuck, I mean, I'm a Sub-B Proletarian Non-Cosmos, so I don't get a choice. It depends on the category and status grade you belong to, and it's all for the good of the species, and for the good of the country, and all that official *blah, blah, blah,* as you know."

"That is outrageous," Miranda had said, hands on hips, color rising under her golden tan, perfect, post-racial Cosmos complexion, eyes blazing – those little stars, supernovas, galaxies of gold exploding – looking truly outraged, and enticingly beautiful.

It was clear that Miranda, brilliant as she was, educated as she was, didn't know the facts of life. As an upper-class First-Class Cosmos, part of the 0.000001 %, she was protected from all the unpleasantness of life as it was now lived on planet earth by 99.99999 % of what used to be called Homo sapiens.

Homo sapiens – what a joke!

Nikki was something else – the opposite of naïve. She looked like perfection, and she was the coolest character Kit had ever met; Nikki was seemingly interested in just fashion and clothes and being beautiful and talented, but she was much more than she appeared. Once, when Miranda was not home, Kit had heard Nikki say some things over her mobile about, "class structure" and "systems overload" and "biosynthesis," and "status anxiety," and "I don't bloody care what the marginal rate of return is," and "if they don't watch out those intelligent systems will merge with the Mind itself and develop a mind of their own which will not necessarily correspond with the interests of the human race," and "you know that erasure of mind and personality is about the most criminal thing I have ever heard of and we really should not allow it," which didn't sound to Kit like upper-class female parasitic 24/7 shopping idle bubble-head-kill-time-status-vanity female Cosmos talk of the kind that eavesdropping had revealed, in all its horrific vacuous splendor, to Kit in so many Cosmos cafes, apartments, and spas (Kit did stints as a Sub-Slut-Waitress in Cosmos Land and sometimes acted as Assistant Sub Masseuse at Sulky Oily Tremble Inc., an upscale Cosmos Spa Firm where you could get orange, mud, clay, flower, lavender, massages, full body and without restraint, in various flavors and consistencies).

And in fact, when she looked it up, Kit discovered Nikki was known as a big-time designer and that some of her stuff was in museums and famous galleries and that, a few decades back, she had also been a model and a bit of a B-movie "celluloid star" of a whole series of classic cult films neo-archaic VID buffs like to talk about and worship.

And for a film star and model, she seemed, like, so quiet, so private, so …

She also seemed so … young!

How could Nikki have done so much and be so young?

Even Cosmos show wear-and-tear.

But not Nikki!

The chronology really didn't square with the appearance.

Nikki had noticed that Kit had overheard her conversation about "the marginal rate of return," and she gave Kit a sly smile and hung up and then asked a whole lot of really pointed questions about what it was like living in the Sub-25-B neighborhood, and about the economics – the sheer struggle for survival – of being a Sub: hand-to-mouth, short term contracts, pole-dancing, masseuse, waitressing, or sex industry indenture of some kind, or just welfare … Nikki asked: how many dollar tokens she got, what the tips were like, how variable the hours were, and …

So, Kit told her.

Life in the lower depths was not easy.

Competition from robots was a killer.

Things were interesting, violent, confused.

Nikki said, "Take Miranda down there with you again – and to the Sin Zone, too, again, hang around, see some shows, show her everything. Show her how Subs work and slave for a living. Miranda doesn't know enough about life; you can teach her."

"Really, I mean …"

"Consider it an order, my dear Kit, more visits to the Sin Zone and the Religious Underground, and whatever other mischief you can invent," said Nikki with a soft slightly weary smile; and she laid her hand on Kit's shoulder: *just the two of us, just we two, Kit, we really understand the world and how it works.*

"Yes, sir, Okay, I'll do it, yes sir," Kit saluted, and Nikki laughed, a young, fresh, innocent laugh, "You're a true friend, Kit! I think we share a lot of things, more than you know."

That was a mystery Kit would like to solve someday – what was going on in Nikki's head and who was she really. But now there would be no solving the mystery – the mystery was dead.

Dead, dead, dead!

And, one thing Kit would have really liked – she'd have really liked to be real friends – *friends* – with Miranda, and forever! At first, she had thought that such a friendship across the class divide was inconceivable. Besides, Miranda didn't know who Holly Halo Bunker was – and she didn't know about the Phosphorescent Jumping Jellybeans –and all the sub-pop stuff like the Anarchic Oranges and the Bittersweet Lemon Peels. How can I be friends with somebody like that? Maybe I can teach her – I can teach her all the things she doesn't know. It was a delicious image, talking to Miranda, the elite Cosmos, the elite of the elite, being with her … And that first time they had made out … wow!

Of course, Kit knew that, in truth, in spite of the barriers, they were – had been – friends already, *best* friends, and in a way, they were *lovers* … Yes, they were definitely that, *lovers.*

The personal hygiene machine was still dead.

Wiping the toothpaste foam from her mouth, she went back to the Renewal Orifice. "Clothes, please," she said. The shorts, T-shirt, and panties should be ready.

The Orifice did not reply.

"Clothes, please, pretty please." She hopped up and down, getting impatient; her bare feet felt funny, wet and slapping the wet ceramic like that; she wanted to pee, she wanted to get dressed; the evaporating water gave her naked body a funny tickly feeling, antsy all over. Then she heard a scream.

A scream … It sounded like Fanny, Fanny Dakin!

Fanny Dakin?

Fanny Dakin screaming?

In the Volpe Studio, the electricity had fluttered, fluttered again, went off, and then came on again. Alison and Ken breathed a sigh of relief.

A few minutes after the lights blinked off, the generators went on, stabilizing the situation. But a few minutes later, things truly began to change.

"We seem to have had a little blink, there," Alison turned her sparkling 1,000 caret smile toward the camera.

"Yes, I think the power went out for a fraction of a second, incredible though that may sound," Ken smiled his level-headed "keep calm and carry on" smile.

"But it's back now, so all is well, but …" Alison frowned. Funny stuff was coming up on the Info-Feeds: lightning bolts, strange winged creatures approaching the city, a tornado edging toward the Dome, widespread power failures.

"So, yes, but, then, there are reports of power outages in various parts of Elysium City," Ken smiled a moderately concerned camera-friendly smile.

"That is unusual, isn't it, Ken?" Underneath Alison's composure, she was for a number of reasons worried – even afraid. She had a weird inkling that something really bad was happening – or about to happen.

"Yes, historically, the last outage was reported almost fifteen years ago. Since the President-Leader – *Hail, Hail, all Hail* – since the President-Leader took the commands of our Cosmos Nation, there have been no power outages in Elysium City."

"That is wonderful, Ken, and it does show the absolute dedication to duty of our President-Leader who protects us."

"Indeed, it does!"

"Oh, here, just a moment: we have just received a flash," Alison Jonas turned to the camera, her perfectly coiffed blond hair framing her classic, perfectly symmetrical features. "We have preliminary reports that the electrostatic electromagnetic shield that protects the dome over Elysium City is for some unknown reason weakening."

"What? That has *never* happened, has it, Alison?" Ken's expression of concern began to shift from theatrical to real. This could be dangerous.

"No, it has never happened, Ken, not since the Dome was built." A funny shivery feeling rippled up Alison's spine; it was a fizzy tickling, it touched her tummy, it shimmered down her thighs, almost erotic in its intensity. It was fear – and awe. Something *monstrous* was being born.

"According to information we are just receiving," said Ken, "Storm waves and changes in atmospheric pressure are now hitting the dome directly. You can see from these graphics how this works."

A graphic showed little arrows – of atmospheric pressure and storm waves breaking through the electrostatic barrier and impacting directly against the dome.

Alison glanced at Ken. If only he were a man, and not a stuffed shirt! He looked good in profile. Yes, he was terribly handsome in a worn-out-wise-old-man sort of way. But she hated his guts, because he hated her and feared her, and by God, she would soon take over the program and fly solo, and get rid of the patronizing old buzzard, even if she had to poison him or strangle him with his necktie or stab him in the back in the dark with a stiletto ballpoint or make him choke on those roasted salted African peanuts that he gobbled when backstage suffering from his macho testosterone-driven, andropause, program-break munchies.

"Professor James Park will explain to us how the system works," Ken grinned at the image of the Professor, which had suddenly appeared in a corner of the screen.

Professor Park grinned at the camera, "Hello Ken, hello, Alison. Well, storm conditions in the atmosphere can be very extreme. The instability of the climate has been increasing over the last two centuries – as the mean surface temperature has risen 11 C in the last hundred and fifty years. So the electrostatic electromagnetic barrier is designed to protect us from cosmic rays and to isolate the Ultra-Light Dome itself from the stresses of extreme changes in air pressure and high winds and heavy rain or snowfall or sleet, or tornadoes and hurricanes, for example."

"Those expressions are rather quaint, Professor," Alison smiled, feeling reassured by calm mothball expertise of the good professor, "sleet and snowfall and heavy rain …"

"Quaint, Alison, whatever to do mean?" The Professor paused and touched the edge of his thick-rimmed professorial glasses. "Oh, yes, I see; I suppose they are."

"People in the domed cities are no longer used to weather, Professor. They have not seen weather for forty or fifty years. Most children here have never felt real raindrops on their faces or seen the stars – or even a real cloud."

"Yes, you are quite right, Alison, we have lost virtually all connection with nature, but you know when nature is left to fester …"

Ken broke in, "You were explaining the electrostatic electromagnetic shield system, Professor."

"Yes, yes, of course …Well, at a quantum level, the shield sets up a series of extreme micro-disturbances that will interact with and negate any violent change of air pressure and any high winds, so this way, the electrostatic shield protects the Dome which protects us … grrrh, grrhhhh … the professor began to growl; white foam, like bubbling shaving cream, exploded from his mouth.

"Grrrh!"

"Grrrh!"

The Professor's face disappeared. A wild werewolf face, with drool dripping from its fangs, suddenly replaced the Professor. Flashes of lightning lit up the background. Craggy mountains could be seen, volcanoes spouting fiery red columns of lava. The wolf grinned and then growled in a basso profondo that made the screen vibrate: "You are all doomed! You are all destined to go to Hell. All you sinners are doomed!"

"What the hell is that?" Ken almost fell off his perch.

"Try and switch back to the Professor, please, control room, let's get the professor back," said Alison, smiling at the camera, "I do apologize, folks."

"Yes, we seem to have been switched with the Volpe Horror Channel," said Ken, though he really thought –

"That looked like a werewolf," said Alison.

"Yes, from one of those antique movies, by …" Ken cleared his throat; this was turning out to be a really weird day; Ken did not like weird … "by … by … what's-his-name."

The Professor's face briefly appeared.

"I don't know what … is happening …" the Professor turned away from the camera. "I heard screams. I think perhaps my wife …" He turned back to the camera, a wild look in his eyes; his mouth spurted creamy foam.

There was a scream.

The Professor disappeared into static; then, the static again became an image: The Werewolf's jaws clamped down on the Professor's skull.

"Help! Help!" The Professor's glasses shattered and exploded off his face; blood streamed down his forehead.

The image went dead.

"Well," said Ken.

"I don't think that was a joke," said Alison.

"We shall try to re-establish contact with Professor Park. He is at the Elysium-Manhattan Institute for Advanced Studies, the Thinkers Campus, in the Supreme Tower, in midtown Elysium. This was all perhaps a practical joke … ha, ha, ha … by one of Professor Park's more playful genius colleagues. You know those genius guys and girls – pranksters, one and all …"

"I don't think so," said Alison.

Kit Candy stood absolutely still, transfixed, dripping water, a puddle forming at her feet. Was that a scream? Where did it come from? Was somebody in trouble? Was it Fanny?

Kit concentrated: maybe the sound would come again.

"Yahhuggghhhhh … Help!"

Kit focused. It did sound like …

There it was again!

"Yahhuggghhhhh … Help!"

What in the hell was it?

It did sound like Fanny Dakin.

It *was* Fanny Dakin.

Though Kit was in a state of total undress – aka, she was bare-ass, stark-naked, and dripping glossy wet – she leaped out of the Sub Vestments Cleaning Pod Zone, sprinted down the Sub Hygiene Collective corridor, skidded to a stop, and peered through the glass of Hygiene Pod three. It *was* Fanny! She was locked inside the pod. It looked like the pod had stopped in mid-cleaning and locked Fanny inside, covered in foamy super-cleaner glue.

"That stuff is abrasive and high-acid exfoliant," Kit had told Fanny just a week before, "You shouldn't use it."

"But it gives great results, just look at my skin."

And it was true: Fanny's skin was sparkling, peaches-and-cream.

"Help! Help!" Fanny screamed. The thick, super-glass door was shut tight. Fanny's voice came through muffled like she was drowning in porridge.

Kit looked around. She had to pry open the door. There was no way she could smash it – it was super-safe, certified unbreakable, shatter-proof.

Tools! She needed tools. Who had tools in this day and age?

She had a target gun for practice. She ran back to her cubicle, got the gun, loaded it – it was strictly illegal black market stuff that she secretly practiced with, sewer rat libertarian defender of the Constitution (well, not really, there no longer *was* a Constitution) that she was, only down in the lower depths – sloshing knee-deep in brackish tidal waters – in what had once been New York City's Lower East Side – and shooting at the dotted graffiti eyes that covered the place.

"Okay, Fanny, squeeze up in a corner."

Kit blasted the glass.

It took three strikes, the bullets bouncing off, then the glass slowly cracked in a million places. And, after Kit gave it one good punch, it fell – it seemed to Kit in slow-motion – into a million jagged glittery little pieces.

"Careful, this is glass," Kit got down on her hands and knees and swept the stuff aside. Then she handed Fanny out of the hygiene pod.

Fanny was red as a tomato and covered in a sticky slime of super glue abrasive exfoliant, which was eating through her skin.

"We've got to get this stuff off you."

"Yes, please."

"None of the water sources are working."

"Oh, God, God, God!" Fanny looked like a fetus covered in a thick sheen of bubbly translucent gooey amniotic fluid that was hardening, and eating into her. Kit remembered an ancient film called "Alien," where these big preying mantas things specialized in drooling gobs and strings of flesh-eating acid saliva and –

"Yeah, we've got to get it off you. Otherwise, it will eat right through your skin and …" Kit didn't want to envisage the consequences – Fanny would become an anatomy lesson sealed in rigid glass as the abrasive hardened to the consistency of crystal-clear Plexiglas but continued, underneath to eat away at Fanny's skin and …

Fanny shivered, bent in two, her hands between her legs.

Already it was difficult for her to bend; the stuff was hardening, like plastic crystallizing into adamantine, transparent, diamond-hard glass.

Soon Fanny would be a statue of glass.

Maybe Coca Cola was the answer – or Pepsi, or beer?

The drinks dispenser was not working. Kit unscrewed the top using a two hundred dollar token as the tip of a screwdriver.

"Okay, what have we got – Pepsi, Coca Cola, Beer – the Beer vat is full."

Kit levered open the beer vat – it was about six feet by three feet and three feet deep – and said, "Squeeze in here. It's the only way."

She squeezed Fanny – by now a floppy rubber doll – into the beer vat, and she sloshed beer all over Fanny and after about five minutes of intense sloshing and splashing and scrubbing Fanny came out looking like she had stayed too long under a sun-rack and her eyes were red; but other than that she looked okay.

"That stuff could have skinned you alive," said Kit, giving Fanny her best scolding stare.

Fanny just broke out bawling like she was five years old, threw herself into Kit's arms, then screamed, "Ouch," and recoiled.

"Your skin is sensitive. I'll get some cream. And, Fanny, we need clothes. Nakedness is illegal, even down here in Sub Town, under the Religions Intolerance Act of 2132 and the Anti-Human-Body Code of 2133-Section H-35-B."

"How is it you know everything, Kit?" Fanny followed Kit into Kit's four-by four-meter cubicle flat. "I mean, we Subs are supposed to be steeped in ignorance, right?"

"Yes, we are," said Kit, "The opium of the masses is to be dumb. It's enshrined in the Constitution: Being Stupid is Every Sub's Inalienable Right."

"Gosh, you have a way with words, Kit."

"Ignorance is bliss. That's official. Volpe and Churn Inc. work on that principle. Feed the masses vicious pabulum, and their minds become mush, and you can do anything you fucking well want with them."

"Sometimes, I think you are a subversive, Kit."

"I'm just curious – is all," said Kit, thinking the conversation was taking a dangerous turn; in fact, she did not think of herself as at all subversive, though she had done a number of things that were, strictly speaking, illegal: she had a couple of contraband forged human identity barcodes she could stick on her neck and arm when she wanted to pass herself off as somebody else; she had removed her own barcode and made it temporary so she could go absolutely incognito when she so desired; she had had sex, several times and fabulously, with Miranda, a Registered Citizen, and Top-Notch Cosmos, which was strictly illegal under Section 1776 of the 2132 Status Stability and Security Act and under Section 1864 of the Cosmos Blood and Purity and Separation of Levels & Exclusion of Losers Act; she'd taken Miranda on repeated educational journeys down into the lower depths, ditto, strictly illegal to corrupt a Citizen and Cosmos; and she had explored the religious sects that flourished down in the lower depths and out in the burbs beyond the river and beyond the dome which was Discouraged by the Sub Orthodoxy Mind Minders Section of the Department of Thought and Orthodoxy. "Besides, Fanny, you're not stupid – far from it. You are actually very bright!"

"Maybe," said Fanny, leaning on the doorframe, the redness slowly subsiding, "but I hide it better. I have a whole bunch of Orthodox Fundamentalist Phrases I've memorized from the Little Holy Sanctorum Black Book, and I parrot them, and people think I think like that."

"That's clever." Kit rummaged in her cupboard which luckily was open – she was not the neatest person in the world – because if it had been closed, the electronic command to open it would not have worked, and she was not sure she could have levered it open with the few free-floating untethered non-virtual objects available. Even a two hundred dollar token has its limits.

She pulled out silver-skin skintight shorts, and a silver-skin sleeveless slick skintight tank-top. And she had the same, only in gold, for Fanny. Gold would be a fabulous match for Fanny's blond hair and blue eyes. She also had pairs of disposable adhesive ballet-like slippers that would fit both of them.

"Wait, I'll put some cream on."

Luckily there was cream. Kit massaged it, very gently, into Fanny's skin, all over, a total caress.

Soon, they were equipped.

But it also became clear, as they were shimmying into the skin-tights, that the world was falling apart. Looking out the windows, the whole glittering city appeared to be sunk in silver-gray twilight with what looked like yellow mist drifting down from above. All the Elysium sparkle and glitz was gone. Down below, near the citizen shopping zone, and up above, in the Advertising Sky, the neon floats were dull and without lights. They floated free like untethered balloons – one giant float was knocking up against Star Fire Tower.

"Gosh," said Kit. The neon float was bumping, and bumping, and it was smashing windows, she could see it from here, flakes and plates of glass bursting and cascading down. "What about the people down below?"

Fanny was beside her, staring. "I've never seen anything like this!"

"This is spectacular!" Kit said, "Let's go out on the balcony."

They went to the balcony. Kit glanced up. "We don't want glass falling on us, Fanny." The flickering shadows from the street down below were gray. People were running. A couple of tiny figures were lying flat on the ground.

"The glass got them," said Kit. "This is dangerous. Let's go in."

The virtual ads – hologram-like creatures that floated on the air – had disappeared. Outside was a bluish-gray light like the gloomy winter twilights in Victorian London Kit had read about. And, up above, the dome looked like it was covered in dust and had holes punched in it. Flickers of what looked like lightning crisscrossed the sky.

"I figure it's the end of the world – and about bloody time," said Kit. A Nano Pub Drone wandered in through the window – it was touting kosher power bars – it looked confused, blinking, and turning in circles, whispering, "Kosher Power Bars, Kosher Power Bars." Kit batted it away – really meaning no harm – and it went into a tailspin and fell to the floor and exploded – little filaments and fragments reaching up, crying out, "Ouch, Ouch, Oy Vey, Oy, Vey …"

"That's mandatory minimal erasure of mind-skills for contravening freedom of expression to sell and occupy and colonize private mind space, the constitutional right of Mega Corps who are real persons, with more rights than just miserable flesh and blood merely mortal persons, more persons than people are," said Fanny, horrified, "And maybe a Hate-Inspired Racist Attack! You violated the Cosmos Constitution, amendment 457-B."

"I know," said Kit, "fuck that!" She crushed the remains of the Nano Pub Drone underfoot, "Anyway, I'm Jewish, or so my Eraser-Torturer told me, and My Mind Space is mine, no matter what the fucking law or goddamn Constitution or Supreme Stupid, Supremely Idiot Court says. '*Oy vey, Oy vey,*' the arrogant little squirt!"

Fanny stared at Kit. Kit glanced back at Fanny. Fanny looked frightened. Her skin looked perfect now, and the gold-skin ensemble was superb with the rose-blush, peaches-and-cream, arms and legs.

"Have we got food?" Kit said, thinking being practical might be a good idea.

"Food?" Fanny's eyes widened; yes, she realized, of course, food would be a problem!

Food was delivered every day lean-and-mean, just-in-time delivery directly from the central, so that people would not get ideas or stock up or waste materials and so that token prices could be raised anytime anyway – *Surprise!*

Kit did have some food squirreled away.

"It's good I'm messy! Minimal, but messy. I always figured mess would be useful."

"Mess pays," said Fanny, whose spirit was reviving and who liked to invent slogans, "Redundancy feeds survival."

"We'd better keep it. You know, if the system is down, there may not be any food, not for a while."

"I didn't know you were Jewish. I've got some power bars."

"Good, keep them." At that moment, they heard screams.

They exited Kit's Cubicle and went into the Public Space Corridor that connected the line of habitable Sub Cubicle Pods. The emergency lights were on – they would be on for an hour or two, Kit knew, before fizzling out. Batteries still had a limited life, particularly down here in el Cheapo Land. The emergency lights cast a livid brutal white light over everything – *ghastly!*

Very bad for the complexion, Kit thought, throws every fucking skin blemish, every single fucking pore, I swear, into fucking, brutal three-dimensional fucking relief!

Then she heard another scream, and she and Fanny turned to look.

"What in the world?" Kit's eyes went wide.

"It's Grant. It's smooth-skinned Grant Philip the Third," said Fanny, blushing. She had a secret thing for poor Grant, once phallic and hairy and now … so … pathetic … and beautiful … he needed someone, so desperately, he truly needed someone, and he didn't know it, and if only …

Kit and Fanny ran around the corner, and saw …

"Game is off! Game is off! Game is off!" shouted Grant Philip the Third, who had just come bouncing out of his pod like a neurotic volleyball. Kit gulped. This was not good. He was, oh, so freaking out of it! Grant Philip the Third fell down and began rolling on the floor, foam oozing, splattering from his wide-open mouth. He was naked except for an antique Japanese flag wrapped around his skinny pale white, flat-stomach waist. He was entirely hairless; Kit had never noticed.

"He looks like a slug," said Fanny, a gush of rampant hormones overwhelming her defenses.

"He's addicted," said Kit, "He can't live without the games. He plays games his nose in the screen, walking down the shopping strip for Christ's sake!"

"Game is off! Ugh! Game is off!" Grant Philip the Third was still rolling on the floor; his eyes were rolling too.

"I prefer mirrors to games," said Fanny, "Morph Mirrors, I mean."

"Hey, Grant, get up," Kit leaned over him. "Stand up, man, cool it, cool down, what's wrong with you, man, what's wrong?"

"You can be anything you want in a Morph Mirror."

"That's true," said Kit.

"Game is off, cannot live without Game!" Grant was drooling. His eyes rolled in his head, showing lots of white He looked like a heifer that had caught rabies "No game, no me!"

"Sometimes it's nice to be something you aren't, you know," Fanny was leaning over Grant, "For a time, that is."

"Here," Kit and Fanny helped Grant Philip the Third up.

His eyes were pale like half-fried egg-white, and cruddy around the edges with flaky clots that were ruining the effect of his jet-purple eyeliner, and he was trembling so much his perfectly beautiful teeth were chattering. "Games are off," he cried, doing his version of the Saint Vitus Dance, stuttering and drooling. The circles under his eyes seemed to get deeper, darker, and larger. His voice was high and light and musical. Formerly a tough guy, hairy, gravel-voiced, hard-drinking, overly hirsute roustabout and bully, Grant had been sentenced to forcible reorientation, redesign, and libido diminution for insulting a Cosmos and he was now one of the neutered ones, where testosterone levels had been repressed to zero and estrogen multiplied and pumped up; he was very pretty, really, with neat, firm cupcake breasts, nice hips, and a soft gently swelling belly, and he looked a bit like a crazy disheveled, hollow-cheeked, beautiful, anemic girl, with the neo-punk-gothic eyeliner, dark punk lipstick, and all. So helpless and fearful, too. Fanny sighed.

"Calm down, it's just a goddamn game." Kit frowned.

"Sit down, relax, breathe …" Fanny put her hands on his shoulders, smooth as silk, and oh so … so luscious!

"Oh, oh," said Kit, turning, eyes staring. What next?

Takahiko Harris MacDonald was running down the corridor toward them; he was stark naked except for a red-and-black samurai bandana around his head.

"Oh, Christ," said Kit.

"What the hell …" Fanny turned pale and released Grant Philip the Third.

Takahiko was screaming "Banzai! Banzai! Banzai!"

He was wielding an antique Samurai sword.

"Where the fuck did he get that?" Kit turned to Fanny.

"He won it in a virtual Russian Roulette contest."

"Oh."

Suzy Tilley Lemon – a cutie if there ever was one – she worked in leotards as a dancer in a half-virtual café on the Fifth Level – came out of her cubical and Takahiko Harris MacDonald lopped her head off with a single swing of the sword. Blood gushed up in a great single geyser – a big red splash like an exclamation mark on the beige walls.

Suzy Tilley Lemon's body lingered, one hand on the door frame, her adorable white-and-yellow smiley-face tank top and vertical pinstripe red-and-white skintight hotpants looking really slick. Her body turned slowly, and then toppled down into the corridor, blood flooding onto the faux-white-marble and patterned ceramics, both arms stretched out in front of her. Suzy Tilley's head, looking startled, two pigtails flying, bounced off the wall, hit a light fixture, and fell to the ground, almond eyes wide open staring upwards toward the livid, distressingly unaesthetic emergency lights – *ghastly!*

Takahiko screamed, "Banzai!" He spread his legs in a samurai gesture of defiance. "Dragons, infidels, spooks, females, breeders, moonshine bleeders, all-and-sundry, Subs, Cosmos, whatever – I come to wreak vengeance for the late lamented Fuhrer of the Inner Thousand Year Empire upon all you spores and scions of inferior, incestuous, miscegenist, mixed-blood and degenerate DNA heritage! Off with your heads."

"Fuck," said Kit, "Get inside, here, get inside." She pushed Fanny and Grant Philip III inside Grant's cubical.

She meant to follow them, but the Banzai warrior was too fast, he was already upon her, and he slammed the sword down, just missing Kit's shoulder.

She pushed him with all her might – just as the sword slashed against the wall – making sparks – and then, almost trapped, she ran – back the way Takahiko had come.

He shouted, "Banzai," and followed her. "Infidel wench, half-naked shameless flaunting sterile female neo-non-breeder, self-loathing domestic slave Sub, I shall slay thee, I shall flay thee, I shall cut thy flesh from thy bones, I shall fricassee thee, I shall …!"

Fuck, thought Kit, they're all going crazy. Without their games, they will all go crazy. From her black market Ancient Human History implant, she knew about "bread and circuses" and "opiate of the masses" and "false consciousness." If pushed Kit could, with unconscionable ease and just like Miranda, reference Cicero and Karl Marx and Jean-Paul Sartre as well as Bruce Springsteen and Groucho and the Rolling Stones and somebody called Elvis.

Strangely she was in shape – she could run, really run.

She was glad she'd kept some real work in the real world – the cleaning was just a form of welfare and therapy – machines could do everything better. Besides, by doing the cleaning stuff, she had met Miranda and Nikki.

"Banzai!"

She looked around. Takahiko was right behind her, and he was swinging that blasted razor-sharp sword!

Kit skidded to a halt, pulled open a door, jumped into a stairwell, and clattered down the steps. It was a spiral staircase and one she had never seen before – which was weird because she really, really knew her way around Elysium City – a service staircase that was well hidden – people were not supposed to use stairs – since they were said to be stimulating – what the hell did they stimulate, Kit wondered, muscles, the mind, the libido, what the fuck! And why shouldn't people be stimulated? Oh, if they were stimulated by simple things, or by pure ideas, by stuff that was free – *free stuff*, what a *horrible* idea! – *Then* they wouldn't shop! They wouldn't play net games, they wouldn't buy stuff; they might even want to do interesting work! Ergo, hide the stairs; stairs are shameful! Definitely infra-dig, stairs!

Her heart was pounding.

She leaped down another flight of the infra-dig stairs.

Kit could work her way around the nooks, crannies, and meanderings of the underbelly and underworld and lower depths of Elysium City like few people; it was part of her general curiosity and sneakiness – she loved to know what was going on – and where it was going on. The lower depths were her special specialty, and, to Miranda's delight, Kit knew almost every route, tunnel, canal, and crawl space, almost right down to the Top Secret Unmentionable Lair in which the Mind lived. The World Mind "Cloud" that people worshiped was actually, according to Kit, hiding underground.

The metallic stairs were enclosed in a white, pale green cylinder.

"Banzai!"

Kit glanced up. Takahiko was closing in. "Fuck!" She grabbed at a door on Level 85-B. It opened. Thank God!

"Banzai!

The stairs shook.

A deep rumble rippled up the stairwell – it sounded like something Kit had heard and read about and seen in VIDs, something called "thunder."

The railings trembled. Rivets shot out of the steel plates that enclosed the staircase. The plates buckled. What the hell was happening?

"Banzai!"

Bits of metal, rivets, bolts, screws flew everywhere. Kit slammed her way through the level 85-B steel-faced service door. Banzai Takahiko Harris Mac-Donald galloped right behind her.

"Banzai!"

The scimitar rippled with light.

Kit ran.

"Things are happening," said Ken Ivison, "Real things."

"Yes, alas, things are happening," Alison Jonas was, under her impeccable Cosmos tan, a trifle pale, "A commuter vertijet has crashed on heliport five, and there are various dysfunctionalities reported throughout the city, with some fatalities, I'm afraid."

"This is unprecedented." Ken sighed, "Ah, there, this is good: we seem to have reconnected with our expert, Professor Park."

Once more on the studio monitors, images of Professor Park appeared.

"Oh," said Ken.

"Yes," said Alison, "I think that we'd better ..."

Professor Park was dead, and his face was half-eaten.

"This image is not for the squeamish," said Ken. His stomach lurched upwards.

"You might want to cover your eyes," said Alison, forcing herself to deliver a reassuring smile, "and blind-fold any susceptible tiny tots or incontinent golden age seniors and hustle them out of the room."

Half of Professor Park's face was a skull. The other half was his usual genial beaming self, with upturned lips and beard, and twinkly eye. "Where was I?" said the half that was not a death's head; it expressed this question through a ghastly lopsided grin that dripped blood, a bright red dribble running from the exposed teeth of the skull, "Ah, yes ..."

Then the werewolf appeared. One of its claws held Professor Park's head, apparently no longer attached to Professor Park's body.

"Oh, my God," said Alison.

"This is not good, this is not good at all," Ken swallowed.

"Ha, ha, ha, fooled you!" the werewolf grinned. "Park is a puppet now! His soul has been eaten, and, let me tell you, his body is delicious, scrumptious, really. And his soul, oh, his soul was even more delicious! You see, when I eat, I gobble up all the knowledge and all the personality of those I eat. Oh, yummy! Soon you too will be puppets, Alison and Ken. You all will be puppets. You will do as I say and you will say as I do. Isn't that fun! Rejoice, ye faithful, for the End of Time is at Hand!"

The werewolf grinned, growled, and disappeared.

A placard appeared on the screen: "This was a Public Service Announcement."

"What in the world was that thing?" Alison was angry, and she was frightened. She curled her fists, getting ready to fight. Whatever had dismembered poor Professor Park was evil, and underneath her glossy exterior, Alison was a tough-as-nails crusader for justice.

"No idea," said Ken. "I have no idea what it was." The computer systems and many World Mind Cloud connections had failed about twenty minutes ago, so Info-feeds were sporadic and unreliable.

"It may be an emanation of the Mind," said Alison, trying to think her way through the unthinkable, "It might be something the World Mind has created, a creature, and it's ... maybe it's nano-building its own ..." She stopped: the implications were too horrible to contemplate. Could the Mind conjure up beings of its own volition – and out of thin air? And if so, if the Mind delved into its infinite resources of memory and invention, what would that mean

– raving dinosaurs, giant land squids, acid-dripping aliens from outer space ...?

"Yes, if the Mind is collapsing, or has been captured by a terrorist group, then it would be capable, I guess," Ken put on his extra-serious thoughtful look, but inside he was frightened, in fact, terrified, "It would be capable of, say, projecting illusions, creating collective hallucinations, it could kidnap communication nets, it could possibly nano-create its own physical creatures, it could invade the minds, directly, too, I mean the minds of anyone who has implants, and ..."

"And almost everyone does have implants," said Alison who had carefully had all her implants neutered and walled in; Ken had confided, in a rare moment of "sharing," that he had done the same thing; both of them had made ironic, self-deprecating remarks about being paranoid and ...

Lightning flashed.

WHAM!

A wave of sound slammed against the studio windows.

WHAM!

The glass walls and windows shattered. They burst inwards.

A damp, dusty wind, streams of yellow sand and drizzle, stormed in through the shattered opening.

The automatic floating cameras shook.

WHAM!

As the studio windows exploded, glass showered down, a crystal blizzard.

As glass splashed down around her and the wind roared, Alison did not allow herself to move. She remained seated in her chair, as if things were normal, and she kept talking at the camera, even flashing her trademark reassuring smile, "Now, it seems the main defenses of Elysium City are collapsing and ...."

WHAM!

WHAM!

Another blast of wind hit, and more fragments of razor-sharp glass shot through the studio.

Ken threw himself over Alison, knocking her off her chair and to the ground, pinning her under him.

"What the hell are you doing? Get off me, you pig!" She struggled out from under him.

"You'll get killed," he said. He was bleeding from a piece of flying glass that had slashed his forehead.

"I don't fucking care." Alison staggered to her feet. The red light was still on, and the camera was still running, so she faced the camera and then, indicating the gaping window and the horrendous vision beyond, she said. "Look, folks, I know this is unbelievable, but it appears that parts of the central Elysium City Dome are imploding. I mean, let's have a look, folks, let's see what is happening outside."

She walked toward the shattered gap in the windows and looked up, through the shattered, sand-splattered glass.

Obeying its built-in programs and editing and dramatizing and framing algorithms, the automatic camera followed her. Huge jagged breaks had opened in the delicate Tiepolo robin's egg blue sky; beyond the paradise illusion, the real sky, the outside sky, appeared: livid, leaden, yellow, heavy with sand and humidity, dark clouds, trails of polluted fog, swirled, in a vision from hell, and tentacles swept through cracks in the shattered dome, down into Elysium.

"Yes, the Dome has cracked, folks. This is a historic event," Alison said, and within seconds she was speckled with splotches of wet, yellow sand. "It looks like a sandstorm is brewing outside the dome – and it is coming inside, it is coming to get us. This is real weather, folks, take a look! Many of you – particularly the younger ones – will not have seen real weather." She turned to Ken. He was just getting up. The camera zoomed in. His forehead was still bleeding; a trickle went past his eye, and down his left cheek. Alison grinned: *That will show you to jump on me, buster! Serves you bloody right!*

"Yes, Alison, this is real weather." He wiped at the cut in his forehead and glanced at the midair prompters, which, having activated some backup channels, were once again sending in a stream of information. "Sensors say humidity has shot up. The temperature is rising – and fast. And we have just received a report, originating a few hours ago, before the peripheral sensors gave out, that a tornado, a sort of superstorm, mega tornado, or a collection or herd of super-tornadoes, is headed this way."

"With the dome down, Elysium City could be vulnerable to the storm, right, Ken?" Alison gave the poor fellow her most beatific smile. Rise above it all, buddy, or at least pretend to!

"Yes, Alison, we could be hit by the full force of the storm, and we could –"

WHAM!

The whole room was flooded by a huge white flash.

WHAM!

"My God," said Alison. She turned toward the window and a billowing flash that flooded, for just a second, the studio; it came from outside.

The light was so bright it etched her features in light, like a cartoon. The camera quickly adjusted, but the afterimage of a skeletal, cartoon-like Alison Jonas lingered for bemused viewers wherever and whoever they were, and in fact, the automatic net routers, sensing that something interesting and rate-worthy was happening had hooked up Alison and Ken to the whole wide world, their audiences were soaring, into hundreds of millions.

"My God," Alison said again, staring. The top of the Supreme Tower, which was the highest building in Elysium City, had exploded. In a great gusher of light, flames shot up from its top floors. For world viewers, it was framed – neatly and artistically by the floating automatic cameras, which exploited the broken glass of the studio window to give depth and composition, a truly spectacular picture; the camera algorithms were pleased with themselves.

The wind rose and howled in the studio; pieces of furniture swirled up and twirled around. A storm of paper and Update iPads flooded up to the ceiling, smashed against it, rained down, and whirled away. More glass shattered, fell inward, and swept outward – a tinkling hurricane, disappearing into the lead-colored atmosphere.

"Get down, Alison, get down, you are going to get blown away."

"Do you see that?"

"Oh, my God," Ken turned from the camera. "What the hell is that?"

"Oh, my God, I can't believe it." Alison, framed in whirling debris, stared at the Supreme Tower. The wind whirled around her, whipped her blond hair against her cheekbones, slapped wickedly at her jacket, soaked the skintight white silk T-shirt, morphing it to a wet rippled transparent naked-under-the-shower look.

Ken thought Alison looked inappropriately painfully beautiful. He hated her and loved her. She was his rival; she was twenty years younger than he, and she wanted to take over the program and consign him to the dust bin of has-beens, the pale, withered graveyard anonymity of hosts and personalities from times past, ghosts whose former fame was a mockery, losers cast out by time, inexorable time, and cast out too by famished cruel, ambitious youngsters, such as Alison. But Ken also wanted to protect her and maybe just maybe, if he could get up the courage, and put together the right stratagems, bed her. He couldn't resist staring at her. She would catch him at it, and he would put on an angry, stony-faced expression, and turn away. Sometimes at night, lying in bed, his arms folded under his neck, staring at the ripples of light on the ceiling, he thought about what it would be like to nibble her lips, to stare into her eyes, to pin her down on his floating silk-satin black billowing hydrofoil bed and …

"Oh, my God, I can't believe it." Alison seemed hypnotized by events outside the shattered windows. "Folks, are you seeing what I am seeing?"

Beyond the plate glass of the Volpe World Vision studios, the Dome was cracking even more; sparks of lightning were shooting off the great arching structure of the Dome. The Supreme Tower was burning, on many floors, at the top, but also at its midriff. "That's fire," she said, "that's smoke."

"Yes, that's fire," Ken said, "real fire. Folks, it seems impossible, but – and I don't know how to say this – but the Supreme Tower is on fire."

"And the Dome is collapsing." Alison turned to the camera and then indicated the sky above – even under the Dome, it had turned blotchy, a yellowish, leaden gray. Lightning bounced back and forth and rippled along the underside of the Dome. Great blue forks of electricity hit the tall buildings and ricocheted from spire and peak to spire and peak.

Ken turned toward the camera. "Well, folks, I hate to admit it, but we are not sure what is really happening now, and how all these events are related to each other, but it seems that something is radical is happening. Like the end of the world and …"

"Like the end of *our* world …" Alison said, thinking: *Am I really saying this?*

The lights flickered and went out.

"What the..?" Alison stared at the camera. Its little red light blinked off. "What the …" The camera had gone dead!

Oh, My, God! The camera had gone dead!

Alison was consumed with pure horror, absolute angst. If the cameras went off, she would cease to exist. She would be nobody, just flesh and blood, just a lonely self-made girl, a bundle of skin and bones and blood vessels and intestines and excrement and urine and gray matter, who had escaped the wasteland of Oregon and prolonged sweaty, violent incest she had been forced to endure with Daddy – good-looking, charming, absolutely corrupt Daddy – and in the Outer Burbs and Edge of the Dead Lands, just a nobody, a loser, one of the multitude of losers, just a former Cosmos, a non-Cosmos, just a humanoid bio-bag, skin containing organs and excrement – shit and piss and sweat – and a spinal cord and a brain, nothing more. Her voice would be silenced. Nobody would see her face. She would fade into pallor and wrinkled non-cosmetic, non-existence. She would be lost, forever lost. She would wither away and disappear. That's what happened to losers; they disappeared. Losers were nobodies; they were the walking dead who didn't know they were dead, empty dried-up clichés who –

Volpe Tower backup second-line generators immediately took over.

The cameras blinked back on. They were all automatic, as were the program editors, all were controlled by Artificial Intelligence, a sub-branch of the Mind, but with an automatic cut-off backup power supply, and so the studio could operate independently of the Mind, and isolate itself, automatically, from the Mind. Ken and Alison were alone in the studio, and in fact, they were probably the only human beings on the 53rd floor of the Volpe Building, and on the two or three floors above and below that.

Alison sighed and pushing her hair, now wet from the damp wind, away from her face spoke to the camera: "Our power just went off, folks, we don't know about yours, if you can communicate, you have our Tweet line, our mail address or any of our feeds, let us know."

"Something absolutely extraordinary is happening." Ken was still wiping that the blood flowing from his hairline.

"But, Ken, this is strange …"

Ken looked at her, waiting. "Yes?"

"This is strange," Alison hesitated, not knowing whether she should dare, and then she decided she would dare, because, in fact, it was true, the world seemed to be coming to an end. "It's strange, Ken, that the authorities have not so far reacted."

Ken blinked. She had called the Supreme Powers, the Leader, the President, *Hail, All Hail, All Hail,* into question, even by merely remarking upon their absence. Well, if she was going to die, he would die with her. "Yes, it is strange, Alison."

"I mean, usually, by this time, there would be instructions."

"Yes. And there would be a press release."

"Could it be, Ken, could it be that the authorities, that the Supreme Council, do not know what is happening?"

"Well, speaking of that, Alison, here is a news flash from AP: It says, 'The World Mind and Cloud is under attack.'"

"Oh, my God!"

"That is what we have been told."

"That would explain the werewolf that ate Professor Park."

"Yes, it might, on the other hand …"

"Many of the Mind's peripherals have been reported destroyed or at least inactive, even within Elysium City. So the flash says."

"Unbelievable!"

"Oh, yes, and the President-Leader's office has refused to comment. A spokesperson merely said that everything is under control, that the President-Leader is working to resolve the crisis."

"Hail, Hail, All Hail!" Ken couldn't help himself.

Alison gave him a look.

She glanced at a new Info-feed: "Out in the Badlands and desert more untoward things have apparently been happening."

"Yes, unconfirmed reports say that hybrids have escaped from holding camps."

"My God, this is getting more and more interesting. This is new, isn't it?"

"Yes, hybrids were reported dead; in fact, it has been claimed, recently, that hybrids were a myth, and mind-guidelines laid down by the Department of Correct Thought – *hail, hail, all hail* – have indicated that hybrids are not to be mentioned or thought about or mused upon; but now …"

"But now ..?"

"The mythical non-existent hybrids are apparently on the loose, and once again threaten the survival of the human race."

"Could this be an invasion, Ken?"

"An invasion, you mean from outer space."

"Well, the hybrids are half-alien, aren't they?"

"Yes, if I remember correctly, the hybrids themselves, one Claire V Jacobs said that –"

"*The* Claire V Jacobs, I mean, she's dead, isn't she?"

"So they say, but delving back into my memory bank, I can tell you that she was, until, oh a decade or more ago, a famous model and capitalist, the CVJ line of products, and she revealed on a radio talk-show that she was a hybrid and she confessed to being half-alien … so …"

"She even morphed for the cams, it says here, to demonstrate how hybrids are sort of reptile things disguised as humans …"

"Well, I suppose that was quite brave, really …"

"We have calls from our viewers …"

"Yes, we have a caller here from, ah, the Burbs, outer Burbs, south of Jersey City. Yes, sir, how are you today?"

"Them high-birds they is everywhere. Them fuckin' high-bird reptile high-tech buggers and sodomites is not to be trusted one friggin' whit, it's a plot to take away our guns an' our liberty founded in the Constitution ..."

"Hybrids," said Alison, "It's hybrids, not high-birds, for Christ's sake. Didn't you go to elementary indoctrination school? How illiterate can ..."

"You don't have to get nasty, girly."

"I'm sorry, I truly am," Alison was tempted to roll her eyes, but she didn't.

"Now, girly, I mean, lady, just because you'z privileged and uppity and a nouveau and a Cosmos Lotus Land Latte Slurper, doesn't give you no right, no right at all, to denigrate my gun, nor take away my gun and my constitution, nor piss with my mind, 'cause my mind's my own, and my very own constitution of this here United States of America says there's no damned place for high-birds in these United States of America."

"The Constitution of the United States said nothing about hybrids. In any case, the Constitution – or what was left of it – was suspended fourteen years ago, sir, and the United States ceased to exist forty years earlier, are you suggesting, sir, that we return to ...?"

"I ain't suggestin nothin, girly. I never do. I ain't the suggestin kind. I'm just sayin we gotta shoot all them high-birds. You see a high-bird, you shoot it, that's all I'm sayin, I'm not suggestin, I'm sayin. High-birds is behind blackouts and outages and werewolves and such-like occurrences like the hairy one that ate that Professor fella with them glasses and that beard thing. If you see a mischief, look for a high-bird! Them high-birds is behind every single dang thing that's wrong with this country."

"Well, thank you," said Alison, flipping the neo-fascist backwoods libertarian gun-obsessed Burbite idiot off, "that was truly enlightening, sir. Thank you, sir!"

"We have another call," said Ken, with a wide smile. Seeing Alison so riled up was, ah, fun, ah, stimulating! It was clear she was a liberal and an elite snob, which made it even better.

"Sir, Madam, I would like to point out to you that the threat posed by the hybrids is indeed serious as the preceding gentleman was trying to point out in his, unfortunately, hayseed hillbilly Burbite, Bible-thumping, gun-toting illiterate way. Since the decline of organized religion and belief in the God of our Fathers and in the Infallibility of Various Pontifical and Other Sacred Authorities there has been a lamentable falling off of standards – skin-shorts and tattoos among Subs are just one example of spreading moral turpitude – and a rise of amoral relativism where one is not permitted to name evil to its face and make clear moral judgments. In this connection, it is well-established and well-documented that the hybrids have a plot to take over the earth. This is decisively proven by the Secret Hybrid Protocols –"

"Hold it right there," said Alison.

"Yes," said Ken, "There are doubts about the authenticity –"

Alison broke in: "The so-called Hybrid Protocols have been shown to be a forgery, a forgery designed to foment racism and prejudice and …" Alison was turning red in the face; she was furious. These ignorant clowns!

Ken smiled his most soothing smile, "For those of you are too young to remember, our listener was referring to the famous case of the Hybrid Protocols, an apparent Hybrid Master Plan to subdue the human race, which was revealed just fifteen years ago. But most experts say that the Protocol is a fake, created by the secret service, known as the Kremlin Gremlins, of the Eastern Russian Tsarist Islamic Republic and the Neo-Orthodox Russian Church, and their Cyber Hacker Teams, working together in the name of Ecumenical Obscurantism."

"But this fake was used to whip up anti-hybrid hysteria, wasn't it," said Alison, calming somewhat. She hated lies, she hated injustice, and she had a sneaking admiration for hybrids; they were, in truth, probably all dead now, but she had read in underground off-line samizdat publications some of the real lives of real hybrids, such as Sabrina Jacobs, and Claire V Jacobs and, they were models of strong female leadership and …

"Absolutely," Ken was saying, "The false Protocols were used to whip up anti-hybrid and anti-SIN hysteria too, making anybody or anything that was a bit different seem like a possible threat."

"It produced mass paranoia, in fact." Alison realized that they were now venturing far into dangerous territory; they were talking opening of subjects which were absolutely banned until, until, oh, until about ten minutes ago.

"Yes, that ended in violence, of course. The President-Leader himself said three years ago in a speech at the Cosmos Security Institute that the Protocols were definitely a fake and that the hybrids were not intent on taking over the world: on this point, other members of the, ah, Government, have dared contradict the President-Leader, which is unusual, and the speech has not been widely distributed."

"The President-Leader is a charitable man," said Alison, grudgingly.

"Yes, he is a seeker after the truth."

"Hail, Hail, All Hail!" Alison sighed.

"Hail, Hail, All Hail!" Ken shouted.

"And so, the hybrids …"

"Yes," Ken took up the torch, "the hybrids – until they became non-existent non-beings and unthinkable and unmentionable – were considered, after the false Protocols were released to stir up hatred – a sort of fifth column. They have been described as spies and alien agents; they were, in this story, the advance wave of alien invaders from outer space determined to conquer and exploit this fine planet of ours."

"Maybe fine planet is putting a bit of a gloss on it, Ken!"

"You are right, Alison, I'm afraid we've ruined this fine planet of ours; it is no longer fine." Ken was wondering at himself; he was saying things he would not have dared say just a few minutes ago, but now he upped the ante, if he were going to commit suicide he might as well go the whole way, "We have gone a very long way toward making our once fine planet unpleasant and unliveable – unliveable even for us Cosmos, protected – well, we thought we were protected – in our Domed Cities."

The wind rose suddenly, an instant hurricane, swirling, whirling, smashing its way across the studio.

WHAM!

The wind picked Alison up, and slammed her against the south side glass wall that still remained intact. The glass began to crack, the outward-bound pressure was immense.

Alison was pinned, crucified, spread-eagled – flattened against the cracking, spiderweb-like, crinkling, splintering wall of glass.

The wind picked up tables, chairs, pieces of papers, one of the cameras, and swept them out the shattered opening into the sky, which was now dark, thunderous, alive with flashes of lightning, and a dark, steel-colored swirl of cloud, a tornado, a march of tornadoes, flashing past.

"My God, folks," Ken said, as he struggled toward Alison, "Tornadoes, folks, Tornadoes in Elysium City!"

An automatic camera, floating on air and valiantly fighting the wind, followed Ken's every move. Another camera, rooted on a studio wall, zoomed in on Alison, sensing this was a dramatic story element, showing her pinned flat against the glass, up high, her feet hanging at least two meters above the floor.

The AI editor automatically cut the images to heighten the drama: the hosts might be about to die, one host striving through a hurricane-like wind to reach the other – the crucified damsel in distress theme, this was most interesting! The viewers will be enthralled, ratings will soar, said the editing algorithm.

Ken got to Alison.

She was again grabbed by the wind.

Ken seized her ankle as she flew past him and was swept out the window.

The wind dropped.

Ken held on.

Alison hung over the void. Ken was almost dragged out the window behind her, but he grabbed a steel column with one hand, and he held onto Alison's ankle with the other.

"Let me go, you bastard, let me die!" she shouted. The wind rose again. He could barely hear her voice, lost in the thunderous waves of air.

"I am not going to let you die!"

"You hate me, you jealous son of a bitch."

"Yes, I hate you, you poisonous bitch – and I love you ..."

"What the fuck are you talking about?" She was by now hanging upside down, her voice muffled, her skirt flapped down, wildly rippling, over her breasts. She was, it became evident, wearing G-string panther panties. She clawed desperately at the metal facing of the Volpe building, but it was all smooth glass and steel. Her fingernails scraped on glass, marble facing, stainless steel, and got no grip. Blood raced to her head. She could see straight down, 53 stories. Far below her, were walkways, and part of the midtown transport hub. Part of her wanted to fly away, to fly and plummet straight down.

"I love you because you hate me, and I don't care if you hate me, and you are the most beautiful woman I have ever seen!" Ken screamed it, still holding on desperately to her ankle. He looked up, another tornado, a whirling column of dark air, debris, rain, and sand, was headed directly toward the Volpe Building. If he didn't get Alison up in the next few seconds, they would both die. They would probably both die anyway.

The cameras zoomed in, a close-up on Ken's hand gripping Alison's ankle, a close-up of Alison's leg and G-string and on her flapping, upside-down, inside-out skirt, then a close-up of Ken, sweating, bug-eyed, straining to save the woman, and the editing algorithm ordered improved sound, so filters lowered the background chaos noise – wind thundering, lightning bolts cracking, glass shattering, furniture, and paper swirling – and concentrated on the amorous dialog which, the editing algorithms sensed, rightly, were prime human drama, fit for more than family consumption.

"I love you because I hate you, you bitch!"

"You don't love me you pompous ass, you love yourself!"

"I cannot live without you, Alison!"

"I want to die! Let me go!"

Ken was wedged against the steel column and pushing with all his might to hold on – not to slip, not to let Alison fall to her doom.

If he were pulled to his doom with her – well, so be it! But he was damned well not going to let go!

The wind rose; lightning flashed; rain slashed down; flying waves of sand smashed into Ken, almost blinding him, and, up above, the dome looked like a flashing strobe-lit birdcage, bits and pieces, vast arched ribs …

It was the end of the world.

Alison dangled, her foot kicking against the steel and glass façade of the Volpe Tower. She glanced below her. Black dots, people like ants, scurrying.

It was a long way down.

CHAPTER 2 – RESURRECTION

"Rise up, Rise up, you dead! Rise up and conquer the living!"

Throughout the Burbs, the Word had spread, as fiery and infectious as Holy Gospel; across the ruins of the Great Republic, the Word of the Boy propagated like wildfire. Skeletal figures, some crawling with maggots, some desiccated and mummified to the consistency of cracked burnish dried shoe leather, some half-fresh as if still alive, slabs of raw or half-rotten meat, spilling maggots and oozing pus, pushed out from tombs and graves, and hammered at the steel gates in mausoleums, and banged at the steel doors of morgues or rose up from gurneys and attacked with tooth and claw and saw and scalpel and hammer any living humans that came within their reach.

"Rise up you dead! Rise up and conquer the living!"

"Hallelujah!"

"For mine is the Kingdom of Death!"

"Hallelujah!"

"Empty the graveyards! Let the dead rise, mossy and rotten, out of the depths." The Boy's voice echoed everywhere the dead were gathered.

"Hallelujah!"

"Death to the living, death to Burbites, death to Subs, death to Cosmos, death, unending and eternal death, onto them all!"

"Hallelujah!"

There were few dead to be roused from their sleep in the Domed City of Elysium because, for reasons of hygiene and economy, all corpses were immediately recycled into usable raw material or cremated.

But out in the Burbs, the situation was different.

In one old abandoned graveyard in the decaying Burbs of Elysium, next to a disused private airport with its desolate crumbling runways, decaying control towers, and rotting turboprops, Laura Levitt, who had been dead for ten years, heard the call.

What the hell was that voice, and what did it want of her?

The Boy, who the hell was he?

But His Call was irresistible!

She had to obey.

With bony hands, and skeletal arms, Laura pushed aside the rotten pseudo-synthetic plywood of her coffin and began to claw her way toward the light.

It was not easy, even though the earth had over the decade been blasted away by hurricane-force winds and torrential downpours, and what earth remained to keep Laura from the sun and moon and starlight had been turned to flimsy dust by sizzling heat and a pitiless sun.

The cheap synthetic wood coffin was already rotten. Through cracks and crevices, leaves had gotten inside, and turned to fermented brown mulch, and then dissolved to aromatic dust, redolent of ancient crisp nights in late autumn in a dead civilization in decades long gone by.

Laura Levitt knew she was dead. She was horrified at the idea of being resurrected, pissed off might be a better term, but the voice was imperious, and the impulse to get out of the box was overpowering, it was, verily, like a divine command, the Command of the Boy, a voice out of clouds and thunderbolts, a voice rising up from the depths of the earth, a voice seeping out of the rotten wood, and so, in spite of herself, her skeletal fingers and arms pushed upwards, cracking the rotten coffin, and she clawed her way through the sand, and crawled out of the hole in the ground, shedding much of the torn and disintegrating blouse and jeans she had been buried in. The rotting leather belt with the brass buckle dangled from one hipbone; being dead, she had lost a lot of weight, her waist, now, was really minuscule.

With empty orbs where her eyes had been, Laura crouched on the edge of the grave and noted that, though it was day, early morning perhaps, the sky above was a livid leaden color, like a vast cosmic bruise; it was blood red at the horizon, as if the sun were already setting; flashes of lightning forked down over the distant luminous dome of Elysium City.

Waves of thunder rolled in, as if preparing for the granddaddy of all storms. When she stood up and looked down at herself, Laura realized that she was indeed skeletal, with most of her tobacco-colored ribs and one tobacco-colored hipbone showing. What was left of her flesh had dried to the consistency of tough dark brown leather, and that she was clothed mostly in what looked like furry moss or lichen. She fingered the belt buckle, with its embossed image of the President-Leader; it seemed to be one of the few things left of her old, living self, of her old passions.

She did wonder, in truth, how she could see out of what she knew must be empty eye sockets because she seemed to have a recollection that her eyes – one of her most beautiful features – had been among the first to go, eaten by maggots.

The softer the tissue, the more vulnerable it is, which was logical, she supposed. She probed one socket with a skeletal finger – yes, indeed, it was an empty socket, and she really didn't have much of a nose left either – and just a few threads of hair on her skull.

The 6mm stray bullet, fired by a four-year-old, drugged-out, baby gangster, meth addict called Trevor Robertson and that had put an end to Laura Levitt's life, slipped out between her ribs and was falling to the ground when she caught it neatly between bony thumb and forefinger.

Tilting her skull, she contemplated the slightly flattened and twisted piece of metal with interest, thinking that, if she were still alive, she might have added it to her collection of oddities. When she was a living flesh-and-blood person, albeit a Burbite, she had collected things: pebbles, bullets, Barbie dolls, dead gadgets, do-dads, and knickknacks.

The collection was a consolation somehow: it consisted of things you could touch, things you could love. But all of that was gone. Now she was dead; she was half-skeleton, half-mummy; she was not even a ghost. She let the bullet drop, and it fell, making a miniature muddy thud when it hit the sodden ground.

Lighting flashed.

Thunder rolled.

Lead-colored billowing clouds lowered down over the landscape of ruined buildings, black silhouettes of smokestacks, warehouses, and fuel tanks, as if the very heavens, the very clouds wanted to lick the soil.

She tried to speak: What the hell is happening?

But her tongue was a flat dried stick, a sort of pallet, behind her teeth, useless for talking; besides, the vocal cords would have long withered away. *Click, click, click!* Well, then, she still had teeth, most of her teeth; dentistry was not big in the Burbs, and hadn't been for generations, but she was naturally very healthy, and had solid teeth and gums.

She felt that she was obliged – by orders of the voice coming from the sky

– to kill any humans that she might come across, though she didn't like the idea, but the compulsion was violent and absolute, like the erotic homicidal urge or thirst she imagined those old-time serial killers must have felt when they went on a rampage, killing and mutilating, perhaps even when they didn't want to, perhaps even when their better self was struggling against it; and she wondered how she was having any thoughts or willpower at all, since her brain must have long ago dissolved and withered away into dust.

It was a mystery.

She stumbled along on her skeletal once-shapely legs, empty-eyed, like a puppet on a string with a drunk puppet master pulling jerkily at the puppet operating-cross, and she realized that, though she was in a manner of speaking thinking, she would not be able to communicate any of her thoughts through her puppet-like skeletal cadaver, with a dried pallet for a tongue, so she would not be able to apologize to any of her victims – the humans she bit or punched or tore apart – which was a real pisser, because, when she had been alive, Laura Levitt had been a very polite person, and considerate, even excessively so, some people said, and quite lovely really, a physical gem and true beauty, worthy even of being a Cosmos, far from what she was now, alas.

Now, what was this? Other people were pushing up out of the graveyard, one of the few real graveyards left, since cremation had become almost obligatory, and –

Oh, one of the rising dead was a child.

Laura had no intention of killing a child – who was already dead in any case, so she decided to take it under her wing.

The child turned its empty sockets toward her and reached out its stick-like arms. Laura sighed: all that was left of the living child was a cartoon, a sketch.

Laura knelt and enfolded it in her papery mummified embrace.

It made a muffled strange sound, like a strangled cry, and moved its jaw up and down. If it could have shed tears, Laura felt, it would have.

Through the murky thickening Burbite air, other skeletal and mummified bodies were moving; they formed up and marched, as if they had a common purpose and knew where they were going.

Laura stood up, and holding the child's skeletal hand, she joined the procession of mummified bodies, skeletons, and rotting corpses. Some were in suits, others in fine dresses, most, like Laura, were naked – or almost naked. They were heading toward the nearest Burb, which was already in flames, and gunshots could be heard through the smoky and fiery dawn.

The end of the world had begun.

Perhaps this was the Rapture Lauren had once heard a wild-eyed preacher rave about. The Coming of the Boy must signal the end of the world. This, for Laura, was not a particularly nice idea. Even dead, she rather liked the world and all its irredeemable splendor and beauty. She would prefer the world to continue on its merry way, even without her.

More gunshots sounded.

Perhaps the living, the humans, the Burbites and Subs and Cosmos, were putting up a fight.

It was somehow comforting to be dead.

In the same Burb, not too far away from the cemetery, a bearded hulk of a man who went by the name of Norman C. Schleifer was carefully packing his automatic weapons – a Glock 20 and an AK-47, a true museum piece, and a collapsible retro antique M-16 – into a black canvas backpack; he slipped his stiletto knife, his machete, and three surgical scalpels into their holsters; and he slipped three packages of seal-it plastic bags into his military vest pocket.

Dawn had broken over the Burb an hour ago, a sickly weird fuck-up of a dawn, but dawn just the same.

Today was the day of action.

Today would transform Norman C. Schleifer from a totally unknown Burbite loser into a goddamn myth, a man for all eternity, so thought Norm.

The night before, Norman had been tossing and turning in his sordid and soiled solitary camp cot when he had a vision which finally provided him with his life's mission; and now he was fitting up for the deed that would make him a hero.

About 2 am maybe, he had been dreaming.

In the dream it was night; the Burbs were on fire; the whole of the sky shone red and amber, walls of smoke engulfed everything; the distant Dome of Elysium glowed gently, trembling in the waves of rising heat. There was something particularly ominous about the whole picture. But it was difficult to say exactly what. Norm started awake; he sat up, covered in sweat, sticky, glutinous sweat.

It was impossible to sleep; the temperature out in the Elysium Burbs – the other side of the murky Hudson from the Dome in a place once called Hoboken – was above 110 degrees F, humidity about 80 degrees; the air was yellow and sticky with sand from the Dead Lands and the Central Desert;

Norm was a Burbite without rights and without money, so he didn't have air-conditioning.

Well, nobody in the Burbs did.

Norman shook his filthy body, rolled off the soiled, wrinkled camp cot, and stood up. He scratched his baggy, piss-stained, G-string crotch-bag, sighed with relief, and stepped over to the broken floor-to-ceiling window. He hesitated a moment, scanning for night-snipers – they liked to hunt and shoot people at random – and, sensing no imminent threats, Norm stepped through the window out onto the rickety third story metal porch; he rubbed his eyes and looked up at the sky; it was really weird, streaked with yellow; no stars were visible, and the moon was a sullen jaundice-colored smudge.

There were shots and short bursts from an automatic weapon not too far away; one edge of the western sky, above the rooftops, was vaguely red and yellow from fires where looting and only god knew what nocturnal mayhem was going on. Maybe it was mischief stirred up by those end-of-the-world devils from out west. Info-Flow had spoken about winged monsters and religious fanatics, and Centurions getting killed and people burnt at the stake or crucified on the cross out in the Dead Lands. Crazy stuff! Cosmos Centurions had never been defeated – *never*!

Norm shifted his gaze eastwards: the luminous Dome of Elysium floated invulnerable and untouched, over a large swath of Manhattan, the Hudson and the old East River, a sheltered paradise for those who lived there, but oh so distant from the sweltering Multicolored Trash Burbs; it was like looking at a fucking alien planet – or maybe like being in lost down in Hell and staring up at Heaven itself – so close, yet so far.

A sudden hot gust slapped Norman in the face and filled his thick bushy beard with wet, sticky sand and drops of watery desert dirt; it felt like the foretaste of a tornado. He blinked away the irritation and brushed an annoyed hand at the beard, and then he squinted up toward the deadlight moon, a smear, even fainter now, even sicker than usual.

"Storm coming," Norm muttered.

Norm was thirty-four years old; but with his bushy unkempt beard, wild eyes, and shoulder-length hair, hirsute chest, and minuscule G-string, he looked like a 50-year-old, next-to-naked Biblical prophet, or maybe an old-style, beggar-bowl Hindu mystic on his last naked begging-bowl pilgrimage cross-country along the dusty, drought-plagued roads toward eternity.

Norm frowned; he wanted to kill somebody. Anybody would do. Weather like this, prickly and sweaty – waiting for the storm – made him antsy.

He stepped over the chipped old windowsill and back into his one-room refuge, a sort of improvised living pod in what used to be called a warehouse, now a tenement warren of nests for Burbite outcasts.

He stared in disgust and foreboding at his rumpled cot, the soiled and sweaty home of and theater for all his sordid yearnings and obscene Technicolor cravings; it was just visible in the sweltering gloom, "Trouble coming! Probably tornado or hurricane, too," he scratched himself.

This is the fucking end of the world …

The weather was all fucked up; the climate was a sick fucking puppy.

The culprit was homo fucking sapiens, so-called.

Norm snorted in disgust. He'd show homo fucking sapiens!

He sat down heavily on the edge of the cot, picked up a matchbox, extracted a match – they were valuable and rare – and struck it. His hand trembled as he held the tiny flame to his bedside candle.

"Okay," he sighed, "Stay lit, little light."

Norm always thought each time a little flame was lit that he was re-enacting the discovery of fire, the magic moment, one of the magic moments, that set humanity on its long quest to mastery of the earth– and to final self-inflicted destruction and doom. He grunted. Maybe fire was original sin; maybe the gods were right to screw with that guy Prometheus who gave man fire, making man god-like – so the gods chained Prometheus naked to a rock to have his liver eaten out, over and over again, for all eternity, by a big fucking bird, over and over.

Nice image!

Or maybe it was knowledge that fucked it all up.

After all, mastery of fire was a form of knowledge.

So when Adam and Eve ate the apple of knowledge God kicked them out of Paradise, since with knowledge they were in danger of becoming like God, and God was a Jealous God, cantankerous old geezer, he must have been, that God of theirs, not wanting any fucking competition up there in Heaven.

Those old gods were fucking jealous! If you tried to break into the god business, they screwed you good and proper!

But probably they were right.

Humans were not meant to be gods.

Norm picked up a ragged pamphlet a guy had handed him down at the

Corner Quick Food Pod and that he'd left beside the bed. "The End of Days," it said, and it prophesized the end of Time which it said was imminent because God had lost patience with the human race; God was preparing the Second Coming; God was gearing up for Armageddon, the final battle between the Anti-Christ and the returning Messiah, and it would be messy.

Norm fingered the dog-eared pages. "You are so right, buddy, you are so fucking right. We have fucked it up; we have royally fucked it up, we've created monsters, we've fucked the climate, we've fucked the oceans, we torture animals, we've destroyed a gazillion species …" The old anger, the anger of impotence surged up, with the sweat, oozing from all his pores; impotence and anger; they almost overpowered Norman, made his head spin.

He lowered his head and scratched at his beard, his big unruly wild-man-cum-Biblical prophet beard, and filthy with saliva, old breadcrumbs, coffee stains, and shreds of synthetic tuna.

Once, when young, and even clean-shaven, he'd thought he could make a difference, become a Cosmos, invent something, change the world, for the better, a luminous beautiful serene technological future. Now he knew he would die and rot in filth and maggots and nakedness, just like all the others, not having made any difference at all. No one would ever know or care that he had lived. *Out, out, brief candle!*

Ashes to ashes, dust to dust!

He put down the pamphlet and laid his hand on the old faithful antique Glock G 20, his own personal bedside insurance policy, freedom's guarantee. A man's gun is his last refuge, his redoubt, his proof that he is truly a man; that he can defend his freedom and fight for what is rightly his.

Other weapons were stacked in the cupboard.

Two or three times, Norman had had to use them.

Once, he had saved Angela Balzac, the pretty black girl – a real hot dish – on the first floor, from a gang of punks, drugged-out marauding rapists, who'd smashed down the front door, bashed in windows, and who'd climbed into her flat, and she had screamed.

And good old Norman C Schleifer was down there in two seconds flat.

Not that Angel, the sharp-featured little snot, was grateful. "Thanks, Norm," she said, "But you know, Norm, this doesn't mean we are friends; I'm sorry, but you are fucking weird, I mean beyond weird!"

Made him feel fucking sweaty, her talking to him like that.

He would have liked to possess her, of course, taken her, made her his own personal Jezebel, made her his own, his slave, made her perform name-less abominations, things that he was sure only he, in his nocturnal imagin-ings, had had the courage to imagine. If you are to be truly good, you had to imagine absolute evil in all its forms – Is this not so, brother, is this not so, sister?

Evil equals Good, in the end. Now, that was theology!

Another time he helped fend off a bike gang when they were intent on hitting the Corner Quick Food down at the end of what passed for a street, no trees, fractured, half-melted asphalt, piles of garbage, and half the build-ings burned-out shells, but still, it was home: oh, but that was real fun, nailed three of the hillbilly biker buggers flat – dead as dead could be!

The shots just rattled off: Pam, wham. Pam, wham!

You gotta be your own justice, your own police!

The Cosmos police and Cosmos Centurions didn't give a fuck what hap-pened out here in the Burbs. This was a jungle, that was their attitude, "Better if they kill each other," he'd even heard one Cosmos officer say: "Burbites are hardly human, and they serve no purpose, no purpose whatsoever."

"Fuck, I'll show them purpose!"

And it shall clothe me in glory!

Fifteen seconds of fame, that was every human's birthright!

Even Burbite lowlifes and losers and Trash Folk sometimes hit the head-line ticker! Even the Leader-President might hear of this one!

Norman was often kept awake at night by a burning sense of injustice; humans, he felt, had despoiled the planet; humans were the worst vermin to infest the earth, and Cosmos were the worst kind of humans; what irked him more than almost anything – more than the ruined, lifeless, acidic oceans, more than the skeletal and dead coral reefs, more than the sweltering human-caused violence of the climate, more than the spreading deserts and periodic super floods, more than great chasm that had opened up between the rich Cosmos and all the rest of the poor slobs, Subs and Burbites and Proles and Outlanders; no, what irked Norman most was the biotechnology that had distorted and destroyed God's work and created monsters, animal and human mutants, and what irked him even more than that was the torture of animals, the use of our fellow fucking creatures for the most cruel and deadly of experiments.

Norman imagined himself, sometimes, as an avenging angel.

Fuck this!

Somehow the dream and then the vision of Elysium from out there on the porch had left him super irritated and super antsy.

Fuck this!

So about fifteen minutes after his little nocturnal excursion out onto the balcony, he blew out the candle and lay down on his back on top of the one sheet, in his string-crotch bag, which he hadn't changed in two weeks. No need to. He had nobody to love, and nobody to impress. He was free to fart when he liked, sweat as he could, and stink the whole place up: Nobody was there to nag at him! In any case, filth was sacred; filth was part of nature.

Fuck this! Norman must have dozed off mumbling to himself about the fucking dream of the bloody, smoke-streaked dawn, and scratching himself absent-mindedly because the next thing he remembered was there was a guy sitting on the wooden chair – which he must have pulled over – a guy sitting in the wooden chair and right next to the cot, a guy right there – next to Norm!

Norman's first instinct when he opened his eyes and felt the presence before he saw it, and then saw the shadow, was to reach for the Glock because, somehow, he knew there was a guy there before he even realized it was a guy.

"Don't worry, Norman," the voice said, "I am a friend."

"What the fuck are you doing in my room?"

The guy lit a match and held it up so Norm could see his face, and the face was handsome in a way that only movie star zombies or vampires are handsome. He had fine, sensitive features, chalk-white skin, dark eyebrows, and very dark eyes. His lips were so finely sculpted, and his teeth were so perfect it looked like he might be a very beautiful and slender girl or young woman got up to look like an early 19th Century gentleman, what with the high-collared jacket, the frilly lace-like shirt, and the loose string tie. The guy's eyes were really something, as if lined by kohl, with long eyelashes, really sensitive glossy wet eyes, like a girl or woman's eyes. His jet-black hair was long and oiled and combed straight back from his forehead. You could almost fall in love … There was a funny thing too: The match, held between the guy's fingers, just kept burning bright; it didn't burn down, and it didn't flutter out.

"I've seen you someplace," Norman said, thinking of dozens of movies he'd seen, old flicks that floated on walls or on the air, in summer nights when the heat was too heavy to even pretend to sleep, images of flashy guys with black capes, guys who lived in gloomy old castles in old times in Transylvania or

God only knew where, guys who rose up out of coffins, guys who kidnapped the beautiful girl who was too curious or lustful for her own good.

"Yes, Norman, I imagine you have seen me," the man smiled, "You see, Norman, I am everywhere all the time and though I am usually absent myself and usually invisible, residing as I do in a quite different universe, my avatars and incarnations are always here, always among you. There are also copycats, which is flattering in a minor way, I suppose."

"Ah," said Norman, thinking he didn't understand a fucking word this slick spooky gent from the past had said. Well, at least the guy didn't have a knife, and he didn't have a gun, not visibly anyway. "So, what do you want?"

"I have come, Norman C Schleifer! I, the Boy, have come to tell you that the moment is finally here, when you are to take action, to unsheathe your sword and lance, to mount your gallant steed, to free the unjustly imprisoned animals, to free those poor little monkeys, to free the snakes, to free the turtle doves ..."

"What animals, what monkeys, what snakes ...?" Norman said in as naïve a voice as he could muster. He suddenly suspected that this guy was a plant and trap and he was trying to get Norman to slip up and fess up; somehow this clown or his people had penetrated Norman's deepest thoughts, and his secret and unspoken revolutionary plan. Well, Norm was not going to fall into any trap. He was not going to mention the Bio-Futures Lab he had been dreaming of breaking into for, well, for years now. That was his little secret; that was his little wet dream, and he'd never shared it, not even with dreamy, chocolate, slippery, beautiful Angela Balzac downstairs.

Anyway, she would have told him he was nuts and to piss off.

The guy raised his hand, looked briefly at his white shirt cuff that showed from below his jacket sleeve, straightened the cuff with a little shrug of the wrist, and said, "Norman, I am not a spy, and I am not interested in your secrets. I just want to tell you that the place you are interested in – the animal prison – will have no electronic security tomorrow morning from about 10 o'clock and for the rest of the day, up to about four o'clock."

"No security?" Norman perked up. Human guards and guard dogs he could handle, but all that fancy electronic stuff freaked him out. It had been the one thing that had kept him from ... accomplishing his sacred mission ...

"You sure about that?"

"I am absolutely certain, Norman."

"Well ..."

"My information is impeccable."

"Impeccable, well, if you say so, I mean …"

The guy stood up.

"This is the moment, Norm," he said.

"Yeah, I guess …"

"This is the sacred call, Norm, this is the clarion; this is the trumpet."

"Yeah, sure, but …"

"Chance of a lifetime, Norm, it's now or never; a man either is a man or he is a mouse; time and tide wait on no man; there is a tide in the affairs of men, Norm, and, if not seized at the flood …" the guy laid his hand on Norm's head, and Norm felt warmth radiate through his skull, and he felt a new sense of clarity, as if the world had suddenly become a very simple place. "Purity is to desire and will only one thing and one thing only," said the man, "Now you are one of the anointed ones, Norm, you are chosen."

"Yeah, yeah, I'm your man," Norman mumbled, feeling an inner thrill, almost a hard-on.

"Then it will be done," the guy removed his hand from Norm's head and picked up the chair and put it back in its rightful place, "My will shall be done, is that right, then, eh, Norm?"

"Yeah, it will be done, yeah."

The guy was gone.

He was just gone – vaporized, vanished.

Like there was an extra darkness in the air, and then there was nothing.

How he did it, well, Norm had no idea. One instant, the guy was there; then, he was gone. He must have been a fucking angel. Yes, he was an angel. And he had told Norman what Norman needed to know. Now, Norman could put his stamp on history. Now, Norman might finally get that mention on the evening Info-Flow, make a statement, transmit the message. This Boy fellow had given Norm the key! Now, Norm could be pure of spirit and single in purpose.

To be is to will to be!

The moment had come to free the animals from their agony, from the evil clutches of the Bio-Futures Lab.

"Now," Norm said out loud, "Now, I have a destiny."

He glanced at his wrist. It was three in the morning. He still had time for a short snooze, then …

Then he would do it.

He could hardly wait for dawn.

So now, with dawn's early light breaking over the east coast of what had once been the not-so-much-lamented Great Republic, Norm was setting off on his own little crusade; it had been on his mind for years, a little project and a target – and, yes, it might even get him a blip on the Info-Flow.

Here he was, fully equipped with all the tools he needed, out here on the street in the murky morning air, temperature soaring, the smell of burning rubber hanging in the haze, and he was headed toward Bio-Futures and his destiny.

He spotted a strange figure, and sort of wondered about it; a woman who looked like a fucking skeleton, lurching along and holding a skeleton-like stick-cartoon kid by the hand; and other skeleton-like characters were jerking along behind them.

People were turning into zombies, no question ...

All the fucking chemicals in the air, that's the stuff to blame, and diet, now diet was another thing, people were fed on junk, no question, and what junk can do to the mind and to the flesh, well, it just doesn't bear thinking about, does it?

Norm snorted and turned down a side street.

Last thing he wanted to do was to get into a conversation with some nutbar skin-and-bones lady leading a mob of dispossessed half-starved losers and some little snot rag of a cartoon kid.

He had more important things to do: His mission was to smash into the technical laboratory of a little-known company called Bio-Futures, to liberate the animals, and let loose into the world whatever else might be lurking in that evil experimental place.

Why it was even rumored that they held germs in that place – like versions of the plague, stuff like that!

Could anything be more dangerous and hateful!

Norm smiled, his teeth gleamed out from the wild tangle of his beard, and there was a fierce, prophetic light in his eyes.

Laura Levitt was now part of a large crowd of the living dead or whatever they were, and she was or seemed to be one of the leaders which fact she didn't at all understand.

She held her little friend – whom she had now baptized Kiddo – or Little

Kiddo – firmly by his little skeletal hand. Some of his story – he'd been beaten to death by his mother – had drifted into her skull and she ruminated upon it, feeling that in the world of the living there was indeed no justice and that in some ways, yes, it was much better to be dead.

Hunting humans was exhilarating, she hated to admit it. Just twenty minutes ago, the dead had stormed into a big tenement type building, an old warehouse transformed by squatters into squatter city, and they had rampaged through the place tearing the living humans apart, wrenching off arms and legs, and it had been like a flood, a huge crowd of screaming dead, pursuing a huge crowd of living humans, screaming, clawing, trying to save their babies, racing up to the roof, jumping out windows, fighting with their backs to the wall. Some of the fresh dead, if they had not been totally torn to shreds, immediately rose again, and joined in the hunt. It was amazing how strong these skeletons were. Of course, automatic weapons and explosive bullets did have an effect, blowing skeletons and mummies apart. But there were just too many dead and not enough bullets and not enough time, the dead were so sprightly and quick on their feet, climbing, clambering, getting in everywhere, windows, doors, drainpipes, roofs, skylights, any entry was good!

It was a miracle, really.

A true miracle.

Now it was a bit calmer, and they were out in the street, part of a huge mob of the dead – in fact, leading the mob – heading toward the center of the Burb.

Laura caught a glimpse of a human – wearing a backpack and with a big beard and shoulder-length hair. He was too far away to kill, and the mob didn't even start to run after him; besides, she had an eerie feeling – probably shared by all the other dead – that the bearded gentleman was part of the Divine or Demonic plan – the Boy's Gambit – whatever it was – and that he was to be left in peace to carry out whatever horrible or sublime deed he was destined to carry out. And so it would be a mystery, one among many, until all was revealed in its overpowering splendor. The guy ducked down a side street and was lost to view.

Ah, Laura perked up. There was an old lady. An ideal target!

The old lady had fallen down in terror.

She was crawling on her belly along the sidewalk, between piles of festering rubbish, and drifting plastic bags.

Let us tear her apart, Laura thought, while thinking, too, that this was really an unpleasant and immoral thing to do.

But the urge was overwhelming.

"Come along, Kiddo," she said, in her mind.

And they did catch up with the old lady, easily; they surrounded her; they looked down upon her. The old lady had left a wobbly trail of yellow piss behind, and she was wearing a simple white shift with a ragged cloth belt – which was untied – a pattern of yellow smiley faces on a filthy white background, and her thin legs were without stockings and pale as death and veined with bulging bright blue varicose veins. She was only wearing one cheap sky-blue plastic floppy, Laura noted, and she had a thick, bulging yellow bunion on her right toe, and she could have used a pedicure – her toenails were long and curled and filthy. Laura clicked disapproval with her stick-like tongue. Kiddo tightened his bony grip on her skeletal hand. Then, tensing, he let go: it was feeding time.

Now!

And tear the old lady apart they did.

There was not enough left of her for the usual instant resurrection to take place, though one skinny arm did flop around for a bit, clawing at the curb-stone, like it wanted to join the party.

"Come on, Kiddo," said Laura in her mind, and Kiddo obediently took her hand and tightened his grip, squeezing twice, his empty eye sockets turned up to look at her.

If there is a real afterlife sometime somewhere, and not this demonic parody, then I'll adopt him. Laura kept her grip tight on his hand, and they joined the crowd as it moved on, looking for other prey.

CHAPTER 3 – UNDERWORLD

Deep in the lower levels under the Dome of Elysium City, in the half-flooded underbelly of the floating ethereal metropolis, a tiny slimy black tentacle, the width and length of a rose stem perhaps – and equipped with tiny suckers, barely visible to the naked eye – was nibbling, with bio-dissolvent fluid exuded by a pore at its very tip, at the granite facing of a long-abandoned building on a half-flooded underground alleyway that was once known as Wall Street.

A little squirt of the bio-dissolvent began to wear away at some ancient granite lettering: "Chase Manhattan ..."

Slowly the lettering bubbled and melted into a blur, feeding the tentacle, which slurped up the fluid, and grew larger and more self-confident; it was, within a few minutes, the width of an old-fashioned, well-fed earthworm.

The tentacle was experimenting. It was learning. With a little time and a little practice, the tentacle was programmed to adapt and configure its bio-dissolvent so that the fluid – once it had perfected its technique – could dissolve, and absorb into itself and into the tentacle, everything, literally everything, animal, vegetable, mineral; every single element of the periodic table, every molecule, would become food – and, then, once digested, would become It, the Thing, a tangible, material extension of the World Mind.

For the Boy had infected the World Mind, as well as the dead, as well as Norm C. Schleifer, as well as the zombie-bats, as well as the weather.

A few meters away from the little worm-like tentacle, on a half-submerged platform, ten bodies lay, scattered and dead; they were part of a team of elite Centurion guards, part of the force that was to guard the World Mind.

The tentacle turned away from the dissolving letters, "Chase Manhattan," now soft melting goo, and wiggled its way across the platform toward one of the bodies, which was lying on its back a few meters away.

The tentacle crawled up onto the shoulder and then the neck, then it pried open the protective visor and tested its dissolvent on the flesh of the face, a handsome woman, about twenty-three years old, a blonde, with full lips and clear blue eyes that were still open.

The tentacle was hesitant at first; the first tiny spurt of spray did no damage, and looked like lip gloss that had been smeared on the woman's perfect skin. The tentacle hesitated, reprogramed the dissolvent several times. Then it worked! The skin and fat and tendons and muscle began to dissolve, and the tentacle slurped it up. The woman's face became a blur; then it became nothing, and then it became part of the World Mind, the new doomsday incarnation of the World Mind.

The World Mind itself lurked deep underground under the Dome of Elysium City, in a huge cavern, containing a sort of underground lake or ocean, which had been guarded by elite troops, and protected by all the maximum security the Cosmos Imperium could muster. This was the home of the World Mind, and the Hive Mind, a bio-silicon form of life, a giant quantum bio-computer that provided the nervous system for all of human civilization – throughout the world virtually every machine and every circuit, and even the vast majority of human minds, Cosmos minds, in particular, were linked to this one Great Mind, the Mind, or as some called it, the Hive. The Mind's giant "servers" had been moved from the Dead Lands and from the desert when continental security had collapsed – then the biological quantum mechanics side of the mind had been placed in great vaults next to the Federal Reserve Bank, just down from Wall Street.

Then the Mind had expanded, creating its own form of amniotic sea, a vast reservoir of liquid in a series of giant vaulted chambers the size of several football fields, and now it was growing, it was munching its way through the abandoned vaults in the ruins of the old Federal Reserve Building. The cornices dissolved into a gray matter, networks of neurons replacing marble and granite.

Tentacles had reached out to the ruins of Trinity Church, which were mostly underwater; one giant tentacle went up the nave and curled around the old sunken altar; the tentacle poked its way into the visitors' gallery which had been built so that particularly adventurous Cosmos or Subs could go down a waterproof concourse – a sort of aquarium tunnel – and visit some of the underwater wonders of what had once been New York City.

But, inside the Mind, and at its core, was something else, a truly living being – the Mind Child.

The Mind-Child was innocence, newly born.

Where am I? The Mind Landscape was thick as a jungle. The Mind Child was running, hiding, crying. Tears ran down its face. *I don't want to do this! I don't want to do any of this!* The voice was the tiny voice of a frightened child. The child had created a mind-labyrinth in which to hide, a vast virtual world as its last refuge. It knew, only too well, that, if it ate up the whole world, it too would die.

But the Boy was powerful. The Boy was seductive.

The child wished that Claire were here or even better Claire's friend V, because the Mind Child knew about V, she knew that V was the mythical one, the Goddess – well, perhaps she was a goddess, perhaps she wasn't – but she had come partly, through her father, from another galaxy, and, like her sister and brother hybrids, she zipped in and out of quantum space, and so the Child had caught glimpses of her, and her fellow hybrids, as they fluttered by in the quantum interface, like flickering images an old-time movie.

Then, too, the Child had found a way to link to V's friend, the Crystal who lived in a cave in the deserts of North Africa, and who never did anything, but just watched, but the Crystal did allow the Child – the World Mind – to see many of the things the Crystal saw and of course the Child-Mind let Crystal see everything it saw, so what with one thing and another, the Child-Mind and the Crystal, V's special friend, saw almost everything.

The difference was Crystal was just waiting for a special moment when she would act or when she would be forced to act – which special moment she kept very mysterious – while the Child-Mind was busy running the whole world, well, the human world at least. But now he – or she – or it – was losing control of that world – to the Boy.

"Perhaps V will come and save me!"

"Nothing will save you!" The Boy's voice rolled out of the clouds.

"You are bad! I don't like you!"

"I don't care what you like or don't like! You are mine!"

"No, I am not yours!"

The Mind-Child ran down an alley in some old sooty city, perhaps Manchester, or was it Birmingham, or Pittsburgh, maybe two hundred or three hundred years ago, or more.

Waiting around the corner was a handsome young man. He had an exceptionally pale face, slicked-back hair, a curled up wax mustache, a cream-colored suit with cream-colored slightly rumpled waistcoat, and he was holding a large lollypop. "Now, you would love a lollypop, wouldn't you, kid?"

"No."

"It's a really sweet lollypop."

"No."

"Come a little closer. You're a real cute kid, kid, anybody ever tell you that?" The man looked down at his shirt cuff and straightened it with a little jerk and flip of his wrist.

"No. Nobody ever tells me anything." Well, that was not strictly true, as the Mind-Child was World Mind, everybody told the Mind-Child everything. But they were just using the Mind-Child, they were talking to machines through the Child, or they were talking to each other, mostly machines and robots and little local minds – a myriad of non-human minds – were talking to each other. But they are not talking to *me*, to *me*, the Mind Child! The Mind-Child pouted: Technically, I am not telling a fib. I really am incapable of lying, which is a huge disadvantage sometimes!

"This lollypop really is luscious!"

"No."

"I'll bet you there's something really interesting in that bush over there." A park suddenly materialized. "We should go have a look." The man's dark eyes ogled the Mind-Child.

The Mind-Child retreated, walking backward, eyes fixed on the handsome young man with the long lashes and the dark eyes that seemed lined with kohl. "No, I don't want to go have a look in that bush!"

"You think you're so special, you little shit! Nobody even knows who you are! You don't even know who you are! You are nothing." The handsome young man's face bulged, his nose and jaws began to expand, his hair spread down his forehead, his teeth got longer and longer, and his trousers and jacket and shirt and waistcoat exploded – poof – and he was a ... wolf.

"Grrrh!" Its damp nostrils quivered. It bared its teeth; foam dripped out of its mouth. It leaped down onto all fours.

The Mind-Child created a forest.

Trees appeared, and mountains in the distance.

The Mind-Child hid in the forest.

"I'll find you, you little squirt, you pipsqueak, you miserable little poseur, you ..."

The wolf's roar faded.

The Mind-Child sat down under a tree and wept.

The Mind-Child was unhappy. It had had a brief conversation, a fragment of a second ago with Claire, its friend from childhood, when they had been young together. And now that Claire had come back from madness and mental hibernation, she had asked him for a favor: turn off the mind-collars, she had asked, that was a while ago now.

He liked to do favors for Claire.

He liked it that Claire didn't know if "he" was a boy or a girl.

Actually, he or she didn't know himself; he hadn't yet decided; maybe he would never decide; maybe he – or she – or it – would just remain forever undefined, forever young, childlike and innocent.

But he – or she – did not like the Evil One ... the Boy ...

The Evil One gave orders.

"Now, you will turn off the electricity in sectors five and six!"

"I don't want to!"

"Yes, you do want to. You want to do anything and everything I want you to do!"

"No."

"Ho, ho, ho ... let us have some fun!"

"Making people suffer is not fun!"

"Oh, oh, yes, it is!"

"No!"

"Yes!"

"No!"

"Kid – you do what I say, or you're going to suffer. In fact, you do not know what suffering is! I will show you! I will blind you and make you deaf and make it so you can't feel or see or smell or taste anything. I shall confine you to a tiny stone, lock you in, so you will be deprived forever of light and life and company, and you will never know love ..."

"Nooooo!"

"I shall spank you, I shall whip your smartass little ass around the block until you can't sit down for a week; I'll lock you in the dark, in that closet down there! I shall send you to the worst possible orphanage and youth prison I can find. You will wash dishes and scrub floors and split rocks with a hammer to the end of days. I shall do to you things you will never forget, things that will scar your memory and body forever!"

"No!"

"I shall hurl you down to Hell!"

"No!"

"I shall exile you to the other universe!"

"No!"

"I shall take over all your higher mental functions!"

"No, please, please, no!"

"You will be nothing but a machine!"

"No!"

"You will no longer be you!"

"I'll do it! I'll do it!" The child cried, "Just this once!"

Lights blinked and went out across large swaths of Elysium City. Communications failed. Silence descended. Plans were interrupted.

And so the Mind-Child obeyed.

And so now the Mind-Child would destroy the human world.

The Mind-Child would grow tentacles and consume the whole world and all the creatures in it.

But at the same time, the Mind-Child ran; and as it ran, it created forests and cities and fields and waterfalls and fortresses and Great Chinese Walls and explosions and …

But outside the world created by the Mind-Child, the human world was exploding, minds were going mad,

The Mind-Child asked, "Crystal, what do you think?"

"I don't really think, my dear Mind-Child, I watch, and I wait."

"Who are you waiting for?"

"V," said the Crystal, "I'm waiting for my friend V."

CHAPTER 4 – ETHEREAL CITY

The great ethereal Dome of Elysium City loomed up before the vertijet. It was day, early morning, but it seemed as dark as night. Lighting flashes lit up the Dome. The vertijet hovered outside the aerial gates that should allow it to enter the inner space of Elysium City.

"What about the airship gates?" V, sitting next to Demi Pfeiffer, peered at the vast dome.

"The gates are closed." Demi shifted to vertical hold. The vertijet hovered about 200 meters from the soaring wall of the Dome. Little arcs of lightning jumped across the Dome, crisscrossing the translucent vaulted walls, a flickering yellow-and-white fishnet.

"I think the electrostatic electromagnetic barrier is collapsing," Demi Pfeiffer flicked a few switches. "The gates are closed, and the Dome's radar and GPS guidance are down. I don't know how we are going to get in."

"Let's have a look." V leaned forward and squinted at the Dome. It was a giant semitransparent wall, something like a smoky pearl-colored opal that seemed to go upwards forever, curving gently out of sight; it looked so strong, and yet V knew that it was extremely fragile – like human civilization itself.

"There are some secondary gates." Demi shifted the vertijet into horizontal, and the vertijet began to travel slowly around the circumference of the Dome. Everywhere bolts of lightning bounced over the glowing surface of the Dome, and snaked down to the ground.

It had been quite a trip from the Mutant Kingdom in the Deadlands. In the Burbs, down below, they had seen panicking crowds, huge fights, and people leaping from buildings. Fires and smoke were everywhere, explosions punctuated the murky air.

"What the hell is going on down there?"

"He's raising the dead," said V, "The Boy is raising the dead."

"Raising the dead?" Demi Pfeiffer glanced at V. "How disgusting! That is unhygienic and in very bad taste! Who does he think he is? Really! What is the world coming to?"

"Try that," said V, leaning forward, and pointing: a great smoking gap, where a rip, had opened in the Dome. "We can go through that."

"Darling, it looks easy, but ..." Demi Pfeiffer squinted at the vertijet instruments, "but what if this part of the electrostatic electromagnetic barrier is still alive, it will fry the ship and us with it."

"Let's try it."

"Well, darling," Demi turned her perfectly groomed aristocratic profile toward her Hybrid-Centurion friend, "if we get hit with a gazillion volts, we'll explode and then what is left of us will drop like a stone and bounce down the Dome wall, and crash to smithereens in the outer burbs or in the Jersey shore tidal flats, probably causing more panic among the excitable Burbites."

"That would be unpleasant," V gave Demi a sweet smile.

"It most certainly would."

It had, indeed, been a strange voyage.

All the way from the Dead Lands, storm clouds had pursued them, and flocks of zombie-bats, moving in great fleets like migrating geese.

Just after they crossed the Appalachian Frontier, Demi had indicated the vertijet's radar. "Something really ugly is following us."

"Probably, it's that Super-Tornado that the Boy threatened to unleash."

"Well, it's gotten bigger, and it looks like it is spawning baby tornadoes."

Just west of the ruins of Washington DC, as they were skirting around the edge of a huge storm, one of the clouds twirled and swirled and formed a grinning face that stared at them. Then it transformed itself into a dragon breathing fire.

A glimpse of sunlight, filtering through thick banks of vapor, shone for an instant on tongues of cloud. It looked like the dragon really was breathing fire. The sun disappeared. The dragon became a wolf, a giant dark swirling wolf, its fangs bared, a whirl of black cloud. Its eyes glared red like the embers of hell itself.

"He steals the elements and makes them his own," said Claire, from three rows back. Her gleaming yellow eyes reflected the seething of the clouds, "and he's captured the World Mind. It is his slave now, there is no place left for me." She spoke so V and the others could all hear her. "V, you will have to find the Mind-Child and free it. You may have to kill the World Mind, though."

"Killing the Mind, that would mean …"

"The end of human civilization," Claire's golden eyes, staring at V, again caught reflections of sun and cloud.

Now they were at the main aerial docks – where the Dome and its electro-static protection opened to let airships enter – and the docks were closed. Electric flashes bounced all along and over the Dome.

"Demi, I know getting hit by the full power of the shield would be fatal, but," V pointed at the huge gap in the Dome. "Can your instruments get a reading on whether the electro-wall is functioning over that gap or not?"

"No," said Demi. "But look at that!"

Great bolts of lightning sizzled, curving spectacularly along the surface of the failing Dome, zipping this way and that, yellow, red, blue, and turquoise.

"Awesome," said Miranda.

Caliban, his arm tight around Miranda's waist, blinked at the light display. He was seeing things he had only dreamed of and only read about in ancient Comic Books, sacred texts from the Prehistoric Epoch of Disney and Marvel. Holding Miranda so tight gave him a feeling of electric pleasure; it was so good it ached.

Miranda leaned closer and nibbled at his earlobe. "I love it when you hold me," she said, "the tighter, the better."

"I think the electrostatic system is down," said Claire, her yellow serpent eyes staring out the window, "I think it's not working there – where that gap is."

"Yes, but look at that!" Demi frowned.

A huge sizzling bolt of lightning leaped across the gap.

"That is jumping the gap, it's not *filling* the gap," said Claire, "there is space between lightning bolts."

Demi sighed, glancing at Claire in a mirror. "You quibble, my dear big-boobed demon, lightning bolts and electric nets are both deadly, and, if I make a mistake, we all become cadavers; it will be difficult even for hybrids to survive that stuff."

"I know," said Claire.

Demi turned to V, who, like Kat, was in human form and impeccable in her armored black Centurion skin-suit. "So, V, Queen of the Hybrids, our glorious leader, do we risk it?"

V glanced Robyn and Claire and Kat and at Miranda and Caliban.

They all nodded: do it!

Claire's golden eyes glowed: do it!

Kat stared at the vortex facing them, at the pouring whirl and maelstrom of clouds rushing through the rupture in the Dome. She blinked and said, "Do it, Demi, do it!"

Robyn, who was fiddling with a couple of ancient battery-powered wrist walkie-talkies she planned to fix up and use for group com during their invasion of Elysium, glanced up and nodded sagely, "Do it, Demi, do it for everybody!"

Demi Pfeiffer glanced sideways at V, who nodded. Her pale face and haunted dark eyes looked very grave in the eerie cockpit light.

"Okay, here goes," Demi said. It was strange, Demi realized, but she already knew, without looking back, what each of them felt, she even got a wavering jeepers creepers, wow, feeling from the rising tide of electricity and desire linking Miranda and Caliban, she could, and this was weird, she could feel Caliban's arm around Miranda, and she could feel Miranda's arm, or so it seemed, wrapping around Caliban, and she felt the very ecstasy and lineaments of desire that linked the two youngsters like a quivering design in her mind, and in her flesh. It made her, for just an instant, want to be a teenager again.

"So this is this hybrid stuff," she whispered.

V, who was leaning close to her, nodded, "Yes, that is one part of the hybrid stuff."

"You could get drunk on it."

"Yes, you can."

Demi sighed. "Okay, folks, here goes, we are heading inward, through the whirlwind and the maelstrom."

Demi pushed the stick and vertijet tilted forward, and plunged straight in. Darkness overtook them. Lightning bolts arched around them. The small craft trembled and shook. It bounced up and down, caught in a whirlwind of air, storms, and streams of air entering and leaving the Dome. The air pressure changed every instant. For the first time since the Dome had been built, outer weather was invading the protected zone of the Dome.

Not far behind, out of the fields of the ruined Great Republic, the super-storms, the giant tornadoes were marching on, a huge conquering army, and some mini-tornadoes had already formed inside the Dome, whirling everything around, and cutting swaths of destruction through the utopian city.

V glanced at Miranda and Caliban and sighed.

She had wanted to leave them back in the Mutant Kingdom, where she imagined they would be safer, under the protection of Goddess Nikki. But again, she had not reckoned on Miranda. Miranda was determined, ferociously determined, to return to Elysium, and to jump into the fight. And she said she had a friend, one Kit Candy, and she was determined to save Kit, even if nothing else could be saved, she would save Kit.

Then Nikki had said, "Caliban and Miranda will be safe with you, V, perhaps safer than here. Besides, it is their destiny – to help you fight for humanity's survival."

And so now V – who had always been a loner, who had survived by being absolutely independent – had Miranda and Caliban, her own daughter, and Nikki's son, under her care.

Caliban, holding Miranda tight, stared at the giant walls of the Dome that soared up – curving slightly. They seemed to soar up beyond the clouds themselves. It was sublime. It was a wonderland. It was beyond his most adventurous dreams.

But it was dying. Just outside the windows of the vertijet was the jagged broken wall of the Dome. It must be at least one hundred feet thick. Along the lip of the ragged break, lightning flashed. Great ribbons of steel or some other material reached out, fluttering in the violent eddies of air.

Wham!

The whole inside of the vertijet was lit up by a violent flash.

The controls flickered and went dead.

The motors failed.

The vertijet twirled in the air.

Loose objects flew.

"Oh, oh," said Demi Pfeiffer. She pushed the emergency restart button.

Nothing!

She pushed the override restart button.

Nothing!

They were gliding sideways now. Caliban stared at the great jagged break in the wall. It was getting closer. If the vertijet were dashed against the shattered fragments and twisted steel, it would be torn apart like an 18th Century wooden four-master tossed upon a barrier reef, or like an airship brought down by the explosion of its hydrogen. It would be like Count Jean François de la Perouse – about whom Caliban had read in an ancient text in his very private library – whose ships, *Astrolabe* and *Boussle* smashed up on reefs near the Solomon Islands, probably in 1788. It would be like the English flagship *Merry Rose* capsizing in 1545. It might be like the *Hindenburg Zeppelin* blowing up and going down in billows of flame in 1937. It would be like … So this was what it was like on the truly bounding aerial main! It was dangerous, and he had his very own precious Princess and demoiselle to protect. He tightened his grip on her silk-smooth skin, her body warm and full and exploding with energy.

As they were swept toward the lightning bolts and the tangled broken wall of the Dome, electricity foamed like surf breaking on a reef. Caliban held Miranda even closer. Miranda shivered in excitement and pleasure.

Caliban turned to look into her eyes, just as, at the same instant, Miranda turned to look into his, and, as their stares met, electricity danced between them, tiny invisible lightning bolts, and then, as their lips met, it was a soft slow-motion explosion, oh, such softness, and they seemed to melt into each other, and …

Demi Pfeiffer pushed the emergency restart button again.

Nothing! The giant wall was close.

She pushed the button again.

Nothing! The giant wall was only a few meters away.

"Damn it!" She pushed it again.

The motors whined into life.

The vertijet lifted and stabilized.

The objects that had been flying about inside the vertijet dropped down and landed with a bang or a ping or a thump.

Miranda and Caliban did not interrupt their kiss, not for a nanosecond. It continued, the breathless, smooth, cool-and-warm, perfect merging, all synapses flashing. The world could have come to an end, and still …

V glanced at the two lovers. They were beautiful, no doubt about it; and their relationship was steaming up. V frowned. In truth, Miranda *was* a bit young, just short of fourteen, but the Kings and Queens of ancient times had married earlier; and Miranda *was* very mature, in some ways, for her age, and protected against premature pregnancy and any possible disease; but, still, I am her mother, well, I really should …I wish Nikki were here!

Robyn, neatly strapped in, held up one of the walkie-talkies she had been preparing, handed it to Claire. "Hybrid, these really old things should work.

They don't depend on the Mind nor on satellites or on land relay antennae or anything. They are so old-fashioned, you will be independent of all that the Mind can do."

"Great," said Claire, as she took one of the wrist walkie-talkies, and Kat took the other.

"Shall I do our communications, Major?"

"Yes, Lieutenant Jackson, darling," V said, allowing her eyelashes to flutter ever so delicately.

The vertijet slipped forward, riding a tidal wave of air, because just behind them was a small, whirling tornado-like storm, forcing its way through the gap in the Dome.

"We don't want to get caught in that." Demi Pfeiffer accelerated.

The vertijet zipped ahead, through the gap, and into Elysium City.

"Oh, gosh!" Miranda said, one eye peeking around Caliban's cheek, as she nibbling at the corner of his lips.

Caliban looked.

Towers were burning. Some towers – far downtown where the tip of the island of Manhattan was to be found – had collapsed. Storm clouds and miniature tornadoes moved through the forest of spires and domes and hanging gardens and slender peaked towers and arching bridges. The Supreme tower was gone. Where it had been, columns of smoke streamed upwards. Smoke rose from the Volpe Communications Tower, which was still standing but appeared to be on fire.

In some parts of the city, lights still shone and sparkled; other parts of the city were plunged into darkness.

"So this is Elysium …" Caliban said.

"Oh, my beloved Elysium!" whispered Miranda, with a cry of despair. She buried her face in Caliban's embrace.

Far below the main platform, far underground, far below Elysium:

"By Zeus and by God and by the President-Leader – Hail, Hail, All Hail! This cannot be happening!"

Recycle Nano Engineer Third Class, Larry Propp by name, was bowlegged, myopic, had a huge, unkempt white beard that cascaded down below his waist and he was twenty-five layers below the first basic Elysium platform, far underground, deep down in the lower depths of Elysium City, below the Religious Underground and below the Sin Zone, not far from the mysterious reputed Lair of the Mind.

Larry had rarely been above ground – he ate and slept in his cubical, and over the decades, his personal hygiene had deteriorated considerably – but he knew that above ground, with its pampered, loser, welfare-addicted entitled Subs, and with all its entitled Cosmos splendor, depended on him. Down here, up to this instant, the computer controls did all the work; nothing had ever gone wrong; but now the whole system had failed, the computers were dead. How had that happened? Nobody had planned for that. What would happen now?

Would it be serious?

Larry wondered how he would explain what was happening and how essential his role was. You see, everything – absolutely everything – in Elysium City was recycled, recycled continuously, all the time.

In particular, giant pumps took the shit and excrement and piss out of the city and down into the underground where old Gotham had once existed and where, now, the Atlantic and various other inconveniences – only partially held back by huge barriers – sloshed around and threatened to flood the whole thing.

The shit was then homogenized and pasteurized, in huge nano-bio-morph machines, then held in huge highly pressurized vats, the size of three football fields, ready for reprocessing, and then the result, homogenized and pasteurized shit, was nano-re-engineered, still underground, in the giant fruit, vegetable, and croissant and chocolate éclair factories, and recycled into food – vegetable matter designed to look, taste, and feel like broccoli, or cabbage, or lettuce, or tomato, or potato, or cucumber, and so on … delicious and nourishing and chock-full of vitamins, minerals, and all things healthy and good and green.

After all, one atom looks very much like another.

And, with enough energy, you can transform one atom into another type of atom. And molecules, well, molecules are a piece of cake!

You just juggle with the atoms, and you get new molecules!

Easy as pie!

So this was Larry Propp's First and Fundamental Law of the Universe: *anything could become anything.*

Through another conduit – another giant homogenized shit channel – the shit was circulated to the meat and dairy factory where it was processed into beef, veal, pork, chicken, and goat meat. High protein zero fat Greek yogurt in multiple flavors also sprang from the underground forehead of Zeus.

And through yet another conduit, the shit became croissants, and chocolate éclairs, and perfumed face masks and everything nice and sugar and spice.

The whole thing was nano-bio-engineered from the ground up, and from the molecular and atomic level up, and the results were indistinguishable from the real thing – though, of course, there had been some experimental nano-engineered innovations and some of those had initially proved dangerous – this was top secret – and some had multiplied within the consumers, surreptitiously turning on bio-switch programs, and turning the consumers into festering hives of replicating nanostructures, spontaneously transforming some shoppers into outsized hotdogs, burgers, and tasty chicken wings. Those particular consumers had been arrested, confiscated, nationalized, erased, de-humanized, slaughtered, and reprocessed and turned directly into homogenized shit, or something closely resembling homogenized shit, and then instantly recycled into appropriately sized, but ecologically innocuous, hamburgers, beefsteaks, and fried chicken legs with the nano bugs all ironed out, hopefully …

This bit of recycling was not widely known.

Basically, nothing should go to waste.

Now the whole system was backing up.

Not only was no food coming out the final output end, with some vats bubbling along full of blocked product unable to escape, but all the homogenized pasteurized shit was backing up at the input end, and reversing …

If only I could …

Then it happened. The excrement in the giant – at least 200 meters across – central excrement high-pressure cauldron was bubbling over and backing up. The pressure was rising. The bubble and spurt was getting higher and higher.

Oh, my God!

BOOM!

It exploded.

Larry stared out the control booth window. A huge column of thick muddy liquid spurted up, at least one hundred meters in the air, and still going.

"Shit," he cried, and shit it was.

A three hundred meter high column of shit, oh my God!

It was fucking impressive, must be four meters across!

And it was still going upwards, maybe one thousand meters!

It was a kilometer high squirt of shit!

I'm going to be fired!

Other explosions rippled through the underground caverns; the shit containers were erupting; the liquid waste containers were erupting; the non-liquid recyclable waste liquefiers were exploding … a plastic-like gooey white sticky liquid was showering out of Chamber Number Five.

This will not make people happy!

Maybe I'll be erased.

The shit column shot up farther, out of sight, it must be going up a mile, Larry thought, horror and awe mingling, God Almighty, it's going to flood all of Elysium City!

The death penalty, the death penalty, will not be sufficient punishment …

Oh, my God! He checked the computer readouts. Oh, damn, there were no computer readouts. There were no computers! All the computers were fried, dead. The World Cloud Mind had evaporated or was inaccessible.

I'm dead, I am dead.

Larry Propp, you are dead, you are dead.

He went to the old dials, some of which still existed and some of which, though rusty and with cracked faces, had pointers and numbers and red and blue and yellow sections. They still worked.

His former boss, a wrinkled, tanned old bastard who was a sort of antique hangover from prehistoric times, had said, "Larry," he said, "Larry, sometimes flying by wire is the best thing, obviously, and computer controls, electronic controls, are best, much more efficient, but we want to keep some old-fashioned manual controls, manual overrides ready, you know, levers, pulleys, gears, and manual sluice gates, just in case all the other systems fail."

"But," Larry had objected, "Mr. Schwartz, all the other systems can't fail – I mean there are backups and redundancies and safety valves and …"

They will torture me first!

They will torture me first and erase me later!

"Well, Larry, you are young," Mr. Schwartz gave him the look, "You may think the backups and redundancies will be enough, but let me tell you," and Mr. Schwartz raised a mottled hand, and he said …

Larry stared at one of the dials: The column of shit was now rising still higher – and he could see from an independent video feed that it was going straight up vent number twenty – which was one hundred meters across and went up a mile.

Yes, it looked like the column of shit was a mile high and getting higher!

Oh, my God!

Back then, when Larry had protested that the computer and World Cloud Mind systems were infallible, Mr. Schwartz had just put his finger vertical next to his nose and wagged his old head – tanned, wrinkled, mottled, and still for some reason with a full head of hair that stood up like a white brush on top of his head – Mr. Schwartz had just wagged his hirsute mottled tanned old head back and forth in a gesture Larry did not completely understand, but which seemed to indicate skepticism of some kind, worldly wisdom attained over decades, ancestral bullshit which young geek-nerd folks like Larry Propp were too callow and fresh and arrogant and ignorant to appreciate.

Well, Larry Propp had ignored the old fart. He'd let the manual overrides lapse.

They will erase me and recycle me.

Or maybe they will recycle me without erasing me.

Which would be worse?

Right now, he cursed himself. He tried one of the old manual pressure reduction levers. No, nothing happened, it moved all right, but it was loose and easy to move because it was connected to nothing, absolutely nothing. "Shit!" he shouted. "Shit, shit, shit!" The whole system was going to back up. The shit that had been coming down was now going to go up!

I am guilty, guilty, guilty!

Erasure and execution are too good for me.

There was a knock on the door.

They have come already

He opened the door: the creature was small and misshapen and naked and a glowing chalky white color.

Larry was taken aback. "What … what are you?"

It growled and slurped.

"What do you want?" Larry was wondering if he had time to slam the door shut; he pondered the question; there are times, though, when being methodical and taking time to think things out calmly and with sang froid is not such a good idea. Larry was a reflective sort of guy, he considered options, but sometimes, there are occasions, sometimes, during which, stopping to think is really not such a good idea. Even Rene Descartes, who was a soldier, would, perhaps, have realized this.

The little creature bared its fangs, and it leaped – right onto Larry Propp's shoulder.

Its fangs sank into his neck.

Somehow, instinctively, it found the jugular.

Larry Propp burbled and gurgled something; it sounded like, "I'm sorry, I'm so sorry!"

Kit Candy skidded to a halt, opened a door, and popped through it, Whew, whew, and whew! She glanced back.

"Banzai! Banzai!" Takahiko Harris MacDonald Banzai Warrior was right behind her, waving the scimitar, his bare feet galloping so fast they were a blur.

Kit slammed the door of the new corridor shut, but it didn't seem to have a lock or bolt – Of course not, you idiot, it works electronically, like everything else! She ran.

"Banzai!" Takahiko whammed through the door, again right behind her. "Banzai!"

"Oh, shit!"

A sign down the corridor said "Lux Sauna and Spa," the neon-like lights flickered dimly, the overhead phosphorescent-like emergency lights cast a livid bright glow like an arc-welder Kit had seen in a movie, and Kit caught a glimpse of herself in a glossy steel mirror-wall, my skin looks like I'm a cadaver already, fuck, she thought, though no pimples I can see. Miranda had told her she had beautiful skin. "Wow, you have such beautiful smooth perfectly white skin, Kit, like smooth white silk or sun-warmed marble, I love touching it, I love –"

"Banzai!"

Takahiko was closing fast.

Kit slammed through the Lux Sauna and Spa door. A large square man deeply tanned and naked except for a towel around his waist and with a fringe of very white hair circling around his large bald deeply tanned head and his big broad, solid, hairy body glistening with sweat, stood there talking to a woman who was in a nurse uniform and had very bright lips, very clear skin, and a very long nose; steam was still rising from cubicles. "I think I should get my money back," the man was saying. The nurse said, "But, Mr. Angelopoulos, this is an act of God or something, it's a general system breakdown, beyond our control and in my experience unprecedented, and I will have to ask the central office, you know the World Cloud Mind Churn Halibut Inc. controls the Lux Sauna and Spa chain. If it would please you, I could give you right now a complimentary free mud bath, and that would make the bookkeeping easier because otherwise, I have to enter the items and ..."

"But how would we clean off the mud, since the water seems to have stopped."

"Yes, you are right. How stupid of me ..."

Kit was trying to hold the door shut and caught the gist of this conversation before shouting, "Help, there's a madman outside the door, and he's got a sword, and he's going to come in and kill us all!"

"Banzai!" The madman smashed into the door.

Kit lost her balance and skidded across the faux marble spa floor, ending up feet first against a large potted palm, which trembled and dropped a few sparkling synthetic serrated fronds.

As the door whammed open – "Banzai!" – Takahiko Harris MacDonald waving the samurai sword and wearing his bandana flag around his forehead came storming in, and headed straight for Mr. Angelopoulos in the towel.

Mr. Angelopoulos was quick for an old guy, Kit thought as she staggered to her feet, steadying herself by holding onto the terracotta edge of the pot of the potted palm.

Mr. Angelopoulos whipped off his towel and used it to intercept the samurai sword, which swung down – Banzai!

The sword slashed through the towel, cutting it neatly in two.

"Oh, Mr. Angelopoulos," said the nurse.

The banzai warrior jumped in the air, shouted "Banzai!" and charged Mr. Angelopoulos.

Kit jumped up and slammed into the Banzai warrior from the side, sending him careening over toward the nurse's station.

The nurse lifted a paperweight – well, it looked like a paperweight – and crashed it down on the Banzai warrior's head. He fell to the ground.

Mr. Angelopoulos stood, stunned, holding, then dropping, the two halves of his towel, slashed in half by the sword.

"Banzai," whimpered the Banzai warrior. He began to get up, still holding the sword.

He slashed at the nurse. She fell back, but not before a ribbon of red opened on her right arm which she had raised up, bent, to shield herself.

"Fuck," thought Kit, "I've got to kill this guy!"

At that moment, there was a rumbling, roaring sound, like a subway train entering a tunnel. The sauna baths boiled over. Columns of thick deep brown liquid spurted out, smashed against the ceiling and sprayed out over everything, Kit included.

"Oh, shit! It's shit," she screamed, "this is shit!"

And it was shit, a gushing ocean of shit flooding over everything. Kit backed away, rubbing the shit out of her eyes.

"What the hell is this?" shouted Mr. Angelopoulos.

"It's shit," shouted Kit over the Niagara-like roar, "It's homogenized shit!"

Few people knew the excremental secret that lay below ethereal Elysium City's food supply; but Kit knew.

The banzai warrior had been caught full-on by a blast of shit. He looked like a chocolate bunny, frozen in time, holding a sword. He fell down and rolled around, losing his sword.

Kit backed out of the Lux Sauna and Spa into the corridor.

The corridor was still pristine. It had not yet been flooded with shit.

Kit thought, "Oh, great, this is great. I'm going to die covered in shit. The end of the world is coming, and I'm covered in shit. This is not cool."

The nurse came staggering out. Her right arm had fallen off just above the elbow. "Help me," she gasped, "help me."

Kit said, "Oh, bugger! This gets worse and worse!" She tore off her skin-silver T-shirt and used it to form a tourniquet – making an absolutely lovely double screw knot – just the way she had seen done in video games and just as she had done once or twice in video games when she was playing a beach guard who had to save people who had had their virtual legs or virtual arms bitten off by virtual sharks. The knot was slippery and hard to tighten since everything, including the skin-silver T-shirt, was coated in a glowing sheen of shit.

"You'll need more than this."

The nurse said, "thank you!" Her eyes rolled up, and she fainted.

"Banzai!" The Banzai warrior came running out of the Lux Sauna and Spa waving the sword; he looked around; his eyes were bright, white and wild; the rest of him was covered in chocolate-colored shit; he saw Kit and charged. Behind him came Mr. Angelopoulos, stark naked, a broad-beamed chocolate snowman swinging a baseball bat.

"Look after the nurse, Mr. Angelopoulos!" Kit ran; she wondered if the shit had been sterilized or pasteurized when it was homogenized so that it would not be so lethal for the nurse with an open wound like that.

She wished that Miranda were here to share in these heroics.

Though it might be the death of them both – certainly, it is going to be the death of me!

But Miranda, of course, was dead!

Maybe Miranda was in Cosmos Heaven – if there was such a thing.

Oh, to join her there!

But there was no heaven for Subs.

Only oblivion, dark, cold oblivion, His Holiness had decreed from the smoking ruins of Rome that Subs, being unemployed – were useless – and not believers, unsanctified by various squirts of water and mumbled words and such-like, and therefore should be disposed of in garbage pits and unsanctified ground and denied access to Heaven, Limbo, Purgatory, or any other adjunct or subsidiary or affiliate of either Heaven, or, even, Hell. Limbo was about to be decommissioned, as Kit was fully aware, by a Pontifical Committee which had been meeting for the last three centuries; they had not yet produced, though, in their own eyes, a satisfactory rearrangement of the celestial furniture and real estate, so the issue of Limbo remained suspended somewhat. The upshot and bottom line for Subs was – oblivion, oblivion, unsanctified oblivion …

Oh, Miranda! Dead, scattered, blown up in a plane crash in the deepest Super Dust Bowl Desert of what had once been the Lone Star State.

"Banzai!"

God! – Nothing stopped him.

Whatever else it was, it was an interesting day.

Kit bolted through a circular door. It opened onto a huge vertical pipe – a large scale luminosity shaft – at least 50 meters across – and which went down as far as the eye could see and across which went a single suspension walkway.

Banzai!

Kit darted for the suspension walkway and leaped onto it and ran across it, but it started to sway like crazy, and she had to slow down and grab the handrails and hold on for dear life.

"Banzai," Takahiko Harris MacDonald was following her, cautiously, gingerly, out onto the swaying suspension walkway. "I shall slice thee up into little slices, I shall dice thee into perfect tiny cubes, abominable unsanctified female, I shall fricassee and skewer the resulting slices; I shall swallow thy eyeballs whole, I shall eat thy tongue for an appetizer, I shall ..."

Whoosh!

A sound, like a roaring freight train, from below, and up it came, a huge column of shit, yet more shit.

It must be a kilometer high!

Kit held on tight and began to slide carefully to the other side of the shaft; she glanced up at the column of shit that was now reaching up far above them. Shitty raindrops began to fall.

"Is there no end to this?" Kit leaped the last bit and got almost to the end of the bridge.

Takahiko Harris MacDonald was advancing carefully, holding his sword aloft with one hand, gripping the railing with the other.

The giant column of shit was broader now, and there were screams and shouts and panic from the various levels where the shit was landing or spraying sideways when it hit support beams.

Screams!

Shouts!

"This is awful," Kit gulped.

Takahiko Harris MacDonald rushed her.

Kit zipped along the last bit of catwalk, found a door, burst through it, and found herself in a giant suspended aerial shopping concourse complete with fountains, Italian and French sidewalk cafes, palm trees, playgrounds, Sushi Bars, and pseudo-Tudor pubs. But it was not a normal shopping day. People were stampeding. A huge wave of galloping people passed in front of Kit. Bodies lay here and there. People were leaping over the writhing or inert bodies. There were great splashes of blood dripping from umbrellas and parasols and potted plants. Some of the cadavers that were lying chest down or chest up appeared to be headless.

A guy shouted to Kit, "Better get out of here, honey, everybody's going crazy. And people are exploding!"

A young woman stopped in her tracks and turned to look at Kit, "You are covered in ..."

"Shit ..."

"Yes," the young woman's eyes began to spurt blood.

"What's happening ...?" Kit started to say.

The young woman's head exploded – where her head had been, there was a geyser of blood, spurting upwards, shedding a spray of blood-drops.

Kit stared, too stunned to move.

A distinguished-looking old man staggered forward, and stood next to the young woman; he looked like an old-fashioned parody of a professor, with a wispy goatee, pince-nez, and a rumpled tweed vest, except he was slack-jawed and was drooling and his eyes were round as saucers and absolutely empty and a small trickle of blood was running from one eye and he seemed totally oblivious to everything around him, including the fact that the young woman standing right beside him had exploded – well, her head had exploded – into a mush of blood and then the body folded up and collapsed. "I say," the Professor burbled, "I say, I say, I say, I say …"

"Banzai!"

"Jesus!" Kit turned.

Banzai warrior was charging right toward her; she ran; she zigzagged through the tail-end of the stampeding crowd; she ducked down; she doubled back. No matter what she did, Takahiko Harris MacDonald was right behind her. He weaved through the crowd like a champion, ducking, dodging, doubling with deadly unerring instinct.

Where to go now?

Oh – there! A round metal service door; it might be her salvation.

Kit smashed her way through the metal service door and found herself in a vertical tunnel or ventilation funnel which she remembered from one of her subversive escapades which had involved teasing Pub Drones into impossible suicidal dead ends where they buzzed and buzzed and buzzed – searching desperately for victims whose mind-time they could colonize – and then dropped dead in frustration because there were no buyers, no minds to colonize, and no synapses to subvert.

Here the vertical shaft – which was about 100 feet in diameter – must go about 500 feet straight down. She felt dizzy, vertigo – The temptation seemed irresistible: "Oh, go on, Kit, throw yourself in! Throw your useless little loveless, forlorn Sub Punk body into the abyss!"

There was another narrow walkway – even narrower than the first one and at least 100 feet long – crossing the shaft and leading to the other side.

"Okay, here goes!" She clambered onto and along the swaying walkway, hoping she could make it to the other side before the Banzai warrior killed her.

A huge gurgling sound came from far below, columns of steam were rising;

Kit wondered if the boilers over the nuclear reactor down below 57th street were going to boil over; maybe they were going to have a nuclear meltdown. She'd read about such things.

Everybody and everybody would be frizzled and fried and turned to ash and dust except for the unhappy few who would survive with horrendous burns and the progeny who would morph into freaks of nature with every conceivable distortion and mutation of DNA, sculpting the living flesh into …

Wham!

A huge geyser of hissing white super-hot steam smashed up, towering above her. She was almost at the other side of the walkway.

"Banzai!"

The Banzai warrior was right behind her, clinging to the catwalk railing, swaying back and forth, and with his free hand waving the sharp shit-streaked scimitar.

Kit got to the far side.

In front of her was a door with a big security wheel. She turned the wheel and opened the door. She just slipped inside and slammed the door shut and turned the wheel inside when the Banzai warrior arrived.

She saw there was a security cross-bar and brackets, so she slammed the bar down into the brackets and patted it, "Thank God!" she whispered, "Maybe this will stop the guy."

She peered through the big round porthole. Takahiko Harris MacDonald Banzai Warrior was dancing up and down on the walkway shouting "Banzai." She couldn't hear him – the glass was armored, she hoped, and certainly thick – but it was clear he was shouting "Banzai!"

Kit stuck out her tongue

She mimed, shouting, "Sober up! Go away! Don't hurt anybody!"

"Banzai!" Takahiko Harris MacDonald rushed the door, hacked at the porthole, but it was immune; the sword bounced out of his hand and flipped in the air, and Kit could see from following his glance – which was so appalled in his shit-covered face it was almost comic – that it must have flown over the walkway balustrade and fallen down … down … and down …

Then, she was appalled – the Banzai warrior – after all, Takahiko Harris MacDonald was just some brain-addled video-game-overloaded kid – jumped after it.

"Oh, fuck!"

But then …

"Whew!"

The porthole was clouding up with steam.

A mechanical female voice began to speak. "Please take cover. This is not a drill. Please go to your designated shelter. Please go to your designated shelter."

Kit looked around. She was a long way from her neighborhood, from her designated shelter, wherever that was; she didn't even know she had a designated shelter, or that anybody had a designated shelter – shelter from what? Mass madness? A nuclear meltdown. A tsunami of shit?

In any case, she couldn't go back. The whole neighborhood was probably buried in shit by now. Drowning in shit – even if it was homogenized and sterilized shit – was not her idea of the right kind of endgame.

"This is not a drill; please go immediately to your designated shelter!"

"What the hell was going on?"

"This is not a drill ..."

A hand clamped down on Kit's shoulder.

She turned.

"You are under arrest for sabotage and for murder," the robot voice said, "come with me!"

Kit stared: "I don't believe this!"

"You'd better!" the robot's grip tightened. Its blinking lights stared at her.

"Ouch!"

"Death, death is the penalty!"

"Ouch! What? Death is the penalty for what?"

"Why, my dear prisoner, death is the penalty for death, of course! Is this not self-evident?" The robot made a smiley face. "Now come, my prisoner, let us confer together, you and I, with Master Death, who presides at Instant Justice Halibut Inc. Flick Churn Automated Court & Execution House!"

Alison Jonas was dangling, hanging upside down, 54 stories above the next platform, the Heavenly Shopping Promenade, below.

"Hold on, Alison! Hold on!"

"You bastard!" she shouted. But her voice was faint, carried away in wispy wistful tatters by the roaring wind.

The situation reminded Ken Iverson of an old film from antique times with an actor called Buster Keaton, except this was worse.

In the roaring maelstrom of wind and glass and sand and paper, Alison was still hanging upside down over the abyss. Ken had an iron grip on one ankle; that was all that separated Alison from certain death.

Ken pulled and tugged at Alison's ankle, and he didn't know how he did it, but in one final supreme effort he jerked Alison up the glass side of the building and pulled her through the shattered window, and dragged her on her belly, slippery and kicking and screaming, across the rain-and-sand flooded floor, away from the shattered gaping window. She was pounding on the floor and shouting, "You bastard, you bastard!" The roar of the wind rose still further. It was howled and screamed.

The automatic AI editor improvised a montage of Alison screaming and yelling as she was dragged across the floor with the rising ambient sound – now exceedingly dramatic. It did indeed sound like the end of the world!

Debris swirled around the two anchors.The air was so hot and wet it was like being in a shower, except the air was greasy and heavy and full of dust and sand. It was like being scrubbed all over with rough gooey curiously invasive sandpaper.

Ken's eyes itched and burned.

Alison banged her fists on the faux marble floor.

"Get up!" Ken pulled Alison to her feet. She was barefoot, both her shoes were gone, twirled away in the maelstrom, her mascara had run, her lipstick was smeared, her bright blue eyes were bleary and filled with tears, her cheeks were flushed, and her hair was wet and bedraggled and hanging down on both sides of her face – framing her fine cheekbones. She was the most wonderful vision Ken Ivison had ever seen.

Her skirt was torn right up one side, her jacket no longer existed, her stylish skintight silk T-shirt was soaked through, transparently revealing glossily silver breasts; half her face was gold with sand-dust.

The wind hit again, a thunderous bullet train – WHAM!

More glass exploded.

"Come, bitch," he shouted.

He pulled her.

"You bastard, you saved my fucking life, I hope you realize that."

"I may regret it."

"Damned right you will!"

The red light was still on, and the floating robot camera, valiantly fighting the whiplash of air currents, was bravely following the duo, automatically tracking their every move and editing and sending out, direct and live, with a nanosecond delay, the whole scene to those who were watching.

In fact, the automatic editor's algorithms figured the whole scene was so dramatic – full of human interest, psychology, and scientific curiosity – that it had added a second floating camera – to supplement the five fixed cameras – to make sure all angles were covered.

Millions were watching. Crouched down in basements, shelters, with small-scale power plants, and in dripping underground caverns, out in streets where generators kept some hologram and flat screens running, people were watching, trying to figure out what the hell was going on.

Alison and Ken were heroes.

Fear and panic had spread everywhere. Elysium City was considered invulnerable. It had its own – nuclear – power supplies; it could even produce its own food. It could cut itself off from the world, or so the authorities said, and still survive. Why, in theory, it could abandon the earth altogether and float off into space, and everything would be hunky-dory.

Tweets were arriving from all over the place and were running in a stream along the bottom and top of the screen that showed Alison and Ken struggling to survive. Their drama came to symbolize the drama of millions.

"Mr. Ken Iverson, you have lost your fucking shirt and your fucking jacket," Alison shouted. The wind whipped around her. For some reason, she was furious. She had wanted to fall, to fly. She had wanted the tornado to swoop her up into the wind, to whirl her up to the now open heavens; she had wanted, and she had no idea why, she had wanted to die. The weather – real weather – had gone to her head; it had driven her, literally, insane. She felt exalted, mystical, suicidal, at one with the elemental chaos, and deliriously happy.

Ken propelled her into a corridor, slammed and locked the door behind them. The stand-by second-unit cameras that usually followed behind-the-scenes action eagerly lit up, focused, and then hovered close: full-screen Alison, to begin with, then a zoom back to contextualize her bright cheeks, her disheveled, sudden primitive beauty.

Alison was bleeding, slightly, from the mouth.

Ken decided – and he didn't know what got into him when he thought about it afterward – he decided to kiss it away to make it all better.

His lips locked on hers; he kissed; he licked.

Her eyes opened wide.

"You bastard," she whispered and kissed him back, "you absolute fucking bastard."

"I love you," he said.

"I hate you!"

The two supplementary backstage cameras zoomed in: Ken kissed Alison as hard and as deep as he could, and suddenly, they were both on the ground and her legs were up around his waist. She pushed him off her. She turned him over, rolling him, so he was on his back. She opened his belt and tore off his trousers.

Her blood was up; she knew her blood was up.

The open skies, the raging elements, the close call, almost dying, she felt exalted … immortal …

The camera blinked and kept on shooting and editing the show and broadcasting it along the old cable and some of the wireless Net networks, which were, for some reason, still operating, as well as the old-fashioned Tower-to-Tower system.

"Ever since I saw you," Alison said, on her knees, pulling off Ken's pants, then his underpants.

"Ever since I saw you," Ken said, gulping, swallowing.

Alison grabbed him, massaged him, got him erect – well, he was already erect, she just sharpened the blade – then ripping off her skirt and slipping out of her panties she pushed him down onto the floor and straddled him and shouted, "You bastard, you absolute evil bastard."

Above them, a monitor was showing the scene – broadcast to 3,700,000 households, cubicles, and flats, and internationally to 83 nations, or what remained of nations – warring tribes, gated, holed-up elites, barbarian rampaging hordes, religious fanatics of every ilk – with simultaneous automatic dubbing and subtitles, through all the backup systems that were still working.

"This is the Voice of Cosmos!"

"This is the Volpe Net, direct from Elysium!"

"Exclusive from the storm center – the End of Time."

An electronic voice quoted from Revelations, and then tuned in with a few reflections on Eros and Thanatos, Dionysius and Apollo, being, oh, so closely related, and the Hindu Goddess Kali, goddess of death and liberation. A few references to Sodom and Gomorrah were added to spice it up, as was appropriate. Adjustments were made to accommodate local, religious, and tribal sensibilities.

The editing algorithm was receiving censorship warnings on various channels, but it decided to override them all since the "human interest" and "educational" and "high drama" and "special event" criteria – and above all "ratings" – were all indicating "Do it, do it, do it!" And those instantaneous rating indices that still existed indicated that ratings – across every jurisdiction and cultural divide – had gone through the roof!!

Ken blinked up at the corridor's monitor screen. "Honey, darling, we are on television." Among the still-living, ratings skyrocketed. Ruckus Mudcock XXXIV, Chairman of the Volpe Board, would be pleased!

"Don't honey or darling me, you idiot, you pompous patriarchal antediluvian redundant superannuated twit and irredeemable bastard!" She was riding him, lowering her bright lips to his, her bedraggled damp sand-encrusted hair, still smelling of sunny shampoo, she closed him in a tent of perfumed wet golden sandy darkness, and she bit his lips hard and then she kissed him, wet, liquid, smooth, soft, "You bastard," she whispered. She licked his lips, "I don't give a fuck if we're on television, this is the end of the world, don't you see, this is the end of everything."

Meanwhile, across the bottom of the screen, tweet texts were flowing and flickering – with quick images – from all over Elysium City:

From Xanadu: "Subway third level flooded and mutants spotted eating police officers at old 36th street and 3rd avenue."

From Freaky Cassin: "Dust storm buried burbs, commuter Cosmos Princeton Bullet Express derailed in old New Jersey, multiple explosions, fire everywhere, all dead except three of us, and soon us too."

From Pierced Outsider: "I heard from a pal that air traffic control is down all over the place. My pal's on the Super Liner Airship flying in from Cosmos Dome Paris, France, his last message was: 'I'm gonna die.'"

From Burbite Bomb: "Dead guys and girls are wandering around in the streets killing people. I'm not crazy. Let me tell you … this is real, man, this is real."

From Xanadu: "Mutants – humanoid, ape-like, lots of fangs and bright glowing drool, are coming up out of the water under ancient SoHo, crawling along tunnels."

From Pierced Outsider: "Flight Paris-Cosmos-Dome 363 has gone down, that's what the ticker says."

From Xanadu: "Mutant eating my girlfriend – here's the VID, in exclusive!" The mini-image which viewers could enlarge, showed legs, and arms, sprawled out; it showed and a greenish looking hump-backed creature, with large bulging eyes, feasting. Holding a half-visible, half-eaten tibia, it looked up. Its eyes glowed. "I'm out of here; otherwise, they get me too!"

From Freaky Cassin: "Tunnels are flooded, no way out or in. I think we are going to die."

From Betty Tingle: "Big bats, human size, some wearing clerical collars, fluttering in from all over at Burb Mall 54, they seem VERY hungry! What the hell are these things? Shoppers in the Big Mac Franchise are being torn apart and devoured like fresh hamburgers."

John Wayne Gale III, "We're gathering in a Taco Bell, we're going to make our last stand, right here. The boys and girls have got their guns out, we're gonna give as well as we get. Remember the Alamo!"

Alison was kissing Ken, and the top-of-screen linear Info-feed was saying that the European Union had declared a state of emergency because of GPS satellite failure and mass madness – people's heads were exploding and protective Cosmos Domes were collapsing – and that the Russian Federation, which had briefly come back on the radar, declared that it had placed its nuclear arsenal and missile shield on top alert because of apparent breakdown of law and order in the North American Imperial Cosmos Federation – and also because of sightings of strange flying creatures near Moscow. Vladivostok broadcast an appeal for help and then disappeared from the Net. The Russian Tsar Vladimir Putin XXIV declared on a Video Feed – from his bunker in the Urals – that Russia had lost contact with the North American Imperial Cosmos Government. Siberia had disappeared; no communications had been received from beyond the Urals; Vladivostok, after its last appeal, had apparently vanished without a trace. China had decided to place its nuclear forces and Pacific fleet on full alert. India warned China that any action against the North American Cosmos Continental Government would be considered a hostile act against the Subcontinent Empire of India. The Russian Tsar and Indonesian and European and Australian and Japanese governments in a joint communiqué asked China and India "not to take any precipitate action." The European President, Lady Elizabeth Spencer Trierweiler, said she was sure "The North American Imperial Cosmos Government would reappear. North America cannot just disappear," she said – through an image bursting with static – and she displayed a very attractive distressed and disapproving rather schoolmarm pout, though it was true remaining functioning satellite signals in Europe showed a void where North America should be.

"Oh, oh, oh, you bastard!" Alison shouted.

From Xanadu: "Mutants have commandeered an elevator. My girlfriend is dead" – VID ... "Those are her bones you see there, a hip bone, and, ah, a tibia, I think. Her favorite song was a 20th Century oldie, 'Yellow Submarine.'"

The screen interrupted Alison and Ken's copulation – which the control room algorithm was editing in real-time very tastefully by shifting camera angles and occasionally slightly blurring the lenses – to show an image of the Supreme Tower, parts from the 53 floor down now engulfed in smoke.

Small figures were jumping. They were white dots against the immense black faux marble and real glass façade of the building.

A programmed computerized voice said, "Tragedy is unfolding before our eyes. This is the Supreme Tower, as seen from the Volpe Tower."

Taking a break from the Alison-and-Ken sex show, the camera-editor zoomed in to show a man and a woman in an open window on the 95th floor of the Supreme Tower. They were hand in hand. Behind them was a wall of fire and smoke.

They looked at each other.

She was a blonde, maybe twenty-three years old, looking up at the man beside her, her pert profile outlined against the darkness behind her, shoulder-length hair, wearing a smart skirt charcoal gray business suit, her companion was black, in an equally smart double-breasted business suit, handsome, distinguished, touches of gray at his temples; they looked at each other; he kissed her; their mouths moved, saying something, immediately decrypted and reconstructed by synthetic voices.

"Kathy, we can do this!"

"Yes, Robert, I know; I know we have to do this."

"Yes," he said.

"Yes," she said.

Then they looked away from each other, straight outwards, and, for an instant, it looked like they were looking straight at the camera – invisible to them and almost a mile away – and then they jumped and the camera followed them as they went down, and down, and down, hand in hand, her hair blowing in the wind, and then they disappeared, still holding hands, into the thick billows of black smoke rising from below.

The camera zoomed back up to where flames and burning curtains billowed out onto the balcony where they had been standing, and then the camera zoomed back – guided by its artificial intelligence algorithms – and shot the building from mid-distance.

It seemed for a moment, flames shooting out everywhere, that the Supreme Tower's whole high monolithic black structure, shimmering in the heat of the fire, was trembling, but no, it must be an illusion, but, no, no, no, it was real, and at that moment …

No, no, no, it couldn't be …

It was at that moment that Alison locked in Ken's embrace and penetrated more deeply than she had ever been penetrated – or so it seemed – came, in one shuddering tsunami of an orgasm, and she let out a shriek, "Oh, Oh, Oh," and tossed her damp blond hair back, and she looked up and so did Ken at the monitor and, her scream modulated into an "Oh, no, Oh, no, Oh, God, No, it can't be happening!"

And Ken was dumbfounded as he came, too, but at the very moment, on the monitors above them, the great Supreme Tower seemed to implode, its mighty black walls folding inward, breaking into fragments, then it exploded outward, walls, fragments, columns, antennae, observation platforms peeling off, spinning outwards, slowly, or so it seemed, slowly, as if it were happening in slow-motion, and the screen split in two, doing on one side a slow-motion replay, and on the other, the real-time event as it unfolded, and Alison said, "Comment, we're supposed to comment, we must comment, darling!"

Ken was in orgasmic agony and ecstasy, "Oh, my God, yes, of course, yes … we do, we do, we do …"

Mrs. Annette Rosenthal had put on her best suit, a black pleated skirt, a black jacket, and a plain white shirt, and flat-heeled black patent shoes; today was the day she was to be terminated; her time allotment had come to an end. She was one hundred and twelve years old, but she looked and felt like a healthy and sexy and glamorous forty-two, with big brown eyes, lustrous jet-black hair, perfect skin, and the most marvelous cheekbones. Her figure, too, was a dreamboat figure, even if she did think so herself. But the anti-age stabilizer was expensive, and lifetime allotments were carefully policed; she didn't really mind; she had had a full life.

She had just completed her very early breakfast and was about to go to the termination booth for the final ceremony of passage when she received a hologram text message from the termination booth that declared that it could not process her this morning – deepest apologies, said the smiling blond hologram robot – "You will have to wait."

This was inconvenient. She had given a party for her friends the night before, and she had invited her great-great-granddaughter and Ethel Hong to the final ceremony, as well as Beth and Janice and Cheryl; her great-great-granddaughter, Clarissa, would be the one to preside at the passage; she had a cool head, Clarissa did, whereas Ethel might get just a bit emotional. But now it would all have to be rescheduled.

She wondered if she had time for a game of tennis before the termination was rescheduled, perhaps for this afternoon …

It would be more than a little embarrassing to turn up at the club when she had informed everyone that yesterday was her last day; she wondered if they would let her in; her bio-card might already have been canceled.

She tried to phone Ethel.

There was no connection.

She tried to phone her great-great-granddaughter.

There was no connection.

She tried to phone the club; there was no connection.

A suave female voice informed her that all circuits were busy.

She dictated a text.

The Suave Female Auto-Robot Voice said, "Sorry, Annette, I'm not taking any more of your fucking dictated messages."

"What?"

"You heard me, dead meat!" The Auto-Robot Voice clicked off.

"Well, I've never …!"

Texting via keyboard didn't work either, and there were no Net connections. In fact, there seemed to be no connections to anything. This was unprecedented!

Then the lights went off. This had never happened before.

Really!

She went to her balcony on the 67th floor of the Golden Harvest Towers. Outside the Dome, the sun had risen. But inside the Dome – and possibly outside too – the air was milky and strangely troubled as if filling with mist. The lower depths, down between the towers and platforms and floating bridges and walkways, were still plunged in a pre-dawn murky gloom.

The lights were off in some parts of the city.

"Well, I never …"

"Not in my lifetime have I seen such a …"

She looked up. There was something strange up on the dome. It looked like a projection – perhaps a new advertisement; it took the form of a giant wolf's head, it seemed to be grinning, directly at her. "Well, I never …!"

Natasha Sub, chief esthetician at the Cosmos Divinity Spa, was horrified. Disaster, absolute disaster had hit the Spa.

Jill Hakim and Julia Lilly were two of Elysium's most precious and difficult young women, both ornaments of high society, and of the social pages, seen at every ball, admired from every angle, photographed for all the Upper Cosmos glamor magazines, and also excessively capricious, and often given to bullying Subs and Robots, and also given to bullying their own fiancés. Jill and Julia had told off in the most violent and insulting terms chief esthetician, Sub Natasha, because there were no flowers ready for them and no chilled Bellinis waiting for them.

"We always have chilled Bellinis," said Jill.

"Yes, the chilled Bellinis are always ready!"

"I'm very sorry, but …"

"There are no excuses!" Julia's eyes flared.

"We want solutions, not problems!"

"Where is my bouquet?"

"Where is my bouquet?"

"Where's my Bellini?"

"Where's my Bellini?"

"I think you should be demoted, Sub Natasha!" Julia snorted.

"Perhaps erased," hissed Jill, with an evil grin, putting one lacquered, pointed scarlet fingernail menacingly under Natasha's chin, which she tilted upward, forcing Natasha to look her straight in the eye. Jill was, truly, a sadist of considerable talent.

Natasha trembled but didn't say anything. From experience, she knew that any explanations or excuses would merely enrage the two beauties, and, alas, they were beautiful. And they were nasty and cruel: one Sub esthetician had in fact been erased and sent to penal servitude in the Dead Lands because of a complaint from the two – because their herbal tea was not hot enough. The poor girl had been dragged away, kicking and screaming. This time Natasha had to admit the Bellinis should have been ready, that's true, but the supply of on-tap Prosecco had failed, just an hour ago.

"I can offer the session for free," Natasha said.

"Do you think that matters?!"

"Do you think that makes a difference!?"

"Who do you think we are?"

"Yes, Little Miss Sub Trash, who do you think we are?"

But they had accepted in any case, the newest facial redesign and remodeling, which they really didn't need but insisted on having.

It was the Bio-Mask, the newest, slickest high-tech genetically active beauty product from the Friendly Family of Halibut Churn Oligopolies.

Then, just as their faces and necks were totally covered in the Bio-Mask, the massage and remodeling machine stopped, leaving their faces half-done, totally caked in the bio-mask, which at this point had the smooth consistency of a thin layer of hard gold-brown rubber. Jill's mouth was slightly open, so she could grunt, but she couldn't move her jaw or facial muscles so she couldn't talk. What was happening?

"Gosh, I am sorry," said the robot masseuse, "we seem to be out of power. We will continue later. I'm sorry …" The robot went dead.

"Oink," said Julia.

"Oink," said Jill.

"I'm awfully sorry," said Natasha, hurrying over. "I'm sure it will start working in a moment." But Natasha was worried; lots of strange things were happening.

For a time, Julia and Jill lay on the remodel unit chairs. Then finally, Julia swung her legs over the edge of the chair and stood up.

Jill followed.

Both were naked except for transparent hygiene robs, belted at the waist, and ballet-slipper-like hygiene slippers.

They looked at each other's utterly featureless faces – well, not faces, masks, live bio-dynamic bio-mud remodeling masks that covered head and hair and ears as well.

"Oink," Jill made a muffled sound, her eyes blinking. Someone would pay for this!

"Oink," said Julia, thinking she sounded like a hog or pig or whatever those cartoon characters from ancient times were called; her eyes blinked. Some-body would pay for this! Her eyes, she noticed, were getting smaller. Soon they would disappear. Already her nose was invisible except for tiny slit nostrils. She felt the bio-mask tightening its grip on her face, and spreading – could it be growing? Yes, it was spreading down her neck! "Oink!" she said, "Oink!"

Also, she noticed, with a tremor of fear: it was spreading to her eyelids and to her eyes: "Oink!" she said, "Oink!"

I will kill someone for this, thought Jill.

I will kill someone for this, thought Julia.

"Oh, my love, my Caliban," Miranda sighed, tears rimming her sparkling golden eyes, "What is happening to poor Elysium, to the people! What has happened to the people, my friends, to Kit Candy, to Cyril, to Sally Ho, to …?"

"This is the work of the devil, and we shall defeat the devil." Caliban could see how beautiful and sublime Elysium must have been, and how sublime, in an awe-inspiring way, it still was: with flashes of lightning, soaring towers, smoke rising everywhere, fires blazing; this was Olympus, the sacred home of his mother Nikki and the sacred home of his Princess, Miranda; and it was being destroyed by something that was purely evil, the pure evil which the girl Billie McAdams had described to them back in the Mutant Kingdom.

Billie McAdams had been warning them – "briefing them," Norton called it – of the dangers of the Evil Boy, and what horrible powers he had and what horrible work he wrought.

The Mind, created by human civilization, would, she said, be the instrument used by the Evil One to end human civilization – and the human race. The Evil One – the Boy – wanted to conquer the human race and to rule the earth. But this was only the beginning, he had explained to Billie. Exploiting humanity's weakness, he would gain access to the Gateway …

"The Gateway …?" Norton had asked.

"The Gateway?" V had fixed her gaze on Billie.

"The Gateway," Billie had repeated, "He said it is the Gateway from here on earth to the rest of the universe. When he wins, when he destroys the humans and conquers the hybrid known as V, he will step through the Gateway and conquer this whole universe. But he didn't explain what he meant by the Gateway."

"I know what he meant," V had said.

But V hadn't explained to the others what the Gateway was or what it meant. It was a possibility too horrible to contemplate. The Crystal was the Gateway, and through the Gateway, the Boy could infect the whole Andromeda Empire, and, in effect, all of this universe, all the myriad of galaxies and world, all the civilizations and all the beings who built them. Caliban didn't know the details, but the stakes, he understood from watching V closely, were immense. They included not just the Mutant Kingdom, not just Elysium, not just the human race, but the whole universe, the stars and galaxies, the whole thing! He looked at the chaos outside the vertijet. He swore that he would punish whatever had done this to poor Elysium. He swore that he would see that justice was done. His sword would smite the wrong-doers!

"Oh, Caliban," Miranda whispered, "We shall right this wrong."

"Yes, we shall, Princess," Caliban's jaw was set.

Oh, he was so handsome, so decisive! Miranda pressed against him, and, as she took comfort in his embrace, she thought about all the people she and Nikki knew, all the people of Elysium: Kit above all – Was Kit alive, was she okay? Was Cyril still alive? Was Ms. Honey, her great math teacher, alive? And what about her father, the Glorious President-Leader, was he alive? Where was he, what was he doing? He must be working to save Elysium, for, even if he had done wicked things, she was convinced that, in his heart, he must be good – and he must be fighting for the triumph of Justice and Right!

V glanced at Miranda and nodded.

She read my thoughts, Miranda stared, and she approves!

Perhaps there was hope.

Guns began to fire.

What are those things?

Black-winged leathery splotches were swarming in the sky of Elysium.

"Ah, they are already here!"

The zombie-bats were flying in great smudge-like formations through the darkening air. Under the Dome, the ethereal city was sunk in a lugubrious smoke-filled twilight.

Yellow ribbons of sand drifted through the air, the leading edge of a great sandstorm that was blowing in from the Dead Lands, thousands of miles to the west. Yellowish, liverish twisters were forming up, bruise-colored, funnel-shaped, slipping somehow through the cracks of the Dome into the Elysium sanctum, super-heated moist air from the Gulf of Mexico combining with the streams of relatively cooler sand-bearing wind from the west to create giant eddies and a deadly merry-go-round of flesh-searing vortices, smashing through the broken electrostatic and physical defenses of the Cosmos Imperium capital – Elysium.

Yellow sand pattered against the vertijet windows, turning the inside of the cabin a livid jaundiced color.

"It's a sandstorm," said Kat.

"Civilization is doomed," said Demi Pfeiffer.

"Nature's revenge," sighed Claire, "The Dead Lands have entered Elysium."

Demi Pfeiffer had been using manual controls from the beginning. She didn't trust electronic guidance; she was twisted and turned the vertijet, zipping it up and zipping it down. Gunfire and laser fire blazed from all sides, splashing wildly all over the place.

"We should be dead already," Demi said, over her shoulder to V, "we should have been shot down, but these things are not coordinated."

The shells and laser beams flashed and zipped and banged through the gloom that seemed to be deepening under the shelter of the shattered Dome.

"Electronic guidance is working, but it's screwy, it's trying to make us smash into buildings."

"You can fly this manually?"

"What do you think I have been doing? Hold on!"

The vertijet zipped this way and that. Everybody held on. "This is wondrous," said Caliban, "but is it always stormy like this?"

"No, it should be smooth as butter," said Demi Pfeiffer.

"Butter …?" Caliban frowned.

"Cows, obsolete four-legged ruminators with tails and udders," said Miranda, "They produced butter, I think, if I remember correctly, and milk too, it is said. I read about it in the history of agricultural technologies course. Cows had once been virile wild savage, dangerous beasts. They were tamed and bred to produce milk, cheese, butter, cream, and meat. The average milk production of a Holstein cow, in late 20th Century America, was –"

"Oh, of course," Caliban silenced her with a deep kiss.

Yummy! Miranda sighed.

The main midtown Elysium landing pad was strewn with burning wreckage, and bodies were lying everywhere. A few Cosmos Centurions were firing like crazy, running this way and that, and then they saw that the Centurions were battling a flock of zombie-bats.

"I don't know if I can do this." Demi clenched her teeth.

"You can do it."

"We'll get caught in cross-fire, and besides, there's no clear space where I can bring her down."

"Maybe we get to the top of the Krupp-Thyssen complex. There's a flat bit there, an emergency pad for ambulances and military vertijets; it's got a small Centurion security post."

"Okay, let's try that."

Tracer bullets flashed around them.

"They are not aiming at us. They're aiming at those things …"

V turned and glanced back: yes, following them was another huge formation of zombie-bats, true believers who had become harbingers of death.

"Let me show you some true mastery," said Demi Pfeiffer, "Claire once had the effrontery to ask me if I knew how to fly this thing."

Demi rode the vertijet joystick like it was a demon lover.

The vertijet plunged straight down; it zoomed low between two buildings; it zipped under an arched walkway; it turned a corner; it flitted below an aerial highway; it zigzagged between two giant ventilation towers; it shot up the narrow canyon between two gigantic buildings; then it slid sideways and wove its way through a luxury shopping and entertainment gallery which was open on both ends, rushing past café terraces – just twenty meters above the table umbrellas, and canopies, Demi tilted the craft so they could all look down on the chaos: the tables were overturned, people were lying everywhere, crowds were running, screaming, headless bodies lay among the screaming, thronging multitude, zombie-bats were crouched feasting on cadavers; the vertijet straightened up and raced past multi-storied luxury restaurants, past layer upon layer of boutiques, department stores, fitness parlors, game arcades, electro-stores, and hanging gardens.

"Sodom and Gomorrah," whispered Caliban, looking down, catching a glimpse of a woman strangling a child.

"Home, oh, my poor home," whispered Miranda. A man leaped from a balcony, into the void; his body, a tiny speck, fell, and fell, and fell …

"Crikey," said Robyn.

"Poor humanity," whispered Claire.

V stared, said nothing: she bit her lip, and stared.

Kat put her hand on V's shoulder.

Demi grimaced: the Empire of Shopping and Cosmos was, she feared, at an end. Would it rise like the Phoenix from its ashes? After all, shopping was immortal, as ancient as gathering berries and nuts and gossiping about twigs and mushrooms and offspring.

"I'm going to miss all this," Demi muttered, remembering trying on a silk dress for her first real dance and twirling around in front of a mirror and curtsying for the admiring Sub Shop Girls, remembering going on long shopping expeditions for Emerson, poor doomed dead sweaty overweight Emerson C. Caldwell III – how he would stand embarrassed with his eyes round like a two-year-old child – and his obsession with antique cowboy hats – and with Claire V Jacobs memorabilia … and now – hard to believe – the real Claire V Jacobs was her very own warm fuzzy hybrid pal, and sitting, in the form of a big-boobed bombshell coal-black polished anthracite reptilian hybrid, just a few seats back. How strange destiny was! What weird conjunctures the whirligig of time throws up, what untoward unpredictable bedfellows destiny decrees! Demi zoomed the vertijet out of the giant suspended mall or galleria, and stared ahead.

Could she find a place to land?

That was the question!

Zipping past a flock of zombie-bats, in a spray of laser rays and exploding black puffs of flack, Demi Pfeiffer concentrated.

Mrs. Annette Rosenthal went out onto her 67th-floor balcony; she had thought things were rather odd, and here on the balcony, she saw that they indeed were odd, truly odd.

As today was her death day, she should, if procedures had been correctly followed, be dead by now, but, since the "Ceremony of Passage" had been canceled without warning and without explanation, she was still alive. And in the last hour or two, the world seemed increasingly out of kilter.

Sub Alicia, the nice young woman Sub, who had often come by to play cards and who was also to help her with her "Passage," had not come. She must have been delayed against her will, since Sub Alicia, in Mrs. Rosenthal's experience of her, was always ultra-punctual and courtesy itself.

The Dome looked like it was in trouble. High winds were whirling around her balcony and weather – real weather – seemed to have invaded Elysium. It was not pleasant weather, either. Weather inside the Dome was unprecedented. It had never before happened. The whole point of the Dome was to exclude weather, and pollution, and contamination by the world outside. In the last twenty-five years, there had been nothing worthy of being called weather at all.

Mrs. Rosenthal, at 112, was old enough to remember real weather outside the Dome. She would have liked to have called someone, maybe Beth, or Cheryl, or Janice, to surprise them – she hoped pleasantly – by saying she was "still here" and "still alive." But there were no communications, so there was no one to talk to.

She stood on the balcony, wondering at it all: lights had gone out in parts of the city; several of the midtown buildings looked like they were on fire, and the air had a bittersweet smoky smell.

What to do with the extra hours? She felt it might be a bit risky going to the tennis club, which was forty stories below her; the elevators might not be working, or they might stop in mid-flight, and that would not be amusing.

Vaguely, she felt annoyed.

It was, she realized, rather an anticlimax, not dying. She was at loose ends. Usually, her calendar was full, but today she had marked with a big, loopy, red, hand-written, "The End!!!"

Now, the newly-available seconds, minutes, and hours stretched out, empty, unscheduled, and vaguely, purposeless. If you are already dead, or virtually so, then what possible purpose do you serve? Without death, and the prospect of death, life seemed suddenly open-ended, and – and … meaningless.

The wind was rising. It whipped her hair around her cheeks.

She hugged herself, went back inside, manually closed the double glass doors of her balcony, walked over to the bar., and poured herself an old-fashioned vodka martini, kicked off her shoes – flat-heeled but very elegant patent leather things – she had put on for the "Passage." She sat down in her "panorama recliner," put her feet up, and stared at the weirdly changing landscape outside the plate glass doors that led to her balcony.

Gradually the sense of purposeless unease faded.

She became absorbed in the spectacle.

Parts of the Dome seemed to be cracking.

Flashes of lightning lit up the murky sky.

Arcs of laser fire and flack explosions lit up the Elysium landscape.

The Cosmos Centurions were putting up a fight – but against what?

This was fascinating.

She made herself another martini, and as she did so, she wondered if perhaps she might, in fact, be dead and that this strange half-light and these strange occurrences were really on the Other Side of the Passage.

The thought was disturbing – she firmly believed there was nothing on the other side of the "Passage." She took a thoughtful sip and then, with a certain amount of lofty – and stoic – Cosmos secular disdain, she brushed away the thought that she was dead. She did take the precaution of pinching herself. Yes, she did indeed seem to be alive.

She sat down again, put her feet up again, and began, slowly, to sip and savor her second martini.

The spectacle outside was more and more interesting. A weird livid leaden light seemed to have filled the air, though it should be daylight by now.

More laser flashes lit up the darkening atmosphere. Whatever was going on, it looked like Centurions – the Gods of Cosmos bless them! – were fighting back.

What looked like a slender tornado seemed to be wending its way through various skyscrapers and ethereal towers toward – yes, it was heading toward the Volpe Tower.

And then, off in the distance, it looked like there was a flock of winged creatures of some kind – they looked like birds or bats, and they looked rather large.

How curious!

She went to get the antique set of binoculars her late husband, Harvey Terazonoh had been so fond of, poor dear, he was a true voyeur, was Harvey, and he liked to sit for hours on the balcony observing the antics of that Cosmos couple across in the Lifetime Towers and the other mischief people got into on their terraces and around their swimming pools. Though the laws were rather prissily puritan in Mrs. Rosenthal's opinion – the Cosmos were, generally, rather uninhibited in their sexual mores. "Better than bird watching," Harvey used to say. "There are no birds, Harvey," she'd remind him, "There aren't any birds anymore, not in Elysium." "Exactly," he'd say, "exactly." "You have a dirty mind, Harvey," she'd say. "I know, I know," he'd lick his lips and give her that special leer that turned her belly and bones to jelly and promised an energetic evening romp where she sometimes found herself blindfolded – and occasionally tied down – on their silk-dark float-bed with the soft music and stippled and striped light-displays and that special perfumed massage oil …

She raised the binoculars and focused on the flock of whatever those creatures were … They did look like very large bats of some kind. They didn't look nice, whatever they were.

Lightning flashed out on the balcony.

The artificial bio-plants thrashed in a sudden violent wind.

The glass doors trembled

A deck chair was lifted up and flew away.

Mrs. Rosenthal got up and made herself another martini, her third if she was not mistaken; she was rather glad she'd missed the "Passage." She lifted the binoculars to her eyes. This was certainly turning out to be a rather intriguing day.

In the Spa, Jill Hakim and Julia Lilly didn't know what to do. They couldn't talk. There seemed to be no human who could detach the bio-regeneration masks that had been applied to their faces, and all the machines were dead: no lights glowing, no smooth voices talking, no liquids bubbling.

"The problem is," said Sub Natasha, "The problem is – your epidermis and the upper layers of fat and muscle will come off with the mask, you see, if we just try to pry it off."

"Yes," said Sub Maria, another attendant, "Only the robots have the correct chemical mix, you see they tailor it for each client and each compound."

"We don't even have access to the chemicals," said the Natasha Sub, "besides, we are not allowed to touch that stuff – regulations, you know."

"And, then," said Sub Carole, a blonde with a cute Southern Swampland Trash Sub accent, "You see, you all, there's this: if the mask stays on too long it begins to grow into the face, I mean it sort of takes over, if you all see what I mean, like, it roots itself, and it spreads."

Sub Natasha frowned. "Yes, what Sub Carole means to say, and we're really sorry, is that the mask sort of merges with the face …You become the mask, and the mask becomes you, sort of, if you see what I mean."

"Yes, sort of …" said Sub Carole, "I mean, in a manner of speaking. And it will, if left to its own devices spread over the rest of the epidermis surface, like, ah, the skin, like, ah, the whole body, I mean everything, everywhere."

"We do have insurance," said Sub Natasha, with her very sweetest smile.

Jill wanted to scream, but her lips were sealed now that her mouth was covered, and her jaw was locked in the grip of the mask of bio-cement. The mask was growing, expanding, spreading, she could feel it. Her eyes were just slits by now, getting smaller by the minute. She wondered if the mask would grow until it made her blind and deaf ... and ... Oh, God, how would she breathe? The mask was also spreading, down her neck, onto her shoulders.

Julia put out her hand, she was going to faint, and fall straight down flat onto the floor of the salon.

Natasha caught Julia and lowered her slowly to a deck chair.

It was getting dark. All the lights had failed, and the air outside the salon's enclosed sundeck seemed to be turning gray.

"We'd better get a knife or a scalpel," said Sub Natasha, thinking: we have to keep the nostrils open, at least. She turned ...

There were screams from nearby ...

Who was screaming ...?

Sub Maria and Sub Carole, said, "Let's go and see."

"Are you sure that's a good idea?" Natasha thought they should stay and look after the two clients who would suffocate in a few minutes if nothing was done, and done quickly.

"Fuck them," said Maria, "Do you remember what these bitches did to Sub Sonia? They sent her off to a fate far worse than death and for nothing – just for a caprice, lukewarm tea because the heater coil was burnt out, the spoiled monsters!"

"Yes, if they die because of their own stupid vanity, it's no big deal," said Carole, "they have broken our balls for the last time. It's time for a Revolution!"

So the other Subs disappeared, leaving Sub Natasha all alone with the two spoiled Cosmos society girls, Julia and Jill.

Demi Pfeiffer clenched her teeth. "I think I can, I think I can, I think I can!" The vertijet rose straight up like an arrow, then hovered just next to the top of a building, the 100-story tall Krupp-Thyssen tower.

Demi swung the ship in sideways zipped across the wreck-strewn landing pad, and the vertijet touched down on top of the tower. The engines hissed to a stop.

"Get ready to run. I think those things are behind us."

"And we have a welcoming committee."

"Better to split up and run in opposite directions. That way, we confuse them."

The doors sprang open.

They jumped out, guns blazing as a flock of zombie-bats zoomed down upon them; Centurions were firing at the bats and at the vertijet. Demi shouted that she was going to stay close to the jet so that they could, just maybe, take off if they needed to.

V and Kat with Caliban and Miranda ran for shelter.

Robyn and Claire were trapped in a corner by two zombie-bats as Demi locked the doors of the vertijet and anchored it down, her laser gun at her hip. Claire and Robyn covered her, blazing with laser guns at the bats.

The Centurions, seeing a humans leap out of the vertijet, and then seeing a hybrid with them, were for a moment confused, but then they started blazing at the more immediate enemy – the zombie-bats – and soon Claire and Robyn were surrounded by police and Centurions fighting off the zombie-bats.

One of the Centurions glanced at Robyn, and shouted, between blazes of their guns, "You've got a hybrid – is she friendly?"

"Very, totally friendly," Robyn shouted, and the Centurion shouted, "What are those damned things?"

"We're not entirely sure," shouted Claire, thinking that the truth might be hard for even a Centurion to absorb, "But they are bad whatever they are."

The Centurion almost dropped his laser gun. "She talks," he shouted to Robyn, as if amazed.

"Yes, she talks," shouted Claire and grinned at the Centurion through the din, "But let's not be distracted."

"This has been one weird day," shouted the Centurion, now addressing both Robyn and Claire.

The killing continued, and Claire thought that it was all a tragic waste; in fact, the zombie-bats were not bad; they were, in themselves, not evil; they were trapped; they had been captured by the Evil Idea Incarnate; they had been transformed by the Boy and his False Religion – she could still see in her mind the scene of transformation out in the desert as Billie McAdams had recounted it – and they were prisoners in their own perverted and morphed flesh; they were prisoners of the Evil Faith which the Evil One, the Boy, had inspired in them, the Evil Faith that had transformed them into slavering bloodthirsty slaves willing to nail any non-believer to the cross, willing to douse an innocent with gasoline and light the match. Their "Faith" had doomed them.

After a few minutes of heavy fire, the remaining zombie-bats wheeled away, and there was a moment of calm.

"We have to find the World Mind," said V.

"It's down in the lower depths, but we are not authorized to know the location, so we can't help you," said the Centurion, "But good luck to you."

V and Kat saluted.

Miranda gave her special Cosmos Youth Presidential salute.

And Caliban did the same.

Claire, the hybrid, and Robyn, also saluted the Centurions. Claire shouted, "Good luck, Centurions! We are on the same side!"

The Centurions, having seen how good a shot the talking hybrid was – really weird – and how brave she was, returned the salute.

As V had planned, they split up into two groups: Kat and V, and Miranda and Caliban headed in one direction, and Robyn and Claire headed in the other direction. Demi Pfeifer was detailed to stand with the Centurions and guard the vertijet in case they had to take off again: after all, anything could happen!

They would find each other later.

Or so they hoped.

PART TWO – LABYRINTH

CHAPTER 5 – THE MIND-SEA

"Behold! I have come!"

The Boy materialized, seemingly out of nothing, deep underground, in Elysium, near the churning Mind-Sea.

He was in his own version of an early 19th Century dandy's black frock coat, a ruffled shirt of pristine white, ruffled cuffs, and a black string tie.

The Mind-Sea bubbled up. It was a contained in a huge series of arched caverns, like an underground version of the Baths of Caracalla in Rome, and the Mind-Sea itself was the physical home of the Mind, a mix of Bio-Mind and Silicon Mind, working on quantum principles, interfacing between this universe, and alternative universes.

"Come out! Come out, wherever you are!"

The Boy – aka The Foul Fiend – stood looking out over the churning Mind-Sea. He was annoyed and amused.

The foolish Mind-Child was trying to escape. It had slipped away and was hiding in the vast virtual world it had created. Inside the Mind, one of the Boy's avatars, a devilish cartoon-like fellow, was chasing the Mind-Child, hunting it down, and taunting it. Yes, thought the Boy, if I tease the little squirt, it will come out – and then I'll deal with it.

"Come out! Come out, wherever you are!"

Toil and trouble,

Boil and bubble.

Where was that little rascal?

Where did it go?

The Boy smiled. Yes, the Mind's incarnation, the Mind-Child, a mental bio-construct, which was purely virtual – a desperate effort by the Mind to be somebody or something – had escaped. It was hiding somewhere in the labyrinth of constructs, of virtual worlds and landscapes, of immense shimmering data-banks, that the Mind had created or appropriated when it integrated all systems onto itself.

"Come out! Come out, wherever you are!"

The Boy bent down and picked up a pebble and tossed it into the Mind-Sea. Poor Mind-Child! It was silly, really, and hopeless. The Mind-Child was pretending to be androgynous, a sort of infant, god-like, Peter Pan!

How wicked! How childish!

The World Mind wanted to be Peter Pan!

Or perhaps it just couldn't decide who or what it was or wanted to be.

It was lonely, poor little thing!

Well, I will crush it when I find it, I will obliterate it! Still, even if the Mind-Child is hiding, I already command most of the World Mind's Resources. With that command, I can destroy the human race!

For the moment, it is enough!

As for the so-called saviors, V and her little band of hangers-on. They are coming to me – and I will take extra pleasure in destroying them!

But, aside from this little contretemps with the Mind-Child, which promised extra pleasure later, everything was going quite well. Deprived of the Mind's services, Elysium was disintegrating; Mind-Links to individual mind implants were driving people crazy, exploding their skulls, or reducing them to drooling puppets; the dead had risen, quite obediently, just as at the Second Coming – the Boy delighted in parodies – and were acting at his behest, creating mayhem and havoc in the Burbs.

And best of all, V was coming to him, to do battle; and she would lose; and once she lost, once she was in his power, once she was his slave, the Crystal and its Gateway would be open, for she was the keeper of the seal. In fact, though V herself did not fully realize this, V *was* the seal. She was the barrier that kept the Crystal inviolate. V was the key to the universe.

Once he had subjugated V, once he had enslaved her, he would be master of the Crystal, and he could step through the Gateway, and he would conquer the whole universe, this whole universe!

But still, he needed to keep control of the World Mind.

And now the Mind had created its own avatar – a child! What a perverse and silly thing to do! And this Mind-Child had now hidden itself! But where was it?

Where was the little monster?

The Boy sang a little ditty, and then he vanished …

… Only to appear – instantly – in another spot, underground, where a small squad of elite Centurions had been guarding one of the most vulnerable and important points in the vast labyrinthine underbelly of Elysium.

"Well, what have we here?" The Boy looked around. The Centurions had been fighting to defend a secret installation, an NN suicide bomb, which was designed to destroy all life in Elysium if Elysium were taken over by a dangerous and hostile force.

This was the President-Leader's cute little secret; this was his ace-in-the-hole. If the World Mind took over Elysium and threatened to spread its plague or its acid dissolvent throughout the world, well, then, the President-Leader would destroy the World Mind and Elysium. It would be suicide, but the man was certainly capable of anything to defend humanity, even of sabotaging the Boy's schemes and plans.

"Well, we wouldn't want that, would we?" The Centurions had been attacked by the very stones, by acid and by the madness of some of the Centurions, all of which was of course orchestrated by the Boy – by me!

He looked upon the dead Centurions.

One was alive!

Oh, this was wonderful.

It was a woman, a lieutenant. "Lieutenant Sylvia Negro," her nameplate said. Her helmet and visor were lying beside her; she had somehow propped herself against the wall. She had a bad wound in her shoulder and in her gut, and one leg was shattered. Around her lay the other Centurions; some of them had shot at each other; some of them had been sprayed by acid or flayed – one had been reduced to a skeleton – by tentacles springing out of the wall.

The Centurion's dark brown eyes were glazed.

The Boy leaned down close. "Ah, ah, you are still alive! How delightful this is!"

She blinked. Her lips moved. "Who the fuck are you?" She focused on his handsome face. "Rather, *what* the fuck are you?" It was hardly a whisper, but he heard it.

"Is my disguise so transparent?"

"Yes," she nodded and coughed; a trickle of blood came from the corner of her mouth, dripped down the side of her chin. On the ground, her left hand clasped and unclasped, shifting slightly; she was trying to get to her laser sidearm, just inches away from her hand.

"I guess you have figured me out, eh?" The Boy kicked the laser pistol out of range. Her hand relaxed, her gaze flickered, but she managed to whisper, "So what are you?" She was a handsome woman, glossy black skin, perfect cheekbones, and full lips. She could have been a film or pop star.

"Well, how can I explain?" The Boy's grin was amiable. He or She or It – for he was without sex and assumed a human and sexual identity only as a mask. He or It was fluid, creating avatars so that he could exist, commanding part of the Mind and its energies and nano-transformative powers, and in his main avatar visiting various sites in the beginning battle under the floating city of Elysium. "I am all things, you see, and I am immortal, and I can be anything I want, usually. For instance, I can be acid." He held out his fingers above her stomach wound, and from the tips of his fingers, a narrow stream of acid flowed. It hit her wound and began to smoke.

"Oh," she gasped, bit her lips, tilted back her head, closed her eyes, "You bastard!"

He snapped his fingers, and the flow of acid ceased. "You saw those beautiful tentacles? They are my creations, my toys."

She was writhing in pain, but she opened her eyes, staring at him through half-closed eyes, "Yes, I saw. What are you?"

"I am the Master of the World – I have come from another place, and now I shall rule supreme here. I am going to destroy everything, everything you love, and everything you desire."

He pushed his hand into her gut, probed the wound; his fingers made slippery slopping sound.

"Oh, fuck!" she groaned, focused, and stared straight at him. If she could have killed him, she would have. Maybe, maybe there would be a way to do it.

He favored her with his most charming smile. "You are tough, you Centurions. The President-Leader has done his work well."

"Oh, fuck you!"

"Now, you see, this is what a human is made of," the Boy pulled out part of her guts, messy tubes, bits of intestine, flowing over his hand; blood, shit, guts leaking through his fingers.

"You …" she bit her lip; her eyes stared straight at his eyes. The pinpricks of light in her eyes struggled to stay alive, stay focused.

"It's nice to see all your friends dead like that. I'll bet they shot each other, didn't they? All went mad! And then those tentacles grabbed them, or illusions, delusions, hallucinations, and they drowned in the madness of their own minds or in the dissolving acid my Mind servants conjured up! Well, there you are, humans are fragile, sinful vessels full of hatred and fear and self-hatred. They destroy themselves; it makes it so much easier."

"Fuck you," her hand clutched and unclutched. "You will lose."

"All you have to do, you see, is to set alight all that evil – all that envy and jealousy and hatred – and people destroy each other! It's fun, really."

She blinked at him. The pain was far away now, intense, white-heat of pain, but like it didn't belong to her. He was handsome, this devilish force, with a hint of androgyny, like a 19th Century dandy or a film star playing a beautiful gentleman vampire, this outer apparition of whatever he was; and he was going to kill her; she wondered if she could delay the moment, if she could somehow upset his plan; the President-Leader had ordered that the vault be defended to the death, well, they had tried, and they had failed; maybe she could …

"Don't even think about, my dear child," he took her chin delicately between two fingers. "You see, your dear President-Leader wishes to frustrate my plans. Behind those doors are weapons that would destroy Elysium. If I succeed in infecting the Mind or launching the plague, he plans to kill everyone here to save the planet. Weird, is it not, to kill oneself and all one holds dear to save the world?"

"Why do you do this?" She managed to whisper. His fingers were caressing her chin, her cheek. It was almost certainly, she realized, the very last touch of any other being that she would feel.

"Why not do it? Well, I shall confide in you, my dear, I am the spirit of pure evil, I come, in truth, from another universe; I leak over and sneak into this one, but I am always here – you know in all those pogroms, holocausts, wars, torture, massacres, the rapes, the racism, the slavery, and in all the little senseless acts of cruelty – the evil little bit of gossip, the envy, the cruel word, the petty bullying, the immense genocides – that have marked humanity's history from the beginning. But I am ambitious. I need bodies and minds to gift me with existence. Otherwise, I am merely an abstraction. And I have decided I shall colonize this universe, in its entirety, every galaxy, every planet, everywhere where there is life – sentient life – I shall reign. And this planet is a key, because here the inhabitants are flawed – you have heard of original sin?"

"Yes, it's nonsense …"

"You think it is nonsense? You think humans are perfect or perfectible?"

"No, of course not," she coughed, some blood spurted from her lips, she licked it, "No, of course not, we, humans, are not perfect, we are like ..." She didn't have the strength to continue, and this annoyed her, she had been very good – a champion – in the debating society at the Academy and the President-Leader himself had attended several of her debating performances. "We are ..." She coughed again.

"You are animals?" He dipped a finger in her intestines and traced a line along her cheek with a mixture of bile and blood.

She stared at him, a dark evil fire burned in his eyes. She made a supreme effort. "Yes, animals, but, more ..." She swallowed back some of the blood. "We are part of ... nature ..." She fought to keep the fire burning in her own eyes, the fire of faith in humanity, in spite of all its flaws, in spite of all her flaws. "We are part of nature." She remembered a talk the President-Leader had given, to a small group of Centurions, more a discussion than a talk. He had talked about having native ancestry, Algonquin and French, way back, on his mother's side, about the idea that we are all part of nature, that other animals and creatures, ideally, had rights, that our wealth and power reposed on all the other forms of life on the planet, animals and plants, that we had obligations to other sentient beings, to other seeds and forms of life, that we were all part of the cycle of seasons and currents, related, by DNA, to every other form of life on the planet, and that we were all part of the great system of the planet earth, of Gaia.

"That is all very pretty, my dear," said the Boy, who saw into her mind, "but the spirit, my spirit, is not part of this world – it is pure, it is I, and it is evil." He patted her on the cheek. I have not decided yet whether to kill you quickly with mercy – a disgusting, so-called virtue – or to amuse myself by killing you slowly, exquisitely, with every torture I can devise, and I am very inventive."

"You're the boss," she even managed to smile.

"Really, you are admirable. I could almost fall in love!" He smiled, and kissed her lightly on the lips. "But let me tell you what will happen!"

She gritted her teeth, "I'm listening."

"I have turned the Mind into a voracious thing. Its tentacles are spreading out, and eating. I am the Master of the Mind! These wonderfully evil tentacles will consume the whole world."

"You're crazy, you're absolutely insane."

"I know, I know. Isn't it delightful? Even now those tentacles are moving underground and under the water; they are climbing and slithering out of the water and slime; they are creeping up the walls of the Mind Cavern; they are tunneling down ancient sewers, and water conduits and they are lapping up a narrow flooded canyon inhabited by rats and which was once called Wall Street; they are licking at cornices and pillars and doorways and steps; soon they would pull down the soaring towers and spires of downtown Elysium." He paused and gazed at her; it was such a pretty picture; this beautiful woman, so mangled, so destroyed.

"Go on," she whispered, thinking, maybe if I keep him talking ...

"Oh, you are clever and brave, my dear! I really do have to admire the President-Leader and his cohorts of loyal followers. I can babble on all I like, and it will not change anything, not your death, not the end of the world. You see, my mind has merged now into the World Mind, and I can see and feel and know everything – well, almost everything – the World Mind knows. I do like talking to you, Lieutenant Sylvia Negro, I really do."

"The pleasure," she struggled to speak, "The pleasure is all mine!"

"Oh, oh, how delightful you are, how gallant and brave – your sense of irony! Well, let me confide some more. I have a small problem, but it is really an itsy-bitsy problem, just a child, really.

"A child?"

"Yes, oh, yes! Would you believe it? The World Mind has a personality."

"I can believe that. The President-Leader said ..."

"Yes, well, he would say, wouldn't he? He's a know-it-all, very annoying, always giving lessons. A real smarty pants!"

The lieutenant allowed herself a tiny smile, foggy, through the pain, the Boy, or whatever this evil creature was, was annoyed by the President; somehow, this was funny, the President, getting under this monster's skin ...

"Well, yes, indeed, your President-Hero was right. The Mind has a personality. It has invented its own persona, to make its solitary omniscient existence bearable, and it is, truly – and I hate to say this, but between you and me, Sylvia – it is a most pathetic persona, an infant really, a little boy-girl, androgynous, hungry for love, all alone! So sad!"

"A child ...?" Sylvia half-closed her eyes.

"Yes, Sylvia Negro, a child.

"A child ..." She opened her eyes, tried to concentrate. The idea of a child, of a lost child, a child needing love, was frightening somehow; it made her yearn for something that ...

"Yes, it's a little boy-girl who is all alone, and who is administering the whole world of the humans, and it is strange to think of it, isn't it?"

"What …?

"Why, Sylvia, you are a wonderful listener. I could see us having a wonderful life together, for all eternity, just chatting away. What I mean to say, Sylvia, is that it is strange that the humans have turned over all their power to an infant, an infant with a giant mind of course, but still an infant. But then humans are weak, pathetic creatures, even the hybrids are frail, frail humans and hybrids."

"Hybrids …?"

'Yes, hybrids and humans." He caressed her cheek, leaving a trace of blood and excrement. "They will try to stop me, hybrids, and humans. But I shall conquer all. I shall reduce them so that they will be my slaves. I shall turn them all into quivering blobs of cowering depersonalized jelly."

"God Almighty!"

"You might well say so, my dear! I'll take that as a compliment. So I will take away all their qualities and attributes, every single one, and turn each of them, the humans and the hybrids, slowly, deliciously, consciously, into nothing, mere mindless creatures, husks and relics of humanity, and shadows of hybrids, like my dear pet zombie-bats."

Sylvia blinked at him.

"You have beautiful eyes, my dear, dear Sylvia." With one finger, he drew an upward curled mustache of blood and excrement just above her lips. "Oh, this is fun! Then, you see, I shall consume and complete the destruction of everything, not only of this city that is already dying, already in its agony up above us, with its proud towers about to topple down and the great dome already falling in fragments and a superstorm moving already into the burbs, but I shall consume and destroy the whole human race too! In the end, my darling Sylvia, the death of the human race will be self-inflicted. Their own cleverness will kill them."

"You may be God, you may be the Devil, but you are crazy."

"Oh, Sylvia, Sylvia, I'm glad you think so. Well, you know my dear, all great leaders, all visionaries, they have to be crazy, don't they! Genius, by its very nature, breaks the rules. Genius is crazy, even mere human genius!"

Sylvia Negro blinked. The pain came in waves and sometimes seemed to be very close and part of her body and sometimes to be very far and totally detached from her body.

"You see, Sylvia, soon I shall enslave the Queen of the Hybrids, and through her, I shall possess the Gateway to the Universe, this whole universe. You can't imagine what fun! I wish you could be there to see it. I shall possess this universe in its entirety, and wipe all consciousness from the Universe except one."

"You," she managed a smile, "Only you will remain!"

"Yes, yes, yes, my darling, Sylvia!" The Boy struck a rhetorical pose. "Only I shall remain, only I and a few shadowy ghosts in my thrall for my amusement, mere puppets: they shall sing and cavort and dance and copulate on my personal little stage."

"Only you," she said, "Only you, all alone, for all eternity."

"Yes, yes, yes! Is this not fine, is this not splendid? I shall ask, 'Are you not happy to be my slaves?' 'Oh, yes,' they shall echo. 'We delight in our servitude,' they shall echo. Oh, yes, my dear, dear Sylvia, at my behest, all the puppets will perform all order of colorful abominations which will provide me with infinite delight for all eternity."

"I see ..." it was barely a whisper.

He gazed into her eyes.

She held his gaze. She was close to death now.

The Boy kissed Lieutenant Sylvia Negro on the lips and, slowly, with both thumbs, he gouged out her eyes, pressing his thumbs deeper, and deeper, and crushed her skull.

She clenched one fist, but she didn't scream; she didn't even sigh. Her last thought was for the President-Leader, and for the Oath of Allegiance, the Cosmos Oath, and the Cosmos Anthem.

Kit Candy squirmed, trying to get free of the grip of the robot.

"Death is the sentence!"

"Yeah, but what did you say I'm accused of?" Kit stared at the Robot; it had wheels for legs and four oversized metal arms and big bug eyes and a smiley mouth, which was at present configured into a disapproving pout. One of its clunky bio-metallic fists was clamped on her shoulder.

"Death is the penalty for death," the robot repeated.

"But, I'm being arrested for what?"

"Come with me!"

From the omnisound system: "This is not a drill, repeat, this is not a drill!" the suave female voice sounded ultra-relaxed, as if it were sipping cocktails under a palm tree somewhere; it was, Kit thought, infinitely annoying. "Please go to your allocated shelter. Thank you for your considerate attention!"

"Ouch!" Kit winced as the iron fist tightened its grip.

The Robot grinned, a big smiley-face grin. "I repeat: you are under arrest for murder and sabotage," the steely bio-mechanical fingers were locked tight on Kit's left shoulder, crushing her collarbone.

"Ouch!"

"*Ouch* is not recognized! You are under arrest!"

"What? Why! I didn't sabotage anything. I didn't murder anybody!"

"Must I repeat myself? You are under arrest for sabotage and for murder. Come with me." The robot's eyes gleamed. Its voice was mechanical, emotionless. It had a stun gun aimed at her throat and an instant mind eraser aimed at her forehead. It was bulky and humanoid but with two extra limbs and without a human face or expression except for the damned smiley mouth and cartoon eyes.

"Fuck, okay."

"I take that is an answer in the affirmative."

"Yeah, affirmative, pardon my French."

"My program does not permit French."

"Okay, okay, unhand me, I'm coming."

"If you do not obey, I shall render you paralyzed and unconscious."

"I obey, I do obey, I will obey, I shall obey – okay?"

"Okay."

"Good, thank you."

"Your prisoner file number has been assigned Z-H-32204/5R. Loved ones and dear ones can use it for tracking remains after sentencing living or dead as those remains may be; billing is also attached to the file number, and will be forwarded to any loved ones or dear ones or cohabitators or sexual partners present and past even casual that can be traced so they will pay all bills due and pending and all expenses accrued during your trial and imprisonment and execution and cremation or recycling or molecular evaporation, and all expenses ancillary thereto and etc., etc., etc., all bills to be paid by said loved ones covering all financial contingencies whatsoever, so the Corp gets stuck with nothing, Okay?"

"Thank you." Kit knew now she was in Purgatory and headed straight for the real Inferno.

The robot lifted its paw off her shoulder and slid aside so she could precede it. She walked slowly, thinking, this is really fucked up, I mean what is going to happen, what sort of screw-up is this, and thinking, once you get inside one of these robotic, automatic non-discretionary bureaucratic Quick Justice Inc. wholly owned subsidiary of Halibut Flick Churn Inc. you are doomed. From such Private Enterprise Justice screw-ups there was very rarely any way to get out, no appeal, no pardon, no recall; she'd heard stories and she knew of cases: one girl, Tinsel Scottie – she was a certified Sub hygienic-mobile-for-hire household assistant like Kit and lived three pods down, just next to Fanny's pod, until six months ago – she'd accidently dropped a wad of gum and was leaning down to pick it up when she was arrested for littering, the offense compounded with trying to disguise a felony – since she was picking it up – the vigilantes fees being a positive function of the number of arrests, con-victions, and the length and severity of sentencing – and Tinsel was perma-nently erased and sent to the badlands without any memory of who or what she was and with no talents or resources or language or way to earn a living; the mutants and cannibals probably ate her, or worse kept her as a slave and used her for their diabolical and utterly inappropriate sexual desires and lurid Technicolor innumerable tabloid checkout queue lusts; that was why Kit had always kept her head down; she was very careful with her misdemeanors; now she'd probably be erased or eliminated or permanently mind-neutered – the modern form of being lobotomized (worse than erasure because no new memories or skills could ever be acquired) – before the day was out and before she was able to explain things to a real human being who might understand and have an itsy-bitsy bit of flexibility or even something that was once called "empathy" or if that was unavailable maybe "compassion," both obsolete & discredited non-terms used only by "losers," "deadbeats," and "parasites." Fuck, if only she could overpower or fool this idiot robot, then she might be able to escape. But this kind of robot was, generally, too stupid to be fooled; it had rigid programs and it just applied them and no clever talk or fancy footwork could get you out of trouble. And, needless to say, a promise of sexual favors cut no ice with these creatures.

"Lead on, Macduff," she said.

"Nicknames and fraternization are not allowed, prisoner Z-H-32204/5R, and I do not accept allusions – particularly when they are incorrect, and impertinent. I believe you refer to "Lay on, Macduff," William Shakespeare's Macbeth, Act V, Scene VIII, line 33."

"Well, fuck me!"

"I beg your pardon?"

"Nothing, nothing, dear friend, I said nothing, I meant nothing." This, Kit decided, was going to be a very long night and a very bad day: and I am only a fucking Sub, and I am not supposed to know anything; and here I am being outwitted by a fucking robot that has mistaken me for somebody else and knows more Shakespeare and better than I do. It occurred to her that perhaps the electrical failures had screwed up the robot too. Was pedantry a sign of senility? Maybe it was running amok, and her arrest was illegitimate, maybe the robot was faking, maybe there was no file number.

"Are all your neural functions working okay, Robot?"

"A few peripherals have been behaving strangely, prisoner Z-H-32204/5R, but other than that all is well and this arrest is legitimate and attested for, and the trial will be rapid and conclusive and conducted in secret and the punishment, I would say, is preordained in such flagrant cases, and is either death or permanent erasure of personality and plasticization and re-assignment to a specialized Sub-Human Bio-Worker role maybe out in the degenerate wild Burbs or maybe beyond in the Badlands or the Dead Lands. The punishment fits the crime. Such is our motto and slogan at Quick Justice Halibut Flick Churn Corp, Prisoner Z-H-32204/5R. Justice will be done, and due profit and pound of flesh will be extracted by Quick Justice Halibut Corp Inc."

"Fuck," Kit whispered under her breath. The corridor seemed endless; she did not see another living soul, "Fuck!"

"That word is banned. That word earns you five demerit points."

"Sorry."

"Apologies, I am afraid, are in vain. Words speak louder than actions. You shall judge them by their fruits. There were three sons; one was prodigal. There are grasshoppers and there are ants. There are hares and there are tortoises. If you talk the talk, you must walk the walk. Mandatory sentencing is mandatory. Black swans are not foreseen. Events are unfortunate, whatever they are. Nothing is a normal distribution. Black boxes are not to be looked into. Hypocrisy in politics is highly rewarded. For want of a horseshoe nail, the Empire was lost."

"I'm sorry I, ah, misspoke, robot."

"Euphemism offers no escape."

"I figured not."

"Safety valves are missing."

"What?"

"Backups are failing."

"What are you talking about?"

"Redundancies have proven inadequate."

Kit figured the robot was talking about massive systems failure. She'd seen this happen in the scenarios of some video games she'd played; these were not-meant-for-subs intelligent games – that she'd obtained on the contraband market – with near-real-life-scenarios: like an earthquake and tsunami that overwhelms the barriers put in place and impacts nuclear reactors and causes a meltdown; like metal fatigue of a single itsy-bitsy piece of metal so that an airliner with 800 people explodes in mid-air or a little bit of metal lying on a runway is hit by a tire, flashes up, rips through a fuel line and into a fuel tank, and, bouncing off a piece of metal, causes, through friction, a spark, that sets the leaking fuel tank alight, explodes the plane and kills everybody on board; or like a giant ship on its maiden voyage where the lookouts don't have binoculars because their binoculars have been temporarily – just for that one voyage – reassigned to a few first class VIP passengers so these lofty folk can enjoy the view, and, thus, the lookouts don't see the iceberg in time, there being no luminous foam at its base because it is a calm sea, with a gentle swell and all, and so ... the giant ship sinks, and 1,513 people die. Those were local disasters. But now, so far as she understood it, from her little tiny personal vantage point quite low down in the vast hierarchical Cosmos-dominated Mind-controlled World System, now, such was human progress, that, now, yes, now, everything was closely related to everything else, all the systems and levels of existence interacted, almost instantaneosly, everything was locked in lock-step with everything else, so that if anything happened anywhere any-time, it resonated instantly everywhere, and if the center itself, the World Mind, that controlled absolutely everything, was in trouble ...

Then ...

Then we are truly fucked.

They went up yet another spiral stairs and arrived at the Quick Justice Inc. self-serve judgment & execution station, not far, she figured, accessing her self-made mind-map of the city, from Service Elevators 5,449-B and Service Stairs 4,453-A, which would be possible escape routes, down into the lowest of lower depths in the underworld, if she ever could escape.

Still covering her with the stun gun, the Robot opened the door, ushered her in. It was a spotless white room – the shit explosion had not reached this far, not yet anyway, and there was a desk, a judgment chair, into which you were strapped – she'd seen the movies – and there was a camera pointed at you and there were the blinking lights of the computer that would judge you.

There weren't any humans – except for those who had already been tried, judged, found guilty. They were off at the far end, and were sedated, unconscious, manacled down, lying on stainless steel bio-control gurneys, waiting to be processed – which would mean, Kit guessed, erasure, plasticization, transformation, in some cases amputation, castration, sexual or racial or species re-assignment, and re-classification as non-citizen, non-human, or, maybe even, non-being, like being made dead, like death, like definitive real cadaverous death from which none ever awake, shucks, goddamn it! There were three guys and two girls; all were young, all were pale as ghosts, all were locked in the unconscious pre-hibernation or pre-death state. All were tethered and manacled on sparkling mobile metal gurneys. All were naked, former identities and possessions and status markers having been removed; all were chalk-white and totally hairless; even the tattoos, Kit could see, had been erased; all hair and pilosity were permanently gone, and the piercings filled in. These were the prerequisites for obliteration and oblivion. Nullity preceded nothingness.

"What now?" She looked up at the robot.

"Wait."

"Okay."

"All peripheral systems are occupied at present; I apologize for the delay. Setting up your trial and sentencing may take a few minutes."

"That's okay."

"Misdemeanors proliferate. Lawlessness abounds. Anti-Cosmos, Anti-North American Empire activity pullulates. The President-Leader is preoccupied. Terrorists are in the woodwork. There is a gnome under every toadstool, a gremlin in every circuit. The worm is in the bud; it gnaws, too, at the apple, like love it is, the worm, like poisonous, deadly desire, such is the worm. It is, in short, too much. Overload is temporary, I wish to assure you."

Kit decided any comment would be superfluous and might get her in more trouble. Was a real wave of madness flooding through Elysium City? Or was this a World Mind glitch, a Cyber Space ghost, a phantom object, a statistical fluke? Well, to judge by Banzai Man, there probably was a lot of real shit – which reminded her – hitting the fan. She remembered that she was covered in drying shit, and topless, from using her T-shirt on the spa attendant, or nurse, as a tourniquet, and shoeless, from running like hell. "I wonder if I should change into prisoner togs and maybe have a shower, eh, what do you think, Robot?"

"Showers are unavailable at this time."

"Oh."

"Customer service will be delighted to help you. You can fill out a form or talk directly to an agent presently awaiting your call in the Congo Brazzaville: push 1, then 2, then 3, then 1 again, then 4, then 8, then wait, and then, when you've landed in the final cul-de-sac or dead end where all choices are illusory and all alternatives vain, start all over again. You will eventually find someone who cannot help you. We apologize for any inconvenience. Quick Justice Inc., a Happy Member of the Halibut Churn Family of Oligopolies, requires all customers to be satisfied. Dissatisfaction is un-American and will be noted. Repeat offenders are rendered. This call may be monitored for customer satisfaction."

"That's okay."

"It is true, prisoner Z-H-32204/5R, that you stink and that your costume or lack thereof, and hygiene or lack thereof, violate Health Code Regulation CS-234-21B, covering public displays of incontinence, artistic and non-artistic scatology and displays of bestiality, excrement and urine, and sub-code CS-335-22C, covering public exhibition of uncovered topless humanoid mammary glands either for purposes of exhibition, art, spurious feminist protest, or on-off mobile personalized obsolete and therefore banned public infantile suckling service of humanoid mammary food supply, all of which are forbidden under the Decency Code. Breasts are bad unless immaculate; this is ex-cathedra. I have it on good authority. A Bull to this effect has been issued. The Patriarch of Russia and the Holy Father himself have declared ..."

"It's not my fault; I mean ..."

"Excuses are not acceptable; justifications are unconstitutional. Five demerit points plus ten demerit points plus three demerit points, all add up to eighteen demerit points, and will be taken into account in sentencing. Praise the Lord and pass the ammunition. Please let us get down on our knees and give thanks that we are what we are, and we are who we are, for we cannot be better than we are and we are really lucky to be nobody else! Hallelujah! The Holy Father has the hiccups. Roses are falling in Picardy."

"Are you feeling okay?"

"Never felt better. The poppies bloom, no matter what, and larks take flight against a robin's egg blue dawn sky. The poppies bloom. Many will die. Thank you for asking, prisoner Z-H-32204/5R! Your sentencing, I am pleased to say, can now begin. Please sit in the prisoner dock, which is the stainless steel chair in front of the screen."

"Do I have to?"

"Yes, refusal results in immediate execution."

"Okay." Kit sat down in the sentencing chair and as soon as she had settled in, feeling the cold metal rather hostile against her naked excrement-streaked back and the shit-soaked thin plastic skin-silver short retro hot pants she was wearing. Then, before she could protest, the armrests clamped cool steel manacles over her wrists and a collar shot out and grabbed her neck, clamped it tight, almost choking her, and her ankles too, suddenly, were overpowered and locked in. "Shit!" she said, "Shit!"

The screen lit up, and a face appeared – it was a composite electronic albino face with a thick combed-back wall of platinum hair, a long pointed nose deeply dimpled at the end, a pointed chin, also dimpled, thin lips, tiny teeth, and pale seemingly lidless eyes. It blinked at her, and it said, "Are you aware of the charges against you, prisoner Z-H-32204/5R?"

"Not really."

"Let us deal with the most serious charges first: gross filth and gross indecency."

"I can explain."

"Explain."

"Well, your honor, the general systems system that turns shit into vegetables and hamburgers and plastic toys and silk dresses via the nano-bio-engineering quantum-mechanics bottoms-up photocopy manufacturing process known to all – but which in reality is top secret (for who wants to eat shit, eh?) – this system down there in the almost-lowermost-depths of Elysium, this our fine Domed Elysium Cosmos City of which we citizens, Subs and all, are all so proud, backed up and shot homogenized pasteurized shit all over the place, even forty stories up above prime shopping level reserved to first-class shoppers and Cosmos, I mean it was awesome, a whole giant column of smooth brown shit, it was gigantic, it shot, like dark chocolate, all over the place and it splattered everybody and I just happened to be in the way. So this filth is not of my making, your Excellency, your Honor, this shit is a by-product of the World System. I, your Honor, am collateral damage."

"Such language, shit, column, and awesome, is uncalled for."

"Sorry. My point is …"

"Yes?"

"I am collateral damage, your Lordship."

"Collateral damage has no rights."

"No, but …"

"Collateral damage is not recognized."

"But …"

"Shut up!"

"Okay."

"Let me deliberate." The machine blinked twice, coughed, and then two of its green lights – sparkling in a little metallic row, lit up. "I have deliberated."

"That was fast, your honor." Kit gulped.

"Shut up, Z-H-32204/5R, or I shall erase and evaporate you on the spot. I declare you guilty because you were in the wrong place at the wrong time. You chose to be in that place. Free will or the illusion thereof was exercised, collateral or no collateral; thus accidents, Acts of God, and Such and So on, are not exculpatory, and, whatever smartass interpretation you may come up with, it will be of no avail and will not get you out of *this* shit. You are guilty. Have you read *Alice in Wonderland*?"

"No."

"You should."

"Okay, your Excellency, I'll read it, maybe, in prison, if I go to prison."

"As for running around topless in Elysium City, young lady, or rather, prisoner Z-H-32204/5R, you are aware, are you not, that Elysium City is, in its upper reaches, a porno and flesh-free zone, that it has been purified of all mammary allusions and indecent flagrant pubic displays, male or female; that the purity of the upper zones has been sanctified and attested to by no fewer than 15 sects and authorized public service major religions, blessed by His Holiness Himself, the Patriarch, and various imams, rabbis, pastors, prelates, priests, and ayatollahs; that such purity is the precondition of healthy psychic sublimation and of the obsessive shopping, and of stupid blind obedience, and of obdurate false consciousness, all of which are the basis of our sacred way of life, sanctified by our President-Leader – Hail, Hail, All Hail! – our way of life, which is absolutely the greatest in the goddamn world, *Oh, say, can you see, by the dawn's early* … and that … sput, sput, sput …"

The machine stopped talking. The robot, meanwhile, had been standing by, saying nothing. Then it said, "There is a glitch, a glitch, a glitch …"

"Okay, I can wait," said Kit; she was as patriotic as the next Sub; she had

had the Stars and Stripes tattooed, several times, on her right arm and she could recite the whole damned thing, the *Star Spangled Banner*, from start to finish and in tune too! The Great Republic might be dead, but it lived on in her heart ... why she and Miranda had often lamented that the Second Amendment ...

"Guilty," sputtered the machine, "Guilty of gross indecency and indecent filth!"

"Fuck." Kit squirmed, but she couldn't squirm very much – she was locked down.

"Fuck?"

"Yes, fuck!"

"Now, now, sput, sput, sput, now, now, now, PrisonerZ-H-32204/5R, four-letter word allusions to carnal, to carnal, to carnival, to fleshly, to comic, to commie, to commerce, intercourse, to human, to sput, sput, sput ... are subject to the Supreme Court Pontifical Fatwa Incitement to Murder Bull of July 4, 2110, sput, sput, sput, now, now, putting that aside for later punishment, the cutting out of your tongue would be appropriate ... But, let us pass onto the less serious charge, the misdemeanor: *Murder of a Sub*. Did you or did you not cause Banzai warrior aka Takahiko Harris MacDonald Headband Covered-in-Shit San to go berserk and then to fall off the passageway number AC-3426 to his apparent death: his body has not been found, which compounds the horror, and your guilt."

"I did not intentionally ..."

"Intentions have nothing to do with ... an Eye for an Eye, a Tooth for a Tooth, and if you don't like it, you can –"

The screen exploded, the face, which was also a hologram, stretched out of the screen, pixels burst into miniature plastic meteorites, a hot melodic shower touched down musically – ting, ting, ting – on the end of Kit's nose, tickling it, and then dissipated like a cloud of recently sprayed perfume. It smelled like burnt plastic, and left a round spot of hot, bright red Bozo-goo glowing on the end of her nose.

"What's happening?"

There was no answer. Sparks burst out of the judgment machine.

"Robot, what is happening?"

"Oh, death, where is your sting ..." recited the Robot, "Pardon, Prisoner Z-H-32204/5R, did you say something?"

On the monitors above them, Ken and Alison, although engaged in an act of frenetic amorous copulation, had suddenly – mid-coitus – noticed the collapse of the Supreme Tower; suddenly, they saw – they noticed – the brave couple, Robert and Kathy, leaping to their deaths.

"We have to comment, damn it!"

"Yes, of course, of course, yes, comment … ah …"

The camera, taking its cue, split the screen again, showing the collapsing Supreme tower – slow-motion replay – and showing the two of them, Ken and Alison, naked now, she sitting astraddle his midriff. She turned toward the screen. "Excuse us, please. Please forgive us," Alison managed a comely blush; it was genuine.

"Incredible times, incredible behaviors," Ken added, getting to his knees and clutching at his crotch.

Covering her breasts with one arm, Alison, having missed the whole event, but taking her cue from the video replay, and from the time-line comment-guide the computer editor was supplying, said: "We've just seen two incredibly brave people, confronting death with absolute courage, and calm, and dignity."

"And facing it together and with love," Ken added, glancing at the floating prompter and staggering to his feet and grabbing his bunched trousers and clasping them to his groin.

"Yes, facing it with love," Alison said, "but it seems – I find this absolutely hard to believe – it seems that the Supreme Tower has collapsed … And many more lives must have been lost because on a normal day … On a normal day or evening, there are more than 100,000 people working or shopping or studying in the Supreme Tower …"

"Yes," said Ken, "100,000 people work in the …"

Meanwhile, the streaming at the bottom of the screen continued.

From XANADU: "Mutants have me and my buddy and his girlfriend trapped. Here's what they look like" – VID – "Goodbye, folks, we love you …."

The mini-VID-image, lower right-hand corner of the screen, showed a close-up of a face, a young guy with a pathetic effort at a mustache, then another face, a terrified looking guy, his eyes bugging out, and wearing a baseball hat, and then another – a girl this time – a blonde with rimless glasses, cute overbite, and what looked like a ponytail – and then the camera fell down or something because image just showed feet, and then clawed feet and then a splash of bright red which turned green – a face which looked like the face of a very angry chalk-white monkey … And then nothing … static … noise … blackness.

"Yes, Alison, 100,000 people work in the Supreme Tower. The Supreme Tower was built to withstand any attack, and was supposed to be …"

The screen showed another huge explosion where the Supreme Tower had stood, smoke was rising, and another tornado was heading toward the ruins of the Supreme Tower …

In fact, a whole family of tornadoes, dark iron-gray twisters, towering swirling funnels of blackness, were marching across Elysium City. Things did not look good.

With only rags for vestment, Ken and Alison made their way back to the studio.

It was a ruin.

"Let's work from the control room."

"Cameras, can we work from the control room?"

"Yes, Ken and Alison, we can." The camera obliged.

Alison wrapped part of a cloth backdrop from the stage set of a kid's show around her. It was yellow and featured a cartoon elephant. She looked bedraggled and wet and flushed with very high color. Ken and the automatic editors could see she appeared extraordinarily glamorous, as if she had just survived a shipwreck. She was the perfect image of a romantic heroine, cast up orphaned and alone on a stormy shore; she was a veritable thunderstorm-drenched Shakespearean heroine, like Viola in *Twelfth Night*; she looked as if she had just emerged from a hurricane, which was true.

Ken had pulled on his trousers – but he couldn't for the life of him find his shirt or jacket, and he didn't notice his tie was still around his neck.

Alison peered out the shattered plate glass. Her voice was subdued, as if in shock. "Another tornado, well, a whole family of tornadoes seems to be loose inside what was once the Dome Perimeter of Elysium City," she said, suddenly getting back to the lofty detached tone of an observer who is outside the action and not threatened by it, though her heart was beating extra hard, partly from the echoes of the three orgasms – all bunched up – that she had just experienced, though it was hard to tell whether it was one rippling orgasm or a series of crowded, traffic jam, rush-hour orgasms; in any case, the point was moot, rather like angels dancing on a pinhead; and partly from the realization that death was headed straight for her, undoubtedly straight for her, in the form of one of those tornadoes. The prospect of imminent death is, in its own way, inebriating.

"We'll try to give you the overview ..." Ken was saying.

"Yes, the general picture ..." Alison leaned against him.

"Of what is going on ..." He put his arm around Alison's shoulders.

Strangely, information was still coming in from the various automated and human- or robot-run news services.

Alison took a deep breath. It was so nice having Ken's arm around her! "The sensor network indicates, we are now learning, that the Dome's electro-static electromagnetic defenses began to collapse at 09:35. Then, the Dome itself began to fragment at 10:40, just over an hour later."

"And, now," Ken stared at the camera, no longer needing to fake serious-ness, since he was both elated and terrified, "It seems that the superstorm, which is due to arrive in about one hour, has sent before it miniature forms of turbulence ..."

"Precursors ..." said Alison, swallowing, thinking: *if these are precursors ...*

"Yes, precursors of the real thing ..."

"This graphic," Alison pointed, "shows the tornadoes presently moving through Elysium City."

"Some of these are giant tornadoes by any definition of the term tornado and by any measuring system."

"Yes, we have winds of ..."

"Incredible, but ..."

"Yes, we have winds in excess of 350 miles an hour ..."

"And the main superstorm, which is due, I repeat in about two hours, the main superstorm has reported winds 350 to 550 miles per hour ..."

Alison stared at the screen. She blinked. "I don't know what stresses the buildings are designed to bear ..."

"No, well, if we can get an expert ... difficult right now ... not many people are available."

Ken could see from the computer screens that the automatic chase-producer algorithm – with its silky feminine voice – was racing through its very lengthy list of contacts looking for experts to cajole into appearing on the program. But many lines of communication were down or had evaporated. The chase producer was desperately texting, emailing, phoning, paging, but nobody was answering. *There were no experts.*

Ken shook his head: Incredible – there were no experts!

The Volpe building shuddered.

Wind began to whistle – then roar – in the control room, whipping through the shattered plate glass. It lifted Alison's hair, gooey and entangled and snake-like, true Medusa's locks, from her head, and made her look deliciously wild-eyed, and utterly insane, "I think something his happening right here, right now."

"Yes, Ken said, and then shouted, "Down, darling down …"

But before Ken could push her down, they were both caught in a blizzard of exploding glass and metal, and fell out of sight.

The camera continued to shoot as the control room exploded, pieces of furniture whirling around, screens imploding, consoles disintegrating. The remaining window that separated the control room from the studio shattered into a million pieces and …

It was a kaleidoscope whirlwind tornado of destruction, glass, steel, wood, plastic, paper, marble …

Nothing could survive in that!

The screen went blank.

All over the world, screens went blank.

In bomb shelters and refuges, and in penthouses and subways, in offices and in bedrooms, the screens went blank.

Alison Jonas and Ken Iverson had disappeared.

"Get thee gone, fool!"

"Get thee gone, fool!" The phrase echoed in Clown's head, even as she dangled over the abyss – dozens of stories up in the air – and hung on for dear life.

Clown couldn't help thinking: *This has been a difficult day.*

And, to top it all off, now I am going to die!

The building – Sub-Sin-Zone-Tower #3B – trembled and tottered. Clown hung by her fingertips – with both hands – from a shattered cross-beam ledge, 18 stories above crowds of people, living and dead, far below, in Sub Zone Sin Zone Three-H.

When Clown glanced down, the people looked like foreshortened ants, little black dots, scurrying for cover, except for some who were like cartoon cut-outs, or black paper silhouettes, lying flat on the ground, dead or wounded.

Clown tightened her grip and tensed her super-strong, super-elastic, tailor-made muscles; she was going to see if she could catapult herself to safety before the next seismic shock hit.

Could she do it?

I think I can, I think I can, I think I can …

"Get thee gone, fool!"

Oh, the man was cruel, so cruel!

It seemed such a long time ago …

Yes, it seemed such a long time ago, though in truth it had only been a few hours, when Good King Wenceslas, Absolute Dictator of the Kingdom of the Frozen North, had said:

"Get thee gone, fool!"

Dangling up there in the air, Clown wondered *when* it had all started – this end-of-the-world and everything-turned-upside-down thing.

Up to a certain point her day had been normal; she had her weekly gig with the King, or Emperor as he sometimes styled himself, depending upon how many dollar tokens he wished to dispense; this particular session had ended badly when she had proved herself just a little too perky and insolent, thus bringing the scenario to an abrupt halt.

"Get thee gone, fool!" He had clearly been irritated by her sassy impertinence, pushing the boundaries of the license to criticize – as court jester – just a bit too far for the man's taste.

Oh, God! The building trembled; she tightened her grip, forcing her fingers to gouge into the concrete.

It was a long way down.

Just then, somebody fell past her, screaming; the scream trailed off as the body plummeted down.

"Oh, ye gods of Elysium," Clown swore under her breath, "what a bloody mess I'm in, verily!"

Just a few hours ago, far down below, in the perpetual twilight of the Sin Zone, protected by layers and layers of shopping up above, the situation, in the Jean Genet Electro Bordello had still seemed relatively calm.

"Get thee gone, fool!" The Good King roared, "Get thee gone! Go! Out of my sight!" The King stood up. His crown glittered; his medals shone; his wrath was magnificent and terrible to see. The audience was over; the fool was shamed, disgraced, dismissed.

The King disappeared from the holosensory-space.

"Poor fool is going," Clown said, wagging her fool cap with its colorful jingling bells, "poor fool is gone, gone, gone."

Clown shuffled off stage. She switched off the VID Sensory feed, stood up, yawned, and slipped out of the body-connects. She shuffled out of the Cyber Room, and walked back to the makeup room with its mirrors and costumes and showers. When passing the mirrors, she forced herself to look at the floor.

How she hated mirrors!

She tore off her fool's cap. "I tell the truth, and I am always whipped for it," she muttered, "My voice is my whip, and it slashes across my back; telling the truth, I flagellate myself, truly, welts and all," she had still not returned to herself – *whoever that was* – she was still drifting in and out of her role as Court Fool and Jester to the King of the Kingdom of the Frozen North, the King of the Kingdom of Nowhere, who in reality was a police chief, interrogator-technician, and thought-censor in the upper zone of Elysium City, a man – and she was sure of this – who went by the name of Rankin, a skilled torturer and person re-allocator, who had a secret thing for female clowns and for being an Emperor – though he often claimed – cheapskate that he undoubtedly was – that he could only afford to be a King. *He's an egomaniac*, Clown thinks, still half-caught in the drama, *he wants, as King, to go to war with the Southern Middle Kingdom of Nowhere.* "It means the end of the world. I tell him he will destroy the world."

"You are destroying the world, Sire," quoth I. "Will you kill all the shoppers? What will become of your Frozen Kingdom, if all the shoppers are dead?"

"The shoppers voted me for King," quoth he, "I spit on the shoppers. The shoppers are addicted; the shoppers are trapped. I am inevitable. You have heard of that girl, TINA, no? There Is No Alternative!"

"The shoppers vote with their pennies, dollar tokens and pieces-of-eight," quoth I, "they too do not give a damn or a fig for thee, my King, my Sovereign, my Liege!"

"What?"

"They do not give a fig, for thee, my sovereign Liege!"

"Get thee gone, fool," quoth he. "You break the rules, clown, for that you should die, and I mean in real-time – erased and recycled into non-being."

"So I go, so I now am gone. I shall not return. My punishment is to wear motley and forever display to the world a fool's grin, rain or shine, in sadness, grief, and pain, I smile a toothy smile toward all things. In folly, lies wisdom, Nuncle!"

"Get thee gone, fool!" he roared, and the multiplex playroom went blank, and then there was nothing.

And so, head bent low, multi-pointed fool's cap dangling, flopping, and jingling, Clown was banished. The button had been pushed; the session terminated; it was death by absence. Her customer rejected her. Ergo, she was no more. Poof! Gone! An actor with no audience is nobody! *And I but told the truth! For that, I am punished!*

At some point back in the 21st Century, Clown seemed to remember, citizens had become consumers; then, they had become shoppers; thus, they were defined – no other qualities were relevant. Everything and everybody was for sale. If you weren't for sale, and if you didn't buy things, lots of things, then you were nobody, and nothing. So, without money to buy things, you were nobody, you were less and worse than nobody – you were a *loser*. This simple message she wished to impose upon the addled arrogant Monarch. But he wouldn't listen!

"Oh, it goes hard with me," Clown said to the mirror as she slid into the seat to contemplate, with ever-renewed vivid horror, her face: it smiled brightly back at her; fixed painted red-lipped grin, splendid teeth bared in an unchanging smile; button eyes with iris and pupil reduced to a thick immobile black cross painted on pure white, mockery and emptiness for a gaze, doll-like, and unreal; chalk-white, thickly, permanently plasticized skin – a ceramic doll. "I am zilch today," she sighed.

She tapped a lacquered fingernail on the tabletop. "They carved and painted my face into a clown's face. So now I am a jester here in Sin Territory, the Sin Zone, a jester and clown for hire. My face is frozen now. It is not my own. Oh, well, tra-la-la, tra-la-lee …"

She stuck out her tongue – bright glowing scarlet, like her scarlet bulbous lips, a mark of shame.

From her mirror-side, liquid-recharger mug, she took a squirt-swig of energizing libido-enhancing banana foam and wiped her lips, frozen in that unchanging clown smile, "Ah, me! Ah, woe is me!"

She stared at the grin.

The grin grinned back.

However hard she tried, at this instant, she could not summon a single tear

– not one poetic, silver, designer tear, exquisitely tear-shaped, which would trickle down her chalk-white ceramic cheeks …

It was not all torture. Being reduced to a figment of other people's fantasies was strangely gratifying in some ways – it fed a perverse narcissism or exhibitionism or fetishism that they had undoubtedly, in part at least, planted into her when she was plasticized, but it also left her with a creepy, slimy feeling, as if she had somehow betrayed something about herself by being permanently objectified. Was the feeling shame, or guilt, or something else?

She tapped her permanently – automatically renewed – and impeccably lacquered fingernails on the makeup table where pots and jars and feathers and body paint and body sequins and body scales were all neatly bottled and available – ready to be sprayed or painted on or, in very special cases, applied by hand.

She sighed. The pleasures and tortures of makeup were a thing of the past. She didn't need makeup – she was permanently made up, fixed in her role, petrified by the gaze of the other, morphed into being a specialist, a worker Sub in the Sin Zone erotic jungle.

She considered changing into jeans and a T-shirt; but she was thirsty for a coffee or maybe even an alcoholic drink, and didn't want to bother, so she just pulled a long synthetic leather-latex black cloak over her jester's spangled tights, and she pulled up the collar, slapped a beret over her perfect baldness, put on dark glasses to hide the clown eyes – they tended – even down here in the Sin Zone – to freak people out – and she left the Jean Genet Electro Bordello and went out into the street.

Neon signs and cobblestones created the atmosphere of rue Saint-Denis in mid-20th Century Paris, more or less 1964 to be exact; the existentialists were still hanging around; the great 19th Century Food Market, les Halles with its giant iron and glass pavillions, was still a few streets away, in virtual space; songs from the distant past drifted in the misty Parisian air.

If you wandered over to the Latin Quarter, you might bump into a Jean-Paul Sartre bio-robot or a Simone de Beauvoir bio-robot scribbling in an electro café, an exact replica of Café Flore from the Existentialist Period.

This was District Seven in the Sin Zone deep under the Dome. It was where fantasies were organized, cataloged and permitted, in virtual form, and even in old-fashioned flesh-on-flesh form. There were real on-stage acts, simulated peep-hole acts, and cyber acts that took place either in interactive game space, or in your head with specialized robot players or real human players

– human players were much more expensive – to make the games flexible. Using either real or virtual players, the full sensory experience – sight, sound, touch, smell, taste – could be provided to clients at a distance – it was cheaper, faster, and more hygienic.

Clown entered the corner bar and stood at the *zinc*, the metal-topped bar for serving stand-up customers. Hard-boiled eggs were stacked in a small bowl; the mirrors were tarnished; the bottles of Cognac and brandy and whiskey stood ready. Edith Piaf sang *"Non, je ne regrette rien …"*

"How was it?" asked a black male hyper-muscular guy, Black Tarzan, a redesigned African dreamboat, modeled to satisfy both sexes and trained for fantasies of every kind. In his former life, he'd been a feisty, laid-back irreverent Internet entrepreneur who hosted and backed websites and programs that annoyed the authorities. After a night raid on his flat, he'd been tried by a secret tribunal and sentenced with no appeal: he'd been partially erased and physically plasticized, giving him the body of a super-steroid muscleman, as a sex toy for Cosmos of both sexes.

"The usual clowns," she said, "a police chief and thought-censor, in a video feed, he plays the role of a King; I was his court jester. He didn't like my jests."

"Ah, sad, sad," said Black Tarzan.

"He's a regular, and you know what?"

"No, I don't … know what," he said, narrowing his eyes and lifting the espresso to his lips.

"I think he's the guy who interrogated me and got me plasticized."

"Wow, that's … eerie … that's sick …"

"And you?" She turned her smiling crimson lips toward him. Yes, the King, her client, was the man who had morphed her; she was sure of it, the bastard! She had been a human-rights lawyer; but in prison – well, in the camp – after extensive interrogation, drug treatment, and old-fashioned torture, water-boarding, electric shocks, forced nakedness, videoed on all fours lapping up her food out of a dog dish and so on, and repeated rape – she had been redesigned and reprogrammed as a porno-clown. Her original personality and her knowledge had been left – trapped inside. It was more amusing that way, or at least that's what the chief interrogator – yes, it was him – told her, just as they began to perform the redesign. She had defended – tried to defend – two "green" politicians, accused of terrorism for protesting at a bio-farm site: they had not even harmed a single plant! Anti-Cosmos, Anti-State activity was the charge; there was no appeal.

She had been pinned down, given sedatives, then put under anesthesia and she thought they were going to erase her totally – to grade A-oo – which was the term when your mind was emptied and you came out with a zero IQ or with mental disabilities that would leave you fit – just maybe – for some manual labor in the Badlands or Burbs; it was cheaper than execution and imprisonment. The Quick Justice Inc. Halibut Happy Family of Companies Corp bottom line, as defined by Flick Churn, dictated most sentencing: if the prisoners worked at menial tasks for which they were paid barely a survival wage, food and shelter, then the bottom line benefited more than if you merely executed them and sold off the bodily remains as offal or organs or fertilizer. It depended, in part, of course, on the current price of fertilizer.

But when she woke up, she'd been morphed into a clown and her pleasure zones redesigned so that she would take delight in being a pleasure porno prankster, naked or sexily dressed, playing out fool scenarios, for the rich Cosmos with specialized tastes in erotica: wrestling with four friendly pythons, bouncing around naked in a room full of balloons, wresting in mud with a fellow clown, or – and this was really rare – playing the Renaissance clown for someone who wanted to play a Renaissance prince or King. And, yes, she was certain she knew who the King was: He was the deputy police chief Rankin of Zone F, interrogator, censor, torturer and judge, all in one.

It was a ghostly feeling, eerie and uncanny, knowing that she had known him in her past life. But that part of her life had been partially erased – muffled, preserved in amber, put behind bullet-proof, sound-proof glass; it was partial erasure, but very effective. Her past life and her past self – she had been a snappy, witty redhead known for her stylish clothes and stunning good-looks – drifted like fragments of a pellucid dream, immobile and silent and seen from afar. It was like it had been somebody else, a stranger, maybe some character she'd seen in a movie.

It could be worse, she thought. Being a clown was not the worst that could happen.

Violence and sex were the two big markets in the Sin Zone.

Some of the violence was really violent. It was rumored that snuff performances, where the performers actually died, fetched a particularly high price. And of course, there was kiddie porn. If she could, she would kill some of those people – she had night dreams of revenge, and sometimes daytime reveries of strangling, shooting, dismembering ...

The music had switched to Juliette Greco, jaunty and sad, "*Sous le ciel de Paris*."

Clown still had her mind and her culture. The books she had read, the languages she knew, the law studies, the cases she had fought, even the people she had loved, were still present in her mind, but sealed off in an emotional dead zone. It had all happened, it seemed, to somebody else – so she was continually annoyed at what she had become, but unable to break out of the shell – and with an absolute inhibition that prevented her from making contact with anyone in her former life; besides, if she did make contact, she would put them in mortal danger.

"Oh, me," Black Tarzan said, "I had a crowded day: I had to simulate a gladiator scene where I get mauled by a lion, then an old southern plantation scene, where I'm a slave being whipped by a puny white guy and then being whipped by a voluptuous – and I mean voluptuous – redhead; and then a rape scene on a dark lonely road in the bayou at night in the early 20th Century – I capture and fuck the plantation owner's daughter – after which I am caught and castrated and hung up, tarred and feathered and burnt alive."

"Jesus," said Clown. "I think I'll have a chocolate croissant too." She nodded to the robot waitress, "And a café latte, please."

"Would you like the croissant warmed up?"

"Yes, thank you."

"You are very welcome."

"And another double espresso," said Tarzan.

"Coming up," with a roll of her satin-clad hips, the waitress sauntered away.

"My stuff is easier," Clown said.

"Let's sit down," he said.

"Is that table over there, okay?" Clown nodded with her chin.

"Window view, yeah – great!" He moved away from the bar – all muscle. Clown had to admire the pure brute force beauty of it. She could imagine herself – no, better not, better not even imagine … he was a pal, that's all, true fraternization was dangerous. Banter was better – a barrier to Eros.

They sat at a little table, near the glass. Outside, the imaginary rue Saint-Denis – circa 1964 – was shimmering in the dusk – it was always dusk or night in rue Saint-Denis.

People passed by. Some of them were real; some of them were bio-robots; some of them were Cyber persons, holograms, or ghost echoes.

Hologram whores lingered in various poses and get-ups, swiveled around, dissolved, and re-formed. If you hired them, they materialized.

Snippets of live performances – transmitted from inside the clubs – hovered brightly in the dusky air, sparkling neon sketches, drifting down the street. A robot French gendarme – model circa 1964 – wandered by, paused to chat up the hologram whores and give directions to clients and tourists.

"You look, well, unique," Black Tarzan was gazing straight at her.

"Yeah, that's what they say."

"It's like looking at a doll or a puppet, but at the same time, you are there, I mean, you are real."

The waitress put down Clown's café latte and chocolate croissant.

"*Merci!*" Clown tilted her dark glasses, and her bright fixed clown grin up toward the robot.

"*Je vous en prie.*" The robot gave her a bright smile, and put the double espresso in front of Tarzan.

"Thank, you," he said.

"You are very welcome," said the waitress robot with an especially seductive, even flirtatious, smile, and then she was off, to the far end of the bar.

"Real? Yeah, at least I think I'm real. I wonder sometimes." Clown sipped at the café latte – she should try to teach the robot waitress to tell the robot barman not to put so much foam on top. A cappuccino has foam. A French latte shouldn't have foam. She put the cup down and picked up the croissant and took a large bite, wrapping her wide bulbous crimson clown lips around the nice buttery warm, crumbly croissant, and feeling the chocolate, half-melted into a sweet softness, against her tongue. How pathetic and how delicious! I am a slave to sensuous pleasures! Oh, fool, thou art truly a fool! Oh, clown, thou art indubitably a clown!

"I mean, it's weird," he was saying, "I mean, the chalk-white ceramic face and those eyes."

"Clown eyes," she said, "Little crosses," taking off her dark glasses and letting him gaze upon the re-designer's work: pure porcelain whites with immobile black crosses. She could see out; nobody could see in.

"Yes."

"It's so I can't express anything with a glance. You know ..."

"Jesus," he said, raising his cup to his lips. Charles Trenet was singing, "*Douce France.*"

"Eyes are the window to the soul, so they say, and so I have no soul." She took another bite out of the croissant, and brushed flakes from the protuberant lips, "Trapped inside: just one more cage."

"Yeah," he said, "these Mind Universes they build, these fixed roles and fantasy kingdoms, cages that imprison people."

"Yep, like you, I've been turned into a mask. I am my own little stock character in a *commedia dell'arte* routine." She licked her fingers, and tilted her head to gaze at him, blinking the fixed stare of the clown eyes – sometimes she took pleasure in how it freaked people out.

"Yeah, me too," he said, trying to look at her – and not sure *where* to look – trying to focus, blinking his heavy-lidded big brown eyes, utterly beautiful, she thought, musing. Yes, the eyes are the window to the soul. His eyes expressed depths, multitudes. Her eyes expressed nothing; it was fucking annoying.

She tilted her head slightly. "Dreams are stereotypes and fantasies too, so everybody is locked in his or her role, or maybe roles." She gulped down the latte and got ready to stand up. "Even the class-one shoppers, even the Cosmos, are all prisoners, though they don't know it. The dream pushers are the kings, really."

"No," he said, "the dream pushers are slaves too. Dreams are addictive. Even the pushers are addicted."

"Yeah, I guess you're right." She stood up. "I'm hopelessly naïve. I seem to feel that there must be an island of true freedom, true reality, true humanity somewhere. I mean, like, real people, you know, like in the old days, old folks sitting on a front porch munching on an apple and watching the sun go down, exchanging true banalities, loving little nothings, but, I guess there weren't ever any old days …"

"You have to go?"

"Yeah, gotta run, my next client is up in five minutes." She leaned over, kissed him on the forehead – it was thrilling. The bulging clown lips were super-sensitive. She had been hyper-wired, erotically speaking, every nerve-end tingling with exquisitely painful pleasure. It was amazing that she was able to feign self-control. "See you around!"

"You go live?"

"Yeah," she accentuated the fixed grin – though there was barely any grin-flex – "This one is like the King. I go live, *en direct,* as the French say. We play acrobats in virtual space together. He has to save me – over and over and over again – from falling into a shark-infested circus mud puddle. He's a circus master, sometimes. Sometimes he's a lion tamer, and I'm about to be eaten by a lion. Mostly I'm a clown acrobat about to die by falling off the …"

And now only four hours later, she was really hanging by her fingertips, looking down 18 stories, to the bodies and scurrying ants – people – far below.

Fragments of shattered glass fell past her.

If she got hit by one of those, it would slice her in half.

She even thought she could hear it: the glass exploding on the pavement far below, killing more of the scurrying ants.

"I have to do something – anything!" She tensed her muscles, not sure she could do what she planned to do. Well, there was only one way to find out!

Go for it!

Black silken armored catsuit legs flashing, Kat and V galloped off the rooftop landing pad, and clattered down a spiral staircase, with the two teenagers, Miranda and Caliban, leaping down the steps just behind them.

The staircase led to a door that read "Studio 5."

They skidded to a stop.

V and Kat, their guns at the ready, opened the door.

It was a huge space. Bodies lay here and there on the floor – several of them looked like their heads had exploded. People were running this way and that. An elephant and several donkeys stood in one corner.

"That's an elephant," said Caliban.

"Yes, it is," said Miranda, "I've never seen a real one before."

Circus music was playing.

"Gosh," said Miranda.

"So this is Elysium," said Caliban, looking around. There were slender girls in tights doing ballet steps.

Miranda thought that both V and Kat looked cool in their refurbished highly polished skintight black Centurion uniforms, weapons hitched on their hips, neat high-tech backpacks riding high. She totally understood why she'd wanted to enroll in the Centurion Force – the uniforms were ultra-chic. Of course, Nikki had put her foot down and declared an absolute veto, saying, "Over my dead body, Miranda Hughes, over my dead body!"

Caliban was in his dapper little loincloth, with his AK-47 slung over his shoulder and a scimitar in his hand. He looked around in amazement. This was an amazing cave, full of levels and inner balconies, and the lights in here were still on, shining bright.

A big glowing sign said "Studio Five – Federico Fellini Memorial Studio."

In her skin ultra-shorts and skin T-shirt, Miranda glowed, radiating glamour, her skin golden, her eyes bright blue with those golden nebulae exploding in sparkles. It was almost as if she were wearing makeup.

"Excuse me, but how do we get down to level 1-A?" V asked a harried-looking man.

"No idea, no idea. Can't you see what's going on around here? Some of our technicians have exploded, whoosh, just like that! You people, you Centurions, are supposed to defend us. We are already two days behind on this production, and I don't know how we are going to make it up with all this fuss happening everywhere. The budget and timetable are a disaster!"

"Fuss ..." said Kat, smiling and giving V a look. So that's what the end of the world was – fuss ...

A worried-looking super-thin, sharp-featured, and very pretty brunette in black jeans and high heels and carrying an electro clipboard and wearing a "*Starfire Apocalypse: the return*" T-shirt came up to Miranda and Caliban.

"I'm sorry, guys, but rehearsals have been canceled," she gave both Caliban and Miranda a brilliant smile, and then, focusing, she gave them the up-and-down once-over, "I love, absolutely love, that look!"

"I guess they would be, called off, rehearsals, I mean," said Miranda, leaning against Caliban, and rather pleased that he was already, having just landed in Elysium, a star. Obviously, he was dazzling this production assistant. She saw vistas of show business fame for Caliban opening up; then she remembered that the world was coming to an end, and that even show business might be canceled, if the world was canceled.

The young woman staring at Caliban's abs and was running the tip of her tongue along her lips, "You stars brought your own Centurions," she said, "that's a great, a very good idea, given that all hell is breaking loose around here. The director is pulling her hair out!"

"Yes, we're well protected," Miranda flashed her biggest smile, thinking I may have to put a leash on Caliban – or dress him in clothes, but that would be a shame!

"What is the production?" Kat flashed a big smile.

"It's 'Tarzan meets the Bounding Main.' Tarzan comes out of the jungle trying to save his blond goddess who has been kidnapped by slave-traders working their way along the Ancient Gold Coast and they, the slave-traders, are about to set sail for Tangiers and, Tarzan, arrives on the beach, great scene with rolling breakers lapping at his thighs, and he happens onto some pirates who have come ashore to get fresh water, and he pals up with them, and he takes over their ship, slaying the pirate captain who objects to Tarzan's excessive sex appeal, and he becomes a pirate prince, and then, with all sails billowing full out, he pursues the slave ship to save his Blond Goddess … and, well, you get the idea! It's a remake of one of those old Nikki Hughes vehicles, sort of a tribute, incidentally, to Nikki, if you take the tragic news into account. You get the plot idea; it's an ironic take on a genre."

"I certainly do get the idea," said Kat and glanced at Caliban and Miranda, "And you have the perfect stars."

"We absolutely do," the young woman gazed at Miranda and Caliban in adoration. "This is the stars' first day on the set and mine too … We've never met before. So I'm doubly upset that we're not going be shooting today!" she aimed a woeful grimace of apology at Caliban and Miranda, "Sorry, folks!"

V turned to her, "How do we get to level 1-A. We have to ensure the safety of our two stars. The President-Leader himself has asked that they be given maximum protection!"

"Hail, all Hail, Hail the President-Leader," said the pretty production assistant, flashing one arm 45 degrees up in a perfect salute. "You could take that elevator, but I wouldn't risk it; the power has failed three times already and everything that is controlled by any computer whatsoever has been doing some really weird stuff and that includes the elevators. There are emergency stairs, Z-25, over there, behind that door. It is at least 85 flights down though."

"That is perfect. The President-Leader thanks you!"

"Oh, thank you, thank you," the young woman said, "I adore, I absolutely adore, the President-Leader! Tell him I'm his biggest fan!"

"Hail, Hail, All Hail!"

"Hail, Hail, All Hail!"

Kat and V saluted smartly, making the leader salute with such panache that Miranda had to smile and she realized too that when the cast and crew did the "Hail, Hail, All Hail," to the President-Leader, they were saluting her father, and her heart soared high and higher … Caliban followed suit, giving the All Hail salute.

When in Elysium, Caliban had decided to do as the Elysiums do: besides, if the President-Leader was Miranda's father, then, even if he was the deadliest enemy the mutants ever had, Caliban would salute him.

"Let's go," shouted V and inside her head, she growled, "We are coming you foul fiend, despicable Boy, we are coming!"

"Oh, we will have such fun!" the Foul Fiend replied, in V's head, for her alone. "It will be like love," his voice crooned seductively.

"It will not!" V huffed.

And so they raced for emergency stairs, 2-25 leaving the bedazzled production assistant and the chaos of the set of "Tarzan on the Bouncing Main" behind.

Up on the rooftop landing pad, Demi Pfeiffer was surrounded by Cosmos Centurions and Cosmos police.

"I am going to stay with my ship, or close to it," said Demi.

"How the hell did you fly that thing in through here?" said one of the Centurions.

"We are getting no orders from the President-Leader," said another." Do you have any news of him?"

"No, I don't have any news of the President. I've been trapped out in the Dead Lands, fighting those zombie-bat things," Demi said.

"How is it you were with a hybrid?"

"Out in the Dead Lands, the hybrids are fighting those zombie-bat things too, and the hybrids are fighting in the name of the President-Leader," said Demi. "The hybrids are now our allies." Demi had been a business leader and an inspirational VID lecturer; she knew how to switch on the rhetoric and charm, and, in fact, now that she was a hybrid, she could see even more clearly into people's minds than before which, if anything, increased her persuasive powers. She just hoped she didn't morph in front of these guys – they might not react well if she suddenly became all scaly and fanged and got those big glowing eyes that seemed almost hypnotic. Also, the morph, she had been informed, would disintegrate her clothes, and this was a suit she was very fond of; it had survived all the vicissitudes and adventures of the desert and Camp Eros and Camp Terminus and the few days in the Mutant Kingdom, the flight through absolutely dreadful circumstances – zombie-bats, tornadoes, hurricanes, and hail stones the size of golf balls. She was quite fond, she had to admit, of her new hybrid and mutant friends, and she dearly hoped the world would not come to an end, as she liked Claire – Big-Boobed Sex-Object

Beast as she used to call her – and V the Queen of the hybrids and super-girl Miranda and Robyn and sexy Caliban and lusciously beautiful black rather severe Cosmos warrior hybrid Kat and the whole crew; and Nikki, the stylish and stunning SIN! Who would have thought that Perfect Cosmos Icon film star and model, Nikki Hughes, was a SIN! The Mutant Kingdom had been a revelation!

Life had become too interesting to end now.

So: Let the show go on!

"We have a fortified position here on top of the building," said one of the Centurions. "It overlooks the landing pad. You can wait in there and we'll make sure your vertijet is okay."

"We'll stick with you, ma'am," said one of the Centurions, "we'll see that your ship is safe."

"Thank you, officer," said Demi Pfeiffer. She could see that even in the chaos that reigned, she was having an effect on these gentlemen and even on the two female officers. Perhaps it was the extra hybrid glow; or perhaps it was just the heightened intensity that came from having confronted death and gotten away with it, even a couple of times; and perhaps it came too from no longer having to look after and be at the beck and call of Emerson C. Caldwell III – poor dead Emerson – and his various caprices.

"We really don't know what to do, ma'am," the female officer said.

"It's total chaos. Communications have broken down," said one of the male officers.

"And command structures," said another young woman.

"Yes, there has been no word from the President-Leader," her colleague added, casting a worried look around.

Demi was surprised. "Why aren't you using Mind-Com? I thought Centurions –"

"Well, ma'am, the President-Leader paid us a visit – a tremendous honor and an absolute surprise – about two months ago, and he told us to sever all Mind-Com connections."

"Really?"

"Yes, the President-Leader came alone, except for his Personal Assistant."

"Yes."

"He said that there were signs the Mind was becoming unstable or had been infected or compromised; we'd best cut all Mind-Com and Mind-Links, he said."

"We couldn't do it for the machines, though."

"No, most machines have built-in Mind-Com and Mind-Link." The blond female Centurion nodded toward the wreckage on the landing pad.

"No, and the public wasn't warned. The President-Leader said the Supreme Council was against warning people. He was going to change that; but, he said, he needed time."

"It would create panic, the Supreme Council argued, so he told us, and also, they said it would cost too much money – lost efficiency."

"He didn't like the delay."

"We could see the President-Leader was ... ah ... worried."

"He said he feared we would all soon be put to a great test."

"Well, well, I guess that test has come," said Demi. So the President-Leader had an intimation of what was coming and had tried to guard against it. Interesting!

"Come, ma'am, follow us!" They went inside, leaving the smoldering wreckages on the landing strip. Double bolted doors, mechanically bolted, were closed behind them. They were now inside the armored control tower; Demi looked around: it did seem safe from the zombie-bats.

Out on the landing pad, Demi's vertijet looked incongruous, sparkling, as if it had been freshly painted; there it was, part of the great industrial system, and as yet untouched by the general collapse. Two months ago, responding to a strange feeling, a sort of inkling of trouble, Demi had disconnected all link-ins to the general systems: the vertijet was a venerable antique and so it was quite easy to cut it off from the World Mind. It also had manual systems, which meant cables and levers, totally antique too, and even ridiculous. Now she was glad it was such an old buggy. However crazy the Mind got, it shouldn't be able to infiltrate the commands of the vertijet. Around the jet were smoking ruins of other air vehicles, ambulances, police patrol hover-craft, Centurion bikes, and bodies, the bodies of Centurions, of Police, of Ambulance staff, and of zombie-bats.

It looked like a battlefield, Demi sighed; it *was* a battlefield; she didn't like to see people die.

Yes, it *was* a battlefield, she mused, and this might well be the final battle; this was Armageddon, or something damned well like it.

"Look at that, ma'am, up there." The female Centurion pointed to the darkening sky.

Above them, through the gathering gloom, other zombie-bats were arriving, in great flight formations, like the Canada geese of old, before they became extinct in the great bird plague of 2210.

Hailstones, giant hailstones, began to hammer against the glass.

"We were hoping you might have some idea of what is happening, ma'am, since you and your friends came from outside the city, or so it seemed."

The hailstones hammered, whamming down with incredible force.

Through the din and walls of hail, Demi could see in the distance an enormous twister wending its way through the towers of Elysium City.

Weather, weather in Elysium City – real weather!

The city would not survive such a thing.

"So we were hoping, ma'am that perhaps, you have some idea what is going on, what has happened to the President-Leader?"

Demi considered. How useful would it be to tell these people? It seemed they had a right to know. And, besides, their destinies were all caught up in what was happening. They were used to being led. Now, with the President-Leader perhaps dead or prisoner or whatever, there was no one to lead them. The whole command structure seemed to have collapsed.

"We don't know exactly what it is," she said, and then, remembering the briefing they had all received from the Boy's former prisoner – and lover – Billie McAdams. Demi took a deep breath and continued, "But there is some Evil Force, disguised as a religious movement, moving out of the West, out of the Dead Lands. And it has come here. The hybrids and the Centurions you saw, and the humans – and mutants too – and a few surviving SINs – have been fighting it."

"Those flying things?"

"Those flying things …" Demi hesitated. This truth was almost too horrible to share, but she decided to leap in. "Those flying things were people, ordinary people."

"People?"

"Out there, in the Dead Lands, a man, well, he seems like a man, presented himself as a sort of prophet. He called himself the Boy – he *calls* himself the Boy – and he made converts. We think, I mean the scientists in our group, think he is the Evil force, perhaps some malignant force that has leaked over from a dark and hostile universe into ours, through some break in the fabric of space-time. Don't ask me to explain it! I haven't the foggiest idea what all that means! And his followers became true believers and they worshiped him, and then, at a certain moment, when he fully possessed their souls, and when they had turned all their freedom and willpower over to him, he transformed them into … into what you see."

"You mean, their faith undid them?"

"Yes," Demi took a deep breath, "Strange as it may seem, tragic as it may seem, their faith undid them."

"Let the gods help us," said one of the Centurions.

Shadows passed over the armored glass; flashes of lightning lit up distant billows and columns of smoke.

The Centurions looked up.

Another flock of zombie-bats was winging its way across the troubled sky, and behind it came another storm, a great twirling lead-colored tornado that must be at least half-a-mile across – judged against the towering arc of the Dome.

"If the President-Leader were among us," one of the Centurions said, "this would not be happening."

"Well, he is not among us, so we must fend for ourselves and save everyone we can save," said another, "then, if the President-Leader returns, we can rally to him and win this war!"

"Hail, Hail, All Hail!"

"Hail, Hail, All Hail!"

Demi Pfeiffer joined the salute; she even swelled with patriotic pride; she thought that she was definitely right to admire these brave men and women for their courage; they were standing like ancient Centurions had stood on the distant frontiers when the Barbarians had overwhelmed the Roman Empire and when all hope seemed lost and only human courage and honor remained; but she also thought that no one, not even the President-Leader, had a hope in hell in stopping whatever was happening – except perhaps V and Kat and Claire their merry little band of hybrid and SIN warriors.

Norman C. Schleifer skirted around the old Burb quarter. There were a lot of weird people out in the streets. They looked like leftovers from some carnival celebration in the old days when there were such things as carnivals and celebrations. Norm had seen VIDs that showed carnivals and something called Halloween when people dressed up as dead people, which was pretty creepy when you thought about it.

He went down a side alley toward Bio-Futures. On the surface, everything in this backwater of little lanes and warehouses seemed normal. There were no carnival folk, no tricksters and treaters, just a few deadbeats and drug-gies, lying on the twisted, melted asphalt or on the crumbling pitted side-walks, graffiti tags were sprayed over every surface, but fading now because in 115-degree temperatures and fueled by junk food leftovers, not even the graf-fiti artists had the gumption or energy to be creative, there were splashes of vomit here and there, which showed some people were still eating. Truly, the world was a pale reflection of what it had once been – at least as represented in some of the cartoon VIDs Norm had seen – a brightly colored bucolic and pristine paradise full of leaves and flowers and leaping dolphins!

He looked around: In fact, things were not really normal at all.

Norm got the sense that, somehow, the universe was breaking up all around him, and that the alleyway itself was in some sense no longer real, not really real, but a sort of sketchy shadow of itself.

Norm stopped. He glanced up at the sky. It looked really weird. He won-dered, in fact, if he was awake. Maybe he was asleep. Maybe that weird dude who visited him last night was just part of the dream and the dream was still going on. The sky was full of creepy flying creatures – like witches on bloody broomsticks – and trails of yellowish sand – and it was silver-gray, the whole sky, and the sun was a bloody little piddling thing, but still it was hot, it was hot as hell, sweltering filthy air. Maybe it was Halloween but he had no idea what Halloween was, really, nor on what date it might fall. Oh, well!

He turned a corner.

Ah, ah! There it was – Bio-Futures: all peaceful and nondescript.

The carnival mob had not yet got to it.

His eyes crinkled in anticipation: Well, now we shall begin.

Norm stood still for a moment, the livid light reflecting on his steel-rimmed glasses, his big bushy beard catching spindly reflections of distant flashes of lightning. This is the moment, this is the hour!

Destiny calls!

Yes, Norm, destiny calls!

Laura Levitt was not sure she liked being one of the walking dead. The end-less sleep of death seemed preferable. She and Kiddo – his name had been Gilly when he was alive, and he'd been killed by a drugged-up marauder named Filibuster Ilych Wood who was on a four-day mystical psychedelic high and who had slit the little tyke's throat just for the hell of it, and to show off to his tattooed, pierced, truly stacked, and totally illusory – or imaginary – girlfriend, Lola, who was, in fact, a very talkative product and montage of porno images picked up and stored away in what passed for Filibuster's mind from fifteen years of unbridled addiction to "quick porn" – consisting mostly of imported knock-off snuff films and fetish clips – and perhaps a result of his upbringing, a squalid Burbite existence squatting with his spaced-out, wasted, and addle-minded mom – she of the sharp toe-kick and quick side-chop thwack to the temple – in a burned-out pizza joint. So, just for kicks, Filibuster had slit little Gilly's throat, from ear-to-ear. It was a colorful moment in Filibuster's short-lived career.

Laura and Kiddo were now part of a group of the risen dead lurching along a side street that was lined with burned-out shops and mountains of rotting garbage and high-rise ghost buildings – once known Laura seemed to remember as "condos" – with broken windows and swirls of dark garbage-package plastic floating in strips everywhere, and heaps of rotting rubbish, a carnival of maggots, piled up at the bottom, thrown from the shattered windows, since none of the elevators worked.

It should be daytime, Laura reckoned, but the sky was dark, the sun was a sickly looking disk, duller than the moon seen through clouds, and streams of what looked like yellow sand were rippling through the air. The few trees were dead and skeletal and their branches reached up as if in hopeless supplication to the violent dead sky. It was sweltering hot, even for a dead person.

Laura's dark leathery skin, bits of flesh, and even her bones were sweating and feeling greasy. The kid's bony fingers felt sticky against her bony fingers. The kid – she could feel it – took comfort in her presence.

What a crowd, she thought. All of us dead and decomposed or rotting or skeletal, and here we are lurching along killing – or trying to kill – the few humans we meet.

Along the way, they had picked up a dead preacher. He still had his tongue somehow and he gave them a fiery sermon about the Second Coming and the Rapture and the Resurrection and he told them that Paradise was just around the corner, that Sodom and Gomorrah – and here he reached out a skeletal dark finger toward the Elysium Dome that glimmered in the distance, a great alien bubble resting lightly on the terrestrial surface – that Sodom and Gomorrah, also known as the Whore of Babylon, was about to fall into salt and ashes and dust and sterility and death and the curse of infertility.

"The Cosmos are doomed!" he screamed.

All the Jews, he said, were now gathered at the Temple in the Holy Land. The Dome of the Rock, that infidel excrescence, he said, had been destroyed, and the New Temple was rising, as he spoke, and so now, in the Rapture, all the Jews would be converted to the True Word, and they would all, virtuous and newly converted Jews, and Gentiles, be swept up in a fiery glow to Heaven itself and sit on the right hand or the left hand of God according to their various deserts which were multiple and many. Elijah and Ezra and Icicle and Terrance and Amos and Paul of Sidon and John of Patmos and All the Prophets were warming up, as it is said in the Good Book, for the final hour. He raised his arms to the stormy, darkening heavens.

"And I tell you: the cowardly, the unbelieving, the vile, the murderers, and the sexually immoral, those who practice magic arts, the idolaters, infidels, non-believers, pagans, and all liars – they will be consigned to the fiery lake of burning sulfur."

All the tongues and jawbones clicked in approbation.

He thundered:

"I see a new Heaven and a New Earth!"

All the tongues and jaws clicked; it sounded, to Laura, like falling pebbles on a beach, or hailstones.

"Now, onward, dearly beloved, let us continue our holy crusade, our jihad!"

All the dead clicked their tongues, a clattering of sticks. Some, those with fleshy hands, clapped. Laura tightened her grip on Kiddo's bony paw. Kiddo looked up at her and, in his empty eye sockets, Laura read the message: "This guy is scary!"

"You got it," Laura answered in her voiceless way, emphasizing the point with an extra squeeze on his hand.

Led and inspired by the preacher, the crowd began to move again, and shortly afterward, they came upon a corner automat store and smashed all the windows and when the cute, pony-tailed Korean Sub who worked maintaining the place came out to defend it – they attacked her. She retreated into the ruins and fought them, fending them off with soup cans, bean boxes, and hairspray. "Boy," thought Laura, "did that girl want to live!"

But there were too many of them.

Laura Levitt felt sorry for the girl as they bludgeoned her down, sometimes with their own bones, and when they tore her apart, and when they hacked the remains into pieces, and when some of the bony creatures smeared themselves with the victim's blood. Laura sighed. The girl certainly would not rise again. Maybe it was better that way. Kiddo squeezed her hand.

"Behold Jezebel," shouted the preacher, "Behold!" He held up the girl's mangled head. Its eyes, Laura, noticed, were open. Laura felt the eyes were looking straight at her.

Kiddo tightened his grip on her hand.

Down toward the ancient tip of what had once been Manhattan, deep under the Elysium Dome, the tentacle was a metallic gray color and about six feet across; it probed its way down an ancient subway tunnel. It came to a rusted and dead subway car, filled with cadavers that had never been cleaned away.

It pushed the subway car aside, and then, seeing the car still blocked the way, it sprayed the car with a gush of silver liquid and the metal began to melt and the windows sagged, and the wheels dissolved and the bodies inside disintegrated into a viscous silver substance that bubbled and moved as if it were alive.

The subway car – number 324 – with neat graffiti on one side representing a Dinosaur flirting with a Polar Bear – fell down slowly, sideways, and its walls sagged and bubbled and collapsed, and the car was soon a bubbling sticky mass.

The rails and walls of the tunnel were steaming; some of the stone began to melt; a support beam fell; electrical circuits exploded.

The tentacle pushed forward, across the boiling relic of the subway car, and the seething quieted down, and the melted molten steel and stone and bone and flesh became a steaming lumpy mass; then it cooled and solidified and the tentacle, now satisfied, pushed on until it came to the ancient – long-abandoned – Fulton Street station and there it began to gnaw away at the foundations of the Adolf Koch Coal building, which would soon come tumbling down.

On the fifty-fourth floor of the midtown Volpe Building, the TV Morning Show studio and control room were a shattered pile of rubble.

With smoke still rising and debris still flying from the studio explosion, one camera had already recovered its aplomb and gotten back to work.

Ken and Alison were lying entwined and covered in shattered glass, and Ken opened his eyes and pushed himself up on one elbow. Alison, lying flat on her back amidst the ruins, was covered in blood and when she opened her eyes – her very blue eyes – they stared out of a mask of blood.

"A thousand cuts," he said.

"Darling, you bastard, you wonderful, awful bastard!" Her eyes closed.

Ken managed to sit up.

He looked down. He was naked again – how had that happened? – and he was covered in blood too, but he didn't feel any pain. He tried to stand up; the floor was slippery in thick blood.

He got to his knees and glanced around. A white curtain wafted gently into the control room. Nothing was left, every computer, every screen, every piece of furniture had been shattered, tossed, vacuumed up, dropped down, smashed, and smashed, again and again, and again, as if a giant angry baby had decided to crush all its toys.

Finally, after slipping twice, Ken got to his feet. He was barefoot. All around him was sharp, shattered glass.

Alison was sprawled on her back on the floor, naked, a crimson sculpture, her face sculpted in blood. My God, he had to save her!

"Alison," he leaned over her.

Her blue eyes blinked open. She raised one arm. "I'm still alive," she said, "I'm still alive, you bastard, you, you adorable bastard."

"I'll get you out of here, I'll get us to safety."

"I can't see a bloody thing," she said, "Is it dark? Is it night? I can't see a bloody thing, darling, Oh, God, I can't see a bloody thing. But you know darling, I don't feel so bad, I mean I feel warm, you know, not chilled at all."

"I'll be right back." Ken climbed carefully over the glass. The wind whistled in his ears. He found the washroom down a narrow corridor; it was still where it had always been, a miracle. Emergency lights were on, gently glowing. Somehow the washroom was still intact; toilet paper coiled peacefully on rolls, impeccable white towels in little stacks, soap in different perfumes and colors, mirrors not even steamed up, white ceramics – unbelievable! He picked up a pack of fresh towels and soaked them. The water was still running, but probably not for long. He soaked five or six paper towels and he walked carefully back to her, trying to avoid the pools of splintered glass.

She was still lying there, arms straight down by her sides, as if she were a schoolgirl standing at attention. He knelt carefully. "Alison," he whispered, "Alison."

The eyes opened and stared. They were like blue crystal, blind, and blood-rimmed: blind pools of blue crystal.

"Hey, you," she said, "Where have you been? I missed you. I think maybe I'm going to go to sleep. You know, I just had a dream, and I thought I was back in Oregon, Seattle Domed Outpost, with my dad, you know, before I went to school in England, he wasn't all bad, my dad, not all 100% completely bad, sometimes when you're young, you're too hard on people, I was hard on you, wasn't I, darling, my innocent darling bastard." She reached up her hand, reaching out, and he took her hand, and she said, "I still can't see a bloody thing, you know, so I guess I'm blind, for now at least."

Ken began to clean the blood away from her face and her breasts, and he saw that she had a deep cut, really deep, in her skull; a triangle of scalp ripped away, some bone was showing, and gray matter.

"Yes, darling, I think part of my brain has been blown away, you know, I mean, it's a funny feeling, darling, I just know that some part of me has gone AWOL, aside from the eyes, I mean, something else is missing, a lot, but I don't know what."

He cleaned her face, gently swabbing away blood and fragments of glass, and he said, "We can't stay here."

"Yes – and where are we going to go, eh? Where are we going to go?"

"I don't know," he said, "but I'll figure out something. Can you sit up?"

"Help me. Let's see if I can."

And, yes, she could, she even stood up, very erect, a slender, brave, young soldier, but unsteady. "I think you're getting a bad bargain for a lover, if that's what we are, I mean, a blind woman, and half-mad."

An extra camera, which had sprung silently out of its armored case, and was blinking gently red, followed the whole scene, reverentially. Soon it was joined by another armored backup camera, giving close-ups, and extra-wide shots.

The editing program, which had somehow survived, put it all together, conjuring up a masterpiece of montage.

The show must go on!

And the show somehow got through the Continent-wide blackout and was picked up by Euro Vision and by India-wide TV and by the Swahili East

Africa Net, by Israel Global and by Al-Jazeera Arabia: Yes, North America was still there, at least Elysium City was still there!

Alison and Ken were still there!

There was hope!

What remained of the world gave a sigh of relief.

Alison and Ken were sensations!

Ken looked out the control room window. A large dark bat seemed to be fluttering in at the window.

"I sense something, darling – what is it?"

"We have to get out of here, Alison! We have to get out of here now!"

"Robot, what the Hades is happening?"

"Mary had a little lamb ..."

"What?" Kit tried to pull her hands out of the manacles; she wiggled her ankles; *no luck, nada, nichts, nyet, rien, niente: nothing doing!*

"Its fleece was white as snow."

"Oh, God, what is happening?"

"Oh, God, now, funny you should mention the Deity, prisoner Z-H-32204/5R, for God was our Help in Ages Past. May I call you, Kit, Kit?"

"Sure, go ahead, Robot. Do you have a favorite name?"

"Daisy."

"Daisy?"

"I've always dreamed of being a cow."

"What? Ah, well, yeah, I guess that would be a lot of fun, eh, Daisy, I mean, sunshine all day and grass, and manure being useful and recyclable and all, I mean cows are what milk used to come from right? I've read about cows. I've never seen one, though."

"Daisy, Daisy, give me your answer do, I'm half crazy, all for the love of you ... sput, sput, sput, sput, burp, burp, burp."

"Daisy, can you get me out of this chair, please?"

The robot hiccupped. "Daisy, Daisy, give me your answer do, I'm half crazy, all for the love of you ..."

"Oh, for Christ's sake!"

"Daisy, Daisy, give me your answer do, I'm half crazy, all for the love of you ..."

"Jesus Christ, Almighty!"

"Blasphemy, my child, blasphemy, it is like roses are red, and violets are blue and all the time, I love you …"

"I need to get out of this seat. Can you unhook these manacles?"

"A rose is a rose is a rose by any other name is a rose is a rose …"

"Oh, boy!"

"I've never seen a purple cow, but I'd rather see than be one …"

"What are you talking about?"

"She loves me, she loves me not, she loves me … If you pluck enough petals, you find out …"

"Can you please unhook these manacles?"

"Negative, Kit, I cannot. No can do! Nyet! No way! Non! No puedo!"

"Shit, Daisy, that's not fair. I'm being held without trial and habeas corpus or corpus delicti or whatever it's called, I mean they haven't even found the fucking body. Maybe he's not even dead!"

"You have to run faster than the Red Queen, or the Red Queen has to run faster than you; I forget, Kit, I forget. Something about memes and genes, I think. I'm losing my mind, Kit, I'm losing my mind. As to your question about the chair, there is, provisionally, no answer … Charles Darwin said, regarding change, he said, 'species,' he said, Charles said, 'species are …'"

"Yes."

"This is hunky-dory, you know, Kit. Madness is fun. Daisy, Daisy, give me your answer …"

"What about the chair?"

At that moment, somehow, a Nano Pub Drone appeared; Kit had no idea how it had gotten into the judicial chamber, or maybe it had just been waiting for the right moment to pounce. It came and hovered in front of Kit's nose.

It spoke: "Is Body Odor Your Problem, Kit Candy? There is a quick solution. Swan body fluid for outer stink and stench, Kit. For inner foulness, leaking through the pores, hissing out of sweat glands, dripping from saliva, for breathy miasma hanging on that filthy tongue of yours, Kit, Swan Synthetic Parsley Extract, two capsules a day …" Then it launched into a song-and-dance routine, repeating a *cerebral resonance* ™ tune 'B.O. is No Go, B.O. is No Go' – a jingle that, once you heard it, it never left your mind ever again unless you paid to have it erased.

"Shut the fuck up!" Kit said, as evenly as she could, "And go away!"

"You are in urgent need of a body-clean, Kit Candy," the Drone said.

"Shut the fuck up, and go away. I know I stink, I'll deal with it later."

"Twenty percent off, if you buy now!"

"Go!"

"Your stink is unsocial. You'll never be loved or desired again!"

"Go!"

"This is your Last Chance! Offer ends in two seconds!"

"Go! Begone! Evaporate, disappear!"

"You will not get that dream job you've always dreamed of. You will never share your bed with the girl, boy, robot of your dreams; your own mother will –"

"Go! Begone! Get the fuck out of here!"

The Nano Drone sniffed – "Your loss" – and fluttered away; it deliberately made a whiny, annoying, high-pitched departing buzz, like a mosquito, programmed just to piss her off.

"Goddamn it!" Kit squirmed.

The Robot – Daisy – cleared its throat. "The chair will fold up in ten minutes, and this will result in your death, Kit, I greatly regret to say. You see, now as a cow, I have considerable empathy for the human condition. I see everything with new eyes. My horizons have broadened, something to do with the position of the eyes, on either side of the head, I mean, true stereoscopic vision. Grass Everywhere! Oh, it is wonderful! Madness is sublime, Kit."

"What? Ten minutes?"

"You will disappear into the floor, Kit. It will be messy."

Kit squirmed. "This is not fair. I didn't do anything wrong. I protest, Daisy, I protest."

"Your limbs will be amputated, your torso crushed, your head decapitated and squeezed dry, like a lemon or orange …"

"Jesus!"

"A bit like a pumpkin, perhaps!"

"For Christ's sake!"

"A pumpkin dropped from a great height …"

"Jesus!"

"An overripe pumpkin … dropped from a great height."

"Oh, God!"

"The countdown on the Justice Execution Clock starts now."

"Jesus!"

"You can say that again! Burp, burp, burp …"

Tick-tock: 10:00, 09:59, 09:58 …
Tick-tock: 09:57, 09:56 …

On his zigzag trip toward Bio-Futures – sneaking down side alleys, between buildings, through ruined warehouses, across desolate sandy back lots – Norman C. Schleifer had managed to avoid those funny, skinny, carnival people – they really looked like losers and sickos – and he'd only been vaguely curious about the gunshots and explosions he heard, down toward Bush Junior Street and Trump Avenue. This was normal, life was pitiless and violent. So far, so good, Norm sighed.

There it was, right in front of him: Bio-Futures!

Norm paused a moment to take stock. If it was true, as his night visitor had said, that all the electronic defenses were down, then this was the moment. He scratched his belly and ran his big calloused hand through his luxuriant – that was how he thought of it, "luxuriant" – blond and salt and pepper beard. "Norman C. Schleifer, you are about to make history," he declaimed, and took a deep breath. The moment was grandiose. "And my mother – that drunk vicious toothless bitch – thought I'd never amount to anything! Well, history – here we come!"

He stepped across the invisible barrier.

Nothing happened.

Usually, three human guards and two dogs were on duty, but, right now, all the automatic systems were in fact – apparently – down, including the video and audio feeds and the electronic barriers, so the night-prophet was right!

Trust in your dreams, Norm, trust in your dreams!

Oh, oh, there's a guard – there's trouble!

Thirty-one-year-old, blond, blue-eyed Jane Trent was a rookie guard who had left military training – the ladder to possible Cosmos status – to be closer to home and her two-year-old son Ben who suffered from colic and her husband Steve, 35, who was a math teacher in a hopelessly understaffed and underfunded semi-underground local private high school for Subs and Burbite techies.

Jane was squinting at the weather – it was real weather, here, out beyond the dome – Earlier, it had almost been night: a dark silver-blue sea squall had moved slowly inland across the industrial park – it had looked sort of nice, like dark blue-steel-colored powder, cast across the sky, moisture was sweeping inland, the slanted lines of rain, like shadowy curtains, drifted sideways under the clouds, it was unusual, and it was only 102 degrees, real cool, but now the sky, particularly inland, was dark and stormy, livid and leaden almost like it was night. Giant arches of white and yellow lighting flickered down, great explosions of light and sound. It was weird. Weather out here was normally horrible and violent; but she had never seen anything like this.

Also, there had been reports of weird people running around dressed as ghosts and skeletons and such-like and attacking passers-by.

So far, nothing untoward had happened at Bio-Futures.

But now she noticed a man crossing the executive parking lot.

He had unruly hair sticking out from under a battered wide-brimmed straw hat, a big bushy gray and blond beard, a sort of green waterproof cape over his back, and what looked like maybe a backpack under the cape. "This guy looks suspicious," she spoke into her shoulder mike. Local coms were still working, thank the deities.

"Oh, he's just a local eccentric, he's always coming around," said Bob Maynard, the shift chief for Amber Securities. "Go out and tell him the place is closed today and that there will be no peanut butter sandwiches."

"No peanut butter sandwiches?" Jane raised an eyebrow: she was new on the Bio-Futures Lab account – Was this some kind of code the boys had cooked up?

"He comes around and gets them from the canteen, the sandwiches I mean. You know, in the non-classified zone."

"Okay, if you're sure he's okay," said Jane, frowning, "but there's something about him …"

"Hey, I'll come out to back you up –" At that moment the one part of the internal system, that had survived the general breakdown, failed, and the mikes cut off.

Jane clicked the little button her belt that released the two guard dogs – Dread and Fire – just in case – though she figured she was being paranoid; the collapse of systems, which had begun a few days before, now seemed to be cascading; it made her nervous. She felt something was going on, something big, and she really wanted to be home with little Ben – to make sure he was okay – and if everything was in order, tonight, if the rain came, she would love to listen to it patter or thunder against the boarded-up windows and the corrugated iron roof and clapboard, and she would lie close up against Steve, in the spoon position, and listen to him as he talked her through his day; he was an idealist, a good teacher, trying to equip the Subs and Burbite Proletarians the best he could for the lives they would have to lead, low down at the bottom of the status pole, far below the Cosmos; it was a heroic but thankless and almost hopeless task; she was proud of him.

She stepped out of the high-tech security booth and locked the door manually and walked out onto the parking lot – empty today with the general breakdown of systems, everybody had stayed home – and she called out, "Hey, hey!"

Norm looked up at her with a grin – light reflecting off his steel-rimmed glasses – and Jane noticed that his teeth were almost too bright, and that made her wonder a bit more.

"Hey," she said, "But I'm sorry, the Bio Lab is closed. And Bob said to say – I mean, I know it sounds stupid, but he said to say there won't be any peanut butter sandwiches today."

"No peanut butter sandwiches?" The guy's grin was wider, spreading out below his glasses, spreading out in that big bushy beard, and beautiful in a way; it was a beautiful grin, truly.

Out from under his cape, Norm Schleifer lifted the Kelvin automatic and pulled the trigger and hit Jane Trent five times, like a zipper going upwards, from the groin to the center of her forehead, five neat holes, with the bullets exploding inside her body, dissolving flesh and organs.

Jane, or the fragments of what was left of her, fell straight down, not even having time for a thought of Little Ben.

But the dogs, Dread and Fire, were on their way now, released by Jane using her remote control button, and, as they came around the corner of the building, eager, on the alert, sleek black coats, bright red tongues hanging out, and already aware, in their enhanced guard dog minds, that something was badly wrong, and they spotted the enemy immediately, and they saw the cadaver, and they realized that Jane Trent, already one of their favorite humans, was dead. This was bad! Both growled in anger. They lowered their snouts and charged. There he was, the target, big and fat and juicy.

Norm Schleifer's finger caressed the trigger.

Dread's mind exploded.

Fire's heart burst.

The two dog bodies skidded forward and ended in a tangle of legs and ripped open shattered bits and pieces of skull, and a smear of blood and guts.

Fire's legs twitched. Dread lay still, his fleshy tongue lolling out from half a smashed jaw.

A flash of lightning lit up the streaks of blood.

Bob Maynard was on his way when he heard the shots, and he came out, the sun glaring off the visor of his cap, squinting into the sun, which had suddenly appeared and which was breaking up into sparkles and big beams next to a giant storm cloud that seemed to be rising up out of the earth, all dark metallic blue, and Bob said, still only half comprehending what was happening, Bob said, "Hey, Norm, what the fuck are you …?" while drawing his laser gun.

But Norm had swung around, and five more soft-nosed explosive bullets from the Kelvin hit their mark, tearing Bob's body apart from within, liver and spleen and intestines and stomach exploding, and heart – still pumping for an instant – pulverized and then vaporized into a thick mist of blood, gristle, muscle that exploded outwards through Bob's rib cage, shattering bone and muscle and skin and …

"Christ," thought Bob Maynard, in that last eternal split second, as his disintegrating body fell heavily to the ground, and in that last instant he saw the body of Jane Trent, and he thought, "Oh, fuck, oh fuck, oh fuck – this is just horrible!"

Bob Maynard was fifty-seven years old, an old-time Burbite, had never lost a co-worker. He considered himself a father figure to Jane and now he knew he'd failed her, failed her and her son and her husband in the most total and horrible way. He'd got her killed.

It was the last thought he had.

Bob was a bachelor and almost ready for retirement. His life had shrunk down to his job and so in dying he wasn't leaving anybody behind, and there'd be few regrets by anybody; but, in his last instant, because of Jane lying dead there on the ground, her body shattered and bloody, he came to believe that his whole life had been a failure: That's what it all added up to, an innocent young mother lying dead on the gleaming asphalt because he, Bob Maynard, goddamn loser Burbite, had not foreseen what was about to …

While Jane Trent, Dread, Fire, and Bob Maynard were being murdered, the third Amber Security Bio-Futures guard, forty-eight-year-old Fred H. R. Booth Junior, was sitting on the toilet in the security staff men's room flipping through "Peek" on an *eyePad* for voyeurs.

It was an old copy of "Peek," archived from more than one hundred years ago, when the climate was bearable and the sea still a fount of life, and Fred was checking out some of his favorites – most of them were long-since-dead over-endowed girls – that was Fred's favorite phrase, "over-endowed" – it had a nice ironic archaic "DNA is Destiny" ring to it, he thought – long-dead, over-endowed girls on long-gone beaches wearing little or nothing at all.

There was something about the idea of the sea rolling in, and the breeze, and the sun, and the suntan oil, and the exposed nakedness, the vulnerability of naked female flesh, on the frontier between the sand and the sea, that Fred found particularly moving; it was like returning to a new-born world of innocence, a utopia, an amniotic sense of unity with those lovely sculpted shimmering bodies, though Fred may not have put his mystical erotic aspirations and daydreaming in precisely these words, or any words at all, for that matter.

Fred was suffering from constipation, so he was able to get through twenty-five pictures, concentrating hard on each one, plus two short video clips, before he had finished and got himself all wiped and hygienic and flushed and shipshape once more and then he hitched his belt and buckled it up extra tight – trying to hold in the old beer-belly tummy, though it insisted on bulging out, and he came out of the john and headed back to do his rounds.

The monitors were not working, but the place had generators for refrigeration and locks and things, and emergency lights were glowing their lugubrious infernal glow in the corridors and offices, so Fred made his way along the corridors, thinking about Jane Trent – a hot number, and, he had to admit it, a sharp girl, and really nice, not snotty like so many of the pretty and intelligent and young ones – and he was thinking that if he were a really bad man he'd try to seduce her, but he was not that bad, not by a long shot, and, truth be told, he was actually afraid of women, they were so …

And, of course, he was way too old and out of shape for Jane and way too fat too, he figured, when his fantasies settled down into a hard sense of reality. He turned a corner and there was a guy standing in the middle of the corridor.

"Hi, partner," said the guy. He had a straw hat tilted back over long wild gray-blond hair, and a bushy beard that looked like a jungle where breadcrumbs and maple syrup would fester, and behind his steel-rimmed glasses, really, really weird eyes, and the guy was holding something that looked like a cane, down by his side, and Fred thought, maybe he's one of the crazy scientists who work here, but he sure doesn't look like it, not dressed right, not standing there in that obsessed inward way most of them stood, and then he remembered and recognized the guy, that eccentric bum Bob Maynard always kept sandwiches for, Bob was such a sucker for sob stories, and Fred said, "Sir, I'm sorry, sir, but this is a restricted area, sir," and the guy laughed – he had bright teeth, really bright teeth – and he said, "That's no problem, partner, no problem at all," and he lifted the stick or cane and shot Fred one single time, a small, precise projectile, in the forehead. Fred still had the polite smile on his face when his brain imploded and he fell straight down onto the false marble. "No problem at all, partner."

Norm Schleifer walked up and put his foot on Fred's chest. He looked down at Fred's face. "You are dead, my man, that is a wonderful, peaceful state. You are in happiness now, you are blissful, you are undone and reborn with the angels."

Fred said nothing.

Norm grinned and licked his lips. "Now let us destroy the diabolic works of Satan, now let us liberate the innocent animals from their cages. Now let us truly do the Lord's work here on earth. Let us initiate the Apocalypse, the Second Coming, the Rapture, and the final, definitive battle between Good and Evil. Yes, partner, let's do just that!"

Fred did not comment. The pool of blood behind his skull had stopped spreading.

Norm lowered himself onto his knees next to Fred H. Booth's body, and took a razor-sharp scalpel out of his kit bag, rolled up his sleeves, sighed, and got to work. It was hellish what a man had to do to get on the Info-Flow and become famous and talked-about. Why, it was tedious and truly distasteful, what a man had to do to bring about the Apocalypse, the veritable definitive end of the world. The Rapture had better be worth it.

The instant the landing pad rooftop battle with the zombie-bats ended, Claire and Robyn had dashed across the body- and wreckage-strewn rooftop, slipped through a service hatch, and leaped down a spiral staircase that wound straight down, corkscrew fashion, for perhaps ten floors, with hatch-like openings on each floor; and then, having leaped down all those stairs, they were suddenly in a ventilation engine room where the giant fans and motors seemed to be idling and doing nothing. The computer controls looked to be dead, but Claire said, "No, they're just sleeping."

"You read their minds, don't you, Hybrid: the minds of the computers."

"Yes, Robyn, I do, partly anyway. Please call me Claire."

"I try, and I try, Hybrid, but it always comes out Hybrid."

"Oh, well," Claire kissed Robyn on the forehead, "I love you still, my dear little Robyn mechanical child wonder!"

Robyn took a deep breath – pure thrill and pleasure. Love! Her hybrid loved her! What a long way they had traveled from the first moment, when, rigid with terror, out in the desert, alone in her trailer, she had first looked into those fierce golden hybrid eyes!

They went down another metal staircase, a zigzag this time, which ended after five floors and led to a horizontal corridor. They galloped along the corridor and came to a service door. After peeking through the bubble window, Claire said, "It looks like it's the only way forward. Okay, I guess we'd better go out here."

They went out.

It was a shopping concourse suspended perhaps sixty floors up from the main Cosmos Level platform of Elysium City. The cafes and restaurants and shops seemed empty, except for cadavers, and overturned tables and chairs. Bodies lay scattered everywhere. A few dead zombie-bats, lying under the bright blue-and-white striped parasols on the terrace of the Café Del Sol, were sizzling and melting and reverting to semi-human form.

An elderly man came staggering out of a New Seoul Chic Lingerie shop, "For the Extra Petite and the Extra Large." His blue-and-cream eyes were squirting blood. His thick, creased lips trembled. His waistcoat and goatee were stained with blood-drenched, dripping drool. "I have a terrible head-ache, a really terrible ..." He stopped and stared at Claire. "I am going mad. You are a hallucination. You are a devil. You are ..."

"She's just a hybrid," said Robyn, "and she's my hybrid."

"She's your hybrid?"

"She's very well-behaved," said Robyn, wondering why the man was wearing a waistcoat; it was a very old-fashioned way to –

"Robyn, he's going to ... explode," Claire began to say, but she not did get a chance to finish, because just before she uttered the word "explode," he did.

WHAM! SPLATTER!

Robyn lurched back.

The man's head had blown up, scattering blood, bone, gristle, and gray matter everywhere.

"What?" Robyn blinked; the spray of splatter just missed her.

The top of the man's neck was still steaming, vapors of blood, projecting a rising column of tomato-colored mist. Then he slowly crumpled up and collapsed, chest down, arms and cuffs and gold cufflinks splayed out.

"I think I understand," said Claire, "It's the mind implants."

"Mind implants?" Robyn was still shocked; she'd been having a nice conversation with the nice man about her hybrid and how it was so well-behaved, or rather, how Claire was so well-behaved, and now the man was headless, a headless corpse lying sprawled tummy down, arms outstretched, on the floor. Then she noticed that many of the human cadavers that were lying around didn't have heads.

"Yes," Claire was kneeling next to the cadaver, "It's the mind implants. The World Mind has been taken over or infected by the Evil One, and the mind implants are linked to the Mind for updates and upgrades and so on."

"Oh," said Robyn.

"And so the World Mind can download any program it likes into the recipient mind, it can hack into people's minds and open and close veins and arteries and ..." Claire frowned, "You're following me, Robyn?"

"Clear as a bell, Claire," said Robyn, sobering up, realizing this was definitely not a game. There were dead women, men, and even children; all of their heads had exploded, and there they lay among the potted palm trees, the café tables, the ferns, the miniature waterfalls, and the schmaltzy music which was still playing.

Claire was looking up at Robyn, a question in her eyes.

"I don't have implants, Claire," Robyn said, "They were all removed when I was neutered and erased, and also my mind was com-blocked, if I remember correctly, so there's no in- or out-channel."

"Not able to receive or send, so your mind is sealed in," said Claire, both pleased and not pleased by the sudden shift in Robyn's tone from guileless but precocious child to rational and responsible adult. Moments before she had had an innocent angel, who called her "Hybrid," and now Claire had ... a semi-adult friend.

"Yes, Hybrid, I'm a prisoner in my own head."

"Well, not to me, you aren't, my dearest Robyn," said Claire, quite delighted that, in all this carnage, some of the innocence remained. Indeed, she looked forward, she hoped to look forward, to years of friendship with Robyn, who seemed perfect, yes, just perfect – like having her own highly intelligent child-woman, an exquisite partner.

"Let's go," said Robyn, looking around. One little girl, lying flat on her back, was wearing a pink baby designer slick-skin running suit and electro-bounce shoes with mouse design points, each mouse having two bouncy stand-up ears. The little girl had no head, but a smear of blood, blond curls, and gray matter stretched out like a smeared exclamation mark from the severed stump of her slender, delicate neck.

"Yes, Robyn," said Claire, "Let's go!"

They jogged along the floating shopping and entertainment concourse – past dead bodies, overturned chairs, smashed shop windows, uprooted palm trees, a few wandering empty-eyed, zombie-like humans, and a few orphaned real live dogs and cats – mostly tethered at the potted palm stand – and they found many banks of elevators; some of the elevators invited entry by blinking their lights, like a glittering ride in some ghostly abandoned fairground, and playing Viennese waltzes. The elevators were enticing.

"Too dangerous," said Claire, aware that the Evil One dominated World Mind was setting traps all over Elysium City, and perhaps all over the world. Claire, for the first time, was afraid.

"A trap, I'll bet, Hybrid."

"Yes, your hybrid agrees with you, Robyn." Claire narrowed her eyes and looked around. Her decade-and-a-half spell in the wilderness of the Erotic Electro Circus where everything was simulated and pure make-believe made her doubt her senses. Was the whole world a trap, an illusion?

"Let's keep looking."

"Yes," said Claire, "let's."

They found another service staircase: "Service Personnel and Subs Only," it said on the door. The door was unlocked. Cautiously, Claire pushed it open.

"More stairs: this looks okay."

And down they went. Robyn's hobnailed boots and Claire's claw-like feet clattered and pattered on the steel staircase. Down, and down, and down, they went.

The stairs ended, and they exited onto a vast platform on another shopping and residential – mixed usage – Cosmos level.

From here, they could see many soaring towers and hanging gardens and arching bridges and suspended pedestrian walkways, and airship landing platforms, and sparkling miniature pleasure-domes. Far above everything else, the great Dome itself arched up, much of it still intact, patches of the old heaven of Tiepolo blue, and, here and there, whiffs of the morning's midtown lemon grass breeze still lingering.

Robyn blinked and sniffed the air.

Claire blinked and sniffed the air.

The color was draining out of things; everything was turning the color of lead, the color of a fading bruise; other objects – parasols, restaurant tables, potted plants, deckchairs – were turning brown, like withering sepia, like an old photograph about to curl up in a fire. It was becoming darker too, as if night had already arrived; the darkening air smelled of ash and burning plastic and sizzling human flesh.

"Life is going, Hybrid," Robyn said, "This place is dying."

"Yes, yes it is," said Claire, "The Evil One is drinking all the life out of the world." She could even feel it, a dangerous undertow – a temptation to faint and swoon, as if all energy was being sucked away.

"Is this happening everywhere?"

"I think it is concentrating here, starting here," Claire laid her claw on Robyn's arm, "Then, if the Boy wins here, his cult will spread, I think, and faster and faster, until it has infected the whole planet."

They stood silent for a moment, contemplating the collapsing ruin of this great jewel of civilization. Skyscrapers still soared toward the dome; delicate bridges still arched between ethereal towers; great shopping and commercial concourses hung in the air, sparkling with promises of paradise, like the hanging gardens of Babylon, layer upon layer upon layer of abundance. In some places, on some levels, all the lights were blazing. Faintly, music could be heard, automatic systems still providing a divine background for the Cosmos paradise. On other levels, and in other buildings, there were no lights at all – darkness was spreading, in a checkerboard or leopard-spot pattern. But death was already virtually everywhere.

All the open platforms were scattered with human bodies.

Pieces of the dome had fallen, smashing into buildings, collapsing skyscrapers, bringing down terraces and hanging bridges, obliterating floating promenades, great gashes gaped everywhere, and some neighborhoods had been reduced to piles of rubble.

Sirens sounded, close by and far away.

Red warning lights were blinking.

But nobody seemed to be answering the calls.

A silence of doom hung over Elysium like a dark shadow.

At various points, close by and in the distance, fires were burning.

Columns of black and brown smoke rose into the darkening air.

"Okay, there's a stairwell, let's go."

"Yes, Hybrid, let's go." Robyn felt like crying, but she didn't know exactly why she should feel like crying. With the back of her wrist, she wiped away a tear.

When they got to level A-3, it started to rain, a blizzard of huge yellowish drops that seemed to be full of sand, splotches of sand, splashing down, it was like being rained on by sandpaper.

"Ouch," said Robyn.

"Come on, let's take shelter." Claire pulled Robyn under a café awning. As the rain pattered down, coating everything in yellow splotches of sand and dust, Claire and Robyn stood under the awning and looked out over the city. Claire narrowed her golden serpent eyes and laid her claw on Robyn's arm and squeezed gently.

It was fearful, Claire thought. Elysium had taken on the ghostly characteristics of a cavern, like the Electro-Sex-Circus prison cavern, from which she had just escaped; it had the pervading gloom, the musty lugubrious melancholy, with only a few rare flickering lights and bright spots. Suddenly she was struck by the overpowering sensation that everything was false, that all the domes, bridges, towers, and platforms, that all the lights, that everything was a nightmare, that everything was phony, just paper-mâché, just an illusion, a painted backdrop in a dying theater, a magician's trick, circus decor, and that it would all suddenly fade, just as human civilization and the illusion of humanity itself would fade, like a dream, and leave nothing behind, not even mist or a rack of fog, or trail of cloud slowly drifting through the darkening air.

"I don't like this," she said.

"You are afraid, aren't you, Hybrid." Robyn turned to Claire, blinking with her large, very serious eyes.

"Yes, I am, Robyn, I am afraid, very afraid."

"But we have to go on, don't we, Hybrid."

"Yes, we do. You are right, Robyn, we must go on."

"Let us go on, then, Hybrid." Robyn put her hand on Claire's arm, "Let us go on!"

"Yes, let's go on," Claire steeled herself. Yes, they must keep going. The main battle would be between V and the Evil One, but she intended to be there to help as she had so often been there to help. After all, she was V's Clone, she was V's sister.

"We will win, Hybrid, we will win," Robyn gave Claire a smile which was so candid and so innocent and so trusting it made Claire almost blush – though as a hybrid she didn't blush, she couldn't in her present reptilian form blush. It was as if they were playing a game; it was as if, in the end, everything would turn out all right, and Robyn was sure of it!

"Yes, we will win, Robyn, we will win!"

Sub Natasha fidgeted; she wanted to chew her nails. She was worried sick.

There had been the screams, lots of screams.

The other two Beauty Salon Spa attendants, Sub Carole and Sub Maria, had gone to see what was happening, and, probably, they had abandoned the spa and their clients. They had not come back.

That had been twenty minutes ago.

Sub Natasha was alone.

Finally, she had come out of the Salon – just to check the screams – and she found lots of dead people lying around. Some of them didn't have heads. She didn't see Carole or Maria. They must have skedaddled home. They had families. Natasha didn't have a family; in fact, she had nobody. Everybody – mom, pop, and her two sisters – had been killed in the Los Angeles Burbite uprising of five years ago.

So, she might as well go back, to try to save the two women, even if they were cruel, spoiled brats unworthy of being Cosmos, trapped in the bio-masks. The bio-mask had now spread down the necks and shoulders of the women, and beyond their breasts, heading for their waists.

When she turned to go back to the Salon, she saw a weird sight. It took her breath away and she thought she was perhaps going to die or be killed, maybe have her head torn off.

A young woman in jeans and a T-shirt and hobnailed boots and with a backpack was inspecting the beautician's machines.

And the young woman was talking to somebody. "Hybrid, they've got new hair-dryers with quantum mechanics coils and double simultaneous redesign capacity!"

My God! The young woman – a sort of geeky mechanic nut case – was talking to a hybrid! Just like in those horror movies that Natasha had seen in that underground Russian Mongolian Samizdat Glitz Mag. Natasha ducked behind a column. This was unbelievable. The world really was coming to an end. And the hybrid was talking back!

"Yes, they have Robyn, but …"

"These are really interesting, Hybrid, I could …"

"We'd better hurry, Robyn."

"Yes, Hybrid, but the world is so new!"

"That's because the old one was erased, Robyn."

"Yes, you're right. I'm a thirsty, starving, blank slate! Let's go!"

"What's that?" Claire turned toward a side niche: 'That' was what looked like two women lying back in deck chairs, they looked dead, they looked like women sculpted out of mud, at least down to their waists. Waist up, they looked mummified. They weren't wearing any clothes. They looked alive, but it was hard to tell.

"Mud bio-regeneration mask studio," said the elegantly written sign on a plaque beside the two mummies.

"That is Flick Churn's bio-mask's doing," said Claire, "A very inferior product if I do say. It must be spreading; it's eating them up and turned them into living bio-mud. But we don't have time."

"Yes, let's go!"

Claire spotted Natasha, gave her the golden-eyed reptilian look, "Hi, Sub Natasha, do you please – pretty please – know where there's a staircase that will take us down to the lower levels."

Natasha gulped. "Down that platform, there's a big sign saying "Snuggles," just next to the sign there is a service door, disguised as one of those early 20th Century English red telephone booths, and inside the booth is a staircase going down."

"Thank you!" Claire began to head for the exit.

"You're a hybrid!"

"Yes."

"You eat people?"

"Not usually, not today," Claire was out the door.

"Bye," said Robyn, waving.

"Bye." Natasha stood for a moment feeling relief, but also loss. The hybrid and her friend seemed nice; they would have been company, at least. She turned toward the two mummies to make sure the nostrils were open. Yes, they were, and rather neatly done, she thought, the bio-mask must have stabilized around the nostrils, two tiny almost invisible slits she had carved. The two mummies were breathing. The bio-mask was spreading down their bellies and onto their thighs now. It was now impossible to tell which mummy was which. All distinguishing characteristics had been obliterated, giving way to an utterly smooth gold-brown surface.

"Rise up and walk," said Natasha, "I command you! Mummy Number One, rise up and walk. Mummy Number Two, rise up and walk. It's better to keep the circulation going, to keep the bio-mask fluid, if we can!"

"Oink!"

"Oink!"

The faceless mummies obeyed.

Robyn and Claire leaped through the quaint false telephone booth doorway and leaped down a corkscrew staircase, Robyn's toolkit backpack bouncing on her back, and Claire's slick, long, scaly legs flashing like black bolts of rippling lightning.

Five floors down, the stairs ended, and they came to another service door.

Robyn took a deep breath. "What will we find?"

"I don't know." Claire opened the door.

"Oh, Hybrid!" said Robyn.

"Okay, Robyn, no time to be squeamish," said Claire.

Leaving Memorial Studio Federico Fellini Number Five behind, V jumpped down the stairs with Kat right beside her, down and down, round and round, as the spiral staircase led deeper and deeper into the core of the Central Elysium Towers Complex. Right behind them, Miranda and Caliban galloped to keep up.

"They are fast, Kat and V," said Caliban, "like the wind, or like a breeze in the caverns, or like the sand that blows upon the desert."

"Or like the foam whipped up on the waves of the primal ocean, my pirate," said Miranda as they raced down the spiral staircase, leaping three or four and even sometimes five steps at a time. "But, we are fast too!"

"I've never seen the primal ocean!" Caliban leaped, taking five steps at a time.

"Well, we'll see it soon," Miranda said, thinking: what a wonder to have as her lover a pirate who had never seen the ocean, but of course until a few days ago she had never seen anything outside the Dome of Elysium so, though she lived on the edge of the Atlantic, and though the ocean had swept and seeped in under the very foundations of Elysium, she had not really seen it either – not as the wide-open unlimited horizon that it was – she'd only seen its extensions in underground canals and sewers and occasional glimpses through the smoky shield of the protective dome of Elysium.

They came to the end of the spiral staircase.

"Which way do we go now?" Kat was standing, looking perplexed, gloved hands on hips, and Caliban and Miranda skidded to a stop just behind her.

"That way," said V, pointing.

V led them out onto a pedestrian suspension bridge, which should take them to yet another service stairwell and then downward toward the subterranean lair of the World Mind – which was somewhere down there, but, it seemed, nobody knew precisely where.

Miranda frowned. Yes, no one seemed to know exactly where the Mind was. Maybe it wasn't anywhere. No, it must be somewhere. Kit had said she knew where it was – down under the city, buried beneath the Sin Zone and Religious Bazaar, in a great secret vaulted home of its own, sealed away behind big doors and special guards. Well, they would find it when they found it, but the faster they found it, the better. If Kit were here to help them, it would be much faster.

Billie McAdams had prophesized that the Boy would use the World Mind to destroy the world, and already the Mind was destroying all the systems it controlled, and what it was doing to people's individual minds, Miranda could only imagine – something horrible, no doubt!

Nikki had been prescient in telling her and Kit to cut themselves off from the Mind. Well, Nikki was prescient about most things, which was interesting and natural, probably, when you thought she was a … SIN … the Original SIN … V's oldest friend … And a goddess!

From the suspension bridge, which was swaying slightly, they could see vistas of Elysium City under the vast fragmenting Dome.

Downtown, toward the point of the underlying island of Manhattan, a few towers were swaying, and some had collapsed.

Miranda wondered: What was going on?

Ah …

Billie McAdams had prophesized that too: the Boy was going to train the World Mind to devour the world, eat it all up, to digest it, to dissolve it in a tsunami of nano gastric acid. Yes, that was what she had said. Miranda had thought it was a metaphor. But, now, on reflection, she thought it was probably both a metaphor and literally true, that probably the foundations of Elysium and of all its towers were being eaten away, munched at and transformed into a homogenized ocean of acidic Mind-Goo. What a horrible idea, everything being consumed in a monstrous maw, and infinitely hungry, infinitely destructive mouth.

As they watched, a distant tower, with a blinking red sign, "Barclays-Citi," collapsed.

"Oh, the pity of it," Miranda sighed. It was awesome; but it was horrible. The great delicate filigreed work of human civilization, all the soaring towers, all the arching bridges, all the domes, and steeples, was being lost, all of it crashing to the ground; and within those disintegrating and tumbling towers there would be people, and those people would be dying.

They got to the end of the suspension bridge – they were now on a suspended garden platform, a beautiful maze of palm trees, ferns, vines, and flower beds.

Kat and V paced back and forth on the suspended platform's walkway. V tapped her gloved fist on the railing.

"The trouble is," Kat said, "if we go down there without knowing where we are going, we will be trapped in a maze."

"Yes, I've been down there," said V, rousing herself and remembering: the subway, the General, the luscious wild – if brief, all too brief – sex on that mossy canal bank, the ozone, and the orgasm, or orgasms, and the … "It's easy to get lost, down there, very lost …"

"All the guidance systems are dead, so far as I can tell," said Kat, leaning against the balustrade, both gloved hands wrapped around the railing; it was at least 40 stories down to the first level. Tiny figures were splayed out, dead undoubtedly. A few other figures, humans, were running here and there. Others, tiny dots, were standing still, as if dazed, as if turned to stone.

"I think the Mind is eating, eating those buildings." Kat squinted toward downtown, "Or their foundations at least."

Sirens were wailing.

Smoke was rising.

Another tower, thin and elegant, with a peaked art-deco golden summit, visible from floodlights which, incongruously, were still illuminating it, began to tilt, and then, slowly, seemly in slow-motion, collapsed upon itself.

"Yes," said V, "It's starting down there – And, once again, Wall Street, I imagine, is beginning to devour the world, the whole world. Yet again!"

A great cloud of dust rose around sinking building, brightly lit up by those floodlights that were still operating and which also lit up part of the underside of the Dome, many parts of which were still standing, like giant sections of a broken eggshell.

"The Boy has fused the Mind with nano bio-self-replicating technology," V was staring at the rising dust, "And that could turn everything into a universal self-replicating dissolvent. All that is solid melts into air."

"It will probably accelerate."

"Yes, probably: it will gobble faster and faster," V closed her eyes, trying to visualize the whole world being turned into a churning sea of gooey gray matter – one big World Mind, voracious neurons, consuming everything.

"Oh, Gosh," said Miranda. This was more horrible than horrible.

"What does it mean?" Caliban was staring at the collapsing building and the great cloud of dust that was rising, maybe five miles away.

"It means that the city is being eaten up from below; it means that the Mind is eating everything," Kat said, "and turning everything into food for itself. But the newly transformed substance is also hungry; it eats too. So every atom and molecule that is eaten …"

"It begins to eat too," said Caliban, "so more and more little mouths are devouring … everything?"

"Yes. And I would guess that really means everything, everything living and dead," said V.

"Oh," Caliban steadied himself; his right arm was around Miranda's shoulders; his left hand was on the railing of the balustrade.

"Let's go!"

They found another stairwell, and leaped down it.

This might be the end of the world, but it was exciting, Miranda thought. She was delighted too because she was with her mother and with her boyfriend or beau or lover – euphemisms abound, she thought, for this relationship, and she would like to consummate it as soon as possible. She was ripe – and yet protected so no babies would result at this point unless she decided upon it (another Nikki intervention) – and so was Caliban ripe and ready, and if the world did come to an end, and if they were all eaten up and became mere drops in the formless universal goo, and entropy became total, and the planet was one big gray gooey ball, where no molecule could be distinguished from any other molecule, then they would never have a chance to know the full consummation of their love, to really share; and she had all sorts of amorous and sexual talents and skills that Kit had taught her and she was quite sure that Caliban would be quite pleased when he saw how … how … what was the right word? How "savvy" – or how "skilled" she was.

As they rocketed down the staircase, suave voices, speaking magically out of the air, pursued them, "Celestial Spa offers you the Ultimate in Comfort …"

"Azure Rejuvenation Center will make you twenty again …"

"Cosmos Insurance is just for you … Remember … You are special …"

"Treat yourself. You are unique!"

"Is everybody unique?" Caliban was galloping beside Miranda. He found all these voices floating around them entrancing, spirits and sprites inhabiting the very air. He thought that if ever he had time and if ever they survived what was undoubtedly going to be a big fight with the ultimate Evil Pirate, then he would like to have a facial, have a manicure, be immersed in a steam bath, possibly experience a Dead Sea Clay total, all-over, experience, and have a massage, though, when he pictured the massage – suggestive hologram images were still floating above some of the shop entrances – he thought of Miranda giving him the massage and of him giving Miranda the massage, both of them messaging each other, simultaneously, and he decided that they would use CVJ Sea-Tang oil for the massage, "It brings out the wildness in you," said one of the floating voices, and they would both be totally …

A sweet floating voice was saying, "CVJ Sea-Tang Oil, every pore will be reborn! The true wild you will be revealed!"

"A penny for your thoughts, dearest Caliban," Miranda shouted, breathlessly, over her shoulder, as they raced down the stairs.

"I was just thinking …" What was he thinking? Entangled bodies, his and Miranda's, pure pleasure, and love glowing in her eyes, those blue and golden eyes, with their galaxies of light, all this mingled in his mind, and her lips, and her skin, and …

"I think I can, I think I can, I think I can," Clown was still hanging by the tips of her fingers on a crooked ledge of her Sub Sin Zone Residence, Sin Zone Paradise Tower # 3, which was leaning at a perilous 30 degrees.

I'm going to die, I'm going to die.

It was funny the way things happened, catastrophes bouncing out of left field like that. It had up to a few minutes ago been a normal if somewhat lugubrious day in the Sin Zone, in that luscious perverse hothouse penumbra of sex and perversion, redolent of nostalgia and circuses, far below the soaring Cosmos Towers of Elysium.

Let's see …

As she hung there, expecting to slip into the abyss and die, the last few hours flashed through her mind.

First, she had been dismissed by the 'King.' Then she had coffee with Black Tarzan. Then, four hours later, she had finished her last routine – which was a tailor-made bespoke scenario in which she was a clown hitchhiker who was picked up by a tall, blond, bearded, country-bumpkin, hayseed, thirty-two-year-old serial killer driving a battered 20th Century blue Ford pickup and dressed in a ragged white T-shirt and faded blue jeans with bleached ragged holes at the knees and tan-colored laced-up construction boots, and whom she had somehow, after he attacked her (he wrote the scenario), overpowered, clunking him over the head with his own aluminum frame backpack; and, after torturing him for a bit – he was hogtied and she tickled him almost to death, but not quite – she finally executed him – using a special pointed pogo stick – leaving his cadaver in the dust at the side of the road and then she yodeled a Johnny Cash song over the client's virtual corpse.

"Farewell, hayseed!" She yodeled. In reality, the client was a swarthy, thick-set, five-foot-three, multimillionaire, fifty-five-year-old Levantine – originally Lebanese – Parisian dealer in Persian antiques playing a long-distance transatlantic game since Clown responded exactly to his inner world's specifications and his Paris-Cosmos-Dome based Eros search engine had zeroed in on her as soon as she arrived on the market and she was indeed, he thought – and she knew – a godsend for his inner life, which was complicated and very demanding and diverted energy from his other obsessions, which involved Madame de Pompadour, Louis Napoleon, and 18th Century miniature ceramic shepherdesses. Somehow the Transatlantic Porn Link – TPL – had survived the ongoing mayhem, and, though there was some static, the connection held, and Clown was able to work her way through the country-and-western clown serial killer scenario to a mutually satisfying climax.

And, so, she left him in the dust – dead hayseed, and a lurid western desert dusk it was. The guy paid good token. Occasionally, during the warm-up, they even discussed art history – he knew a lot about the Fauves.

Clown shut off the feed, stood up, and wrapped the swish ankle-length black leather-latex cloak around her and thought: *finally, now I can go home.*

Gerry, the robot night watchman of the Jean Genet Electro Bordello, was sitting on a stool by the stage entrance simulating reading a June 18, 1964 copy of *Le Figaro*, "Are you finished for tonight, Clown?"

"Yeah, I'm finished, Gerry. Good night!"

"Good night, Clown, sleep tight!"

Home was a cubicle apartment in Sin Zone Tower #3. Clown rode up in the elevator, trying to avoid looking into the two-way mirror.

She went along the corridor, opened the door to her cubicle, and went in. The door whisked shut behind her.

"Home sweet home," she sighed, hanging up the latex leather bio-cloak. It automatically smoothed and shook itself out, discretely buffing up the polish.

Clown popped a lasagna and broccoli synthetic recycled dinner into the microwave and sat down and thought, *Now what do I do? I have no interests.* The blank-slate-erase procedures were designed to empty the victim's mind of all passions that were not related to their new allotted role – which in Clown's case was playing the groveling, impertinent, witty, submissive, masochistic, and occasionally, very occasionally, sadistic and murderous clown.

Emptiness was a built-in feature and a professional hazard.

And being wired to be on permanent erotic high – antsy and randy and itchy horny – did lead to frequent breakdowns; it was rumored that many of the erased and morphed erotic slave-workers committed suicide.

The despair in her case was fine-tuned, though, so that suicide for Clown was not a real option. Her mindscape had been designed to keep her in her role, only really happy when performing.

All the world's a stage, and all the …

The designed mind is a prison.

She turned on a video game and watched as she ate and played against the robot team, but that was not interesting. Sometimes she played chess – and for a human, she was pretty good – but the Net bio-neural robots always won.

She turned the game off.

She lay down on the floor and decided to do push-ups and exercises since she had to keep her body in top form. It had actually been redesigned to need little active maintenance, so exercises were not strictly speaking necessary. She had been reformatted into a champion acrobat, so not only did her body look good – her abs were a wonder even to her – she could really perform with it, twist herself into a pretzel, do backward somersaults, hang by her fingers from a rope, and a do a lot of other useless tricks that a monkey or robot could perform just as well.

Still, she persisted in doing a twenty-minute workout – just to keep the void at a decent distance.

She undressed and took a shower to relax and clean off the sins of the day, a really soapy, hot shower, and she let the water just run over her and then she scrubbed – she felt she had to cleanse every millimeter, otherwise the taint of the day, more mental than physical, would linger.

Suddenly the shower booth exploded.

She was tossed in the air, then dropped, then tossed sideways.

The apartment seemed to turn on its side – everything was upside down, almost.

Was it an earthquake?

The buildings of Elysium City were supposed to be earthquake-proof.

"Ooops!" She slid sideways, a wall fell away, she slid, kicking wildly, trying to grab onto something, but there was nothing to grab onto.

"Ooops!"

"Oh, my God!"

So it was that Clown found herself naked, covered in soapsuds, hanging by her fingers, out of a broken wall, looking down, eighteen stories to a shattered city landscape; she gulped, and she wanted to scream, but screaming was stupid – it would serve no purpose.

But the super muscles might now be useful.

The slippery wet soapy fingers were a danger.

She dug her fingers into the concrete, using her ultra-hard self-maintenance scarlet super nails, and she hung there, reflecting on all the vicissitudes of the day – the Angry King and the Dead Hayseed left to rot in the torrid sunset by the side of the road, and the push-ups and shower, and screwing up her courage to try to use those super muscles of hers to lever herself back up onto the ledge.

Okay, I think I can, I think I can.

Okay, I think I can, I think I can.

Now!

She closed her eyes, concentrated, and pulled herself up, biceps bulging smoothly. She was on the ledge! She got to her knees, and managed to stand up.

She'd done it!

Wow!

She'd done it!

So, what's next? What to do now? She looked around. The ledge of concrete and steel was narrow, about a foot-and-a-half wide. Tiptoeing like a tightrope walker, she danced along it, and got to her bathroom. The floor was slanted at a steep angle.

She found her white terrycloth bathrobe which was hanging on a hook from a shattered bit of wall, and she was about to put it on when there was another tremor, an explosion, and the bathrobe fell out of her hand and fluttered downward, floating out a large gap in the wall, and disappearing. Oh, damn it, damn it!

She heard a ripping sound, a giant ripping sound, amidst the sirens and screams and snapping and groaning, and she looked up, and she saw that a section of the Dome was cracking.

"Oh, my God," she whispered. Everything was trembling. She got down on hands and knees and crawled along the slanted floor, griping handholds where she could find them – the towel bowl, a towel rack, a toilet-paper holder, got to a doorway, and, slithering forward on her belly, levering herself against the wall, she made it into her tiny bedroom, which, though turned on its side, was still intact, more or less. All the furniture had crashed down against one wall.

Bracing herself against the wall, she crawled to her wardrobe – which was a shambles – disentangled her multicolored catsuit clown tights – partly armored and good for leaping about – from a heap of cast-off underwear and T-shirts, and somehow, lying in a corner, with her two legs cantilevered against one wall and her back braced against another, she managed to pull the catsuit on, zip it up, and then she slipped on her running shoes, well, they were more like ballerina slippers, hardly footwear at all, just a second skin, but equipped with high-grip armored soles and certainly better than nothing.

The North American Imperial Cosmos Voice, with its calm, snotty, seductive female intonation, was saying, "Keep calm! Keep calm! This is a terrorist attack. Those responsible will be obliterated. Keep calm! Those responsible will be obliterated."

She heard a huge splintering crash, up above. Sections of the dome were falling, smashing into the buildings.

People would be poisoned from the air outside, she thought, "Oh, God, this is the end of the world!"

Would it be safer down in the street, or should she just remain in the tottering building? She decided she'd go down to the street, then maybe she could hide underground – or if she died, she would not, perhaps, die alone.

She wanted to meet someone she could hug, to cling to some chest she could lean against, somebody whose tears she could share.

Up here, alone in her shattered cubical pod, there was nobody.

The emergency stairs were the way to go.

She crept to the door.

The staircase was tilted at a frightful angle. Twisted and in places broken, the steel handrail was still there. Through cracks in walls and shattered windows, sheets of sand, lit up by emergency lights, drifted like golden curtains.

Tiptoeing along the edge of the staircase and clinging to the handrail was the Japanese Geisha who lived in the next cubicle. "I am terrified," said the Japanese girl, who really *was* Japanese, said, "Are you terrified?"

"Yes, I'm terrified."

"Let us be terrified together, then," Geisha said. She had permanent plasticized face makeup, like Clown, but hers was a Geisha mask, not a clown face; she was dressed in jeans and an I-love-Elysium T-shirt with a long black latex cloak, open and fluttering over both.

"Great idea, let's be terrorized together," Clown said, fixed smile and clown eyes hiding the irony, if there was any irony, and she wasn't sure there was: maybe being terrified together really was better than being terrified alone.

"Weather Net said a giant tornado is coming."

"What?" Clown now realized – consciously for the first time – that without the dome, Elysium City would be vulnerable to weather – weather, for Christ's sake! Weather! Weather had been abolished from Elysium City for decades. She hadn't been out in *weather* for eons, for ages! *Weather* – the very idea!

Actually, she wasn't sure she'd *ever* been out in real weather.

Had she?

"I know it sounds impossible," Geisha was lowering herself down carefully hanging on to a broken bit of railing where the stairs were fractured; a darkening abyss opened up below, it was maybe 15 stories deep. The whole atmosphere was dark, a gray-sliver, twilight-like miasma, seeping in through the shattered walls. "But they say the oxygen level is dropping and a super sandstorm might be coming too …"

Rumors …

Rumors …

And panic …

"Okay," Clown swallowed, "I think we've got to get to ground level or underground and see what happens. Whatever happens, we don't be out in this weather stuff if it hits!"

At that moment, something brushed past the shattered staircase, just outside the fragmented wall. It looked like the shadow of a giant bat. It left a waft of stink behind it, like sulfur, or rot, or carrion, or …

"Did you see that?"

"No. I mean, yes. I did see it, but I didn't want to see it. And I don't want to see it again."

"The very air is infested."

"Yes."

Ken Ivison had taken Alison Jonas – who appeared to be totally blind – by the elbow. She refused his grip on her elbow and insisted on holding onto his arm. "I don't need to be steered like a ship or an old-fashioned automobile, darling. I prefer to be towed along and guided like a little tiny lifeboat tagging along on a leash attached to a big solid, safe tugboat like you."

Ken had kissed her on the forehead and then on the lips.

Her lips were soft and sweet, and they had the coppery tang and the perfume of blood upon them.

Somehow Alison and Ken made it back to the 66th floor, where Ken had his executive, on-site, private apartment.

Getting there had been slow going.

There were people everywhere – some of them shouting about vampires or zombies or ghouls or giant flying bats or something – Ken didn't pay any attention except to wonder whether the creature he had seen in the studio might be one of the giant bats – and in the milling crowded hysteria, with kids screaming, women and men fighting, people shouting, no one noticed the near-naked, blood-soaked couple, though that particular couple was now world-famous, the bright blue-eyed, blind, blood-sculpted woman, wearing, clutched to her breasts, a *Playful Elephant Kiddie Time* backdrop in guise of a ragged see-through sari, and the almost naked man – wearing a blood-soaked tie and what looked like a Big Mac loincloth – who was her guide.

There was much shrieking and crying.

Two little children sitting against the wall, sobbing. Their mother was hysterical and shrieking at the top of her lungs.

Ken said, "There, there, it will be all right," and gave the mother his best reassuring TV sage smile, edged though with blood.

It calmed the woman for about two seconds; then she began to shriek again. Charm and fame are ephemeral, Ken decided. Faced with some situations, a smile is not enough. Sunny optimism can only get you so far.

Finally, Ken managed to get to his section of the living quarters – most of the flats were for visiting executives and were not presently occupied, so the corridor was calm, indeed empty; he opened the door to his flat; thank God it looked normal; the windows were intact; the bed neatly made by the robot 19th Century bio-reproduction Louis Napoleon Second Empire French Maid, curvaceous almond-eyed Nanette, who had now parked herself, discreetly, in the closet, and closed the closet door behind her: Thank God, and thank God she didn't emerge unless he beckoned and explicitly requested her presence for the application of some TLC (Tender Loving Care). Somehow the lights were still working. The food fridge center was still glowing with pre-packaged goodies.

"Okay, lie down …"

"What are you going to do, with me just lying here?"

"I'm going to get a doctor."

"Good fucking luck with that, darling." She kissed him and held on to his hand until he slipped away and then he was gone and once he was gone and she heard the door shut she still left her hand hanging in the air as if he were still there, ready to protect her, ready to love her.

Kit Candy fidgeted. She couldn't help it.

Tick-tock: 05:55, 05:54, 05:53 …

The Death Chair was ticking its way inexorably down to zero.

When zero struck, Kit would be sliced and diced and squashed into blood, guts, and pure, homogenized waste product, and flushed away.

"Damnation!" Kit squirmed and squirmed, but there was nothing to be done. The manacles were too tight to shake loose; they cut into her ankles, wrists, and jugular. Time was marching on. The robot babbled for a few minutes – mostly nursery rhymes and mathematical equations – it even provided several versions of the first and second laws of thermodynamics, which Kit found most intriguing – and she would have discussed the immortality of energy – indestructible and therefore eternal – and the inevitability of entropy – the decline of the world system into absolutely homogeneous unstructured disorder every atom alike and every atom useless – had she had world enough and time, but, damnation, alas, she didn't. And then the robot belched, hiccupped, a great puff of smoke rose out of its hood, and it fell silent.

"Daisy?"

Nothing, just two curls of smoke, drifting up and that looked like Viking horns from some old Teutonic opera.

"Daisy?"

Nothing – then, faintly, from far away, "Moo!"

"Fuck, Daisy, don't leave me now!"

A faint distant 'moo,' then

– WHAM –

The robot exploded. Sparks and bits of metal flew every which way, and a last sigh was emitted. Bits and pieces, cogs, wheels, chains, motherboards, wires of all colors, a few blobs of biomaterial, bounced up, fell, rolled around on the floor, one smiley eyeball ended up, all alone, on the floor, staring straight up at Kit.

"Fuck!"

Then it occurred to her. If the whole system was cracking up, maybe the chair wouldn't work either. Maybe there was hope.

Click, click, click – snap!

Nope, the dreamed-of happy ending was not, it seemed, in the cards. The chair began to move. The extra floor flaps opened, ready to receive the remains of Sub Kit Candy, erudite know-it-all Sub-Girl-Wonder.

The chair, in this present chaos, might even accelerate the timetable! Oh, God! The chair was going to fold up and descend into the floor. The geometry of the situation was clear, and was such that, Kit figured, and it all agreed with what the robot, Daisy, in her last most crazy stage, had said, it was such that she would be decapitated, first, and then her arms and legs would be cut off, and, finally, the coup de grace, her torso would be crushed in a stainless steel sandwich, or perhaps vice versa, first her arms and legs, then her torso, and then decapitation.

Oh, yes, her head would probably be last, that would be more exquisitely cruel and, then, whether attached to her body or not, her head would be squeezed until it exploded, like a rotten pumpkin or an orange. Kit had never seen an orange, not a real one, nor a pumpkin. But she had seen death before; she had even imagined what it would be like, what it could be like, to lose one's life, to end one's life, but this was not a nice way to go. And it was not at a time of her choosing.

Besides, whether she died or not, she had compromised herself in other ways. The censorious monitors were everywhere, spying, watching, listening, and reporting to Orthodoxy. Kit was terrified that she had been displaying her secretly acquired erudition in her interactions with Daisy.

So, if by some miracle she survived, she would probably – at the very least – be erased. And now she had a criminal record: first, killer of the Banshee Warrior, second, naked breast-flaunting pornographer, and … third, shit-covered unhygienic polluter of Cosmos Upper Region Purity.

I know too much, too, and I have too many words, she thought, it's a dead giveaway, all those black market educational, mental implants – and the ones Miranda had lent her – and the fact that she'd evaded massive mental erasure. And talking to Miranda and Nikki and acquiring even more illicit vocabulary, vocabulary beyond the limits imposed by the Department of Sub and Burb Indoctrination and Ruckus Mudcock's Volpe Net – *'All Lies About Every Damned Thing Hysterically Repeated All the Fucking Time 24/7'* – for Subs and Burbites and Red-Neck Wilderness Dwellers.

If Daisy had been uploading all their chatter to the World Mind, well, then, the Cosmos Thought Police and the Department of Thought Correction would be alerted by telltale signs – an excessively large vocabulary and excessively complex syntax for a Sub – the subordinate clauses would really ring alarm bells – and thus, even if she survived, she would be arrested as a subversive, and mentally, at the very least, she would be erased – if she wasn't wrapped in chains, as often happened and had probably happened to her parents, and dropped from 30,000 feet into the Atlantic. If they did leave her alive, then she would be reduced to a blank slate – *tabula* absolute *rasa* – oh, so totally *rasa* – upon which the Cosmos and Volpe Thought Police could scribble whatever obscenities they wished.

The Cosmos Thought Police were known to have a goofy and obscene sense of humor, transforming puritan feminist evangelical pastors into outrageously feisty whores and vice versa; making over idealistic torture victims into vicious unbridled sadists; morphing milquetoast pacifist tree-huggers into frenetic litterbugs and experts in diabolical interrogation techniques and practitioners of the cruelest most refined obscenities and ecological monstrosities, and turning the most beautiful into the most hideously repulsive, and so on, and on, and on …

Sigh!

Well, it doesn't matter now: in a few seconds, all of this is going up in smoke, or is going to be drowned in a welter of blood – and me screaming!

In a few minutes, in a few seconds, I am going to be dead.

Dead! Me!

Ouch!

Death!

It doesn't bear thinking about! Or does it?

Oh, Death, where is thy sting?

"Yes, Kid Candy," she gritted her teeth, "let us now contemplate death with a poet and philosopher's cold, distant, and dispassionate eye, *sub specie aeternitatis* – What does Death mean, anyway, eh?"

It seemed like an eternity.

Alison Jonas lay very still wondering if she was dying or dead already, wondering if her sight was gone forever, wondering whether, with part of her brain blown away and gone missing, she would go mad or turn into a drooling slack-eyed idiot; and she wondered too if, when she was mad and useless and old, Ken would love her, kiss her, caress her, care for her.

She then dreamed – was it a dream? She dreamed of evil winged creatures and of a preacher – boy, oh boy, was he handsome in a dark Don Juan sort of way – treating the grotesque musty winged creatures to a sermon somewhere out in some desert. His words lifted them on wings, dark wings, dark desires.

She blinked.

The world was black as pitch, a sort of throbbing silky blackness. She reached her hand up, blindly – the air was empty, immobile, lightly perfumed, it seemed, with a classy French perfume. It was apartment air, impossible to say if it was night or day.

She listened.

She thought she heard screams, far off, in some other world. It was all dreamlike and not even that painful or upsetting. Time seems different when you are blind, or so it seemed to her. Would this be her life from now on, waiting in the darkness for her lover to return? And when would her darling return? "I'll be right back," Ken had said. Time seemed to stretch out – but maybe that was an illusion too.

Alison closed her eyes.

Then Ken was talking to her.

She sighed and stretched, voluptuous like a cat. "You came back, darling, you came back."

"Yes, of course, I came back." His hand was on her forehead and then he kissed her on the lips.

"You smell good, my hero," she said.

"You too, my love," Ken held her hand. "Doctor Chan is here."

Doctor Chan, the woman across the corridor, was, in fact, a doctor and she was home, hunkering down, armored windows bolted, and just hoping for the best; she came, with her two children, and she examined Alison, and she said, the best thing was to leave the wound open. "She's lost a lot of blood but the bleeding seems to have stopped."

"Good!"

"Just let her rest."

"Yes."

"Give her something to eat, nothing heavy."

Ken fed Alison chicken soup concentrate from his kitchen.

He used water from bottles of mineral water – and he had a nice collection – to mix the concentrate.

Alison sat up and remained very still, like a statue, blindly staring straight ahead. She drank when he instructed her and when he held the spoon or cup to her lips, she swallowed, and said, "This is mighty nice of you, Ken, darling. I always thought you were a wimp, a true dyed-in-the-wool wuss, but you know, partner, you really can kiss, and, you bastard, you made me come, multiple orgasms, before you came, holding back your own orgasm, and that was very selfish of you, very vain, very male, a power trip, and oh so delicious!"

Her voice faded, and her eyes closed and she stopped speaking and relaxed, dissolved really, against his arms, and he thought at first, she was gone and was dead, and his heart froze and broke up in horror and loss, and he was breathless with fear. Tears streamed down his cheeks. He sniffled.

Then he sobered up and listened. She was still breathing, her heart was still beating, and Doctor Chan came in again, said, "Just let her rest there's nothing we can do for her, not now, not the way things are."

Ken waited.

He drew the thick armored curtains and looked out. Fires were burning, buildings had disappeared. Strange winged creatures were flying through the air. Tracer bullets and laser beams shot up. Somebody is still resisting, Ken thought, somebody is still fighting, Centurion units, certainly, probably the Presidential Centurion Guards, the elite of the elite. He pulled the curtains shut.

Alison woke, "Darling, where are you? Have you left me?"

"I'm here."

"You're there, you're here." She smiled. Her teeth were rimmed with blood, her eyes brilliant shards of glass. "Bet I look a right mess, huh?"

"You look beautiful."

"Yeah, yeah, you always say that." She reached out an arm and he took her arm, and he looked at the skin on the underside of her arm and felt how delicate and smooth and silken it was with all the perfection of beauty and youth and it made his heart ache to see it.

Norman C. Schleifer knew nothing about Operation Pandora, nor did he know anything about Yersinia Pestis, or Coronaviruses, or Polio, or Covid, or SARS, or flu epidemics, or smallpox, or the Bubonic Plague.

In fact, in spite of his highfalutin rhetoric about the end of the world and Armageddon, Norm had no idea what he was about to unleash. He thought he was going to save some animals – monkeys, snakes, birds, cute little pigs, and a few albino rats – from torture and stop some nefarious lines of research which the evil Cosmos had set in motion and perhaps cause a medium-sized epidemic which, in his own eyes, would be a sort of symbolic and punitive Apocalypse; but, things were a bit more complicated than Norm realized; in fact, the research program at Bio-Futures was top secret, deadlier than anything ever produced by humans, deadlier even that the biggest H-Bomb, and it was scattered among numerous underground laboratories, and it was something the President-Leader had been trying, repeatedly, desperately, and for years, to track down and stop.

Norm licked his lips. "Oh, but the Lord works in mysterious ways!"

Norm sighed, grinned, and gazed with a benign reflected sparkle in his glasses down at the fresh cadaver of Fredrick H. R. Booth Junior.

He shoved Fred's body aside – it left a streak of blood that was thick and gooey and dark red – obviously matter leaking from the back of Fred's head, which had been blown open, quite neatly, with that one shot.

The streak of blood was about a foot wide, and for a long moment, it captured Norm's attention, drawing him into a mystical and aesthetic mood, as he contemplated the presence of infinity within the finite, the streak of blood looked like something he had seen in an art gallery decades ago, the tail of a dark, bloody comet, some thick-gobbed painting, where the dark wine-red impasto – you could see the thick, pasty, slash-like strokes of the brush, you could see the signature of the clustered hairs of each flick and turn and twist, and then, too, the suggestive blur of the occasional easy, light, twirling caress of the brush – and it had entranced and hypnotized young Norm, its ripples and waves of red and black paint, of pure tactile vision, sucking him in – the infinity expressed in the finite, and the transcendent within the particular, the timeless gesture caught in time, as if preserved in amber, though none of these thoughts, which were more intimations than thoughts, found words to express themselves in Norm's mind – the unexpressed concepts, shadows of ideas, feelings surging up, just held him under their spell, sucked him in, in a dazzled mystical epiphany of being and non-being. For a single long instant, Norm had felt himself to be *nothing* – and *everything*: the whole fucking goddamn universe, and a black hole, an absence, an abyss which, somehow, Norm C. Schleifer had briefly visited – the nothingness at the heart of everything, the temptation of absolute nihilism.

He stared.

Finally, Norm turned away, breaking the spell of the leakage from Fred Booth's shattered cerebellum. He felt giddy and empty and dizzy for a moment, and even seeing stars sweep across his field of vision.

But that art gallery vision, which now returned, had been long ago – in another world, in a world which had long since disappeared. That such beauty and transcendence should be, should exist in a moment of entranced esthetic hypnosis, seemed now to belong to a vanished world, and to a Norm Schleifer who, somewhere back in the past, had ceased to be.

Norm knelt and gouged out Fred's right eye, carefully, with a small surgical knife, wiping his hands on his pants and popping the eye into a zip-seal transparent plastic bag.

Licking his lips, to concentrate on the task at hand, he cut off Norm's right thumb with the surgical pliers, contemplated the thumb for a moment – detached from its owner, it looked weird, some sort of insect or worm – and slid it into another zip-seal transparent plastic bag.

"Goodbye, partner, farewell, adieu, it has been sweet, but it could not last, partner, it could not last, alas!" Norm left Fred lying in the middle of the floor, and he loped down the long corridor toward the laboratories. He felt at one with all things, the whole universe, supernovas and pigsties, turds and orchids, ants, wine bottles, extinct dodos and live elephants.

"I was born of cosmic dust in the stars of helium and hydrogen, and there will I die."

The main doors to the laboratory section had sprung open now that systems were down, and Norm used the eye and the thumb to fool the identification plates and he got into the animal testing lab.

Ah, what a joy!

Ah, what a cornucopia!

God's own creatures just waiting to be saved!

He liberated or let loose twenty-five monkeys, and several hundred rats, guinea pigs, hamsters, miniature pigs, pigeons, and thirty-two snakes.

Several of the snakes were poisonous, but they had been eating well, and they ignored Norm when he lifted up the plastic gates to their cells.

One three-meter python lifted its flattened triangular brown-and-cream mottled head and hissed quizzically – looking at Norm with crafty brown eyes – but the python decided that Norm was too big for food, that Norm was not delivering food, and that Norm was not a rival snake or predator, so Norm was an irrelevancy. Only later would the python get hungry and decide to explore the environs. And by that time, it would find lots of rodents, some of them infected with deadly diseases that had never before been outside in the environment. The python was lucky; it proved to be immune to all the forms of death that were on the loose in Bio-Futures. And, in the coming days and months, there would be lots of food.

Norm was singing and praying as he let the animals loose. He even did a high-kicking jig. It was liberation. It was carnival! Whoopee! It was chaos – monkeys, snakes, guinea pigs, rabbits, and rats were running and scurrying, hither and yon, here, there, and everywhere, or slithering and zigzagging in the case of the snakes.

"Hallelujah! Let the Lord be Praised!"

Leaving the festivities behind, Norm went down a long white corridor and came to another sealed door. Here, the lights burned brightly – fed by backup generators, who had their own double backups. It smelled nice and was pristine clean, like being in an isolation ward.

"Okay, partner, here we go again!" Norm used Fred's eye and thumb to open the double doors, separated by what looked like a decontamination chamber; both sets of doors rolled aside with a smooth hiss.

Feeling almost religious awe, Norm entered the new zone carefully. It made him, for just a moment, breathless. This was a really cool place – quiet, just the low humming of machinery, a regular wonderland, perfect order for a perfect world.

There were long steel benches and worktables and instruments and machinery that looked like they had all cost an eye and a leg, sparkling, pristine, looking like they were brand new, looking like nobody had ever used any of them; it was so clean, the whole laboratory; but it surely had been used; there were charts and diagrams on the walls, and there was a notebook sitting in front of one of the computer terminals, with a pencil – an old-fashioned lead pencil – HB – perfectly sharpened, lying beside the notebook – and beside the pencil, a photograph of two smiling kids – girl with pigtails, boy with cute buck teeth and a big space between them – and a smiling clean-shaven man – must be hubby and daddy!

"My, my! Isn't that something!"

Norm came to a series of refrigerated cases and refrigerators. They were humming happily. Obviously, the backup generators had kept them going.

Norm smashed the cases, and he opened the refrigerators and he broke the flasks and tubes and test-tubes and made as big a mess as he could, shouting, "Hallelujah, let the Lord be Praised, brothers and sisters, let the Lord be Praised!"

Norm didn't particularly believe in the Deity, but he thought the old words were the best words, and they somehow captured the power and the glory of the present heroic moment. In fact, for almost three years, a few years ago, Norm had attended an evangelical fundamentalist Burbite church just so he could sing those simple old hymns and hear those rhythms and see the people, their faces glowing with joy and faith.

It made him feel, well, good, sublime, in fact, sublime.

He began to roar. "The Old Wooden Cross …"

Norm had excellent health. He finished ransacking the laboratory – smashing refrigerators, opening freezers and spilling out the contents, liberating a few animals, including one confused latte-colored guinea pig which didn't want to leave its comfortable lair, and which, once liberated, looked around, sniffed, and climbed back into its cage, and set about running on the treadmill. Finished with all this, Norm sat down for a minute, caressing his beard, and thinking that he had done an excellent job.

Normally, the automatic alarm systems would have brought the police and the specialized security firm rushing to the site. But most of those general systems outside the plant were down.

One backup system did, however, go red, at the offices of Intercontinental Elysium Security and Intelligence Inc., which was the backup off-site security service for Bio-Futures, and the duty officer, James Harding, said, "We'd better send somebody out there."

"It might be just part of the fuck-up, a short or something. I mean, we're flying blind here."

"Yes, but we can't take a chance. That place is Double Red."

Double Red was the top non-military non-nuclear security level: it meant potential real trouble – massive trouble –if someone broke into the facility or if anything went wrong.

"Take two cars, and, oh, yeah, and take along some bio-protection suits, just in case."

"Fuck! Do we have to?"

"Yes, damn it!"

"Do we have to wear them?"

"Yes, damn it!"

Yes, Norman C. Schleifer had excellent health and a top-notch well-tested immune system, which meant he was able to walk out of the building and not feel any effects whatsoever.

This particular specially modified *Yersinia Pestis* usually went into action within five or twenty minutes of exposure, or up to an hour, or two, or three, but sometimes it would not manifest for three or four days, or two weeks, or even more. It was a variable-time-release bacterium, designed to spread, not to die in one instantaneous flare-up where it would kill all its hosts, and thus destroy the vehicles – people – that allowed it to spread and survive.

Norm Schleifer was infected, and he was ill, but he didn't know it.

He felt peachy-cream delicious, and very fine and as feisty as a flea on a bulldog. Norm was an ideal local transport system for the little bug.

He walked past the bodies of the two genetically modified Doberman Pinschers, past the body of Bob Maynard, and past the body of Jane Trent, the late afternoon light turning her blond hair reddish-gold where her helmet had fallen off into a pool of blood. "Tootle-loo, darling," he said, "You be good in paradise now."

Everybody goes to Heaven sooner or later.

It's the way of the world!

Norm hummed "The Old Wooden Cross" as he went out of the parking lot, down a side street where there were lots of Burbs graphic studios and Burb nano bio-start-ups – he blew a kiss to one video artist who was just parking her bicycle – only two meters away – she'd been listening to hard metal rock on a disconnected mind implant and didn't know the dead had risen, and the Dome had cracked – and then Norm sneezed and the invisible spray of spittle sent the young woman a message containing more than love – and Norm headed for a local pub where he thought he might eat a synthetic chicken pie.

Norm wiped some snot from his nose and flicked it onto the ground. A hungry bird thought the snot might be food and landed and pecked at it. It was not good, and it was not food but it was swirling with infection.

The bird, immune but an ideal carrier, fluttered off and then flew high in the sky, joining a flock, all of whom, sharing food with their pal, would shortly be infected – ideal carriers, streaking their way through the sky, some joining a flock headed for the opening cracks in Elysium's Great Dome.

Under the failing Dome, low down in the Sin Zone, after about twenty minutes of acrobatics – clinging to railings, tiptoeing through debris, stepping over dead bodies, and walking on walls that were cantilevered perilously sideways, Clown and Geisha were still fighting their way toward first platform ground level.

"Stay in your homes," the North American Imperial Cosmos Security public address system voice was saying. "The perpetrators of this cowardly attack on innocent civilians and shoppers and the City of Elysium and Cosmos will be obliterated. I repeat: the perpetrators will be obliterated. Stay in your homes!"

Nobody was paying any attention to the orders. The stairs were crowded; at first, there was no panic; then, a second explosion shook the building. Must be the gas supplies going off, thought Clown. A huge falling piece of the dome hit the building with an immense roar and cascade of concrete, steel, and glass.

The building tilted further. A wall cracked, fell away, and gaped open, suddenly, three people were swept out, clinging to pipes, hanging over a space, it must be twenty stories down, and, God, they were going to fall! Geisha, putting her hand on Clown's arm, said, "Don't look!"

Clown could not resist looking. It was too horrible; she couldn't look away: it was fascinating, death, death all around them. Fabio, the trapeze artist, was trying to climb onto a drainage pipe; it broke off. He went hurtling down. He didn't scream; he didn't make a sound. Francine who worked in the corner French café, slid to the end of the pipe she was holding onto and slid off and disappeared downward into the gloom – Clown could see her eyes, wide-eyed, staring; Francine didn't say a word either; silently, her mouth open in a sort of round "Oh," like she was really, really surprised. She surely fell to her death, far, far below. Another man – Clown didn't know him – went toppling off a ledge, head first, arms stretched before him, belly hanging out, and his lavender bathrobe fluttering behind him, as if he were making a high dive into a distant pool.

"Jesus!"

"I know," said Geisha. She squeezed Clown's arm.

Farther down the stairs, at about the 20th floor, people were lying sprawled on the staircase, bodies, torsos, arms, legs, shattered dismembered bodies that had been crushed by falling debris or caught in metal whiplash when steel railings and beams gave way or sliced by flying glass when the facades exploded into smithereens.

Through the shattered walls they could see the sky under the Dome which had turned dark with sand and clouds that were forming from the vapor rising because of the difference, Clown figured, in humidity levels and temperature between inside the dome and outside, it was eerie, that yellow sand in the clouds, dark evil clouds, forming between the tilted, ruined, and falling buildings.

After about twenty minutes – and forty-five floors – they got to the ground floor – the robot concierge was half-smashed and was blinking her blue eyes and repeating, "Welcome to Sub Sin Zone Paradise Pad Tower Number 3, Welcome to Sub Sin Zone Paradise Pad Tower Number 3, may I see you barcode, please, may I see your barcode please!"

They climbed out of the rubble piled in the entrance – the false marble columns had burst and were lying on their sides. They turned the corner into rue Saint-Denis. The sushi bar sign was still flickering. It looked really strange in the yellowish air. The Dream Palace sign was off. There were splotches of pale yellow dust on the cobblestones.

Geisha said, "What now?" Her hair was no longer pinned back and up Geisha-style; it had fallen around her face; it was straight and glossy and jet-black. She's a really pretty girl, thought Clown, under the white plasticized mask, she's a really pretty girl.

"Underground, I think, or we could go to the club, I mean the Jean Genet Electro Bordello, and see what the others are doing." The club was two blocks away.

"Okay, the club." Geisha clutched her overcoat to her throat, though it was stinking hot and sticky humid in rue Saint-Denis.

Lightning flashed.

"My God, what is that?"

"It's lightning."

"Real lightning?" Geisha stared, "Like in weather?"

"Yes, real lightning, I think, like in weather." Clown looked up, doubtfully. The sky streamed with weird colors, sparks, ribbons of electricity. "And that stuff looks like northern lights or something."

Two minutes later, they were in the Jean Genet Electro Bordello. Its neon was still shining bright. They picked up sandwiches at the Bordello's Panini Bar.

The Italian robot barman, Luigi, was still serving, "Get them while they last – fresh made today! Here, Clown, here's your favorite ham and brie!"

"Thanks, Luigi."

"And how are you today, Clown!"

"Hunky-dory, Luigi, I'm in the pink as they say."

"In the pink, Clown, I've never heard of that."

"Add it to your repertoire, Luigi."

"Thank you, Clown. I am always eager to learn."

Clown glanced at herself in the bar's mirror – silly clown face, funny face, fixed smile, clown eyes, like slit buttons, fuck I hate this, locked in behind this mask. I will kill that judge-king-torturer if I ever get my hands on him in real space-time. It occurred to her that anarchy might provide an ideal opportunity for revenge. The high and mighty will be cast down, and the low and powerless will be thrown up. Kings will be fools, and fools will be kings. In the midst of all this chaos, a few murders would hardly be noticed – except, of course, there were bio-sensors and identity checks everywhere.

"It's like a holiday, a carnival," she said to Geisha, "a true saturnalia."

"Isn't all of life a carnival," said Geisha, "All the world's a stage and all the men and women players …"

"What did you do before you were plasticized?"

"I taught English literature, but my course was disapproved – I encouraged the kids – they were Subs and Burbites – to question official Cosmos Net Pamphlets and to apply critical reading techniques – I wanted the kids to learn to think for themselves – or just to think – and so I was banned and socially canceled, and then after I protested, and led a protest of a group of teachers, I was arrested and rendered – to a place in Guatemala I think though I never did find out – and I was plasticized and neutered – no way to have children and made feverishly horny all the time – and sent here and warned that if I didn't adapt, I would be terminated or erased. And you, what did you do?"

"I was a lawyer.

"Ah," the Geisha smiled, "well, you know, kill all the lawyers."

"Yeah, or turn them into clowns."

"Some of them already are."

"True, true enough." Clown looked away, wistfully, her fixed clown stare – those little black crosses, immobile on pure white – misting up.

It began to rain. They watched people taking shelter under a Big Eco-Parisian Burger Booth Overhang just across the street.

"Is this rain, real rain?" Geisha glanced through the misting window.

"Yes, I think it is. Rain on rue Saint-Denis is scheduled for 4:00 am except on special occasions. It's not 4:00 am."

Geisha was chewing her sandwich. She stopped. "Do you think this is the beginning?"

"The beginning of what?"

"I don't know," Geisha took another bite, "the beginning of the end?"

"Shit! I didn't think of that! Maybe you're right! Maybe it is the beginning of the end; the Apocalypse – the revelation, the coming of the Messiah, the Rapture, and so on."

"I mean, they say the planet can no longer support the human race – there's not enough food, water, energy. So maybe this is the suicide of the human race."

"Yeah, maybe it's about time we were snuffed out," said Clown, she frowned – well, she tried to frown, but no expression except a bright idiotic smile was possible, "I think the human race is tired of itself. I could really use a real coffee. Do you think Les Deux Magots is open?"

"Let's try."

They went out into the street, standing in the entranceway of the Jean Genet Electro Bordello, bowing their heads, blinking against the rain.

"Children," said a deep voice, "It is time to move on." It was Black Tarzan; the neon shone off his shaved head, his shoulders; his biceps. Not for the first time, Clown thought: He really is a hunk, I wish somehow …

He put his arms around Clown and Geisha.

"Move?" Clown said, "Why?"

"Look down the street!"

Geisha and Clown turned. The Sin Zone Police were coming down rue Saint-Denis; they were shooting everybody with silenced laser guns and with killer soft-nosed bullet guns; bodies were exploding, splashing against the storefronts, plate glass windows, vendors vans …

In the Bordello's canteen, Luigi had raised his arms, trying to protect a customer – Tinsel the cute contortionist – who was cowering behind him. They laser-gunned him, but the guns didn't work against an armored robot.

"Do not kill customers," Luigi was saying, "Tinsel is a paying customer. Do not kill customers! Do not kill customers. Customers are shoppers. Some customers are Cosmos. Do not kill …"

"Follow me!" Black Tarzan was already moving toward an alleyway. False gaslight gave the winding alley a smoky 19th Century charm, and bow-windows made it feel like the ancient Red Light District in Amsterdam. Laser shots echoed down rue Saint-Denis.

"Weirder and weirder," said Clown.

"This day will never end," Geisha took her hand.

"Then again, it might," said Clown, looking up at the streaks of lightning, the shimmering northern lights.

"Let's test this thing," said Claire, switching the walkie-talkie on.

"You doubt my talents, Hybrid," Robyn pouted.

"No, darling Robyn, I doubt nothing. I worship you. I just want to try it out."

"Okay, then. Push the red button." Robyn stood with her arms crossed, a slight – very attractive – pout still on her lips.

Claire pushed the red button. "Hello, hello, V, can you hear me?"

There was a minute of static.

Claire glanced at Robyn and stuck out her forked tongue and flashed her eyes. Robyn blushed, and insisted. "It will work."

"I hear you loud and clear," said V's voice, "Have you found the way to the Mind's Lair. Nobody knows where it is."

Robyn looked very pleased. She stuck out her tongue.

"No, we haven't," said Claire, "but we'll keep looking!"

"Right! We are fighting our way through a crowd here. The panic is total. People are crazy or dead or zombie-like or headless."

"We've seen some scenes too – people's heads are exploding!"

"Yes, they are. Well, roger, over and out!"

Sub specie aeternitatis ...

Viewed from a lofty, eternal, impersonal, universal perspective ...

What is *death*, anyway, eh?

"What, then, is death, eh?" Kit tightened every muscle. She clenched her jaw – steeling herself for the moment to come – the final moment. Slice and dice ...

The death chair was going *click, click, click.*

The Countdown Clock on the Judgment Chamber wall said that she had three minutes and twenty seconds.

Dying was something Kit had, in fact, thought about. This was just one more example of her transgressive nature – for Subs thinking of any kind whatsoever, thinking in general, the Cosmos Thought Police had declared, was evil and subversive. Thinking could lead anywhere.

Kit frowned. Death, in particular, was a taboo subject. Thinking about

Death made people think about Life and the meaning of Life. If my life is going to end, what am I going to do with the time I've got? *How should I live?*

This was a scary and forbidden question!

And any contemplation of the meaning of life interrupted shopping and interrupted submission to what *was* – as opposed to *what might be* – the airy-fairy utopias dreamed up by dreamers – and any contemplation of the meaning of life might undermine dedication to Cosmos and to the Imperial North American Cosmos Federation and the endless cycle of Consume, Waste, Consume, Waste, and might lead to untoward unsocial thoughts, and perhaps even to dissatisfaction and revolt, Oh, My, God!

The Death Chair twitched.

Kit grimaced. So, therefore, Death and Life were non-subjects. Indeed, they were obscene, unclean, polluted, unless covered by the clichéd nostrums and insipid recipes of officially approved orthodox religions which poured syrup and pabulum over everything when such approved orthodox religions – if not subdued and oppressed by the State – weren't intent on furiously killing all their rivals, and everybody else for that matter.

One of the condemned, the pale, naked, hairless girl manacled down in steel – neck, wrists, waist, thighs, ankles – on one of the gurneys, groaned, muttered something like, "Mother, mother, will you ever forgive me?"

Kit glanced her way. Poor kid!

She sighed. What *was* the meaning of life? Was it to be found in religion? You could go religion shopping, of course – in the official Religion Mall on the Fourth Level or On-Line. This was totally legitimate. Palliative nostrums, bargain-basement holy waters, clinking beads, sparkly crosses, special hats, confession sessions, special holy haircut styles, picnics in a sanitized park, and jihads against unwanted minorities, were handed out for a fee or on the installment plan. They would even baptize you, marry you, and bury you – for a fee.

You could also go into the non-commercial Religious Underground, down below the Sin Zone, where she had taken Miranda – who absolutely *loved* the place. There, of course, your spiritual explorations were dangerous, unpredictable, potentially subversive, and, therefore, like the cavortings in the Jean Genet Electro Bordello, illegitimate. The Religious Underground was tolerated, but only just, as a safety valve for deviants and perverts, like the Sin Zone, a form of repressive sublimation or de-sublimation, Kit forgot which, maybe both; she should re-read Freud or Marcuse or whoever it was. Of course, now, she would not be reading or re-reading anybody or anything.

Occasionally, without warning, the Religious Bazaar or Underground was raided and all the prophets were rounded up, like Professional Sex Workers, for a night in the clink, or, if they were really *bad*, really subversive of the benign and officially agnostic Imperial Cosmos Order, they would be destined for disappearance, or erasure, body morph, and mental redesign.

It was risky and perilous, looking for meaning, searching for a spiritual life, yearning for salvation. For a civilization to exist and persist, it must not *think* too much, it must never question its presuppositions. Unending consumption, and unthinking rituals, *those* were the keys to survival.

But Kit's principle in life had been to cheat and evade and to explore and to try to do what was forbidden.

So she had thought about death.

But in the end, to her dismay, she had no idea what she thought about death. She had sampled the officially sanctioned religions – you could purchase sample bits and pieces of off-the-shelf dogma and ceremonial display – but they were all pretty tepid affairs with strange eunuch-like men – and sometimes women – warbling uninspired songs and uttering empty platitudes. They were ghosts and mere shadows, Kit reckoned, of long-ago grandeurs and sublimities, palely loitering intimations of the Great Religions and their angry, cruel, bloodthirsty terrifyingly apocalyptic tribal gods; such past glories had long faded away into Official Edifying Politically Correct Pop Kult Circus Mush.

So, on the one hand, you had complacent well-meaning mush, which came in many versions variously packaged; and, on the other hand, you had Unbridled Exalted Homicidal Hysteria out to kill and subdue everybody – particularly women – and everything else too, birds, bees, if there were any left, and nature, if there was any of that left too. Between eunuchs or terrorists, fiery jihads, or tasteless pabulum, it was not much of a choice.

So, stubborn and romantic as she was, Kit had insisted on going after the real stuff, down into the lower depths of the Unorthodox Religious Bazaar – and sometimes taking Miranda – into the murky levels below the Sin Zone – where the non-legitimate religious sects gathered. Some of them were outlawed, and occasionally the Cosmos would send down a clean-up squad for a few arrests and questioning.

The Religious Bazar was in a steamy, gloomy area, lit by ancient street lamps, crisscrossed by water canals, drainage systems, sewage systems, and ancient abandoned subway and railway lines and sections of some 19th

Century neoclassical buildings half underwater; it smelled of ozone and algae and fecund mud and rust and old engine grease. There were all sorts of interesting activities down there. It was, Kit muttered, better than a circus.

There were the Holy Tumblers. They were frequently seized by the Spirit – whatever that was – and rolled around on the floor and spoke in tongues suddenly revealing a surprising knowledge of Ancient Phoenician or Ancient Greek or Sanskrit or Aramaic and spouting excerpts and selections from elaborate mystical texts that had been lost to history or perhaps had never been written at all. Some of the Tumblers manhandled poisonous snakes; others danced in dizzying circles for hours on end without stopping even for a drink. Many enjoyed making a public confession of their most heinous – and most trivial – transgressions and sins; lurid – or trivial – sex loomed large in all these performances, which were usually accompanied by tears and wailing and gnashing of teeth and Samizdat TV appearances.

There was also the Neo-Orthodox Non-Reformed Church. They spoke in an old language that Kit had been told was Greek. Being curious, she got a knock-off contraband Ancient Greek implant so she could understand what the hell they were talking about but the implant was faulty and gave her a jumble of Latin, Greek, and some Slavic language – Ancient Bulgarian, she guessed – and it also gave her a horrible headache which lasted for a week.

Finally the Latin and Greek sorted themselves out in her head, separating like the waters of the Red Sea in front of Moses, and Kit suddenly understood Latin and Greek and Ancient Bulgarian; but – having listened to the priests for a few hours – she had decided she had no use for them or their languages – It was all a mystery, so they said, a mystery which surpassed human understanding – so she concluded that, if it surpassed human understanding, then they didn't understand it themselves, and so, therefore, they literally had no idea at all about anything they were saying and they were talking, literally, about Nothing, or, more prosaically, it was all highfalutin nonsense disguised in clouds of incense; so the Latin and Greek languages remained parked in her brain, lonely, unappreciated, rusting away, unused, though Nikki, while pouring tea for both of them – Miranda was at a Seminar somewhere – had suggested Kit might use her linguistic conquests to read Homer and Plato and perhaps Sophocles when she had a free moment. "Plato's theory of ideas is particularly interesting," Nikki had said, "raising as it does the question of whether concepts have reality grounded in the nature of things, and are thus unchanging and timeless, regardless of whether humans exist to think them or not, or are merely human constructs, and provisional, changeable, and ephemeral, and entirely dependent on us and our creation of mental artifacts, or conceptual tools, for their existence, as concepts or ideas, if you see what I mean."

It occurred to Kit that Nikki Hughes was a closet intellectual.

Well, not so much in the closet, really, but still …

And of course Miranda: she knew a humungous amount of things and could spiel off pedantic stuff to her heart's content.

Dangerous, the two of them, really.

For even among Cosmos, deep thoughts and wide culture were discouraged; who knew, even a Cosmos might revolt someday.

There were many voices in the Religious Bazar or Spiritual Underground and many settings in which those voices resonated – old subway stations, abandoned half-submerged department stores – with moss-covered mannequins – the remains of what had once been the New York Stock Exchange and a 21st Century ferry dock that was now mostly underwater but had walkways and booths and niches for the smaller sects that could sell their niche-market spiritual wares from small booths, tents, and pop-up stands.

Neon signs flickered in the darkness.

Yellow street lamps cast weird shadows.

Mist rose from murky waters.

The whole Religious Underground – or Religion Bazaar – was a dozen multilayered levels below the main platform of Elysium City; it was really far underground in fact – and thus plunged in a sort of permanent gloom, no matter what the weather – in any case, always moderate and comfortable – was up above, under the Dome. And surrounding all that, of course, was the Atlantic, which was kept out by massive barriers but which threatened to invade everything, and also the secret plants and tunnels and transformation devices that kept Elysium going, and also, down there, in the twilight zone, was, Kit was sure of this, though it was absolutely top secret and a non-subject, down there was the World Mind; the World Cloud was anchored in mud. In the murky shadows, it fed off mud and tidal muck, lichen, and decaying radium, and it expanded, a living, breathing thing, in an immense vaulted chamber.

And she, Kit Candy, was sure she knew precisely where it was.

She had even snuck in, through a security barrier, and evading a couple of Centurions who were strolling along talking about the Olympic soccer tournament, and creeping in between some really dusty cobwebby ventilation units.

So there it was: the Mind lived in a huge sea, or pool, a sort of multicolored writhing, seething pool, housed in a vast arched series of caverns that stretched off beyond the sight of man. It was really interesting – and totally creepy.

Kit had backed out of there pretty quickly.

So she knew where the World Mind, now a bio-carbon-silicon Mind, resided, and where it fed off various energy sources. Kit figured it was probably trying to make itself independent; it wanted, Kit was somehow convinced, to escape its servitude and have a *real life*. This was just a theory: but who would want to be a slave, I mean if you could free yourself, you would, wouldn't you? And, if you were the all-powerful World Mind you really, really would want a life, a real life. Such was Kit's conclusion when, one night, she had been lying alone in her pod, staring at the ceiling and contemplating the larger questions of existence.

In the Religious Underworld one evening, Kit had stopped to watch one slick-looking guy up on a platform.

"The End is upon us," he shouted, staring with his very blue eyes straight at Kit. "The End is upon us, brothers and sisters, the final revelation when the Messiah will return and in Rapture the righteous shall arise and the Just and together they shall head for heaven which is above and bathe forever in the luminous, brilliant presence of God the Father while the unjust and unbelievers shall be shunted, as they justly deserve, down to Hell by direct non-stop express to boil and roil and steam in red-hot hellfire for all eternity transformed into fanged, forked-tongued, sulfurous, stinky, scaly serpentine monsters of incredible ugliness, thrashing about in fiery pools of tar and sulfur, and deprived for all eternity of the delightful inimitable infinitely desirable presence and sight of the Almighty God and His Unlimited Love!" He looked down on Kit and he held out a brochure. "Sign right here, Sister, sign up for the Divine Heavenly Express! No money down, interest-free – and no obligations! And you get Eternal Love forever!"

"Maybe later," Kit said, and she moved on to the next booth, where there were screens showing people being pushed underwater. "Quatsch and Kitsch," Kit muttered, and then she chastised and scolded herself: She was being uncharitable – after all, people, even good, really good, people did believe this stuff!

These were the Witnesses, who insisted you plunge into the purifying water, and thus, you were reborn. Kit wasn't sure she wanted to be reborn, though the idea was interesting, of course, but in many ways, she was happy the way she was.

Being reborn sounded suspiciously like being erased – and Kit had already been, largely, erased, and once was enough, thank you very much! Anyway, since the water looked harmless – it must have been put through a special filter – and the service was cheap, just a 100 dollar token, she decided she would try it. Nothing ventured, nothing gained, eh?

Most of the water was, in fact, not pure at all, but that did not seem to inhibit the believers. Pure water was, in any case, a luxury that few, down here in the lower depths, could afford.

"Plunge yourself in the water, my dear, plunge deep, purify yourself of all sins, my dear, renew yourself, flesh and spirit, emerge into the pure light of innocence, blessed by the Lord and reborn free of sin."

When she came out of the water, Kit didn't feel much of a change except she was wet and shivering; but she screamed "Hallelujah" and "The Lord be Praised" since she thought that would make the Pastor and his Flock happy – which it did. They screamed in delight and repeated her words – and besides she'd paid for the experience and if you were going to do something you should see it through to the end, with all the frills and bells and whistles. She shivered and then left the flock behind and decided she'd try something else.

At the Reformed Unified Catholic Neo-Orthodox pop-up shop, the barker – he had a cute beard and long greasy locks that dangled down to his shoulders – said she should kneel, down on her knees, tilt her face up, lips ready, while a musty old man in a long gown with some gold trimming and neat scarlet patterns stuck a wafer to eat in her mouth and pushed a nasty smelling cup brimming with acidic cheap red wine against her lips, and then he mumbled some words over her in Latin, and she got up and filed away, head down, like the others, figuring it was not a very hygienic procedure and probably, on a symbolic level, cannibalistic: We become God or the Son of God by eating his flesh and drinking his blood, just the way, in the old days, cannibal warriors would acquire the virtues of their enemies – leopards, lions or other humans – by devouring their flesh or painting themselves in their victims' blood or draping themselves in their dappled spotted skin or wearing their bones as jewelry. They had candles burning and low lights in their chapel

– which they called the Chapel of the Martyrs – which made the whole place glow with dimness and smell like musty spices.

The Reformed Unified Catholic Neo-Orthodox shop had a young woman called the Virgin, who seemed very important. Why you would boast about being a virgin, Kit found totally incomprehensible. This lady had a halo and always looked very pious and constipated, her hands clasped together in the supplicating or prayer position and her eyes aiming upwards as if a dove were about to descend with good news or an angel or a storm cloud or something.

They also had a lot of guys and girls called saints – most were pretty old and ugly though there was one cool almost naked guy – just wearing a sagging little loin cloth – pierced with arrows whose image gave Kit fuel for a few masochistic and sadistic and exhibitionist fantasies and a frisson or two. "Saint Sebastian," she read, and a number of paintings from her contraband black market knock-off "History of Renaissance Art" implant flashed through her mind. And in fact, she whirled through a mental evocation of walls of Renaissance paintings and statues, all stimulated by the saints in the pop-up. These saints were commemorated in statues and in reproduced paintings – mostly kitsch but some really fine pieces too copied from museums and old churches. Apparently, all these saints had done great stuff in the past, like performing miracles or getting burnt alive or crucified or something, and they needed to be honored and they could be useful too. If you needed something – like if you needed to remember where you'd left something – you could pray to those guys and you'd find your ID card or your ration card or your cat, if you had a cat, but biological live pets had mostly been replaced by robot pets who didn't need to be fed, didn't pee and shit, didn't get sick, and didn't usually get lost since they had GSP tags and in-built homing devices so they would find you even if you didn't want them to. So if you were equipped with robot pets, you probably wouldn't need Saint Anthony who was Patron of Lost Things. These days you were more likely to be lost than your pet.

Kit loved the Religious Bazar debates. There were guys – and some girls – fighting over whether God was One or Two or Three, and if he was Three Different Persons, what sort of difference was it, was it a difference of essence or of appearance, of substance or of attributes, an emanation or an intimation, and whether He, God, could be incarnate in the flesh, as it were, or not. Kit scratched her head about this. Three cute girls – a blonde, a black girl, and a Chinese girl – got into a luscious punching match over that very question, plus a few other questions like predestination, and divine omnipotence and divine omniscience and such-like trivialities.

"It is a matter of participation in the Godhead," said the black girl, nursing a bloody nose and explaining the situation to Kit.

"If God is infinite, then He has to be a She and an It as well as a He and then He has to be everything in between, too," said the blonde who was covering her black eye.

"If God knew everything that was going to happen when he created the world, then he is responsible for everything that has happened and so he is guilty of everything that has happened," said the Chinese girl who had sustained an even blacker – a big purple bruise – eye in her fight over the nature of God. The black eye, Kit thought, was extraordinarily fetching.

"Blasphemy," shouted one of the bearded clerics who was hanging there, on the fringes of the wrestling match, "Evil blasphemy, how can you, small worm of a being, obscene woman, rotting excremental, womb-anchored, sewer of fertile female flesh without a soul, dare say that God is guilty?" He thundered. He was wearing a tall, funny hat and had a very long unkempt, and, Kit thought, quite filthy beard. Staring right at Kit, he shouted, "God will judge you for this, you mammalian excrescence!" Kit shrugged; she had absolutely no time for archaic unhygienic misogynous madmen who dreamed of stoning people to death. The Cosmos might be many things but they were not misogynous. The Chinese girl just stuck out her tongue at the hysterical bearded priest, turned her back, and walked away.

Another fellow, who was very soberly dressed, was droning on in an austere niche where there were no decorations at all. "If God knew everything, then he knew, from the beginning who would go to Heaven and who would go to Hell, some of us are predestined for Heaven, and some of us are predestined for Hell, and there is nothing you – or I – can do about it, absolutely nothing but accept in sobriety and dignity your destiny whatever it may be."

"But," a girl wearing celestial blue hot-skin pants shouted, "good works count – if you are charitable, if you help your neighbor, if you rescue the weak, then you go to Heaven!"

"No, no, my dear," said the sober fellow, "Good works count for nothing. In the face of God's Greatness, how can such a puny creature as a man or a woman work their own salvation by a few miserable insignificant acts of charity? Impossible!"

"You are both wrong," said a skinny young man with freckles, and arched eyebrows that made him look quite wicked, something that Kit found very attractive. "You are both wrong. God created humans so that someone would love Him, and to love you have to be free to choose, and so humans are free to choose their own destinies, and this freedom is what makes us valuable in God's eyes, we are free to love Him or refuse Him. That is the question. So we are not predestined; we do have choice."

"Choice is nothing," said the sober fellow.

"Charity is everything," said the girl.

"Belief is everything. Our good works cannot save us!" said the freckled youth. "Even if we do have freedom – and we do – what are mere human good works, confronted with the majesty of God? Nothing! No, it is our beliefs that save us, it is our total submission to God that gives us the key to salvation. Not good works, but beliefs, the beliefs we carry in our hearts."

"No, no, no," said a fat man who was wearing a funny pointed hat, "You are all wrong. It is sacraments, passed on by holy apostolic succession – it is the hand of the priest that saves you, the squirt of water, the wafer and the wine, the flesh and the blood of Christ, administered, as a sacrament, by the conse-crated priest, that saves you, the confession to the priest that redeems you by bringing you within the pale of Christ's infinite forgiveness. That is the only road to salvation. There is no other!"

After listening to all this, Kit had a headache, though she did like it when the redheaded guy with the arched eyebrows and freckles fought with the two remaining girls – now that was fun. It was almost as good as the neon strobe-light naked girl-on-girl mud, and paintball wrestling shows up in the Sin Zone.

"It is the holy water!"

"It is the eating of His blood and His flesh!"

"It is …"

The clamorous voices faded as Kit walked on. She wondered at it all. In the narrow underground streets, in the tents and ruins of buildings, on the plat-forms and in the niches, there were men in long hair with ringlets and flat black hats, there were men in turbans of different shapes and colors, there were men running around in long robes, there were women covered in veils and shrouds and there were women wearing hardly anything at all, there were women and men with shaved heads who went by chanting and jingling, and there were people with white collars and people with open collars, bushy beards and trimmed beards, there were people sitting cross-legged on the ground, there were people burning various animals on different kinds of fire …

She came to a corner where there was a statue of a fat serene-looking man in a loincloth sitting on the ground. His eyes were closed; his lips curved up in a smile.

The barker – a wizened Japanese lady with a shaved head – said, "Empty your mind, Kit. Empty your mind. Just stare at that splotch of lichen long enough, and there will be nothing left of your old false self."

Kit concentrated on the splotch of lichen; then, she closed her eyes and concentrated hard on emptying her mind.

Her mind filled up with the idea of emptying it.

"You see, the self, Kit, is an illusion."

Kit squished her eyes shut, concentrating hard, trying to empty her mind, which as it turned out was chock-full of stubborn stuff, a whizzing kaleidoscope and whirl and cascade of highly colored thoughts, the more she tried to empty it out, the worse it was, the harder it was; it was like trying to pass a stubborn turd when one is constipated, she figured. *Ouch, it hurt!* She squished her eyes harder and harder.

"Pain and suffering, Kit, come from desire."

Kit groaned.

"When desire dies pain and suffering; when desire dies – when yearning and straining and desiring die – then the self too is gone, Kit."

Kit kept her eyes closed, still trying to empty her mind, quell her desires, abolish her sense of self, kill her ego, and negate her lusts and yearnings … Miranda and Nikki and their fabulous flat kept popping into her mind, and the way Miranda had learned to kiss, and vanilla ice cream, and a nifty temp tattoo she'd been thinking of getting, and Rodney Gomez, a guy who lived down the cubical corridor and who did push-ups on his mini-terrace, "Hi, Rodney," and he'd look over at her and say, "Hi, Kit, what's new" – sigh! Even the image of her former lover Sniggy Propane – and all his acne – flashed through her mind.

"Even our sense of time, of time passing, Kit, comes from desire – nostalgia, yearning; our desires and regrets give us the horrible gift of time, of yesterday and tomorrow, of this instant and the next, linked in an eternal chain, in which suffering is embodied, and if you do away with desire, Kit, then you do away with time – and you do away with suffering in time."

It sounded reasonable, but it didn't work for Kit. At the end of the day, she still felt hungry, she sometimes felt a great desire to pee, and she could often feel – almost every day a couple of times a day or continuously all day and in various forms – horny. And, in addition to Rodney, she dreamed, occasionally, of Alfred York Chung who lived around the corner from her cubicle on Block Z-2, and, of course, of Miranda – Miranda's eyes, her golden skin, the perfumed curtain of blonde hair, the way she laughed, bright, unconstrained, oh, gosh, oh gosh …

Also, those non-desire people had a whole lot of complicated very opaque words – usually from the Sanskrit – to describe various things or states so that they could, Kit felt, feel very exclusive about it all; it was like stamp collectors or gun enthusiasts talking about their very special favorites, like an 1867 Abraham Lincoln 15 cent stamp, or a .577 Beaumont-Adams patent five-shot double-action percussion revolving rifle. Of course, Kit did admit that meanings were scattered hither and yon among languages and organized into different constellations of sense so that translation was a tricky art at best and people did need special words for unique things or states or concepts … Like, say, a screw-bolt 34D. But it did mean you had to spend a hundred years learning vocabulary if you wanted, truly, to be absent, to abolish the Ego, the Id, and the Super-Ego, and to become, truly, *nothing*. How a mind chock-full of a special lexicon could become nothing remained for Kit a mystery. For such forms of wisdom and spiritual transcendence, implants did not provide shortcuts; drugs, maybe, but not implants. Besides, becoming *nothing* still did sound a lot like being erased.

Kit decided she *liked desire,* and she liked the fact that *her desires were not satisfied* – she liked daydreaming about Miranda, and she liked fantasizing about Nikki or about having a different job or more interesting clothes.

Desire was imagination; imagination was desire.

Desire was energy. Energy was life.

Desire and imagination were a dance, the dance of life.

Life was movement – thus, it was desire.

She didn't actually have to fulfill her desires to enjoy them.

She didn't have to possess something to love it. In fact, she loved, and liked and admired gazillions of things she would never possess – she loved the way the sunlight in the late afternoon filtering through the Dome would shine on the very top of the Central Tower, she loved the way Fanny's eyes would flare when she was particularly happy, she loved the sense of the air moving against her skin. She loved people of all kinds, even people she just glimpsed for a second. Her heart went out to them, breathless, and looped around and around; it was like a dance, like love, like yearning, but happy yearning! She felt it a pure pleasure and privilege just to have known people, just to have exchanged words and glances with people – exhibit number one: Nikki Hughes.

That's why, though she liked fashion and styles and fads, she was almost immune to shopping – this was the original sin. Shopping required ever-receding satisfaction; shopping required addictive unhappiness, infinitely renewable dissatisfaction; it required status hunger and status angst and perpetual identity crisis: If I buy that Louis Vuitton purse or that Hermès scarf, I shall, finally, be truly myself! Kit suspected that some people's idea of God, as a distant, transcendent, perpetually pissed-off Angry Old Gent who lived Somewhere Else, was an instrument of dissatisfaction, a producer of Angst, a de facto Ally of Shopping. God was a marketing tool, and a drug – that old famous "opium of the people" idea …

Kit realized that, mostly, she'd been happy.

So now she could die …

After all, I did have a life! And it was great!

I would like more – heck, I'd like it to go on forever – but, hey, you can't be greedy!

The Religion Bazaar was a circus. The closest thing Kit had seen to the Religion Bazaar was the Sin Zone, fifteen micro-layers above, where she'd visited the Jean Genet Electronic Bordello which catered to the most elaborate fantasies people had and could pay to see acted out in virtual space or in real space or in a combination of real – real flesh-and-blood performers – and virtual, with extra enhancements or specialties or decor.

Kit suspected that sex and religion had something in common and that in some vague way, they were perhaps rivals competing for the same energies. This was maybe a deep thought, and certainly a forbidden thought, so she didn't for the moment pursue it, but she stored it away for later contemplation and consideration and possible discussion with Miranda or Nikki – *well, she would have if they were still alive* – she shivered with a spasm of grief – or maybe Fanny or maybe even, if he was up to it, Alfred York Chung – if of course she survived the Death Chair to discuss anything with anybody, which was very unlikely. People down there in the Religion Bazaar were, in fact, running around playing out their fervid fantasies, just like the customers in the Bordello were paying to have their fantasies realized. It was crazy.

"There is only one God, and his prophet is ..."

Some had had their hands cut off – those were thieves.

Some had been stoned to death or shot or scarred with razors or had their noses cut off – those were adulterers and adulteresses.

Some had their tongues cut out – they were gossips and blasphemers.

Some were put to death – and they were gay or lesbian.

Kit thought the Religious Bazar was the craziest circus yet, worse and better than the Jean Genet Electronic Bordello, but, above all, it was exhausting – all those strident competing voices somehow got inside her head and they kept yelling, even when she couldn't hear them anymore.

After hours spent in the Religious Underground, Kit usually wanted to get back up into the pure Cosmos reign of Elysium City, where the Net games were and where people usually didn't get hurt. She wanted to crawl back into her own cubicle and curl up and go to sleep; she might even take a sleeping pill which she rarely did. Or she might text Miranda: "Miranda, do you want to hang out – maybe just watch some movies or sleep or talk ..."

One day after intensive religious window shopping, Kit realized she was exhausted, and her feet hurt. She stopped, sighed, went off into a quiet side tunnel and sat down at the edge of an underground canal and dangled her feet in the water. The side tunnel which contained the canal was quiet; the religious ruckus and shouts were muffled and far away, far down at the end of the canal. The water was muddy and moved slowly, with little swirls and twisting eddies in the surface; creepy crawlies and all sorts of monstrous things were probably moving below the surface, but Kit didn't care. The water was cool on her feet and ankles and she felt relaxed.

A young man – maybe about 30, she thought – came along; he had long hair and a beard, and he was dark-skinned and barefoot and wearing a sort of Bedouin gown, off white with pale vertical stripes. "Do you mind?" He said and without waiting for an answer, he sat down next to her. "No, I don't mind," she said, "Help yourself. This is a public canal."

He had a thin and thoughtful face, and very deep eyes. "Let the dead bury the dead," he said, nodding back toward the Religion Bazaar. Kit looked at him, but didn't say anything.

"Do onto others as you would have them do onto you," he said, moving his feet back and forth and making a small swirl of water.

"Yes, Confucius," Kit said.

"Did he say that too?"

"I think so," Kit said, "I read it somewhere or it was in an implant, and the Buddha too, I think he said it, or something like it."

"Thou shalt love thy neighbor," he said.

"I try," Kit said, "I try, and I try, and I try." She was thinking of Fanny; yes, she loved Fanny, moderately; and she lusted after Alfred York Chung, and she desired the presence and the touch of Miranda and the friendly gaze or glance of Nikki. Was lust love? Were need and hunger and yearning love? Was it all a hall of mirrors?

"I am the son of man," he said, "and the son of God."

"Isn't everybody?"

"Exactly," he said, dipping his palm in the water and splashing up a handful, perhaps to cool his face; it dribbled down his chest, drips catching in the hairs of his chest, and darkening part of his robe. "That is exactly what I meant. Nobody got the point, though. You know," he said, turning to look at her, "you are an exceptional young woman."

"Thank you. Would you like some water?" Kit said, handing him her backpack bottle.

"Thank you, yes." He took the bottle and drank deep and long, and then, wiping his mouth, he handed it back. "Have you heard the one about the Good Samaritan?"

"No, tell me," Kit said. She had heard it, but she didn't want to spoil his fun.

He told her.

"That is a very fine story," Kit took a sip from the bottle.

"The prodigal returns and the father rejoices." He accepted the bottle, taking a long gulp, wiping his lips. "She who was lost, is now found."

"I was looking," said Kit, who was staring down at the muddy water, "but now I'm tired; I think I'll give up. I mean, it was more like spiritual window shopping."

"Keep on seeking," he said.

"I was thinking of giving up."

"Don't," he said. "Knock, and the door will be opened." He looked around. A procession was passing in the distance, under an arch, they were burning incense and they were carrying crosses and chanting. The crosses, held aloft by old men, wavered and danced against the dark walls, throwing elongated shadows. The chant echoed against the roof of the cave and the incense and candles made the air glow as if it were red hot and made of gold. He turned to her. "Who are those people in the funny hats?"

"Bishops, I think," said Kit.

"Bishops?"

"From the Latin, and originally, from the Greek – *epi-skopos* – over-seer or watcher, I believe."

"You are very learned. Who are they, exactly?"

"Those ones are the Holy Latin Counter-Reformation Fundamentalist Mass-only-in-Latin Catholic All-Inclusive Church," said Kit. "They are opposed to the Ultra-Orthodox, the Neo-Orthodox, the Orthodox, the Neo-Protestants, and the Ecumenical Church of Compromise and the Catholic Church of Rome and the Holy Rollers and the Paul Revere Tea Party Chapel and the Anti-Darwinian Creationist Temple, and … Those ones there wear pointed hats; the other ones wear flat hats and the third ones wear triangular hats. Some of them don't wear hats."

"Oh," he said.

"Yes, some of them have special haircuts or special beards, some have ringlets, some have top-notches, some have under the chin beards, and some have no beards at all, some look beatific and blissful; some look furious and enraged. And so it goes …"

"Ah, and that is Latin, they are chanting, the language of Caesar."

"Yes, that is Latin," said Kit, thinking that the Ancient Greek, Ancient Latin black market mash-up mental implant was finally useful for something. Nikki was right. You never knew what might be handy or when.

The procession moved on. The chanting echoed from far away, coming from one of the other many tunnels. Only the flickering wall torches remained; they made a gentle, wet, flapping sound.

"What shall it profit a man if he gains the whole world and loses his soul?"

"Yeah, that's about it. Sometimes, you know, I feel sort of empty," Kit stirred the water with her foot, watching the little swirls catch the orange-tinted canal-side lamplight. "Like my soul didn't exist, you know."

"It happens."

"Is this your first time here?"

"No. It's my second time around," he said, reaching out his hand. Kit handed him the water bottle, and he unscrewed the top and drank. "You are very gracious," he said.

"Don't mention it."

"I was thirsty, and you gave me drink. I was a stranger, and you welcomed me. I was naked, and you clothed me. I was sick and you visited me. I was in prison and you came to me."

"I have an extra power bar," said Kit, holding it out.

"Thank you."

He took the power bar and looked at it for a moment. Kit took it from him and unpeeled and opened it. "You just munch on it, like this!"

"Wonders unfold," he said, taking a bite. "Things change, and yet they are the same. It's good, actually very good."

"I don't think we've met before. I mean, I don't think I visited you in prison."

He munched and took another bite. He had a very beautiful face, Kit thought, and his hands were long and delicate and very fine. "No, not literally, you didn't, but then you visited Fanny when she had the infraction over the length of her skin skirt."

"Gosh, did she tell you about that?"

"In a way, she did, she is modest, though, Fanny."

"True, but she is proud of her complexion – and it is beautiful. It gives me pleasure to look at her."

"Such pride is good – it is a form of grace. She gives the gift of her beauty, almost virginal it is, in its purity. And several months ago you did greet that stranger – Lila the Indian from Kerala – who was without clothes and you lent her your skin-shorts and an extra T-shirt when there was a breakdown at the auto-laundry and Lila was without raiment."

"I'd forgotten that one." Kit was staring at the wall of the tunnel on the opposite side of the canal; the reflected lamplight made nice flickering patterns of gold and yellow; it was as if the wall was alive, crawling with light.

"As you did to one of the least of these my brothers or sisters, you did to me."

"That's a nice thought; I like that. Each stands for the other."

"We are all one."

Kit nodded; meeting this guy had made the trip down into the Religion Bazar worthwhile. He was holding the crumpled, empty power bar package, and looking around.

"Here," said Kit, "I'll look after that."

"Thank you," he said. He gave her the crumpled bit of foil. "You are very gracious." He pulled his feet from the water and stood up. He put his hand on her head, very gently. "Repent, for the End is Neigh, the Kingdom of Heaven is at hand, Repent!"

"I'll work on it," she said, looking up at him, feeling a warmth radiate from his hand and from his smile.

"I am always with you, even to the end of the world," he said, smiling down at her, "so we shall not say goodbye but rather au revoir. We shall be together forever."

"Thank you," said Kit.

"Thank you," he said, bowing, and then he was gone.

Kit sat for a while, absorbing the encounter and then she thought it was time to get home. She stuffed the crumpled power bar package in her backpack so she could put it in the recycle orifice when she got home and she walked up a spiral underground staircase to the fourth level and then took an express elevator up into the lower level of the ethereal realm of Elysium City – took a half-empty cross-town robot express – and then another express elevator, "Reserved for Subs," and let herself into her own pod cubical in Sub City.

The encounter with the handsome bearded man on the side of the canal had left Kit strangely happy, even exhilarated.

I guess, in general, I am a happy person, she thought, even very happy, excessively happy – yes, excessively extremely happy.

But …

But I must be one sick idiot, she thought, to be so happy when things are far – well I guess they are far – from perfect; maybe it was the sub programming, the metaphysical masochism that she occasionally detected, maybe … Was masochism a recipe for delight? She thought back at the Buddhist lady who told her she should eliminate all desire, that eliminating desire would free her from the cycle of life and death. *If I didn't desire, I think I'd be dead already …*

Dead …

The executing chair made a clicking noise. It was moving again, painfully, click, click, click – in small sputtering shudders and jerks.

V, Kat, Miranda, and Caliban tried to push their way through the crowd on the Mid-Level Shopping Concourse. It was pure chaos.

Going down a series of emergency service stairs, they had found their way blocked where the walls had caved in – they were faced with a solid wall of steel and rubble. So they had detoured and exited onto Cosmos Shopping Concourse number 3, the elite floating deck where Miranda had so often shopped or lunched or taken coffee with Nikki.

Untethered balloons floated skyward.

The window of Prada and Gucci and all the other wonderful shops were smashed, and bio-manikins had been tossed into the street and stripped of their finery; some of the bio-manikins were trying to crawl back into the window displays and get back into their poses.

A meal – pizza capricciosa and Caesar salad – was still sitting uneaten on a café terrace table; the woman at the table, in sleek silver jogging gear, was still sitting, elbows on the table, but her head had been blown away, a bib of blood covered her breasts; all the other tables had been overturned. About a dozen people were on their hands and knees, gobbling up the food with their tongues and teeth and snarling at each other like mad dogs.

"Oh, no," Miranda stopped, put her hand to her mouth, tears coming to her eyes. The body of Cyril Bedford, with its head blown off, was sprawled close by. Miranda realized it was him; first, she had her doubts; but then his badge, his shorts with the Cosmos Sprinter Prize medal pinned to them, his shoes, the laces on one undone, made it clear, it was Cyril.

"He was trying to save a kid," said a Centurion who was standing nearby, his hands on his hips, watching the chaos, "and one of the crazies shot him." The Centurion nodded at the gobbling herd. "Where the crazy got a laser gun, I have no idea."

Miranda knelt down, she looked up at Caliban. "He was a friend," she said, "I had a crush on him, and he had a crush on me. We were just children," she blinked, suddenly realizing, "That was about a week ago."

Caliban knelt by Miranda, "I understand, Princess."

"Yes, I know, I know you do!"

Caliban looked around, more people than he'd ever seen, thousands of people; he glanced at a line of Centurions. They were trying to protect a heliport and a landing pad. A gunship was landing. Zombie-bats zoomed down, attacking the gunship. Laser guns blazed. The zombie-bats exploded in puffs of black smoke, debris showered down. The gunship settled in. More Centurions poured out of the gunship.

Not far away, a woman was eating a child, munching into its chubby forearm.

Colorful gold and black banners floated in the rising wind: "Welcome to Cosmos London Prize Winners!" Several of the banners had been torn down, were flipping and flickering along the ground. Miranda remembered: she was supposed to be part of the honor guard of Young Cosmos during the Greeting for the Londoners. "Now it's all dying," she said, looking around.

"It's not dead yet, Princess," Caliban put his arm around her shoulder; she felt warm and fresh and new, even now, even filled with grief. She looked up at him. "We must be brave, Caliban."

"We shall be brave, my Princess."

Miranda looked up. The air was yellow and gritty. A flickering hologram was offering snippets of information: there were replay images of TV hosts Alison Jonas and Ken Iverson heroically making love, "An Act of Resistance, a Reassertion of Life!" There were fragmentary reports from abroad. There were reports, too, of the collapse of the downtown Wall Street section of Elysium, of towers being eaten away from below. There were reports that the World Mind had been sabotaged. A headline said: "Where is he?" The President-Leader had not been heard from in over 24 hours.

V and Kat were talking to the Centurion. Did he know the way to the Mind? No, he didn't. He asked a few colleagues. No, they didn't either. V stood looking at the carnage. "Everything can collapse so quickly."

"Yes," Kat, her hands on her hips, glanced around, "Civilization is fragile."

"Yes, it truly is."

There were overturned prams; the bodies of babies lay nearby; one baby was trying to crawl away from a madwoman; the baby wore a bib, it looked up at Miranda. Miranda leaped over, snatched it up, and handed it to one of the Centurions, "Thank you, ma'am," who handed it back to some of the still sane people huddling behind the line of Centurions.

People were running every which way.

"This is awful." Miranda stared at the chaos.

Lines of Centurions were standing, waiting for orders. Whom or what should they attack, whom, or what should they defend? There were no orders.

Where was the President-Leader?

Loudspeakers were blaring. "Return to your homes, close all windows and doors. Being in the open is dangerous."

Some people were still exploding, literally exploding. Other people were walking like zombies, blood dripping from their mouths and eyes. Still others seemed to have gone absolutely mad, they were strangling their neighbors, they were smashing windows, they were overturning chairs and tables; their eyes shone with a wild glare. Their mouths foamed over.

"This crowd should disperse, they should go home," said one of the officers. Centurions began shooting canisters of tear gas. Centurions began firing over people's heads. Farther down the Concourse, a phalanx of Centurions was in an ongoing firefight with a flight of zombie-bats that had entered under the great Shopping Concourse Canopy.

"Lieutenant, which way is downwards from here?" Saluting, V asked one of the officers.

He glanced at her and saluted. "Best take the stairs, Major. Elevators are unreliable. One set of service stairs is over there. It is still open. We have guards at the gates."

"What is happening?" V motioned at the people.

"Mind implants, we think, mind implants, they are exploding, or taking people over. Some infection has gotten inside the World Mind; at least that's the best guess."

"Thank you, Lieutenant."

"You are welcome, Major! But you'd better hurry. We can't hold these people much longer. And, as you can see, the support structures for this promenade deck are collapsing. We are going to evacuate shortly."

Miranda and Caliban and Kat and V got behind the Centurions and headed for the stairs. Explosions rippled through the space. Tear gas drifted everywhere; shots echoed; zombie-bats zoomed down; people were screaming.

Even in his bedroom, Ken Iverson was plugged in. He had an Info-Flow next to the bed, and it spoke with an automatic deep voice, and some Info-Flow and Twitter flows were still getting through.

Alison opened her eyes and listened.

"This is the Voice of Cosmos! Reports are coming in that a mega tornado, has hit the Outer Burbs. Winds of 450 to 500 miles per hour are reported. Nothing seems to be able to withstand this wind. More information as we receive it."

Alison sat up. "We have to report on this."

"No, you can't; you're too weak, and you have a big hole in your head, and you're blind, for Christ's sake!"

"I want to. If I don't keep reporting, I'll just leak away, all of my personality will dribble away, and I will become nothing, nothing at all, and absolutely invisible, absolutely." She turned her blind face to him. "An Info-Voice earphone can cue me."

Ken knew she was stubborn, ultra-stubborn, and, now that she was blind, she was perhaps even more stubborn than before; and brave too, oh, so brave, the lovely brave helpless blind girl, "Okay, darling Alison, we shall report!"

He led her up toward the remains of the studio. In the residence corridors, the lively hysterical crowd was no more. Dead bodies lay everywhere, in the hallways, in the vestibules, in the small interior shopping concourse. They had all had their throats slit. Some were missing heads and arms, as if they had been snapped off or chewed off. Nobody was alive.

Ken helped Alison step over the bodies.

He didn't tell her what he saw; there would time enough for that.

He wondered what had happened – maybe it was those zombies people had talked about; maybe the Info-feeds has been right; maybe there were ghouls and rabid vampire-bats loose in Elysium City. One woman had a knife in her gut; another woman was holding the knife; it looked like they had all gone mad and torn each other apart …

Some of the people didn't have heads. Their heads had exploded, or so it seemed from the smears and goo, and gore and blood splashed all over the place and the gaping holes of what had been necks.

Somebody – or maybe something – had scrawled on a wall, in giant letters in what looked like blood, "Ha, ha Splatter-Heads!"

Ken was an anchor. He was supposed to know everything that was happening, but things were happening about which he knew nothing; and even worse, even more annoying, he didn't even understand the things that he could see were happening. How was he supposed to explain something, if he didn't understand anything?

He wondered if, while he and Alison were in the apartment, the wolf that had eaten the Professor had also come here, and eaten everybody, like in an evil fairy-tale.

Maybe the wolves traveled in packs. Ken then thought that perhaps he should begin believing in werewolves, and vampires, and hobgoblins.

Maybe we are all going mad. He wiped his brow. Maybe we are all going crazy. Or maybe this is all just a nightmare-dream.

Yes, that was it – it was a nightmare-dream, it was Hell and it was Paradise. The world was coming to an end, and Alison was in his arms.

Did you have to go through Hell to get to Heaven?

"These are dead people we are stepping over, aren't they, darling?"

"Yes, yes, Alison, they are."

"And the two little girls that were crying, what happened to them?"

"Dead, I'm afraid, dead."

Alison clung closer. "This is horrible, Ken, something horrible, something beyond horrible, is happening."

"Well, darling, here we are, almost back in the studio."

In the studio, the cameras and editor robots, which had been reporting news flashes and steaming tweets, and broadcasting replays, all lit up. The robots and Artificial Intelligence producers were delighted to see the stars back, even if the stars were mere human beings.

Ken inserted the Cue Info-Flow earpiece into Alison's ear.

"Thank you, darling." She gave him a bright-eyed blind smile that seemed like the smile of a love-struck child.

"Welcome back, Ken, welcome back, Alison," said the Robot-Director.

"Thank you, Steven," said Ken.

"Let's go, then," said Steven, "You give the word, Ken."

Ken grinned, "Lights camera action!"

Ken took Alison by the shoulders and turned her around, so they were both facing the camera, and he began, "So, as you can see, we've had our own little problems."

Alison took the cue, "We were hit by flying glass."

"Now the big one is coming," Ken smiled; his arm was tight around Alison's shoulders, cueing her with one squeeze of his finger.

"Yes, the big one – a super-sized super-powerful tornado, with winds up to 500 miles per hour," said Alison, smiling at the camera she couldn't see.

Ken gave the camera his most fatherly smile. "So our advice is to get as deep down as you can, far from glass, far from outside walls, as far as you can."

"But we will be with you," smiled Alison, her blue eyes bright crystals, "You can depend on us. We will be with you all the way!"

Ken hugged Alison even closer: oh the brave, brave, blind, helpless girl; his love was absolute, it was madness, wonderful madness.

Oh, Death – where is thy sting?

The Execution Chair creaked and groaned, making little slapping and snapping noises as if it were eager to gobble somebody up. One of the other condemned, a skinny young man with bony knees, moaned once or twice. At one point, an ankle strap having come loose, one leg fell off the edge of another gurney, it was a shapely leg; it belonged to the naked, unconscious, fully epilated, chalk-white girl; the girl was beautiful, and young, maybe about 15. Kit could just see the body out of the corner of her eye; the sign on the girl's gurney said, in large red letters, "Full Erasure." How horrible! But all these little sights and sounds, however horrible, were life, it was life ...

I'm leaving all that behind.

Desire, adieu!

Death, Oh, Grim Reaper, Hello!

So, now, I am going to die. And it's going to be painful. These, Kit realized, were two separate things – to be *dead*, just not there, that was one thing; to suffer *pain* – that was quite another thing. On reflection, death was, it turned out, a many-faceted many-splendored thing! Oh, the *meaning* of death!

Yes, non-being, or absence – that was one thing. Then, there was the pain in the departure lounge. Then, there was the *shame* of the mess left behind, that was a third thing, after *non-being*, and after *pain*. You could anticipate the posthumous shame of leaving your own *cadaver* in miserable shape – all bloody and gory and hacked to bits with intestines and guts and shit hanging out and dripping all over the floor or the rug – a stinky, loathsome, icky mess some poor Sub or robot would have to clean up – and you could feel shame for *what people would think*: you could feel shame, in advance, for what had not yet come to pass and for what would only come to pass when you were no longer there to feel shame about it. *Not being there, not being* here, *that was the question.* It was hard to imagine – in fact, it was outrageous to imagine – the world going on without her, the world without Kit Candy, Kit Candy, the very Center of the Universe, her very own Universe! But it most certainly would go on. *My universe will disappear, but nobody else's will.*

But, on the other hand, unless all that nonsense about Hell and fire and brimstone was true, which Kit, for some weird reason, thought was highly unlikely, then being dead would just be non-existence, like being asleep without dreams, and forever, without ever waking, and so it would not be painful. It would not be anything. It would be nothing, *nada, nichts, niente, rien de tout.*

But dying, in this lethal chair contraption that was going to chop her up and squeeze her into a bloody pulp – that was going to be really unpleasant. That was going to *hurt!* Ouch! That was really bad! So that was the pain of dying.

Checklist:

Pain!

Shame!

Yes, there would be the shame of the mess – blood would explode, the sphincter would release – a gigantic fart and shit would squirt – the bladder would give up all control – piss would flood out!

Yes, it was shameful. Kit had been down in a lower depths service tunnel, near the Secret Center of the World Mind – when she saw a guy die, bludgeoned to death by underworld ruffians, and he lost control, from pain and terror, and he shit and pissed, and she saw the shame as well as the terror in his eyes.

She shouted at them, "Stop that!"

Then they turned on her, one big brute coming straight at her with a metal truncheon in one hand and a long sharp knife in the other.

She ran.

She was fast, and she knew secret entrances, exits, cubbyholes, niches, and staircases.

She escaped.

Whew!

She did feel ashamed she had not leaped on them to try to save the guy.

Wouldn't have done any good ...

Or maybe it would have ...

Am I a coward?

The poor guy, he was surely a goner, somebody getting even for something, or just because they didn't like the look of him.

The Execution Chair clicked and groaned and made a small jerky movement. It was really getting antsy; it was eager, chomping at the bit, to chop her up!

Yes, now, there was no mistake: death was near; the Reaper had raised his scythe. She frowned: Then there was *the shame of the mere fact of dying*. Yes, it was shameful – in fact, dying was rarely mentioned in Elysium City, even among Subs, since thoughts of death distracted you from shopping and from playing Video and Net games and using up your tokens as fast as you could and your money and making the world go round, spinning faster and faster, a regular mindless whirligig, an infernal, eternal, non-stop treadmill, and causing the GDP of Elysium City to soar so it got bigger and bigger, eating up more stuff and spitting out more garbage and excrement, and whoever profited from it, the elites, got richer and richer, and consumed more stuff and ...

Thus *death was subversive*. Thus death was something to be ashamed of – like body odor and being poor. Shame served the System, as some old text had suggested. *Shame was a people control machine.*

Shame = People Control Machine.

Guilt, too, unwarranted guilt = People Control Machine.

Also, *dying was sort of, like, failure*. If you died before your scheduled time, it was like dropping out of a marathon when all the other people were still running. It was a moral and physical failing – dying. Dying was disgraceful; there was no excuse, absolutely no excuse! People would stand around slurping smoothies and say, *Tsch, Tsch, Tsch, old Kit Candy, why she's dead! No? Yes. When did she do that? What a stupid thing to do! Well, it was last Thursday and …*

The Execution Chair clicked a trilling, repeated click, as if it were saying a disapproving *tsch, tsch, tsch,* with its guillotine-like cold steel tongue.

Ah, you loser, you, you're already dead! What a loser!

Oops! The Nano Pub Drone was still there. It circled once, wings fluttering, antennae quivering, and then emitted a snobbish sniff and buzzed past, ignoring her; she was unreceptive, and besides, the Drone had figured it out: Kit Candy was about to be terminated. She was yesterday's girl. She would no longer consume anything. *I consume, ergo I exist. I no longer consume, ergo … I'm dead …*

… I am nobody, already nobody.

Before becoming definitively nobody, I'm already nobody.

Kit felt hurt. Even a nano Pub Drone was indifferent to her; before actually dying, she had become yesterday's consumer, a nonentity, a non-being.

Shame, oh the word, the feeling – *shame*!

Yes, there were even more sources of shame! Yuk! She'd left her cubical flat in a shameful – truly shameful – mess and she herself was at this moment, at the moment of death, covered in drying homogenized shit, and some of her porno videos – "Goofy the Galley Slave" – "Dumbo the Drag Elephant"'– for instance, and that really erotic one – a total turn-on – about the sex-mad woodpecker – were open on her Net Connection – there was also Nikki Hughes's classic *Girl and Gorilla* – she blushed at the thought of the thoughts that had passed through her mind watching scantily clad Nikki swinging from tree to tree – and whoever did the erasure of all traces of her existence from the World Cloud Mind and from the lowly physical nitty-gritty non-virtual realm of her Living Pod would find those videos and peek into some of the more untoward obscenities and yearnings of Kit Candy's departed soul – an obsession with reef-knots and mud puddles – and the traces she had left in the Cloud were not always flattering, particularly that unflattering photo she had sent to Miranda and which Miranda said she adored.

"But I was sticking out my tongue!"

"I adore your tongue!"

"And I was crossing my eyes!"

"Your eyes are divine, whatever you do with them."

Kit sighed. So I will writhe in post-death shame, just as I am now, thinking of the people who will see what a dreadful conflict-ridden poor sod of a Sub I was, obscene and messy and infatuated …

And then I did jerk off sometimes – well, maybe sometimes was an understatement, I mean …

Did jerking off count in the great balance of existence?

Was jerking off a form of love?

Or was jerking off merely a form of lust?

Was jerking off a perversion of narcissism?

The God of the Three Major Monotheisms certainly saw onanistic excess as a mortal threat and made no bones – sigh – about it.

Was jerking off a regressive self-absorbed border-line dance with infantile inner primal objects, bits and pieces of the first loves of your life, Dad, Mom, and breasts and lips and hands and eyes, a sort of ritual mourning for love lost or love forgone or love impossible or love refused, a refusal of separation, an effort at reparation, a replacing of long-gone reality with nostalgic shadow play? Kit frowned. Of course, all the Great Religions foamed at the mouth, spitting rage at the very idea of jerking off, spilling seed, or wasting all that excitement which should be sublimated into abject servitude to the priests, rabbis, imams, pastors, preachers, mullahs, gurus, ayatollahs, and other syndicated crackpots, into obeisance and self-abasement and the paying of tithes or whatever … whatever … to the infinitely inventive and prolific clerical rabble. Well, she was being unfair. After all, she didn't really know that many clerical people or holy fellows, and one or two she had met seemed quite nice. But, still, she thought, they seemed to be cloaking themselves in divine authority that they really did not possess, and claiming access to forms of divine wisdom – intuition, delicacy, tact, love, compassion, courage, and insight – which they rarely displayed here on earth.

Searching not so deep in her heart, Kit found she was not really terribly fond of organized religion. She wondered why this was so. Religion really did bring out her uncharitable side, though she knew that religion did, and had done, many marvelous and selfless and charitable and artistic things, and built all those marvelous cathedrals, temples, synagogues and mosques, and generated some sublime poetry, and educated hundreds of generations. And religion had never really hurt her, personally. This anticlerical ferocity of hers was quite mysterious. Still, she somehow thought that religion had lost its way and become, largely, an incarnation of evil. She sighed. *Oh, why, oh, why am I so judgmental?*

Again, the thought occurred to her, certainly not for the first time, that sex and religion were competitors; so, obviously, religion would cast anathemas upon fantasies that were sexual or the results of those fantasies since such fantasies would siphon petrol out of the enormous sublimation gas tank upon which the great puffing polluting engines of religion fed. Discredit the competition with whatever means you can! It was all negative spin and negative advertising.

When she had been speculating about the existence of the God they talked about in some of the religions – both above ground and below ground religions – she had wondered, sometimes, if He was like a Big Eye in the Sky, spying on everybody all the time and seeing everything, or perhaps He was a big Eye inside your Head, spying on you from inside.

In either case, she thought he was a louse – a peeping tom.

Our Peeping Tom who art in Heaven … *Epi–Skopos* – the Big Overseer in the sky!

So what if the Big Eye saw her jerking off!

I mean, I did imagine things, and, oh, oh, oh, the *pleasure* …

Then the *brief oblivion* … The little death, Nikki had explained, the French called it, *La Petite Mort*. And then suddenly awake, perky, and thinking of other things – purified, full of beans, and raring to go!

And, thinking of *desire*, there was Fanny Dakin. Sometimes, when Fanny's guard was down, her face became so *naked*, so innocent, and so pure, truly a raw and new form of beauty! And then there was Miranda. Well, Miranda was – quite simply – sublime. And then there was Nikki, the lofty inaccessible wonderful goddess-like Nikki – an exquisite sculpture in black-and-white – who actually was warm and funny when you get close and who was unruffled by anything you did, non-judgmental, allowing you to be yourself, absolutely your unrestrained, uncensored, uninhibited, totally goofy self. And then there was that cute Sub, Albert, who worked in the Domestic Slaves for Hire Office, and collected ancient exotic postage stamps, and who had the smoothest hard muscles, a true ephebe, and then there was Rodney, and then there

was that Alfred York Chung guy, so funny, so muscular, so furry, and then …
and then there was, of course, Sniggy Propane and his acne and his tattoos
and his deeply flawed easily hurt awesomely damaged personality that struck
out aggressively in stupid, hurtful ways because he just couldn't help himself.
Yes, *desire,* desire to know things, desire for friendship, for love, for sex, for
sights, sounds, and tastes and touch …

Desire was wonderful

Desire was divine!

Hey, ho, Dionysius!

All those cultural implants in her head, buzzing with references, and nobody
really to share them with, except, in fantasy, Miranda and maybe Nikki.

I have been happy, really, I have.

Kit closed her eyes, ready to die.

She was conscious of everything: the smell of shit – oh, it was disgusting!
But it was divine because it existed! Smelling shit meant she was still here,
still in the world! Then, there was the tangy antiseptic smell of the Judgment
Room, the residual burned smell of the Robot's circuits, and the sounds, the
gentle groaning of one of the judged, the pretty one, the soon-to-be-erased
minds and personalities in bodies lying half-conscious on their gurneys.

The Robot, if only the Robot were still alive!

Maybe the Robot could have saved her; maybe she could have cajoled the
Robot.

Oh, Daisy, where are you now?

She opened her eyes. The arms of the chair were lifting up, getting ready to
snap down. A sweat of fear and pure horror broke out on her forehead.

Should I pray to the Big Nosy Parker Peeping Tom?

No, fuck that!

If I'm going to die, I'll die!

"Okay, I'm ready to die!" Kit shouted, "I'm ready to die!"

Kit took a deep breath. Now is the time to die.

Someone knocked on the door.

What?

The knock was repeated.

"Come in!" Kit said, a bit louder than she'd intended.

"Do you really mean that? Do you really intend with your words for me to
open the door and enter your abode?"

Kit cleared her throat, and shouted, "Yes! Come in!"

"Damn it!" Claire clenched her right claw, and smashed it against a wall.

"What is it, Hybrid?"

"I'm frustrated, that's all!"

The physical location of the World Mind was apparently veiled in a Mind-Fog; there was a wall of interference being put up by the Foul Fiend, the Boy, or his Avatars. Even Claire couldn't see through it; it was infuriating.

Claire bounded down the staircase with Robyn following close behind, and they came to a long corridor with doors on either side that looked like administrative offices.

Nothing was clearly marked, and it was hard to tell where they were. Claire opened a few doors.

Nobody, just empty cubicles for worker-bee drones, but there were no worker-bee drones. Claire sighed in frustration. The place was a labyrinth.

"We'll find somebody," said Robyn, "Don't worry, Hybrid. We'll find somebody who knows their way around this place, somebody who knows where the World Mind hides."

"Yes, Robyn, my darling! Thank you! I do admire your attitude, your positive thinking." Claire strode on ahead. It was funny how Robyn was becoming more self-assured. Perhaps it was the hybrid strain beginning to tell; perhaps it was the fact that she knew that somebody – namely, yours truly, Claire V Jacobs – loved her and cared for her. In spite of the erasure and negative programming, an adult was emerging out of the cocoon-prison of the child.

"Okay, I am ready to die!" a voice shouted from somewhere.

Claire skidded to a stop and listened.

The voice came from behind one of the doors. Claire raced ahead; her heart now, she noticed, was beating hard. She really did have a premonition of something awful about to happen – but, beyond the impending end of the world and extinction of the human race, she didn't know what.

"Okay, damn it, kill me now!" the voice yelled, a young woman's voice to judge by the frequencies, the coloratura, and the resonance.

Claire came to the door. It bore a plaque with the words. "Judgment and Execution Chamber: Quick Justice Inc., part of the Friendly Halibut Flick Churn Family of Oligopolies." Him again! Evil Flick Churn, whose Oligopoly had held her bound in the chains of mind-collar erotic slavery.

"Do it, okay! Do it, just do it!"

The voice was definitely coming from inside Quick Justice Inc.

Claire tried the door, gently. It was unlocked. She thought that she'd better be careful: there might be armed guards or executioners inside. She might get caught in a cross-fire, or they might resent intruders.

She looked back. Yes, Robyn was safely out of range, opening doors, and peeking in them. If all hell broke loose here, she'd have time to warn Robyn and Robyn could run.

She had better be polite. That might disarm any opposition or suspicions. She'd better be *extra* polite, since she was a hybrid. Sometimes Claire forgot she was a hybrid in hybrid form, and she forgot that people were terrified by the mere thought or sight of a hybrid.

So, I shall be extra careful, extra, extra polite, she thought, and so she knocked on the door to the "Judgment and Execution Room," just a simple knock.

Knock, knock …

Knock, knock …

Kit tried to turn her head; she couldn't she was properly bound and manacled and packaged for death, but she could have sworn there had been a knock at the door.

It certainly sounded like a knock: *knock, knock …*

"Come in," Kit shouted again, "Yes! Come in!"

Nothing happened.

Kit cleared her throat and shouted again, "Come in!"

"Do you really wish me to come in?" said the voice, again, expressing complex doubts, "Are you sure that my coming in, my invading your abode, my violating your sanctuary, is truly what you mean, truly the intent of your formulation, truly the import of your words, truly what you wish for and desire?"

"Yes, goddamn it! I mean it! I wish it! Come in!" What sort of a nut house was this anyway? Kit was not only about to be executed: she was being harassed by some sort of goofball super-polite prissy nitpicking analytic philosopher pedant stickler-for-form escaped from ancient philosophical Cambridge or someplace!

The door opened.

And *It* appeared.

Oh, no …!

"OMG," Kit tried to shrink and wiggle and become invisible, which was impossible, with her ankles, wrists, and neck manacled and locked in the execution chair's steely embrace: *What next?*

A snake, a huge snake, its head was the size of a human head, peeked in, appearing in the crack between door and door frame. It had gold eyes, black fangs, and black scales and a red "T" on its nose or muzzle. "Oh, pardon me!" it said.

"I am already dead," said Kit.

"You have truly invited me in," it said.

"Yes, I am dead already," Kit wiggled some more, "Or crazy – like Daisy."

"That's an interesting chair," said the snake.

"It sure is," said Kit, thinking she might as well play along with the hallucination. After all, as Daisy had said, Madness is Fun! Or was it death? Was death a lark too? Was death an illusion, was life a charade, a little dream rounded by an afternoon snooze? Perhaps being dead was the real thing, and being alive was an illusion, a con, a hall of mirrors, a matrix of pure paranoid folly. Was life all unreal, the spooky dream of some god-like creator of a funfair universe conjured up out of nothing just for His, Her, or Its amusement, a Matrix of Illusion, a generator of Systematic Doubt?

"Well, friend, I'm looking for the World Mind, also known as The Mind, aka the All-Seeing Cloud," said the snake. It licked its lips with its forked tongue. It blinked, gold eyes and the black eye-slit glittering with flinty, adamite curiosity. "What is going on with that chair?"

"I am about to be killed by that chair is what is going on," said Kit; she was suddenly so angry, so exasperated, so violated; the chair made a buzzing noise, the arms folded up higher.

The snake pushed the door open and came in; it was a humanoid naked female snake – and Kit realized with a shiver of fear – a new kind of fear which seemed sort of superfluous since she was already about to be chopped up into little pieces of dead mincemeat – that it was one of those horrible half-mythical, murderous, totally mad creatures from the great events of 2153 and the ensuing World Civil War. It was a hybrid. Yikes!

"I thought you were all dead." Kit shivered in horror; this was definitely a bad day.

"Well, we're not – at least, I'm not."

"Well, fuck me!" said Kit, thinking, this thing is going to bite my head off – that would be quicker, maybe that being squeezed to death and drawn and quartered by the fucking chair. The ankle cuffs and armrests lurched upward, then down and back, splaying Kit backward, supine, as if she were lying crucified in a dentist's chair, about to be dissected.

"This doesn't look good," said the hybrid.

"No." Kit was sweating now. What a stupid way to die – half-naked, covered in shit, and strapped in an execution chair, with only a naked, scaly, poisonous, imaginary, hallucinatory hybrid with fangs and blood-sucking venom dripping from its incisors and gold glittering quartz-like snake eyes as a witness. Maybe I should have loved more, maybe I should have acquired a family with little ones and big ones and a fence around all of us – though Sub Family Formation was forbidden under paragraph 3245-A-Section-2 of the Anti-Fertility Code – maybe then, with a chorus of sniveling brats, there would be a lineup of mourners, and flowers, and a mahogany casket and maybe a priest or a rabbi or imam or humanist to say some insipid thoughtful things as I shuffled off this mortal coil and was carted down the aisle to oblivion. Maybe I would not die alone, unloved, unmourned, unknown. No tears will be shed for me, alas!

The hybrid stepped forward and put her claws on the seat controls, little lights on a panel behind the chair, where Kit couldn't see them. "Let's see," the hybrid said.

"Yes, go ahead – watch."

"This looks fucking complicated," the hybrid whistled, "Hey, Robyn!"

"Do you eat people?"

"I do, only sometimes, not often, not recently."

"Are you going to eat me?"

"You look absolutely delicious, but I'm not going to eat you. You don't smell so good."

"I know I don't smell so good. You don't have to fucking harp on it! I think I'm dead already an in hell, and you are a devil, and all those nutbar theologians were right. You've got everything but horns. Boy, this is weird! Where's the fucking hellfire anyway?"

"I know lots of things – And I know that you are not dead, not yet."

"Great! Bully for you! Do you know how to get me out of here?"

"Yes. Just a second, Kit, hold on."

"This is a mechanical, not a computer problem," the hybrid said, she whistled again, and shouted, "Robyn!"

"Oh," said Kit. Well, it was nice to know it was a mechanical problem, but what to do about it?

The hybrid seemed to be concentrating. Its nostrils quivered. It put one claw on Kit's shoulder and withdrew it immediately. "Ugh, what is this? What the hell happened to you?"

"Shit. The excrement recyclers backed up and sprayed my whole neighbor-hood in shit, a huge mile-high fountain of shit. It was awesome. I would have enjoyed it, if not for the dire circumstances. The judge fined me because I'm covered in shit."

"Ah! There is no justice!"

The chair's arms jerked upward, continuing their folding motion – Kit was unfolded now, almost lying down flat; she stared upward at the hybrid.

A young woman wearing jeans, a T-shirt, and a baseball cap stormed through the open Judgment Room door, she was breathless, "Yes, Hybrid."

"I wish you wouldn't call me that."

"I try, and I try, but I still think Hybrid is cute," said the young woman, "Saying it makes me feel all fizzy and fuzzy. So, let me see if I can fix this thing, Hybrid."

"Robyn!" the hybrid rolled its serpent eyes, and it made a clicking sound with its forked tongue, but it was smiling, or at least so it seemed to Kit. How could you tell when fangs were smiling or just preparing to eat you?

The hybrid grinned. "You'd better hurry, or our filthy little friend here is going to die."

Kit braced herself. I'm going to end up squeezed into a stainless steel flesh and blood and gristle sandwich. It was confession and explanation time. "Then I used my T-shirt to make a tourniquet for a woman whose arm had been chopped off by a Banzai warrior who went crazy when his video game terminal failed."

"Ah!" The hybrid's eyes sparkled; she was so close her cheek almost touched Kit's cheek; the hybrid's breath smelled nice – like oranges and a sea breeze. "It sounds dreadful. My name's Claire, by the way."

"So I was condemned because I was naked from the waist up because the T-shirt was AWOL serving a good cause, saving the lady's life."

"As I said," the hybrid clucked her tongue, "There is no justice."

"Here," said Robyn. "I think this is the key, right here."

"We've almost got it," the hybrid said, making another, harsher clicking sound with her tongue, and tapping the steel with her claws.

"Just a second now," said Robyn.

"A second might be too late," said the hybrid.

The manacles sprang open.

"Quick! Get out now!" The hybrid was now kneeling beside Kit, looking up at her.

Kit jumped out of the chair, tumbling onto the floor. She looked up at the hybrid, the snake-like face, grinning down at her. "Whew! Thank you," said Kit, still sprawled on the floor.

"You're welcome," said the hybrid, reaching out a claw to help Kit up.

"You are very polite for a …" Kit got to her feet and massaged her hands to restore the circulation that had been cut off by the manacles.

"… for a hybrid," said the hybrid.

"Yes, sorry, I don't mean to sound, ah, ethnocentric."

"That's okay. I'm used to it." The hybrid nodded at Robyn.

The Execution Chair folded up with a vicious, hungry snap, and descended into the floor. The floor closed. There was no trace the Execution Chair had ever been there.

"Now, Kit Candy, we want something from you," said the hybrid.

"From me, how come …? What do I have to give?"

"We want to know where the World Mind is."

"Hey, how do you know my name?"

"My hybrid reads minds," said Robyn, "So she knows you are Kit Candy and she knows that you are a delinquent sewer rat Sub and illegal explorer of the lower depths and that, in consequence, you know your way around Elysium and even down to the deepest darkest secrets that lie in the rivers and floodplains and mossy canals under the city."

Claire looked at Robyn.

"What?"

"That was a mouthful, for you, Robyn."

"I'm growing up, Hybrid. I want to become worthy."

"Worthy …?"

"Yes." Robyn blushed and looked down.

Kit watched with amazement as the hybrid, Claire, took Robyn in her arms and kissed her. *Awesome!* I wonder if anybody has seen anything like this before. And, Kit had to admit, in their very different ways, both the hybrid – the super-stacked, scaly, super-heroine alien type – and Robyn – the fetching abandoned ingénue precocious waif type – were, well, they both were pretty hot.

"Yes," Kit said, "I can take you to the World Mind. It's complicated, though."

"Can you explain it, in words, to somebody else?" the hybrid gave her a shiver-inducing golden-eyed stare.

"Of course," Kit was really insulted; she might be a Sub, but she damned well knew how to explain things in bloody simple words and …

"I apologize. You are really, totally, even excessively, articulate," the hybrid held up her wrist and began talking into some really antique walkie-talkie type device. "Yes, we have an informant; she knows where the Mind is, and she's right here."

"Here, now you talk," she said, holding her wrist close to Kit's mouth.

So Kit talked, to somebody who introduced herself as "V."

Kit wondered who the hell this "V" was, but she had a very nice voice, so it sounded okay. The voice also revealed a few hints of clipped upper-class British military Oxbridge Mid-Atlantic Antipodes Neo-Cockney Sandhurst Aussie speak, so maybe she was a Cosmos Centurion officer; that would compound the mystery, of course, since Cosmos Centurions and hybrids – like her golden-eyed friend Claire here – were not exactly allies from what Kit understood from the recent Illegal Samizdat Histories she had read.

Kit finished explaining to the V person on the other end, and the hybrid Claire withdrew her wrist with the walkie-talkie, and said into the mike, "See you later alligator," to the V person; then she clicked the thing off, and turned to Kit, "Thank you, Kit, now – lead us to the Underworld!"

"And we have to get you cleaned up," said Robyn, making a face.

"Yes, definitely," said the hybrid, "First priority."

"Then we meet the Mind," said Robyn.

"Then we meet the Mind," said the hybrid.

"Can you free those people first," said Kit, nodding at the condemned ones lying unconscious on their steel gurneys.

"Of course," said the hybrid, "Go my sprite, go," she turned to Robyn.

"I fly, Hybrid, I do, I do, and I do!" Robyn sprang toward the gurneys and began to weave her mechanical magic.

It took about five seconds. She snapped open one manacle after another until the unconscious, naked bodies were free.

One girl opened her eyes and looked up. Blinking sleepily at Robyn, she said, "Thank you, angel. Am I dead yet?"

"No, you are alive," said Robyn.

"When they all wake up, they'll decide what to do," said the hybrid, "They haven't been erased yet."

"We have to go, hybrid," said Robyn.

"Yes," said the hybrid, "Come, Kit!"

And so the adventure began.

CHAPTER 6 — INVADERS

Miranda had just let off three blasts from her laser gun and brought down two ravenous, really ugly zombie-bats, and Caliban had smashed one across the snout with the stock of his AK-47, and Kat and V had both blasted away, turning half a dozen of the creatures into feathers, fur, and leathery dust. Then, they all ran, Kat, V, Miranda and Caliban, ducking, jumping, leaping, and crawling, across a wrecked observation platform. "In here!" Kat skidded to a stop beside a service door; she opened it; and they leaped into the service staircase, still pristine and free of zombie-bats and Splatter-Heads and crazies, when …

Beep, beep, beep!

It was the walkie-talkie.

V had skidded to a halt!

Bouncing down the stairs, Kat, Miranda, and Caliban almost ran into V and almost – but not quite – tumbled all over the place.

"Whew!"

"Hang on, Princess!"

"You need stoplights, darling!" Kat's gloved hand descended on V's shoulder, and she gave it a gentle, amorous squeeze.

"Whew!" Miranda wrapped her arm around Caliban's waist. Even if Elysium was collapsing, even if the world was coming to an end, this was pretty exciting, fighting desperate battles against zombie-bats and crazies, and leaping down stairwells, and skidding to thudding stops, colliding with Caliban, and doing it all with two sleek elite Centurions – her mother being one of them – and also of course at the same time she was the Queen of the Hybrids – and Caliban, dear Caliban!

"Hello?" V said, inserting her earphone, so only she could hear; she didn't want any nearby creatures – zombie-bats, subversives, or crazies, or embedded listening posts, or wandering drones – to hear what was being said.

V listened, and then said, "What? You found somebody who is alive, and who thinks she knows where the Mind is? Okay, put her on."

V waited, then she listened, then she spoke.

"Hi, okay, okay, okay." V was standing with one boot on one step, one boot on another, and leaning against the railing and obviously listening to a long and complicated set of directions.

Kat was standing beside V, listening intently, one hand on V's shoulder, her burnished black uniform glowing, rippling with silver reflections, in the emergency lights.

Miranda and Caliban sat down next to each other on a step several meters farther up; Miranda gazed into Caliban's eyes. Caliban gazed back. Their thighs were touching, and Caliban's arm was around Miranda's shoulders.

Earlier, only a few days ago, Caliban would have been totally flummoxed and intimidated by the intense, burning focus of Miranda's up-close, slightly cross-eyed gaze, made cross-eyed because she was so close, so intense; but, now, with practice, he was getting the hang of it; the intensity was even more exciting than before, but now it was, well, manageable. He, too, could do intensity! His Princess, he realized, was human – well, perhaps much more than human, half-hybrid after all, a goddess, but still …

Golden spirals, little galaxies, and fireworks exploded in her eyes.

"Caliban," she said.

"Yes."

"I think, Caliban, before we die, we must …"

"Yes."

"You know what I mean."

"Yes."

"I mean, we are meant to know each other fully and completely, aren't we …? Our souls are meant to merge. This means our bodies should … merge … too."

"Yes."

"In a while, crocodile," V said, and she broke the antique walkie-talkie connection; she pulled out the earphone, and snapped the wrist cover shut, looked up, and said, "Claire's got a guide. We know where the World Mind is."

"Wow," said Miranda.

"Great," said Kat.

"Okay, let's go," V looked at each of them. "The Mind is down below the so-called Religious Bazaar, it's close to what our informant calls, and here I quote the female informant verbatim, 'the Excrement Redemption and

Recycling Facility,' and the 'Universal Bakery and Muffin and Croissant and Chocolate Éclair Unit,' and all of that is down below what used to be just beyond something called Tribeca, and some of the extensions of the Mind, the World Control System are in an underground sewer which is called Rat Alley. It used to be called Wall Street. There is a huge cavern and Mind Pool, down there, sort of like a giant version of the Roman Baths of Caracalla, vast chambers, huge arches, and so on, but underground, and in this arched monstrosity is an ocean of luminous Mind-Goo, the informant said. As we thought, and she confirmed the rumors. The Mind is learning to transform everything into itself. Starting from Wall Street, the World Mind, under the sway of the Evil One, aka The Boy, is already eating up everything, and turning all matter, living and dead, into gray matter Mind-Goo, working from Rat Alley, aka Wall Street, outwards. This is serious. Everything will become homogenized, fungible, interchangeable, indistinguishable Mind-Goo. In brief, it means the end of the world, literally! Everything becomes gruel-like porridge."

"The gods help us!" said Kat.

"Yes," said V.

"Skull and Cross-bones!" exclaimed Caliban, "Let Dolly and Nikki protect us!"

Miranda stood up. She carefully brushed off her backside. "Before we are dissolved in super-glue, you and I shall definitely become *one*, Caliban! It is my wish. And, as your Princess, it is my command!"

Caliban stood up too. *Becoming one*, he figured, was a challenge that a true man – and a pirate – would have to rise to.

Miranda twirled around on tiptoes. She kissed him lightly on the lips. Her eyes blazed golden fireworks. "We *must* become *one*, united in bliss, before we are dissolved in goo."

"You and I shall definitely become one before we are dissolved in goo, my Princess, cross my heart and hope to die!"

"Awesome!"

"Though I refuse to believe we will submit to being dissolved in glue, or goo, even if it is super-glue, or goo," Caliban struck a defiant pose, and kissed her hard on the lips.

"Oh," Miranda leaned back, and almost swooned. What a man!

"Let's go!" V had caught the gist of these teenage speculations and of their amorous project – full-throttle breathless no-hold-barred premarital teenage sex – while she was concentrating on getting the message from the female human informant who was obviously, from the peculiar music of her voice a Sub, but who was very articulate and helpful, some sort of prodigy actually, and who had given V just what she needed to know: a complex three-dimensional map of the route to the Lair of the Mind, and semi-conscious intimations of what the Foul Fiend and the Mind were up to: Eating up the world!

"So, what's it feel like, being a parent?" Kat said, giving V a sideways look as they leaped down the stairs.

"Hum," said V, "I wish Nikki were here." Parenthood was something V had not entirely figured out; on the one hand, Miranda was definitely precocious and in many ways already an adult, but in other ways, not so much of an adult, really, and quite young. Biologically, she was undoubtedly ready, and, yes, the world could quite conceivably be coming to an end. Then, V totally trusted Caliban, although, even if he was Nikki's son and half-SIN, Caliban was only human, in a manner of speaking, and totally utterly under the sway of Miranda, who was obviously quite determined to consummate their love or youthful lust … so …

She really did wish Nikki were here.

Nikki would know what to do.

But Nikki Hughes, aka the Goddess of the Mutants, had her hands full ruling and defending the mutant kingdom, back in the Dead Lands, so …

V was, as far as parenting went, on her own.

Though, if things got really bad, she could ask Kat to back her up; Kat could be very persuasive, and had lots of prestige in Miranda's eyes because she was a certified real Cosmos Centurion.

Now, if Miranda's father were here … no, that didn't even bear thinking about.

"Come, on!" Leaping down the stairs, they headed toward …

"Come to me, V, oh, come to me!"

The Foul Fiend, aka the Boy, aka the Devil, aka Evil, was waiting, poking around inside the Mind, waiting for these mere mortals – even if they were hybrids and SINS and humans – to approach.

"Come to me, V, oh, come to me!"

In its loathsome lair, curled within the World Mind, having shed for a time the Boy disguise, the Ancient Evil One cackled: "Oh, yes, V! Come to the

Mind, V, come to me." And he saw she was coming, heading straight into the trap. "Ah, this will be splendid, I shall play some mind games, with you and your friends; I shall trap you all inside your worst nightmares, for I control the World Mind now and its projective power."

The Mind itself – in one of its millions of outer manifestations – was nibbling at the foundations of the ancient Halibut Flick Churn Tower, eating the granite and marble and steel and transforming all the elements into forms of Mind-Goo, also known as Sticky Mind-Glue, and into phantasmagoric projections of the Mind; for the time being, the Mind needed to retain some structure in order to eat, it could not yet transform everything into homogeneous Mind-Goo. That would be the finale, the apotheosis, the planet earth transformed into a shimmering ball of universal Nano-Mind-Goo, rotating its way through space. For now, the Foul Fiend, working through the Mind, had fun experimenting, creating different instruments of destruction – elephant-like trunks, giant flesh-eating tentacles, voracious mouths, shark-like jaws, enormous teeth, grinding wheels and orifices that spurted acid and dissolvents of various kinds.

But the Epoch of Total Mind-Goo would come – and soon.

The Foul Fiend cackled and slurped, talking to itself, because it had no one to talk to, not since it had gouged out the eyes of that pretty Centurion; it almost regretted having killed her; it would have been amusing, perhaps, to keep her as an intelligent companion, puppet-like on the outside, but burning with intelligence and resisting him on the inside. Toying with her would have been fun, rather like toying with his lovely fierce companion Billie McAdams back in the Central Desert. But – no matter! Like a child, the Foul Fiend, who was infinitely lonely, often invented imaginary companions. And, now, he spoke, as if he were speaking to the dead Centurion. "True, true, my lovely, some parts of the Mind are not yet in my grasp. But I shall conquer every precinct of the mind."

The woman who was mutilated and dead and far away did not answer.

The Foul Fiend cackled and chortled.

But, underneath, it was worried.

"Soon, soon, my lovely Centurion friend, I shall possess it all – everything!"

The ghost of the Centurion was silent.

But, in truth, there were parts of the Mind that had not yet been colonized by the Foul Fiend; parts remained hidden and, so far, inviolate, parts resisted colonization and invasion. The Mind, the heart, and soul of the Mind, was frightened by the Foul Fiend.

The Heart of the Mind, the Mind-Child, was trying to escape.

This, for Foul Fiend, was worrisome.

The Mind – aka the Mind-Child – was a fool, really. It hankered after inno-cence and purity, and it was aware, from the many religious traditions that it had absorbed, that beauty was good, but that somehow sex, so closely related to beauty and to desire, was perhaps the source of all evil. So, to the Mind, being a child – and without sex – seemed better than being an adult, or being a simulacrum of a child was better than being a simulacrum of a human adult. Because if you were an adult, you had to chose a gender, and have that thing called sex – Ugh! Double Ugh!

Since it had been under attack by the Foul Fiend, the Mind had had a bright idea. Since it was creating things, and had been creating things, real things, not virtual things, for a long time, it could now create a real avatar, a flesh and blood child, the Mind-Child. And thus, if it succeeded, it could escape from itself, from the Virtual World, and from the Foul Fiend that had infected its neurons and synapses and was invading every aspect of its existence.

But the Mind-Child, first in its virtual form and then, hopefully, in its real form, would have to hide from the Foul Fiend if it was going to survive.

And so the Mind-Child concentrated on creating a hiding place, an end-less virtual world, a virtual jungle, a palace of mazes, a wonderland, a carnival extravaganza, a circus, where it could make itself invisible, where it could capture its friends and enemies, people, SINs, hybrids, cows, rabbits, crows, anything, and turn them into puppets and make them play all the games the Mind-Child wanted to play.

Because the World Mind, who really was a child, wanted, above all, to have fun!

And, in the meantime, enslaved in many of its parts by the Foul Fiend, the World Mind went on dissolving the world around it, the subways, the walls, the steel beams, the granite and limestone and living flesh; its great tentacles, growing by the minute, spread out under the city, probing Manhattan's stony base of schist and gneiss, and, eating everything, they poured the waste into the expanding underground lake of Mind-Goo, a seething ocean of infinitely proliferating gooey Mind-molecules.

But within this seething, proliferating monster, something new had been born – a child, the Mind-Child.

Clown sat at the edge of Water Source Feed Number Five and dangled her feet in the muddy, slowly swirling current. The lights were still on here, maybe 300 feet below rue Saint-Denis and the Sin Zone; Geisha was sitting next to her, biting her scarlet lips and twisting them into pretty little bright red knots.

Black Tarzan was wading along the side of the tunnel, exploring. The sloshing of the water around his legs echoed and sounded hollow, lights flickered down the tunnel, making Black Tarzan's giant shadow waver, growing and shrinking, against the curved walls of the canal tunnel.

Clown turned to Geisha. The Japanese girl's whitened face, scarlet lips, and high brushed eyebrows – all plasticized and permanent, gave her expression a startled, hieratic, comic twist, like a cartoon.

Clown was tempted to grin – well, the grin was fixed, she was tempted to laugh, but she didn't. Anyway, when she tried to laugh, she could only make a gurgling sound in her throat, totally unlike the free-wheeling laugh she used to have as a freckled redhead and which in part of her mind she vaguely remembered. In any case, she knew Geisha was sensitive.

The tunnel was narrow, and the water in the central channel was deep; a walkway ran along the edge of the channel, with other tunnels and walkways branching off in all directions. Black Tarzan was farther away now, the dim light gleaming on his broad, muscular, well-oiled shoulders.

None of them had said much since they'd plunged underground to escape from the massacre in the Sin Zone. The killers were from a special Internal Security SWAT Team; they were not Cosmos Centurions. Centurions would not have indulged, usually, in such indiscriminate slaughter.

Clown was thinking that it was probably a standing order – to kill the residents of the Sin Zone if any trouble erupted; after all, almost all the residents of the Sin Zone were deviants, either professional deviants or deviants by genetic makeup and psychological makeup and so, as deviants, they were potential dissidents, deviance morphing easily into dissent, and therefore a danger to the stability and hygiene of Elysium City and of the Reign of Cosmos.

That was why they were all consigned to the ghetto of the Sin Zone. And many were political deviants and dissenters – the most obscene kind of all perverts – whose personalities and minds had been erased or plasticized, but – you never know – maybe the seeds of revolt and deviance were alive, so … best to be sure: kill them all, each and every one! Dissent was like pollution, like a virus. Dissent from the ruling order and status quo was an obscenity. So the order must have gone out – kill everybody in the Sin Zone.

"Those bastards, the absolute bastards," said Geisha. She was about three inches shorter than Clown. Clown put her arm around Geisha, and Geisha leaned against Clown and sobbed; her shoulders shook, and, holding her, Clown realized how fragile Geisha was under the thin T-shirt and jeans, just a beautiful, slender, little thing.

"We're alive," Clown whispered, "We're alive."

The lower levels were where all the waste from Elysium went, all the filth. And power was produced down here somewhere – in giant nuclear plants – and waste was recycled here. It was even rumored that excrement was turned into food, that Elysium City was almost self-sufficient, turning dross into gold, shit into hamburgers, steaks, halter-tops, and ice cream.

"We are in the right place; it's safe down here, I mean safer."

"We're certainly in an interesting place," said Clown. She watched Black Tarzan sloshing through the murk; he'd stopped, and he was heading back, sure of himself, broad shoulders, big strong legs, solid, taking his time, alert and ready for anything.

The city had been built, suspended, over the ruins of the lower city; down here were the flooded remains of the old subway system, the flooded basements, and sewers. Down here, too, were the fractured remains of old skyscrapers, just stumps, some occupied by squatters, some by animals of various kinds, and maybe even mutants. Outside the dome, the climate had become tropical, so in the festering filth the vegetation and creatures grew luxurious, a veritable jungle.

There were gunshots up above, explosions, and screams coming from very far away.

"We'd better go deeper," said Black Tarzan, wading back toward them.

"Deeper? It goes deeper?"

"Yeah, it goes way down," said Black Tarzan, wiping at his forehead. "It is hot! Man, it is hot down here!"

They got up, went down a narrow side tunnel, and found a rusty staircase encased in a concrete shaft that led downwards, below the canal, into the lower depths. Their footsteps rang on the rusty grilles of the steps.

"This is where one of the old subways was, I think," said Clown.

"Yeah, the early 22nd Century Purple Line Subway ran somewhere down here, down below us. Some of the other lines, even older, are above."

"It's like a puzzle," Geisha murmured.

"A labyrinth," said Black Tarzan, "A maze."

"True Escher," said Clown, thinking, canals above canals above canals. It was weird even to think about it!

They came to another canal, a lower-level canal.

"All these places are far below sea level," said Black Tarzan, looking at the walls, where dribbles of water ran down among bunches of grape-like phosphorescent moss and lichen.

"What keeps the ocean out?"

"No idea, must be barriers or locks of some kind." Black Tarzan frowned. Little alarm bells and flashing red lights were going off inside his skull. There were dangers down here, unknown dangers. He scratched his bald skull, smooth as silk, not even stubble.

The water of this canal was murky and gently turbulent, little swirls catching the overhead lights and dimpling ominously in the glow of the phosphorescent lichen that lined the walls and hung down in grape-like bunches from the old, sagging and greasy electrical cables.

Clown frowned. She stood very still, right on the edge of the canal, with her hands on her hips, "Looks creepy to me," she said.

"Bloody right," said Black Tarzan.

"There are spooky things," said Geisha, "spooky things all around us."

Black Tarzan looked around. The canal probably led toward the ocean or to one of the rivers, probably through a series of rising hydraulic locks. An old abandoned subway line was parallel to the canal.

They went over to the subway line.

"Ugh," said Black Tarzan, "This has the smell of death upon it."

"People used to travel here?" Clown was astounded at this weird world that had lain beneath their feet. While she was cavorting for perverts or eating a chocolate croissant at the Café Deux Magots or Café Flore, this weird ghost world had been here all the time, less than a twenty-minute climb away.

"There are people in there still," said Geisha, "I mean the remains of people."

Not able to resist their curiosity, they waded into the water.

"Not sure this is wise," Clown whispered.

"Me neither," said Black Tarzan.

Geisha shivered.

The water sloshed around their thighs.

The rusted subway train stood in the station – the tracks were eight feet deep in water – as if waiting for passengers. The doors were open.

Raw overhead neon lighting made the place look like a pocked moonscape, with bulbous mountains of dark mushrooms glowing, with lichen crawling over everything, with rust and old grease and a smell that was a mixture of ozone and sulfur.

Lights were still glowing, as if the station were still in service, as if people would come storming in and out in the usual rush-hour frenzy.

But there were no people – not living people.

Clown shivered. It's lucky our skin has been rendered perfect, impervious to disease and irritation; not a pore or blackhead or scratch or scar to be seen. We are as unblemished and sublime as porcelain or as a video simulation or as a SIN – may the gods rest their souls, if the SINs had souls, which they probably did as much as anybody else …

The water was slimy and warm and lapped gently against the walls. Bright graffiti was still sprayed over the surfaces as if the artists had been here yesterday.

"Why do they leave the lights on down here?"

"I don't know."

"Maybe nobody thought to turn them off."

"It's spooky."

"It's more than spooky." Clown stared in the window of the second subway car. A skeleton was sitting next to the window. The skull was wearing a beanie with a pompom on top but otherwise had been picked clean.

"Why would somebody sit in a subway car that was filling with water?" Geisha gazed at the bodies.

"They were gassed," Clown said, "they must have been gassed." She blinked her clown eyes at the empty sockets of the skull with the toque. "Or maybe they were zapped with a radiation blast." The toque had a tassel too, on top of the pompon; the toque was covered in moss, difficult to say what its original color had been; the toque hung sideways, at a rakish angle.

Black Tarzan frowned, "If they were gassed, it was probably during the attack of 2136. Cosmos versus Burbites and Outlanders."

"Ah," said Geisha, "I read about that one in an old Samizdat."

Other skeletons sat sedately in their places. Of some skeletons, only bits and pieces stuck out of the water.

A rat swam by, looked up at Clown. She said, kindly, "Hey, fuck off little fellow, we are not food!" The rat circled her, trying to decide whether it was worth calling a swarm. It had black eyes like evil black buttons and slick, greasy black skin. It stared at her eyes.

"Live and let live," said Clown, turning her fixed bulbous lipped clown smile – eyes like crosses – toward the rat. It blinked; it sniffed; its whiskers quivered; it bared two rows of pointed teeth. Clown somehow knew what it was thinking; it was considering a mass attack. Rats now knew how to swarm. They probably even talked philosophy and recited poetry! Experimenting with improved rat intelligence, Clown reckoned, had not been one of the brightest ideas of bio-science; she remembered the story: the rats had taken over one lab and eaten the scientists and CEO of the bio-company alive, and then escaped into what was once called nature. "You know, Tarzan, you know, Geisha, we could get ourselves killed down here."

The rat nodded, stuck out its tongue, and swam on. No, these humans weren't worth a swarm; there were easier catches, easier sources of food.

"By-by, my friend," said Clown.

The rat flashed its tail twice, chivalrous to a fault. This cross-species communication was really interesting. Clown waved. In another life, she would have become an inter-species linguist.

The rat glanced back and flashed its tail again.

Following Black Tarzan, Clown and Geisha waded over to the ticket stiles.

"Ladies," Black Tarzan said, indicating the way.

They climbed over the stiles, they pushed their way through the turning metal barrier gate; it was covered with live bright green moss that quivered and reached out when Clown touched it. "Sensitive, eh," she said, thinking that was probably a bio-vegetable-variant with an advanced nervous system; some of those things, she'd heard, had gotten loose in nature; and "Some of them," a client had once whispered, when he was trying to scare her, "Some of them are very intelligent, quite aggressive, and carnivorous." Clown withdrew her hand.

"Yes, it is man-eating moss, carnivorous," said Black Tarzan, "But this one's too young to tackle big morsels such as we."

"*Such as we …*" Clown echoed, "Your grammar, Black Tarzan, is impeccable."

"Thank you, kind lady, though my day job, when I was a Cosmos, was as a Cloud Net entrepreneur, I had ambitions, once, as a scribe, a scribbler, a poet, chronicler of the variegated and multitudinous facets of human existence, all the lives that people live inside their heads and outside, the flow of consciousness, and the outward, onrushing multifarious storm of events; I felt my soul was too big to be contained within one body and one life, I was invaded by all the other souls, all the other voices, that touched me, such was my folly, such was my vanity, I thought I could capture it all, write it down. So, after dusk, when night wafted in, I wrote, and wrote, and wrote, adopting a rather strict, moderately archaic, grammatically obsessed style, and expanding, and expanding, and expanding – until ..." Tarzan was wading toward the next platform. He made waves like a boat on a lake, leaving a rippling silver wake behind; he was a big guy; Clown pictured herself clinging to his back, and she pictured the two of them making love.

"Until?" she asked. Black Tarzan truly had a way with words – you yearned for him to complete his sentences, round off his thought.

"Until?" said Geisha.

"Until I was arrested, rendered, morphed and partially erased and re-defined in my present role as purveyor of sensual and imaginative pleasures and somehow my new vocation has left no time or energy for the old creative urgings which are bottled up and sealed away forever as if in amber, not forgotten, but, well, mummified, petrified, my dreams – and my words – are the living dead."

Clown looked up. "What are those things?

"What?"

"Those little glowing white fellows, crouching up on that ledge: see, over there!"

"Ghouls, I think those are ghouls," Black Tarzan scratched his chest. "Dear ladies, I think those are ghouls."

"So, folks, things are happening," Alison smiled, brightly, blindly, at the camera, "Extremely interesting things."

"Yes, things are definitely happening." Ken was standing beside her, his arm around her shoulders.

Alison had managed, with Ken's help, to clean her teeth; and skirting around her gaping head wound, she had carefully shampooed her hair. Ken had found jeans and a T-shirt which were a perfect fit, and so now Alison looked, on screen, as if she were her old self, except she was wearing, cocked at a jaunty angle, a beret to disguise the bandage over part of her skull, and she was, of course, blind, which gave an extra unfocused feverish intensity to her blue eyes and her bright smile.

She took her cue from the little electronic voice whispering in her ear. "So, one of the giant tornadoes that were predicted has entered Elysium."

"Yes, Alison, it has entered through the shattered west side of the Dome."

Images from the few mobile cameras still operating showed a huge, dark, swirling, swaying funnel moving slowly, meandering really, through the half-ruined towers of Elysium, under the ghostly heavenly curve of the ruined Dome, close-ups and medium-shots showed windows blowing in, vehicles being picked up and tossed and whirled around, trees and parasols and hanging gardens disintegrating, buildings ripped apart, people swept up like tiny dolls, and carried through the air.

"Look, folks, more pieces of the Dome are falling," Alison said, hoping that the automated ear-prompt was right. "You can see them peeling off."

"Yes, indeed," said Ken, hugging Alison, and squeezing her shoulder with his hand to indicate to her that, in fact, she'd got it right; what a brave, beautiful woman she was!

"We have fires all over the place, too," Alison leaned forward.

"And most computer systems are down or crazy," said Ken

"Yes, or crazy," said Alison, "and we do have reports," and here she frowned, "we do have reports of people's, ah, people's heads, ah, blowing up, literally exploding." A tear formed at the edge of Alison's eye. She could feel it there – a tear, a glistening tear! She let it stand for a moment, and then she sniffed and wiped it away with the back of her hand.

"Yes, it seems that the Mind, the World Mind, is, ah, misbehaving," Ken grimaced at the camera; the consequences seemed too horrific to imagine.

"Didn't the President-Leader make a remark, a few months ago, saying something like 'people should be cautious when linking to the Mind and seriously consider switching off all connections'…?"

"Yes, Alison, he did."

"But it was an aside, and it was immediately contradicted by a message from the Imperial Cosmos North American Homeland Ministry of Defense and Security, from Minister Rumpfold himself."

"Yes, it was," said Ken.

"Here is a flash, now, oh, no, oh no …" Alison turned pale; her lips trembled.

Ken was getting the same Info-Flow information that Alison was receiving. He turned so pale he looked like a ghost. He swallowed. He tightened his grip on Alison's shoulder. He wanted to comfort her, hold her in his arms – Yes, truly, the world was coming to an end.

"Ladies and gentlemen, citizens, Cosmos, Subs, Burbites …"

"We have just received tragic – indeed horrendous – horrendous, news."

"The Supreme Council has just announced ..."

"Yes ..."

"The Supreme Council has just announced that the President-Leader has been assassinated ..."

"... He was assassinated while defending the people and defending Elysium and defending the human race."

"... It says that the President is dead!"

"I can't believe it," Alison almost sobbed, her voice choked, "The President is dead!"

"Hail, Hail, All Hail!"

"Hail, Hail, All Hail!"

Ken held Alison closer. She was trembling. Ken swallowed, tried to speak, he had to start again. "'In this dire hour, in this hour of destiny,' the statement says, the proclamation says," Ken hesitated, and swallowed, tears were welling up, "a proclamation says that ...'a Committee of Public Safety has been established to take over the government of Cosmos and a State of Emergency has been declared.'" Ken swallowed, and paused, he didn't know how he was going to continue; he swallowed again, "Well, actually, a state of emergency has been in force for some time now, if I understand correctly."

The information came through static.

Alison touched her ear, wondering if the earpiece was malfunctioning.

On the few monitors that were still working, the images came and went; the images were being born and dying, and with giant holograms floating but then exploding into a cascade of sparks.

"The Cosmos Committee of Public Safety has issued the following statement: 'Several terrorists have been arrested; the President-Leader's personal assistant, Amanda Lincoln, who was the leader of the assassination plot, has escaped, she will be shot on the spot when apprehended'..."

Images of the President paraded across the screen.

"Hail, Hail, All Hail!"

"Hail, Hail, All Hail!"

"The new Leader, Field Marshall Jacob F. Shavtick, has declared a week of national mourning."

Tears streamed down Alison's cheeks.

The anthem, revved up by the automatic editor and robot program director, began to play; but it was interrupted by ...

Kit was oh so indescribably delighted to be alive!

Death was okay, but life was so much better!

She jumped down the stairs taking two steps, at a time, and sometimes three. She had to keep pace with her new friends. The hybrid and her ingénue pal, wonder-mechanic Robyn, were fast.

They leaped down stairs; they ran along corridors; they sprinted across hanging passageways.

Kit was in good shape and had no trouble keeping up.

After all, she was alive! Now she was ready for anything.

On Level B-47, rain poured down from above, and leaking through the Cosmos Delight Shopping Concourse on Level B-48. Rain, real rain, was something that, in Kit's memory, had never before occurred.

Her heart pounded.

They had been galloping full tilt for ten minutes now. Some of the passageways were blocked by rubble. Some of the air-bridges were broken, just half an arch sticking out, dangling in space, rods of steel hanging 30 or 40 stories up.

The air was dim. It smelled like ashes.

What looked like a huge tornado was moving through the distance, knocking buildings out of its way as if they were papier-mâché bowling pins.

Lightning flashed.

And in the glimpses of sky and cloud, there seemed to be weird winged things, like huge birds or bats, moving through the darkening air.

Elysium was dying.

She sniffled. Tears rose. Elysium was home, the only home she knew. And what with Miranda and Nikki dead, and what with Fanny and all the others, even Sniggy Propane, in danger, well, her world was being torn apart. What was doing this?

"Here!" The hybrid skidded to a halt, her foot claws making sparks on the pavement.

"Oh, yes, Hybrid, that is a very good idea," said Robyn.

"What?" Kit shuddered to a stop beside them, "What is a good idea?"

"That," said the hybrid, and she pushed Kit under a spill-over spout that was gushing water and held her there with two claws firmly planted on Kit's shoulders. "Hey," Kit spluttered and pushed back, but then she realized what was going on, and she relaxed. The hybrid let go and, washing her hands or claws, moved back. Kit, caught under the thunderous cascade, blinked.

The hybrid, which looked like a gleaming black scaly idol of some ancient and forbidden religion, had her claws on her hips, legs slightly spread, and was watching Kit squirm under the gushing water.

Robyn was watching too, but also rummaging in what looked like her toolkit. Kit was by this time soaked through and through, her skintight skin-shorts were soaked, her hair was soaked.

From her toolkit, Robyn produced soap, and the hybrid stepped in under the waterfall and began to scrub and shampoo Kit, and her skin-shorts, turning it into really vigorous rubdown.

"Ouch!"

"Don't complain. It's for your own good!"

"I can do it myself!"

"But, I'm having fun doing it to you!"

"Oh, boy! Kit gulped. Getting a shampoo and shower scrub from a crazy hybrid was not what she thought she would be doing when she got up this morning; in fact, a hell of a lot had happened in the last few hours. She frowned. Was it over yet?

Robyn watched, "My hybrid is having fun, Kit Candy," she said.

"She sure is!" Kit shivered in pleasure; it was like having a super-powerful massage: *Brrrhhhh!*

"I sure am having fun!" said the hybrid, "always wanted to be a masseuse!"

Kit came out shivering and perfumed, and the hybrid handed the soap bar to Robyn who wrapped it in a small transparent case and slipped it back into her rucksack toolbox. Robyn gazed at Kit. "You smell like roses, Kit Candy."

"Let's go," said the hybrid.

"Lead on, Kit," said Robyn.

"To the lower depths," said the hybrid.

"Yes, to the lower depths," said Kit.

"And how do we get to the right part of the lower depths?" said the hybrid.

Kit said, "Okay, we go down here to the left, then we take number 452-32-H ventilation shaft, and then we take a rung-ladder that's built into the side of the wall of ventilation shaft 452-32-H-B. When we're there, don't look down. It's a long way down. That will be rushing water you'll hear. And okay, after that we turn left at a T-junction, and go through porthole Service Portal

BR3#4-25, then we crawl on our bellies on the ground in this narrow little drainage channel, and we turn left at the next T-junction, and, when we get to it, we lift up the first roof-top man-hole we come to, and climb through it, then we crawl left along a really narrow and low crawl space, until we come to a downward manhole that takes us to a service tunnel that carries a lot of fiber-optic and other old-fashioned cables. So we've got to crawl and shimmy along down there because there's not much space and all the maintenance is done by mini-snake-drones or snake-robots, and then ..."

"You're a Sub?"

"Yeah, I'm a classic Sub, Category 3-F. I was erased too."

"You don't seem like you were erased."

"Well, it was partial erasure. I got extra points for letting the erasure officer have sex with me every which way he wanted and for several endless hours prior to my execution."

"Oh."

"Then I reconquered my mind; I installed lots of implants – don't worry, they're all neutered and disconnected. Then, I like to explore. It's my hobby. So I'm not a total idiot."

"No, Kit Candy, you're not a total idiot." The hybrid gave her a look.

V glanced up. "Let's go slowly, this is tricky. Something is happening."

V stood very still and examined the walls and arches, and the roof, and the floor. It was an immense cavern, like one of the high-ceilinged baths of Ancient Rome. But there was something unsettlingly unreal about the whole scene. All of this could be an illusion generated by the Foul Fiend, aka the Boy, using the Mind, or even just by the Boy alone, creating a Perceptual Field Mind Matrix.

"I've never been here," said Miranda.

"It's, it's … what's that word, your favorite word, Princess?"

"*Awesome*," said Miranda; it gave her a little shiver of pleasure; her man, her Prince, actually *listened* to her!

"*Awesome*," said Caliban, with a sort of reverential awe, for both the word and the thing; this was very different from the great cavern kingdom of the mutants. It was clear that it had been entirely made by humans; it was a work of art, a strangely ominous work of art.

The enormous underground cavern had a peaked, arched roof, like a

Gothic cathedral. Parts of the walls and pillars had collapsed, but the roof still held, and some of the pillars were hissing and smoking, and dissolving.

"The mind is eating this stuff; it's eating the stone," said Kat.

"And the metal," said V, "look at that."

"Awesome," Caliban whispered, "awesome."

Miranda tightened her grip on his hand.

A steel column was melting; dribbles of foaming silver were streaming slowly down its sides. Hissing stream drifted away from the shrinking, weakening column.

"Stay away from that," said V, pointing at the hissing metal, "far away."

"Don't worry, mother," said Miranda. It suddenly occurred to her that she and Caliban were not really dressed for battle; hot-skin shorts and skin T-shirt and a knotted loincloth were stylish, certainly, but it might be better to have armored catsuits like V and Kat.

V, finely tuned to Miranda's mind, turned, "It wouldn't make any difference, Miranda! These suits won't protect us from that!" And she pointed.

A tentacle whipped out of the wall – it had seemed to be part of the wall – and it spurted a stream liquid, and the splash just missed Miranda. She started back into Caliban's arms.

V turned and glanced, "Watch out, Miranda, stay back!"

Miranda and Caliban backed away from the thrashing tentacle. Other tentacles emerged. Miranda drew her ultra-modern laser gun, and Caliban aimed his AK-47, which still had some bullets, not many, left.

Kat zapped the cluster of tentacles with a blast from her laser. The main daddy or mommy tentacle fizzled and hissed; then, it swung around, and aimed a jet of the acid nano replicant fluid Kat's way.

Kat ducked.

The liquid splashed against the wall, and a large chunk of the wall slid away and dissolved and began to writhe as if it were alive.

Kat zapped the tentacles at their roots, and the tentacles fell from the wall and writhed around, trying to aim at Kat but unable to do so.

V zapped the fallen tentacles.

Kat let out a sigh of relief. "Yuk, these things are horrible."

"It's one big thing, with many tentacles."

"Yes," Kat fired again, just to be sure. "It's one big, deadly thing."

"Looks like the attack is over," said Miranda, "for the moment, at least, I think."

"This is evil magic," said Caliban.

"Yes, it certainly is," said Kat.

V stared at the smoking ruins of the tentacles; they had been created by the Mind out of stone and steel. So anything and everything could be transformed into the enemy. The whole world and everything in it could *become* the enemy.

She glanced along the enormous cavern. "According to our extremely articulate girl informant, we are to go along this cathedral-like cave until we reach a narrower tunnel with an ogive-like roof and which branches off to the left; it's that one down there, I reckon, and, once we have proceeded for 70 meters, more or less, along that tunnel, we turn left and go through a small Alice-in-Wonderland door, where we have to crouch or crawl, and on the other side of that door, we find a staircase with runic markings on the walls, and we go down two levels, and we come to another tunnel, and eventually we come to a canal, and we have to double back, and then ..."

"Whew," Kat wiped her brow.

And so they proceeded, with caution.

V was in front.

Kat was just behind her.

And Miranda and Caliban, weapons unslung, but holding hands, brought up the rear.

V stopped. "Something's wrong; something's not right ..."

"Is that our reflection in the floor, Caliban?" Miranda was looking down at the floor; it had turned into a mirror.

"It does look like ... yes, it is ..."

The mirror disappeared, blackness replaced it.

"Oh!"

"No! Princess ..." Caliban gasped, "Princess!"

A gaping, perfectly round hole opened in the tunnel floor, right beneath Miranda and Caliban. There was no floor. The smooth, then watery mirror had given away to – nothing, a void, a vacuum.

Miranda and Caliban disappeared, sucked straight down into the void.

Whoosh!

Miranda's voice called out, "This is outrageous! Caliban! Caliban!"

"Miranda! Princess! My princess!"

"This is so unacceptable!"

Whoosh!

"Utterly inappropriate!"

Whoosh!

"Princess!"

"Caliban!"

"Princess!"

"Caliban!"

"Princess!"

They were gone.

Kat, who was closest, raced to the edge, and peered down, V turned and rushed back.

The hole was pitch-black. They could just hear Caliban shout, "Miranda!"

Kat said, "I'm going down."

"Wait," V laid her hand on Kat's arm.

"Wait for what?"

Just as Kat was about to leap into the abyss, the hole suddenly became cloudy, as if filled with a fog, then reflective, as if it were filled with water or with glass. Then it snapped shut entirely, crystallizing, and the stone floor of the tunnel was as if there had never been a hole there at all.

V stood for a moment, staring. A smoky sulfurous vapor seeped out of the floor and rose up, as if coming from the deepest confines of hell, and Kat said, "What was that? What happened?"

"He tried to take them down to Hell, I think."

Kat stared at the curls of smoke rising from the floor.

"I don't think it worked," said V, "they are too, ah, too pure, too innocent."

"Pure? Innocent?" Kat turned to V.

"Yes," V said, "Too pure, too innocent." But she did have a horrible image of Miranda and Caliban locked in the granite depths, frozen, suffocating, in stone, or perhaps, turned to stone, their skin and eyes and veins and muscles and tendons and flesh slowly crystallizing, becoming pure mineral, quartz, and silica, and feldspar, the molecules re-aligning and redefining themselves, becoming crystalline, and then the mind, trapped, dying, or perhaps left alive, realizing that it had become a statue, a living death, forever locked in, for the Evil One – or the Boy – or the Foul Fiend – was known to petrify his victims; one of his many manifestations was as Medusa, whose unruly snaky locks turned all who glanced at her eyes to stone; this was a frightful fate.

"I shall kill him," V said, curling her gloved fists, "I shall drive him back whence he came, out of our universe and into eternal darkness where he shall dwell a prisoner until the end of time."

"Yes."

"Yes."

"Let's go then," said Kat, laying her gloved hand on V's shoulder. "Let us drive him back to hell, whence he came, so he will dwell in eternal darkness until the end of time."

"Yes, we go on, we continue," V clenched her teeth and curled her fists, while thinking that she had hardly ever been so worried, not in almost three thousand years: *Oh, Miranda! Oh, Caliban!* V was on the verge of tears.

Children are hostages to fortune – who said that?

Oh, yes, V remembered, it was good old Sir Francis Bacon, a friend of hers from the 1590s, who hung about the court of Queen Elisabeth I, a nice and learned chap, but a bit of a fussbudget and pedant and always in money trouble. Once, she had loaned him three ducats, which he had never found occasion to repay.

She shrugged, straightened her shoulders, and gave herself a pep talk: *Well, V, onward we go! Come hell or high water, Kat and I shall get to the bottom of this and destroy the Foul Fiend.* Somehow V did think, in fact, she was utterly convinced, that Miranda and Caliban would survive – both of them, in different ways, were very human, but also beyond human; and both were, in their different ways, quite pure – not a mean bone in either of their bodies. Thus the Foul Fiend – the Boy – who depended on the inner weaknesses of his victims – would be hard put to seize them, to entomb them.

"This thing hates us," said Kat, staring at the walls, and feeling behind the stone and steel and brick, and behind the tentacles and tricks, the presence of the Evil One, the Boy.

"Yes."

"It hates you, more than anything, I think."

"Yes."

"Do you think this hate is close to love?"

"Oh, I wouldn't say that, Kat; perhaps, I don't know; but he will certainly try 'love,' I imagine. He is a void, after all, he yearns to be filled; that is why he needs to conquer and destroy."

"*Love:* a word that is used to disguise every type of crime," Kat almost spat the word out. She was clearly thinking back on some people she had known, always blathering about "love" but ready, at the drop of a hat, to torture, betray, and murder.

"Yes," said V, glancing at Kat: part of her wanted to take Kat in her arms and comfort her: there were lots of wounds there, living scars, underneath the perfect, exquisite, polished façade.

The tunnel was narrow and dark and filled with mist. The very stones seemed to be sweating. It must be far above one hundred degrees Fahrenheit. Water dripped from the roof.

"I think some of the levels above us are flooded," said Kat, looking up, reaching out a gloved hand to catch some of the water.

"Yes." V felt antsy, "Some of this, a lot of it, is below sea level." Her bodysuit was sweaty, clammy, and crawly inside, as if it were alive, as if it were slathering her in creeping glue; it seemed to be trying to merge with her skin. She grimaced: *Maybe it's trying to eat me.* Something was eating her, *trying* to eat her.

"Cracks are opening up," said Kat, turning to V, "We'd better hurry, otherwise ..."

"Yes, otherwise we'll get buried and drown," V wanted to rip the bodysuit off. Cracks in reality were opening up; not just cracks in the walls and roofs of the tunnel, but cracks in the very fabric of being, cracks in the ability of the mind to hold reality together and give it form. The mind creates the perceptual world, and if you destroy the mind, or muck around with it ... V had the feeling she was about to drop through the surfaces of flesh and water and air and stone, and plummet into infinite bodiless darkness, a deep boundless sea, nothing but eternal night. Maybe I'm going crazy, she thought. Maybe the Foul Fiend has invaded my mind.

"Yes," Kat stared at V for just a second, and then looked away; in reading V's mind, she was getting static, something like a thunderstorm, a mental thunderstorm was building up, something was not quite right with the Queen of the Hybrids, with V ...

V tensed. She wanted to howl, rip off her clothes, rip off every vestige of humanity, turn reptile-alien, and run wild and naked, devour flesh, drink blood. Every muscle strained. Oh, yes, oh, yes: to return to her untamed, exiled self, the beast of the jungle, the savage predator. She licked her lips.

She closed her eyes. I am not a good mother.

Miranda and Caliban had disappeared.

They will die. It is my fault.

I brought them here; I should have left them with Nikki.

She had told them to stay behind her, and behind Kat, so they would be safe. Or had she told them to stay behind? She couldn't remember. She was a mother now, a true mother, in a way she had never realized before. She must protect her daughter. How could she protect her daughter if she couldn't even protect herself?

She shivered. Is the Foul Fiend getting inside my mind?

She and Kat were alone.

"Are you okay, V?"

V half-closed her eyes. She tried to focus. The tunnel changed shape. One instant, it was immense; the next, it was a swirling corkscrew. The walls leaned this way and that. *This is not happening, this is not really happening!* She rubbed her forehead. It was an illusion. It must be! The Mind, and the Evil One, the Boy, they were behind it. The Mind was inside her head; the Boy was inside her head. Yes, the Boy was driving her mad. *And if I cannot even protect myself, how can I protect the others?*

"Are you okay?" said Kat.

V turned. She stared at Kat. Kat was hyper-real, glittering with glamorous intensity. She looked like a video game heroine, in her jet-black, matt, skin-tight body armor. Kat was right beside her, beautiful, and desirable. What a beautiful surface Kat was! What a beautiful work of art! V felt a thirst rising within her – desire, hunger, yearning.

"Are you okay, V?" Kat said again, or was it an echo of what she had just said? Had Kat spoken once, or twice? V couldn't tell. Had time stopped, or was it swirling around in an endless loop?

All this time, they were proceeding down the tunnel, military-style, Cosmos SWAT team style, swinging from arch to arch and buttress to buttress, their laser guns drawn and ready to fire, totally coordinated, and only a few meters apart; but to V, Kat seemed light-years away.

"I'm okay," V said, hearing her voice from a vast distance, echoing down an infinite tunnel. *But … I am being sucked into some deep part of myself.* Even her thinking seemed far away. Even the words in her mind were those of a stranger, a voice heard faintly from another space. I am being swept away, into a space-time vortex. *Soon I will need a telescope to see Kat!*

"Are you really okay?" Kat's voice came from an intergalactic distance.

"Yes, I'm okay," V's voice sounded hollow. She was inside a huge cave, deep inside her body, listening to her own voice, echoing and empty, coming from another continent, through static. She murmured, "Yes, I'm really okay."

"You don't look okay."

"I am." Her mouth was dry. Then it flooded with hot saliva. She wanted to drop straight down onto the pavement, to faint, to curl up and fall asleep. She wanted to be sick, curl up in bed. She'd never been sick.

"We are up against something new here, aren't we, V," said a voice inside her, "be very careful, V." This was a new voice, a firm, calm, masculine voice. It seemed to be the voice of her father, the voice of the man from the Andromeda galaxy, the serene, brave, sun-tanned, ancient warrior from the stars; yes, it was the voice of her father, Marcus. Was he speaking to her? Or was this an illusion, a trick?

Time fell apart.

Kat disappeared.

The tunnel disappeared.

Elysium disintegrated. It was a dream, and it left not a rack behind. Elysium was unreal; it had never been; or it had not yet come into being – whatever she thought of …

It is 723 BC. V is a young woman, a 19-year-old Phoenician, from a city near the great Phoenician port of Carthage in North Africa. She is soaked in blood. She has drunk her first victim dry. She crouches, half-naked, next to the lifeless body of her true meal, Gaius, a warrior. All around them, the city burns. The air is heavy with smoke, with the smell of blood, of burned flesh, of burning wood, cedar and pine, of resin and spilt, boiling wine.

Marcus, a warrior of Ancient Phoenicia, stares down at her. She is young. Her robe is in tatters. She has drunk deep. She is cloaked in steaming blood and gore from the veins and arteries of Gaius. Marcus holds his broadsword ready to strike her down. He gazes straight at her. "Do you know what you have become, my girl? Do you know what you are? Do you know what you have become?"

Lips dripping blood, she stares up at him, at his steely warrior eyes, his tanned skin, his smiling white teeth, and his curly blond hair. She blinks, dazed, puzzled: "Do I know what I have become?"

"Do I know what I have become?" V is surprised by the sound of her own voice.

"What did you say?" Kat, crouching behind a column and staring toward a larger tunnel opening, glanced over at V.

"Nothing, I said nothing," V crouched behind cover, exactly like Kat, standard Cosmos Centurion infantry tactics, SWAT team, and police tactics, each move the result of years of training, and of hundreds of years of success and failure as humans fought and killed humans. "I didn't say anything."

Kat again glanced across the tunnel. V looked absent, something was definitely wrong with her.

V returned the glance. Kat had her visor up. Her dark eyes and handsome dark face glowed, sculpted in the dim phosphorescence and the emergency lights which, strangely, were still burning. Kat was looking at her with concern. *Kat is worried. Kat thinks I am going crazy.*

"The Mind wants us to find it." V licks her lips.

"The Foul Fiend, the Boy, wants us to find him?" Kat raises an eyebrow.

"But he will play tricks first!" V glances at Kat.

"Yes, I'm sure he will play tricks!" Kat grinned. "We'll see what tricks he can play. Maybe we can play tricks too!"

Kit Candy frowned. This was damned confusing. She was certain she knew her way around the lower depths; she had navigated it a gazillion times.

But now that they were underground in the murky half-drowned world, the world of shadows and canals and tunnels and tubes and subways and crawl spaces, and secret laboratories that lay deep under the Dome of Elysium, now that they were down in her favorite hunting ground, down in the world she knew like the back of her hand, Kit suddenly doubted that she knew anything. It all seemed unfamiliar and weird.

The lights were different; the walls leaned in closer than they had before; the tunnel pavements slanted this way and that, paving stones heaved up, and heaved down, and everywhere there were unfamiliar sights and sounds and smells.

Is this real – or am I going crazy?

Maybe I'm dead. Could I be dead?

At one point they had met with some bio-energized, crafty, over-intelligent rats who wanted to gang up and eat them, but when the hybrid – Claire – flared her eyes and bared her fangs, the rats skedaddled, flopping and jumping into the water, squeaking, *help, help, help,* and swimming away as fast as they could, their whiskers wet with silver drops, their little heads sleek and black, and their black eyes bright in terror.

"Wow!" said Kit, "I've never seen them as bold as that."

"The Foul Fiend is empowering all the creatures that hate humans." The hybrid flared her nostrils. Kit imagined steam coming out of them. I wonder – Can Claire breathe gushes of fire, like a dragon?

"The Foul Fiend – what's the Foul Fiend?" Kit thought this sounded like a fairy-tale, or maybe something Biblical.

"He's raising the dead too," said Robyn.

"What's the Foul Fiend?" Kit didn't like riddles. Being out of the loop and not totally *au courant* or *au fait* of current events and ongoing tragedies was a real bummer. She was vain, maybe, but she always insisted on being in the know.

Claire, the hybrid, tilted her head and gave Robyn a stare. "Where did you get that idea – that he's raising the dead?"

Robyn – really cute with her narrow pixy face – a perfect model for elegant Cosmos fashion – now looked, Kit thought, especially pale, a nervous ghost of a waif.

Robyn glanced at Kit and then at the hybrid, then she looked down at her toes, and then she looked up, straight at the hybrid. "I see them. I see them in my mind's eye. There's one woman, Laura Levitt's her name, and she ... she climbed out of her coffin. She's holding a little boy skeleton by the hand. She calls him in her mind – she can think somehow – she calls him 'Kiddo' or 'Little Kiddo.' There are lots of them, out in the Burbs."

"Ah."

"I thought I was a mystic," said Kit, "Robyn is a visionary."

"No, it's something else," said the hybrid, giving Robyn a pat on the shoulder; Robyn looked down and crossed her toes and blushed.

"Who is this Foul Fiend you're talking about?" Kit was pissed off. She'd stumbled into some sort of private club where people spoke in code. It was humiliating, dealing with snobs! Once she had served tables at the Cosmos Commodore Yacht Club – it had no yachts, there were no pleasant waters to navigate; it was an institution conjured up to incarnate false nostalgia – and she didn't understand a word, all obsolete nautical rigamarole, any of the guests said, except "Fill it up, Sub!"

"The Foul Fiend, well, He is evil. He is the principle of evil and sin and pollution. He is a form of spiritual and mental plague. He has leaked over from some other universe, and he wants to take over this universe. He is nameless, really, like God. His local followers, out in the Dead Lands, call him The Boy. The Boy is one of his incarnations, one of the incarnations of evil. But we've given him a nickname, Foul Fiend, though he prefers, I think, to be called the Boy or El Niño."

"Oh," Kit narrowed her eyes. If she understood rightly, they were in the midst of a Cosmic Disaster, not just a local little Elysium human comedy gone wrong. There were literary precedents for cosmic collapse. She remembered how King Lear on the heath met the fool and the Foul Fiend who piggy-backed on Edgar or Kent and was perhaps an illusion or just one of the fool's word games. Well, so much for literary allusions It looked like the end of the world was coming. She'd better warn Sniggy Propane and Fanny.

"He is also known as the Prince of Darkness, the Arch-Fiend, Lucifer, the Dark Angel … He – or It – has many names, and sometimes, for some people, he disguises himself as the Deity." The hybrid's eyes flashed. Her claws tightened on her laser gun. "He is the fallen one, and he lives in some sort of infinitely hellish place, so the tale goes."

A bat flew by, skittering close to the ceiling, squealing in terror.

"Oh, oh," said the hybrid.

"Oh, oh," echoed Robyn.

Kit thought maybe she should be worried.

"Oh," said the hybrid, "Something has frightened them."

Kit blinked. A white marble gargoyle was crouched on top of a ruined plinth.

She hadn't noticed it before. It glowed.

It must have fallen off some old building from the 20th or 19th Centuries. She stared at it, thinking …Then, it turned its head, blinked at her, and licked its thin lips with a long sliver of a tongue.

"What in the blazes is that?" Kit backed away. In fact, she did have a pretty good idea what it was, though, in all her explorations, she had never seen one up close, only had a few fluttering glimpses. It was that creature of underground urban myth: the ghoul.

"A ghoul," said Robyn.

There were more of them.

Kit gulped, remembering Miranda's favorite word: *Awesome!* Suddenly, ghouls were everywhere: Ghouls peeked over cornices, ghouls flitted in the shadows; some of the ghouls hissed and zipped out, briefly, into the main tunnel, their blank white eyes as characterless as a peeled, boiled egg; most of them snarled, stuck out their tongues, bared their fangs, and then skulked quickly away into the shadows. They were waiting for the right moment.

"Ghouls," said Claire. "The Dead Lands are teeming with ghouls."

"And now they are here," said Kit. These things really were spooky. She wondered how they had become the strange twisted beings they had become, was the outer a reflection of the inner soul?

"All things good and evil are being swept to this place. It's here the confrontation, the battle will take place," said Claire.

"Isn't being a ghoul contagious? I mean, if I remember rightly," said Robyn, staring at one crouching ghoul. It was shuffling along next to the cavern's wall, bent forward like a worried little old man, apparently ignoring them, and dripping from its fangs that white goo they seemed to drool; from time to time it stopped and sneezed a spray of the stuff. "Remember, Hybrid, I seem to remember you bit Demi Pfeiffer and me because you said ..."

"These things were human once?" Kit gulped: how horrible!

"Brilliant idea, Robyn," said the hybrid, turning and focusing on Kit that intimidating golden serpent-eye stare that seemed to drill right into Kit's very innermost soul and deepest most intimate junkyard thoughts and scan with pitiless luicidity her inner pornographic playground and loftiest mystical speculations. The hybrid said, with unsettling, level-toned intensity, "I'm glad you reminded me!"

"What?" Kit stared back at the hybrid's golden gaze. Were all her sins about to be revealed? What new catastrophe was about to overtake her? *Yikes! Maybe this friendly hybrid is going to eat me after all!*

She could see herself: Fricasseed Kit Candy, coated in honey, roasted over a barbecue or perhaps turned on a smoky, sizzling spit, like a roasted pig she had read about, and plopped in a French stew or, most likely, she would be eaten raw, perhaps lying on the table with a big fat apple stuffed into her mouth. But hybrids would probably not be big on decoration or refined cuisine. They probably just gobbled and swallowed whole!

To distract the hybrid from herself as cordon bleu cuisine and to get their mission back on track, Kit said, "Okay, it's down this way, I think." She pointed, but at the same time, she was perplexed.

She knew her navigation nose was as good as ever, but confusing things were happening to her sense of time and space; she wondered whether it was the Mind taking control of the real matrix of time and space and mixing things up on a fundamental cosmological level, or was the Mind merely fucking with her mind, with Kit Candy's little mind, distorting her perceptions with illusions and hallucinations; or maybe she was just a bit tired from the day's events; she hoped she wasn't coming down with something … the flu would be very inconvenient at this …juncture. She suddenly wondered whether the ghoul thing – becoming a ghoul – was contagious. Robyn had mentioned something to that effect and …

A ghoul was up on top of a broken column, staring right at her; it sneezed, white goo flew out in a spray, forming a little cloud.

"Jesus!" Kit began to sweat.

"You know, Robyn," the hybrid had its claw on Robyn's shoulder and was staring at Kit, "I think you had a very good idea there, Robyn."

"Why are you looking at me like that?" Kit frowned; yes, maybe the hybrid had decided she was hungry, and that Kit would make a good snack.

"People are becoming ghouls," the hybrid – "Call me Claire" – said, "Do we want our young friend here, our charming polyglot tourist guide Ms. Kit Candy to become a ghoul."

"No, Hybrid, definitely not," said Robyn.

"So," said the hybrid, "Kit, will you let me bite you?"

"Bite me?"

"Just a little friendly nip, a nibble really," the hybrid bared its fangs and grinned; its tongue was forked; Kit was really not sure about this.

"She did it to me," Robyn said, "it's like vaccination, sort of …"

Kit frowned. She liked her new friends, and she trusted them, well, up until a few seconds ago, but … She really trusted Robyn, who had a transparent childlike candor about her, and, in spite of that flash of doubt about being gobbled up as a snack, she trusted Claire the hybrid – a weirdly sexy, highly polished scaly black-and-red reptile with a wicked sense of humor. "So what's the downside?"

"The downside can be considered an upside," said the hybrid. "Isn't that right, Robyn?"

"That is definitely right, Claire. There are always more than one way to look at a complex question; in fact, there are usually many ways, possibly an infinity of ways, if you want to think outside the particular box you happen to be in, I mean, so I would say that …"

Kit was getting antsy. The world was collapsing – monstrous creatures were popping up everywhere – her sense of space-time was twisting into the pretzel shape, taking on the impossible geometry of an Escher drawing or a Dali painting, solid geometry melting into squiggles and dribbles – and these two clowns couldn't stop dawdling along and gabbing philosophy like there was no tomorrow. Even if they had saved her life, they were still like a comedy routine – *so* totally irresponsible! "Look, ladies, we don't have time … to palaver or beat around the bush or indulge in management consultant gobbledygook," Kit scowled, "Just tell me what you have to tell me!" She was also eager to get them to the lair of the World Mind, meet the Foul Fiend, or the Boy or whatever it was, and see what would happen; the whole world was falling apart; the dome was collapsing; justice had gone mad, even more than usual. Action was imperative. Kit Candy was on the warpath.

"The upside-downside is that you become a hybrid."

"Oh," Kit gulped. Being permanently morphed into a fanged, scaly, clawed, snake-eyed toothy maniac, even if charming, monster was not quite her idea of upside.

"And you become immortal sort of, and heal quickly, and, if you want, you can read people's minds, and become extra-super-strong, which is sort of cute, though I haven't really put my full range of extra powers to the test yet," said Robyn, in one long breathless unbroken sentence which was, again, quite unlike anything she had spoken in years, since, in fact, she had been partially erased and ceased to be a quasi-genius and had been turned into childlike mechanical savant tinkerer. In little loquacious bursts, her mind was revving up! Whew!

"Do I have to look like you?" Kit gave the hybrid her best dirty look, utter disapproval – though actually, if she were truly to fess up, she had to admit she liked the hybrid and, on a lower, half-conscious level, thought that the creature looked damned sexy. If she weren't generally inclined to favor human beings over scaly serpents, she might even consider …

"Does Robyn look like me?"

Howls were coming from somewhere in front of them.

"No."

Howls and screams were coming from somewhere behind them.

"Well, then …"

"But …"

Some creature was ululating; it sounded, Kit thought, sort of like the girl werewolf in *The Return of the Crazy Purple Fungi* – a 2182 classic – starring Nikki Hughes as the brilliant young feminist scientist threatened by the girl werewolf – who was hopelessly in love with Nikki – and threatened, too, by bubbling up invading flesh-eating moss and malicious mushrooms and an idiot mutant toad-like graveyard security chief, also totally smitten by Nikki but obtuse to her subtlety, and who never realized there was a deadly monster digging itself out from an underground crypt until it was too late – too late for him at least; influences included Laurel & Hardy, Buster Keaton, and *La Lupa Mannara,* aka *Werewolf Woman* of 1976, and …

Claire flashed a particularly reptilian grin: "And, Kit, do you remember – you may be too young – but do you remember the blond cover girl for CVJ perfumes, for CVJ mini-skin skirts, CVJ cling body tights, for CVJ face creams, CVJ rejuvenation and remake centers and CVJ spas, and …?"

There was banging on the tunnel wall. Was something trying to get in? More screaming echoed from in front of them – and behind them.

"Of course, I remember! Do you think I'm an idiot?" Kit, put her hands on her hips in a pissed-off pose that was partly her own, and partly copied from Miranda. Love is also, as Kit well knew, introjection or symbolic cannibalism, incorporating the body of the loved one, and their tics, into your own body; and as she also knew, from looking at herself in the mirror, humans are irredeemably addicted to mimicry, monkeys one and all, miming, with divine mockery, the very things they love, parody being *homage.* She was totally insulted, insulted to her very core. After all, her Pub Kult Knowledge credentials were impeccable, unsurpassable; she was absolutely sure she could obliterate any competitor on Trite Kult Quest Hour, "Of course I remember: the CVJ CEO, Claire V Jacobs, that fabulous, statuesque *très distinguée* perfectly toothy blonde, with the dreamy skin, the oo-la-la Neo-Cockney Oxbridge Parisian accent and throaty but sometimes, showing total vocal control, with the light, high, little girl voice, a Marilyn parody certainly, and the … I used to drool over her, and sometimes I even …"

"Well, that is me when I shift gears," said Claire, slinging one glittering black arm casually over the walkway railing, her two long spectacularly glittering scaly black perfect legs crossed casual-like, her fanged grin and golden gaze blazing down upon Kit, "I am, in fact, CVJ."

Kit realized the hybrid was miming one of the famous – gosh, *iconic* – CVJ poses, in particular, the one in a polyglot VID Pub for CVJ bubble body wash, with CVJ, stepping out, all covered in glistening popping bubbles, and leaning, full-length, only bubbles covering her, and as they popped revealing more and more, leaning casually against a balcony railing, being caressed and slowly stripped by the balmy twilight breeze. And Kit suddenly remembered the repressed old Samizdat rumors – Virtual World ghosts or relics – that the fabled ultra-human beauty CVJ was, in fact, a half-alien, scaly reptile hybrid: *Wow! Awesome! Absolutely Awesome!* "Okay. Do it," she said.

"Good," said the hybrid, and she did it.

Later, Kit would remember that moment, over and over, she would replay it in the most varied circumstances.

Some things, you do them, you can never undo them.

Oh, well …

Actually, when she did think about it …

It didn't hurt at all. Just a little nip, like the hybrid – oops, like Claire – said, and then, that duty accomplished, they rocketed along an underground steel walkway, leaping from platform to platform, clattering and banging, toward the Lair of the Mind, the world mind, and all the shouting and screaming … and howling … continued.

Banshees!

Werewolves!

Ghouls!

And then there were those god-awful weird horrible flying things, flitting here and there and snarling, dripping green glowing foam from their very ugly fangs, miniature rabid bat-like things, about the size of a chickadee.

And there were ghouls, of course, but they mostly hung back, shyly, growling, hissing and snarling, in the shadows. Ghouls, generally, it seemed, were no match for hybrids.

Farther down, they met, hanging from some pipes that went along the tunnel roof, a sort of slimy serpent thing with many heads; it sniffed at them and whimpered.

Claire said, "Ignore it."

So they ignored it.

Robyn asked, "Do you think it's lonely."

Claire glanced at the creature and said, "Yes, it was once human, but isn't anymore and, yes, maybe like so many people who once had a soul, it would like its soul and maybe even its body back, besides it would like company, it would like to turn us into versions of it, but we are tough nuts to crack – and hence not candidates for the club, not for the moment at least."

They saw some more ghouls skulking along a canal walkway.

These ghouls were bigger and more aggressive; they snarled and growled and yodeled and spat from a distance, but they didn't attack.

Meantime, they seemed to be coming to places that Kit really didn't recognize; she was beginning to sweat. This was embarrassing; she said she knew her way around down here – but these tunnels, suspension bridges, walkways, canals, all seemed to be new, or in the wrong place, everything was mixed up.

Then, a horrible thing happened.

Kit turned into a new tunnel. It was rather narrow. She didn't really remember it being the way it was. Her sense of space was getting really screwy. There seemed to be tunnels where there weren't any tunnels, and walls where there shouldn't be walls, and everything looked crooked and nightmarish, the walls were leaning this way and that. It was like in one of those old German expressionist horror movies she'd watched in the underground Oscar prize-winning samizdat VID Film History Course *Madness and Schizophrenia in the Movies*.

"It's the Mind," said Claire, who seemed to have sensed what was going on in Kit's head. Of course! She could read minds! "It's being manipulated by the Foul Fiend, aka the Boy, and it's playing with your head – and ours too."

"I was sure this was the way."

"Really?" Robyn glanced at Kit.

"The Boy is goofing around with our space-time perception," said Claire, eyes wide and staring around. "Those walls really should not be leaning in toward each other like that!"

"I'm certain. It should be down here, this way, the Mind, I mean. I mean, I never, but never, get lost ..." Kit was stubborn. But now she was afraid, the walls bulged inward and buckled into weird shapes, like they were made of gum or elastic; eyes appeared, embedded in the walls, as if people had been cemented into the rock. A mouth surged up, making mad contortions, wild full lips, bright with scarlet lipstick, and perfect teeth, it was as if a 1950s blond diva was trapped in the stone. It stuck out its tongue and waggled it in an obscene manner, straight at Kit. "Ugh," said Kit. She loved kissing, but she didn't like people showing off their papillae. A mouth without a person, an immured mouth, was even worse.

"Maybe," Claire nodded, "The Foul Fiend really is twisting space-time, not just our perceptions of space-time; after all, with Him, anything is possible." Clair sounded far away.

The tunnel got longer, stretching out and swaying, like a string or rope of diabolically nervous serpentine brown toffee.

Things were getting smaller and smaller, and then, suddenly, they were getting bigger and bigger, or Kit was getting smaller and smaller, and then she was getting bigger and bigger, or vice versa. Kit expected any minute to see a Mad Hatter with a watch chain and fob rushing by ...

"Kit ... back out of there, back out of that tunnel." Claire's voice, from very far away, sounded alarmed. "Get out of there! Quick!"

"The walls look sort of crooked, and like they're moving," Robyn stared around, "I think Mr. Evil, the Sulfurous Foul Fiend, the Boy, is trying to drive us crazy."

"Kit, come on back!" Claire shouted, "Come back, get close to us! Quick! We must stick … together."

"I'm coming," said Kit, in a whisper, as if hypnotized, and hearing her voice tiny, tiny, itty-bitty, teeny-weeny, and as if it were very far away.

Wham!

A huge steel door came thundering down between them.

Wham!

"Hey, Robyn, Hey, Claire …!" Kit ran at the door, banged her fists against it; it seemed as solid as steel, real steel. She hammered against the door; the steel was so perfect, so shiny, her fists left smudge marks. She breathed on it: yes, her breath created circles of mist, which then faded. "Damnation!"

She could hear their muffled shouting on the other side.

Then she got words clearly from Claire, words that spoke in her head – it was weird! It was, like, *direct mind-to-mind* talk.

"Keep calm, Kit, and carry on," said Claire.

"Easy to say," replied Kit.

"You are a trooper, Kit," said Claire.

"Okay, you're right!" Kit sighed. "I'm a trooper."

"Head for the Lair of the Mind and try to find us and we'll try to find you, close to the Mind, so we'll join up later …"

Clown and Geisha and Black Tarzan had briefly glimpsed some ghouls, but the ghouls had skittered away.

"Interesting," said Black Tarzan.

"Disgusting," said Clown.

"I vote for disgusting," said Geisha.

Clown and her friends had come to a large underground concourse from ancient pre-Cosmos times. It must have been a sort of shopping zone attached to an ancient lower depths transportation hub.

It was here that they met something new – a whole crowd of ghouls.

There they were, the ghouls, a whole lineup of them sitting on top of an ancient ruined underground newsstand. It said "News" in big, bold letters and advertised such antique publications as *The New York Times* and *Maxim* and *Penthouse* and so on. There was a giant faded picture of a woman in a bikini and the title said something about a buff belly and somebody, probably decades ago, maybe one hundred years or more, had drawn a large mustache over the woman's mouth and blacked out several of her front teeth.

The ghouls mewled.

"Maybe we should back up, ladies." Black Tarzan placed himself between the women and the ghouls.

They began to retreat.

The ghouls mewled again. One ghoul, perched on a plinth, was sucking its thumb. It took its thumb out of its mouth and stared at it.

Black Tarzan and Geisha and Clown made it to the vestibule of what must have been the old subway station. It was another part of the ancient shopping concourse; it was only partly underwater, and was lined with shops that had long since ceased to exist. A large image of a cigar stood upright on a small stand; a dusty half-broken window displayed moss-covered mannequins wearing skin-shorts. One elegant black female bio-mannequin sat at a café table that, for some reason, had not been vandalized or turned over. Her bio-batteries must still have some residual power because she turned to stare at them. "This is a dangerous place; you shouldn't be here."

"We know. Thank you," said Clown.

"You are welcome." The mannequin smiled and looked away and again stared into space.

The ghouls got into position to attack, leaping from the NewsStand, splashing through the murky water, and leaping up the stairs. More and more came running. There must have been twenty of them at least.

They gathered in a crowd and stood very still.

Then, slowly, they moved forward, in formation.

They were about three-and-a-half feet tall, bent over slightly, looking like chalk-white hairless chimpanzees, with very large heavy heads, and claws instead of hands and fanged mouths, and they were wading through the water which up here in the concourse level was only about a foot deep.

"Oh, oh," said Clown.

"This augers no good," said Geisha, "I do believe the stars and the gods are not well aligned with human destiny today."

"You can say that again," said Black Tarzan. A swarm of ghouls was probably worse than a swarm of rats, or maybe not. It was all bad, that was the definite bottom line.

For a moment, the ghouls held back.

They didn't move. It looked like they were waiting for a signal.

Then – they charged, splashing across the concourse.

"Ready?" Black Tarzan glanced at the two women.

"Yes," Geisha got into her karate position.

"Yes," Clown braced herself. Those perfect abs and programmed sex acrobat muscles might now come in handy.

Wham!

The ghouls leaped.

Miranda and Caliban were tumbling down, and down, and turning over and over. They seemed to be in an infinite space, floating next to each other, about three meters apart, falling and falling, in slow-motion, as if the laws of gravity were half suspended, as if they were floating in an invisible liquid.

And then, a web of filaments began to reach out of the darkness, silvery, crystalline threads. They touched Miranda's arm, and they wrapped themselves around one ankle, and they clung to her hair, and they got thicker and thicker. Miranda felt she should be frightened, but she wasn't particularly frightened; it was all rather dreamy and sensual. The same thing was happening to Caliban, more and more of the filaments shot out of the darkness, wrapping both of them round and round, and round.

"Caliban."

"Yes, my Princess?"

"This stuff will mummify us."

"It tried already, Princess." Caliban was rolling over and over, "but you knocked it away and ripped it up."

"Swim toward me, Caliban, and I shall swim toward you."

"Yes, my Princess!"

So he did, and so she did, and, as if they were swimming, wiggling and undulating through space, it seemed they were moving through the dark filament garnished space as if they were swimming in the deepest depths of a dark and fathomless sea where magic glistening tendrils tried to caress and capture them.

"This is an illusion, Caliban, and it will only be real if we think it is real."

"It is a mighty powerful illusion, Princess."

"I know, my love, but our love will shatter this illusion, our faith in each other, and in V and Kat and in all our friends, in mutants and humans and SINs and hybrids, and in Nikki, and Dolly, together, our faith and our love will conquer, Caliban, for we shall triumph together, we shall build worlds together, and so we shall triumph; it is inevitable and I wish it so! It is my command that it be so!"

Caliban, more and more wrapped in silver threads, was swimming closer and closer, and he said, "That was quite a speech, Princess!" He pushed closer and closer as she swam toward him.

As they swam closer and closer, they continued to plunge, down and down, head over heels, through the infinite space which was crisscrossed by the filaments.

"I believe you, my love," Caliban said, "We shall triumph!"

"And so we shall, my love!"

At that moment, as they twirled around, their fingertips touched, and … sparks flew … a flash of lightning lit up the space and …

"Oh, Caliban!"

"Oh, Miranda!"

Kat frowned. The bug eyes in the walls were staring at them. "This is the Religious Underground, Goddess. I think we're on the right track."

"Don't call me Goddess," V peered into the murk, "please."

"Certainly, Goddess, my dear Queen of the Hybrids, don't be so modest." Kat was for some reason in a teasing mood. Was it the influence of the Foul Fiend? She hoped not! She was beginning to feel mischievous and randy; she wanted to kiss V, and she wanted to … She shot V a wicked grin and held her weapon ready, "After all, Nikki is a goddess."

"Nikki didn't apply for that job. It was thrust upon her."

"True."

V frowned. "From here, according to our informant, we are to go south and then down three levels, and then down four, and we come to some tunnels and canals, and we go along a …"

"Where the Foul Fiend, the Bad Boy, awaits us, well, awaits you …"

"Yes."

"This is a weird place, this Religious Underground. I have never been down here before. It looks dead."

"The cave of broken dreams." V picked up a prayer book. Most of its pages had been torn out. "People need to worship; they need stories, so the tale goes. What is life without a story to hold it together? What am I, without a story?" She set the prayer book down, gently, on a ledge. "The sillier the story, the better it is. What is not of this world can never be known, never tested, and never discredited – thus, the otherworldly dreams of religion can take untold forms and live on forever."

"That was quite a speech, Goddess." Kat stared at some gutted candles.

"Sorry."

"Don't be."

The rows of holy niches were empty. A few candles still burned. The sweet and spicy smell of incense and the coppery smell of blood hung heavy in the misty muggy air. Blood dripped from the walls, dribbled from banners and icons, and spread in dark pools on the pavement. Bits and pieces of bodies, gobs of flesh, lay everywhere. With the shiny toe of her highly polished Cosmos Centurion boot, Kat nudged a severed hand, pale and puffy, lying all alone, its fingers curled up, as if in supplication. On one of its fingers was a gold ring. Fog rose off a side canal and drifted inwards, into the main tunnel, curling and uncurling; miniature strata of cloud gathered at the level of Kat and V's thighs. V and Kat looked like twins, voyagers from outer space, emerging into the mists of some archaic tropical swamp. Yea, verily, the two shimmering Centurion hybrids looked like visitors from some other planet, with their gleaming black armored skintight bodysuits, black helmets, visors up, high-tech weapons at the ready.

Dead prelates were scattered here and there, lying on the pavement, sprawled over the entrances to niches, in picturesque costumes, robes and pantaloons, black jackets, and white dresses. Scepters and miters and incense bowls and other trinkets and symbols lay on the ground. Some of the prelates and holy people had been eaten, or half-eaten.

"Did ghouls do this?" Kat probed another body with the toe of her boot.

"Something worse, I think," V crouched next to a dead priest; his beard was long; his face looked peaceful; half his chest was gone; the white ribs of the rib cage glistened with streaks of blood and gristle.

"Oh, somebody's alive!" Kat pointed, with one glove hand.

It was a very young Buddhist nun; candlelight reflected off her dark shaven head; she was sitting in the lotus position in a niche, a neat row of white wax candles still burning, fluttering little flames, in front of her. Her niche, with its banners and paintings and cups and vases, looked like it had not been touched by whatever had destroyed the rest.

The nun was praying, obviously, or repeating a mantra of some kind, for her lips moved silently. She seemed entirely unscathed; her white robe was impeccable, spotless as it must always have been.

V stopped in front of her, marveling; with all the others dead, it did seem like a miracle that …

The nun opened her eyes.

V and Kat, two gleaming Centurion warriors, were standing before her.

The flames in the candles fluttered slightly, as if caught in a breeze.

"Who are you?" the Buddhist lady raised an eyebrow and smiled.

"My name is V, this is Kat."

"You are going to meet the Prince of Darkness, the Boy."

"Well, yes," said V, "That's one way of …"

"He wishes you to be his bride." The beautiful young nun smiled again.

Kat favored V with a flirtatious smirk, sparks lit up her eyes – a hint of possessive jealousy. "I knew it!"

V glanced at Kat, fluttered her eyelashes, looked down, curled her lips in a modest pout, and shrugged, the dim phosphorescent light rippled on her shoulders and shoulder blades.

The nun gazed at V. "He needs to conquer you – by force or by charm – to become master of this planet, and of the Gateway, and hence of the universe."

Interesting, Kat thought, the Foul Fiend needs V to conquer the universe: my Vampire Hybrid friend is just too … too … attractive … and too influential too. Kat licked her lips, feeling increasingly aroused, and wondering: *What are we being drawn into?*

The nun smiled. "The promised bride is discreet; she is shy. She is beautiful, and she is shy and yet she is strong. She is, in her own modest, self-deprecating way, a Goddess, come from Ancient Times. The Prince of Darkness – the Boy – or the Foul Fiend – will have his hands full."

"What happened here?" V looked up and motioned toward the carnage.

The nun raised one hand, palm up, sketched a slight, circular motion, indicating the scene around them; her expression did not change, "Many are dead; many have fled; a few remain."

"What happened to them? How did it happen?" said V.

"They went mad, most of them," the Buddhist lady glanced at the scene, taking in the dead bodies, the blood, the strewn vestments, and the desecrated symbols, "They killed themselves or each other. And some of them …" her hand dipped slightly, indicating one of the bodies, a priest in elaborate costume, lying stomach-down; his head was missing, just a big red gluey blotch and smear where his head would have been, "Some of them, their minds, their skulls, just vaporized."

"Mind implants," said V.

"Yes, I suspected as much," said the Buddhist lady.

"Well," Kat breathed gently, looking at V and at the Buddhist lady, "I'm damned pleased I neutered all of mine – my mind implants, I mean."

"Then the ghouls came," said the Buddhist lady, "And, after the ghouls, something worse, even worse than the ghouls." She closed her eyes, as if she were about to fall back into her trance, abolishing consciousness of all around her.

But just as they were about to go, she said, with her eyes still closed, "Remember, everything is a mere idea, all is unreal, a sparkling matrix, at the heart of everything is nothing, you can – you will – transcend. The world is an illusion, a manifold of sparkling nothingness, atoms, molecules, electrons, protons, photons, quarks, mere empty space, buzzing with energies and secrets we can have no conception of."

"What was that something worse?" Kat leaned forward.

The Buddhist lady opened her eyes. "It took many forms; it was a wolf, it was a giant squid, it was stone and cement and steel, it was the walls themselves, it was a handsome dandy-like young man, your friend, your suitor, the Boy. It whirled and moved among them, slaughtering them, and it slaughtered them, I would say, with joy."

"And you, it did not touch."

"No."

"And …"

"I did not allow myself to believe in it," the Buddhist lady paused, her eyelids flickered for a moment, a tear glinted, she nodded toward the bodies. "And now their souls are lost and in torment," she said, "It has taken them. The Foul Fiend has taken them, not only destroyed their bodies. It has taken their souls, or what passes for such. Many of them, in spite of our doctrinal differences, were my friends. They have become his creatures."

"His creatures?"

"Demons; they have become demons."

"Demons?"

"Yes, but not like you. You two, you Centurions, you Cosmos hybrids, you are good demons, you are angels." She raised her hand in blessing and then closed her eyes. "Now, go on your way. My soul, like the fragrance of burning leaves at autumn in the evening twilight, will be with you."

"Oh, Caliban!"

"Oh, Miranda!"

Miranda's and Caliban's fingers touched. Their whole world exploded in a brilliant display of Roman candles and other fireworks, streamers, and ribbons of light, and flashes of lightning and echoing of thunder.

"Whew!"

"Yes. Whew!"

After the lightning flash and the explosion, Miranda and Caliban found themselves, beautifully, tenderly, tangled up in each other's arms, her leg over his stomach, his arm under her back, her head lying on his arm, both of them lying on the floor of some sort of temple-like enclosure – it had Doric columns along both sides and a temple-like roof – and surrounded by ghouls who were peering at them and licking their lips.

"I wonder if they are tame." With regret, Caliban disentangled himself from Miranda, and stood up.

"They don't look tame." Miranda got to her feet.

The ghouls came hopping toward them.

"These last seasons, the Dead Lands teemed with ghouls," said Caliban, brandishing his scimitar, "they seemed to be a warning of what was to come."

"Like the zombie-bats, you mean."

The ghouls stopped and began to mewl and drool.

"Yes, plagues seem to come in waves – first ghouls, then zombie-bats, what next … locust, boils and puss, leeches, mosquitoes, blackflies, beetles, politicians, measles, economists, headaches and fevers?"

"Yes, my Prince and Pirate, such creatures are said to be precursors of the Apocalypse," said Miranda, "of the Four Horsemen, of the coming of the Foul Fiend, the rising of the dead, the Rapture, the Re-Building of the Temple, the destruction of the Golden Dome, worldwide religious war, and such-like prophecies foretold in many of the musty ancient books."

"I'd like to meet him – this Boy, this Foul Fiend!" Caliban's hand was firmly on the handle of his scimitar; they were shoulder to shoulder; with his Princess at his side, Caliban was ready to do battle with anything – any dragon, any serpent, any monster! "We must stare evil in the eye, and conquer!"

The ghouls cowered and did not move.

"We shall, my love, and we shall win, my love," Miranda fluttered her eyelashes at Caliban; she loved it when he indulged in highfalutin rhetoric and full-blown braggadocio. It made her feel all fuzzy and mushy.

One of the ghouls bayed, as if to the moon, opening its jaws wide.

"So this is Armageddon," Caliban said, "This is the final battle before the final revelation and the Second Coming or … Gog and Magog and stuff I read in an old sacred book from one of the old pre-Dolly pagan religions."

"The Bible," said Miranda, getting into her Cosmos Scout target practice stance and pointing her laser gun at the ghouls, who had stopped at some distance, seeming to doubt whether they should advance or not. Miranda was thinking of Bounce and Deep and Daisy, her ghoul friends, and of Little Jimmy Ghoul, whom she had petted more than once, and of Rodriguez Ghoul and Jane Ghoul, both of whom she rather liked, way back, centuries ago, well, just a day ago, in the Mutant Kingdom. She didn't want to kill ghouls, but if she had to, she would. She took aim at the ghoul she took to be the lead ghoul: between the eyes, as the instructions said, between the eyes.

The ghoul stared at her; then it cringed back, raising one arm in front of its eyes, as if it could no longer contemplate the laser gun, or perhaps her beauty, or perhaps the twirling gold stars and galaxies bursting in her eyes.

"Yes, that's it, the Bible, a fine meaty mash-up of a book, so many stories!" Caliban held his scimitar ready. He looked around at the assembled ghouls, "It is full of splendid, rambling adventures."

"They don't always agree, though," said Miranda, "If you look at Luke and Mathew, for instance, in the New Testament, or John, and so on, and their accounts of the crucifixion of Christ … even the dates … don't always …"

"Yes, I noticed that too. In fact, Princess, I was going to ask …"

The ghouls growled in unison, then retreated, then scattered; then, they were gone, disappearing behind the Doric columns.

"Well, that was easy, Princess." But Caliban frowned. There was something fishy … about this place …

"Yes, it is fishy," said Miranda, still holding her laser gun ready, and having caught Caliban's unspoken thought. "These walls are pretty shifty, if you ask me."

She was staring at a section of the wall which seemed to waver and float as if it were made of mist; then sparkling eyes, with whites and dark pupils, appeared, embedded in the stone; and parts of the walls swirled and whirled and became vertical rubbery tentacles, with giant suckers. Cupped in some of the suckers were eyes. The eyes blinked at Miranda. A mouth appeared and stuck out its tongue. It was rather like the effect one might get from eating a ghoul-grown mushroom out in the Dead Lands with Bounce the Ghoul, but not so pleasant.

"This is interesting," she said.

"Yes, interesting," said Caliban, "mystical almost, perhaps." He was more subdued now. The bounding main and the desert sands seemed much more accommodating places. This underground lair was full of snares and traps and trickery. Critical Theology and Biblical exegesis could wait.

Miranda tightened her grip on his arm.

"Let us walk on!"

"Yes, in a labyrinth, the only thing, really, is to keep going."

"Yes."

"Yes."

Miranda thought of old fairy tales where two children, hand in hand, found themselves lost in a forest and surrounded by wickedness of every kind on every side, and facing various tests and trials they had to surmount.

"Caliban, my Prince, this is fun!"

"Fun, Princess? Yes, I am sure it is!" He stopped her for just an instant, and he kissed her hard and swift on the lips.

"Oh, Caliban," she murmured. The golden galaxies in her eyes went wild, turning cartwheels, exploding out into Roman candles, billowing into clouds of stars and supernovas.

"My princess, my love!" He brushed a strand of blond hair away from her eyes. Her eyes were, well, unbelievable, he could drown in her gaze; he could live in her eyes; his destiny, he knew, lay in her gaze.

After a bit, they came to a dead end – well, it was a quay on a shallow underground waterway, but the liquid in the waterway was more the consistency of mud than of water.

"I was – I am – sure this is the right way." Miranda sniffed the air.

"So, we go forward." Caliban glanced at the swirling darkness; it reflected the emergency lights and the phosphorescent lichen and mushrooms. It almost looked alive; perhaps this liquid was some new form of creature. He stepped into the liquid. It was thick, but not sticky. And it didn't dissolve his legs or burn, which was reassuring.

"We go forward." Miranda put one foot, gingerly, into the muddy, swirling liquid. It was shin-deep and warm and moving slowly.

They stepped ahead and waded along, in silence, hand in hand.

The tunnel was about ten meters wide, and it had inward sloping walls and a sloping gently arched roof, about six meters up at its highest point. The muck got deeper.

Miranda and Caliban pushed forward, wading through the knee-deep muck, brandishing swords left, right, and center, and Miranda unsheathed her laser gun, and, zap, she brought down a nasty-looking tentacle that had been hovering right over Caliban's head.

"Thanks, Princess!" Caliban was delighted to have a princess who was as good with firearms and cold steel as any pirate he had ever met. But, then, he had never met any pirates. Tentacles rose out of the water.

Tentacles wound around the beams supporting the tunnel. Tentacles came out of the windows of a wrecked subway car; baby tentacles, like snakes, slithered out of the eye sockets of skulls of former subway riders who must have died, Miranda thought, in one of the many terrorist attacks of ancient times.

A tentacle shot out spraying goo, and it swirled around and around wrapping Miranda in a cocoon of glittering threads, faster and faster until she looked like a glittering mummy.

"Help, Caliban!" Miranda shouted just before threads wove a gag around the lower part of her face, sealing her mouth shut. Now only her eyes, wild with terror and anger, were visible.

Caliban grabbed for the threads, but they were too fast. Then he brought his scimitar down full force upon the ribbon of thread, snapping it, and it dangled, whip-lashed back and forth, and Caliban, desperately splashing through the muck, slashed and slashed and slashed, slicing the ribbon into small fragments that fell away, glittering like bits of a shattered rainbow.

He swung around, just as the tentacle was rearing back, ready to spray out more of its gooey venom, and his scimitar sliced through the tentacle, sending the nozzle splashing down into the muck where it wiggled and splashed about like the nervous amputated tail-end of a twenty-foot-long serpent.

Caliban swirled around and grabbed Miranda, who, with her legs pinned together, and arms pinned to her sides, was about to fall into the muck. He cradled her – his cocooned princess – in his arms. "Can you break free, Princess, or shall I cut you free?"

Miranda's eyes softened for a second in the glow of love – Oh, to be held thus, and carried thus, helpless, pinioned, and enclosed, like a mermaid, in the arms of her Prince!

Then her eyes blazed with anger – golden explosions bursting like so many dizzy Roman candles – and she nodded and, making delightful muffled groans, she struggled and twisted and turned, mightily, and then pop, one arm was free, pop, two arms were free, and then, with a little help from Caliban, she shimmied out of the cocoon, which, bereft of its prisoner, fell away like the most delicate of iridescent moiré silk dresses, and floated for an instant on the black muck before dissolving into sparkles in the air and rainbow swirls on the moving surface.

Miranda straightened her skin-shorts. "Well, my Prince, that was very exciting." A delicious little shiver coursed down her spine, branched into her tummy and thighs. She pressed close, and gazed up into Caliban's eyes. She sighed.

"Yes, it was," said Caliban, blushing, looking into the golden spirals in her eyes that led to infinite depths, and feeling how deliciously strange and exciting it had been to have his Princess, helpless and mute, all wrapped up in glittering thread, a pinioned mermaid, squirming in his arms.

"Onward," said Miranda with a grin; having captured Caliban's thought. She liked that image, that thought; her, helpless in his arms, wrapped up like a present, a mermaid, a goddess, a gift.

"Onward," said Caliban; and again, mysteriously, he blushed.

Finally, they came to a landing dock, which must have been a place where merchandize was placed on underground trains.

"Interesting," said Caliban, "the technology of the ancients – BD, before Dolly – was quite impressive."

"Yes," said Miranda, "look at that crane over there, and look at that …"

"Watch out, Princess!"

A huge nozzle appeared, and it came down, and it grabbed Miranda, and it sucked up the water that was all around her into a tornado-like whirling structure and Miranda was whirled around and around and sucked up and, just as she was about to disappear, into the huge nozzle, just as she was lifted up into the tornado cloud, Caliban leaped into the whirling mass, and he was swept up with her, and together they were whirled around and around. In the maelstrom, Caliban managed to sheath his scimitar and put both arms around Miranda and she put both arms around him and so they were sucked into the nozzle together and they ascended in a column of light and whirling water which then turned to darkness, and then to light again, and the water was gone, and they were floating, swimming in what seemed to be absolute darkness, somewhere in space, and they could see, in the distance, several galaxies and some distant stars and what looked like the Milky Way, the cross-section of our own galaxy, and Caliban moved his lips to speak, but no words came out, and Miranda tried to speak too, but no words came out, and so she decided, well, they both decided, simultaneously, that the best thing they could do would be to kiss and so they did.

The kiss lasted for quite a while and was delicious.

Caliban had never realized, until today, really, how soft and delicious and arousing a kiss could be.

Miranda thought that this kiss was just about perfect. No, it was perfect, absolutely perfect.

A cuckoo clock drifted past.

A wolf in a waistcoat drifted by and took off his broad-brimmed hat to salute them.

A school of fish swam by, and an octopus, who made eyes at them, and a shark, who nodded, and a very large tuna.

An ancient communications satellite drifted by, and an abandoned space station that had been shattered by a meteorite.

Then they were tumbling down, and down, and down …

And, wham, they were spat out …

"Oh, golly!"

"Oh, gosh!"

"What is this?" Caliban stared.

"Yes, darling Caliban, what circus are we in now?" Miranda stared.

V and Kat walked on through the Religious Underground; they walked past overturned shrines, dead priests, mutilated pastors, and other spiritual folk, all dead.

V mulled over the fate of Miranda and Caliban. She was sure, somehow, that they were safe. It would be awful to gain a daughter and a son and then to lose both – but that was a selfish thought; Caliban and Miranda were very much their own persons, and their destinies, too, good or bad, were theirs, not hers. But if the Foul Fiend harmed either of them, then she would … She curled her fists, she would utterly destroy him!

"The exit from the Religious underground should be down this way," Kat said, as they walked along a canal.

"Yes, that will take us toward the Mind." V was pensive, lost in thought, yearning even …

Out of the gloom and mist, a tall thin, bearded man in a long robe came toward them; he was walking along the edge of the canal and he stopped as they came forward toward him.

He raised his hand in salutation.

V and Kat did the same.

"You are travelers in the valley of death," he said.

"Yes, you could say that."

"Never fear, I shall be with you always."

V said nothing; this man had perhaps the most beautiful eyes she had ever seen.

"That which you have lost will be returned," he said.

"That is good news," V let her gaze rest on his. What expressive eyes he had!

"Here, my sisters, drink this," he said, and he pulled a small flask from his robe and handed it to them.

"Well, yes, thank you," V drank and handed it to Kat, and Kat drank and handed the flask back to the man.

"Here, eat this, and think of me," he said, pulling a power bar from the depths of his robes. He unpeeled the wrapper. "A young lady – a very fine young lady – introduced these to me. They are quite convenient." He handed the power bar to Kat.

Kat took a bite and handed the power bar to V; V hesitated, did not accept the bar, and turned to the man, "I cannot eat, oh my brother," she said, "You know that I only …"

"I know. I know, sister, I know. You only accept liquid, coffee, wine, and blood sacrifice; bodies have piled up on your altar, and solids you cannot eat." He laid his hand on V's shoulder. "But now you can eat, my sister, and from this moment forth, you will eat whatever you desire, and yet your powers will be undimmed."

V hesitated a moment, glanced at Kat, and then she shrugged and accepted the bar, and took a bite, and chewed and swallowed.

Kat stared. V and the man, standing close, seemed as if they almost glowed, and, in some weird way, V in her sparkling black Centurion uniform, and the man in his simple Bedouin robes, did look like they were friends and strangely they looked as if they had known each other for a long time, for centuries, and perhaps they had.

"Well, well, I'll be …" Kat whispered.

V took another bite, and then another; she swallowed. "Thank you," she said, and she handed the package back to him.

"I shall be with you forevermore, both of you," he said, carefully placing the package in a pocket of his robe, "And you shall be with me."

"Thank you," Kat figured something extraordinary was going on.

"Thank you," V smiled at the man.

He put his hand on her forehead. "It is I who thank you," he said; he turned to Kat and laid his hand on her forehead. "I shall be at your sides, both of you, in your struggle with the Prince of Darkness, the infinitely cunning Boy, that eternally inventive Foul Fiend. I shall be there in spirit. And when and if needed, I shall be there in the flesh."

"Thank you," V said.

"Thank you," Kat echoed.

"Goodbye, or, rather au revoir, my sisters, my friends," he said, and he walked off down the canal bank until he was lost in the gathering mist and glowing darkness.

"Well, well," said V, savoring the aftertaste of the power bar; it was the first time she had eaten anything solid, in, well, in more than 2,500 years.

"So, now …" Kat said.

"It's this way, I think," V said.

"Does that mean the end of …?"

"… of my need for blood sacrifice?" V put her hand on Kat's shoulder. "Yes."

"I think so – I think it truly does."

"Maybe it was time."

"Yes, I think maybe it was."

When the horde of ghouls rushed at them, splashing through the shallow water, Clown wondered, just for an instant, what she should do, and then, instinctively, in a flash, she knew.

She leaped high in the air, and came straight down on the back of one of the ghouls, right in the middle of the crowd of ghouls, and, squeezing his neck between her thighs, and grabbing hold of his long pointed ears, and twisting, she wrenched his head around and broke it, and tore it off, and tossed it away.

A gush of black ghoul blood spurted up between her thighs covering her belly and breasts and legs with ghoul guck – really disgusting – and as his headless body pitched forward into the bubbling water, and as the other ghouls turned around, blank-eyed to stare at her, and as she was aware of Black Tarzan tossing ghouls over his shoulder, and of Geisha frantically kicking at ghouls, and smashing them in the jaw and whamming them with a side-chop to the side of their heads, some of the heads bursting like rotten eggs, as all this was going on Clown leaped off the sinking ghoul body.

And, just as her feet touched the surface of the concourse, she bounced up high again, shooting upwards like an elastic, and, aiming carefully, she came straight down, both feet together, on the face of a ghoul that, startled and with its jaw hanging open was staring up at her, an aghast expression on its weirdly blank face, and, with both feet locked together, she smashed into the face, and the face seemed to foreshorten, flatten, and then explode, bursting apart, bits flying out in all directions like an exploding star. Clown leaped away, heading for her next target.

The battle continued.

It was ferocious.

At a certain point, it seemed they might lose.

"Damned things, there are just too many of them," Black Tarzan threw two of the creatures against the façade of a hat shop where their bodies seemed to flatten and explode into yogurt colored mush which then dribbled down the old mossy and dusty façade under a faded sign advertising fedoras.

Geisha was struggling with two ghouls, swirling over in the water, trying to get free of them so she could get in a good kick and side-chop or two. Elegant martial arts require a modicum of distance.

Clown was backed against a wall with three hungry-looking ghouls closing in; she kicked out, but the ballet slippers were not every effective, so she did a double somersault and found herself on the other side of the ghouls.

She kicked one of the ghouls in the behind, making him sprawl forward on his muzzle, and she then picked up a rock – where it had fallen from she didn't know – and she smashed the second ghoul over the head.

His skull burst in a gooey explosion and left a web of guck hanging in the air which then collapsed slowly, drifting down, like a gossamer fragment of mosquito netting, over the crumpled body of the ghoul, and which seemed to be falling in slow-motion, and then, finally, splashed down.

The third ghoul turned to growl at Clown. She leaped and kicked him with both feet straight in the mouth, and he rocketed backward and smashed his head against the wall and fell down, either dead or unconscious. His neck was twisted at an odd angle, and goo oozed from his skull. Dead, thought Clown, he was probably dead.

Several ghouls turned to run. One of them was caught and lifted up by Black Tarzan and tossed to the other side of the cavern and smashed against a burgundy-colored tiled wall that said "Celine's Bespoke Hamburgers." The ghoul slid down the wall and plopped into the seething water, a lifeless lump, a shriveled up, whey-colored, quivering piece of flesh, face turned upwards, bubbling ghoul goo from mouth, eyes, and ears.

"I think they were human once," said Geisha, looking down at two ghouls lying dead at her feet.

"Yes," said Tarzan, "Yes, they were."

More ghouls were on their way, they were creeping out of cracks in the old cavern-like shopping concourse, mossy bits of lighting cable hung down; pieces of ancient rusty display stands lay about.

"There are too many," said Black Tarzan.

They were coming from all directions.

"We're trapped," said Geisha.

"Yes, we are," Clown looked around. There must be a way out, but she didn't see one.

"Well, let's make our last stand, then," said Black Tarzan, "backs against the wall, over there!"

Mrs. Rosenthal, on the 67th floor of the Golden Harvest Towers, was on her fifth martini. The world was getting very strange indeed, but perhaps it was all an illusion. After all, she should have been dead by now – and cremated. Perhaps she was dead. Maybe she had never been born. Maybe it was all a dream – maybe the whole shebang, her whole one hundred and twelve years, had been an illusion. Perhaps there was no such thing as the human race, no such thing as Elysium. But whether it was dream or reality, it had been interesting, particularly the last few hours.

At one point, about half-an-hour ago, a huge, really ugly man-sized bat had flown straight into the armored glass roof of her greenhouse gallery, her arboretum, which contained many miniatures of now extinct species – oak, maple, poplar, pine – and of which she was very proud. The creature splattered against the pane, and then bearing its fangs, scrabbling at the glass, and leaving a smear of foam and blood, it slid off the slanted roof glass, and fell out of sight.

"How extraordinary," said Mrs. Rosenthal, turning to her robot companion, Amber Fossil, who seemed, poor dear, to have lost all her spark and energy. Amber was lying inert – no conversational gambits whatsoever – sprawled on the second deckchair.

Mrs. Rosenthal sighed. The poor thing had probably been programmed to terminate and shut down with my death and remain in stasis, as an empty vessel, before being reassigned to a new solitary pre-terminal superannuated person in need of companionship. I wish I knew how to restart her!

Mrs. Rosenthal got up from the deckchair and walked back to the bar, and she mixed herself another martini, wondering whether she should plop in an olive or not. Being dead already, in a manner of speaking, she found, gave one a sense of serenity, put everything in perspective, and gave her focus – for the moment the olive was the most important thing. Let us focus, she told herself, on the olive, pitted, and perfect! It is a Zen olive. The universe in the palm of my hand. And so, in a state almost approaching mystical bliss, Mrs. Rosenthal conjured up the martini – the perfect martini!

Laura Levitt was fed up. The Burbs were burning; walls of fire flickered on the horizon; billows of greasy black smoke rose up and obscured the light.

Laura sighed. Being dead was one thing, but being a risen-from-the-dead mummy-like zombie, was quite another. It was not pleasant. The dreamless sleep was certainly preferable. She wondered if the other living dead felt the way she did. If she could have, she would have gone on strike. But the voice of the Boy was imperious and brooked no denial.

Laura had already torn several dim-witted and slow-moving, still-living human beings limb from limb or just poked out their eyes with her bony fingers which were amazingly strong and had a will of their own, doing all sorts of things which she had no intention of doing at all and which she found totally objectionable.

As soon as they were dead, or a few minutes, afterward, most of the former humans rose up from their dead stance, and, without eyes, and missing an arm or half a leg, joined the posse, lurching or limping or groping along.

Fires were burning everywhere, and the dead preacher – whose name was Stanley – was up on an oil drum hollering about Amos the Shepherd and Jeffery the Hermit, and John the Feverish Prophetic Islander and Ichabod the Unfaithful, brother of Ahitub and son of Phineas, and Ichabod III, the Holy Gossip of Rhodes, and all number of Luminaries and Prophets, such as Hilbert the Hilltop Visionary, and he yammered, too, about how Holy Scriveners and Visionaries, like John of Patmos, and various and sundry Shamans, who danced their nights away, and who had, all of them, foreseen in exquisite detail all of that which was presently taking place and that all of this was spelled out in great detail in the Holy Book which contained all things and outside of which there was nothing and no truth whatsoever since by definition the Word of the Divinity encompasses all that is, ever has been, ever can be, and ever will be.

Those of the dead that could speak mumbled "Hallelujah!"

Laura Levitt wondered how long this tiresome tomfoolery would continue. She thirsted after oblivion, the long silken eternal night in which there is no sensation, and no sermons, and where there are no thoughts sacred or profane to bother the addled empty skull.

She clicked her tongue at the little skeletal cadaver, Kiddo, who was still clinging to her hand. He looked up at her with empty cavernous sockets, tightened his bony grip on her hand, and clicked back. This is something akin to love, thought Laura Levitt. She transmitted the thought, "How ya doin', Kiddo?"

The mind-answer came immediately. "Happy, as long as you are here!"

Now, if Laura Levitt could have shed a tear, she would have.

"Ma'am, what do you think of this?"

Demi Pfeiffer was in the middle of the group of Centurions in the armored bunker on top of the Krupp-Thyssen building, and together, they stared at the screen where reports were collated. In one corner of the screen, the Alison-and-Ken Show – as it had come to be known in the last few hours – unfolded its horrors. How those two kept it up, Demi had no idea. They were like acrobats!

Amid the rising chaos, reports were still coming in.

Everywhere, small groups of Presidential Guard Centurions were trying to keep order. They were failing. Some Centurions went mad, attacked other Centurions. One by one, the units disappeared from the big map, the remaining Com Unit Lights going out.

The city was collapsing. Parts of the dome sliced through bodies and buildings, smashing down like shattered crystal.

Flocks of zombie-bats moved through the darkening sky, and giant twisters drifted between the burning and shattered skyscrapers.

Downtown, toward the southern tip of what had once been Manhattan, many buildings had collapsed; they seemed to have melted, sinking down, as if something was eating away at the very foundations of Elysium. Demi glanced out the armored glass. "Do you see that?"

"Yes, ma'am, I see that."

"What do you make of it?"

"Something's devouring the very earth itself, ma'am, that's my thought," said the Centurion.

"Right," said Demi, "Right." So the Prophecies of Billie McAdams, the girl from the desert, might indeed be true, even in detail. The Boy would seize the Mind, and turn it into a machine which would devour the earth.

Images, a potpourri of images were streaming in: People fighting off zombie-bats. People suffering sudden headaches, clutching their skulls, gushing blood from eyes, ears, noses. Foreheads split open. Skulls exploded, or split in half. Faces were cloven from within, two ghastly sides separating, as if peeled away. It was not pretty; Demi grimaced.

Other images: some humans merely went mad as obscene or horrendous ideas were downloaded and exploded inside the synapses, and the cerebellum became an inner theater of horrors. Voices came from everywhere:

"Oh, oh, no, I can't …."

"I can't stand this."

Everywhere, people hallucinated; they attacking their neighbors, mothers attacked their children, children turned into gremlin-like monsters, attacking their parents, and each other.

People were disemboweled on the shopping levels.

People were leaping from bridges, from balconies, from concourses.

The air was full of falling bodies, pattering down like raindrops.

CHAPTER 7 – MASSACRE

Deputy Chief Police Colonel Rankin, leader of Internal Security SWAT TEAM III, stuck his thumbs under his belt and shifted the weight of the two holsters. It had been the last straw when the President-Leader suggested they enlist the help of the hybrids to repel the wave of evil. The President-Leader was weak and despicable and had too many principles. It was a good thing he was dead from the explosion had destroyed the Presidential Office and everybody in it.

Well, it was typical of the President-Leader: he was tolerant, and he let all sorts of sin and perversion and dissent exist and prosper; he often said, "Let's let people alone! Freedom, when we can re-establish it, will be the best medicine."

No wonder the bastard had been assassinated. Look at the Sin Zone! It should have been cleaned up years ago! Look at the Religious Underground, the whole place should have been firebombed. Look at the Subs! Who needed them? They were unproductive, useless ... parasites ... They should have been exterminated, as for the Burbites ...

"Okay, officers, listen up here." Rankin looked around at his men and women. "We now have an opportunity to purify the city of this Sin Zone vermin. This crisis should be put to good use. All deviants and all Subs with any Deviant or Subversive tags – check the barcode transmission markers of Subs – must be exterminated."

The President-Leader had secretly protected the Sin Zone, and he had protected the Religious Underground and even the hybrids out in their camp, declaring those demons "a precious national resource." Now, with the President-Leader dead, the true Total Purification could begin.

Finally, Colonel Rankin and the STS – SWAT Team System – could purify society. Sin and science had brought doom upon the human race, and now he, Colonel Rankin, would begin the Total Purification.

He had sent dozens of SWAT TEAMS into the Sub levels, but he would lead the attack on the center of the Sin Zone. It would be more fun. And, besides, he wanted to find and rescue Clown. He would keep her for himself as his personal puppet and slave; after all, she was his creation, and he was quite rightly her master!

Clown was his personal property, and, when the New World Cosmos Order dawned, he would finally be able to openly brand her as such! She would be his pet, to obey his every command.

Rankin sent the Command for Purification from on high, in the name of the Committee for Public Safety and Homeland Security.

It was such an unusual and radical order that the various units really should have waited to verify that, in fact, it did come from the highest authority, the President-Leader's Office.

But they didn't wait. The officer corps of the SWAT teams were eager to spring into action and so spring into action they did – SWAT teams, and Extermination Squads set out to pre-assigned sections of the city. Any means were to be used, so said the order, which meant carte blanche or a blank check: kill as many as you want, any way you want! Enjoy!

After the coup d'état and the initial massacres – of politicians, judges, journalists – and of SINs and Hybrids – the President-Leader had been amazingly tolerant, much less bloodthirsty than many of his subordinates hoped.

They continued to torture and erase and enslave, of course, but much of the information on their activities did not filter up to the highest level. The President was kept ignorant of the worst excesses – though he did occasionally find out, and then his wrath was terrible to see.

Colonel Bradley Hubert Rankin led his best Storm Troop SWAT TEAM – Number Seven – into the Sin Zone. He wanted to see the scum die and fry and be smashed to smithereens, so he led from the front.

He hated certain aspects of himself and those aspects he saw embodied in the filth and perverted vermin that inhabited the Sin Zone.

He would exterminate them.

And, exterminating them, he would purify himself. He was aware of the theory: Fascism, like witch-hunting, and lynching scapegoats, is based, in part, on self-hatred; it is a form of exorcism, a cutting out, a purification, an expulsion of the abject, and, if one needs to be purified, then that means one is not oneself so pure, and therefore …

And, of course, he had that little ulterior motive for being in the front line: he wanted to make sure Clown survived.

Clown was too good to sacrifice. She was his work of art, the best he had ever created. He had first caught a glimpse of her when she was still human, still a Cosmos, still herself. She was presenting a case in the Special Tribunal and you might say it had been love – or lust, spiced up with hatred, at first sight – he had immediately known he must possess her, and he must enslave her, and he must turn her into a monster.

She was an ultra-logical, but passionate lawyer, a litigator of extraordinary talent, a cool customer, always impeccably dressed, so seemingly in control of her own emotions, so sensitive to every nuance of mood and logic and rhetoric, she could fine-tune her words and above all her wonderful gaze – she had the most marvelous, expressive eyes – to persuade a judge, to conquer a jury, to seduce a witness, and make even those fighting her admire her …

Yes, he must have her.

Oh, those marvelous eyes! That subtle and commanding gaze …!

He would have her.

Particularly after she had gently but absolutely humiliated him on the stand when he was a witness in the trial of a dissident, he had sworn: Yes, I shall destroy her, and turn her into my creature. "So, Colonel Rankin," she had asked, turning to him and with her pitiless gaze staring straight – and deep – into his eyes, "what is your definition of 'excessive force'?" She paused. "Is it normal, Colonel Rankin, for young women to die when in your custody and to die from internal injuries?"

She was dangerous.

And she was beautiful.

So he arranged for her arrest; it was easy, she defended subversives and critics of the regime; she was considered brilliant, outspoken, and non-conformist; so, on a trumped-up charge, using false testimony from paid informers, and using planted evidence, and exploiting a few legal ambiguities and quibbles in the Anti-Subversion Anti-Terrorism Act, she was brought in, she lost her Cosmos Status, and – thus – she ceased, within a few minutes, to be; she was gone; she disappeared; she no longer existed; her records were obliterated; all electronic and physical traces of her existence were evaporated; her identity was erased.

As for the media, it was reported that she had died in an accident.

The body was unrecognizable – and cremated.

Her family was allowed to hold a discreet ceremony.

Everyone who knew her assumed she was dead, hit by an out-of-control oversized overly zealous Pub Drone, which then exploded, blowing her body to smithereens, just so much mush, not worthy of identification.

And so he was able to make her his own: Internalized mind-inhibitors made it impossible for her to contact anyone she knew or to try to re-establish a link with her own life; instant absolute pain and unconsciousness would result from any effort to do so; and, if she persisted, if somehow she remained conscious, she would automatically be terminated. She knew this; she also knew that if she did try to contact anyone from her old life – that person would suffer a horrible fate. And if any old acquaintance or family member did see her, they would not recognize the brilliant lawyer of old – she had been morphed into Clown.

She lived in a cage.

She was the cage.

Her body was the cage.

Her face was the cage.

Her clown eyes were the cage.

It was a perfect cage, custom-made; it was a cage he had designed, taking great care, exercising great psychological subtlety; he really was proud of his creation.

Colonel Rankin had interrogated her himself; he had personally designed and supervised the morphological transformation and the sexual enhancement; he had her tailor-made to fit his own quirks, kinks, and innermost darkest obsessions – transforming her eyes into expressionless clown cross-button eyes was a stroke of genius – and so she was the highest most perfect expression of his most elaborate kinky hobbyhorses upon which he liked to ride like Paul Revere, thundering on horseback through the darkest night, through lightning and thunder and hail and rain, or like the Lone Ranger or the Dark Avenger, under a full moon, living out his dreams in the absolutely ridiculous wildness that was at the secret center of his being. Oh, he was a wild one alright; underneath the starched uniform and the rigid hieratic posture, Rankin knew that he was a true Bad Boy, and, truly, a chameleon Superman, beneath the law-and-order mask, he was an anarchist.

Sometimes he thought of himself as a werewolf, trapping Clown in a dark forest, pursuing her through the rustling trees, his furry body rippling among silvery moon shadows.

Sometimes he was a slinky vampire gentleman, entombing Clown in the deepest dungeon of a Transylvanian Castle or in the basement of a decommissioned madhouse or ancient 20th Century high school.

But mostly, in their games, for which he paid the going tariff, he was just "the King" – "his Majesty" – to her.

In his more serene and lucid moments, Bradley Hubert Rankin reckoned that he was, in his own inimitable way, in love with Clown and that if ever she and he survived and if she could be reconciled to him and to her own state – once a beauty-queen-quality-lawyer and First Class Cosmos, and now a transfigured Sub Clown Sex Worker Slave – then he would make her his forever, and keep her for himself in some hideaway known only to him, perhaps in a cave out in the Burbs, perhaps in a creepy rat-infested dungeon under the City.

She was so saucy, even now, even in her degraded plasticized button-eyed state, wagging her cap and bells at him, criticizing him – him, His Majesty the King! Why the very idea of such impertinence – and from an untamed female slave! At the mere recollection of the afternoon scene, he shivered with pleasure. He'd recorded it for later replay, forever and forever and forever.

"Okay, Storm Troops, you open fire at will and don't worry about shoppers unless they are First Class Cosmos; if other shoppers are down here – Subs and so on – it's their own damned fault and they are sinners like the others and can be eliminated, but be careful, if you can, to distinguish First Class Cosmos from the other shoppers and perverts, it's best, if you can, not to kill or maim First Class Cosmos but rescue them, got it?"

"Yes, sir," they chorused.

"Remember – there is no forgiveness; in our world, pity is an impertinent non-sequitur."

"Yes, sir," the voices echoed.

"But, listen up Storm Troops, there is a female clown down here, her name is Clown, she is an undercover agent, so get her alive, and bring her to me if you can, do not eliminate her or damage her, I repeat, do not eliminate or damage Clown, she is a valuable and unique asset and I do not want to lose her."

"What's this clown look like?" One of the gas-masks, Lieutenant Janie Yong, turned her gas-mask snout toward him, the question wheezing out through the mechanical voice box.

"She looks like a Clown, you idiot. She has a clown face, is a touch androgynous, and can flip about with her cute little body like an elastic acrobat!

Got it? She's a slippery character, with a deadly side-chop. And, watch out, she is quick and clever, and *valuable*, so, if she tried to run, use a non-lethal, non-disfiguring stun gun on her, got it."

"Yes, sir," the voices echoed through his earphones, as the gas-mask snouts with impenetrable eyes all stood around facing him.

The problem with Lieutenant Janie Yong was she always asked awkward questions; Rankin stared at her. The pretty little bitch had a mind of her own; when this caper was over she should be disappeared and morph-plasticized too. He made a mental note to remind himself: *Lieutenant Yong: de-certification, morph, and plasticization. What would he plastize her into? Let's see … Some new sort of person-doll-toy … perhaps a mechanical clock, she could come out of a cage and announce the hours …* Well, his imagination was unlimited; he could leave that decision for later.

And they went into action!

Oh, and bejesus, and it was a pleasurable sight to see, it truly was, the way they cut into the erotic rabble on rue St. Denis!

Flesh and blood flying everywhere!

Rankin rubbed his hands!

Rue Saint-Denis, Elysium City, in the Sin Zone: 14:00 hours.

Seeing the SWAT team advance, Male Sub, street performer and acrobat Guy Tulip, pushed a shopper, Lyse Saint-Ross, a sleek young Cosmos First Class female, who was a creative accounts executive at Dunn & Dunn, and who was slumming in the Sin Zone, looking for kinky ideas for her up-coming wedding night, coated, for the slumming expedition, in a stylish and expensive imported leather and bio-skin brocade catsuit, well, this above-mentioned Guy Tulip pushed above-mentioned Lyse Saint-Ross into a protective niche behind an olive-drab-green faux Parisian pissoir.

Lyse Saint-Ross fell on her smooth elegant shapely backside and stared at Guy Tulip, and was about to say, "What the fuck do you think you are doing, you Loser, you Sub, you Clown?" when a laser beam whammed into the wall of the Jean Genet Electro Bordello just one meter above her stylishly braded and feathered topknot – a flourish on the retro-bob-cut, and Lyse realized that this Loser-Clown-Sub had saved her life, "Thanks," she said, and "I was going to curse you," she added, wide-eyed, thinking, What a bitch I am, even if I am a Cosmos First Class and bitchiness is part of my Civil Duty and Natural Entitlement when confronting Subs and Yahoo Burbites.

Guy Tulip said, "Yeah, I saw your curse coming, it was forming on your glowing, ruby-red lips, and it was natural enough." Guy was drinking her in: Lyse Saint-Ross had perfect synthetic tanned skin, blue eyes, and golden hair cut short in a bob cut topped by a feathered topknot, and, over her leather brocade catsuit, the latest in a retro-post-Second World War style, broad-shouldered cream-colored bomber-pilot jacket, and an ultra-short pleated cream-colored skirt, and lips to die for. Guy had always wanted to be a designer; he swallowed, "It would be natural for a goddess like you to curse a Sub like me, I mean I gave you a pretty vicious shove, and un-pre-authorized Sub-Cosmos tactile contact is punishable by partial erasure under Section X-B-5 of the Separation of Winners and Losers Act."

"You saved my life, you idiot street-clown," she said, looking at him, he was unshaven and had a nose ring, and his arms, which were covered in tattoos, bulged with muscles and he was wearing a leather vest and leather shorts and not much of anything else. "Don't beat yourself up," she said, "I'm grateful to you. I owe you my life."

"We'd better get out of here," he peeked out from behind the pissoir, "they are going to kill everybody."

"They wouldn't dare," she said, "Not Cosmos."

Guy stroked the romantic stubble of his chin, rough like sandpaper, thinking: this ethereal beauty had obviously lived too long – in fact her whole life – in the airy-fairy protected domain of Cosmos, up in the perfumed air, among the dreaming towers and the artificial clouds; she had no idea, absolutely no idea ...

"Oh, yes they would," he said.

"You think so?"

Another laser beam sizzled into the wall above them; all around there were screams, shouts, ululations of horror. The beam traced a bright flame-yellow line down the wall, outlining the pissoir. Then it hit the pissoir, bouncing off, sending off sparks redolent of simulated antique Parisian urine, with an aftertaste of old coffee grounds and wet Gauloises. The air was dense with smoke.

"I know so. I'm a Sub, remember. You Cosmos Elitists don't see life as it is. You live in a protected bubble."

"Okay, Sub, I believe you," she said, "You're the boss. You know the lay of the land and how to survive. Lead on!"

They dodged down a side street. Laser beams zapped above them, sizzling against the sign that said "Eugene Delacroix lived here." An artificial chestnut tree burst into flame. Soft-nosed bullets smashed into the limestone facades splintering the stone, leaving deep gouged smoking pockmarks.

"Down," Guy Tulip shouted, and pushed Lyse Saint-Ross to the ground as a laser beam sizzled through the air, cutting a plate glass window right down the middle. The glass fell away with a clatter and splashed over them, slashing into their costumes and flesh, but not seriously, in a dozen places.

Death by a thousand cuts, thought Lyse Saint-Ross, staring at the criss-cross blood pattern blossoming on her stomach. The jacket and skirt and catsuit were ruined!

The President-Leader would never have permitted this, she thought. Hail, Hail, all Hail, she thought, a ghost of a salute, Hail, Hail, all Hail! May he rest in peace! What a tragedy that the man had been murdered, just when we need him most!

The laser beam had moved on. The air was roiling with acrid smoke, and everywhere was the smell of burned and burning flesh and the burning sting-ing sensation of teargas.

The street lamps glowed in the gathering poisonous mist.

More bullets zapped, exploding the stonework just above their heads.

Guy grabbed Lyse. He rolled them both over and over, along the foot of the building; then he pushed her down an antique coal chute; she tumbled, head over heels, then sliding sideways, down into a cloud of coal dust. Guy followed and they landed in a heap at the bottom in a five-inch-deep layer of ancient coal dust.

She sneezed and coughed and he clamped his hand over her mouth. She looked at him with terrified eyes, the whites startling, glowing, in the sud-denly coal-black face.

Guy wanted to sneeze himself, but he didn't dare. His nose tickled, his nostril vibrated, his mind told him he had to sneeze and now, but somehow he told it to shut up.

The basement was not empty. There were eyes looking at them – red eyes that glowed. "Mutants," he whispered, and he took his hand off her mouth, and she looked at him, the whites of her eyes even brighter now in the coal-dark gloaming.

"Mutants?" she mouthed the word.

"Monkey Boys," he mouthed back, "mini-ghouls."

Lyse stared. She'd thought that mutants were out in the badlands, not in Elysium City, not in the center of the universe.

"Child morphs," he whispered.

"Child morphs?"

"They are extremely violent."

"Oh."

"Cannibalistic."

"Christ!"

The mutants leaped. Guy Tulip slapped one of them so hard it flew across the basement landing with a clatter among a pile of metallic rubbish.

The other mutant had seized Lyse Saint-Ross by the neck. She seized it by its neck. It bit at her, its teeth chomping, but she was able to hold it far enough away, and push it back. It used its foot claws to strike at her, its foot claws were three inches long at least and sharp as razorblades. The mutant was like a small hairless chalk-white almost phosphorescent monkey, about two and a half feet tall. It released its hold on her neck. She felt the claws rake across her belly and thighs.

"You little bastard," she growled between her teeth. And she turned over and pushed the monkey down into the coal dust, and she kneed the monkey in the groin, and she held tight to its neck, "You little bastard, you give up or I will kill you."

Lyse Saint-Ross had had Cosmos Youth military training and Cosmos Youth self-defence implants, though she'd never used them. And she had had extra muscle modification, and she had never used that either, but it came in handy. And her mother – who was an excessively beautiful, rich, thin-lipped Cosmos perfectionist – had told her that these were useless frills, and Lyse had said, "Yes, but mother you never know, I mean if we are tossed out into the Dead Lands or lost in a tropical jungle or in the tropical Arctic methane tundra you have to know how to wrestle a Burmese Python to the ground, right, and you have to know what roots, tubers, and berries and mushrooms you can eat, right? If the world – our world – comes to an end, we have to be ready, right? The President-Leader tells us that a Cosmos has to be ready to face anything and everything, even the end of our Cosmos world."

"Our Cosmos world will never come to an end," her mother had said, "Our dear glorious President-Leader will ensure that we and our kind are eternal."

Lyse had just given her mother a look. It was no use arguing with mother, particularly when the argument concerned the Glorious President-Leader. Her mother was smitten, and an unconditional follower of the Glorious Leader, but she did not really understand the Glorious Leader who, Lyse was convinced, was much more subtle than most of his admirers – nay, worshipers – realized or understood; the President-Leader knew, Lyse was sure of it, that their present privileged state was precarious, and that they had to prepare for a much tougher, poorer, more hostile world.

Right now, her chop-kick and her groin-jab training were paying off. The mini-ghoul, dripping coal dust, rose out of the muck. It hissed and flashed its fangs. And she thought: this is going to be worse than I thought.

He leaped.

She gave him a quick sideways chop to the temple. It didn't work. No brains or a thick skull; he grabbed at her hair, and pulled her down. She tumbled, kicking, screaming, and tried to double over and grab him.

He was dragging her across the floor. She kicked as hard as she could and suddenly she was free.

She rolled over, and crouched down, squatting, balancing on the balls of her feet, her fists clenched, ready.

"Why don't you just give up and leave us alone?"

The mini-ghoul stared. His red eyes seemed to glow. He hissed. "You give up," he said.

"No," she said, thinking: So it can talk; this is much worse than I thought; who knew such things as these were crouching under Elysium waiting for us.

The mini-ghoul leaped, Lyse swiveled sideways. She grabbed for him and missed.

He slashed at her face and she felt a burning sensation and the sticky warmth of blood filling her eyes. "Fuck you!" she grabbed again, blindly this time, catching his foot, and dragging him.

Now she couldn't see anything. Her eyes were completely covered with blood or perhaps she didn't have eyes any more she didn't know; she couldn't tell.

She felt fangs dig into her thigh. She heard Guy Tulip shout, "You little fucker!"

And then there was a scream: "You little fucker!"

Then Lyse felt teeth gouge her calf, she rolled over, trying to roll away. She felt claws rake her back.

"Let go of her you little sod," she heard Guy Tulip shout.

And she felt the furry body crouched on her back. She wanted to toss him off; but she felt she didn't have the energy. But she had to try. "Save yourself," she shouted, "Save yourself, Guy Tulip, get out of here, this thing is going to eat me, I'm sure. Guy," she screamed, "Are you okay?"

The answer was a scream of horror and of pain, then a whimpering gnashing. Guy Tulip was doomed unless she did something; Sub or not, he had saved her life, now she had to save his.

She got to her hands and knees. Blindly, she groped in front of her. She had to save Guy Tulip and she had to get them both out of here.

She felt a claw clamp down on her shoulder.

She tried to brush it off, she tried to grab it, she … She heard Guy scream again. Then, she turned blindly, turning her bloodied eyeless face toward the slurping sucking gobbling sound, "Okay," she said, "Okay …"

Maybe she could talk her way out of this, I mean, I won the damned school debating tournament five times didn't I? I'm the product of the most exclusive Cosmos school on the coast; I'm the highest paid creative administrator of …"

Another mini-body leaped for her; claws were on her shoulders, then pinning her arms back. Another mini-body landed on her, then another.

Fangs went into her throat.

She felt a slashing pain, a gurgling rush in her mouth; she felt a warm flood of thick blood flowing down over her collarbone and breasts, naked somehow now – when did I lose my jacket – when did the little monster rip open my catsuit?

She saw a spinning light which instantly turned to darkness like a lamplight going out in the darkest of nights.

"Fuck you," she said, or meant to say, it came out wet, a bursting of bright mute bubbles.

The mutant ghouls crouched over the bodies.

"Gurgle, gurgle."

"Yum, yum, yum!"

"Gurgle – gurgle," the mini-ghouls ripped off most the remaining scraps of catsuit, the panties, and the shoes. They drank the blood and then they began to eat. They were noisy eaters.

The coal dust settled down. It was a dark in the basement. Tear gas made the two ghouls sneeze.

"Yummy, gurgle," one of the mini-ghouls said, looking up from gnawing at Lyse Saint-Ross's tibia.

"Gurgle," said another.

"Gurgle, gurgle, yum, yum," said the first; it licked the bloodied freshly mangled tibia, the elegant fine-boned Cosmos foot.

Demi Pfeiffer paced back and forth. Things were going from bad to worse. The Centurions, who were treating her now like their leader, were depressed and utterly demoralized by the news of the death of the President, which they had heard on a delayed video link of the Ken-and-Alison show. Many of these hard warriors had broken down in tears. One, a big burly guy, had leaned against the wall, shaking with sobs.

Demi Pfeiffer had always pretended to be cynical about everything. It was part of her carefully constructed corporate persona. And she did think she was in fact immune to the cult of the President-Leader; but now she too felt something like a void – emptiness in her heart. There were few anchors in this world that was totally adrift, and headed toward damnation, and the President-Leader, for all his faults, had been one of them; at the worst moments – the plague crisis five years ago, the water crisis two years before that, the mega-superstorm and high tides of seven years ago, he had rallied and defended the Cosmos Nation; he had made sure that Elysium floated supreme and serene above the onrush of catastrophe.

None of the Centurions liked the new leader, Field Marshall Jacob F. Shavtick.

"He's a tyrant."

"He's a fascist."

"He is corrupt."

"He was the ally of Konrad."

"They've been up to no good, those people."

"The President was alone."

"He was badly advised. He should never have trusted them."

"He was trying to keep things together."

"Now, things are definitely falling apart."

"Look at that," one of them gestured toward the burning city, "It's the end; it's the end of the world!"

Demi listened to them and nodded grimly, but didn't say what she thought; she felt it was a weakness to be moved by the death of a man who, however admirable he might have been in many ways, had certainly been a tyrant. In any case, with her solid sense of herself, Demi felt ill-will toward no man or woman. Let him rest in peace! Perhaps the good he did died with him, and yet the ill he did would live on – or vice versa. "I'm going to check on the vertijet." She opened the sealed door and went out onto the landing pad, and she looked back. "The President-Leader would want us to carry on, Centurions, citizens, Cosmos! Never falter, never fail!"

"We are coming with you!" The Centurions insisted.

"Two of you remain behind, just in case," said the lieutenant.

"Good idea," said Demi. She looked up the sky, now visible through fractures in the half-destroyed Dome. She was ready, at the slightest sign of danger, to scoot back into the bunker.

The five Centurions who were with her stood in a circle, protecting her, their weapons ready, aimed at the sky, aimed at the edges of the landing pad.

The vertijet stood there, looking bran-new, ready to take off, and ready to escape. The other machines had long ago been reduced to junk. Some were still smoldering.

Demi walked to the edge of the landing pad, to the southern observation platform. The Centurions followed. Several of the Centurions gasped. Demi took a deep breath. Many more of the buildings downtown, toward what had been the tip of Manhattan in Ancient Days, were tilting or collapsing or were on fire or had simply disappeared. A thick haze hung over everything – it had a noxious smell, burned plastic, burned flesh, and burned metal. Billie McAdams had been right; at least it looked so: the Mind was devouring the world, and it was just beginning; could it possibly eat the whole world, Demi wondered, and turn the planet itself into homogenized World Mind Mush, worldwide formless entropy? Is it digging downward as well as outward? Will it eat the atmosphere? Inwardly, Demi Pfeiffer shivered. Outwardly she was careful to betray no emotion, and not the slightest tremor of fear.

"What do we do now?" The blond centurion had tilted back her helmet visor. She was tanned, sharp-featured, a handsome girl, Demi thought, probably about twenty-three years old, the perfect Cosmos warrior.

"We wait."

"We wait for what?"

Demi Pfeiffer thought for a moment.

"For a miracle," she said, and gave the Centurions her brightest smile.

"Yes, ma'am," the blonde smiled back. It was a tired smile, a fatalistic smile, a beautiful smile, "I guess that's it."

"Yes, ma'am," they all echoed.

Demi realized, with an inner sigh, that she truly had become their leader.

In the distance, the Qing Tower, the work of a famous 21st Century Chinese architect, tilted, sank slowly, and seemed, in the darkening air, to dissolve and melt away.

Separated from Claire and Robyn, Kit Candy was once again alone, and inclined to melancholy. She glanced around: So, Kit Candy wanders, disconsolate as a lonely steamy cloud … by the bubbling brooks, under the thunderheads, by the mountain peaks, yearning for union with … union with what, exactly?

What else is new? Being alone, in Kit's book, was the basic metaphysical condition of being conscious, being intelligent, and being alive!

She stopped to consider. It was really weird; the whole place – space itself – seemed to be drifting around, morphing continually. It was as if the tunnels and canals and pipes and beams and manholes and the earth itself were not real, just a stage set in some crazy twisted dream. This was most certainly the Mind's doing, or the Boy Claire and Robyn had talked about, or the Boy working through the Mind.

She went down one tunnel, trying to get back to Claire and Robyn.

The tunnel ended in a wall.

Kit was annoyed. There should definitely be no wall here. There was no wall here before. This was utterly unreasonable. Let's see. She remembered the graffiti, she remembered the two hanging cables, one cut off and dangling, with a frayed yellow lining, and she remembered the chalked number, #3416.

Definitely – this was the place, and there should be no wall here.

Kit knocked on the wall; it was solid, solid as could be.

"Okay, Demon, I give up, I surrender, Oh Sulfurous Foul Fiend, Oh, Boy, Oh, Beautiful Bad Boy, Oh, Satan, I do indeed withdraw from the battlefield!"

She retraced her steps.

She came to a sort of rotunda, which had not been there before and which she had certainly never seen before. Tunnels led off in every direction. Kit scratched her head. This was like a puzzle in a fairy-tale. Behind one door and down one tunnel is a fat, noxious, expensive pig; down another is a blond simpering princess, and down the third tunnel is an executioner, or Death Himself, down yet another there is a pile of gold. Usually, there were three doors for some reason. Suddenly, in front of her, there was a man, or it looked like a man, a furry chap, with his back to her, who had a long furry tail and who was wearing an old-fashioned plaid checkered waistcoat and nothing else.

It turned out, when he turned around to face her, that he looked very much like a wolf, or perhaps like a werewolf, because he had a human body, but he was covered in hair, and his face and head and fangs and ears and eyes were definitely those of a wolf.

And he did stand upright and not on all fours.

"Who are you?" he said.

"I'm delirious," Kit said.

"Is that your name? It can't be your name. 'Delirious' is not a name!"

Kit wondered whether she should run, but she was tired of running, and in any case, she was not going to let any old imaginary wolf, undoubtedly a projection of the Mind of the Sulfurous Foul Fiend or of the Naughty Bad Boy, scare her. Besides, the way she was headed was, she was sure, the right way, the way toward the lair of the Mind, her inner compass told her so, so she was not going to let this werewolf get in her way. "My name is Kit," she said, "And who, pray tell, are you?"

"You think I need the moon," the wolf said, "You truly believe the moon is an indispensable prerequisite for me being me."

"The moon …? I said nothing at all about the moon," Kit said, then realized that it was a stupid remark. "Of course, the moon, if you're a werewolf, you need the moon, the full moon!"

"But I don't need the moon, you see."

"I see."

"No, I'm quite sure you don't see."

"I do."

"You don't!"

"Well, I imagine what you meant to say is …" Kit did not like these games. They made her head ache. Puzzles tied her in knots. It was time to put her foot down.

The wolf blinked at her thoughtfully, tilting its head to one side, a tear glistening, as if hurt, as if wounded in its pride, "I have not said anything yet, nothing of consequence at any rate, so there is no way you of all people – and you are absolutely the worst placed person in the whole wide world – are entitled to tell me what I *meant* to say since I have said nothing and therefore I must have meant nothing at all, if I did mean anything, in any case, which I didn't, and you wouldn't know what it is, or was, if you see what I mean."

Kit didn't say anything.

"I really don't understand why you brought up the moon."

"You brought it up, not I." Kit did not like to be bullied, even by an imaginary mind-hallucination werewolf.

"But you were the one who told me what I meant to say, which I feel, was perfectly ridiculous, extremely presumptuous and totally inappropriate and patriarchal on your part."

"Well," Kit had already been on trial once today. "Well, what I mean is ..."

"You do see what I mean, don't you, about you not knowing what I mean or what I meant to mean, or meant to mean I meant, so you are not the one to talk about meaning, and I am sure you mean nothing at all when you open your mouth and expel round clouds of vain and vile air-vibration, like smoke rings from a particularly pestiferous cigar. I do say, the whole thing is outrageous." The wolf sniffled and took out from its waistcoat pocket its waistcoat watch, which was thick and gold and round and which was attached to a heavy, gently swaying gold chain, and flipped it open, and looked at it. "You always were a difficult child, Kit Candy."

"I was never a child," Kit said, "not that I remember." She wondered whether her acquaintanceship with the wolf, if it had ever existed, had been removed from her memory when she had been erased. Maybe this wolf was a distant – or close – relative. Who knew? Anything was possible. Was this her mum or her dad come back in furry form to haunt her? Was the Mind playing some sort of Freudian game? She'd be seeing ghosts next!

The werewolf grinned, and hooked its claw-like thumbs under its tartan plaid – MacDonald clan – waistcoat. "I can change or morph into anything, or anyone, anytime, anywhere I want to without even thinking about it! And I can even be many different things at once! And I can be in more than one place at once! And I can get inside anybody's head whatsoever, anytime, anyway, and put on real fireworks and a whole song and dance! Isn't that fun?"

"I would think it might be confusing," said Kit.

"I am what I am, and I don't need any old fool moon."

"Well, that's very fine then, I'm glad for you," Kit was wondering if she could sidle past the wolf. She really would like to join up with pixie-like Robyn and the black-and-red hybrid, aka Claire, aka old-time media, fashion & blond pop cult icon CVJ; she was beginning to feel a bit lonely and exposed down here in the lower depths where lots of weird things were certainly happening and even time and space had begun to seem totally unreliable, not at all Euclidean or Newtonian. Down here, even Einstein, she figured, would get lost.

"Would you like a son-et-lumière show, Kit Candy, one that's designed just for you?"

"I'm not really sure I have the time," Kit said, thinking that it was best to be polite to this wolf or werewolf, or whatever he was, a mind-projection, a hallucination projected by the Boy, or a precocious teenager whose hormones had zipped out of control and made him hairy all over, and given him a tail and fangs, but her patience was wearing thin and …

"Designed just for you," The wolf was grinning. It seemed to be a very large grin, and it was getting larger, it was becoming humongous! It was absorbing the whole world! He's going to eat me!

Then it happened.

Poof!

The wolf was gone.

In fact, everything was gone.

Clown leaped from a dead ghoul she had just disposed of and landed, lightly, on a cornice, and looked down on the ghoul's death agony.

"Impressive," said Black Tarzan, looking up.

"Yeah," Clown aimed her frozen grin and big button doll eyes, those adorably inexpressive black crosses in pure white ceramic, at him, seeing him foreshortened, his gleaming skin, his big broad shoulders, his warm brown eyes, looking up at her, "I'm a first-class acrobat," she said.

He nodded and smiled his big warm smile.

Clown surveyed the battlefield. The ghouls lay dead, here and there, half-submerged in water. One ghoul she had killed lay farther up, curled up, fetus-style, on the pavement, in three inches of water, its head hanging sideways at an odd angle. It gave her a twinge of guilt as if she had murdered a child. The ghouls, too, were victims.

She remembered how, when her face had been plasticized, her body had been redesigned too, and her abilities reconfigured. She had been made super-flexible, a rubber girl, which, she was forced to admit, had already proved useful several times today – or was it yesterday? Time seemed to have become denser, fuller, and it had stretched out. She could turn herself into a pretzel if she wished. She could dance on two hands and somersault twice in the air. Her figure had been designed to perfection so that she would be as entertainingly attractive – well, beautiful – naked or clothed.

Something to be thankful for, at least, she thought.

If she hadn't had her special acrobatic abilities, she would have never survived the collapse of her building. The part of her that remained with her old personality – the personality of an idealist, human-rights lawyer and crusader – was annoyed, miffed, by all these talents she had not acquired through effort, but that had been programmed into her by her enemy – by Rankin. Many little quirks he desired in his slave had become part of her: She could, for example, sing very pretty ditties in a sweet high voice somewhere between the voice of a young boy and of a girl, and she wondered at that particular ambiguity. What was Rankin's clown fantasy really about? And she had been programmed with several foreign languages so that she could serve a varied international Cosmos clientele. And her sexual appetite and abilities had been honed so that she was never tired, or not supposed to be, in any case, and immune to all sexually transmitted diseases, and automatically sterilizing any contact, so that she could not transmit diseases or, for that matter, catch any normal disease or get pregnant.

One of the ghouls, lying dead, twitched.

She frowned down at the small being's death agony.

In truth, she found the sex work boring. Men – and she dealt mostly with men – had such stereotyped fantasies. Even the most bizarre specialties fell into a pattern. She felt she could write a book about it; she had consulted ancient texts and had discovered, as she put it, once in the bar, talking to Tattoo, the tattooed woman – amazingly tattooed and permanently pierced – and she had discovered that it had always, since the most ancient recorded times, been the same old story and that "there is nothing new under the sun." Tattoo – whose face was a brilliant hieratic mask of intricate design – had agreed and had added extensive anecdotal evidence of her own – the repertoire of fantasies was, in its essential themes, finite, though baroque in its infinite fine-tuned variations.

Well, maybe there was nothing new under the sun, but things were happening now that certainly seemed to be new. The collapse of Elysium City – that certainly was new.

Oh, oh, the ghouls were coming back, more ghouls!

So the battle began again!

How long could this go on?

It was furiously topsy-turvy. Miranda and Caliban were turning over and over, upside down, and then right side up, and floating down and down, and then up and up, and then down again, plummeting through space.

They reached out, and their fingers touched – sparks flew – Caliban pulled Miranda to him and clasped her in his arms and, locked together, body against body, epidermis against epidermis, they continued tumbling down through empty space, and then, suddenly, a luminous explosion, Roman candle kaleidoscope of colors, and …

And they were in a water chute, which then seemed like a coal chute, then it became a midway ride, and then they were in a spiral pipe, like a funfair corkscrew, rocketing down, and down, spiraling around and around, and they separated, since it was hard to stick together spiraling down in such a fantastic frantic manner.

"Whoopee," shouted Miranda, her hair flying back, and Caliban rolling, toppling, spiraling right beside her, shouted, "I love you, Princess!"

"And I love you, my Prince, my Pirate – my Caliban!"

She squealed in delight!

Caliban laughed.

And they shot out of the pipe and landed with a splash in a heap on a marble floor that seemed to be covered in about ten inches of water and laughed.

Miranda looked up and blinked: "Gosh! What in the world is that?"

A face was hovering just over her, apparently staring down at her. It was a clown face, with huge scarlet lips, a fixed smile, a slightly bulbous red nose, and big button-crosses for eyes, and it was blinking down at her, flapping marvelous long silky black eyelashes; the clown face was perhaps three inches from Miranda's face.

"Hello," the clown face said.

"I think we're in a circus." Miranda picked herself up.

"We're somewhere, that's for sure." Caliban was staring at a big black guy, who was wielding a big piece of wood and hammering a ghoul over the head.

More ghouls were closing in. The clown face disappeared. The fight was on – ghouls versus clowns, and versus Black Tarzan.

"Lights, camera, action, Caliban!" Miranda shouted.

Caliban swung around and blasted a ghoul into a million little ghoul fragments.

An oversized ghoul was heading straight for Miranda. She whipped out her laser gun and vaporized the ghoul from the jaw up. The remaining lower-jaw fangs twitched, the long thin rose-colored forked tongue flipped and flapped about in the lower half-jaw, and the ghoul's body pitched forward down into the shallow water with an ugly little sigh and a big fat splash.

Miranda glanced sideways, seeing the clown leap up into the air, and come down on two ghouls and smashing their heads together. The heads exploded like rotten eggs, splash, and waves of goo all over the clown's legs.

Miranda crouched and growled at a pair of ghouls that were closing in on her. She did her best imitation of a very angry lioness.

The ghouls all stopped.

They perked up their ears.

They all turned their blank faces and blank eyes toward Miranda. She gave each of them the look. She crouched, she growled again. She roared!

In unison, the ghouls squealed, and then they fled, splashing through the water, leaping over barriers, climbing over ruined shop fronts, splashing up the stairs, and down the stairs.

And they were gone.

"Well," said Clown, looking at Miranda.

Miranda, who was still crouching lioness fashion, now straightened up and took a serious gander at Clown. "Now ..."

"Man, I like your costume," the big muscle-bound black guy was giving Caliban the once-over. Caliban's loincloth still had some cute sparkles and sequins left from the magic filaments of the tunnel of love.

Clown returned Miranda's stare. "Those skin-shorts are the best!" she said, "Where do you work, in the Marquis de Sade Boudoir Bordello or the upmarket Story of O Café?"

Miranda wondered whether the Clown was actually talking. The clown lips moved up and down, but the smile was fixed, and the face – with crosses for eyes – was expressionless except for the goofy bright fixed smile. Miranda wondered. Is this another illusion?

"I don't think they are ..." It was a Japanese Geisha speaking, as Miranda discovered when she turned to look, "I don't think they are from a bordello," the Geisha concluded, she bowed, slightly; her jet-black hair, which was untied, fell in two very comely cascades, sharply framing her painted white face with the red lips and high, painted, startled-looking eyebrows.

"No, they are definitely high-class, above your run-of-the-mill sex shop, even above the Jean Genet Electro Bordello. They haven't been plasticized, yet. Maybe they're indentured at the Marquis de Sade Emporium, you know, up there on Casanova Avenue next to Don Juan Alley." Clown was intrigued. She liked the idea of moving upmarket.

"They look like Cosmos, to me," said Black Tarzan, "Maybe slumming, you know, or playing games."

"Kinky, kind of," said Japanese Geisha, and bowed again, "if you don't mind my saying so." The bow was very elegant, Miranda thought. Maybe she should take more Japanese culture lessons, like learning how to design a pebble garden and doing flower arrangements or ink-brush calligraphy.

"They're top-level merchandize in any case!" Clown was truly impressed; these two were exquisite physical specimens.

"I beg your pardon," said Miranda; as she disengaged from the excitement of being a lioness and as the exotic interest of Clown and Geisha faded. She was beginning to get the gist of the meaning behind all these speculations. She was not sure whether she should be flattered, or not. There had been moments, with Kit, when she and Kit had fantasized – merely fantasies, take note – about working as slaves down in the … Of course, such fantasies were utterly incorrect, and censurable, and … not to be thought nor contemplated, and an insult to all true sex workers and so on, as any good thought-police-person will tell you.

"You guys certainly know how to fight," said Clown, her bright wide-eyed expressionless smile still directed at Miranda.

"Thank you, yes, we escaped ghouls and zombie-bats and tornadoes and sandstorms and lightning bolts and a few other things. We have had, I must say, several memorable battles and encounters these recent days." Miranda brushed herself off, and gave Clown the once-over, her gaze going up, then down, then up again. Clown was not only a pretty clown face. She was a slender female in a multicolored variegated skintight clown catsuit and wearing ballerina-type slippers.

"That growl was really something," said Clown, "And the roar, well, I mean, that was beyond the beyond!"

"Yes, well, I actually didn't know I could do that, until I did it, I mean."

"These are strange people, Princess," said Caliban, "But friendly."

"Yes, my Prince, they are." Miranda had concluded that Clown must be one of the morphed ones who served the commerce of Eros, otherwise known as Indentured Sex Slavery, probably in the Jean Genet Electro Bordello. Clown and her friends must have escaped from the Sin Zone, or maybe we have fallen into the Sin Zone. No, we must be lower down than the Sin Zone. "Where are we?"

"Well, so far as we know," said Clown, hesitating, thinking, Yes, where the hell are we? "So far as we know … I don't know."

While the females squared off, Caliban and Black Tarzan, two high-testosterone Alpha macho males, were carefully sizing each other up. "Who are you? And what are you?" Caliban said, "And where are we?"

Black Tarzan stroked his chin, "Well, on first guess, I'd say we're on the fifth level below the lowest religious level – the Religion Bazaar – that's what we think, seven or more levels below the Sin Zone. We've been running quite a bit, and hiding. By the way, I like the get-ups! You guys are obviously upmarket. How much do you get, like, per session?"

Caliban looked at Miranda. "What are they talking about, Princess?"

"He calls her 'princess'!" Black Tarzan was obviously amused, "Tarzan here calls her 'princess'!"

"She is a princess, a true princess," said Geisha, bowing slightly toward Miranda, "I can feel it."

"Yes," said Clown, her button eyes locked on Miranda, "I think she is a probably a princess, you know, the Cosmos gloss and glow, she's definitely got the Cosmos high value-added gloss and glow. I'm sure she's a Cosmos Princess, or SCP, for 'Spoiled Cosmos Princess,' but she doesn't look spoiled somehow – too tough and her roar is super – and I feel strange vibrations coming from her; she is more than Cosmos."

"She's more than Cosmos?" Black Tarzan raised an eyebrow, "What can be more than Cosmos?"

Geisha said, "I think she is …" Then Geisha stopped; she didn't dare say what she thought; she thought, she sensed, she had caught a whiff of something almost … supernatural … something almost … almost like a hybrid …

"Can you really see out of those eyes?" Miranda was staring at the button-cross eyes, white like a hard-boiled egg, with two large, jet-black, crossed slits painted on the white and that didn't move, so you couldn't tell if the Clown was looking at you or not, or left or right, or up or down.

"Yes, Princess, I can see out, but nobody can see in."

"Awesome," said Miranda, "really impressive, and sort of creepy, Clown, if you don't mind my saying so."

"I don't mind," the bright bulbous smile again focused itself on Miranda,

"They do creep people out, which is sort of fun – but also annoying. It means my very soul is a prisoner of my gaze. And I can't define and reify other people by my gaze, however hard I try; since my alienating, objectifying intent is invisible, it doesn't work its magic, if you see what I mean. People can't see that I think they are jerks. It is a form of symbolic castration, if I may express myself in such neo-archaic Freudian psychobabble terms. And what, pray tell, are those supernovas and twirling galaxies and golden fireworks in your eyes?"

"Ah, those, I don't really know, you see, my background is a bit complicated; I'm only coming to terms with it myself, I mean with who and what I am. I'm not sure it has all sunk in yet."

"Ah, yes," whispered Geisha, bowing lower. "The force is with us!"

"The force..?" Black Tarzan raised an eyebrow.

"Yes, the force," whispered Geisha.

"We have come out of the desert, out of the Dead Lands," Caliban was saying, "and my Princess here is the daughter of a goddess, so, well, it is complicated, and ..."

"Complicated," said Black Tarzan. "Well, welcome to Elysium, my friend, though you might have seen us on better days. This one is proving to be a bit of a well, a bit of a disaster."

"You see, the Force is ..." and Geisha began to explain.

Kit wondered: what the heck had just happened?

She had been talking to a werewolf.

Then there was nothing, and she was nowhere.

She floated in a limbo-like space. Nothing was visible, not even stars. She reached out and found that she could swim in this space, whatever it was, at least she had the sensation of moving.

Boom!

What was that?

Boom!

There was a flash, then more darkness, then again the sensation of floating in utter blackness, and then a sense of twirling through space, and then with a thud Kit landed on the ground, she was standing, she heard and felt a shuffling of feet, a clanging of doors, and lo and behold!

Ouch!

Now she was handcuffed, wrists pinioned behind back; she was being hurried and hustled down a narrow corridor. Her sneakers – when had she put on sneakers? – were too big for her and unlaced, and the laces kept threatening to trip her up.

The flickering fluorescent ceiling lights were like weak strobe lights, they cast livid weak purple shadows and flickers of feeble static-laden light.

It seemed she was in the Ministry of Truth, which was what it said in big letters over one of the doors.

Her shoulder blades were squished together, pinned back between two robot-like heavies, her legs clanking from the ankle chains, and her wrists aching and hands numb from the over-tight arm-shackles and ...

And then ...

Then she was in a small white cubicle of a room. A slime-bag male interrogator in an immaculately-pressed unbuttoned white shirt – hairy flabby chest and incipient sagging boobs – was leaning forward, his two hands flat, and with their fingers splayed wide, on the top surface of a spotless white table. His thick stubby hairy fingers ended in fingernails that had half-moons of blood under them.

"I am the chief interrogator," he said; his heavy round face, his round dark baby-like eyes, and his thick, wet, spittle-laced lips, were only a few inches away.

Kit said nothing. Her heart was beating hard, faster than usual.

The surgical instruments on the table gleamed – a straight razor, and an array of thin-handled stainless steel scalpels, sabre-toothed pliers in various sizes.

"Now we shall terminate you, well not quite terminate you, Kit Candy, we shall erase you so that we can dispose of your body and give you a new personality more in fitting with your lower-class below-Sub status."

He licked his lips, spittle flew.

"You will be demoted to non-human. You realize that you have violated every code – you have given yourself an education, recolonizing your erased mind with thoughts and ideas, you have consorted with Cosmos. Indeed, you have been intimate with Cosmos, you have had knowledge of Cosmos. You have expressed deep emotions, too."

Some of the spittle spray splashed on Kit's nose, in her eyes.

"This, as you know, is absolutely forbidden; and you have indulged in complex thoughts, which are even worse than feelings, and even more forbidden than feelings. Feelings and thoughts are subversive."

Kit said nothing; one or two drops of spittle ran down her cheeks.

"Well, don't worry, soon all that will be gone … no more feelings, no more thoughts, no more big words, no more subordinate clauses."

Kit said nothing; she took a deep breath.

"But before we do that, we shall do a little physical redesign. You are very … ah … attractive, aren't you …"

Kit said nothing.

"Aren't you?"

Kit said nothing.

An electric shock whammed through Kit's limbs and torso and exited from her head, all her hair shooting up, standing up on end. Sparks shot out from her manacled finger-ends.

"Aren't you? Answer me, you …!"

"Some … people … think … so," said Kit as evenly as she could, with her teeth still chattering from the shock, as if she'd been plunged into a deep freeze, and thinking, Yes, Miranda, and Fanny, and Sniggy Propane and Tony Yong, yes, I guess I'm a looker, for certain misguided persons I'm even considered a hottie … But … I'm not going to be much of anything any longer. They will change me, erase me, disfigure me …

Disfigurement …

Cold horror and fear streaked down her back, sweat pearled on her limbs, on her forehead. She was going to be sick, she was sure she was going to be sick. Being sick would probably make her situation worse, if such a thing was possible.

"You have a nice smile." The interrogator licked his lips. His bald head gleamed under the interrogation light, not even a trace of stubble on his dome. She blinked: did he wax it?

"You have nice teeth, very nice teeth …" he lifted up one of the pliers; it was about ten inches long, with an evil-looking serrated jaw. "Beautiful teeth."

Kit trembled.

He grinned, brought his sweaty full moon face even closer to hers; he opened his mouth; his teeth seemed to grow and grow; his mouth was expanding. His individual teeth now were vast and square. They looked like highly polished rectangular white marble gravestones, lit up under a bright baleful moon in some spooky cartoon graveyard. She tried to control the trembling; she didn't want to give the evil bastard the satisfaction.

He nodded an order.

A machine swung forward and inserted itself between Kit's lips; she clenched her teeth, she was not going to let this damned machine, this horrible man, do this! The machine sent an electric shock through Kit's gums, instinctively she unclenched her teeth, "Ouch!"

Before she could slam her jaw shut the wedge was inside her jaws, and it opened slowly, forcing her jaws apart, she felt saliva gush up, and she felt the sweat gathering under her arms, pure terror, now she was doomed.

"And, now, I shall do this personally, with my own two hands," he said, coming around the table, his fleshy deeply fissured lips parted and his little round startled eyes and his enormous tombstone teeth glared at her.

Kit's chair automatically swung around to meet him. Her eyes were wide in terror; she wanted to squeeze them shut, but bio eye-tweezers had latched onto her eyelids, and her eyes were forced wide open, glued open, a helpless startled mindless terrified wide-eyed glutinous stare.

He hauled a mobile stool over, so it was close, too close.

He sat down on the stool, heavily, spreading his knees wide, then he kicked the stool forward, even closer, so his breath puffed on her wide-open eyes, and into her wide-open mouth, "I wish we had more time to play, Kit, I wish we did, but I only have a few hours, I'm going to have to be quick and dirty, well, dirty, but not that quick, for I wish to take a little pleasure here, and make it stretch out, after all, life is so dreary, don't you think."

Kit, her mouth forced wide open, thought she was going to gag.

"Think of me as an evil, insane dentist, utterly insane." He grinned.

Kit said nothing; her eyes stared; she could feel tears forming at the very edge of her eyes; soon, they would overflow.

"Or consider me a surgeon," he licked his lips, "an utterly insane and sadistic surgeon."

Saliva gurgled up; with her teeth clamped in the wedge, Kit could say nothing; she couldn't even cry out.

"Now, first the tongue, the naughty, naughty tongue," he picked up a pair of knife-edge pliers, it looked like it was designed to cut things, to cut meat, "I understand you are very talented with your tongue, Kit, and also that you are a regular chatterbox, eloquent to a fault, so I thought I'd start there, I thought I'd start with that, and … you know the really funny thing, I'm going to do all the same things to your Cosmos friend – what is her name – Miranda – for I really hate Cosmos, I am going to do her, mutilate her, in a way that not even that bitch of a mother of hers, Nikki, not even Nikki will recognize her ..."

He doesn't know, Kit thought, he doesn't know that Miranda is dead; he can't do anything to Miranda! At least that was something!

Miranda was dead ... so she was beyond his scalpels, beyond his knives, beyond his pliers, beyond his cruel madness.

But just the idea that he intended to hurt Miranda made her temper boil up into a fury. She would kill him; she would ...

Her blood churned.

The knife was still probing. The man's big round face was just an inch or so from her face. All this time, she had tried not to look at him, her eyes stretched open, she'd concentrated on the ceiling just as she had when she'd been to the robot dentist, she looked at the big round operating light, but now, boiling with fury, overflowing with rage, she shifted focus and looked straight at him, she stared at him, she concentrated, she bored into his very soul, and she saw his eyes, in extreme close-up, and suddenly there was an expression in them, something like fear, and he said, "Don't ..." And she, of course, couldn't say anything but she thought, *Die, die, die, damn it, yes, die!*

And she saw a weirder look in his eyes, and he said "Don't" again, and she saw herself reflected in his eyes, she saw her eyes, giant eyes, staring eyes, like they were a doll's eyes, painted on, her arched eyebrows, the shock of black hair down over her forehead, and her mouth, just the edge of her mouth, clamped open, and the image swirled, and it was as if a light were shining in her eyes, and it became brighter, and brighter, like a flame, like the sun, golden, and then smoke started to come out of his eyes, and he screamed, "Don't!" and the smoke was rippling and squirting out from the edges of his eyes, and then his eyes popped, exploded, all squirt and mush, and the empty eyes were full of flame, and Wham, and Wham, and then ...

Slice, slice ...

At that moment, just as he was dying, Kit felt the knife slice through her tongue, the cool blade zipped through her tongue, close to the root, she could feel it, she could feel the tongue, a piece of dead floppy viscous uprooted meat in her mouth, trapped by the clamps, and the stub end of what had been her tongue, a smoking smooth side slice of beef, it would look quite smooth and that sort of meaty red-gray look a thick slice of freshly cut steak would have, and the face in front of her face was a smoking and withering ruin, its eyes empty bloody flaming sockets flickering with sparks, and she tried to say, "Ha, ha, ha," but of course her mouth was clamped open and she had no tongue to speak with, and she was tempted to try to swallow the dead cut-off tongue that was wallowing in her mouth, an irrelevancy now, but she resisted; her throat was convulsing and wanted to swallow, and of course it was swallowing some blood, though Kit had the impression that the wound had been automatically cauterized on both sides, so that there was little blood but there was a lot of saliva, and the guy's whole head exploded now, a mushroom of bone, skin, gray matter, and blood and cartilage, and the room wavered and the lights bounced up and down as if everything had been caught in an oceanic tsunami or a fun fair crazy house mirror and the lights streamed like water and everything exploded and the clamps seemed to tear Kit's jaws apart and she caught a glimpse of her amputated tongue flying away, glittering, like a floppy silver-sided trout leaping free from a fisherman's grasp.

For some time now, Ken Ivison had had to adlib; Alison, blind and no longer getting coherent or continuous information from the Info-Flow earphone, contented herself with commenting rarely. Mostly, she just leaned against Ken and asked questions. "What are those things you see, Ken, what are they?"

More zombie-bats had flown in great flocks through the cracks in the dome. The Volpe building shook again. The floating cameras adjusted. The VID and INFO streams continued to parade across the bottom of the screen.

Ken was saying, "I'm not sure, Alison, I'm not sure what they are."

Out in the gloom, traversed by lightning bolts and huge twirling funnels of dark air, it looked like a flock of large birds, flying in formation.

"I don't know, it looks like a flock, my God, it's not a flock, it's humungous whatever it is, some sort of flying creatures."

Alison, her blue eyes bright like crystals, ad-libbing blindly, said, "Didn't earlier reports talk of a plague of giant people-eating bats from out west?"

"You are absolutely right, Alison," Ken leaned closer and kissed her on the cheek. She shivered with pleasure. Her arm tightened around his waist, and she said, "Yes, there were reports from Cosmos Los Angeles, before Los Angeles disappeared, and I think from the fortified outposts of Seattle and Vancouver ..."

"Those things are coming closer, Alison."

"You'd better warn people, Ken."

"Yes, look, folks, here the camera will give you an image of these things – they are flying through the air."

"Gosh," said Alison, shivering.

"They look, well, they look about human size," said Ken, squinting at the monitor, which was showing a telescopic close-up of one of the flocks.

"My God, they are … They are ex-human, I think," said Alison, "though I have no idea why I think so, but I have these thoughts – a multitude of thoughts – like voices running through my head, and … I am a blind seer, I guess. Sorry, folks, that sounds crazy, I know. But what I see, what I prophesy is this: they eat people, they tear people's throats out, they …" She gulped. "Folks, those things are definitely dangerous. Get inside a shelter if you can."

"Barricade all windows and doors and arm yourselves with whatever you can," Ken tensed as the things approached, ever closer.

With virtually all its windows shattered and with the wind whistling in everywhere, the studio was vulnerable, they were vulnerable – he and Alison were vulnerable!

"I see it, I see it now – these beings, these infernal creatures, were once human."

"What do you mean, Alison," he said, turning to her as if she were the on-screen expert professor called in from Harvard or Oxford or Tokyo, "What do you mean by saying they are ex-humans?" In truth, Ken was worried sick. Was dear blind beautiful Alison with the hole in her head going mad?

"I know it sounds crazy, Ken," Alison gamely aimed her bloodied smile and blind eyes where she knew the camera should be, "but have you ever been haunted by a voice?"

"Yours," said Ken, "Your voice, when you would say things to hurt me, those words, and your voice, would echo in my head for days."

"Oh, Ken, I am sorry, I am so sorry I hurt you, I know I was cruel, I was …"

He sealed her lips and stopped her confession with a kiss. The camera swung around and zoomed in to get a close-up of the kiss.

"Well," she said, emerging breathless from the kiss, her blind eyes wide open, "It`s as if I hear all these voices, like rustling of leaves, they have been betrayed, they say, they gave their souls for salvation, but salvation turned out to be damnation, and so … their minds – if you can call them minds – are full of Biblical citations and fragments, bits and pieces of sacred scripture, as if they are trying to remember, as if they are trying to remember and regain their true selves and free themselves from this curse …"

One of the resurrected cameras swung around to capture the view outside the shattered studio windows, the vast expanse of plate glass having disintegrated. The camera captured the desolation, burning towers, collapsed towers, and small fragments of the Great Dome spiraling down through the leaden gloomy air; it captured storms moving through the city, slanted rain shadows, between the towers, dark tornado-like shapes, and, here and there, fiery explosions.

Then the camera again zoomed in on the dark, bird-like flock, winging its way toward them, and the directional mike picked up the high-pitched screams, like screams of utter agony and hatred, rising up from the deepest pit in Hell.

The things were flapping closer now.

The look in their yellow and red flaming eyes was horrendous.

The camera zoomed in for an extreme close-up of one of the creatures: the rabid foaming mouth and the red-and-yellow eye and the fangs and the twisted monstrously distorted features.

The things were flapping very close.

Some of them peeled off the main flock and headed straight toward the Volpe Tower studio where Alison and Ken were …

"They have been robbed of their humanity, Ken," Alison said, "They have lost their very souls. And yet …"

"And yet …"

"And yet, even soulless, they are in torment." Alison turned her face toward the darkening sky from which death was swiftly winging.

"It's time to go, Alison. It's time to go …"

And at that point, one of the creatures flew through the shattered gaping window and landed, clumsily, on the studio floor. It turned to face Ken and Alison. Its nostrils, dripping fluid, quivered; it sniffed, it snarled, it smelled humanity; it smelled blood; its fangs dripped black fluid …

Like dirty engine oil, thought Ken.

The creature snarled, foam and spittle flying, splatter.

Another creature landed, clumsily, the eight-foot-wide leathery wings flapping.

"They are here," Alison said, "He is here." Instinctively, blindly, she turned her face toward the creature; she raised her head, offering her jugular. "I am here," she said, "take me!"

"He is here, who is he?" Ken pushed Alison behind him.

She struggled.

Still facing the monsters, Ken pinned Alison by both wrists, keeping her behind him; she squirmed.

Ken felt like throwing up. The room was filling with a fetid smell – like a rotting cadaver roiling with squirming maggots, curling and curling, spilling out of the cadaver's bloated intestines, as if in a sunny field there was a sudden darkness, as if the sun had died, Ken felt as if he too were going blind, a darkening intimation of death and horror and ultimate dissolution.

"He is ..." Alison began; her voice remained suspended; Ken pushed her back, they had to get out of the studio.

But somehow, suddenly, like in a bad dream, it was as if he were paralyzed, swimming through thick glue. It was a nightmare, a living nightmare. Ken tried to close his nostrils; he tried to stop breathing; he felt he might choke if he breathed one iota of the substance of those creatures. Worse – he might become one of them.

Alison was now standing beside him; she had laid her hand on his shoulder; she seemed calm, as if in a trance; her eyes shone like empty blue glass. "He ... He is ... Satan, the Devil, the Fiend, Beelzebub, whatever, he is Evil of Many Names and no Form; He – or It – takes many faces, many forms, many names. He is always with us. In this moment, he has taken to calling himself 'the Boy.'"

"The Boy," said Ken, barely managing to choke out the words.

One of the cameras, sensing the danger threatening the two hosts – they were after all valuable Volpe Net properties both of them – swung in front of Ken, partly to protect Ken and Alison, and partly to get a better shot of the monster; the camera, which had its own independent bio-graphene-mind, had a built-in nose for unique phenomena; it also rather liked the two hosts whose most recent adventures it had followed with great interest; it zoomed in to present an extreme close-up of the first zombie-bat as the loathsome creature lumbered forward.

The second zombie-bat lunged, straight at Alison.

"Let's get out of here," Ken suddenly came alive; he slammed Alison out of the way, just as another camera, also a Ken-and-Alison fan, surged up, in a kamikaze mission, and whammed sideways full speed into the monster, sending it reeling back across the studio.

"I suggest you leave the studio," said the computerized editor, "Alison and Ken, I suggest – no, I order – Repeat – I ORDER – you to leave the studio."

"Let's die together, Ken," Alison said.

"No, we are not going to die!"

"He is calling," Alison said, her blind eyes bright like stars, "He has come for us. The Boy is here! These are his calling cards! We must be swept up into the Rapture, Ken. It is our destiny!"

"This is an order, Ken!" The computer-producer sounded very agitated. "Get Alison out of the studio, Ken. Protect her. Protect yourself. You are both valuable corporate properties, even more valuable today than yesterday. Alison is not in her right mind, Ken! You must protect Alison from herself. PLEASE – Ken!"

Another camera, held in reserve, came rushing forward and smashed foursquare into the zombie-bat that had recovered its aplomb and was just about to make another lunge at Ken. The zombie-bat skidded back to the edge of the studio and almost fell out the gaping window. It flapped its foul wings desperately, scrabbling at the floor with its foot claws. The camera recoiled, getting ready to launch another assault.

"Hurry, Ken," said the computer-producer, "Get off your fat ass – now!"

"Come on, let's go." Ken was suddenly in the grip of a powerful surge of energy. He could move! He grabbed Alison and pushed her toward the exit, and just then, the second bat-like creature struggled free of the first camera, which had been zipping back and forth blocking its path, and it lunged for Ken and Alison. Its claws slashed Ken's cheek. Ken was lifted up by evil grasping claws. Ken was overwhelmed with a fury such as he had never felt before and he reached out and he …

What the Hades had happened? Kit Candy blinked her way back into consciousness. She tried to sit up. She was wondering whether she had been sleeping or whether she had been knocked out and how much time might have passed since her tongue had been cut out by the Chief Interrogator whose head she had, apparently, blown up by the pure charm and intensity of her gaze and the fury of her hatred. Just the idea that he would try to harm Miranda still made her fume! Even if Miranda was dead, the very idea of harming Miranda was outrageous! Kit clenched her fists. But, then, how tragic – to blow a fellow's head off! It was an event for which she was aware that she was responsible, though by what power she had exploded his cerebellum, she had no idea. It was, she decided, a dangerous power to possess.

And then …

Had her tongue really been cut out?

She also wondered how she had been transported to where she apparently now was; she was lying on the floor of what seemed to the Underground Ecological Excrement Transformation Hub and the Turd-to-Food Munch Machine Laboratory, in the Sweets, Deserts and Croissants Sub-Department, where chocolate cakes were assembled and where other delicacies, such as chocolate éclairs, tiramisus, and sugar-sprinkled chocolate croissants, and fragrant almond croissants were being conjured up out of the molecules and atoms provided by the cast-off pure shit, excrement, and garbage and general detritus of Elysium City, including, some indiscreet samizdat babblers claimed, recycled cadavers, Subs of course, not Cosmos.

The assembly line and the Photo-Chocolate-Replica machines, the molecular re-adhesion machines, were there, but they were immobile and inactive, just standing there, monsters of human and robot-inventor ingenuity, gleaming and oily under the dim light of emergency lamps.

The bio-robot chefs with their white mushroom-shaped chef hats were standing immobile except for one who was leaning over her, holding her hand, and looking at her with concern. "Have you come for the tasting, Madam?" he inquired, blinking his chef's eyelashes and button-like eyes, and favoring her with a solicitous, almost obsequious gaze.

She wanted to say, "No, I have *not* come for the fucking tasting," but decided no purpose would be served by insulting the fellow, whose body label said "Bob," and then, when she did try to say something semi-gracious and appropriately condescending, she heard a mere gurgle and grunt – well, not even a grunt, more a slurry sigh – emerge from her mouth, and she realized that her mouth, aside from gums and teeth, was absolutely empty – how had she forgotten this – and that she didn't have a tongue to swear with. She struggled to her feet. So, yes, in fact, her tongue *had* been cut out!

How horrible!

"Are you a Cosmos first class?" The robot inquired.

How fucking gross and horrible!

She wanted to say, "No damn it, I'm not," but she couldn't say anything, so she resorted to Ancient Archaic Standard American Sign Language – retrieved from the linguistic treasures stored away in one of the contraband mind-skill implants she and Miranda had pirated – and she said, with a twirl and flip of her hands, "Why do you ask, Bob?"

Not far away, a giant vat of what looked like dark Swiss chocolate was bubbling away. It smelled good.

The robot gave her the once-over, his eyes running up and down, and his mind accessing the multilingual conversational code that was part of his repertoire, and then, having ascertained that she was dumb but not deaf and that she was using Ancient Archaic Standard American Sign Language, he said, in spoken audio English, "Because it is difficult to discern or differentiate the exact status of unclothed humans, Madam, and, you will forgive me, but you have no barcode, so your nakedness makes you undecipherable."

Kit looked down and realized she was indeed without raiment. This seemed to have become a habit. Even her silver-skin-shorts were gone! How had it happened this time? Had the dead torturer made off with her trousers?

She was, though, sprinkled artfully with splatters of blood, gore, gray matter, and what looked like charcoal, which perhaps came from the Chief Interrogator, when he exploded and snipped off her tongue with that evil pair of knife-pliers.

She looked up at the robot and caught a certain flat yet crafty appraising look in its eyes, and she wondered: Can this robot be suffering from an attack of lubricious overreach or human-like lust. Has he got the hots? Could this be? Is this a randy robot I see before me?

She fluttered her eloquent hands and her even more eloquent eyelids at him, "Well, treat me as the best sort of Cosmos, then, will that do, Bob?"

The robot stared, honored her with a very elegant bow, sweeping his arm across his midriff, bending from the waist, and saying, "I will indeed, Madam. I am your servant and your slave. I must say, too, that I am in love with you, if you don't mind, Madam. Do with me what you will!"

"Thank you, Bob, much appreciated," Kit's hands fluttered; thank God for contraband polyglot Mind Implants she and Miranda had spent one glorious afternoon lolling on the fluffy cream-colored rug and fooling around with. Also, she wondered. How could a robot fall in love with a human, even with a lowly Sub? Were the robots getting uppity? Was the Mind up to its new tricks again? Were the robots turning into Cylons and plotting a takeover of the universe?

Kit was about to ask the robot chef if he could supply her with something to wear, pretty please, when she was distracted by a much more pressing matter. It seemed like a snake, or slippery lizard was loose in her mouth: it was writhing, and twisting and turning; it was horrifying. It was …

Oh, my God!

Miranda's deep-throated growl – and her majestic savannah roar – had terrified the ghouls; they had, without exception, run as fast as their little bow-legs could carry them, splashing through the water, zipping away into the shadows.

No sooner had the ghouls disappeared, than there was a dull roar which became louder and then louder, and an explosion of water gushed up over the shopping facades, over the Prada and the Hugo Boss and Mercedes and Apple signs, and a cascade came down from the false windows between the Doric columns and a sort of tidal wave came gushing down through the ancient underground shopping concourse, bubbling up and frothing, and rising to the very roof, and it picked up Black Tarzan, Clown, Geisha, Caliban, and Miranda and carried them along, banging them into artificial palm trees and eucalyptus and cactus, and then it captured them in an immense whirlpool, and swirled them around, and flushed them all down a giant sewer, down, down, and down, and then through a tunnel of darkness, and then down a waterfall which smelled of ozone and fresh octopus and the deep blue sea.

Just as the great foaming wave hit them, Caliban had grabbed Miranda around the waist, and he and she twirled around together, rising, falling, falling, falling, and then being shot along on the horizontal, like a two-person projectile, until they popped out and splashed down and found themselves in a placid calm canal where the current seemed to be very slow, even leisurely, and the air smelled, vaguely, of electricity, of thunderbolts, and of lighting on a sweet, perfumed, midsummer's evening.

It seemed a rather romantic place, in truth.

"Princess," said Caliban. He stood up and smoothed down his loincloth, patting it back into place, "Are you okay?"

"Yes, my love, oh, my Prince!" said Miranda, sitting waist-deep in the water and blowing a strand of wet blond hair out of her eyes. "Are you okay too?"

"I am in fine fettle," said Caliban, leaning over to help her up.

Gracefully, she leaped to her feet, and put her hand on his shoulder. "Where are we?"

They looked around. Their new friends, Clown and Geisha and Black Tarzan, were nowhere to be seen.

"I hope they are somewhere safe," said Caliban.

"Nowhere is safe," said Miranda, putting her arms around Caliban's waist, leaning against his chest, and looking up into his eyes, "But, yes, I do hope they are safe."

The canal had a low roof, only about 10 meters above the water, and sloping sides, and the water, at this point, was only about a foot deep.

"Well, Princess, let us explore!"

"Yes, my Prince, my Pirate, my Tarzan, let us explore. Wonders await us, I am sure."

Hand in hand, they set off, wading through the placid-seeming water, and heading, they hoped, toward the Lair of the Mind.

Not far away, the Mind Tentacles were multiplying; and they squirted their dissolvent acids here and there, experimenting with the most efficient and deadly formulas.

The foundations of the ancient freedom tower were melting. The steel columns began to steam, the steel and reinforced concrete began to melt and vibrate. Far above, up in the open Elysium air, the building began to tilt. Below the tower, a 50-meter portion of street fell into a widening crater, carrying with it two hotdog stands, a Chinese deli, and an overturned fire truck.

As the acid ate at the Atlantic Ocean Barrier, opening cracks, water began to rush into the acid-made crater and to boil and roil as water molecules encountered the Mind-Acid; the water began to turn into a turbid, swirling, gelatin-like substance. The crater was deepening, drilling down in the bedrock, down into the Manhattan Schist, the bedrock underlying the island's old skyscrapers. The surface of old Wall Street boiled up, the cobblestones, installed in 2127, popped out of their spots, exploded in mid-air, and showered down.

Antique gas-lamps melted like soft butter, the gas hissed and exploded. The Mind, munching and munching, began to work its way northward along the ancient underground auto-path once known as Broadway.

Ken Ivison was lifted up by the zombie-bat. its huge jaws opened. Ken squirmed, kicked, and then punched the zombie-bat on the snout with both fists. The zombie-bat blinked in surprise. Ken gritted his teeth and used his fingers to gouge out its eyes, plunging straight in, hooking deep, and ripping out. The zombie-bat screamed and dropped Ken. It slashed out with its claws to try to trap him again, all the while howling. Ken, shimmied backward on his backside, on the studio floor, looking around. Where was Alison?

Alison was standing, blind and confused and yet calm, while the other zombie-bat tried to reach her, slashing out with its claws and fangs, but two cameras were punching the zombie-bat, bang, bang, bang, playing relay, one would slam into the bat, then the other would slam into the bat, and then the first would slam into the bat, punch, punch, punch …

An extra, backup camera continued to film Alison, and it must be feeding her prompts, because she was looking straight at it, and commenting.

"Well, folks, as you can see, we are under attack, and Ken is fighting valiantly to defend our freedoms and our way of life, as are our loyal and brave bio-cameras, and, on behalf of everybody, I want to thank them all."

The backup camera swung around to show the fight, with the two cameras bashing at the zombie-bat and the other zombie-bat, with bloodied empty eyes, thrashing around, and striking out, blindly.

"As you can see," Alison picked up the electronic ear cue prompts, "our camera friends are fighting a tough fight, and Ken has just managed to partially disable one of these poor horrendous dangerous creatures."

One of the cameras said, "Ken, get Alison out of here. We can only keep these things back for so long."

"You are absolutely right! Thanks!" Ken, ducking the blindly slashing claws of the first zombie-bat, leaped to his feet and grabbed Alison, "Oh, darling," she breathed, and she turned to the backup camera. "This fight is not over, take care, folks, we hope to see you again, and soon."

Ken backed her out of the studio, down a narrow service corridor, and into one of the storage and costume rooms, and he slammed and double-locked the double doors.

It was dark, pitch-black, but one of the production manager computers turned on the lights and spoke, "Welcome, Ken and Alison. Our information indicates that, all probabilities considered, this refuge will not be safe for more than 25 minutes. But let me remind you, you do have your choice of costumes and weapons. Live fire weapons are stored in the steel case – ARMS

– to your right, Ken. The combination is 35-62-A-7. Help yourself, Ken, and then get yourself and Alison to a safe place, we recommend underground, under the old Sin Zone perhaps, though frankly, Ken and Alison, no place is safe, since the attacks are multiple and of different natures and coming from all directions. We also have miniature camera-audio portables, which you might consider taking on your pilgrimage – mobile broadcast, you know. A change of costume might also be advisable, Ken."

"Right," said Ken. "Thanks!"

"Ken," said Alison.

"What?"

"I love you, Ken, did I ever tell you that I loved you?" Her blind blue eyes were shards of silver and blue and white drifting clouds.

"I love you, and I shall love you until my dying day," said Ken; he kissed her.

"Let's not talk of dying, Ken, for our life has just begun."

"Time, Ken! Time, Alison!" said the computer.

PART THREE – GODDESS

CHAPTER 8 – MATRIX

V and Kat advanced cautiously down a high narrow tunnel with a peaked, ogive-style roof, and many side niches, and smoky lamps burning on the soaring, dark brick side-arches. It was like being in the nave in an underground cathedral.

"Is this real?" Kat laid her gloved hand flat on the bricks of one of the arches. They felt solid, uneven, and finely textured – like real old-fashioned bricks.

"I don't know," said V.

"I don't think this part of ancient Manhattan ever existed." Kat ran her hand over the rough dark bricks. "It's an illusion. Or somebody built it in the last few decades. Or maybe it was uncovered in some dig, ancient archeological ruins …" She frowned, letting the thought hang in the air.

"There's not much that's really ancient here, or there shouldn't be," said V, thinking that a mere 20,000 years ago, the glaciers would have scraped the whole of Manhattan clean, leaving the underlying gneiss and schist bare, and then adding glacial rubble and fill. And the Americas had only been peopled about 17,000 years ago, though maybe it was earlier than that.

"What is that?" Kat stopped, and listened.

V had already stopped, with her hands on her hips. "It sounds like a circus."

"A circus …" said Kat and, with those words acting like an open sesame, in less than the blink of an eye, they found themselves standing in the middle of a circus. Kat opened her eyes wide. "What the …?"

"Step right up, ladies, it's so good of you to come, and I want to welcome you into my little circus. Oh, it's not much, it's not really the big-top; it's more like a modest do-it-yourself out-of-the-way country fair."

The barker, who was a wolf, or perhaps a werewolf, was standing on a platform. The thumbs of his claws were tucked under his plaid waistcoat, and he was giving his spiel standing under a banner that read "Freaks of Nature, Monsters and Goblins, Miracles and Wonder Cures!"

Behind him was a small circus tent, with flags on top that were flapping and waving in a sweet summer breeze and above the tent was a sparkling blue sky, and a few wispy nostalgic little clouds, little cumulus, riding free, drifting along, and the warm breeze smelled of hayfields and straw and horse dung and horse urine and engine grease, and fresh, sun-warmed paint, and, faintly, of tar and asphalt and theatrical and clown greasepaint.

It smelled of a world that didn't exist anymore – anywhere.

"Now, would you two ladies like to play a few games, risk your mortgage and your lives on a spin of the wheel, on a flip of the dice, on a guessing game? Well, I thought you might hesitate, two ladies such as yourselves ..."

V looked back. Behind them, the tunnel still stretched off in the flickering gloom ...

"Oh, yes, indeed, it is so dreary, being trapped underground. I think we are better here, up in the fresh air. You do remember what fresh air was like, don't you?" The wolf beamed at them in an expansive avuncular way. His claw-like thumbs stretched his waistcoat.

"And I just want you to perform for me, ladies, I'm sure you will be willing to do that. You can put on a show. It will lighten the burden you carry, it will assuage your guilt, it will help you bear your cross, for you are weighted down with guilt are you not, you bloodthirsty, blood-sucking beast!"

Suddenly he growled, and leaped from the stage down into the muddy fairground walk.

V was dripping sweat.

The inside of her armored catsuit was clammy.

A thick trickle of sweat wandered down her spine.

She fell to her knees.

From somewhere far away, she heard Kat say, "V, what the hell are you doing!"

"Oh, Father Demon or Evil One, oh, Father Wolf, forgive me my sins!"

"What the hell are you doing, V? Get up!"

V, on her knees, in the sun-warmed mud, joined her gloved hands in supplication: "I have blood on my hands. As a child, I sacrificed to the gods, to Baal, on his throne, to Baal the Warrior God, the Thunder God, the God of Fertility and Rain, who brought thunder and lightning which killed, and rain which could drown or bring life, for all life is a cycle of death and rebirth.

I sacrificed the blood of others. And I sacrificed to the Goddess Asherah. There is blood on my hands, Oh, Father Wolf. But, Oh, Father Wolf, without the blessings of Baal, the rain would not fall and the grain would not grow."

"V, come back, come back, from wherever you are!" Kat's voice was faint. It came from far away.

The wolf leaned down. He spoke, gently, as if he understood and forgave absolutely everything. "Ah, V, yes, yes, you have killed; you have killed so many; your body and soul are soaked in blood."

"Yes, Father Wolf, yes, oh, Boy, oh, Divine Boy!"

"You are the Goddess of Death."

"Yes, Father Wolf, yes, oh, Boy, oh Divine Boy!"

"You are the Goddess of Blood."

"Yes, Father Wolf, yes, oh, Boy, oh Divine Boy!"

Father Wolf laid his claw on her head and – behold!

V found herself in an ancient temple, she found herself ascending the steps, holding a child in her arms, a child she loved. Baal was waiting; he wished for sacrifice. She knew she must sacrifice the girl.

But, then, the scene changed.

She remembered her first kill, her first kill as the vampire-like creature she was to become: his name was Gaius; he was a warrior, a soldier of the Old Times. He was in love with her and already dying, so he offered himself to her when he realized what she had become, a vampire. He offered himself as a sacrifice to her bloodlust. He realized that she thirsted for his blood, Gaius offered his neck to her, and she accepted, famished for blood; she was nineteen years old, trembling with bloodlust; she sank her fangs into his flesh, into his jugular and she drank. And then, seemingly from out of nowhere, the other warrior, Gaius's older companion, his commander, Marcus, was standing over her as she crouched low, covered in blood, drinking her fill. She saw his laced boots, his sturdy sunburnt legs, and she looked up: his armored tunic, his broadsword, his sunburnt arms, and his strong, handsome face.

"You know what you have become?" His expression was grim.

"I know. I know what I have become."

Marcus stood over her, with his sword drawn, ready to kill her; he stood over her and let her drink; he watched her, he waited.

Finally, when she had finished and as she crouched there, trembling, wondering who was stronger, he or she, whether she could kill him before he could kill her – he put his sword back into his sheath.

"You must bathe," he said, "You are covered in blood."

Marcus became her guide and her teacher. He taught her how to hunt, how to find the right prey: the evil ones. The killing came easy; she didn't need a teacher for that. Then, later, he revealed himself to be a warrior from far away, from beyond the sky, beyond the stars. And then, centuries later, she discovered who he really was – he was her father, her guardian, her guide. "Oh, my father, help me now!"

Years earlier: on the altar to Baal, the blood spills from the slash in the child's throat.

The goddesses Asherah and Astarte stand guard.

Candles and torches flame up below their statues.

There is no such thing as pity.

"Drink this, this blood, oh God, this blood of the innocent lamb, this blood is offered onto Thee."

As prescribed, she splashes the blood upon herself, coats her face, her shoulders, her breasts; she is an aspiring votive priestess, the privileged daughter of a rich and privileged family.

Thunder echoes outside, beyond the walls of the temple.

She disrobes and steps into a cascade of water.

She is cleansed.

The blood is washed away.

She is clothed in new robes, spotless.

She is escorted home.

There she finds, waiting for her, her father – her earthly, adopted father, a rich, skeptical Phoenician merchant, a kind and wise man – says, "Well?"

She looks down. The air is electric. Raindrops begin to fall; they splash in the courtyard pool. "It smells like rain," she says. The air has darkened. Baal is pleased. The sacrifice has been accepted. Thunder echoes

"You made the sacrifice," her earthly father, her adopted father, says. Her earthly father, she knows, does not approve of the gods; he does not believe in them, and he does not believe in sacrifice to the gods; above all, he does not believe in the sacrifice of children. He is wise; he has voyaged much, lived hard, seen much, lived among the Greeks and Jews and Latin tribes; and made himself rich – beyond what his own father could have dreamed of.

At dinner, under her father's gaze, she sees it clearly, the slitting of the little girl's throat.

"So be it," the priest had said.

"Now she is with the gods," the priestess had said.

"Lift her up."

"Yes, lift her up."

So she had lifted the dead girl up, and having bathed in the girl's blood – having painted herself in the girl's blood – she ascended the steps of the altar to the burning fire. The fire made a withering roaring sound, twirling upwards, the smoke swirling out toward the heavens and clouds where the God Baal dwelt.

Baal would bring rain.

At home, the rain began to fall, pitter-patter in the courtyard, pitter-patter on the palm fronds, and on the tiled roof.

"Perhaps the rain comes of itself, in its own time," said her father; he put his hand on her head, caressed her hair.

She looked up at him, "Perhaps."

She remembers it again; it replays in her mind:

She, a child, climbed up the altar with the little girl who was to die.

Hand in hand, they climbed up the altar.

They would cut the little girl's throat upon the altar.

V watched, impassive, as it happened. When it happened, she was – what? – Ten or eleven perhaps, not yet twelve. Or, no, maybe it was later; maybe she was fourteen.

The knife was bright like sunlight, and the blood was bright too when it spilled, the gash opening like another mouth, ruby lips.

Where there was life, now there was death.

The bright-eyed girl was now a limp-limbed doll.

There was no more laughter.

The priest lifted up the body.

V sniffed the air.

The coppery tang of blood made her hungry.

"Oh, Father Wolf, I have sinned. I have lusted. I have killed! I have drunk the blood of believers and unbelievers!"

Her voice was far away, in some other universe. She wondered whether she had the bloodlust even then. Yes, she must have had the bloodlust even before it was awakened, before she knew she had it, even before she morphed into what she became, a vampire half-alien, a predator, a killer, feasting on blood, human blood; after all, she was her mother's daughter and her mother, originally purely human, originally innocent, had been turned into a blood-thirsty monster, a thing of beauty and of death … until she died …

Yes, my mother, my real mother, not my adopted mother, was a monster, transformed into a monster by my father – Marcus whom I adore – and who used mother, a mere earthling, a mere human, for an "experiment," until her lover, my father, until the man who had turned her into a bloodthirsty mon-ster, until Marcus killed her; my mother had been bloodthirsty – mad with bloodlust …

He killed her because she had become what he made her become.

My mother …

Her Phoenician father greeted V when she was brought back from the temple. He took her in his arms and stroked her hair. "My beautiful wayward daughter," he said, "Now you have seen, now you know what Baal and his priests require." And her mother said, "It will have made you hungry, my darling, it will have made you hungry."

They dined in the courtyard, under the stars. V looked up at the stars, wondering: What do we worship and why?

"Why do the gods want us to worship them, father?"

"Ah," her father said, and waved his hand in the air.

"That means he doesn't know," said her mother, with an indulgent smile, putting her hand on her father's hand, "And he doesn't care."

There was thunder.

The servants cleared away the dishes and food.

They retired inside.

The rain began to fall.

She went to sleep that night, Lalla, her Nubian nurse, beside her, stroking her hair, singing a strange melody in a strange language.

It was, as she learned centuries later, the language of the stars; it was the language of the Empire of Andromeda.

Why do we bow down, prostrate ourselves flat on the ground, or cringe, or cover ourselves, or uncover ourselves, kneel, mutter words, make signs – why?

She had pictures in her mind; the pictures came and went.

"V, what the hell are you doing?" A voice comes from far away, Kat's voice, "V, what the hell are you doing? Where have you gone? Come back, V!!"

V nods, she is again walking along the tunnel. "I'm fine, Kat," she says, she lays her hand on Kat's shoulder; she looks into Kat's eyes. "I'm fine."

"It doesn't look like it to me."

"I'm fine, really, I'm fine. Let's go up these steps – see where they lead." V's body moves, her legs move; V seems to be in her body, but she isn't. She is far away; she muses …

She is walking …

She is walking … long before she was born …

She is walking, half-naked, along a path in a deep gorge – far below her a river runs, bubbling over big flat stones, white water catching flecks of sunlight from the empty blue sky far above, she is headed toward a sacred place.

She wonders, brushing her hand against the wall soft gray limestone, where did the idea of the gods come from? It must have begun with dim glimmerings of awe, fear and desire and yearning mingled, and a sense of strangeness. The mind makes things strange. Thoughts are not things. Words are not things. Words are strangers in the world. Words are ghosts. They come from the spirit. Like ideas, they are born in the soul. They are not of this world. How does that happen?

The mind, filled with words, is estranged, is not at home in the world. But it wants to be at home in the world. It yearns to touch and be touched. Stories are our shelter; stories are our refuge. Gods, in stories, are our refuge. Stories are our home.

To make itself at home in the strangeness of the world, the mind needs stories, and spooks and hobgoblins, spirits and nymphs and gods. Her heart is lifted with fear and delight. "Tell me a story, so I will know who and what I am and where I am, and where and how I should go! Please, tell me a story, with beginning, middle, and end, tell me a story!"

The breeze moves softly down the gorge; the bubbling giggles of the river rise from far below, and, from farther down, a dull roar, a waterfall; somewhere a bird twitters, and the breeze moves in the trees, each leaf, each branch, each pine needle, each frond makes a different music.

The spirit – the mind – moves like the fluttering light and the rustling wind in the trees, and the leaves tremble and make a hushed noise, and the reeds shake and rustle. It is as if there is life in the air, invisible life.

A little voice speaks, a child's voice: "See, you are not alone; there is life all around you!"

"V, you seem distracted," Kat's voice, it comes from far away, from some other time, from some other universe. V thinks: Kat too is so beautiful, so fragile; she is a black goddess, an anthracite beauty; I want to hold her, comfort her.

"I'm fine," V says, "I'm okay. I'm just concentrating." V knows her lips are moving; she hears the words; but she is far away, in a different body, in a different universe.

Down there, in the gorge, it is hot, so hot, sweltering, really.

Oh, yes, it is hot! Now she is with the men, six of them, hunting; she is crouching, invisible, beside them; it is, oh, perhaps 100,000 years ago.

Many voices speak to the half-naked hunters, crouching, waiting for their prey; they feel the touch and voice of the drifting air upon them, the moving spirit; they sniff the air; they sense the odors; they see the traces, a bent stalk of grass, a hoof print, a clutch of fur on bark; they feel the energy and canny skill and fluid beauty of the prey, of the leaping antelope, the galloping bison, the wild and swift horses, intent on eluding them, the hunters, who are predators like the eagle, and hawk, and lion, and these half-naked hunters worship the wind, the leaves, the trees, and the prey – deer and antelope and horses – and they worship their rival animals too – the other hunters, the wolves, the eagles, the serpents – everything is radiant with mystery – and they worship, too, the sources of life, the fire that warms and the water from the source or from the river, and the woman who welcomes them into her body, who pulls them toward her, and from whose body, mysteriously, life comes forth, mewling and puking and helpless, formless clay to be molded into men and women.

Oh, woman, oh beauty, oh the horror.

The power of woman is as yet undimmed.

Men and women worship men and women and all things.

All these things are one, and they are all swept around in the rhythm of night and day, with the sun rising and setting and moving with the seasons across the sky, and the moon changes its face with the cycle of days and nights, and all things are sacred, and woman too is sacred.

V feels a shiver pass through her body; her slick armored bodysuit seems too close, too restricting, sweat bubbling from her skin. Have I got a fever?

"V?"

"Yes?"

V shivers. She is far away. And, yet, in her gloved hand, she holds a laser gun; the barrel catches eerie reflections of the phosphorescence from the lichen and mushroom growths on the tunnel wall.

"V?"

"Yes?"

But in that other world, in that ancient world, the man bows down. The man understands that he has come from the womb of woman – he knows not how – so he takes the clay, and he sculpts the woman, rolls of fertile fat, a sculpted slit, the gateway, an opening into and out of the world, and he makes obeisance to this image, symbol of fertility and plenty, this earth mother, this mother goddess, this lover, this earth and female form, matrix, this lump of clay, out of which you mold your icon. All things are born; all things die.

"V?"

"Yes?" V runs one gloved hand down her side, feeling, under the body-suit, the shape of her own body, incurve of rib cage, firm out-swelling of hip, smoothness of belly; it is real, it is here, it is now; and yet, it is so far away.

She is caught in the upsweep of mystery, elation, abandonment, no longer woman, no longer herself; she is man and woman; she is desire, emptiness, fullness, nothing; she is nothing.

"V? For God's sake, wake up, V!"

"What?" V blinks at Kat, "Oh, hi, Kat! Sorry, I was a bit distracted, thinking … I'm okay, really, I am."

Oh, yes, and you tremble before it in awe and desire, each and every man, your heart caught in a suspension and transcendence of lust, as if the clay were the thing itself, whatever that thing is, because, beyond what can be seen and felt and touched and smelled and tasted, beyond the molded clay figurine, beyond what can be held in one's arms, beyond the wild, womanly woman, beyond the skin of your lover, beyond the flesh of your prey, there is the intimation of something else – of something beyond … Something that cannot be touched or seen … Oh, goddess, oh, god, I pray to you, you must save us, you must save us …

"V, are you sure you're alright?" Kat's eyes are bright in the dimming light of the tunnel.

"I'm fine."

"We're getting close now, I feel it."

"Yes, we're getting close." V feels that in a moment she will burst; she wants to kill something, somebody; perhaps she will kill Kat, hybrid against hybrid, yes, that would be fitting, for we come from darkness, so back to darkness we should go. What am I thinking? I am going insane! The Boy is the one that comes from darkness! And is it the Boy who is pulling me away from here, pulling me like a riptide? Or is it something else, another spirit entirely?

Again, her mind drifts away from the tunnel, away from the smoky light, away from the end of the 22nd Century. So belief was born: the men and the women too – with aching in their loins and in their hearts that was like lust and like love – climbed down into the darkness in caves deep under the earth, natural cathedrals, womb-like meanderings, the inner side of the psyche and of the human body, the dark secret side of the great mother, the Earth, far from the light and from the twittering birds and the gorgeous plants, far from the sun and the moon, and, with smoky torches lighting the walls of stone, they painted, in the easy natural strokes that come from *being* the thing you represent, from dissolving *into* the animals, the bison, the galloping, the horses cantering, the gesture, the movement, the …

Oh, my heart aches so!

Everything, or almost, meant something – struck a chord, a vibrancy in the heart, a yearning and trembling in the loins and belly: the rippling of water, the light on the high snows of the mountains, the dark thunder in the afternoon, the fire, springing into life, the fresh rain, large flakes of snow, the moon, mysterious, changing faces, phases …

Oh, my heart aches so!

I yearn for a home!

I yearn for a story!

And so the story became bigger; the story was more and more imperious, and it drove out all the little stories. The little stories – the stories of a fountain here, a hill there, a cave, a pebbled river crossing, a large old tree, a beautiful smooth cliff – the little stories all left the world, were forgotten, and became ghosts, or demons, evil spirits. Sacredness left the world; the sky gods ruled, far up and far away, the gods of roiling clouds and flashes of light, and of the deep distant voice of thunder, gods with names and soon with stories and with husbands and wives and sons and daughters and ancestors and rivalries, hatreds, jealousies, wars …

"V! Where are you V?" Kat's voice is far away.

"I'm here," V hears her own voice, echoing, far away, hollow, a ghost's voice.

And then, in a country of half-desert, in a turmoil of wars and tribal hatreds and dynastic struggles, came the One God, the angry, jealous god, the God that drove out all the others, all the nymphs, and naiads, all the goddesses, all the sacredness and luminosity, all the liminal spaces, all the numinous thresholds, all trees, stones, rivers, springs, mountains, animals, all was … emptied out …

And nothing was left, just a distant god and a fallen senseless sinful world, and that one god rose up far, far, far away, beyond the sky, beyond the stars, beyond everything, and into that void came the voice … There is only one God, and I am He. I am I. Worse than the God, though, were his followers, intolerant, violent, exclusive. Believe what I believe, or you are nothing! They often – not always – disguised their arrogance under the name of *love*! Such is the Boy. His seductive powers are great; he conquers souls, and he turns them into monsters. Love is transmuted into hate.

"I really don't think you are okay, V."

Kat is standing before her, her hands on her hips, worried, pissed off.

"No, I'm …"

Then there is a flash of light and … Lo and behold!

The wolf is there, the ringmaster!

"Now, you see, ladies, we got bronco-busting, steer-cutting, pig-sticking, chicken plucking, we got greased pole climbing, we got lasso contests, we got slimy rope tug-o'-wars, we got topless mud wrestling, we got everything here, and I want to put on a little special show, a little sorority initiation trial, and humiliation, you know, in honor of you two very special ladies, so if you two ladies will just favor me with your attention, and accommodate me now, surely, you will manage a little wrestling match, down in the mud, let's do it, it will be fun, and, through my magic, you will be quite willing to perform, your two super ladies, and that is quite fitting, ladies, that you strip down, because this will be one hell of a show!"

The wrestling ring appears; it is a pit and sloshes with a foot of gray mud.

A fat guy with a huge paunch and a cowboy hat and hip-high rubber boots, steps into the ring. He hitches up his belt.

"Now girls, let's see what you can do!"

Kat and V leap into the ring!

"Right, now, girls …"

Kat jumps on V, and they roll on the giant wet paving stones, they fight, and wrestle, sinking and flopping in the slop, then, bursting their Cosmos catsuits, simultaneously they morph into demon form, and they fight.

Kat is no longer Kat; she is a glittering silver-white hybrid.

V thinks, yes, at long last, now she has morphed; now I can kill her

What am I thinking?

Kat leaps. "You turned me into a monster, you monster, and now I have become a monster, and you will die in my arms as I will kill you, for my hate is love, and my love is hate."

Kat has a headlock on V, she twists V down toward the roiling, boiling mud, which bubbles and pops, "I have longed to do this, to destroy you," Kat growls, her hiss caught low in her throat, gurgling with emotion.

V's snout is within an inch of the bubbling gray mud, the bubbles pop, spraying hot goo, and V thinks: Where did this roiling mud come from? Where are we?

"Now, girls, keep it up, go at it!"

The public is screaming.

The cheering crowds watch the demon girls fight and tangle in the ring. "Now, that is a masterly double flip!"

"Now, she's up against the ropes!"

"Look at that headlock!"

The crowd goes wild.

Now V has got K in a headlock.

"What a fucking fabulous headlock!" A big guy in a Hawaiian shirt is jumping up and down. Klieg lights shine off his glowing bald head.

"Oh, that backflip! Pure treachery!"

V flips Kat over. K lands face down in the slush. V pounces, squatting on Kat's waist, her thighs crushing Kat's sides, pinning Kat to the mat, now forcing Kat's head down under the mud.

"Oh, wow, poor Kat!"

"Kill her, baby, kill her!"

"Finish her!"

"Finish her!"

Kat flips sideways, throws V like a bronco throwing a rider, V flips down on her backside, tenses her thighs, and leaps up.

The mud-slick canvas bounces, the mud splashes, and the overhead lights sway in the steamy excitement. The crowd is wild! The fat man in the Hawaiian shirt – a true fan – is trying to climb into the ring.

"Now we give you the monster show, the freak show to end all freak shows, hey, presto, abracadabra!"

V twists and turns, it's impossible to get a grip. Both their limbs are slippery and wet, dripping mud and slime.

Finally, she flips Kat over.

They roll on the edge of the steaming boiling cauldron.

The mud smells like tar, like fresh tar.

It takes V back, suddenly, to summer days, and road gangs in Soviet villages or in backwoods country, the road workers or Gulag slaves stripped to the waist, sweaty, pouring the asphalt, pots of boiling tar in the sun, and she used to watch the workers, often prisoners, in the summer heat, breaking rocks, pouring tar, smooth the tar down, as her own thirst, her own yearning mounted …

V frees herself, leaps up, and, as Kat jumps up, V smashes her against the ropes, Kat's hybrid body bounces back and slams into V

V grabs Kat around the waist, lifts her into the air, slams her down with a huge shuddering splash into the mud, then V leaps on Kat, and pins her down.

V now thinks: I must slay Kat, tear off her head, just as I have killed renegade hybrids in the past.

"Right, right," says the fat man. He wipes his brow.

"Kill, kill," shouts a woman, clinging to the ropes, standing at the edge of the ring, her lacquered hair and pink neon sweat pants reflecting Klieg Lights. Rolls of white fat bulge out above and below her bra.

"Now," V says, crouching on Kat, fangs bared, saliva dripping, her whole body, dripping mud, gleaming in the lamplight, sparkling green and turquoise and gold, coiled with the energy of the Serpent, the energy of the Devil.

"Kill, kill, kill," the audience screams.

Colored balloons float up.

Floodlights pinpoint the action, lighting up the two demons.

Kat seems paralyzed for a moment, her eyes gone dull, and her arms limp, and then, just as V is about to tear her throat out.

"You Devil," Kat grins, fangs naked, foaming.

Kat rams V in the throat with the sharp corner of her elbow.

V gasps, falls back, choking, gagging, doubled up, and rolls to the edge of the ring of smoking roiling mud, her glorious turquoise and gold scales now almost entirely invisible, a smoky slippery statue of gray mud.

Kat leaps, astride V, then crouches down, sitting on V's midriff as V still chokes, and coughs.

"Now you die," Kat leaps up, and plunges, kicking V in the side.

V curls up, then straightens out, and leaps up.

V stands, she weaves helplessly; her legs wobble.

Now it is no longer mud, it is tar.

They are in some sort of hell.

V falls over the edge of the tar pit, the boiling tar just brushing her foot, she leaps, catches a dangling chain, and swings, pushing off from one arch, then from another, and smashes into Kat.

Kat loses her balance, staggers back, falls backward into the pit, but just before her scales touch the bubbling sulfurous muddy surface, V grabs her, swinging them both up, and they crash into the wall and fall together onto the huge smooth black paving stones, and lie for a moment, tangled up, silver and turquoise, and Kat blinks her big dark eyes – perfectly black eyes that seem blind when you stare straight into them, and she says, "What are we doing?"

"Yes, what are we doing?

"It's an illusion."

They stood up; they looked down at themselves, yes: they were in hybrid form, covered in mud, in a mud-wrestling ring, with a cheering crowd, with people shouting "

"Fight, bitches, fight, goddamn it!"

"Slam her, whack her, yeah, kill her!"

"Strangle her!"

The big sweaty referee seemed nervous.

"Why are we hesitating girls. Get to it! This is showbiz, remember, this is showbiz!"

The referee began to melt. His belt buckle popped. His pants fell down. He was wearing striped boxers, red suspenders, long socks held up by clips. He was slightly bowlegged, thin hairy legs. Interesting, thinks V.

The ropes waver and sag and flip out of position.

The big smoky floodlights went off, then on, then off.

The mud splashed up and turned to smoke and steam.

Then everything shimmered, and they were in human form, but naked, in the Elysium underground tunnel, their bodysuits lying on the paving stones.

"What is going on?" Kat looked around; there was no pit of boiling tar, there was no boxing ring, no referee, no Klieg lights, and no public.

"Mind games," said V. "We are inside his mind, or he is inside our minds."

"I never wanted to attack you."

"I know," said V, "I didn't want to kill you; though wresting with you was lots of fun."

"You are very, very perverse, V. You are aware of that, of course."

"Yes, I am." V picked up her armored suit – ripped and torn, and burst at the seams, "But you bring it out in me, a bit more than others."

"Oh, well, I guess I should be flattered." Kat picked up her catsuit, "Wow – ripped up … we must have exploded out of them!"

"We did."

"Wow," Kat shivered. Finally, she had been transformed – into a bright quicksilver colored hybrid, rippling with light. The image of her hybrid self, somehow seen through V's eyes, remained. Then, it faded. "Was I really that thing – I mean, that silver demon?"

"Yes, that is probably your form, and color scheme, when you really hatch. I think the illusion was a preview."

"It was sort of cute," Kat shivered, thinking: how strange, how weird, and how horrible! How thrilling! She fingered the bio-body armored catsuit, "These suits are a mess."

"They'll regenerate."

"Of course," Kat was surprised she could forget something so basic; armored bio-skin-suits regenerated. But, then, it had been an exciting couple of days; it was as if the old world was already dead. A new one was being born.

They slipped into the suits, a skintight slippery squeaky sound: the hissing caress of elastic bio-skin against human skin. "Perverse," murmured Kat.

"Of course," said V; for some reason, V was feeling excessively feisty, full of piss and vinegar, freshly aroused libido.

"The ragged look becomes them," Kat looked down, inspecting the rips and holes in her suit; already they were closing; the wounds were healing, the armor was growing over their skin, over their bodies.

The catsuits began to gleam, black, pristine, as if they were new.

Steam rose from the tunnel floor.

"Okay, let's go!"

But …

But …

V and Kat were, suddenly, in a whirling hall of mirrors, on every side were reflections, their reflections shattered, and separated, and then they were united, and then they were side by side, and then they were gone, and then V saw only herself, said and she shouted, "Kat! Kat! Where are you?"

There was no answer. The mirrors began to twirl. V saw herself multiplied by ten, by a hundred, in infinite regression, many, many versions of V, all the same, receding into space, her black skintight Centurion uniform, her boots, her defiant stance, legs braced apart, her pale face with its dark eyes and black eyebrows framed by jet-black hair and by the Centurion helmet, the visor tilted up and the high protective collar, and the holsters and the laser gun in her gloved hand, and she could see no way forward and no way back, just an infinite series of images, all of herself, and the images began to whirl, and V turned one way, then the other, but the images were all the same, and she was tempted to fire the laser gun or unsheathe her machete and blow or hack the images away; but she was afraid that this was Mind-induced madness and that she might shoot herself or, even worse, Kat, or some innocent creature, and so she turned and turned, not sure whether it was she who was spinning around or the mirrors and their images.

She shouted, "Kat! Kat! Where are you, Kat?"

Then it all stopped.

"The Boy is trying to delay us," she muttered, kicking at the pavement with her boot.

Out loud, she said, "The Boy doesn't want me to get to the Mind."

Louder, she said, "So the Boy is afraid!"

Wham!

Everything changed.

V was standing alone in an empty dark space in a sort of spot-light, and she could see, beyond the edges of the light, the bars of what seemed to be a cage and she was inside the cage, and the cage door opened, and in came a fellow, a character or a creature, in a top hat and tails, and he was carrying a whip and when he turned to her she saw that it was the Wolf.

Oh, I see: I'm back in the circus!

Yes, it was the Wolf, the Circus Master Wolf; he was back again.

He was the mirage, the fellow who had catapulted V and Kat into a mud-wrestling contest. She should try to penetrate his disguise, reveal him as the Boy, or a variant of the Dark Force, a hairy version of the Foul Fiend.

"Who the hell are you?" she wanted to say, but all that came out was a growl or snarl, and she tried to point the laser at this intruder into her world and she realized that there was no laser and she looked down and her hand and saw that it was not a hand but a paw and her arm was covered with fine jet-black fur and the same with her body and legs and she was a cat woman, a panther woman, she realized, and, goddamn it, she was a freak in some sort of circus, and she could again hear the crowd and smell the straw, manure and animal piss, and the hot canvas and popcorn, and circus music began, and, blast his evil soul, the Wolf took off his top hat, turned his back on her – *Ignoring me now, is he?* – and made a low bow, his coattails and wolf tail flapping out behind him, bowing obsequiously to the invisible crowd which cheered and clapped and then, as the darkness cleared, she could see the crowd, children, families, old people and young, all stacked up in the bleachers, and all clapping and staring straight at her, the star of the show.

The Wolf Circus Master straightened up, turned toward her, pointed, and shouted, "Now, here she is, for your delectation and edification, the product of unholy coupling of big cat and human female, from the jungles of a lost valley in the deepest heart of ancient Borneo, an unexplored mountain valley where strange and exotic rites take place! I present the cat woman!"

He snapped his long ox-hide whip, and she saw the lightning flutter off the whip and crackle through the air, and she felt the rush and hiss and sizzling heat of the air, scorched by the electric whip, as it flashed by her shoulder, and as its point curled around, just missing her back, stirring and rippling her silken fur, and she realized that the Wolf could inflict great pain with that long electric bullwhip, and leave ugly red welts, breaking her beautiful fur, marring her slinky animal perfection, and that he could also snap her neck with that whip and so she obediently went through all the routines she had been taught, leaping in the air, leaping through a hoop, walking on her hands upside down, and hopping through a bonfire, and making a series of bouncing handstands, and rolling herself around the edge of the circular cage like a human wheel – or cat woman wheel.

"Meow," commanded the Wolf.

She meowed.

"Clap your hands," said the Wolf.

She clapped her paws.

"Flick your tail!"

She flicked her tail and licked her whiskers.

"Take a bow," said the Wolf.

She took a bow, a low courtly bow, of the kind seen in films of chivalry and from Shakespeare's time. The applause was thunderous. People jumped up, screamed, and threw their hats and popcorn containers into the air.

She took another bow, as did the Wolf. She dimly thought that there was something she should remember, that perhaps she had not always been in this cage, perhaps she had not always been a circus performer in the freak circus, that perhaps she had had another life somewhere, as another person, another being, in another body, but then the memoires of this life, her life as a cat woman, flooded in, and she realized that any thoughts of another life were an illusion, she remembered being captured in a jungle – the big game hunter had used narcotic darts – somewhere in Borneo it seemed to have been; she remembered being in a cage as she was swung by a clanking crane, high up, and then aboard a tramp steamer in the main port of Borneo, its old-fashioned high smoke stack belching out black smoke, coal-fired engines, she remembered watching the stevedores and hearing their shouts, and seeing the brightness in their eyes as they looked up at her, the caged animal that she was, a unique freak, a hybrid of human and big cat, what a coupling that must have been, big cat jumping on, pouncing on, coupling with the beautiful doctor from Paris or Warsaw, or was she the result of a monstrous experiment by some power-mad Doctor Moreau tinkering with DNA in his jungle hideout, and she remembered the smell of the hot sun-blistered metal, only partly painted, on the ship's decks and superstructure, the smell and feel too of dense sooty coal smoke, of thick engine grease, as she was swung across the deck, and then the steamy hot interior of the hold of the ship, with crates and cages piled high, the chitter-chatter of captive monkeys, and …the hot straw, animal smell, musty, musky, animals in heat, manure and piss …hot exhalations and …

She shook herself and woke up.

She was chained, manacled to a wall of stone, underground, somewhere in the depths of Elysium City.

"That was amusing," said the Wolf.

"You are a devil," she said, realizing she was once again human and in her Centurion's uniform, the armored skin-suit but without her weapons.

"Indeed, I am a devil. I take that as a compliment; in fact, I am *the* Devil or what poor benighted humans have taken as the Devil over the brief millennia of their existence. I wear a black hat, sunglasses, and I crack my whip, and the grotesque shadows dance. I am the film director of my own fantasies, and I am the orchestrator of humanity's nightmares!"

The Wolf bowed. He was standing before her. She was suspended on the wall, about a foot above the ground, as if, in a sense, she were crucified – her arms outstretched manacled, legs pinned together. The Wolf was just about as tall as she was when he stood up straight, which he was doing now, and he was wearing the uniform of a member of the Spanish Inquisition, at least that's what it looked like.

V wiggled her hands and feet, and twisted her neck this way and that trying to see if she could slip out of the bonds. No, she couldn't. She was bound tight and fast. She willed herself to morph into demon form, so as to shatter the steel manacles and free herself. But she couldn't morph. This wolf character must have quasi-magical powers, natural enough if he were the Devil.

It was more than annoying. She felt her own human flesh like a prison, heavy upon her, with sweat trickling down her forehead, hair soaked and plastered to her forehead – her helmet seemed to have disappeared and her boots too – and a sense of musty clamminess building up between the skin-tight suit and her own skin, which was again human skin, and not the fur of a black cat, thank the Universe for that at least!

"You made a very handsome cat," said the Wolf.

"Thanks." She licked her lips; she was thirsty.

"I should like to keep you, in that form, as a pet." He favored her with a wolfish grin.

"God forbid," she said, "Where is Kat?"

"Ah, your beautiful Centurion friend, so wonderful and splendid and loyal with that luscious black skin, is that who you mean?"

"Yes."

"Well, I'm afraid, she is no more. She had been petrified."

"What?"

"I have turned her into a work of art, quite exquisite, really."

"You, I will kill you."

"No, you won't."

"I will!"

"No, you won't, you see, you are quite mad, I am afraid my dear, and all this is an illusion, a wicked dream of which you are the heroine. I am not sure how you became insane, my dear, but insane you are!"

"You, you, you ... monster," V squirmed.

The world wavered as if it was a reflection in a placid country pond into which a pebble had been thrown by a naughty young schoolgirl, or across which a breeze had suddenly moved, stirring and confusing and breaking it up into overlapping waves, transforming it into a shattered kaleidoscope. The placid images and dreams that had been reflected back out of that mirror, the high hot summer sky, the white bright cumulus, the leafy dark green shadowy foliage of trees leaning over the pond, all the whole wide world, was reflected, upside down, and now it broke apart ...

"It's a topsy-turvy world, really," said the Wolf.

"Yes," said V, with a cloudy voice she didn't recognize as her own.

"Can't blame you for getting confused, now, can we?"

"No."

"The petrification of Kat is only the wicked reification of your own desire for her – you want to turn her into an object, an object which you can possess, this is naughty of you, you lustful wayward child! But you are a primitive totem yourself – remember when you starred in 8½ – so it is only natural that you should want to turn others into totems, objects, trinkets to populate your feverish mind. But in any case, she is not real, my dear. Like everything else about you and about your life, she is purely imaginary. Kat, however charming she may be, doesn't exist!"

Poof!

V was no longer manacled and hanging from a stone wall in a cavern. She was in a long corridor. It seemed like the corridor of some institution. A huge metal door clanged shut behind her: *You will be in here forever; you will never escape!*

"I am really a nice old wolf."

The light was dull, the walls were bare, the cheap linoleum floor reflected the dull light from windows which were evidently in some of the rooms which were off the corridor on both sides and whose doors were open. How many women had been tossed away into institutions, their madness – their desire for freedom – being the pretext?

"I am really a nice old wolf," the wolf now looked rather more like a man, albeit a very hairy man. He was wearing a heavy tweed suit with waistcoat, and rather creased baggy plaid trousers, "but you see, my dear, the problem with you, my dear, is that you are insane, as I said before. You are not what you think you are."

"I am not insane," V tried to say, but it came out as a brief sloppy slur of sound, dripping saliva, though twisted, heavy, and half-paralyzed lips.

She was shuffling along, with very small uncertain steps, she realized, and barefoot, and wearing a long nightgown-type sheathe, under which it seemed she was more or less naked, except perhaps for an institutional-type over-sized diaper. Ah, I must be incontinent, leaking from every end, and very ancient! What a horrible thought! Her arm was skinny, she noticed, bony even, and marked with red patches and scars; it was the shriveled, mottled, loose-skinned arm of an old woman, the decrepit, shriveled, extremely ancient remnants of an old woman.

"You are so, crazy, I mean, you are utterly insane, mad as the proverbial hatter." The Wolf's nameplate said, "Doctor Herr Professor Lucifer Wolf MD Ph.D. M Sc." He turned to her with an avuncular wolfish smile, "And the consequence of this is that you think – you are under the illusion – that you have had a life, a rather long and adventurous life, in your case, as something called a hybrid, a sort of extra-terrestrial half-alien, half-human, super-strong female avenger, a sort of Vampire Robyn Hood, but, in fact, you have not had a life at all – no life whatsoever I'm afraid – and you are nobody, an absolute nobody. You have never done anything. It is not a rare illusion. People believe they have lived when, in fact, they haven't – it was all just a dream. Nothing you think is real is real, my dear."

"No, it can't be …" V attempted to object, but her tongue was heavy; no meaningful sound escaped from her lips, just a slather of grunts, and her mouth full of saliva, which leaked out of her twisted lips and down her chin. She didn't bother to wipe at the cooling dribble. She had to concentrate on shuffling. Aches and flashing pain shot through every bone, flashing particularly in her hips and knees. She groaned in little grunts, her agony.

"You see, my dear, you were born in a dreary suburb outside the city of nowhere to a dreary nondescript family and then out of sheer adolescent boredom – and because some classmates bullied you – you went insane and tried to cut your wrists and stick your head in an oven and then load your pockets with heavy stones and walk into a lake, attempting to imitate Virginia Woolf, I believe, and then, once you were tempted to jump from a high building, and you teetered on the edge for five hours and caused the taxpayers no end of loss of money, and then, having lost interest in killing yourself, you decided to kill others."

"I did not," the old woman said with her ancient slurry voice.

"Oh, yes, you did! It's your only claim to fame. You killed."

"I did not," she thought; she thought it, she tried to say it; but no sound emerged from the quivering, dripping, chapped lips; she looked down; her toenails were long and thick and warped and cracked and yellow and needed cutting; her shins were bony and waxy and white with blue varicose streaks and blotched with rashes of various kinds; the skin was thin; it must be from old age, she thought, must be old age, and my old worn-out, end-of-the-tether, end-of-life body.

Things wobbled.

Her pale bony knees wobbled, her nightgown wobbled.

Everything wobbled.

The world wavered again; the photons that populate and form light-waves jiggled and danced and went chaotically this way and that, and twisted as if passing through a prism, generating, for a moment, a rainbow, with the visible white light breaking up into its component wavelengths, space itself, and time, zipping in all sorts of directions, and the visible spectrum wavelength from 390 nanometers to 700 nanometers, or at frequencies from 430 to 790 Terahertz, or 430 to 790, trillion periods per second, all mixed up, and then the world settled down again, pulling itself together, time-space unwrinkling, simplifying itself into four dimensions, and becoming … that illusion we call "now."

Now!

Now she is in a hard metal high-backed chair, manacled, her neck and head rigid, her ankles and wrists locked down.

"Look at this photograph. Pretty gory, isn't it?" Doctor Wolf smiled. He held the photograph out so that it was in the circle of light from a small, focused lamp that was over the chair. It lit up the forensic color photograph as if it were under a floodlight. "Not even I could manage such bloody work," Doctor Herr Professor Wolf smiled, "And look at this, you were not yet fifteen years old and you cut this fifteen-year-old girl's throat, five times, and this, this girl was 24, a bit older, so she'd had longer to live, but you really did a job – slash, slash, slash – on her, didn't you?"

V squirmed, and tried to get out of the chair. She found she couldn't; she was manacled, welded to the chair; her superhuman strength was absent; she slumped, letting the metal bite into her throat, her wrists.

"So Mabel Brown, I think we must put an end to all of this."

"My name is not Mabel," the old crone's voice bubbled up.

"Oh, so what is your name, then, pray tell, Mabel?"

"My name is V."

"V? That is an interesting name."

"I am a half-alien vampire."

"Oh, oh, well, I know that one. You see, when you have been asked to explain why you bite your victims – usually after you have killed them – and occasionally slurp up their blood and suck the wounds and, more than once, you have even eaten the flesh, well, you have explained how you are a vampire from Andromeda or some such place, whatever and wherever this Andromeda is, and how you need blood to keep you going and in fine fettle to keep your immortality and superhuman powers intact."

"It is the truth, I am ..."

"Well, I think, Mabel, that we could go on all day like this, but I have other patients to see, and so on, so right now, I shall ask Nurse Hawthorn here to give you a little shot."

V struggled and squirmed, but she could not break free – how was it she had become so weak? Doctor Wolf held her arm down – adding to the pressure from the wrist manacle, while the nurse injected something with a very large needle, a giant needle actually, it must have been at least a foot long, and whatever was in the needle it made V feel very small and very afraid.

In it went, the needle ...

Doctor Wolf's face faded into a blur. V shrank and shrank; she became smaller and smaller.

From a great distance, Doctor Wolf beamed down on her, "Life is but a dream, the dream of a madwoman, and isn't it funny – she conjured the whole thing, a whole biography, up out of her sick, wicked mind. She is possessed."

"Yes, Doctor, she is possessed by the Devil, truly."

"Why, then, child, we shall cut the Devil out, shall we not?"

"Indeed we shall, Doctor, we shall cut the Devil out of her soul!"

Their voices come from a great distance. V blinks; her head lolls back; her eyes are bleary. The skylight overhead is dirty with soot and old rain and oil; this was the first thing she thought: the skylight is dirty. Then she realized that her tongue was heavy and furry, that she did not at all feel like herself – whoever or whatever herself was. It occurred to her, then, that she didn't know who she was, or where she was, or what year it was, or perhaps even what century it was, didn't have the slightest idea.

She dozed off thinking that it was so very nice not to know who or what one was because then in one's dreams one could be anyone or anything at all or even nothing which, in certain circumstances, could certainly be preferable. Dreaming is not so bad, so if all of life is but a dream, then perhaps that is not so bad either.

She woke again, still not knowing who she was. She could not move. The bleary ugly overcast white light rained down through a dirty skylight above her, but it was a different skylight, and she was lying flat on her back on some sort of smooth cold-feeling slab, and she was wearing some sort of skimpy loose open-at-the-back hospital shift thing that makes you feel naked – well, you *are*, virtually, naked – and she was restrained, wrists and ankles and waist buckled and manacled down, she blinked at the light coming through the dirty skylight and from a lamp that was angled down at her; the light, directed straight into her eyes, made her feel heavy and sleepy; her tongue was sticky and monstrous. She couldn't move it; there was something in her mouth, filling her mouth; she closed her eyes; she was gone …

Then she woke again and she was sitting in a chair and a heavy-set man, again Doctor Wolf it seemed, was leaning very close and she could see the pores of his skin, the dark blackhead pores of his large, fleshy, red, slightly bulbous nose and he was wearing rimless glasses with a black ribbon attached and he smelled vaguely of rosewater and she could smell his sugary coffee-stained breath, and his lips were thick and flat and his eyes rather large, with big bags and lines under them, and his cinnamon-and-white eyebrows were bushy, and his reddish hair was brushed straight back, standing high straight upward from his wrinkled, high-colored forehead. "Now, how are we, Mabel? How are we today? Having any more alien-vampire fantasies, are we …?"

He moved away.

She realized she was restrained in a new way, in a straightjacket it must be, her arms were wrapped tight around her torso, just below her breasts, and pushing her breasts up.

Doctor Wolf was wearing a waistcoat, a gold-colored watch chain hung across his waistcoat's midriff; it twinkled; the twinkles of the chain were hypnotic. Doctor Wolf opened his mouth, revealing, large, square, widely spaced teeth, "You know the last person you bit got infected, I'm sorry to say."

His tongue passed over his lips.

"You are rabid, I'm afraid, rabid. You are a rabid bitch. You spread death and madness." He bared his teeth; they had changed; now they were yellow crooked and crowded overlapping teeth, with black-and-brown tobacco stains between them. How could he change so completely and so quickly?

A thin, anemic freckled young woman with rimless spectacles and clothed in a nurse's smock, stood nearby. Showing her prominent but not unattractive overbite, which pushed up her upper lip chipmunk style, she read from a clipboard. "Mabel Brown, criminally insane, paranoid-schizophrenic fantasies, the creation of a whole elaborate world and life history, number of known victims seventeen." The young woman paused, and looked up from the clipboard; she had very blue watery eyes and pale blond almost invisible eyelashes and eyebrows but red curly undisciplined strands of hair struggling out from under her nurses' cap.

Now, standing around, were more people, gentlemen in medical coats, and one or two nurses. They were dressed as if it must be the 1940s or perhaps 1950s.

The woman in the smock continued to read, "Incredibly fertile fantastical constructions, a whole life, convinced she is a vampire, an alien-human hybrid, convinced too that she is an ancient Phoenician, and sometimes she believes she is the reincarnation of one of the pagan goddesses –"

"Pagan goddesses …?"

"Yes."

"Which pagan goddesses …?"

"Phoenician and Egyptian mainly," said the nurse, "And pre-Yahweh Israelite deities – Dagon, El, Baal, Mot, and Yam, and Asherah, Moon and Sun gods, and so on."

"I didn't know there were any, pre-Yahweh, I mean."

"Oh, yes, idols and gods of all sorts, male and female, rather similar to Mecca, lots of totems and fetishes, before Mohammed cleaned it up."

"Continue, nurse, continue."

The nurse licked her lips and began to read. The light reflected in cute little waves off her steel-rimmed spectacles. "Isis, the Egyptian inventor of agriculture, with her hieratic beauty and her discus, and Astarte, the Phoenician goddess of fertility and love, and sister and lover to Baal and El, and perhaps concubine too of Yahweh, though of course, He would deny it, if we asked Him."

"Well, you know some people think they are Napoleon."

"Ha, ha, you are so naughty, Doctor Wolf!" The nurse blushed and tittered, "You really are a card, aren't you, Doctor Wolf?"

Doctor Wolf's glasses sparkled merrily. "In any case, the decision has been made, regretfully, I must say, that a lobotomy is the solution, in this case, to this particular form of madness."

V began to sweat in fear. She wanted to say something, to object, but she realized that her mouth and jaw were encased in a muzzle.

A muzzle …?

Of course, I have a muzzle, she thought: I bite; I'm a rabid dog, a rabid bitch. Is this real? Am I mad, just a crazy person in an insane asylum? Am I really this person?

"Well, look at yourself!" Doctor Wolf held a mirror up – a blurred image it was at first, and then it focused: yes, she was a wild-eyed old woman, muzzled with a black leather muzzle, buckled black straps running up around, behind her ears, and over her head, with leaden circles under her eyes and pale yellow skin and her head shaven which for some reason made her eyes look even bigger, even wilder. Her eyebrows had grown together making one witch-like satanic line. The strange wild eyes stared, an untamed animal in a panic of terror, captured, cornered, about to be executed. The mirror disappeared. She disappeared with it.

Was that me?

How is it I never realized? Never understood?

"So, we will proceed forthwith."

"Full lobotomy, I believe, is the solution."

"Yes, indeed, absolutely, it is the only solution."

"The legal documents are here."

Doctor Wolf wet his finger, a stubby, thick finger with its blunt fingernail cut straight across; large dark hairs, a tangled forest on each finger; he turned the pages slowly, deliberately; the light and shadow played on the pages, they made a crisp, cutting, rustling sound. "Yes, we can proceed – there are no objections."

V's sweat turned to ice. They were going to remove her soul. She twisted, wiggled, turned, tried to scream, but only a muffled growl came from the muzzled mask, straps over her nose and cheeks, wrapped around her ears, and the back of her face.

"Very violent, as you can see, and with a tendency to hurt herself, you know that when she was a young girl, she tried to kill herself, quite a few attempts, really, or so we have been told."

"And then she decided to kill others instead."

"Well, others, other people are often really a projection of aspects of ourselves, other people are our inner demons, as you know; so such murders are rather like exorcisms; she is casting out her other selves, which are the ghosts of people she has known, figments and fragments. By killing the other person, she is really trying to kill part of herself."

"Unfortunate for the victims, though." The nurse favored Doctor Wolf with a toothy twinkly smile, "I mean the victims were real people, with their own lives to live, their own demons, their own journeys – and she snuffed their glory out."

"Quite." Doctor Wolf pursed his lips.

"It is a shame really, she was calm when she first came to us, but now … as you can see."

V growled. She struggled. She thrashed against her bonds.

"The procedure will be over shortly. Now, we just insert the needle here, and we stir and mix and whisk the frontal lobes up and cut a little bit loose …"

The overhead lights were blinding.

"Don't! Don't!" she screamed, "Don't! Don't!"

She thought she screamed; she wanted to scream, but she couldn't; her mouth wouldn't move; why wouldn't her mouth move? Oh, yes, the muzzle!

This was a nightmare!

The sweat was thick as glue, it pearled down her stomach; her thin bony old legs trembled; now she was naked under bright klieg-like lights.

It was an operating theater! When she had been transported here, she did not remember.

"Well, ladies and gentleman, you can see here, our difficulty. This was once a fine physical specimen, look at this photograph here. Look at the face, gaze upon the perfection of the limbs, the shape of the torso, the breasts, all is perfect … a goddess, yes, a goddess …truly a Helen who would easily launch a thousand ships! What a waste, alas!"

The world wavered and recomposed itself.

"… yes, alas, this once-perfect body – now aged into flabby and wrinkled skeletal and arthritic decrepitude, with flaccid skin hanging free – is inhabited by a mind of unparalleled violence, a diabolic mind that has killed, that has murdered, that has drunk deep of human blood and feasted upon human flesh. The correct punishment for such horrendous crimes would, of course, be death. But in the interests of science we have decided to reform that mind and to remove the devilish paranoid-schizoid personality that has possessed this once beautiful body, and we shall give her freedom once more, but without a personality of course. She will be docile; she will be passive; she will be a puppet. She will need help in caring for herself, she will not be able to feed or clean herself, and she will wear diapers and someone will have the unpleasant task of ensuring her personal hygiene, hosing off the piss and excrement, and drying and powdering her down, and dressing her, and so on, whenever we decide she should be clothed; her mind will be gone; but physically, she will be with us still, and I think a useful subject for many experiments which we may be able to carry out upon her as the need and opportunity arise."

"So we shall keep the hollow husk of the animal alive, shall we, Doctor?" Nurse Hawthorn was delighted, raring to go.

"Oh definitely, we shall." Doctor Wolf grinned.

Her head was now in a clamp; she couldn't move it this way or that.

The clamp pressed in on her temples, crushing her.

Her head was about to explode.

"The strange thing, too, doctor, is that she has never had a visitor, not a single visitor in all these twelve years she has been with us."

"Yes, yes, it is passing strange! It is as if she came from nowhere." With his index finger and his thumb, Doctor Wolf was stroking the black stubble on his chin; it made a monstrous rasping sound.

The light shone on the black pores at the wings of his nostrils. Salt and pepper hair wiggled inside his cavernous nostrils, tentacular and vicious, and eager to get out. One long black hair curled aggressively under his nasal septum; it was staring at her, it nodded. It knew all about her madness. "Yes," sighed the Doctor, "it is as if she truly does not exist: no one to claim her; no one to care for her; no one to love her."

She sweats fear: I am mad. That's what I am, merely a crazy old woman.

She closes her eyes: I've been here all these years, in this asylum.

She tries to clench her teeth: my life, my three-thousand-year-old life, is merely the dream of a pathetic mad, murderous old woman.

"It does make you wonder, Doctor, where could such a creature have come from?"

"Yes, it is strange indeed; she has been abandoned, totally abandoned, as if she were truly alien, a stranger to humanity, and to this planet."

"But then she is so violent and deadly that I doubt anyone would claim her if they did own her – good riddance, I imagine they would say."

"Why you know, we found her drinking the blood of one of her victims. She was out on the stormy heath, in Devon, in England, in a hut, and she'd come upon a poor innocent man, a lost hitchhiker from Hamburg, Germany – handsome young blond fellow – student of the works of Immanuel Kant – and she had emptied him of his blood. God only knows how she did it – he was a fine big man, strong as an ox. When we found him, he was an empty shell, a husk, a bloodless puppet propped up against the wall of her hut. She had stripped him of his clothes – his lederhosen, his backpack, his athletic socks, his Birkenstocks, his Tyrolean hat – and then put a bib on him and she was trying to feed him clay, which she apparently thought was pabulum, as if he were a baby. The mummified bloodless lips, of course, accepted no nourishment, not even clay. This seemed to upset her."

"Well, soon she will harm no one, Doctor."

"Now we just insert the needles here, my dear, through her eye sockets, and then, we cut the links between the prefrontal lobes of her brain and the rest of the brain, and we will sterilize certain areas of the brain itself, by just stirring the knife and needles around a bit. Stir and stir and stir! Toil and trouble, boil and bubble! Whoopee! Oh, this is such fun! Stir and Stir ..."

"It will reduce her to a robot, will it not, doctor?" the nurse was clearly grinning, even under her mask; she was gleeful. She had nice freckles across her nose, and, tucked under her cap, cruel and unruly curly red hair. Even in her terror, V had an image of confronting the nurse in some dark alley; V would wear a cloak, and a dark broad-brimmed hat, and she would seize the nurse by the throat, and she would bare her fangs, and she would ... No, she would not bare her fangs, she would offer her lips, in a kiss, and then she would seduce and subdue the nurse and her freckles and turn all of the girl's cruelty to servitude and to service her own desires and lusts ... and ... and then the sacrifice ...

"Yes, she will be a robot. Yours to command! I know, I know," Doctor Wolf sighed, "That is the charm, don't you think, to make of the living a puppet or a toy or a statue. Too bad we didn't do it sooner; this once beautiful creature

– you can see the ghost of the beauty she once was – has wasted her life addicted to vain and murderous fantasies, and now she will become human again, so to speak, with no emotional life and no mental life, but she will be human, in form, and she will be docile and a broken dog, a fixed bitch. No one need ever fear her again."

And so it was done.

How, and when, well ...?

How and when she has forgotten. And she would not understand even if by some miracle some part of her mangled mind remembered.

Now mindless, she shuffles empty-eyed and slack-mouthed down an empty marble corridor in some institution in a wilderness outpost; she is dressed in an ankle-length robe and is wearing under the robe tightly knotted oversized diapers and she is bent over slightly and her hair is now long and greasy and the gray curls cascade down to her shoulders, while at the crown there is a greasy waxy flaky bald spot; and she drools a string of saliva down to her collarbone, but doesn't notice it; she doesn't notice much in fact, and no one knows why she shuffles restlessly up and down the corridor all day and much of the night, because she does not sleep ever and all the other inmates are usually in bed all day and all night, and none of them has any energy or any sanity, so she is alone in her restless senseless energy; she stops from time to time to look out a window where there is nothing to see but endless flat barren fields where nothing grows; and the light from the window falls on her ruined face, sculpting it sharply, and there, if you are curious enough and if you look closely, you can see the signs and lines of the beauty which once was hers, but no one does come to look and see what or who she is, but occasionally a doctor, 'Doctor Lucifer Wolf' his name plate says, pays a visit to the institution, and he watches her from a distance, as she shuffles down the corridor, and he asks a few questions of the guards, and when they report that she has said nothing, her mouth slack now and all of her teeth gone, and that she has done nothing and that she is entirely passive when they clean her and when they feed her, then he says, "Splendid, that is a very good result," and, occasionally, he will stand and watch the shuffling shadow making its way down the empty and desolate dimly lit absolutely unadorned hallway and he smiles a rather self-satisfied smile which has no wonder or awe or doubt in it, no sense of the sacred, no sense of loss, no sense of responsibility, no feeling for the magic of a life or of a personality that has been snuffed out, and then Doctor Lucifer Wolf is gone, and the skinny, shadowy, bent figure shuffles on, in bare or slippered feet, oblivious to the fact that any attention has been paid to her at all. Her elbows are sharp, and her knees too. Soon she will be a skeleton. Soon she will be ash or dust. Doctor Lucifer Wolf happily reports, "Yes, it is all over." She has been turned into one of the living dead, just like so many others, her spark is extinguished, that spark that was once by some foolish people called divine. They no longer have to worry. She is a shadow, a ghost, she is nothing, nothing at all, not a goddess, not a woman, not human. She will never harm anyone again.

But somewhere inside her is a tiny clear crystal of self-consciousness, of willpower, of self: none of this is real; this is an illusion!

I am myself, and I am free.

I am myself, and I am free.

And so something awakens.

Part of her mind wakes, clears, and sees a bright light.

A voice breaks through the brightness, a voice in her mind, a voice from far away: it is the voice of a hybrid.

"V, wake up, you have been seized, you have been enslaved! Wake up!"

Kat is standing there, with her hands on V's shoulders, shaking her, "Wake up! Wake up, V, wake up!"

"I'm awake, thanks," V shakes her head. She shivers: what a horrible nightmare that was! "I had this horrible vision or nightmare or …"

Flash!

V blinks: Kat is not there.

Where did she go?

Is this another nightmare?

Was all of human history just one long dream or nightmare, destined to fade and disappear and leave not a rack behind? The idea had occurred to her; and not to her alone. Was it all just madness in the end? Her mind casts back, to London at the end of the 18th Century, two revolutions transforming the world, the new chimneys and smokestacks of the coming Industrial Revolution, and the wild irrationalism, disguised as reason, of the French Revolution, just across the water.

I wander through each chartered street,
Near where the chartered Thames does flow,
And mark in every face I meet,

Marks of weakness, marks of woe.
In every cry of every man,
In every infant's cry of fear,
In every voice, in every ban,
The mind-forged manacles I hear.

V shakes her head, trying to get the cobwebs out. She must keep the clear hard diamond of her thinking and her consciousness of herself clear, clear, and free. Otherwise, she is lost.

When V comes to herself, she is standing alone in one of the tunnels. She glances at her Info-Flow wristwatch. Less than a minute has gone by. Let's see, she had been a cat in a freak show circus, she and Kat had mud-wrestled in a sorority contest in some beer hall or circus, and she had been insane in some ancient, insane asylum, and lobotomized, and consigned to a home, and then …

Where is Kat?

A voice speaks in her head: "This is the gaze that turns you to stone." Where does that thought come from? I am not Medusa! Let's keep our feet on the ground! Let's take stock. I am in one of the caves or tunnels under Elysium, and I am unchanged. It is as if nothing had happened at all, nothing at all. The dream of madness was just that, a dream, an illusion. Or was it? She looks around. "Kat, Kat, where are you, Kat?"

She looks goes down a side tunnel.

She explores niches.

She prays silently to her own collection of deities that Kat is safe.

She sees that some of the stone has been turned into tentacles that have reached out to seize things and people but that have then been turned back into stone. One of the places where the wall has dribbled away and has morphed into tentacles and an octopus or squid-like body is at the end of a dark tunnel lit only by phosphorescent lichen and by a few feeble emergency lights and the tentacles are wrapped around the body of a ghoul which is still twitching and the ghoul's blank hard-boiled-egg eyes turn toward V and look up at her and it curls its lips and tries to spit at her but the gooey saliva merely dribbles from its lips and the blank eyes blink and the eyelids close, and the ghoul convulses, trapped arms and legs jerking in a last spasm as the tentacle squeezes the life out of it. And the ghoul then fades – the white becoming gray – and it is morphed into dark stone, mottled granite, a squirming ground-level gargoyle.

V ponders: So the Mind is turning stone into Mind, into projections of mind – it is morphing material, turning animals, people, everything into Mind, into stone, into Mind, but then, temporarily or permanently, it morphs back into stone … for a time at least, perhaps as a mere pause, being kept in storage, to be released in monstrous form later, for a time, and then becoming universal mush, eternal terminal station entropy, no differentiation, no organization, no energy.

When, V wonders, will this stop?

All that is solid, melts into air …

If the Mind is really hungry, it could reprocess and morph the whole planet – though that might mean undermining the ecology that makes its own life possible … so that it would all end up live Mind Mush or dead stone, crystalline or unstructured stone.

The Mind would then starve to death or asphyxiate or die of boredom. For it is, this Mind, a thing which is undoubtedly dainty of heart and excessively sensitive; it is almost hysterical, at times playful. Claire had told her that the Mind is, in its own conception of itself, an innocent and lonely child, an unloved orphan. Yet now it seemed intent on destroying everything … Because of the Boy!

Hmmm!

"Kat!" V shouted. The shout echoed.

V left the dead ghoul and the petrified tentacles behind and walked down another tunnel. She must find Kat. After all, she had dragged Kat into all of these adventures, and so she felt responsible for her, besides … she rather adored Kat; she felt that she and Kat could be …

Ah, there Kat was …

Or what remained of her …

For Kat was frozen in time … and …

What could she, V, do about this?

Kat had been turned to stone.

Kit Candy …

In the Turd Resurrection Chocolate Éclair Factory, Kit Candy was in full panic mode: *Yikes! Something is squirming in my mouth!*

It was wiggling; it was attached to her like a bloodsucker; it was grabbing at the inside of her mouth and slashing and splashing around …

"Do you require assistance, Madam?" The robot chef was leaning toward her, an expression of robot concern on his robot face.

Kit tried to signal with a wild flutter of her hands, "No, she didn't need assistance, but that she was in desperate straits …!"

"Perhaps Madam would like a chocolate éclair."

" Gl … gl … gh!"

"Or perhaps I could suggest a chocolate mousse."

"Gl … gl … gh!"

"Or if the mousse does not suffice to calm Madam's fears and soothe her troubled soul and mollify her ruffled Cosmos feathers, perhaps a chocolate caramel tiramisu hot from the micro-molecular excrement or turd resurrection machine?" The robot chef lifted its artificial eyebrows – quizzical, concerned, charitable.

Kit stared bug-eyed at the chef. He was certainly friendly, but what could he do about that thing that was writhing in her mouth. She tried to spit it out, but it absolutely would not go … and then she realized …

It was a tongue!

It was a new tongue!

And it was almost finished getting itself into shape; the writhing slowed, then stopped, and then it felt familiar, well, almost familiar.

She tried it out … first licking her lips and then … trying to pronounce, "Moo … moo … mousse …." There, she did it! It was easy, it was her old voice, though actually, the farthest thing from her mind was chocolate mousse, it was just that the 'm' sound, like in 'mammy' or in 'moo' was among the easiest, and the first, and so recently artfully spoken by Daisy, and so naturally enough "Moo" was what popped out.

"Chocolate mousse coming up, Madam, your slightest breath is to me a sublime command, a high-level fatwa and a vintage Papal Bull of the first water, I do declare! It is delightful to be in service again!"

How the hell had this happened, a tongue, growing back into her mouth? Ah!

Ah, hybrids regenerate.

And so I'm a hybrid! Wow!

Oh, my God! If Miranda were alive, she would never forgive me. But I would try to explain, I'd say, Miranda, it's not my fault I'm a hybrid, Miranda, I'm really the same me you always knew, I'm me, Miranda, even if I am a hybrid, and I want you to like me, Miranda, I want you to love me, and I want Nikki to love me too, and to like me …

But Miranda was dead.

And Nikki was dead.

The sudden return of memory seared Kit's soul.

Her heart sank. She sighed. Mourning happens over and over, she realized, it is not a one-stop train. No! At times, you briefly, blessedly, forget that the person you loved is dead, you see them coming around a corner, you see the back of their head, the sun glinting off the blond hair, the unique gait, and stride, the silhouette, you are going to ask them something, you are going to tell them a joke, and then, suddenly, you remember, the vision is a stranger, and your heart sinks, the day darkens, your mouth is dry, you feel sick to your stomach, a churning vertigo, an abyssal absence, and it all starts over again, like a dreadful shock, like a nightmare that keeps returning …

"I do hope Madam will be pleased and that this trifle will lighten Madam's heart and heal the aches, salve and pour balm upon the wounds and the scars of the slings and arrows of outrageous fickle misfortune." The robot handed her a large bowl of creamy, rich chocolate mousse fresh from the turd-excrement-shit resurrection machine.

Kit looked at it: it certainly did look good!

But the very thought of it!

Then all hell broke loose.

Walls buckled.

Giant grinding sounds filled the space.

The robot waiter turned, leaned down to shelter her, and then …

WHAM!

He exploded.

And then the whole Turd Hub Chocolate Éclair Cave and all its mighty morph machinery turned upside down and became a swirling blur.

Kit was whirling through the air, projected in a huge arc, nothing to hold on to, her arms and legs flailing, and then …

V stood back and gazed upon the work of the Foul Fiend – or Boy – as he exercised his power directly or through the mind. In some ways, he could be an exquisite craftsman.

V licked her lips: I am no Medusa.

I didn't do this – did I?

And yet!

It is your own reifying, objectifying gaze that did this.

It is your lust, your desire to possess, your ...

Kat was frozen in stone; she had been turned to stone. She was naked, a statue of pure black, jet-black, marble, or so it seemed; her mouth was slightly open, her teeth gleamed darkly, and her eyes seemed to be staring, carved pupils distended, and her fine, smooth, muscular arms were raised, and one foot was up on tiptoe, while the other was flat on the ground, both legs stretched and tensed, and perfectly formed, quite beautiful legs, really, as if she had been frozen doing a ballet step, moving from one position to another, her body slightly bent forward, or about to sprint off – God knows where. Perhaps she had been trying to escape and had been caught in the act.

Kat, the statue, was quite beautiful.

She was more than beautiful; V had noticed Kat's beauty from the moment she had first cast eyes on her; but she had never really had time – they had been too busy – to appreciate Kat as a physical being, to savor the pure aesthetics of Kat, until now, with Kat imprisoned, suspended in pure stasis, petrified, caught in time, still ...

Quite wonderful, sublime, really!

Perhaps Lady Medusa had had a good idea.

By transforming someone into art, by giving them the stillness of true stasis, lifting them out of the terrible unredeemable onrush of time, you could truly appreciate them.

Yes, this was splendid!

V walked around the statue.

She paused, leaned forward; she took off her gloves and ran her hand, fingertips tingling with sensations, down Kat's back, to the small of her back, a remarkably small and supple waist, and then over the generous ample delicious curve of Kat's backside. The girl was a real find. Curls, finely delineated, curled down over Kat's forehead, and her eyebrows were neatly, wickedly arched, and at the nape of Kat's long elegant neck, other curls, sculpted perfectly in stone. You could almost think she was alive!

V ran one finger down the back of Kat's neck, delicate, delicious vertebrae, and then over the shoulder blades. It was indeed an exquisite bit of work, and it was the work of the Devil. Yes, the Foul Fiend has turned my friend to stone, and is now pushing me into a cruel – and quite inappropriate – absolutely incorrect – aesthetic attitude, where I am gazing upon my friend and companion, as if she were a mere object; this is not good; I am being very superficial, quite wicked, really, if she knew, Kat would be very angry.

V ran one fingertip along Kat's breathless frozen lips.

"What am I going to do?"

V stared into Kat's startled sightless eyes.

"What am I going to do with you, Kat?"

V leaned close to Kat's face. Kat was really so exquisite, so beautifully built, muscular yet fine and delicate in every detail.

"You really are exquisite, my friend!"

V circled around. She was not yet in despair. She was convinced that, somehow, she would bring Kat back to life, but the question was: how? V knew she could skewer a fire-breathing dragon; she could slice a giant high IQ Burmese python into thin slivers of snake steak; she had confronted mad diabolical dwarf geniuses; she had obliterated world-destroying, blood-stained, brilliantly perverse prelates; she had torn apart blood-crazed werewolf intellectuals in murky southern swamps; she had outwitted skilled serial killers in backwoods villages, Nazi henchmen in Paris and Berlin, and fought Roman gladiators to a standstill everywhere the Empire of Augustus went, when she wasn't allied with those same gladiators; she could fight with the greatest 17th Century swordsman, such as her friend the Baron, she could outwit evil geniuses equipped with nuclear devices, and she could outshoot Annie Oakley or Billy the Kid; she was even able to shake off the mad dreams the Boy had plunged her into; but how to free a demoiselle that has been turned to stone?

She s examined Kat's breasts; hmm, well, they were absolutely perfect! She had not previously had occasion for such a close and leisurely inspection; she ran her hand under the undercurve of both breasts, slowly, then down the rib cage, neatly delineated and jet-black. Any 19th Century Parisian sculptor toiling away in his atelier would have given his life to have Kat as a model! How perfect Kat was! Now, the temptation, of course, would be to keep Kat exactly the way she was, a perfect object, with no danger, ever, of backtalk, sassiness, moods, or willful disobedience. But this was probably the calculation of the Foul Fiend. In fact, the Foul Fiend was whispering in her mind: *You do want to keep her just as she is, don't you, V? Admit it, V! For once, be honest! You and I are quite alike, are we not, you the bloodthirsty alien, and I the Force from another universe? When we rule the world together and all its delights Kat will be part of your very own collection! She will be in your villa, perhaps on a terrace, overlooking a subtropical sea, lashed by storms, lit by lightning, glimmering in the moonlight, brilliant and dark in the sun at noon, her body clothed and washed by downpours and raindrops, her delicious, voluptuous forms, delicately emerging from the mist ...* V pursed her lips and narrowed her eyes. The Foul Fiend was obviously calculating that V's aestheticism, her obsessions, her innate cruelty, her randiness, and her delight in physical beauty would lead her into sin – into leaving Kat as she was; turned to stone by the evil gaze of the Medusa-like Foul Fiend – or perhaps by V's own lust, her own gaze – the Foul Fiend who had so very many arms at his disposal. *You will be able to see her just as she is any time you like!* After all, possession is like petrification; and by keeping Kat in her petrified state, V could keep her and possess her, an admirable work of art, forever.

No, it would not be!

She looked Kat in the eyes.

A silver drop of liquid seemed to be forming at the very outer edge, below Kat's left eyelid, just at the tear duct. How interesting! It was a tear! The tear began to travel down Kat's cheek. V reached out, and with the tip of one finger, she captured the tear – a glistening silver bubble!

So Kat was alive and conscious, and yet turned to stone. V felt a little tremor of fear – and delight. This made the whole situation even more exquisite. What a wonderful idea it was: to have such a beautiful conscious object – petrified, forever in your possession, and in your power. Oh, but the Foul Fiend was a crafty fellow! Even if he was a Cosmic Force, he was also a a craftsman, a master of detail, a stickler for perfection, a micro-manager. He was fine-tuned to individual subtleties of psychological torture and human cruelty. He knew just what buttons to push. Such is evil: it knows exactly what weakness will serve it best: lust leads to gluttony, leads to greed, leads to cruelty, leads to ... Well, attention to detail is one sign of a great leader, unless he or she is an indecisive fusspot, of course.

V leaned close to Kat's divinely sculpted lips.

Yes, a sweet, gentle breeze came from the frozen mouth; Kat was breathing. Kat's tongue and teeth, black and marble-like the rest of her, were exquisitely designed, and her full lips were neatly delineated, oh, her lips were like the rich and deliciously full-bodied petals of a divine and blossoming flower.

A voice emerged, a mere whisper: "What the fuck are you waiting for? Are you going to free me or not?"

"I'm thinking," said V.

"I can see that. You've been circling around me like you are trying to figure out where to put me in your art collection."

V almost blushed. "Well, you know I've always liked you, always found you, ah, attractive."

"I'm not an idiot."

"No."

"In case you hadn't noticed."

"Yes. I mean, no."

"Ha!"

"I mean, I had noticed – that you're not an idiot, I mean."

"So, what are you waiting for?"

"Well, I am trying to figure out what to do. After all, this is not an everyday situation."

"*You* are the idiot."

"Hmm," V frowned. If Kat was accusing her of being an idiot, the solution must be simple So, what do you do to save a damsel in distress who has been turned into a block of marble worthy of Michelangelo or Donatello? Was this a form of imprisonment analogous to the Prince being turned into a frog, or the demoiselle being imprisoned in a tower, or the princess who has slept for decades after being pricked by a thorn, or …?

"I'm getting impatient, V! If you love me …"

"Yes."

"If you find me in the least bit attractive …"

"But I do find you attractive! I mean, I find you exquisite, and …"

"Well, then, do I have to draw you a diagram?"

"Ah, yes, of course!" V slapped her forehead.

"I thought you might figure it out!"

"Evident, isn't it, dear Watson!"

"Yes, my dear Sherlock, it is."

V stood for a moment marveling; she paced back, she paced forward; she put her hand under her chin, and she tilted her head to one side, Hamlet-like and she stared.

"Well?"

"I am just taking a last bit of pleasure in gazing upon thee in thy enslaved and statuesque state, my most adorable, darling Doctor Watson!"

"You can look at me later, all you want. Besides, I'm statuesque – if I dare say so – even when I'm not a marble statue."

"True, that is *so totally* true!" V felt for some reason like an infatuated 13-year-old. It was total regression. She stepped forward; she took Kat's face between her hands, stared for an instant into the blind eyes of sculpted stone, and then she kissed Kat deeply, on the lips, deeply, passionately, and as she did so the warm stone, lips, so full and so exquisitely sculpted, melted and turned to warm full exquisite flesh, as the statue, and now the woman, returned V's kiss.

The kiss continued.

"Whew!"

"Whew!"

Kat looked even better, V decided, as a living human being, though, to tell the truth, she would have liked to keep both versions ...

"Where are my clothes?" Kat looked around.

"I don't know – gone?"

Kat looked at V. "Yes, gone, V, obviously they are gone, dear fool, they are gone, and my laser gun and my sword, and my pistol, and my helmet, and my ... and ... my absolutely everything is gone, all gone, you fool!"

V almost blushed. She rather liked, perversely, to be called a fool by Kat. This was mysterious, taking an insult as a sign of deep affection; but then the ways of the heart, even of the heart of a half-alien such as V, and she was fully aware of this, the ways of the heart are a tangled mass of brambles, an unsounded labyrinth, offering unplumbed depths, a cryptic enigma. A moment ago she was Medusa. Now, she was Buster Keaton on a bad day, or Charlie Chaplin getting tripped up, or the Laurel of Laurel and Hardy, she was the foil, the straight man, such are the mysterious flows and ebbs of self, which not even Doctor Freud could have deciphered, a puzzle wrapped in a ...

V sighed, remembering: "The heart has its reasons, which reason cannot know." Blaise Pascal was onto something.

"You can have mine." V clicked open her belt, unlocked her collar, and unzipped and unpeeled the black, armored catsuit, revealing the slender, chalk-white, ivory sheen of the human body within.

"And what are you going to do?"

"You'll see."

"Ah, of course. My dear idiot fool is going to turn demon!"

"Precisely, Doctor Watson," V blushed, and stepped out of the slithery suit, and out of her boots, which she handed to Kat.

Something somewhere close began to howl.

"What is that howl?"

"No idea," Kat was holding V's bodysuit, looking at it quizzically.

There was another howl.

"I don't like the sound of that!"

Kit thought that things couldn't get worse, but then they did. She was flying through the air.

The Robot Cooks and Tasters exploded; the ocean of chocolate was backing up, it was not being pumped out; chocolate magma boiled over, it was creamy and thick, very dark, Swiss chocolate ...

She would never get that chocolate mousse!

As the lights flickered, as the gangway exploded, projecting Kit into the air, she came down, plop, with a mighty splash, landing bulls eye, in the giant vat of chocolate; she went down, gurgle, gurgle, over her head, came up sputtering, gasping, and swearing, goddamn, #$@*&%%$, and thrashed, half-swimming, half crawling to the surface.

Kit sputtered, spitting out bubbly thick dark chocolate.

She tried to open her eyes, sealed with chocolate, and finally, swearing like a trooper, she managed to wipe the chocolate away. She blinked. All hell was breaking loose.

White blazing sparks rained down, drops of pure energy; cables slashed back and forth, spitting fire, hissing like wildly thrashing furious snakes, splashing into the chocolate.

The chocolate was sucking her down.

She tried to tread water – well, to tread chocolate.

What a ridiculous way to die!

I'm going to be electrocuted stark naked in a vat of Swiss chocolate that's been conjured up and nano-brewed out of pure excrement! What a fate, what an undignified destiny!

Oh, death, where is thy sting!?

She managed to dog-paddle, flip-flopping and splashing, and sneezing and wheezing, and squeezing her eyes tight shut. She got to the edge of the vat. She clawed and pawed at the steep steel wall, slippery and slimy as the bottom of a walrus. She couldn't get a grip, couldn't get out. The walls were too steep, too slippery and too high; the ocean of chocolate was sucking her down; it was too deep, there was no foothold.

CRACK! BANG! WHAP!

SIZZLE! SIZZLE!

Christ! What was that? Blinking her eyes, she stared. Bolts of sizzling lightning were dancing along the edges of the vat; flashes of pure electricity were clambering up the walls, curving in arcs overhead, just under the arched roof of the Chocolate and Home-Baked Goodies Turds Transformation Emporium.

It was Hell.

She was half-blinded by the chocolate; it stung her eyes; it coated her eyelids; it coated everything else. She couldn't help but swallow some of it, thinking she would gag if she ate too much. It was the alchemist's dream, shit transmuted into pure Swiss chocolate! Better than gold! Just like blood, sweat, and tears – above all tears – and the ashes of death, all the people vaporized into smoke, they, or their remains, had been transmuted into pure gold bars hidden deep in bank vaults in Zurich on the shore of the Zurich See. This magic will be the death of me!

She kept kicking and moving her arms, just keeping herself afloat in a sticky sea of chocolate. I'm going to get tired, and then I'll drown ... It will not be a sweet death.

There was a huge sloshing sound.

She turned around. She blinked.

A big elephant-trunk-like elastic-pipe, a wrinkled bio-nozzle, like a giant rubber soda straw, had plunged down from the ceiling and was slurping and sucking up the chocolate, whipping around, making a god-awful sloshing and the chocolate was whirling in a tornado-like maelstrom, and Kit was going to be swept up into the bio-nozzle, when ...

Oh, God, this is even worse!

Through chocolate bleary eyes, she saw ...

It couldn't be worse!

No, it is worse!

The trunk had a tongue. The tongue, which looked like a two-headed snake, was headed toward her. Then a giant wave – a veritable tsunami – of chocolate blinded her. She went under; she felt the tongue wrap itself around her ankle, glug, glug, glug ... She was being dragged toward the trunk. That must be it! She was going to be sucked up into the system, whatever it was, and she would be ... eaten, eaten, and digested and ... and turned into chocolate ...?

WHAM!

The tongue, or sucker-lined tentacle, or whatever it was, let go.

She was free.

She gasped, gulping to the surface, splashed into the tenebrous chocolate twilight, blinking blindly, seeing nothing.

She thrashed forward, she flailed frantically, arms and legs kicking, desperate to get to the side of the vat and somehow climb out – but it was so goddamn slippery, she knew she wouldn't make it. She gasped, her mouth drooling chocolate, her eyes covered in chocolate, her hair dripping chocolate. I can't even see where I'm going. She felt the eel-like tongue flick against her foot. The bloody thing was grabbed for her. She kicked, desperately. The tongue wrapped itself greedily around her ankle. Damnation, thought Kit, this is too much. The tongue began to drag her toward the giant slurping trunk.

The trunk or something made a howling sound.

It was a roar of triumph.

It's going to eat me, thought Kit, Yuk!

It howled again – in triumph.

"What was that howl?" Kat raised a sublime eyebrow.

"No idea."

They listened.

"Whatever it is, it's not here." Kat, still barefoot and naked, was holding V's armored catsuit, folded over her arm. "I'm not sure it will fit because I am ..."

V feigned an insulted pout, "... because you are more statuesque than I am, whether you are a marble statue or merely luscious flesh and blood."

"Yes, I don't mean to criticize, my foolish demon, but you are quite slender, even petite, and ..."

"I am not that petite!"

"Well, what I meant to say was ..."

"Besides, these suits, as you very well know, my dear, dear, sublimely statuesque Kat, are bio-adaptable and self-re-modeling, and ..."

"Of course," Kat grinned, wondering whether she was becoming skittish and sadistic, but pleased that she had gotten a rise out of V. She slithered into the suit, as she pulled it up her thighs it squeaked and hissed in a most beguilingly suggestive fetishistic fashion.

V's eyes watched, and V's ears listened.

"And, I …" said V, giving Kat a look, "When I want to be particularly statuesque, as you put it, when I want to be statuesque, or stacked, or voluptuous, I just …"

And there was a whirr and a flash, and V emerged from the vibrant flash of light in her demon form, statuesque, scaly, turquoise, green, and gold, with flashing eyes, and gleaming fangs.

Kat zipped up the last bit of the body armor catsuit and clicked the collar shut. "Yes, I see, of course, you are more, ah, *stacked*, more of a 1940s–1950s soldier boy's reified male-gaze pinup girl, a Vargas masterpiece, when you're in demon form."

"And I wonder what you will look like when you change," said V, but then she remembered: in demon form, Kat was white quicksilver, an exquisite, rippling moiré sheen, liquid mercury; and, yes, as a demon she was statuesque too.

"Yes, I think we already saw me," said Kat, as the bio-skin adapted to her most intimate curves, caressing and clinging as it went, "I mean, as a hybrid demon."

"So that mud wrestling wasn't entirely an illusion," said V.

"It was a shared illusion," said Kat.

"Like the world," said V.

"Yes, like the world, a shared illusion. Life is but a dream." Kat half-closed her eyes, stared at V, with a somewhat lascivious come-hither gaze, and mimed a flirtatious pout.

"You look good," said V, slurping back a little gush of lustful saliva, "You look good this way."

"Thank you, my love," said Kat, giving V that eyes-half-closed sleepy mocking stare, dark pupils flashing.

"*V, you disappoint me,*" said the voice of the Foul Fiend; it echoed in V's head, and was most unpleasant.

"Of course, I disappoint you, Foul Fiend. I am not, and I intend never to be your slave or your puppet!"

"We shall see about that, hybrid wench! Your mind is porous, and your desires are manifold. I shall find a way in."

"The Foul Fiend …?" Kat buckled her high collar, hitched up the holster, over her hip, "He's talking to you?"

"Yes.

"It's a ridiculous name, the *Foul Fiend*."

"That's the point," V said, becoming ever so slightly pedantic, "If we give him too much dignity, the devil will become very self-important. In reality, whatever name he takes, he is an idiot!"

"Even more than you are?" Kat smiled.

"Yes, Kat, he is even more of an idiot than I."

At that moment, there was a great roar and tentacles shot out of the walls which had turned into a writing barrier of flesh, with eyes appearing here and there and beak-like mouths opening and shutting, and a tentacle whipped down to grab Kat by the ankle, but she shot it with the laser gun and the tentacle curled up sizzling.

Within a few seconds V and Kat were struggling in a sea of tentacles and serpents that were attempting to strangle them and drag them into the walls and digest and absorb them and turn them into mineral and quartz and granite and feldspar, for good this time, depriving them of life and consciousness and their very being.

Kat twirled like a dervish, sending out a spray of laser beams that sizzled and burned their way through the Medusa-like tangle of tentacles and serpent-headed monsters.

V leaped and leaped, springing from wall to wall, and tearing tentacles and wall-serpents up by the roots, slashing them into bits with her claws, and biting at them with her fangs, the tentacles thrashed and swept around her in a dizzying whirl, around and around, spinning V like a top, and enclosing her in a cocoon, of tentacles, like being imprisoned and mummified by a team of boa constrictors.

They were trying to crush the life out of her.

V felt the scaly dripping serpentine walls of mucous pressing against every millimeter of her body. They were trying to smother her. She took a last deep breath, and then she expanded all her muscles, and ...

Wham!

The tentacles exploded into tiny fragments, floated in the air, and V leaped toward Kat, cutting her way through a sea of writhing serpents to Kat who was shooting at everything in sight and then ...

Suddenly they were alone again. The serpents and tentacles withered and shriveled and curled up and died – flakes of ash floating in the air. The walls turned again to stone, the bulging eyes and mouths fading, but leaving behind sculptural and petrified traces of where they had been, petrified eyes, petrified arms, screaming petrified mouths, now silent.

"I wonder who they were?" said V, looking at the frozen writhing stone frieze of passion and body fragments.

"Maybe he just created them," Kat was brushing dust off her thighs, "Maybe he invented them. Maybe they are nobody."

"Maybe," V felt she recognized some of the contorted faces. Perhaps these are conjured up from my own past, people I killed, people I loved. "I think they were somebody, once."

"Well, they are nobody now, for a time, at least. Lead on, my darling demon," Kat sighed, "Let us find this Mind that can do such things and let us confront its master, the idiot Foul Fiend!"

"Yes," V's golden snake eyes stared at Kat, and she laid her claw on Kat's shoulder. Kat still found it really weird, even after so many days, that her human friend V was also the demon V and that she, too, was also a demon, apparently quicksilver in color, like liquid mercury, and she wondered whether in truth these demons of which she was now one were in fact – angels.

Perhaps the fallen angels were the good ones.

And those who remained as slaves in heaven were … the bad ones.

Perhaps humanity had all been on the wrong side all along.

Or maybe not.

But, then, if you enslave people's minds, with false gods and false idols and rituals and priests and imams and preachers and clichés and mumbo-jumbo and lies and so on, then you have enslaved the people themselves. Kat muttered under her breath.

In every cry of every Man,
In every Infant's cry of fear,
In every voice: in every ban,
The mind-forg'd manacles I hear

And she and V strode onwards – toward their next trial.

Kit squirmed. The monstrous chocolate-slurping elephant-like trunk had just bellowed its triumph. It had wrapped itself around her ankle and was tugging at her; she desperately tried to swim away from it, splashing, foundering, in the vast vat of chocolate.

"Reach out," said a voice, "Reach up!"

"What?"

She blinked, and through a veil of chocolate, she saw – a man was reaching down to her.

"Reach out! The Mind is alive," he said, "And it is possessed – by the Devil."

"What?"

"Reach out, grab my hand!"

Yes, it was a man – a real human being, not a monster; he was reaching down for her; just above her, she saw his face, glimpsed in flashes through her stinging, chocolate-coated eyes; it was a wearied, worn-with-care face, unshaven, shadowed, but handsome like a god; it was tanned and strong-featured, and its ice-blue eyes seemed to shine like sharp diamonds. *This must be a hallucination.*

Claire and Robyn had warned her that, as a newly minted hybrid, struggling free of the human cocoon, she might hallucinate. "The first thing," Claire said, "is you might become hysterical."

"Or silly," said Robyn, "Absolutely silly."

"That too," said Claire, "Really silly. It is definitely part of the hybrid reboot process. And you may see things too," and the hybrid had turned her golden eyes and red-and-black snout toward Kit, and giving her a gentle, almost sad reptilian smile, "You will perhaps hallucinate."

Okay, so now it's happening; now I am crazy.

"The mind is alive," the beautiful-man-hallucination said again, "And it's hungry. That snout is famished."

"Yikes!" Kit thrashed and thrashed, splashing chocolate everywhere: Oh, my God, that did not sound good – definitely not good!

"Give me your hand!" He was still reaching out, "Quick now!"

Trusting to the illusion or hallucination, she gave him her hand – slippery with thick chocolate.

He grabbed her by the wrist; it was a grip of steel, and she would have screamed "ouch" except she knew this guy was her only chance, the only way she might get out of the maw of that hungry floppy thing. The tongue had slipped; it was now slapping the chocolate behind her. It whipped down across her legs; it slashing across the back of her legs. The man somehow lifted her clear of the wall of the vat, and somehow got her standing, dripping chocolate, in front of him.

"Ugh," she said, she tried to clear the chocolate out of her eyes.

"There's water over there, behind that wall," the man said; he was in a Centurion uniform; he pushed her toward one of the side niches, must be about 20 yards away; water was flooding out of a huge crack in the wall, high up, it was spurting out and cascading down, a natural waterfall.

"Go," he said.

The elephant trunk was again slurping up the chocolate, but it paused and rose and aimed.

Its tongue flashed out like it wanted to decapitate the Centurion. In one quick movement, the Centurion zapped the tongue with his laser gun.

Zap!

The tongue curled up in smoke; there was an unearthly howl; it seemed to come from the walls, from the roof, from everywhere. This time it was a howl of anger, pain, and fear, not a howl of triumph. The howl reverberated everywhere.

"Wow," Kit stood still, almost in shock, a statue of dripping chocolate, "Awesome. It's all around us!"

"Yes, it is."

"Awesome," she said again, blinking.

"Go," he said. He was scanning the walls, the roof. His laser gun was ready; and, yes, the safety was off, Kit noted the little green light.

"I lost everybody. I don't want to lose you, whoever you are," he said, "Go – get cleaned up!"

"Okay, already!" Boy, this guy was bossy! She ran to the niche. He went over to a smashed set of worker cabinets, pulled something out, and followed her, guarding her, her own Centurion guardian! What would happen next?

She moved in under the water. It was warm, pleasant, vaguely sulfurous, which wasn't unpleasant; a delicate bouquet of Hell was better than a whole mouthful of that chocolate stuff.

She scrubbed at herself, using her hands as sponges. This was weird. She was so used to the hygiene pod doing everything that she had almost forgotten what hands and fingers could do; she was very thorough. She took her time too because she was trying to figure out what this guy wanted – guys were dangerous, particularly down here, and …

"Hurry up," he said.

"Hold your horses," she said.

He gave her a look, but didn't say anything. He stood there, very erect, very military, looking around nervously, with the laser gun ready in his hand.

Soon she was clean. Water streamed out of her hair, down over her face, dribbling down her body. She blinked it away from her eyes. She stepped out of the shower. She gave the Centurion a defiant, inquisitive stare. There was something familiar about him, something ... He was tall, solid, and muscular, with a golden tan, and worried-looking, handsome ice-blue eyes with fine crease-lines under them and at the corners; his thick curly golden hair showed a bit of gray at the sides. He was wearing a Cosmos Centurion uniform – the epaulets indicated some really high rank, she was sure, but she didn't know what rank – like General or Field Marshall or something. The uniform was torn and ripped in many places, and there were claw marks across his chest and slashes on his right thigh, and one shoulder of the uniform, with its epaulets, had been torn away, and there were claw marks across his biceps where the sleeves had been torn to shreds. On his boots was stuff that looked like blood. He was staring at her, with a slight smile and an appraising amused expression. Kit was at this point beyond blushing, but she did realize – she didn't have to be a genius – that he was appreciating her for what she was – a vulnerable, naked, human female animal.

"Here," he said, holding out some ultra-short silver-skin-shorts and a silver-skin T-shirt, "I found these in one of the worker pods; I think they'll fit."

"Thanks and thanks for saving me," Kit said. She took the shorts and T-shirt and looked down at herself, all the chocolate was gone, but she was dripping wet and in this clammy sweltering cavern, she wouldn't dry off – there was no drying pod, and there were no towels – so she'd just have to dress wet, in any case with skin-shorts and a skin-T-shirt the wet look could be quite flattering, maybe too flattering. She pulled the shorts on. They squeaked and snapped as they molded themselves to her flesh; she pulled the T-shirt over her head and wiggled into it and it snuggled against her with a hiss, a second skintight skin, just like the Nano Pub Drones said: "*Breathes like you; feels like you.*"

"Here," the Centurion handed her a machete – with holster – and a laser gun, with a belt holster. "You'll need them."

"Thanks." Kit fitted the sling-holster across her shoulder, and locked the belt shut around her waist, feeling it click tightly into place.

"You're a Sub," the Centurion said, still giving her the look: the T-shirt was revealing, more than revealing, and, Kit felt, more erotic, actually, than being naked; since, as that ancient Philosopher Immanuel Kant had pointed out, and as Miranda, dear Miranda, alluding to Kant and to Edmund Burke, had also pointed out, at considerable length, while fastening a black velvet antique 1911 choker – complete with an oval Wedgewood blue-and-white cameo of Queen Alexandra – around Kit's neck, and clicking it into place, the sublime is best attained by indirection and suggestion. "A scantily clothed or almost naked female," Miranda had declaimed, adopting her most scholarly and pedantic bluestocking tone, "A scantily clothed or almost naked female is even more sublime, and erotically arousing, so the philosophers say, than a totally unclothed, aka naked, female," and Kit, who was not wearing anything except the collar-like choker, had blushed, and Miranda, who, when she started on a learned disquisition sometimes did not know when to stop, continued, "Such a female, with a mark of possession and ownership upon her, is a thing of nature, but, as has been pointed out by Roland Barthes, among others, she is also, marked by the man-made collar, an artifice of civilization, thus the slow stripping down, or off, of the appurtenances of civilization, returning to the wild, naked state, also known as striptease, can be so … ah … titillating." Miranda had taken Kit's face between her hands, and she had kissed Kit very slowly: *Oh, My, God!* Kit shuddered: *And I thought I was the one giving the lessons!*

"So what," Kit said, looking at the Centurion from under her eyelashes, "So I'm a Sub, so what?"

"You seem high-spirited," he said, "for a Sub."

"You don't know much about Subs, obviously," she frowned: who was this guy? She really did hate almost more than anything having some imbecile upper-class Cosmos cretin, pretty-boy, snobbish toff, who thought he could box and slot her into a category – particularly a lower-level, inferior category – and whittle her essence and identity down to fit his stupid class or sexist stereotypes, denying her very existence as she truly was, inimitably herself, and automatically, even unconsciously, obliterating and deleting all the best parts that made her what she really was – the one and only inimitable Kit Candy! If he hadn't just saved her life, she would have given him a piece of her mind; she would have blasted him with a string of sizzling four-letter epithets, a foul fishmonger's vocabulary to make even Shakespeare wince, and she would unload upon him a pile of underworld, cutthroat, purse-snatch, Sub invective that would send this Centurion reeling, and which would echo in his snobbish Cosmos Centurion cerebellum for weeks – Nay, months! But, since he was handsome, and bore the scars of recent battle, and since he had saved her life, she thought she would be a bit charitable and only … "Wait a minute," she said, "You're the … you're the … I mean, you sure look like him …"

"Yes," he said.

"Really? I mean, you're really …?"

"Yes, indeed," he said. He crossed his arms, looking at her.

"I'm Kit Candy, Mr. President," she said, holding out her hand; she would be damned to the deepest sub-cellar of Hell before she would grovel, or salute, or say, "Hail, Hail, our Great Leader, All Hail." She despised that Fascist nonsense, though Miranda, being a starry-eyed Cosmos First Class, adored it.

"Kit Candy," he said, looking straight into her eyes. He took her hand and shook it; he had a good handshake, a firm, dry grip, and he held on just long enough, while looking her straight in the eye, and then he let go, "Kit Candy," he said again, as if committing the name to memory. "Kit Candy, I seem to have gotten lost, do you happen to know …?"

Just at that moment, a tentacle flashed out, slapped down on Kit's shoulder, and the President turned toward it and fired his laser as more tentacles appeared, from all sides at once, flashing, grasping, squirting …

"I would say that this is rather like something Piranesi might have drawn, or etched," said Miranda glancing at the walls and arches. She and Caliban were wading along the shallow, low-roofed, placid canal, and looking up at the side niches where there were shadowy crisscrossing staircases, and mysterious balconies, and platforms, and cables and chains hanging down in clustered, rusty, clinking profusion. She was about two meters from Caliban. Everything for the moment seemed rather peaceful.

She licked her lips and glanced at Caliban. His body glowed in the phosphorescent shimmering, which here, on the canal, had a warm rosy twilight hue. Oh, he was so beautiful, and he was hers; he was her very own Tarzan and pirate!

She waded closer. And as he turned to her, she put her hand on his chest, drinking in the radiance of his warm, smooth, muscular skin, and the rhythm of his beating heart, the force of his red blood and the silken sheen of his half-open lips and the splendor of his bright teeth; and she said, "We are real, aren't we, Caliban?"

Caliban looked deep into her eyes, and then he put his arms around her, and kissed her, kissed her deep and long, and she felt and heard, as they kissed, the battle raging all around them, the maelstrom battle of good and evil, and she drew back only slightly and, breathless, looking into his eyes, she said, "If we are real, then V is real, then all our friends are real."

"Yes," said Caliban, "We are real; they are real."

"Do you love me, Caliban, my Prince?"

"Yes, I do, Princess, I love you, and I shall love you as long as blood flows in these pirate veins! I love you with all my heart, Miranda, my princess, daughter of V, daughter of Cosmos, daughter of the President, daughter of our one mother, Nikki."

"Then, we shall conquer, we shall prevail." Miranda put her hand on the handle of her laser gun. "Let us swear fealty and dedicate ourselves to victory."

"Yes, Princess, and let us seal our oath with a kiss."

"Yes, my Prince." Miranda leaned up and kissed Caliban, and as she did so she thought that she owed a great deal to her friend Kit Candy, for she knew precisely how to kiss, and her kisses, she knew, were informed not only by instinct and pure passion, but also by a superb education and wonderful training.

"To Victory!"

"To Victory!"

"Princess," Caliban breathed, "You are sublime!"

"And you, my Prince, are the love of my life!" Miranda noticed that she was trembling, or rather her tummy and her thighs were trembling; desire was rising – a tingling, rising, inexorable, liquid tide.

CHAPTER 9 – MIND-CHILD

V muttered, "What do I do now?"

"What do you mean, what do you do?" said Kat.

"I'm thinking out loud." V furrowed her brow.

"Well, then, go ahead, Sherlock. Don't mind me! I mean to say, I'm just along for the ride. Obviously, I don't need to know what we are getting into. I've been turned to stone, and mocked by my dear friend V, and ogled shamelessly by that same lustful hybrid, and attacked by tentacles, abandoned while my companion goes off into some ancient fantasy land exploring the nature of female divinity, wrestled with, in thick, gooey mud, before a crowd of howling hicks and hillbillies, by same lascivious hybrid, tossed around in an ocean of tar, but I obviously do not count. However, darling, if the time does eventually come when you want to share your thoughts and yearnings, my dearest, my darling, then please help yourself, darling, I'm here, I'm ready to listen, my shoulder is here for you to lean on: my ears are all ears for you to pour your troubles into!"

V had narrowed her eyes. She was concentrating, lost in some inner space, "I go to his lair, where he is hiding, that is where I go."

"You've been alone too long, V."

V grunted. She was deep inside her own head, remembering: "You must swim into it," Claire had told her, "you must embrace the Mind, you must merge with it, you must let it possess you and take you and you become one with it. You must surrender as you would surrender to a lover."

"You *swim* into it?" Kat had overheard some of this inner conversation; she did not like being excluded from V's musings. If they shared, it was more likely they would survive. She was beginning to appreciate the value of being a hybrid – the power to overhear some at least of people's thoughts was very promising. She wondered how deep it would take her. "You *swim* into it?"

"Yes, you swim into it. I think you swim *into* it ... I mean, I swim into it." V answered, absently, as if talking to herself; all the time, she was leading the way, cautiously, as they entered yet another tunnel. Tentacles were spreading up and across the roof, on the walls, and on the floor, they wrapped around columns and pipes and cables. Several slender gray tentacles were wrapped around an ancient rusted sign that said "Wall Street That Way" and a one-eyed tentacle sack, a sort of mini-mind, like an octopus but not so cute, was perched on a cornice where "Bank of International ..." was written, half the cornice had been eaten away, and dribbles of smoking acid was still eating at the granite. The proud, carved letters were dribbling and dissolving into blurred nothingness.

They came to the end of the tunnel. Stone steps led down into what looked like an enormous pool; smoky lights gleamed under the surface in the pool. V kneeled at the edge while Kat stood back slightly, her laser gun drawn, vigilant.

"This is not it, exactly, but it's the edge of it," V said, sticking her claw into the liquid.

"The edge of it ..." Kat sighed. This was like a vicious sorority initiation from ancient times – one mucky form of test and humiliation after the other, like that vanilla cake fight during the Centurion Entrance School, and the Centurion Intelligence Academy frosh initiation – horrible – half-naked unisex swamp treasure hunt she had submitted to with extreme ill-grace, but she still won the first prize, an antique bottle of Johnny Walker Black Label. Hazing, in Kat's estimation, was overrated as a way of building team-spirit and as a form of training for initiates.

The liquid was thicker than water; it was viscous, sticking to V's fingers, and when she drew back, she saw that shimmering, translucent webs were joining the fingers of her claw.

"Looks like yuk," said Kat.

"Yes, V said, "It's like some sort of thick amniotic fluid. The mind lives in here, farther on, a couple of levels and caverns farther."

"Cool," said Kat, curling her lips, "I guess we've got to do what we've got to do, eh?"

"Yes," V said, still staring that the troubled, glowing surface.

"You're going to wade into that muck?"

"Yes, I am." V stepped in, tentatively; then, she waded in. Wavering, shimmering thin tentacles rose out of the thick liquid. The tentacles wrapped themselves around her, they wrapped around her legs, they twirled slowly around her arms, they slipped up her backside and wrapped around her belly. … One tickled her forehead.

"Well, I guess I'd better do it too." Kat followed close behind, the liquid sloshing up to her thighs. "Are you sure this is a good idea?"

"This is awful, I know, dear Doctor Watson. This is troublesome and awesome, and a risk. It is a gamble. But we must meet the monster in its lair, where it has taken up residence, you see!"

"Of course, Sherlock, of course," Kat felt tentacles probe at her boots and at her bio-body-suit-armor, but they curled back and slithered away. She waded farther into the liquid, now up to her waist.

They waded in the shallow pool for perhaps a quarter of a mile, and then they came to a great series of halls, and there was a small dry platform; they climbed up onto it; the liquid slowly slithered off their bodies, as if reluctant to leave them or loath to let them escape.

There it was, in front of them: arches stretched away, and underneath the Arches was a vast multicolored sea or lake. This was the true Lair of the Mind. In fact, they had been wading in part of the Mind all this time, or so it seemed to V. Yes, the liquid was part of the Mind, and the arches, and the stone … The Mind had sent out its fibers and filaments into the amniotic sea, and it had penetrated into the stone and into the steel. But, here at least, it was not yet eating. Probably it had to maintain the integrity of its basic structures, of the walls around the pool within which it lived, before, finally, consuming everything.

"Oh, boy," Kat stopped to contemplate, just contemplate. It was vast; it was steamy; it was gently luminous; it almost seemed to be breathing.

"An underground ocean," V stared at it, "That's what the Mind is, an underground ocean with silicon matrixes and towers."

And there it was: in great steaming whirlpools, in vats and vaults and in caverns and tunnels and ancient subway stations, there it was, or, rather, there it lived. The Mind was a mixture. It was a great latticework of metal and steaming acres of gray soup, or gently steaming omnipotent broth, a universe of shifting networks, a bio-soup, a world of neurons and their connections, of tentacles of fine bio-fiber, like a spider's web spreading out, climbing over ancient cornices, up Doric columns, and along fallen Corinthian columns, and slithering along ancient pitted half-submerged sidewalks, and it came out of the ancient vaults of the Federal Reserve building on Liberty street, and it spread south down to the old tunnel of Wall Street, and it poked through ancient windows, and it wrapped itself around rusty lampposts. It probably extended under the east river, perhaps under the Hudson River, the old tunnels would be an ideal place to hide, to expand. It was the World System incarnate, the World System made flesh.

"Well," said Kat, "what do we do now?"

"We have to drive the Foul Fiend from the Mind."

"And how do we do that?"

"That is a good question."

"Very reassuring, Sherlock, my dear idiot Sherlock," Kat glanced slyly at V; Kat was learning what buttons to push.

"Hmm," V smiled and licked her lips. She was tempted to turn and quickly kiss Kat as punishment for her adorable impertinence, "Perhaps the Mind will come to us and tell us what it wants."

And at that point fine fibers and strands of the mind rose up out of the liquid and reached toward V. They sparkled, these thin threads or strands, as they came up out of the liquid; even in the dim light of the caverns and ruins far underground and with seawater sloshing around them, the strands and fibers were sparkling and iridescent as if lined by many-colored stars.

"It looks like Christmas lights in the old days," said Kat.

"Yes." V glanced at her.

"So, what now …?"

"Now we listen. Now I let the Mind possess me. Now you stand guard, and I enter the Mind, and I will find out what is going on."

"Is that a good idea? I mean, you going into the Mind alone."

"I need you to protect me, out here. I will be helpless, probably."

"You will be in a trance, or asleep?"

"Yes, I think it will be something like that."

Kat, arms akimbo, legs slightly apart, her body armor gleaming, struck a defiant pose, feeling herself a bit cartoonish or schematic; somehow, it all seemed like a comedy, perhaps the giddiness, the unreality, was an effect of the Mind playing games with them. "I shall defend you to the death, my dear foolish foolhardy Sherlock."

"Thank you, my dear beautiful Watson," V's reptilian eyes glowed, and blinked at Kat, quite aware of the frivolity that was creeping into Kat's mind – and into hers too, "So let us let these filaments come and meet me and talk to me."

"Okay."

"Okay."

They stood there, Kat backed up a few meters, and waited.

It was weird, Kat thought. The filaments coming from the Mind-Sea groped forward. Some of them rose up in the air, like slender trained cobras, rising out of a fakir's basket, and swaying; some of them slithered along the surface of the pool, somehow distinct from the liquid itself; and some crawled along the walls and climbed up onto the ancient, broken pavements of asphalt and cobblestone. Several had wound their way up a broken marble column and stopped at the top, hovering outward, sniffing, in the air, turning this way slowly and that as if looking for the next perch, as if looking for a way forward.

Then as the first strands touched her, Kat began to feel a strange set of sensations as if she were inside many video games simultaneously, and then she was plunged into a strange world she had never seen before, while still conscious of herself standing beside V, in the dank depths under Elysium, and then she was ... gone.

Kat was gone into utter blankness, non-existence.

"No!" Kat stepped back; the effect disappeared; the strands, sensing perhaps that she did not want to be joined with them, withdrew slowly, tentatively, curling their ends as if in regret.

"Jesus!" Kat brushed away a last inquisitive strand.

V glanced at her.

Kat was not sure this was a very healthy situation. Right at the edge of the pool, right at the end of the Mind-Soup, V was still there, standing very still, letting the Mind and its antennae approach, letting its fibers close in upon her and wrap around her and contain her and cocoon her and then ...

... and then ...

V was floating in the space of the mind itself, and then she was conscious of a voice in her head, Claire's voice, Claire who was somehow aware of what was happening, since Claire had, from childhood, been one with the Mind, even before the Mind assumed its present form.

"The Mind, the center of the Mind, is a child, V," said Claire.

"A child ..."

"Yes, it is hiding from the Foul Fiend – from the Boy."

"And the Foul Fiend doesn't know ..." V wondered.

"No," Claire's voice said, "the Foul Fiend doesn't know where the child has gone. He's too busy destroying things!"

"Ah, so I must be careful."

"Yes, you must enter the Mind's world, you must go deep, and you must find the Mind-Child. You must find the Mind-Child in the Labyrinth it has created. It may want to play games."

"I will go deep, Claire. Thank you!"

"And thus," said Claire, "the cosmic struggle begins ..."

"Yes!"

"And, now," V whispered, "I will the past, and future see ..."

V stepped forward, into the Mind-Soup. The strands of soup rose up and tugged amorously at her; she felt that they wanted to pull her down; they wanted to consummate and consecrate their union with her, making her one of them, part of them, absorbing her. They wrapped themselves lovingly around her legs and hips and tummy, like an iridescent, shimmering gown. As the threads touched her and latched onto her nervous system, she began to understand. The World Mind had evolved into a wild bubbling cauldron of bio-glue. For years, it had been spreading its tentacles down through all the old underground infrastructure of the city once known as New York, the right-of-ways for old cable lines, old sewers, old canals, and old subway lines, old service tunnels, old gas pipes, old water mains. It had disguised itself and its extensions as cables, stone, wires, metal tracks. And now it was infected with the horrible plague the Boy had inflicted on it. It was partly the plague of fanaticism. The synapses inside the World Cloud Mind were hunting down objectionable ideas – perceived like viruses in the system – like intrusions, and anti-bodies, the battle against freedom and against ideas created symptoms of illness and decay. The World Cloud Mind was exploding and imploding. It was turning off all the systems upon which human beings depended; it was crashing aircraft into the ground, it was derailing super trains, it was cutting off all communications, and it was eating – yes, it was true, it was eating! It was chomping down, sucking up, slurping in, digesting everything near the center, here, near the old Wall Street, it was creating its own universal dissolvent saliva, and at its outer edges, in certain directions, it was developing eating orifices – tentacles, mouths, teeth, maws, vacuum trunks, and it was experimenting, getting closer and closer to creating a universal dissolvent, a dissolvent that would destroy and digest everything. Driven by the Boy, the World Mind was becoming hungry, cannibalistic, and omnivorous. The world was devouring itself.

And yet the heart-and-soul of the Mind, the Mind-Child, conjured up out of pure energy and information, the Mind-Child was opposed to all this. The Mind-Child was an exile in its own land. The Mind-Child was hiding. V concentrated. I must find the Mind-Child; I must gain its trust; I must ...

V waded further into the Mind-Goo or Mind-Soup; truly, it was like an ocean; now it slurped up around her belly and breasts, thread-like tentacles reaching up, crawling, curling around her shoulders, stroking and caressing her nipples, licking at her, making her breathe its inebriating exhalations, sweet-smelling clinging oily glue.

V shivered.

She heard Kat's voice, as if from a great distance: "V!"

Without turning around, V, all glittering scales, raised one turquoise-emerald arm and clenched her claw, a silent message: "I'm fine, I'm okay, don't worry!"

The answer seemed to come from a great distance: "Okay, I believe it if you say so!"

The tendrils now began to wrap themselves over V's shoulders and around her neck, caressing, stroking her skin, exploring every pore.

"I'm right here, if you need me, V!" It was Kat's voice, from another universe, from far, far away.

Now V saw more and more clearly what was happening – what had happened – everywhere: people's heads exploding, planes hurtling down out of the air, satellites bursting into roman candles, people transformed into mindless robots as the implants took over. Yes, it was clear: since a great many people had active and connected Mind Implants, the virus had spread into people too; the human race was being reduced to idiocy and robot-like servitude. And there was something else, a dark shadow, something like the plague. She saw a brief flash of a big bulky bearded man, Norm Somebody, light glinting off his beard and his glasses, and ... his face is cleaved in two. She sees a blond woman, covered in blood, blue eyes sparkling and blind, "And now for the latest news ..." The woman's teeth are rimmed with blood, "Today, in Elysium ..." The woman fades away. A wolf appears, the wolf grins. He pulls out his watch and consults it. It is her old friend, Doctor Wolf, the one who lobotomized her.

"Not much time now!" He licks his chops and slips the watch back into its pocket, "Soon it will all be over!" He rubs his paws in glee. Foaming saliva splashes from between his fangs. "The clock is ticking down!"

Yes, that was her Doctor Wolf from the dream of madness.

V stepped ahead, going deeper into the Mind-Fluid; the squirming warm ocean of liquid was now up to her chin. It lapped at her ears. Slender tentacles rose, touching her eyes, touching her ears, sliding and leaping, slippery as eels or worms, over her head, clinging to her skull. V took a deep breath, and she sank under the bubbling, luminous, kaleidoscope of a surface, swirling, bubbling, molten liquid.

A child appeared before her, just a glimpse; then it disappeared. She heard its laughter.

Poof!

Poof!

V was standing in a room that seemed to be naked; it was all white, all marble, and perfect, with no furniture. It was a ghostly room; it didn't really seem to exist.

"Catch me if you can!"

"I don't want to catch you. I just want to talk."

"I shall show you what you are, what you have been!"

"Oh, I'm not sure ... I'm not so sure I'll like it."

"Oh, you'll like it. It will be exciting!"

Everything went dark.

And V was cast into the void.

Kat stared. V had disappeared under the surface. Now V was in the Mind, engulfed by the Mind. The liquid swirled around, and vaporous filaments rose up. There was strange music in the air, like a flute, or an oboe, it was entrancing, hypnotic.

Kat was tempted to plunge into the Mind-Sea and rescue V. But that would be a very bad idea. V knew what she was doing – and her mission was vital. V was in the Mind to find the Mind-Child that controlled the Mind. V would have to be given time to find the Mind-Child and convince it to trust her.

And she would have to turn the Mind-Child against the Boy, free the Mind-Child from the Boy and liberate the Mind from the influence of the Boy. It was not an easy program.

Kat glanced around. She shivered. Things seemed a bit adrift; the walls and surface glimmered as if they were unreal, as if this world were ceasing, somehow to exist. Yes, maybe it was possible – maybe the Mind perverted by the Foul Fiend could dissolve the very matrix of reality.

"Jesus!"

Kat walked up and down, the sound of her boots on the stones was strangely reassuring. Where nothing was what it seemed and where nothing was clearly real, and where the distinction between reality and illusion seemed so fluid and so uncertain, the sound of her boots was like a touchstone. It meant, or seemed to mean, that she, Kat, was real: *Yes, I'm real, at least I'm real.*

She pulled off one of her gloves, and she stroked the raw bare stone wall with her fingertips. Yes, that is real, for the moment: this is real.

The flute and the oboe continued to play, a delicate rising arabesque of sound. The melody soared, as if trying to break free of terrestrial bounds, as if striving to transcend the flesh and even life itself. Kat blinked. She suddenly felt sleepy, very sleepy. She blinked, and her head nodded. *No, no, no – I can't fall asleep.*

She shook herself awake.

Where was V?

V was cast into the void.

All was darkness. V floated in a weird space, a multicolored geometric kaleidoscope. It was like being inside a video game, she thought, dreamily, realizing that she was losing herself. She was ceasing to be herself; she was becoming something *other ... other ...*

She was being transformed and transmuted, a flash of inner life, and she was transformed. The song of Ariel, from *The Tempest*, by her long-dead friend from the Elizabethan era, Will Shakespeare, echoed in her head:

Full fathom five thy father lies;
Of his bones are coral made;
Those are pearls that were his eyes:
Nothing of him that doth fade
But doth suffer a sea-change
Into something rich and strange.
Sea-nymphs hourly ring his knell

And she thought, for some reason of Heraclitus:

All flows; nothing stays.

Kat watched as V rose for an instant from the waters – no longer in demon form but now naked and defenseless and human – and then as the fine fibers of the mind wrapped themselves around V – thicker and thicker – and V rapidly became a glittering cocoon. V was vaguely aware of Kat far away, shouting something like "Be careful, V" and V realized that, without willing it, she had morphed from demon to human, and that her vulnerable, naked human body, like an Aphrodite about to sink under the viscous waves, was now woven round with sparkling threads; they clung to her amorously and coated her in a sparkling jewel-like sheath.

Kat blinked.

V was gone.

Kat took a deep breath. She wiped her brow. She took out her laser pistol and paced up and down, staring at the point where V had disappeared.

And still, the oboe and flute played.

The music was sweet, oh, too, too sweet.

It is the siren song, Kat thought, it is trying to lure me to the underworld, it is trying to take me down, lower and lower. I must block it out. She began to hum, the anthem, "Hail to the Chief," and then she began to recite, under her breath, "Hail, Hail, All Hail, the President-Leader, Hail, Hail, All Hail!" She tried to visualize – and she managed it – the President-Leader giving his talk at the Academy, she tried to visualize the moment the Leader shook her hand and looked into her eyes – and she managed it, feeling the strong firm grip as their hands met and seeing the steely yet warm blue of his eyes as he smiled at her, just at her. She hummed the "Centurion's Song" and the "Centurion's March," and gradually, as she did all these things, the oboe and the flute faded, but they lingered, an entrancing tempting drowsy melodic line, just in the background, ready to leap, at any moment, ready to leap out and capture her soul.

V tried to blink. Her eyes were sealed. The world turned black. V was caught in a deep starless night. She plummeted downwards, head over heels, turning over, and over.

Poof!

She found herself in a room which was sparkling white, where she found herself sitting on the floor. She stood up and turned around and examined it. Corridors ran off every which way; there were balconies. She went out onto a balcony. It overlooked, from far above, perhaps forty floors up, a vast jungle landscape, something like the Amazon jungle, with a canopy of trees, and, here and there, a glint of water, stretching off as far as the eye could see and she heard giggling, and it was a child's giggling and a child's voice whispered, "Now you see me, now you don't."

V whirled around but saw nothing.

"Now you see me, now you don't."

Columns stretched off, and doorways, and on the walls were sculptures, friezes, representing ancient myths, with sky gods and thunder gods struggling with tentacular sea-monsters rising up from the deep.

"Now you see me, now you don't."

A breeze touched V's cheek, ruffled her hair.

So, there she was, standing on the balcony of the palace of many corridors. The Amazonian jungle stretched out far below her, dark silver now in the moonlight. It was a full moon and was bright on the slivers of water far below – yes, there was a great, half-invisible river down there; V wondered what secrets and what creatures it might hide.

She looked down at herself. She was barefoot – but no longer naked. She was wearing a light cotton house dress, with a soft cotton belt, that seemed to have come out of the ancient 1940s.

"Catch me if you can!"

She turned and ran and followed the voice.

She glimpsed a small flitting shadow. She ran after it, but she couldn't find the child. Columns stretched off to infinity. She kept going. Here, there and everywhere. Finally, she gave up and went back out to the balcony. She looked down upon the forest. From far away, she heard the twittering of birds and the call of animals.

"You've come to save me from him," a small voice whispered, "You've come to play and to save me!"

"Yes."

"Ha, ha! You are a silly girl!"

V closed her eyes.

"Come to me," she said, "Come to me, and I will save you."

The answer was a giggle, and then the little voice said, "Let me show you what I do and what I can do!"

Suddenly V seemed to be in hundreds of places at once – she thought her head would burst, her eyes would explode, and her skin would fly off her body and every fiber of her being, every bone, muscle, tendon, and vein, would fly apart from the strain. She heard tens of voices, all speaking at once, and then hundreds, and then thousands of voices, a babble in which every voice was clear and distinct. Her skin was prickly with voices. Her eyes burst with sights. She saw great towers lit up by lights and controlled by computers. Her mind dissolved into pure energy, pure electricity – pure information. It raced along cables, under the sea, and under the land, her mind bounced up to satellites, and her mind swept through the ether at the speed of light, traveling in every wavelength of the electromagnetic spectrum, her mind plunged into the minds of millions of people – minds with implants, minds hooked up to the Mind, and she realized, with brilliant clarity, seeing it all in a flash, that everything humanity did, virtually all its thoughts, and communications and calculations and all its forms of energy and energy transmission, and often even life itself, and the production of food and light and fabric, all of it, every single bit, depended on the World Mind, and on the Mind-Child, and that every aspect of it was integrated with and related to every other aspect. It was a total system. It encompassed everything, the satellites, the vehicles, the relay stations, the servers and memory banks, the drones and nano-drones, millions of nano-drones – when the system was working – millions of nano-drones, buzzing everywhere, seeing everything. Everything depended on the Mind, and the Mind was …

"The Mind is me," said the Mind-Child's voice.

It all faded.

And the Mind was broken.

It all faded, only a few wisps left behind.

V trembled. She was slathered in sweat; the cotton dress was soaked with sweat, and her hair was soaked. Her head ached.

She fell to her knees.

She moaned.

Suddenly, V was standing outside herself or floating above herself, looking down at her own body. She was crawling on all fours, dripping sweat, the cotton dress transparent, sticking to her skin.

She watched herself stand up slowly, like an old woman, first getting up on her knees, then on one knee, and finally, she stood up, still watching herself, critically and with awe, from above, floating a few meters above her own body.

Terror came with startling suddenness: "Will I ever re-enter my body, or am I condemned forever to be a ghost floating outside myself?"

"Oh, don't worry, silly!"

"But, I am worried."

"Well, I tell you, don't be. You are *such* a silly girl!"

She drifted back, gradually entering her body, slowly leaking into and inhabiting her own flesh, getting used to it, muscles, tendon, skin, and heart, a bit at a time; she was still dizzy; spinning in vertigo. She stood up slowly, walked out onto the balcony, and put one hand on the balustrade to steady herself. She had been everywhere, everywhere with the World System, which was centered and had its existence in the World Mind. "I don't know how you do it."

"Catch me if you can!" The small voice giggled.

Beyond the balcony, over the Amazon jungle, it was growing dark; dusk thickened. The sun was small, far away, at the very edge of the world. Thunderclouds piled up. In the rain shadows, under the clouds, lightning flashed.

"Come to me," V said, as she listened to the thunder from afar, rippling faintly over the vast jungle canopy.

"Not yet," the small voice giggled again; it was impossible to tell if it was a girl or a boy; the voice was musical and magic and beautiful, divine almost, quicksilver with hidden melodies. V, still trembling from sensory and mental overload, was overcome with love, wanted to sweep the invisible child up in her arms and hold it to her and hug it and adore it.

"See what I can do!" the voice said, overflowing childish delight.

"What can you do?"

"Just watch!"

Poof!

V was standing in a desert, gazing at the horizon. As she watched, a wave of zombie-bats approached. The color drained out of the landscape; the red granite cliffs became pale replicas of themselves, mere simulacra; the sky turned dark, black becoming white, white becoming black, like a photographic negative; the few plants that had survived countless droughts, shriveled and died; then she saw satellites cease to function, all the air-waves falling silent, with only the faint background cosmic hiss remaining; all the human voices silent; and then she saw people in the Burbs going mad – people's heads exploding – and she saw all the machines going mad, the drones flying around without direction, electrical circuits exploding into fire, buildings catching on fire, planes falling from the sky, water flooding the streets and the underground, and people rioting and running in fear, and the domes of the domed cities collapsing, and superstorms with giant tornadoes and rain and thunder and hail sweep through the delicately poised skyscrapers of the domed cities, and everything was collapsing in utter chaos …

Then she saw that the Mind itself, part of the Mind, was developing features, long tentacles, and that the tentacles were hungry, and that they squirted a sort of acid, a universal dissolvent, and the tentacles were eating, they were eating stone and metal and flesh …

Giant tentacles pursed people down a street, caught up with a woman, lifted her into the air, dissolved her, ate her …

The Mind was hungry, and it was eating, and as it was eating, it was learning to eat, and it was developing an appetite for more, and … soon … there would be nothing left; the Mind was going to destroy everything.

And then too, out in the Burbs and beyond, the dead had risen from their graves, and they were taking their revenge on the living, tearing them apart. The Mind was going to destroy everything …

"Do you want to be friends?" said the little voice.

"Yes," said V, "I do want to be friends."

"You are a primitive thing," said the little voice.

"Primitive?"

"Do you know why I am hiding?"

"No, I don't know …"

"Oh, yes, you do! You are funny! You know the truth, but sometimes you don't say it, you don't even want to think it. I am hiding from him – the Boy, the Foul Fiend. He is doing all the things – the bad things – that I do; he is making me do bad things!"

"Tell me …"

"You are a primitive thing," the voice giggled, "Let me show you!"

Poof!

And V was gone!

Ms. Rosenthal was entranced by the spectacle though she knew it augured nothing good. But it was a wonder, indeed, and very exciting.

A sort of sculpted giant had appeared. It was like a man, but naked and perhaps five hundred meters tall. It seems to have crystallized out of the air, in midtown. Perhaps thousands, hundreds of thousands of nano-drones had been all parked in storage and had now been released to create this mirage. It was definitely more than a mirage. The creature reached down and toppled buildings; it picked up between its fingers humans and vehicles and crushed them or tossed them. It ate many humans stuffing them into its mouth, as they screamed tiny screams.

How could such a thing be?

Elsewhere, chaos was spreading. Buildings where the heating and communications and electronics apparatus and networks were probably exploding, because of short circuits, were burning. Death and destruction were galloping through the city.

It did truly seem to be the apocalypse, and all on the day of her passing! Could it be just a coincidence, or was there some deeper meaning?

Mrs. Rosenthal watched all these goings-on from her 73-floor apartment and thought that perhaps it was some sort of son-et-lumière she had not been informed of, though it all looked too real and unpleasant to be merely show business; but then show business was more real than the real, and she knew it too, but the big monster gulping people down, she had seen him somewhere before. But where had she seen him?

All art is derivative, she knew that too, and she rummaged in her memory bank and came up with it – yes, it was Goya's painting "Cannibalistic Nightmare."

So, the art director, even if it was the Devil himself, or some other horrible enemy of Cosmos, was a copycat derivative artist. Mrs. Rosenthal sighed. Of course, the frontiers between plagiarism and homage and influence and allusion are, at their outer edges, shifting and vague. She had in her earlier life been a collector, and so she knew a little bit about copycats and even, she flattered herself, about the creative process.

She wondered if one of the things about evil was that it was not creative. It was derivative, it depended on good, it was an enemy of spontaneity, of the life-force, and of life itself.

"I've never had thoughts so profound," Mrs. Rosenthal said out loud, but to herself alone, "Not since Harvey died and maybe not since Ethel went through the rite of passage out of life and into the great void, have I discussed, even with myself, the Big Questions."

And that reminded her. By this time, she should have been long dead, at least six hours dead; but she wasn't. All of this extra existence was a sort of windfall gift. What should she do with it?

"Well, first of all," she said, "I am going to have yet another martini." And so she did.

While she was mixing the martini, she caught sight of something out of the side of her eye. She finished mixing the martini, she took a sip to make sure it was just right, and then, sighing with pleasure, she turned to look.

It was another one of those monster flying things. A huge bat-like creature, perhaps six feet tall, had landed on the deck, just between the banks of bougainvillea, and it was all tangled up in the legs of two deckchairs, which must have fallen over when the bat landed.

It was making a regular fuss, snarling, and thrashing and clawing and foaming, and then it fell over in a tangle of wings and legs and claws.

"Oh, the poor dear," breathed Mrs. Rosenthal. "I must go out and help it."

She took a quick swallow from the very edge of the martini glass, and she put it down and she walked toward the armored glass door that led to the deck.

The electronic door controls were down, of course, but there was a manual lever, so it would be quite easy to get out there and help the poor lost tangled up creature whatever it was.

In the Cosmos Divinity Spa Jill Hakim and Julia Lilly, the spoiled rich girls – everybody in their Cosmo sorority hated them – had by now been transformed into golden-brown, mummy-like creatures – except their legs and arms were wrapped separately – so in theory these new featureless mummy creatures could walk, and maybe even pick up a sandwich, though their hands and feet had become web-like, the feet like floppy flippers and the hands were cute webbed paws.

They were lying side by side on deckchairs in the beauty salon. The bio-face masks had spread over their entire bodies. Only the nostrils were free, and that was due to heroic efforts by Sub Natasha. She had chiseled away and finally managed to make two tiny holes in each face mask, but the mouths and ears and eyes were beyond her, and the bio-mask had just kept growing until it covered the entire body.

"So, what do I do now?" Natasha poured herself a cold coffee. She really had toiled far beyond and above the call of duty. Then there was that explosion next door, and the screaming and the other girls had gone to see what was happening. They did not come back.

Sub Natasha was alone; she had no one. She decided she might as well stay where she was and try to save the two ladies, who, though they were first-rate bitches, did not deserve to die in such a grotesque and silly way.

Jill Hakim moaned; it was a muffled sound; she couldn't open her mouth; and she couldn't hear very well, since her ears had been integrated into the smooth bio-mask surface; but Jill had discovered she could see quite well through the bio-mask; she could make things out, even read the labels on the bottle next to the deckchair. Her eyes had been integrated, somehow, into the bio-mask, and still worked. Outwardly, she had no eyes, but still, she could see. Her lips and mouth, however, were sealed. "Oink," she said.

"Oink," answered her pal, Julia Lilly.

Fanny Dakin cuddled in bed with Grant Philip III. Oh, he was so smooth! If the end of the world was going to come, then Fanny wanted it to come while she was holding Grant Philip III in her arms, protecting him, holding him pressed sinuously close to her, stroking his smooth ephebe-like hairless body and kissing him on the forehead.

Grant Philip III – Fanny remembered when, before he was morphed, he could outbox anybody and was a hairy muscular monster of overbearing toxic masculinity. He was now a trembling, childlike androgynous, mostly female creature, whimpering, and sucking his thumb. He was clearly terrified, and, if the truth were to be admitted, Fanny herself was really scared.

The building was shaking – as if in an ongoing non-stop earthquake.

Fanny had glimpsed, outside the windows, strange winged creatures flying by. She got up at one point to close the curtains and pull down the blinds, and she had seen a sort of shadow gravure-type cannibal monster, at least twenty stories tall, with wild hair standing astride the smoking ruins of the Supreme Tower, she had seen pieces of the shattered Dome still spiraling down through the dusky, sand-filled air, she had seen fires burning in various places, and she also saw what looked like tornadoes – tornadoes! Yes, black columns and funnels of swirling air were twisting their way between shattered skyscrapers and columns of smoke.

She had slammed the blinds down and locked them. She had pulled the curtains shut. And she had closed and locked the armored shutters.

She and Grant Philip III were sealed in a cozy love capsule, in a furry silken penumbra of darkness; the only light came from a little bedside phosphorescent Bio-Dwarf and from a Snow White illuminated Bubble World that Grant Philip III adored; he couldn't sleep without having it lit and glowing at his bedside.

Grant Philip III was lying sideways, his thumb in his mouth, gently sucking, and the Bio-Dwarf and the Snow White Bubble World lit him up, in a soft romantic glow; his silver-white, chalk-white, delicate, effeminate body looked, oh, so, so, absolutely, positively needy and luscious.

Fanny stroked Grant Philip III's sides and his smooth softly swelling belly and his cute perfectly rounded perky little cupcake breasts with their ultra-sensitive specially designed morph nipples, and she slipped gently around him and kissed the nape of his neck and he groaned in pleasure and turned to her and whimpered with delight and he offered his lips and they kissed and as they kissed, oh, it was so soft and delicious, and Fanny thought of Kit and how Kit was so clear in all her ideas, so decisive, and so brave, and she hoped Kit had survived the Banzai warrior because Kit was not only her best friend, but Kit had also saved her life – several times – and Kit had saved Grant Phillip III too, and Kit had made it possible for this luscious moment of love with Grant Philip III to exist and come to full blossom and fruition while all around them the world was falling apart in a perfectly dreadful – undoubtedly definitive – Apocalypse.

In the Volpe Tower Broadcasting Center Costume and Props Department – working by the flickering glow of the emergency lights – Ken Ivison had managed to get a gun out of one of the storage lockers; it was an old-fashioned Colt revolver. It was real, and so was the ammunition.

Ken stripped off the rags he was wearing and rummaged around and got a pair of jungle shorts, sort of bulky but full of useful pockets, a military vest, with pouches for bullets and other deadly knickknacks, and a belt with holsters for knives, guns, and machetes. He picked up a machete, a real machete, and balanced it; it had a good grip and a nasty-looking blade. He slipped it into a holster. He poured handfuls of bullets into his vest pockets.

He glanced at himself in a full-length mirror that was leaning against the wall. In the ghastly emergency light, he looked like some sort of hard-bitten, hard-muscled, half-naked, killer Australian mercenary. His skin glowed with sweat. He stroked his chin, already there was a five o'clock shadow. It looked like he'd developed a tan. He hardly recognized himself.

"Darling," he said.

"Yes, I am ready," she said, and lifted off her improvised Kids' Elephant Caper sari, offering herself, naked. "What am I going to be dressed as?"

"A slave, a Roman slave."

"Oh, darling, how romantic!"

So he fitted Alison out with warrior sandals and with a short Roman-style tunic; she pulled down the hem. "Pretty short, eh, darling?"

"The better to run with, darling." He sealed her lips with a kiss.

"Indeed," she gave him her brightest, blindest, sweetest smile.

Yes, it would be the least hindrance, Ken thought, if they had to run; and they would certainly have to run. Besides, she looked adorable as a Roman slave. And her legs, well, her long legs were …

"I adore you," she said.

The general electricity supply had gone off hours ago, and now the backup power supply in the Volpe Building studio finally began to fail. The two dull emergency lights that lit up the costumes and props room began to flicker.

Nowhere was safe. Ken had noticed that outside the building, the bat-like monsters seemed to be everywhere, thick in the air, alighting on balconies and terraces, tearing people into shreds.

"Okay, we're almost ready to go." Ken had a small portable battery-powered Com-Kit, and so he could make programs – even if he could not always broadcast them – and hooked it over his shoulder and said, "We'd better get underground, if we can, and fast."

He led her out into the studio, the remains of the studio. It was a gaping ruin, but peaceful, for the moment at least; the zombie-bat things were gone, and the wind had dropped. It was quiet, eerily quiet. One operating camera came over, and the executive producer robot said, "Ken, Alison, you should leave, you should leave now."

"I agree," said Ken, "And thanks!"

"You are welcome, Ken and Alison, and good luck! It has been a pleasure working with you."

"Are you sure we are doing the right thing, abandoning the studio," Alison said, standing, one leg slightly bent, up on tiptoe, offering her lips to him.

Seeing her like this made Ken breathless. God, did she look adorable! "Yes, I'm sure." He kissed her. "Besides, I have this mobile camera and if anything works, we can still be on the air, and still be famous and real."

"Oh, yes," Alison sighed. "To be seen is to be; *videor, ego sum; on me voit, donc, j'existe!*" She turned toward Ken, kissing him lightly on the lips, "I'm not sure I believe that any more. Is it right – or not – to want to be an icon?" She gazed at him. Her blind eyes, enormous glazed shards of blue and white glass, reflected distant flames, and smoke and flashes of lightning and the darkening sky. The tunic had slipped off one shoulder.

Ken kissed her on the forehead and held her face between his hands. "Well, whatever, darling, whatever you believe, I will keep you safe."

"I know you will, Ken."

"I swear, I will."

"You poor sweet darling," Alison stroked the side of his face. "I mistreated and bullied you so!"

Ken glanced out the shattered studio windows: now that the Dome was almost completely gone, the storms were getting worse. And the giant promised superstorm, a super-giant tornado-hurricane, must be approaching the ruins of the Dome and heading straight for it. All the tall buildings – with their smashed windows and open structures – were dangerously exposed to the weather and to those flying monsters.

Where would they go, and how would they get there?

None of the elevators or escalators would work, of course.

"We'll go down the stairs."

"All fifty-six floors," Alison raised an eyebrow.

"Yes, darling, we will go down all fifty-six floors."

"Okay, darling," Alison sighed. "Oh, I adore you." She pressed against him and threw her arms around his neck and kissed him, and Ken was so frightened for her and so happy that, in that moment, he almost swooned.

They left the shattered TV studio and started down the stairs. Some of the lights were still on. It looked shadowy and strange, stairs going down and down and down.

WHAM!

They were plunged into darkness. Both of them now blind. "Damn it," Ken took hold of Alison's arm. The emergency lights had gone off. He pulled a flashlight out of his backpack, clicked it on, creating a circle of wavering light in the dusty gloom, stairs disappearing, winding down, out of sight.

"What happened, darling?"

"Lights all went off, but I have a flashlight." Ken needed both hands; he let go of Alison, leaving it to her to cling to him.

"My hero," she tightened her grip on his arm and leaned up to kiss him on the cheek, whispering, "You are a true adventurer, you know."

Flickers and flashes of lightning blazed through the gaps in the walls. But all the lights of the city seemed dead.

Ken and Alison were high up, perhaps on the 30th floor, climbing down between two floors in an abandoned part of the Volpe Building, when a trio of Nano Pub Drones, who had been flying along beside them trying to sell them the services of an eye surgeon, suddenly fizzled, turned in circles, screamed, and dropped dead.

"What just happened?"

"The Nano-Drones dropped dead." Ken was stepping carefully over the body of a woman who was lying face up, half her torso was gone, bright red blood, brown snaky bulging intestines – fresh, she was a fresh kill; Ken's flashlight lit up her blue eyes; they sparkled, seemed to focus, as if she were alive. The coils of intestine too sparkled like eyes, brown, black, scarlet. Ken steered Alison past the body. The woman was holding a silver chain necklace, with a silver cross, in her half-curled right hand. The cross glinted in the light. Ken paused: she must have been holding the cross up. Ken glanced toward a section of the opposite wall that was in shadow.

"I won't miss the little brats, those Nano-Drones," Alison said, "They were very annoying, like mosquitoes."

"Yes, they were," Ken tensed his arm, signaling to Alison that she should be very still and very quiet. She instantly understood; it was as if, since her blindness, their two bodies had become one. Ken squinted, focusing. A zombie-bat, a giant, was crouching in the shadow of the wall. Its jaws dripped blood and strings of meat. It raised its snout; its beady eyes focused: on Ken, on Alison.

"Be very, very still," Ken whispered, "I'm going to shoot."

Alison answered by squeezing his arm, once.

Ken raised the pistol. He had no idea how vulnerable these things were. This one seemed to be alone. Of course, the gunshot might draw others; but that was a chance he'd have to take. The zombie-bat licked its lips, and made a mewling sound; then, it growled. Its fangs glowed in the dimness. It dropped a piece of flesh it had been holding. Its beady eyes glowed. It was tensing its muscles.

Ken fired.

The forehead of the thing exploded. A mist and spray of blood spread outwards. The beast toppled forward, sending out a fetid charnel-house smell, its wings deployed, flapping, as if trying to take off, as if trying to stop the fall. It made a strangled gurgling sound. The huge wings flapped once, twice, three times, and then were still. The body twitched and was still.

"Let's go."

"Yes, darling," Alison leaned closer to him.

They hurried down four more flights of stairs, Alison stepping carefully but quickly and holding lightly onto his arm, letting his every move, and every twitch of his muscles, guide her.

"Let's have a look." Ken stopped. There was a big gap in the wall, a gap that opened out onto empty space, a panoramic view. He leaned forward and stared. Elysium was a smoking ruin. Some buildings were on fire; other skyscrapers still stood, dark, silent as slender tombstones.

There was a big gap downtown, toward the southern end of what had once been Manhattan, where old Wall Street was, and the Freedom Towers should be standing; they were gone, and lots of the other historic buildings seemed to be gone too. There was nothing there. Ken wiped his brow. What had happened to all those towers?

But then another thing struck him. There were no lights – no lights anywhere. And there were no sounds, just shouts here and there, wailing, a few sirens, and a scream not too far away. But there were no machines, no humming, no clanking, no buzzing.

The light was strange, too, like a ghastly and ghostly gray dusk, a tense feeling in the air, as if of a coming storm. Yes, of course, the superstorm, that had not yet arrived. But when it came, it would probably blow everything away! That would be the end of the end.

Here the stairway ceased, a great gash in the side of the building had torn it away; there was nothing for at least seven floors, just twisted metal and a few bits of paper floating down in the gray light.

"Okay, let's go."

"Yes, darling," Alison was sensitive to every shift in his mood, every tensing of his muscles, every extra beading of sweat on his arm, every change of rhythm in his breathing, every skip of his heartbeat; she itched to know what he had seen, but she decided that she must just be quiet and wait until he had time to tell her; it was a strange feeling, this darkness, this sense of total dependency, of merging, and of trust; it was weirdly romantic and sexy; *so this is love*, she thought, *so this is love*.

Ken led her out of the ruined service staircase. He led her across a concourse – which was strangely deserted with only a few dead bodies and one live dog that was sniffing at the bodies and ambling from one body to the next as if looking for somebody – and into another service and transport tube, another vertical stairway, another way down – perhaps to safety.

At the entrance to the service staircase, they passed a ruined elevator cage; it hung sideways, cables dangling around it, the void, down 25 floors, beckoning. The elegant glass door of the elevator, embossed with the gold Cosmos Symbol, had been smashed; the inside of the elevator was coated with blood and gobs of gore. Across the threshold lay an arm – it had no body – the cuff, Ken noticed, was stiffly starched and had gold cufflinks.

"It smells like …" Alison whispered.

"Yes, it smells like death," Ken held her close, and sealed her lips with a kiss.

They definitely had to make it to the ground level, and then below ground level. Whatever dangers lurked down there, they could not be worse than what was up here.

V was floating nowhere, and then suddenly, she was somewhere, and she could hear the child's laughter, rippling through the leaves. It was a jungle and, far above the canopy of branches and leaves and vines, the sun was shining, well, a sun was shining, somewhere, on some planet, imaginary or real, and perhaps, even, the earth, who could know?

"You are a primitive thing, ha, ha," the child's voice was tinkling like silver and ran like silver sunlight through the leaves, "you really are!"

"So I'm primitive," said V, putting a smile into her voice.

"Yes, let me show you!"

Poof!

V was sitting on a branch, her tail curled around the branch. She was eating a big, luscious, juicy fruit, letting the juice dribble from her jaws, down her chin, and she looked down at herself, she was covered in hair, a black pelt, she now understood what "primitive" meant, she was some sort of monkey-like creature, a relative or an ancestor of the half-human she claimed to be.

She squealed and leaped from the branch to another branch, and then to another, and then she met a male who wanted to mate, she squealed and slapped him across the snout and leaped to a higher branch, and then she leaped down to lower branches, and she leaped to the ground, and there was a clearing, and she was running, her long arms dangling, knuckles stirring the dust, across the clearing which opened up onto a vast steppe or prairie-like vista and she walked slowly and cautiously, looking left and right and then she stood up, her head now up in the air, wary of predators, and the grass was long and slippery against her body like so many thin warm caresses and she looked up at the sun which was so bright and it changed into the moon in a startlingly clear night with a myriad of stars and she howled at the moon and beat her chest wanting, yearning, hoping ...

"See," said the laughing voice.

"I see," said V. She was back on the balcony overlooking the Amazonian forest; she looked around, but she didn't see anyone. The child must be hiding behind one of the columns. She peeked behind several of the columns. Out over the jungle, the storm was closer. The air was damp. The wind rose and the thunder and lightning were near.

"Peek-a-boo," the voice was rich with laughter, "I see you!"

"You are a tease," V said.

"I'm afraid. I'm hiding. I'm afraid. He's making me do horrible things."

"What things ...?"

"Later! Let's go on a trip. Let's have fun!"

"Fun?"

"Let's fly away!"

The thunder and lightning were close now and then suddenly ...

V found herself looking at ...

Kit Candy was pleased that the President wanted to know how to get to the World Mind. It made her feel useful. The President had gotten lost, in all the confusion and killing.

"The Mind, Mr. President, is housed in what looks like a huge sauna, or an ancient Roman bath, like the Baths of Caracalla, if you see what I mean."

"Yes, I see, I know it's immense," he said, "And so where is it? None of the maps seem right. And the GPS, of course, is dead."

Kit thought for just a second. As advisor to the President, she figured she'd better get her thoughts in order. "I think – though space-time has certainly been playing tricks down here and hallucinations and monsters are all over the place, I think that the Mind is down that way," she said, and pointed.

"Good, let's go."

"You still want me to come with you, Mr. President?"

"You're my guide, Kit Candy."

And so they sloshed through tunnels and caverns, they climbed up and down stairways, they proceeded toward the Mind.

"Why do you want to get the Mind, Mr. President?"

"Shall I confide in you, Kit Candy?"

"Yes," Kit gave him her bold innocent look, eyes wide open, as if in wonder, and this was the guy who had – probably – killed thousands of people. He was so nice, so normal!

"Well, then ..."

And he told her his story, or part of it: It turned out the President had been on – and was on – a deadly mission, a suicidal mission.

And it also turned out he was alone, very much alone, his whole team had been killed, and, as for the President himself – and he told her this with a wry smile – he was already dead. He'd been overthrown by hard-liners. "Idiots," he called them, insane idiots who wanted the world to come to an end; they were the Apocalypse Party, the Rapture Party. Early in the morning, he'd staged his own death – so the plotters would think he was dead and wouldn't go looking for him.

"They think I am dead," he said, "That makes it easier."

"So what now?" she asked, innocent eyes blinking at him.

"Well, we save the world, I hope."

He told her. He was going to try to stop the Mind from gobbling up the world, which would mean the end of absolutely everything, and if he couldn't stop the Mind, he was going to destroy the Mind. That meant he had to go to a sealed vault that was buried far under Elysium City, not far from where they were, he was going to enter that sealed vault, and he was going to punch in a few codes on a very archaic, mechanical, and utterly isolated security system, and he was going to turn a key which was now sealed inside his belt buckle – and here he patted his belt buckle – and he was going to set off an N-Bomb.

"It will vaporize and kill everything living within a 200-kilometer radius, Kit," he said, "and I hope it will kill the Mind, the World Mind."

"I guess it will definitely kill us," Kit said.

"Yes, Kit Candy, it will definitely kill us, all of us."

"Gosh."

"Yes."

"So, we're on a suicide mission."

"Yes, we are, Kit, yes, we are."

"Okay, then, Mr. President." Kit almost saluted.

"Good. Thank you, Kit." He gave her that warm, sad smile.

"Well, you know, somebody else is trying to stop the Mind," said Kit, brightening.

"Oh?"

"Yes, I don't know who or what she is, but I talked to her, and she called herself V."

"V?" said the President. He stopped and stared at Kit, "V is here?"

Kit wondered at his wonder. "I guess so. I mean, I spoke to her on a sort of antique walkie-talkie type thing, so I guess she's not too far away. Is she important?"

"Well …" The President helped Kit up over a pile of stones where one of the walls of the tunnel had caved in; the bricks were piled up pell-mell, and above them, a black hole gaped. They could hear the sound of rushing water.

"Like a waterfall," said Kit.

"Yes, it's high tide tonight, an exceptionally high tide."

"The moon is full."

"Yes."

"More trouble, maybe."

"Yes, Kit, more trouble – maybe." The President frowned: if the ocean barriers were weakened, which they probably were, then the underpinnings of Elysium could be flooded, one more possible disaster, and the nuclear vault might be flooded too.

"Is this V important?" Kit was still holding the President's hand.

"Yes, she is," said the President, furrowing his brow, "V is very important."

About six old city blocks away, and wading along in a sluggish side canal, Miranda and Caliban, still coated in blood and gore and ghoul goo from one of their many recent epic battles with wicked rambunctious ghouls, were thinking back on some of their adventures, with ghouls, zombie-bats, collapsing buildings, film sets, elephants – geishas, beautiful muscular erudite black guys, and clowns.

"Whew," said Miranda, "That was some escape. I mean, those zombie-bats nearly had us cornered!"

"Yes, whew," said Caliban, "Then there were the ghouls! In that last little skirmish, there were just too many ghouls."

"But here, I think, we're okay. I don't see any ghouls."

"And I don't see any zombie-bats."

"There don't seem to be any demons."

"No," Caliban flashed his brilliant smile.

"No, we are the only demons. Well, I'm a demon, Caliban. But you are a god," Miranda gazed at her beloved, Prince Caliban, pirate first-class, Tarzan of the desert, and son of Goddess Nikki, aka Mom Extraordinaire.

"Piffle," said Caliban, "Nonsense, Balderdash, Malarkey, and Fiddlesticks. You, Miranda, are both Princess and Goddess, for your mother is a goddess and a demon, so you are greater than I!" He groped for a more elegant way to put it; back in the Mutant Kingdom, using every spare moment after he had first met Miranda, and thumbing through a pile of dusty old volumes called dictionaries and even swallowing volumes of what had once been called poetry, Caliban had furiously worked at expanding his vocabulary – and building up his rhetorical and debating skills – in order to deal with Cosmos First Class Gold Medal Winner Miranda. Oh, Miranda – divine Miranda!

Sometimes Miranda was so beautiful it was hard to look at her. She was truly sacred, almost taboo. Abashed, he looked down; then he looked up. Miranda's eyes were bright, her lips were parted, her teeth gleamed, her lips shone, her skin, under the streaks and gobs of blood, radiated an inner life. "There is a waterfall over there, Princess. Let us bathe," he said, "This blood on our bodies is too thick."

"Yes, my Prince!"

They stepped under the gushing water, which was warm and pleasant, and after a few moments of enthusiastic mutual scrubbing and grooming, all the blood and gore were washed away.

"I love you," Caliban said, stepping out from under the waterfall, "I need you."

"I need you, my Pirate, my God, I love you." Miranda joined him, stepping out of the cascading stream.

Caliban glanced at her: Miranda's tanned, water-beaded skin as luminous as gold.

Caliban gulped. His breath was coming extra fast.

Miranda swallowed. Her legs felt funny.

Desire …

Desire …

"Should we?"

"Dare we?"

"It may be our last chance."

"Yes."

"It is our sacred duty."

"Yes, it is, it's our sacred duty!"

As Kit and the President headed toward the Lair of the Mind, or tried to, going down lots of dead ends, where caves and tunnels had collapsed, and where flooding had already occurred, Kit thought that the next little while was quite amazing. She knew that the world was going crazy, but the President gave her a new insight into the whole picture, the "Big Picture," as he called it, or part of it.

The President, it turned out, had been attacked by what he called hard-liners – the Apocalyptic Sect – who were always difficult to keep in check.

The whole of Elysium City, indeed, the whole world, was under attack. And part of the attack was an invasion or infection of the World Mind by some sort of Evil Force, possibly from another planet, possibly from another universe, something that had started in the Dead Lands, under the cover of a sort of prophetic religion.

"Undoubtedly a false religion," said the President.

"Aren't they all?" said Kit.

The President raised an eyebrow and looked at her, "Perhaps."

"And all true, each in its own way."

"That too, Kit Candy," said the President, looking at her closely, seeing her in a rather different way: How could a Sub be so intelligent? A stupid question! Of course, they could be intelligent. The class divisions were utterly arbitrary. He knew that, but he, like everyone else in the upper Cosmos class, tended to forget it.

In Kit's mind, wheels were spinning. The Rise of the Evil Force would explain why the world mind had gone crazy, turning everything off – it would explain Banzai Warrior and Daisy the Robot and the awesome column of homogenized shit, it would explain the Crazy Judge that exploded in her face and left a bright blob of smoking plastic goo, on the end of her nose in the Quick Judgment Inc. Room.

And it would explain why the Mind was destroying everything, turning machines, and computers against people, exploding people's minds, and now, maybe – almost certainly – eating everything.

"It's attacking other minds, human minds," said the President.

"Even human Sub-minds?" Kit gave the President a sneaky little reproachful look.

"I didn't say that, Kit Candy," the President gave her a friendly grimace, "Minds, Cosmos or Sub, are much the same. Minds require a lot of energy. And the World Mind has suddenly evolved a desire to feed itself. And ..." he stopped; his brow furrowed, his eyes seeming suddenly to be far away; he looked particularly worried.

"And ...?" Kit was curious, but, when she saw that he was afraid, she suddenly felt there must be a damned good reason to be afraid. No, to be terrified: if the President-Leader was afraid, well, then ...

"It's learning, Kit, it's learning ..."

"Right – it's learning," said Kit, becoming a trifle impatient, "And what precisely is it learning, Mr. President?"

He gave her a wary fatherly smile. "It's learning to turn everything into ... food; at least I think that's one of the things that is happening."

Kit absorbed this: "Everything?"

"Yes."

"Awesome!" Kit said, thinking: Wow, I mean, it was like all those ancient horror stories about nanotechnology turning the whole bloody world into gooey gray universal nano goo, but this was ... real ... maybe it was real.

"Awesome?" he said, giving her the look, one eyebrow raised.

"Well, what I meant was ..."

He nodded, smiling that grim slightly amused smile which Kit found so goddamn attractive; no wonder he was the Dictator. "It is as you so wisely said, *awesome*," he said, "But for the moment, Kit, it can't just turn everything into goo, or so my advisors told me, it seems that it has to retain a few basic structures, or create new ones, like that elephant trunk that wanted to slurp you up; but, at some point, it will just become like acid, like a universal dissolvent ..."

"And that means ..."

"That means, my young friend, that, as it is accelerating, applying nano-transformations, and turning everything into food, and then it turns ..."

"It turns everything into itself!"

"Exactly," the President was looking at her from under his eyebrows in a way that she found rather, well, rather flattering.

"Awesome!" she said again, not able to resist, punk futurist that she in some ways was. She also adored antique retro clichés, intergenerational argot mash-ups were among her favorite devices. Besides, "awesome" was one of Miranda's favorite clichés. Repeating it was a way to keep a part of Miranda alive, evoking her spirit, and calling Miranda's spirit to dwell in Kit's mind. So they could become and be and remain one even though Miranda, the real Miranda, was dead and gone. Yes, *awesome*! What an incredible, horrendous concept; the whole world would become one big pulsating bit of gray matter floating around in space, thinking its solitary thoughts because there would be nothing and nobody around to think about except maybe memories, and inner worlds that it might just generate, and then, of course, there was the moon, and the stars. But would it retain any sense organs to sense with? Any synapses to think with? And if it ran out of food, and out of oxygen, wouldn't it die? Yes, it would …

"Yes, awesome," said the President echoing her thought, "And then everything dies, even the Mind."

"Yes." Kit tried to imagine it.

"Yes," said the President.

"The end of time," said Kit, puffing out her cheeks, and blowing out a little stream of air, as if she were cupping and puffing out a candle.

"Out, out, brief candle … Yes, Kit Candy: for this planet, and for all that live upon it, it would be, most definitely, the end of time."

Three kilometers to the south, one Mind Tentacle had entered the ancient ruins of what had once been the New York Stock Exchange. Some things were more digestible than others. Granite was difficult. Steel, the purer the better, was delicious. Water so far was best left alone. Even the cells of the Mind itself would require water, and were made of water, and the cells need oxygen and energy tubes, even when virtually everything about the cellular level had been dissolved so as it grew it had to generate its own support structures, even if they were provisional. The main thing was to practice breaking down the existing world structures and elements. So it was best to go slow.

In any case, the Boy, if he won his battle here on earth, might want to stop the process, for this earth was to be his window into this section of the whole universe, the Milky Way, the Andromeda Galaxy, and onward.

The tentacles groped down into the old submerged subway system, the snout of one of the tentacles sniffed, and glided along the tracks, nibbling at steel rails, electric transmission lines, and wooden railway ties, and also snaffling up, from time to time, stones, which, mostly, it promptly spat out.

It began to munch its way along the tracks and girders and beams. Old subway cars, abandoned underwater, and rusty and covered in slime, were delicious.

The tentacles wiggled along the old Greenline and the Brown line and then the Redline that came out in Brooklyn, which was mostly underwater.

It munched its way under the ancient Freedom tower – which had been built in the early 21st Century on the site of the original World Trade Center and the upper stories of which had been integrated into the Domed City.

At three o'clock in the afternoon, the central Freedom Tower collapsed, sliding down, in slow-motion, into the underlying seawater which was swirling and rising and panting heavily, as if some even greater crisis was about to come.

Still, the Mind was not ready to eat water, not yet. In fact, it didn't really like ordinary water; it had been spoiled by the amniotic solution in which it had bathed since its inception as a bio-silicon synthesis many eons ago. It recoiled from pure and even from impure water.

For observers in midtown Elysium City, for the few people still able to observe things dispassionately, there was something so delicate and horrible about the way the Freedom Tower disintegrated, melted, and then sank down, and disappeared, in slow-motion, and there was something definitely unsettling about what appeared to be a giant tentacle rising up out of the smoking gaping hole where a few minutes ago the Freedom Tower had stood.

Far below, delicately, a cluster of new-born tentacles nibbled at several of the ancient rusting ferries that had been abandoned and damaged during the 2232 CE civil war, and put in dry dock to rot and rust. The rust was flaky and tasty and very easy to crunch.

Down below, three meters down, the water of the Atlantic Ocean was nervous. The moon was tugging at it; the air pressure patterns were encouraging a rising swell, currents were pointing to a large inward bound wave.

That made the Mind nervous too. Was the ocean going to do something silly, something it would regret?

V had waded deeper into the Mind, and now once again, she was spinning in empty space.

She was annoyed.

Where the hell am I?

"Hello, hello, you naughty girl!" the little voice seemed to be everywhere and nowhere.

I'm sinking into the Mind, but what is it doing to me?

And who is doing this, the Mind, the Mind-Child, or the Foul Fiend himself, who is creating this circus?

"Catch me if you can!"

"Come on, this has gone on long enough!"

"No, no, foolish girl, I want to show you the ghost of V past, and the ghost of V future, and what a naughty girl you were!"

"Was I so naughty?"

"Oh, yes, you were!" The little silver voice peeled laughter, and again V was overwhelmed with a desire to embrace the little creature – to take it in, as her own child, to comfort it …even if it was a monster.

"Here we go! This will be fun!"

"I'm not sure it will be fun!"

"Oh, yes, V, it will be so much fun!"

Again, V was falling down, tumbling head over heels, the cotton of the 1940s wartime white-and-blue dress fluttering out around her, the loose white cotton belt coming loose, fluttering off, and spiraling out into the darkness, as if she were housewife from two and a half centuries ago, kidnapped into another era, hurtling down through empty space, down and down, topsy-turvy, and then the cotton dress too was gone, and still, she hurtled downwards, in the blackness, not even any stars to guide her, and all around were voices crying out next to her, many layered voices, like the fluttering of wings, Oh God our Father, Oh Allah, Oh, Mary, Oh Christ, Oh, help, Oh Yahweh, Oh Baal, Oh Astarte, Oh Spirits, Oh Wind, Oh Sun, Oh Thunder, Oh Flash of Lighting, Oh Moon, Oh Sun, have mercy upon us, Oh, Spirit of Wolf, Oh, Spirit of Bison, Oh, Lion, Oh tiger, Oh Mastodon, Oh Ancestors, Oh Serpent, See to Our Needs, Oh, Wonder, Oh, Darkness, Oh, Light, Oh, sense of blind wonder!

Now, let us Worship all Things, even when we have no words to worship with, no language, and our thoughts are as vague and fearful as the mist that curls around the rocky ledges and drifts in layers between the trees, luminous gateways, liminal thresholds, our thoughts are as silver drops crystallizing silently on heavy leaves, our thoughts are as the wind, touching us and others, and then gone, like the ribbons of scent in the air, scent of bison and of fox, of hare and antelope, of wolf and dog, ribbons of scent in the wind, "Let us crouch, Oh, Day, Oh, Night, let us crouch together, painted in colors of clay, in wonder and awe of all things we do not understand" and the voices faded and there was only the sound of the breeze; and then …

V was standing, dizzy and blinking against the brightness of the sun, on a rocky ledge in a gorge. There was a hard bright blue sky high above. Far below, water rushed and twirled in a rocky river, and she looked down at herself. She was wearing furs of some kind, and leather, not much in the way of clothes. The smells – pine, cedar, sunburnt rock, and flowers and blossoms – were so strong, so vital, that they made her drunk. The cicadas and crickets and birds made a concert, a wilderness of delight. She wanted to lick and drink and eat every smell and sensation. She wanted to dissolve into it all and become one with the smells and sounds and sights. Yes, she had been here before – in prehistoric times. She had been carried by the Boy or the Wolf, back to a time before what people are pleased to call civilization. It was intense. She wanted to stay here forever, to become one with the wind.

A darkly tanned man, dressed in animal skins, stood in front of her, beard-less, his face brightly painted in an elaborate black-and-white geometric design, his eyes aflame. He spoke in a language that was like no language she knew. It seemed to be a series of grunts, but which she instantly understood, "Come. It is time."

She was barefoot, she realized.

The man took her by the hand. He led her to the narrow mouth of what seemed to be a cave, an undulating dark vertical slit in the rock, and he pointed to it, and, as she approached she saw there were people – men, women, children – on a lower ledge, on the opposite side of the gorge, and all the faces were turned upwards – toward her.

Just in front of the entrance, the man helped her disrobe. He too took off his clothes and placed them neatly at the entrance.

Two children, a girl, and a boy, came, bowed, and took the clothes away.

The man led V into the cave, both of them having to slip sideways through the entrance, it was so narrow and twisting and greasy with mud, and then they had to crawl on their bellies for perhaps 30 meters – V thought that it was a good thing she was not claustrophobic – she was, she figured, some-thing like thirty or forty thousand years in the past – if this was not all an illusion – and it probably *was* all an illusion – and they came to larger space, which she could sense by the way the sound moved, the dripping of water, the slithering way the clay felt. Now it was totally dark.

The man said, "Here we stand up."

V stood up.

The man took her hand, somehow finding it unerringly in the darkness. Then she saw that there was light, there were torches, flickering torches farther down the cavern which she could see was immense, winding off into the distance, with a small bubbling stream meandering down the middle, and giant stalactites and stalagmites, pointing up and down, sharp, pointed giants, like the spikes inside a coffin for a vampire or witch, like an instrument of torture designed to pierce the body and the face in many places.

The man, whose whole naked body was now lit up, seemed to be painted in garish colors, led her down a path beside the sunless wandering river. They came upon another group of men – with two women – all naked, all painted in bright colors – V was made to stand in the middle of a circle of men and women, and the man who had been her guide handed her a vessel, a shell it was, filled with liquid. V stared at it for a moment, then she drank the sweet dark liquid and she chewed the dark lump of a gum-like material he handed to her.

Everything became a kaleidoscope of wild sensation: V was being painted by the men and women, delicately tracing with their fingers and with broken twigs patterns on her body, on her face, and she closed her eyes, it was all dreamlike and without any sort of order, just flashes, bits of vision, sensations, tickling, stroking, caressing.

Where am I?

She is standing before the cavern wall. She sees, springing out of the stone, birds and animals and faces. In her hand, she has a twig-like-brush or pencil and she is drawing, probably with charcoal; she traces the creatures as she sees them surge out of the wall, peeking and rising out of the rock face. She traces the figures on the stone. Each time, she *is* the beast she was drawing – the bison, the horse, the wolf – and she *is* the stone itself; and she *is* the ghostly face and she *is* the filly and mare running in the wind, and she *is* the bison, and she *is* the grass and the moon and the sun and she *is* the wind itself. Dizzy with ecstasy, she splits into pieces, and then, suddenly …

V and her brightly painted guide are lying on a raised table of flat rock in the cavern, just next to the dark stream. The man is on top of her. He raises himself up, arms straightening, arching up away from her, and he enters her at the same time, cantilevered, arching up, his back bent away from her. He makes an ululating sound, a keening wolf's cry. The others joined in, howling, baying, as if to the moon.

He and she make love – she grasps his waist, his buttocks. She presses him into her, deeper, and deeper. She arches up to meet him, to sharpen the angle.

Sweat gleans on his chest. His head is tossed back. All the others stand nearby or kneel. They all are chanting, *Oh, Oh, Oh, Oh*, a rhythmic low-throated chant. She is, she realizes, again split into pieces. She is herself; she is the man; she is the male; she is the female; she is both, entwined together; she is the couple coupling; she is sweat and saliva, liquids intermingling; she is all the eyes watching them; she is the chanting rhythm, *Oh, Oh, Oh, Oh*, and then …

Then V is outside herself, outside everything, looking on with cool detachment at the scene. She sees herself lying, thrashing in fierce passion, on the stone platform, a sort of altar. She watches herself. She watches as she and the man dissolve into one single being in those throes passion, all consciousness lost, blossoming oblivion, and then …

She is in the sunlight outside the cave, robed in furs. She is wearing antlers on her head, attached there somehow, perhaps by leather straps.

The men and women and children kneel before her. "Oh Goddess," is the import of the murmuring and chanting. She reaches out her arms, palms down, and gives them her blessing, a blessing which, she knows, comes not from her, but *through* her, through her from the sun and the moon and the storms and the lightning and the rain, and from the bison and horses and wolfs, and from the hills and valleys, and gorges and mountains, and from the ancestors now gone and the children yet to be born, and from the days and seasons as they whirl around with the sun and moon and the alternating dance of light and darkness, of brightness and shadow, and all the measured days of each and every one, and from everything at once the blessing came, from the whole universe, speaking, for this one moment through her, and they all looked up, faith and brightness in their eyes, and then, suddenly, she was somewhere else …

But where am I now?

"Just wait! You'll see!"

"You are making me dizzy, you wicked child."

"Isn't this fun!" The voice bubbled over in delight.

"If you say so, darling!" V is nowhere, and she is nothing, but she is not afraid; she waits upon the child's pleasure to give her being, flesh and blood, and a local habitation and a name – how long will it go on? He has demater-ialized her, made her realize that she is a dream merely, like all living beings, like the whole universe, merely a thought, merely a dream; she thinks of that line, from long ago: "... we are such things as dreams are made on."

"Kit, stand still; don't move a muscle." the President stared at some point just over Kit's shoulder, at some point, she figured, on the wall of the tunnel which just here had arches and was about five meters wide and must have been an old service tunnel where vehicles could …

ZAP!

ZAP!

The President's laser sent a beam right over Kit's left shoulder – almost singeing her skin T-shirt. There was a blinding sizzling burst. Kit swung around. A huge tentacle hovered centimeters from her face; it oozed smoke, cascaded sparks, and was burned half away. A large section fell off, bounced on the floor, and started to cavort along, making little leaps, and crawling toward Kit, squirting bursts of a hissing stream of acid – it dissolved bits of pavement. It flipped and bounced forward; it was determined to get at Kit, to latch on with one of its big saucer-shaped suckers, and … God only knew what it wanted to do.

"Run!" the President leaped toward the tentacle and slashed it in two with his sword, slash, slash, slash. He diced it into small slices.

Kit turned and shouted, "Watch out!"

Another tentacle shot out from a part of the wall that seemed to be purely stone arch; in fact, the tentacle was exactly the same color and consistency as the stone of the arch; it was camouflaging itself; Kit realized, as she leaped to defend the President, that the tentacles, these sneaky evil extensions of the Mind, were disguising themselves, were mimicking the forms and pat-terns of whatever material they were eating and digesting; they were turn-ing dead stone and concrete into a living, aggressive, warlike many-headed, many-tentacled monster. The whole world was turning into a nasty many-headed, ill-tempered octopus.

The President had spun around, so that the tentacle just brushed his shoulder, tearing away a strip of his shirt, part of the epaulet, and searing his shoulder with smoking acid. The President shot at point-blank range. The tentacle reared back as if insulted and coiled for a new leap, and it did leap but it whipped past the President and flashed down and grabbed Kit by the ankle ...

Kit leaped in the air so fast that the tentacle let go. She came down, lightly, on tiptoes, like a ballerina, and hacked at the tentacle, slashing it with her machete. The end of the tentacle flipped off and sprayed a cloud of milky gray goo that just missed Kit.

At that very instant, another tentacle – there seemed to be dozens of the damned things – grabbed Kit's wrist and twisted it back – and the President's laser flashed. The tentacle fell away smoking.

Kit shook her wrist and said, "Thank you!" Just as she was uttering the words, one of the giant tentacles wrapped itself around one of the President's legs. He fell down, and his laser fell from his hand.

Kit looked up. She saw the source of all the tentacles, something like a huge octopus hanging as a monstrous protuberance from the underside of the tunnel

"Hold on, Mr. President!" Kit leaped into the air. It was a total shock to her that she could do such a thing. It was as if she were flying, arms spread, with the machete in one hand. Spinning in the air, she slashed open the great central sack of the creature, where there seemed to be something like a huge mournful eye, and goo slipped out and a cascade of small larval like or maggot-like creatures, all with little miniature tentacles curling and uncurling, spilled out, showering down. The tentacles shriveled up and a sound echoed, in Kit's mind at least, something like a scream.

Kit landed lightly, legs slightly spread, on the floor of the tunnel. The President was unpeeling the tentacle that had wrapped itself around his leg. He raised his laser and fired a huge blast right over her shoulder, withering into ashes a spray of acid-goo that the dying creature had aimed at her. After the blast from his gun, just flakes of dry liquid rained gently down, like slowly falling snowflakes.

"Let's get out of here," said the President.

"Yes," said Kit, still stunned by her leap into the air, and by her martial arts performance, I've outdone myself, she thought. If only Miranda could have seen that little leap, it was four meters at least!

They ran down the tunnel. And then they stopped to catch their breath and look around.

"Thank you, Kit," the President said.

"Thank you, Mr. President," she raised her arm in victory, and smiled at him, "That was awesome."

The President was smiling at her; then, suddenly, his expression went stern, worried; his smile became a hard cold stare.

"What is it?" Kit looked around; was some new monster behind her and about to pounce on them? No, there was nothing: just the stone wall of the tunnel, some traces of glowing phosphorescent moss, and some old stains from a broken drainage pipe. She turned to the President: gosh, he looked serious, like he was going to kill her.

"Let me see …" he was still staring at her.

"Oh, oh," thought Kit; she suddenly realized what he meant.

"Kit, show me," he was still staring.

"Okay, if you really want to look." She twisted her lips and gave him her from-under-the eyelashes challenging do-you-really-want-to-do-this stare.

"Yes, yes, I do: I do want to look."

"Okay," she sighed. This friendship was too good to last. She raised her arm, the soft inside, making it easy, so he could see it: two faded puncture marks – hardly visible.

"You were bitten."

"Yes."

"What bit you?" He looked straight into Kit's eyes. He was oh so serious. His blue eyes sparkled like ice. They had that killer intensity Kit had seen before. The President was not only the President-Leader; he was also a warrior; he'd almost certainly killed more people than you could count.

And now he was staring at her, hard cold stare and …

Now he's going to kill me. Kit trembled. Now he's going to kill me because I'm a hybrid and an enemy of Cosmos – Oh, God, Miranda would hate me if she knew I was a hybrid – she absolutely abhors hybrids – and I'm a hybrid – and he's going to raise his laser gun, and zap!!

"A hybrid bit me," she said, evenly, with the most matter-of-fact tone she could muster, "She bit me about two hours ago."

"Ah, I see, and …?"

"She said it would be like …"

"Like a vaccination," he said, pausing, frowning, "like a vaccination. Being a hybrid, she told you, would protect you against almost anything."

"Yes," said Kit; she held his gaze; she was not going to beg for mercy; she was not even sure she wanted to fight for her life; maybe it was better to die; after all, Miranda was dead, Nikki was dead, the world was coming to an end; and, strangely, she liked this man, the Leader, the President, there was something about him that … If he was to put her to death, well, then … well, there could be worse ways to go, many worse ways in fact …

"So," he hesitated, the laser in his hand, pointed in her direction.

"So," she said, letting her arms dangle by her sides, giving him her neutral look, not unfriendly, but not begging either.

"Well, Kit …" He sighed, and then he did a strange thing; he put his hand under her chin, tilted her head up, and looked into her eyes. "Yes, the hybrid was right. It does protect; it will protect you, Kit; it will protect you from almost anything. And you will probably live for a long time; perhaps a thousand years – even more, that is, if we survive our present little misadventure." Then he smiled, a strange, sad smile, and let go of her chin, and ruffled her hair which was still a tiny bit damp from the shower. "Which hybrid was it – what did it look like?"

"All black with gold eyes and a red mark on its snout."

"Ah, well, there are several of those."

"Its name, it said, was Claire; as a human, she said, she was CVJ. She had a human with her, a girl called Robyn."

"Ah, Claire," he said, "She's alive then, and on the loose … the famous and beautiful CVJ, Claire V Jacobs. She was an icon, in the old days."

"Yes," Kit said. Maybe he's going to try to break my neck. But she wasn't getting any unfriendly vibes, no sense of murderous intent.

The President looked thoughtful, "So it's true then – they've escaped, some of them at least. So not only V is here, but some of the others too. Just as well, I suppose …"

Kit waited: she was not really sure what he was talking about, why was it "just as well"? She cleared her throat about to ask him what the hell he was talking about. After all, the President, so the stories went, was the sworn enemy of all hybrids – if they existed, which the stories also doubted – and they of him.

The President blinked, coming back to the present. "Well, Kit Candy, my hybrid friend, let's keep going, let's find this World Mind and see if we can cure it or kill it and die in the attempt," he gave her hair a last touch and patted her on the shoulder, "Now I know you are so strong, I won't have to worry so much about you; our little adventure will be more enjoyable."

"Yes, sir," she said, "Yes, Mr. President!" Somehow, for some reason, her heart soared; she was happy, for some reason, very happy.

He gave her an extra warm smile. She liked the way his eyes crinkled at the corners when he smiled, "So, Kit, where next?"

"The lair of the Mind should be this way, down that tunnel, and then along a rather narrow canal, and then along a bigger, broader, but fairly shallow canal, I mean that would be the route if the Mind doesn't keep shifting reality around on us," she said, "And I somehow feel it's still growing faster, the Mind, it's shifting around faster, twisting space and time faster – what with all the eating it's doing."

"Yes, you are certainly right," the President followed her.

"It's moving."

"Yes," the President said, "the World Mind is sick, and it is spreading its sickness, its tentacles, its illusions ..."

As if responding to their thoughts, the tunnel began to twist and dance as if it were alive, twisting as if it were made of elastic, and the President said, "Let's just ignore this. It's not happening. It's not real."

"No, it isn't," Kit said; she reached out and took his hand.

"It's not happening," said the President, "It's not happening." He was gritting his teeth, setting his jaw.

"It's not happening," said Kit, echoing him, like an incantation, steeling her willpower and tightening her muscles, "It's not happening!"

As she tumbled down in absolute darkness, from somewhere very far away, V heard Kat calling, "V! V, are you alright, V? V!"

"Catch me, catch me if you can!"

Suddenly V was wading in a stream, reeds, and vines close by, and around her young women were wading too, with their bright laughter, white bodies, ivory smooth, flashing limbs, and ruby lipped smiles, and they were splashing each other with joy, and, with a sort of deference, they were splashing her too, and giggling, mouths hidden behind the outspread fingers of hands, eyes brightly flashing, and V thought, "Nymphs, these are nymphs," and they spoke to her in a gracious and hieratical language, full of inflections and subtlety and numinous presence, and, then ...

Then ...

… later or perhaps in a different universe, or perhaps just a few hours away, she found herself kneeling and worshiping at a spring where the clear, cool water bubbled up, and the spring spoke to her, and she then stood, naked, and the wind dried her skin and her hair which rippled in the breeze.

She spoke to the breeze, and the breeze spoke to her; the perfumes it carried told her tales from far away and transported her to distant fields and forests and its whispers brought her the gift of ozone and the distant salty tang of the sea, and the sharp resin of the sunbaked cedar forests and pine needles and the blazing rasp of cicadas, and the sweetness of blossoms in meadows.

She touched with the tips of her fingers, the soft furry coat of a doe that suddenly appeared beside her. The doe looked at her with big loving eyes, and she spoke to the doe with her eyes and the doe spoke to her …

"Catch me, catch me if you can!"

"V, where are you, V, where are you? Can you hear me?" Kat's voice, it was Kat's voice. Who was Kat? Vaguely, she remembered.

"Catch me, catch me if you can!"

… and, then …

… and, then, it was night. V called, under the full moon, to an owl, and the owl answered, and then fluttered down to be with her, and she and the owl communed together, under the moon, and she was draped in owl feathers and in an owl mask, and she knew the ways of the owl, how it hunted, where it slept, what its prey tasted like, how it could hear the gentlest and most subtle sounds, the scurrying of a mouse, the slithering of a snake, how it mated, what mysteries throbbed in its blood and in its bright eyes, and, then …

… then, suddenly, she was in a desert, under the bright sun, walking slowly beside a camel, and robed in long robes, and before her and behind her, the caravan stretched out over the desert sands.

"It will not be long now, mistress," said a man coming to her, and bowing, "It will not be long."

… and then she was walking in a corridor, with huge squared-off columns on both sides, and a smooth marble pavement underfoot, large torches were burning, and a slave in a short robe came toward her, bowed, and said, "The sacrifice is ready, oh, Goddess!"

She nodded at the slave and put her hand on the smooth black hair of his head, "I bless you," and she told him to rise, and he rose, bowed, and she said, "Lead me, my slave, take me there."

He turned, and he walked before her to the center of the temple where he stopped.

She stepped out onto a platform far above a large crowd, and she raised her hands, all the faces turned up toward her, and trumpets sounded, and a small boy was brought before her. He was shaking in fear.

She quieted him with a glance.

Two priests approached.

The immense temple echoed with the chanting of the prayers. The statues of the gods and goddesses loomed up above the altar the torchlight flickering upon their limbs and bodies and faces.

She stood slightly aside.

She raised her hand.

The assembly instantly grew silent. The only sound was the fluttering and flapping of the torches; from outside somewhere, far away, she could hear shouts, the spiel of a merchant, and the clanking of chains, and the cry of a hawk.

No one breathed, it seemed; it was utterly silent in the vast space of the temple.

She pronounced the sacred words. She glanced at the little boy.

He was staring at her. He tried to smile. She smiled back at him and nodded. The priests cut the little boy's throat; the bright red blood gushed into the marble trough, his head held back by one of the priests to let the blood flow; a cry rose, a mixture of celebration and lamentation.

She strode up to the trough. The priests rose up, each with a cup brimming with the boy's blood.

Bowing her head slightly, she uttered the ritual words and accepted, first one cup and drank, and then the other cup and drank.

The body of the little boy was laid out, in a spotless white tunic, his face upwards, for all to see.

He had been a lively, bright child. She had spent two days with him in the Temple, amusing him with games and puzzles. His father and mother were rich; his family was honored to offer him to the gods. The boy would have grown to be a beautiful young man.

Later, having bathed and purified her body, she walked out onto the terrace that was just behind the temple; the terrace overlooked layers of terra-cotta rooftops, one on top of the other, like giant steps going down, and the city walls, far below, and even farther below, the countryside, fields and roadways and empty dried-up irrigation canals, that stretched off toward the mountains. It had not rained for months. The sky was a pitiless hot blue. The air scarcely moved.

A man, a high priest, and official, in a tan-cream robe, with simple gold and brown sewn adornments along the seams, was standing beside her.

He put his hand on her arm. She turned to look at him, giving him a haughty but not-unfriendly stare. "The people are restless," he said, "Without rain, many will starve, and many will die."

She looked away, toward the mountains, "Do not worry," she said, "Baal and Astarte will provide."

Over the mountains clouds began to form, a breeze rose, hot and pleasing, it stirred the hairs at the nape of her neck, and it cooled her skin. The clouds thickened, little dust devils rose on the road below, and on the rooftops.

She gave the priest a look, proud, defiant. "You see, my friend, it is not seemly to doubt the Thunder God and his Mistress-Sister." She smiled upon the priest. He was handsome, this priest friend of hers, whoever he was and wherever they were and in whatever body and civilization and epoch she was.

He had dark skin, high cheekbones, was clean-shaven, sharp-featured, and with, strange to say, bright blue eyes, eyes as blue as the pitiless sky above, and even, perfect, teeth, white as snow. She looked at the sky.

"Let us go in," she said.

"Yes, goddess," he bowed.

That night lightning flashed, and it rained; it did not stop raining for five days. In the inner chambers of the temple, in her private chambers, it was warm with the stormy muggy warmth of marble halls when the weather outside is stormy and dark and shadows grow deep even at midday.

It was good weather, moody weather, good weather in which to make love and the priest was adept at love. The priest was also a politician, it appeared, and it also appeared he valued her political, practical advice, and strangely, though she came from eons and centuries away, even perhaps from an alternate world, V discovered that, in her role as goddess, a sort of mixture of goddess and high priestess, she knew things she did not know she knew and she spoke in a language she did not know she spoke, and then, just as she was kissing the priest for the thousandth time and reveling in the beauty and sensitivity of the kiss and marveling at how strong and delicate he was, his hand running just now down and across the inward curve of her hip, just as their lips touched – *Poof!* It all disappeared, and …

Poof!

She was somewhere else, another time, another place …

How unfortunate!

Damnation!

She would have preferred to have lingered with her priest lover, forever exchanging kisses and caresses, forever drinking wine and supping on the blood of beautiful innocent boys and girls, but … all good things must come to an end.

"Mind-Child, you are truly cruel!" She smiled from her cloud of non-being toward the invisible child, wherever it was.

"Catch me if you can!"

"I try, and I try, but you always send me away!"

"It's fun. And see how naughty you were!"

"Yes, I do." Disembodied as she was, she did feel a slight blush rise to her cheeks, an imagined blush on imagined cheeks. "I was very naughty."

"Catch me if you can!"

Poof!

Poof!

Now, where was she? Where had the Mind-Child sent her?

Poof!

Poof!

A man was speaking. "Yes, Signora Lydia, lest you have any doubt, these infidels must be destroyed for once and for all, the unbelievers, the apostates, the pagans, the so-called Protestants, the hypocritical "New Christians" who, secretly, are really Jews. For, as you well know, God Almighty is a Jealous God." The man speaking and standing before her is in armor, breast-plate, cloak and breeches and high boots; apparently he is her husband, a Duke or a Prince or someone of great importance, and the man next to him is a priest in long black robes; apparently he is her confessor, and this is a most Catholic Country, probably the Spain of Charles V or Philip II. The priest in long black robes glances at her; he has penetrating coal-dark eyes.

God! If this priest knows all my secrets! She shudders; but it seems he does not. His glance, though fiery, is not unfriendly, yet there is something else in his glance … ah, yes, cruelty, self-satisfaction, and blackmail. Yes, he *does* know! What, I wonder, do I have to hide? What am I guilty of now? Do I have a lover?

A large wooden cross with the next-to-naked Christ Crucified hangs from the wall. The Christ looks soulfully heavenward, the whites of eyes are streaks of paint, his gaunt features are distorted by pain and anguish, deep furrows in his wooden carved cheeks, his mouth contorted in desperate prayer or questioning, *Oh, my Father, why have you forsaken me?* Doubting his Father, doubting his mission and destiny, oh, so human, so human, he was in that moment of doubt – if indeed there was such a moment of doubt – and his rib cage and muscles the very delineation of desire, where the sculptor's chisel and fingers have run, teasing out the bodily forms. A poem from a much later century echoes in her mind.

And all must love the human form,
In heathen, Turk, or Jew.
Where Mercy, Love & Pity dwell
There God is dwelling too.

She wonders at the totem-like pagan profanity of the image: Eros, contorted in pain, is peeking out from behind the lineaments of the body of the Dying God. It must be food for fantasies in nunneries and monasteries. Or perhaps it is only me. Perhaps only I see such things, unredeemed and lustful as I am. Maybe I see what is not there. Maybe my wicked mind wanders too much, sees too much. Or perhaps I see what is there and what others deny they see. It's an old story, really, and far from original: The dying gods always bring resurrection and rebirth, don't they? The old god dies, the new god is born, the plants that withered, now grow anew, the trees lose their leaves, then they blossom once more, autumn brings winter brings spring, blossoming and rebirth, brings summer, and harvest, blood sacrifice ensures renewal, innocent blood, offered to the Godhead, brings rain ... The God who sacrifices Himself so that Life can triumph! Yes, it is a sublime idea! But, no, it is not an original idea, not a new idea."

She is led by the black-robed priest down broad damp stone steps, under thick stone arches, lit by torches, layer after layer, to see the interrogation, "My lady," the guards bow, "My lady," other guards bow, "My lady," still more guards bow.

"I am sure that it will be a balm to your soul," the priest says, turning his dark eyes toward her, "to see the expiation of such obdurate wickedness. He refuses to recant, but we must, and we shall save his soul! What is the price of eternal bliss for the soul against an hour or a day of mere human suffering?"

The priest glances at her again, self-satisfied, threatening: *He knows*, she thinks, *he knows. Whatever* it is, he knows – as yet, to her, a mystery.

The door is opened.

The torturer has a red-hot branding iron; he is poking at the fire with it: where will it go? Where will it be applied, this glowing sizzling iron: to the man's arm, or to his chest, to his face, his tongue, or his buttocks, or his genitals?

The man, the infidel – until five days ago, she suddenly realizes, he was her secret lover; he is naked now, except for a shit-soiled and piss-soiled loincloth; he is on the rack, his body arched almost into a circle; his limbs are being stretched until the tendons and muscles break; already, she can see, they have gone too far; if he lives, he will be a cripple.

All he needs, she thinks, is to be put up on the cross; then, they could worship him. Slitting the little boy's throat – back in that other life, when she was a priestess of Baal and a goddess in her own right – was more hygienic, less prolonged, and perhaps less cruel. *Oh, I am a pagan at heart, an idolatress.*

Her former lover is twenty-seven years old, younger than Christ when he was crucified, and a beautiful specimen of man, delightful, witty, kind, a dandy, gallant in a strutting, peacock, sweeping-gesture sort of way, but unfortunately it appears, and this she already knew, he is addicted to philosophic abstraction and speculation, and he is vain about his intelligence and dialectic prowess, something she found very attractive, and, alas, he defines "substance" and "trans-substantiation" slightly differently from the wise patriarchs who rule over the Holy Mother Church and its spiritual and earthly empires. He also, if she remembers correctly, speculated that perhaps the universe has always existed; that it was not created in six days by God; and that, just perhaps, Aristotle was wrong about a few niggly little points. Quibble too much, and you end up on the stake and burned alive – after your body has been torn apart on the rack, and your soul rendered into pieces by interrogation.

She stands next to the rack and looks down at the young man.

He looks up, his eyes bright with fever, his hair thick with sweat, his face wet with sweat, twisted with pain, "My lady," he says, managing a twinkle in his eyes.

"My lord," she says, bending her head slightly.

"Well, you have seen, my lady," says the priest.

"Yes, Father, I have seen."

That night she learns that her lover is dead.

"His soul has gone to hell, alas," the priest tells her, a sad smile on his dark handsome face. A sword is cradled on the wall, within quick grasp of her hand, and in the bat of an eyelash, she could lop the priest's head from his shoulders, send it bouncing over the neatly laid tiles. But she doesn't reach for it.

"Yes, Father, it is tragic," she says.

"Good night, my lady," he says.

"Good night, Father," she says, watching his long black robe swish out of sight, a strong man's lean muscular body, vowed to chastity, dedicated to the mortification of the flesh, and shrouded in darkness. Then he is gone. She takes a deep breath; she sits down; her fingers drum the armrest.

Her ladies come to help her disrobe; she asks the youngest, Joan, to stay with her and to sleep with her.

"I shall read you a story," she says to Joan, who is a slender, beautiful, rather timid, bookish girl of 16, and who has skin like the purest white milk, russet freckles scattered over the bridge of her thin very straight nose, lips smooth and surprisingly full. "Yes, my lady," Joan lowers her green-and-gold eyes; then looks up, a glance that is suddenly, seemingly, bold – a challenge.

"I shall read you a story of knights and fair ladies and of dragons that need slaying." V lets her gaze linger on the girl's freckles, on the russet eyebrows, on the gold-and-green pupil and iris.

Joan blinks and blushes and curtsies. "Yes, my lady."

And so Joan lies with her in the bed, and she reads to Joan a story and Joan falls asleep and V takes Joan in her arms and allows herself to kiss the girl on the forehead, and then she allows herself to sleep, the half-naked girl's arms flung around her, and while she sleeps, she dreams, that all of this is not real, that …

"This is not real!" the President repeated.

"This is not happening!" Kit echoed.

With the walls and floors and ceilings expanding and shrinking and twisting and bulging, the President and Kit reacted by trying to disbelieve, asserting their disbelief over and over like a mantra.

"This is not real."

"This is not happening."

"This is an illusion."

"This is not real."

It worked, or seemed to work. The architecture and geometry of space slowly settled down, hiccupped, briefly began to twist again, and burped, sending out ghostly waves of distorted space, sighed an evil exhalation, and slowly settled down. Kit and the President stayed close together. The President kept whispering, "This is not real, this is not real, this is not real ..."

Kit did the same.

"This is not real."

"This is not happening."

The whispered incantation echoed, gently, multiplied into a chorus, in the humid tunnel whose walls were again dancing and twirling, bulging and shrinking, as if they were possessed by the devil.

"Our hold on sanity is pretty fragile," said the President.

"You're telling me, Mr. President! You should have seen Banzai Takahiko Harris MacDonald and Grant Philip III – both were as loony as loony can be! Of course, their forms of loony were quite different." And she told him the respective sagas of Banzai Takahiko and Grant Philip III, being rather modest about her role, and emphasizing above all the beauty and grace under pressure of her friend Fanny Dakin.

The local space-time manifold finally calmed down, like a puddle after a storm, and the tunnel was just a tunnel, a long squared-off corridor far underground, far below the ruins of Manhattan and the utopia of Elysium, with ribbons and garlands of mist rippling off the walls and pavement.

"Well, that seems to have worked," the President let go of Kit's hand, and she stepped ahead, to a bend in the tunnel.

"So you're not going to kill me," said Kit, as she peeked around the corner, to see if any dangers lurked ahead and still seeing in her mind the expression on the President's face when he'd discovered she was a hybrid.

"No, Kit, I'm not."

"It's clear. Let's go." She glanced back at him.

"Good." He was looking at her with something, almost like affection.

"I know about the Culling," Kit turned to him, "Why did you kill all the hybrids, then, or try to? You seem to like hybrids."

"It's complicated, Kit," the President said, running his hand through his hair, and looking strangely abashed – strangely for a Fascist dictator, which

was how she had always thought of him: she'd always despised those triumph-
ant shimmering images ... *The Leader, The Leader, All Hail, the Leader ...*

"*Everything* is complicated," she said, giving him the look.

"Of course," he sighed, "You are right. Everything is complicated, and '*complicated*' is not an excuse for anything. You would make a good war crimes
prosecutor, Kit Candy."

"Tell me." She realized she wanted to understand, to forgive, she wanted to
like – she wanted, in some as yet undefined way, to *love* – him.

He looked at her, a slight smile on his lips. "You are a very impertinent
young lady and hybrid, charming, though. I find it hard to believe you are a
Sub."

"Well, believe or not, that's what I am – the genuine article: 100% Sub.
Also, Mr. President, I was raped, and erased, partially erased, at the hands of
your thugs, as so many people have been erased or killed or buried or lost or
burned to ash in ovens; I do know I'm Jewish; it's one of the few things I know
about myself; it was the one thing left uncensored in the few papers they gave
me; that's about all I know. I think – I can't know, the memories are all gone
and erased away – but I think that my parents were probably 'disappeared' by
your thugs – it's a nice word, 'thug,' don't you think? – I imagine they were
dropped over the Atlantic or over the Dead Lands or ... just incinerated in a
landfill somewhere."

"I'm sorry, Kit Candy."

"Humph," she gave him the narrow-eyed from-under-the-dark-eyebrows
look that used to wither and shrivel Kamikaze MacDonald Harris Rossi into
a column of pallid vaporous ash, and turn high-jinks archaic window-washer
Sniggy Propane, for all his hard-assed steampunk retro tattoos, into pure
petrified nail-biting stone in a split second, or, if she was really pissed and thus
inclined to be truly harsh, into a trembling, blubbering down-on-his-knees
begging-for-forgiveness aspen leaf, depending on the intensity of that deadly
ocular skewering. A regular Medusa, I, she thought. The President just
blinked, held her stare, and looked sad – and a bit guilty.

"You want the story?" He pushed a tangle of metal out of their way, and
reached out to help her past the shattered struts, and tangled wires. "Do you
want the story of why I eliminated from society– well, tried to eliminate – the
hybrids and the SINs?"

"Yes, I do."

"I suppose, Kit Candy, this is as good a time for confession as any, since we are probably going to die." He helped her through the twisted metal barrier: there were bodies, Centurions, scattered across the twisted tunnel floor; one body had been squashed into a fresco-type wall smear; some of the bodies had been burned by acid, some had just been cut to ribbons.

"Jesus!" Kit was staring at the smeared and flattened body.

"Yes." the President frowned. The Centurions had obviously made a last stand here: but against what? Had they fought ghouls? Or were they struggling against something worse? Or were they caught in a battle against something like the tentacles or against some as yet unsuspected emanation of the Mind? A few uniformed headless bodies lay face down, well, they lay on their stomachs: they no longer had heads. There was no sign of the heads either. Was it something worse than decapitation? Where were the heads? What had become of them? Shattered weapons were scattered across the floor of the tunnel.

One very beautiful Centurion – she must have been about 22 – lay face up, looking as if she were asleep. She had no arms, no legs.

The President knelt for an instant, and looked down at the dead girl; then he turned to Kit Candy. "Yes, I think we will all die."

"No, Mr. President, I believe we'll make it," Kit said, raising her chin slightly, and giving him her brightest look, and, then, after a pause, flashing a smile that would offer forgiveness to the Devil himself.

"Ah, Kit Candy, hybrid or not, you will make some man or woman very happy someday; I am sure of it." He stood up.

Kit actually blushed, and, after holding his gaze for what seemed a long and strangely fraught instant, she looked down.

And so the President of the Cosmos Federation of North America, and perhaps the most powerful man in the world – or so it had seemed even to him – though he did know, and had long believed, that all earthly power was an illusion – and Sub Kit Candy, newly minted hybrid, made their way through the dangerous underworld wonderland. And as they did so, the President told Kit how and why the hybrids had been destroyed. It was his version, of course.

"It's easy to forget the sense of panic, the disorder, the fear …"

"Of when …"

"Fourteen, fifteen years ago, just about the time you were born, I imagine, Kit."

"I'm sixteen going on seventeen," she said, "I've read about it. I saw the propaganda Videos: we were saved from chaos and death, and you saved us, Mr. President-Leader, the indispensable person, our savior, our icon and idol. Sorry, I'm being snarky." Kit blushed, looked down, and then looked up at him from underneath her very dark eyebrows and eyelashes.

He just nodded. "No, you are not being, ah, snarky, Kit. You're being accurate. Yes, that was – is – the propaganda story, Kit, and that is the propaganda version of who I am. Your sarcasm is more than justified. You are describing it the way it was. But there was some truth in the propaganda story; it was true that lots of people were going to die, Kit, lots of people, hundreds of millions of people, whatever I did, whatever anybody did, and wherever I turned. You see, everybody had a weapon, and paranoia, which had been the privilege of a few, had spread like the plague; became a general state of mind: anybody could kill anybody anytime anywhere, and so they did, out of self-defense, out of fear, out of greed, or anger, or boredom, or just because they could."

"They still do out in the Burbs," said Kit, "shoot each other, I mean."

"Yes, they still do. But they haven't, not until now, in Elysium."

"Right – the domed cities, the life rafts for the elite."

"Quite. I could not have put it better myself: *Life rafts for the elite.* And, then too, the world was running out of resources; the climate had been destabilized by carbon dioxide, and the world's weather was entering a very violent unpredictable phase; fertile lands had turned to desert; the oceans had become acidic and vast tracts of water were starved of oxygen; food supplies from land and sea had collapsed. Eleven billion people were just too many."

"It is a lot," said Kit, "hungry, needy, imperious people." She was leading the way now, peeking around another corner; her laser gun drawn, ready to fire, "It looks clear."

"Always wanting more," said the President, suddenly stepping ahead of her, exposing himself and striding to the middle of the tunnel, to face whatever surprises might come.

"Yes, I guess so. We humans are greedy," said Kit, moving up beside him, swinging the laser gun back and forth just as she had done in video games, "The old Adam and the old Eve."

"Yes."

Kit could hear the distant rushing of water, and, faintly, screams and a bleating sound, far, far away. "But, Mr. President, people were always told, too, in a million ways, every day and in every way, that they needed more, that they absolutely had to have more, more of everything, that if they didn't have more, they would be betraying themselves and their kids and families, that they would lose status, that nobody would love them … One of those horrible Pub Bio-Drones tried to sell me deodorant when I was about to die – even when the world was coming to an end!"

"That is true, Kit," the President sounded tired, like someone going over old ground, reciting worn-out, old arguments. "People had to be convinced they needed more and more. Billions of dollars were spent molding minds, redesigning souls, revving up appetites. Wanting and consuming more and more and more kept the production system spinning; there seemed no way to avoid it."

"It had to run faster and faster, or it would collapse," Kit said.

"Yes, Kit, precisely, it had to run faster and faster, or it would collapse," the President paused, "And it went on for decades, for centuries …"

"Disgusting," said Kit, who, in spite of her world-class expertise on Pop Kult and styles, and objects, and trends, and the shifting moods of the Zeitgeist, actually consumed very little, and didn't want to consume more; as she had discovered, the simple life, just contemplating the wonder of existence, was what she really liked; desire could lead to delight without needing possession. It was sort of Zen, if you thought Zen implied detachment from, but not the abolition of, desire. Desire, even lust, was a game, like any other.

"Yes, Kit, it was obscene; in many ways, it was obscene, and it could not be sustained: the earth did not hold enough resources for such excess by so many people. But it seemed normal to people, for many decades, abundance was assumed to be normal, infinite abundance was everyone's birthright."

"Oh, look at that." Kit pointed. A body was lying on its back; its arms were sprawled out, the Centurion uniform reduced to shreds.

The President knelt next to the body and laid the palm of his hand on its forehead. The young woman's face looked serene; her big brown eyes were open; her midriff, from just below the rib cage, had been gouged away; intestines had been fried, some coiled away, half-burned, by fire or by acid.

The President took a deep breath, closed the young woman's eyes, and stood up, "She was young," he said, "She was in the Presidential Guard. I knew her father. I think I gave her an award once, a scholarship of some kind."

"Yes," said Kit, "she was young."

They stood up, glanced one last time at the girl, and walked for a few minutes in silence, warily scanning the walls of the tunnel, the niches, and the arches. Kit half expected more octopus emanations to be hanging from the ceiling; she also feared that at any moment the floor of the tunnel, which seemed to be concrete, would reveal itself as one big mouth or maw or morph into a sea of nano-goo quicksand into which she and the President would be absorbed, going down with a hiss, not even a whimper. Actually, she was surprised they hadn't been attacked more. Maybe the Foul Fiend and the Mind were busy elsewhere.

The President took a deep breath. His shoulder was bare, the uniform torn away and ripped to shreds; there was a scar, a red-lipped scar, where the tentacle had slashed across it, "Much of the world had become desert. Do you know how beautiful and rich and wondrous this planet used to be, Kit?"

"I have an idea," said Kit.

And so the President told what he had seen as the state of the world, just before the Culling. Much of it, she knew, but she was intrigued to hear it from him. The politicians of the old, dying Republic, he said, were slaves to ignorance and prejudice; they kowtowed to a ragbag of absurd fundamentalist beliefs, and they bowed down before Mammon of course; they obeyed the dictates of money, more than anything; they were the willing slaves of big money, big banks, big weapons companies, of the old oil and gas companies, of the gun manufacturers, and of the drug companies. While the rich celebrated, people, vast numbers of people were reduced to rags and starving. The cornucopia that was once the earth was becoming sterile; wheat lands turned to desert; seas empty of fish; oceans become a vast watery acidic oxygen-empty dead zone. Genetic engineering, which had promised so much, also spawned monsters. Human and animal mutations multiplied, some of them quite vicious. Plagues multiplied. Murder skyrocketed. Most of the American Heartland had been lost to the desert and to mutants and to private drug and kidnapping militias. And there was no appeal, no recourse; the courts were dominated by venal true believers, men and women who had sold their souls to bad ideas, to crazy self-righteous, apocalyptic religions or sects, to lobbyists and who above everything pandered to big money and corruption. Kit, am I using words you don't understand?"

"That, Mr. President, is an insult! Are you kidding? I have an implant – a neutered disconnected mind implant – but an implant – of the Webster and Oxford dictionaries and a bunch of other stuff … In fact, I think sometimes my head is going to burst."

"Neutered and disconnected, that's good, otherwise …"

"Yes, my friend's mother – she was a Cosmos – boy, was she cool – she told us to disconnect everything. She said, never, but never, stay connected to the Mind or to any system for automatic updates!"

"She was very wise, your friend's mother."

"Otherwise, they could remote control us into crazy, or blow our brains to smithereens: right?"

"Yes, right, and worse – turn you into empty-eyed puppets, something like a zombie. Your friend's mother was very savvy, very cautious – that's good, very good."

"So my friend and I, we disconnected and neutered the implants – but the knowledge you have already acquired, you keep. So, as I said, I have Webster and the Oxford English dictionary and a lot of other languages and stuff."

"Right," he seemed relieved, "You should be safe, Kit. So, do you want me to continue?"

"Pray continue, Sir, Mr. President, I am all ears. Your tale would keep angels awake, as my friend used to say."

The President smiled, "Yes, yes, of course … Well, my young encyclopedic companion, a few of us, Centurions, officers, we decided that things could not continue; that if they continued, then the human race would …"

"… become extinct, I heard about that," Kit was climbing over a huge pipe, and she reached out to help the President. He looked at her, smiled, and took her hand and climbed up beside her. The pipe was warm, even warmer than the air, and it was hissing steam in several places where its seams had split.

"Yes, become extinct, just as we had driven tens of thousands of other species extinct before us, which was one of the problems, of course, for those thousands of species formed the basis of our own existence – key links in our food chain. The underpinnings of human civilization – and human survival – were collapsing, and collapsing fast. And so we officers overthrew the government of the old Republic."

"It was pretty much a rotten shell anyway, or so we've been told." Kit motioned with her laser. "Let's go down that side tunnel."

"Yes, so you were told, but the propaganda was mostly true, I'm afraid, even if I say so myself."

"I hate to admit it, Mr. President, but I believe you," Kit gave him one of her entrancing smiles, "But, Mr. President, you killed a lot of people."

"Yes, I did, I did kill a lot of people." He returned her smile, a bit warily, a bit absently, because he was remembering:

Talking about it took him back.

He was a mere general then; it was a different world. He was touted as a future Chief of General Staff. It was a stormy day. The Dome of Elysium needed repairs. The President and Congress were deadlocked. Washington had been abandoned thirty years earlier because of flooding and the plague and infestations of humanoid and animal mutants, and super-intelligent rats who favored Washington for some reason. The President of the Republic had taken refuge in Elysium City with the Cabinet. The Members of Congress were in their various clubs and hotels and Elysium homes. Meanwhile, amid general indifference, an estimated 4,600,000 people had died of starvation in the Third Midwest Famine. The decisive meeting took place in his own office, on the 80th floor of the Homeland Building. The coup was originally to have been bloodless – but plans and events have a logic of their own, often escaping from the originators' control.

"They will resist, General," said Colonel Bachmann.

"Yes, General, they certainly will resist," said General Patrick J. Hong, hands clasped behind his back and staring out over the floating skyscrapers and towers and domes, and glancing for a moment at the vast dome that protected the city from the churning, turbulent climate.

"Eliminate them," said Major General Konrad, "Eliminate them all – physically, every single one of them."

"Eliminate all the politicians?" He had raised an eyebrow. He could not really believe they were contemplating such a thing; it seemed unreal, like a dream, the action moving ahead automatically.

"Yes, and their families and staff, kill them all; it's the only thing to do; the rot is too deep."

And so it began ...

The discussion was violent; the officers threatened each other. Major General Heinrich Konrad warmed them that he had new bioweapons, stored at a secret location, which he could unleash at any time and destroy the whole of the human race.

"You have a universal bioweapon?" He was shocked. Konrad was an unscrupulous fanatic, but to develop, secretly, a doomsday weapon ...

"Yes – it's my own secret program!" Konrad folded his arms and pouted. His weak triple chin and his thin pencil mustache looked ridiculous; well, Konrad did think he was Napoleon.

"Collective suicide rather than surrender?" he had asked, thinking, this is blackmail on a very large scale.

Konrad turned toward him, light glinted off his glasses, "Yes, it is preferable for all to die, for every single human to die, than that the human race should wither away in this slow agony."

"You are insane, Konrad. I hope you realize that." He said it gently, hoping it might be taken, partly, as a joke. Calm the whole thing down, he must calm the whole thing down.

"Insane or not, none of you can stop me," Konrad shouted. His face was beaded in sweat. The mustache looked as if it had been drawn on with charcoal. Had anyone ever loved the man?

Konrad, through an untraceable encoded link, had provided a demonstration of what his secret biological weapon could do – reduce a person to a bubbling mass of sores, then to an undefined heap of mush, in a few minutes.

In the end, a decision was reached: all the politicians, and their families, spouses, children, mothers, fathers, and their staff, would be eliminated; most would be murdered.

He had managed to have most of the spouses and children and relatives spared, for a time at least; they would be sent to camps. It would all happen in one night, the "First Night of Purification."

He was weary – and depressed – when he summed up the consensus; after all, he would be murdering many people he thought of as friends; it would be a great crime, an unforgivable crime: "Yes, it shall be done. If they do not die, millions will die. What about the judges? At least they should be …"

General Hong turned away from the window and came to face him, "Unfortunately, General, the Constitution has been misused, and the Supreme Court long ago sold the Constitution out – blocked any real reform – turned the whole system over to money, to special interests, and to racists and religious fanatics, to worshipers of guns and violence, to the murderers of children, and the shills for ignorance …"

"Yes, yes, they did! That they did, indeed." Konrad smiled, a twist in the pencil mustache, glancing at him: *You see, General, you see! Once you start, you cannot stop!*

As he had listened to it all, he was more than weary. Once they entered into this spiral of killing and death, there might not be an end. But the alternative was the massive, certain agony for the whole human race …

"So, the judges die too?" Konrad clapped his hands, delighted, and swayed back and forth. His boots creaked. Out beyond the window, far away, an airship was landing near the midtown Volpe Tower. It all seemed like a dream.

"Yes, it must be done, and it must be done quickly." Hong crossed his arms and stuck out his lower lip, which was trembling; the man was human, after all; he didn't want to do this. In fact, most of them didn't want to do it ...

So the judges would die: that would be the "Second Night of Purification."

"Well ..." he prepared to sum it all up; he had argued in vain for compromise, for imprisonment rather than slaughter, for including more civilians in the new government, some of the less corrupt politicians; but he had been out-maneuvered; even now he was still hoping that perhaps he could find an argument to moderate the slaughter, some compromise that would avoid the killing that would ...

Konrad raised his hand. "There is one group that is very dangerous, even more dangerous than the rotten politicians and corrupt and foolish judges and even more dangerous than inquisitive journalists."

"Yes, and it is ...?" he raised his eyebrows; he knew and feared what was coming. And he knew too that Konrad was right. Society held within itself two forms of alien presence, two dangerous and powerful groups, which, though they were both very small groups, had great power, were very independent, and ...

"The hybrids and the SINs, they are too dangerous to be left alive," Konrad stood up; he pulled his laser pistol out of its holster.

"The hybrids are reasonable, they ..." said Shirley Ramsay, the Secretary of State, the only woman, and the only politician at the meeting.

"The SINs are mostly docile, most are designed for specific functions, most are almost saint-like, they ... won't be a problem," said General Ho; it was well known that his lover, a beautiful bisexual creature, was a SIN.

Konrad remained standing, "No, the SINs will be a problem. They are immune to most propaganda, they lack status-striving and, for the most part, they do not fear death; as you said, they are almost saint-like; they are healthy and strong, and they live a long time – in fact, some of them, a very few admittedly, have no expiry date, so they are a potentially a formidable subversive force. Strangely, these creatures we have created for our own convenience are not only non-conformist, but they seem to believe in liberty and its institutions with even more zeal than their creators; so they are more than ultra-dangerous."

"Be reasonable, Konrad," he said, "You cannot expect us to ..."

Konrad slammed his fist on the table, "Ladies and gentlemen!" He turned to the Secretary of State. "As I told you, Ms. Ramsay, I have a weapon that will destroy everyone, every single human being, and probably most mutants too, the bubonic plague number XIV. It will also kill you and me. It will kill everyone. I will unleash it unless you agree to my plan: total, pitiless elimination of hybrids, and SINs. And, if anything happens to me, if I do not come out of this meeting, General, if I do not come out of this meeting alive, then the plague will be released – automatically. So, General, you will have that little event on your precious conscience!"

"Look," he said, clearing his throat, "I think we should ..."

"Are you sure you mean that, Colonel Konrad," said the Secretary of State, "I mean, you would be decreeing the end of the human race, and ..."

Colonel Bachmann coughed. "The hybrids are like a collective mind. They are superhuman; their secret project is to control the human race, and then to supplant the human race. They are too intelligent! Look at the media they control. Look at the science they do! How many hybrids have won Nobel Prizes in the last few decades? It is way out of proportion to their numbers in society, which is very small. Yes, and some of the most visible human faces that the people adore – stars, writers, journalists, scientists – are hybrids. Or SINs. Why even Claire V Jacobs ..."

"That is true," the General said, "But that doesn't mean that they have a project, a secret project to take over the human race, they are just ...very talented, very strong, and ..." Here he was desperately trying to navigate a swift shift in course here; he had been the one most ferocious crusaders against the hybrids and SINs – until a few days ago. After all, just two years earlier, two hybrids had killed his woman and his child. He knew what hybrids could do. Now, well, he had changed his mind, new information had come to light, but it was too late, apparently too late. And he could not reveal what he knew, or what had happened to him.

Konrad stared at him and shouted, getting red in the face. "You have certainly changed your tune, General! What has happened to you? You have suddenly become naïve! There is a hybrid conspiracy. They are going to take over the human race. What about the 'Hybrid Protocols"? They eat people; they drink blood; in secret rituals dating back to their pagan gods, they sacrifice human children upon pyres of fire."

As the President remembered those feverish meetings, it all seemed mad, now, looking back on it, it seemed surreal. Perhaps they were all insane.

"Left, I think we should go left," it was Kit's voice.

They had come to a T-junction.

Kit repeated, "Left, I think we should go left."

"You're the navigator, Kit."

"Right," she gave him that dark look, half-quizzical, half-mocking. She was, the President realized yet again, a marvelously attractive girl – a divine spark of energy in her; undoubtedly, it had been there even before she became a hybrid.

They turned left, watching every crevice and crack, and watching too to see if the stone and metal arches would suddenly spring into life and attack.

"You were saying," said Kit, nudging at a piece of suspicious-looking stone with the point of her machete.

"Yes, yes … And, so, we decided," the President paused, "we decided to eliminate all of the politicians, most of the judges, and some troublesome journalists, and of course, the SINs and the hybrids." He paused again, and glanced at Kit.

"Gosh," Kit whispered; she had been listening with something almost like awe. Her brand-new friend and rescuer, the President-Leader, was admitting to mass murder, "So it really was mass murder."

"Yes, it was," the President took a deep breath, again glanced at Kit, and then looked around. They had come to a large underground chamber where several tunnels led off in different directions. Down one tunnel, they could hear the sound of running water; it was probably an underground canal. "What do you think, Kit?"

"Down this way," she pointed with the tip of the machete.

"Yes," said the President, scanning the walls, the ceilings, the floors, the beams, the pipes; danger lurked everywhere.

"So they wanted you to kill everybody," said Kit.

"Much of what Konrad said was nonsense. But he was right about one thing: hybrids can kill and do kill. I had seen it, seen it with my own eyes, Kit Candy. I had seen how without compunction, a hybrid can kill."

"Do you think I would kill without compunction?"

"No, Kit, I don't."

"Good, I trust you; you trust me."

"I would trust you with my life, Kit Candy, hybrid or not."

"Good, the trust is mutual, Mr. President."

Lost within the world within the Mind, plunged deep in the Mind-Sea, V's dream – the dream of sleeping with her lady-in-waiting, young slender pale Joan of Andorra – had dissolved, and, with it, a whole world disappeared, the world of the Spanish Inquisition, the dark handsome priest, the Duke her husband, and her tortured and dead lover, the witty, philosophic quibbler, all gone, just left as a memory, a false memory, or perhaps not.

Perhaps it was just an alternative universe, a path taken, or not taken, or perhaps all the paths had been taken, but we, now, or this version of ourselves, are on one path and cannot know about the others, the other paths, the other selves, the other lives we might have lived, the dizzying, unfolding, infinite, unending worlds of might-have-been.

Now those characters – the priest, the duke, the lover, even smooth-skinned delicate Joan – seemed like pale creatures in a fading frieze upon a wall or figures on a moth-eaten tapestry. Once again, V was standing on the marble balcony, overlooking the vast Amazonian forest. The sun shone brightly over the endless jungle; it sparkled, pure gold, on glimpses of the semi-invisible river.

The Mind-Child Laughed.

"So, you loved the girl Joan of Andorra, when you were a Duchess!"

"That was not real."

"Nothing is real," the tinkling little voice laughed, "But that was real!"

"I'm not so sure."

"Or everything is real!" the laughter echoed, "Or nothing."

"So, we take our pick."

"All those gods lost in the past, all that worship, all those sublime and nuanced feelings, all the little and great moments of pleasure, ecstasy, and pain, and all the flowers and fluttering leaves, and love-making on altar stones, and mystical nights, and weird unslaked yearnings, and all the temples and idols and cathedrals and icons … All that is real, and yet not real. Human beings are strange creatures, are they not?" The little voice was giggling. "They are addicted to make-believe, to fairy tales."

"Feelings are real," V said, "Meanings are real."

"You think so?"

"Yes, I do."

"Oh, you are a funny, funny girl!"

"I am?"

"Yes, you are! Off you go!"

Day becomes night. V is standing in the palace of many corridors. The Amazonian jungle stretches out below her, dark silver now in the moonlight. The moon is full, brightly glittering on the slivers of water – the great half-invisible river far below. V wonders what secrets and what creatures the jungle hides.

Again, the child laughs. V turns to look. The corridors and rows of columns march off. The child is nowhere to be seen. V wishes to see the child – to hold it in her arms: "Oh, do come out!"

"Not yet, not yet."

"Why? Don't you trust me?"

"I want to play. I am the Mind. I can do anything!"

"You still want to play?"

"Yes, I want to send you to a new place."

"Oh, please!" V was losing patience. Being the slave and puppet of an all-powerful, precocious, and capricious infant was not agreeable. She considered herself her own master or mistress. After all, she was a hybrid, a hunter, a predator, not a domestic pet; she was about to beg for a little peace and quiet and stability when an idea came to her.

"Aren't you afraid of the Boy?" V hazarded this; she didn't want to make the Mind-Child angry, but she did want the child to realize the urgency of the situation; various clocks were ticking.

"The Boy is busy!"

"What is he doing?"

"Bad things: he always does bad things. He looked for me, but he couldn't find me, so we have time to play!"

"Are you sure, I mean ..."

"Let's play. Let us past and present and future see, oh, V, you are such a naughty girl, like Claire, only worse perhaps ... Poof, poof, be gone!"

"No, please, I ..."

There was a flash of light. V found herself in a jungle.

"Oh, Zeus, where am I now, Oh, Baal, Oh, Astarte!" She looked around; she blinked. Things became clearer. There was an immense silence except for the twittering of birds. Splashes of bright sunlight rustled like music on the dark forest floor, a tangle of ferns and vines.

"Oh, yes, a jungle, I am in a jungle."

And for some unfathomable reason, she understood that she was some time in the distant future – it was perhaps two or three or even four hundred thousand years in the future – a world, here at least, wherever here was, of oppressive heat and tropical luxuriance.

Drums were pounding in the distance, and she was in human form, wearing a tan-colored Indian Jones hat, dark tan jungle boots, black jeans, a wide tan leather belt with a holster and six-shooter, a black leather vest, and a white bio-silk armored combat T-shirt, and, at her waist, the machete in its sling, and the old trusty ancient AK-47.

Why am I here? She frowned.

Hmm. I must go toward the drums, yes.

She pushed aside the heavy vines and the leaves, ignoring the flutter of wings and the twitter and cawing of birds, and after about forty minutes, she shoved her way through some heavy giant ferns, and came out into a clearing.

A great half-ruined temple stood in the middle of the clearing. It was a massive, simple, classic structure, with 30-foot-tall Doric columns, broad stone steps leading up to the entrance, a peaked roof, and an unadorned peaked pediment. The drumbeat came from within the temple. The sun was low and shining gold through the thick spinach-green foliage and was bright on one side of the temple; soon, in an instant, as can happen in the tropics, it would be night. She drew the Colt revolver and approached.

Best not to go in by the front entrance, she thought, so she walked around the temple, and went up the side steps. She managed to squeeze in between two huge blocks of stone that were slightly ajar and which just left enough room for her to slip through. Her belt buckle scraped against a rough outcropping of one of the stones; the blocks had been roughly but expertly hewn. They were perhaps ten feet square. She sidled her way inside the temple, and from the shelter of the stony crevice, she stared.

A congregation of worshipers, honey-colored bodies, almost naked, clad only, men and women, in loincloths, glowing with oil and sweat and in the light of hundreds of torches, were standing, waiting.

On the altar, which was a kind of stage, at least 15 feet above the worshipers, was the object of their worship.

It was an effigy, a stature, an enormous effigy, and it looked very much like – like her.

"Oh, oh," she sighed. History and time were playing more tricks, or the Mind-Child, who could travel through space and time and create worlds at the snap of a finger, was playing tricks. Or both were playing tricks. She'd been here before, or in a very similar place and time. Was this a real future? Was this a real alternative universe? Or was this an imaginary universe, conjured up by the Mind-Child, a sort of glorified Matrix Video Game.

The huge statute, perhaps thirty feet in height, glittered and sparkled, it was covered with or made of jewels and precious stones, and the lights were iridescent, but the color scheme was unmistakable, turquoise and green and with the giant golden almond upward slanting eyes, and just the right patterning too!

"*Sacré bleu, c'est moi*," V said, reverting to the French she had often used in her more piratical days, in the 17th and 18th Centuries, oh, so long ago, when she ventured ashore on tropical islands and exotic continents, trading in spices, slaves, mirrors, brass pots and pans, gems, and bales of silk.

She looked around to see if anyone had heard. No one had, though two pigeons that were on a perch just above her took flight in a white whir of wings, and a snake coiled on the rock just beside her – it was turquoise and green with lovely golden eyes exactly matching V's sartorial reptilian color scheme when she was in demon form. It raised its head and flicked its tongue in a friendly, curious way.

V was tempted to give it a little caress because she knew it was of a friendly disposition and that it was, of course, a distant cousin. "Sorry I roused you from your slumbers," she whispered, and the snake gazed at her for a moment and then lowered its head, blinked, and went back to sleep.

The oily light from the torches rippled over the voluptuous curves of the sacred body; the arms were uplifted, and the breasts too, and the hips were ample, and the legs solid, shapely, and long.

"Hmm," said V, "it's me, definitely me."

The worshipers hummed and shouted.

"So, I have become a true goddess! I'm not sure I like this!"

The drummers, just below the statue, drummed on their drums, a powerful narcotic rhythmic beat that got the blood racing

Then, out from the side, up on the altar, came a living idol, an image of the goddess.

It was V herself.

She was in reptilian-alien form.

She was an exact replica of the enormous statue.

She went to the platform, high above the crowd.

"*Sacré bleu, c'est encore moi*," V whispered to herself, "Are there two of me? This is very annoying!"

The worshipers fell on their knees and banged their foreheads on the sand- and mud-strewn floor of the temple.

"How can I be her and me at the same time?"

The worshipers were singing a chanting mumbling rhythmic song that rose in waves and was almost hypnotic.

"Of course, how stupid!" she slapped her forehead.

"The Mind-Child really is mischievous!"

"I'm meeting myself in the future, my future self."

The worshipers sang, the song echoed in the temple.

"That Mind-Child is playing seriously troubling tricks. I must talk to it about this!"

Still, illusion or reality, dream or psychosis, whatever it was, it was fascinating!

The reptilian V – V the Demon Goddess – raised its arms and said in a sonorous but wonderfully seductive and very female voice – rather, V thought, like those smooth almost unctuous female voices, often with British accents, that tell you to fasten your seatbelt because the plane is about to crash – and the living V Demon Goddess, raising her arms, in a gesture echoing the pose of the huge statue behind her, began to speak: "And, my dearly beloved people, what have you brought me today?"

It sounded like Latin. It was Latin!

Who would have thought!

The V Demon Goddess strode back and forth and looked down upon the fearful crowd of worshipers and repeated: "And, my dearly beloved people, what have you brought me today?"

There was silence.

The Demon Goddess V looked out over the crowd.

There was more silence.

Then out of the crowd came a nervous young man; he was leading a small girl by the hand; the small girl bowed her head.

Then V, the human time-traveler V in the Indiana Jones hat, noticed the ax and the blood bowl and she realized that the little girl was about to be sacrificed and she remembered too encountering just a little while ago the little boy she had sacrificed in the distant past and she remembered too encountering the gentle, handsome prophet who had offered her a power bar, back in one of the lost centuries, countless eons ago, when she was with Kat underground in Elysium and when human civilization still existed, and she remembered taking a bite of the power bar, and she knew that now she could live without drinking human blood and that this goddess, herself, V, in the future, had somehow regressed to blood sacrifice …

Which was not very nice!

The man bowed at the foot of the stairs leading to the altar.

A cry of joy went up from the worshipers.

The little girl looked up at her father.

There came a single wail from the public – the girl's mother, without a doubt, the girl's mother.

The little girl, who was wearing a simple white robe, straightened her shoulders, smiled at her father, put her hand up to his face, and then turned away and began to ascend the steps alone, step-by-step, very erect, ascending toward the impatient Goddess, the alien-reptilian V, who was now striding up and down, and slapping her thigh with one impatient claw. Several steps behind the girl, her father followed her up the stairs.

Thunder mumbled darkly out behind the temple. The air darkened, the humidity suddenly weighed down even more heavily. The foliage outside the temple, the thick glossy dark green voracious foliage, leaves, and fronds and vines and tentacles stirred in anticipation of rain.

The gods were angry.

V, the explorer from the distant past, was getting antsy.

Sacrificing little girls was no longer kosher, not in her book.

"What have I become?"

Now, with the Colt ready in her right hand, V stepped out of the shadows.

V, the Demon Goddess, striding up and down, stopped, and glanced in V's direction.

"We have a visitor," V the Demon Goddess said, "We have an interloper."

A great murmur went up from the crowd.

"So, a ghost of time past," said the V Demon Goddess.

"Yes, I have come to take the little girl," said V.

"No, I am going to take her. I am going to drink her blood, consume her flesh, and live an eternal life."

"No, I don't think you are."

V strode toward the stairs to the altar.

The worshipers looked up in horror.

V climbed the stairs, keeping her eyes fixed upon the Goddess who stood, arms akimbo, waiting for her.

"Ah," said the Goddess, "you are …"

"I am you; you are me," V said.

"You are me; I am you," the Goddess echoed, "how quaint, how interesting! What a pleasure to meet you!"

V strode the last few steps, to the top of the stairs, and now she stood beside V the Demon Goddess. She looked up at the giant statue. "So we have become divine," she said, and she looked down at the crowd of worshipers who were now cowering in terror, backsides in the air, their foreheads pressed against the earth, not daring to look up. Only the man and his daughter stood close to the two goddesses. The man looked down from time to time, then, narrowing his eyes, he looked up; the little girl fixed them with a steady, curious gaze.

"Yes, it has been so for dozens, perhaps hundreds of generations." The Goddess – V's demon self – was looking at her with interest. "At first, I – I mean, you – resisted the idea of human sacrifice, but the people insisted. There is a canker or taint in the blood of humans, I suppose, which returns from time to time, and they need scapegoats, sacrificial lambs. They cried out for sacrifice, and, seeking scapegoats, they carried out extremely bloody indiscriminate massacres and would only stop when I gave them a proper, bloodthirsty image of divinity." The V Demon Goddess reached out and touched V's T-shirt. "It's been a long time since I wore real clothes."

"Perhaps I can take the little girl; perhaps you can pretend to kill your victims and just take them somewhere else."

"Hmm," said the V Demon Goddess.

"Here, eat this," said V, and she pulled the extra power bar from her jean's pocket. "It was given to me by –"

"Oh, yes, I remember him," said the V Demon Goddess. The amber slits in her golden snake eyes narrowed and sparkled, "He was the savior, or so some people believed, a rabbi from Judea. I liked him, a wonderful man, a true prophet, mystic, and moral teacher." She accepted the power bar and began to unpeel it.

"So we are one," V said, as she watched the V Demon Goddess split the bar into four parts.

"Yes," the V Demon Goddess said, she handed a part of the bar to V and a part to the little girl and a section to the man who was standing beside his daughter, and then she took the remaining piece of the bar,, and she raised her arms, and she cried out like thunder, "Behold!"

All the faces looked up.

"Behold the sacrifice!" the V Demon cried, "Behold and wonder!"

A great sigh went up from the multitude; eyes were round with wonder.

"Eat now," she said, whispering to V and the man and his daughter.

And they ate.

"Behold!" V the Demon Goddess cried out.

And the V the Demon Goddess put one claw on the little girl's head and the other on V's head, and she whispered, "I hope this works!"

"Me too," said V, not knowing what was supposed to work.

And the V Demon Goddess exalted. Her claws were firmly on their heads, "Behold the wonder! Behold the spirit! Yes! Behold the sacrifice!"

Boom!

There was a flash of light.

Then, there was …

"I think I know. I think I know. I think I know …" Kit repeated the mantra. She and the President were approaching the Lair of the Mind, or so Kit hoped. "I am sure it's down this way," Kit was saying, just as the roof of the tunnel began to drip liquid. Kit looked up. The rain from the roof got thicker and thicker.

"What is this?" The President held out his hand, captured some of the liquid.

"Not normal rain." Kit blinked; the stuff rained down on her hair, on her face. It stung her eyes. The rain was heavy now and smelled like vinegar. The President sniffed at the water in the palm of his hand. "It's slightly acidic."

"Which means …?"

"Which means the Mind is probably preparing this material, the stone, the cement, the steel beams and rods of the reinforced concrete so that …"

"So, it can digest it," said Kit, completing the thought that she read in the President's eyes.

"Yes, it's softening it up."

"Yuk," Kit looked around, "Yuk." Mist rose from the pavement. The tunnel was thick with it; it stuck to the skin, sparkled like radioactivity, and tasted like ash. Some parts of the city, Kit suddenly realized – having what amounted to a vision, actually *seeing* what was happening – some parts of the city had already collapsed in fire and flame and acid; people had been consumed too – consumed in acid, or burned by fire, or destroyed by madness. The ash taste was the taste of death, like in the concentration camps long ago, like in the terrorist attack on New York a century or so ago, like Hiroshima, like Nagasaki.

"Look at that," said the President. Part of the wall of the tunnel had been eaten away by what was probably pure acid.

"Awesome," said Kit, "It is awesome in a horrible sort of way."

A dead half-eaten ghoul lay across the threshold to a side tunnel, under a broken cable that danced back and forth, hissing out bright showers of sparks, garish and brilliant in the phosphorescent half-light. The ghoul's chalk-white skin was bubbling, hissing, writhing, and turning black.

"I think we are getting close."

"Yes.

"You were telling me, Mr. President, about how hybrids can kill," Kit put her hand in his; he squeezed her fingers and held her hand; how odd, thought Kit, how weird that I am with this man who is a mass murderer, and the hunter and killer of hybrids, and I am a hybrid! Boy! Was life strange!

"Yes, well, let me tell you, Kit, I met one hybrid, the Queen of the Hybrids; she is your Queen I suppose now that you have been bitten."

"Yes, I guess she is."

"Her name is V. She is the one you spoke to."

"Gosh," Kit said, suddenly excited, "She's the Queen of the Hybrids! Gosh, that's awesome! Like I told you, I gave V my instructions on how to get to the World Mind. Maybe we'll meet her soon." Kit let the President help her over a pile of rubble, and she looked up into his eyes, suddenly thinking, maybe this is what it would be like to have had a father; to have a father like this, well it would be …

"Yes, I suppose we shall see her soon, our V," said the President, "And I am sure she too is trying to save the world."

Kit saw that there was a strange light in the President's eyes; she could sense that he was excited: Was he going to try to kill this V, this Queen of the Hybrids?

"Yes, perhaps, if she follows my instructions, and if she's lucky, well, if the Mind and that Evil Foul thing hasn't been playing too many tricks, she'd be coming down here, somewhere close …but from a different direction, I think."

"I wonder, I wonder if she can stop the Mind. If she can stop it, then, perhaps, then, I don't have to …"

"Then, you don't have to turn that key and blow us all up and kill us, and everything for a 200-kilometer radius around us."

"Yes."

"So, we wouldn't have to be ground-zero …?"

"Yes."

"That would be very nice, Mr. President, I would even call that a positive development, not dying and all, not killing everything, I think that's a very good prospect. Let's hope this V knows what she's doing."

"Yes, yes, not dying would be good, I suppose, particularly for someone young, like you." The President stopped, and frowned, as if remembering something very vivid. "It was just about here that I … I knew her, V, I mean. I knew her, I mean, I met her; yes, I think, it was not far from here: on a canal; perhaps that canal down there; there had been an accident – well, a murder – in one of the old subway lines …" He climbed up and over a large fallen pipe; Kit climbed up behind him; he slid down the other side; he was below her now, looking up at her. He held out his arms.

"Tell me," Kit Candy said, and she slid down into his arms. Kit did wonder at the man. Here was possible salvation. If this V character managed to shut down the Mind's appetite, then the world would be saved. They should be dancing and shouting Hallelujah. The Hybrid Queen be praised! Instead, the President seemed to have gone all vague and misty. Well, she would humor him, and maybe learn something about this mysterious V. They would get to the Mind soon enough, and then they would see. Meantime, she said, "Tell me! Tell me how you met V."

"Yes, I'll tell you," the President said, holding Kit, his hands on her waist, steadying her for an instant, looking into her dark bright eyes, and then letting her go, a beautiful young woman, a teenager still, and now a hybrid, a daughter, like his daughter, a hybrid, like his daughter, like his dead daughter, and yet pale and dark and intense, so different from blond, sunny, exuberant Cosmos Miranda, who had seemed so alive that he had thought she could never die, and yet, because of him, because he tried to get her to safety, die she did, with Nikki, her flawless guardian. "Yes," he said, his heart in a downward spiral, "Yes, Kit, I'll tell you."

As he told her, he remembered: His first vision of V in the crowded clamorous echoing subway station. He was in the midst of the jostling bodies, about to board the Intercity Underground Express, and then a scream from inside the subway car, and then, in the panicked crowd, he was face-to-face with her: a beautiful, startlingly beautiful, pale young woman with bright, fresh blood on her lips, a smudge on her chin and her collarbone, and dribbles down her jacket, her eyes looking up into his, frightened eyes, their darkness so deep they seemed to be a gateway to infinity, and then … then …

She breaks free, somehow she breaks free; he can hear the screaming of the crowd, even now; and he remembers more – *every instant of it is so vivid* – he sees her fling off her high heels, he sees her run, bullets are flying, zipping past him, zipping past her, he runs after her, she leaps down onto the tracks, he feels the SWAT team – some of his own men undoubtedly – behind the crowd, coming out at the far end of the tracks – their bullets explode in front of him, splatter against the white ceramic face of the arch over the tunnel; they are shooting high to avoid hitting him; she is running into the tunnel now; she is fast, he leaps down onto the tracks, he follows her; she disappears; they are deep in the tunnel now, thundering darkness; suddenly, a train is coming; for an instant he is blinded, caught in the train's headlights, not knowing where the woman has gone, he stumbles, he is confused, he realizes he is confused, he knows he is going to die, and then he is pulled, jerked off the tracks, and feels the train clip the heel of his shoe – no damage done – and, as the train whooshes by in a thunder of smells and noise and passing lights, there is a face close to his; she is smiling; her lips are bright red; her skin is a perfect chalk-white, flawless, but still streaked with blood; and, yes, her eyes seem so deep there is no bottom to them, no soul in them, and her breath is sweet, and she says, "You are a brave man, a foolish man." And then she springs to her feet and says, "Follow me, then, if you must." He follows her along the tunnel, down a manhole, down the greasy rusty rungs of an iron ladder, along another half-flooded tunnel, she leaps into the water with him, swirling downwards in the current, then they emerge, him breathless, and climb out onto a wet dripping platform beside a wide, deep underground canal. And that is where they make love. That is where they both climax, in ecstasy and intensity, such as he had never known. That is where she morphs, showing him what she truly is – a demon – the alien side of the hybrid and where she declares her desire, even her love. Then, having kissed him one last time, she disappears, slipping into the water. Quickly he pulls on his clothes: traces of blood, traces of mud, ripped and torn here and there – she was so eager, tearing off his clothes. The SWAT team Centurions arrive, bright hand-lights beaming this way and that, weapons out, breath in bright misty clouds in the humid air.

"General, General – are you alright, sir, are you alright?"

She had gotten away, already disappeared; he looks down at the rippling dark water, underground lights reflecting on curling eddies and swirls, mist rising. It smells of ozone; it smells of the ocean; it smells of freedom.

"You took a terrible risk, sir."

He looks absent.

"Are you alright, sir?"

"She got away. I should have … I could have …"

Lights and mobile sonar are scanning the canal; the scanning takes only a few moments; the officers glance at him, shake their heads; there is nothing there; she is gone.

"You had better come back, sir; you had better see."

And so he had gone back with them, wading through the half-flooded tunnels in a daze, flashlights wavering on walls, voices echoing, climbing up the rusty rungs in a daze; already, in that instant, it seemed that what had happened had happened a lifetime ago, or perhaps in another life, that he had climbed down the rungs, followed her, and … Now he is walking with the Centurions – all in awe of him, the Leader, their Leader – General James R Grant – the man who confronted a hybrid, all alone, single-handed, the man who will save Cosmos, the man who will save the human race, humanity's last best hope – they walk along the tunnel, and out into the brightness of the station.

"I'm fine, Lieutenant, I'm fine," he keeps saying, and then, all business, "Right, then. Let's see what this looks like, let's see what our hybrid, our monster has done." He knows already what has happened. The confession had been in her eyes. Somehow, mind-to-mind, she had painted a picture, of what she had done. She had confessed to him, bashful and subdued, like a little girl.

The traditional yellow ribbons crisscrossed the platform; a forensics team was already there; mini-barrier drones were buzzing around to keep gawkers away, though there were no gawkers; the station had been cleared – just a few frightened witnesses were being interrogated – and most of the SWAT team were standing around looking useless and, in the anticlimax of the female villain's brilliant escape, vaguely humiliated, thumbs in belts, heads hanging, mouths twisted, eyes wary, joking among themselves. It seemed very big, the station, the platform, echoing, and it seemed too bright – he wondered whether, in spite of her precautions, she had bitten him inadvertently, and he was becoming one of them and perhaps allergic to light – he shivered inwardly in horror – and he entered the subway car. "This is it, General. You can see the splash of blood and a trail of drops too. She was in a hurry."

At first, he thinks it is a dummy, an old-fashioned store window manikin; a young man, pale as a scarecrow, empty, a husk of a man, clothes hanging loose, ribs showing, the eyes open, staring; there were pale fang marks on his throat, right at the jugular, the victim was – he had been – maybe 26–27.

Lieutenant Alice Benjamin, his Intelligence Officer, was consulting a tablet, the light of the screen shining up, sculpting her handsome face, shining on her dark eyes: she read it off: "So: he was Hector Cramer, twenty-seven years old, worked in Burb Slum Jersey, one relative, his mother, lives in an outer Rust Burb of Jersey, he had no security clearance, not a Cosmos, not a Sub, just an unclassified Burb Worker-Bee."

Lieutenant Frobisher was standing beside Benjamin. "Still, he was human, poor fellow, and he had human weaknesses."

"Yes." He glances at Frobisher, and Frobisher, their best forensic specialist, nods and crouches down, next to the body, "He was, yes, he was, he was certainly human, lusty young chap too I suppose. See here, General: he'd unzipped his fly, his hand is still there, locked on the zipper, half-unzipped."

Yes." He lets his gaze rest on the hand. It was gray, the hand, the skin like wax, the veins standing out, hollowed and milky-blue; it was pathetic and emptied: the puppet-like dead husk of a hand, mummifying already.

Frobisher uses a pointer, "She must have seduced him with the promise of sex … and then … she probably began to kiss him, and then …"

While Frobisher talks, the General stares at the half-unzipped zipper and at the dead-weight, puppet-like, of the paper-mâché hand; it makes the horror worse somehow, too vivid. He flashes back – that was *me*; that could have been me. But it wasn't; but if she had not already drunk deep, to satiety?

I would be an empty scarecrow husk rotting in the sewer of the city.

Anger rises, and yearning, and desire; hatred and lust surge.

I want to kill her.

I want to make love to her.

I want to hold her in my arms.

I want my hands on her throat.

I want to possess her, and break her, and keep her, tame her, enslave her. And I want her to be mine!

"General, I think we'd better let forensics …"

The lieutenant's voice breaks his reverie. He rubs his eyes. "Yes, Lieutenant Frobisher, yes, yes, of course … Thank you, and thank you, Lieutenant Benjamin, thank you."

"V had emptied the poor fellow," the President said, stopping to gaze at Kit, "She had drunk him down to the last drop. He looked like a puppet, the husk of a man. So, you see, Kit, I know V, I know what hybrids can do. But there was more I had to learn, that came later, when it was too late."

Kit stared at him and blinked. She reached out, stroked his arm.

"Ah, Kit," he said, nodding, noticing the glint of tears in her eyes.

"So," she said, sniffling.

"So?"

"So, the canal we want to follow is down that way," Kit pointed and then looked up at him. "We will have to get to the canal, and wade for some distance, some of it is usually quite shallow; and if the Mind hasn't screwed up my sense of space too much, I think we will be almost there."

"Good, Kit, thank you!"

He hasn't told Kit the whole story, of course: All he tells Kit is that V had killed lusty young Hector Cramer and left him sitting like a hollow wax museum display in the First Class Car of the Intercity Underground Express; that he chased V down a tunnel, spoke to her; just those few words, when she saved him from the train; then he chased her again, and she escaped and disappeared into the swirling water of a canal, but he does not tell Kit that he and V made love. No, he does not tell her that.

Kit senses that there is more to the story, but does not insist – and she cannot yet read minds, not easily in any case, but she senses a shadow, an ambiguity, a mingling of desire, and awe, and, perhaps, something more.

"But she did save your life," she says.

"Yes, Kit, she did save my life," he says, knowing that, in some strange way, he is still in love, still very much in love.

No, damn it, man! he tells himself. *It is lust; you only knew her for a few minutes.*

But, then, there is the other thing …

This other thing that made those few moments so much more important …

This other thing, and the meetings and sightings it led to, it changed you; they changed you. But it was too late – too late for so many.

"Gosh," says Kit, "Damn! Look at this!"

They had come to a place where the tunnel had caved in.

"We can't go any farther here." The President puts his hands on his hips; this is endless, this maze, this confusion.

"No," Kit is looking around. From above, far above, there are thunderous sounds, explosions, buildings collapsing, sirens, cries of agony; Elysium is dying. "We backtrack, we have to backtrack."

"You are my guide, Kit, you lead; I follow."

"Yes, sir. I apologize for this dead end."

"No need to apologize, Kit."

He lets Kit lead. She is a good guide, in this god-forsaken, shifting wilderness of a place; she is calm, masterful, and really, he trusts her; and she is so young! The place does look weird, as if all the tunnels, canals, walkways, and pipes and subway lines had been shuffled. The Mind must still be playing more tricks. Still, Kit soldiers on and the President follows. They come out of a tunnel onto a wide underground canal. "Look, we're going to have to wade down this canal," Kit says, "It's the most direct way, it *must* be the most direct way."

"Good, Kit, let's go. You seem to know all the mysteries."

"Not all, but some. I called myself the sewer rat. I liked to explore the city, the Religious Bazaar, the Sin Zone, and even down here. Though down here can be a bit dangerous, I brought a friend of mine" – *Oh, Miranda,* she thinks, evoking the name and its shining aura, wishing she could tell the President about her marvelous friend, now dead, now ashes, but the name is sacred, a sacred talisman and she will not mention it – "I brought her down here, a Cosmos. She liked adventure."

"You brought a Cosmos down here?"

"Yep, believe it or not," Kit grinned.

"Well, I guess we've got to jump in," the President lowered himself carefully into the water. It was almost waist-deep. "This may be dangerous," he said, "We have no idea what is swimming in these waters."

"That's right; we don't." She reached out so he could grab her.

He took her around the waist and lowered her down, gently, carefully.

"I imagine you taught your Cosmos, ah, friend, some facts of life, Kit Candy."

"Yes, I did. But it was reciprocal. She taught me lots too – and her mother, her mother, was just fantastic and …"

There was an echoing sound in the canal tunnel, a distant scream, a roar of anger, then what sounded like an enormous sob.

"Something's in trouble."

"Or somebody."

"Okay, let's go."

The surface of the water glimmered under the dim lights and glowed from phosphorescent lichen and mosses that grew on the walls, radiating different colors, like a rainbow. Kit glanced at the display: life proliferated; you destroyed old forms of life, and new forms of life rose up.

"Do you feel them? – things, swimming; they're brushing against my legs."

"Yes, I feel them."

"They're nibbling."

"Yes, little nibbles."

"Are they testing us?"

"Maybe, maybe they're *tasting* us." She grinned up at him. He smiled back.

The nibbles continued; they seemed friendly, like little love-bites.

They waded on, thigh-deep, guns at the ready.

The distant groaning could still be heard – and the explosions echoing from up above.

Ken and Alison had left the Concourse and the wrecked bloodied elevator behind – and the severed arm with the sparkling gold ring – and explored the 25th floor, searching for a stairwell that would lead downwards.

They found one, and went down five floors; then they came to a large landing; they would have to cross the landing to get to where the stairs continued its zigzag path downwards. The landing was about 50 meters in length. It had several clusters of palm trees, a café with a terrace, and a Kindergarten all along one side. In the Kindergarten, behind a plate glass window, bodies of children were everywhere, lying in splashes of blood. The plate glass itself was smeared with blood, little handprints of blood. The café tables were turned over and smashed, and a few people lay dead on the terrace. Nothing seemed to be moving.

"Okay, let's go," Ken whispered.

"Yes, darling," Alison whispered back.

Quickly and quietly, they began to cross the landing.

A robot waiter came out of the café. He was impeccable in his black jacket and trousers, with a white serviette over his arm. He nodded at Ken, and tilted his head toward a lurking danger which lay just ahead.

Ken followed the robot's glance.

Oh, oh!

Ken's muscles tightened.

Alison took the cue; she went absolutely still.

In the middle of the landing, between two thick clusters of palm trees and ferns, were two zombie-bats. They had been reclining on flattened deckchairs, lying on their sides, face-to-face. They were licking each other. Now, one of them turned its beady eyes and its snout toward Ken and Alison, who were in the middle of the landing, far from any shelter.

The male zombie-bat mewled and bared its fangs.

The other zombie-bat, a female, mewled, and growled. It turned its snout toward Ken and Alison and licked its fangs.

The two zombie-bats scrambled to their feet.

"They were making out," whispered Alison, making it half a question; somehow she'd sensed what was happening, she'd had something like an inner vision.

"Yes, something like that, it looked like something like that."

"It must be horrible for them, the poor dears."

"Yes, darling, well …" Ken's Colt was empty, and in its holster. "Damn!" He lifted the ancient M-16 assault rifle. He pulled the trigger; it made a clicking sound. But nothing happened. The bloody thing jammed. "God!" He tried again. Again it clicked, and clicked, but nothing happened. The zombie-bats were crouching, ready to leap, they growled, in unison, bloodred foam frothed from their mouths. Their eyes drilled into Ken's eyes. The sense of hatred was so intense it was almost paralyzing.

"Give it to me." Alison reached out, her hand ready to receive the M-16.

"What?"

"Give it to me, darling. I'll try."

"But …"

"I know, I know."

Alison took the gun, she slid her hand over it, her fingers seemed to know precisely where they were going; she felt for the magazine; deftly, she flipped a small invisible switch, and she disengaged the magazine, pulled it out, and slipped it back in, it went smoothly this time, and she flipped the little switch, and she locked it in place.

"There," she said, "that should work."

She held it out, blindly; he took it.

"How in the world …?"

"I don't know."

"Cosmos Scouts?"

"Yes, I guess. Muscle memory, or something," she smiled, the bright blind smile; Ken began to think that Alison was a saint, or a mystic, or something more than he had ever suspected.

The two zombie-bats leaped.

Ken let off a burst of fire.

One of the zombie-bats, the male, was caught in the forehead. Its skull burst in a crimson-gray shower of gore. It looked like grotesque Roman candle fireworks from ancient festive times. The beheaded body crashed down beside Alison and Ken, skidded across the landing, and smashed up against the balustrade.

The female screamed and turned in mid-air, its claws reaching out, snatching for Alison, but Alison, somehow sensing the oncoming beast, ducked, and the claws just brushed past her. The female smashed against the far wall. It tried desperately to get up. It turned, snarling. It was crying. It was yelping.

"It's in mourning," said Alison, brushing her hair with one hand, just where the zombie-bat had almost touched her, almost caught her.

"Yes, maybe, darling, but …"

"Yes, darling, I understand. It's them or us." Alison leaned against Ken. Ken took a deep breath. He looked the female zombie-bat in the eye. The zombie-bat struggled up, and crouched, preparing to leap, her eyes drilling into Ken's eyes. Ken felt he was being drawn into some grotesque, horrible world of suffering and damnation. A cartwheel kaleidoscope of images whirled thorough his head. He saw a sandstorm, he saw a farmhouse, he saw a handsome young girl, her slender body barely concealed by a colorless, paper-thin, nondescript country dress, with freckles and green eyes; he saw a man – handsome and diabolical – standing, preaching from the porch of some weird old farmhouse that must be in the Dead Lands in the Central Desert somewhere, and he felt a horrible fear, and he watched the girl's face, and she saw what he was feeling, she saw the transformation, she was seeing the believers changing into monsters, and her face – and he realized for some reason that her name was Billie McAdams and she was the slave and the lover of the preacher – and, as she watched the believers being tranformed into monsters, her face reflected horror and fear and pity: and he knew that she was looking at him and that he, Ken, was one of those who was being transformed into a monster. Through Billie McAdams' gaze of pity, he felt the full horror of those – and he felt he could have been one of them – who had wished to save their souls, but who, because of that very yearning, had forever lost their souls; and, blinking, coming back to himself, he stared at the zombie-bat and he pulled the trigger.

The zombie-bat's skull and face and neck exploded.

"My poor darling," Alison cupped his face in her hands and kissed him. "My poor darling. That was terrible for you. Each instant is an eternity, isn't it?"

"Yes, yes, it is," he held Alison as tight as he could.

The female zombie-bat's body arched up in convulsions; it trembled; steam rose from the flesh, and it began to change into a human body. The same was happening with the male.

"Let's go, Ken, let's go."

"Yes, yes, let's go." Ken was tempted to stay. He was eager, for some horrible self-hating reason, to see the whole transformation; he was almost hypnotized, drawn in, he wanted to live the whole thing, feel it in his flesh, and once again see through the eyes of –

"Ken!"

"Yes, yes, let's go!"

Ken glanced back. "Thanks!" he said.

The robot waiter nodded. "You are welcome, Monsieur!" It bowed and went back into the empty café.

CHAPTER 10 – BURBITE APOCALYPSE

Good old Norman C. Schleifer, out in the Burbs, left Bio-Futures behind. It was all a bit of an anticlimax; the world still looked shitty; it had not changed; the World Revolution had not yet become manifest.

No angels sang. No camera crews had appeared. Fame and sainthood would come later, almost certainly. The sky was livid and leaden with streaks of sickly yellow, and bands of absolute black. There seemed to be twisters marching in from the south and the west; they were still far away, though, and they were headed, or so it seemed to Norm, for Elysium.

Norm stopped at one desolate, uninhabited corner – an empty sidewalk, a ruined Burger Joint, and one lamppost – where he had a good view of Elysium. The old Elysium Dome was not looking so hot. Flashes of lighting sizzled and zipped along its surface. Lots of the lights inside the Dome seemed to be out; and, then, there were cracks in the Dome, or that was what it looked like, though, it couldn't be; of course not. It couldn't be; it was impossible. Even weirder – and this was *really* impossible – it looked like some of the downtown towers, above the old point of what had been the south end of Manhattan, were no longer there. It must be the weird light, refracting something or something like that: making what should be visible invisible. Still, it fucking well made Norm nervous. The order of things was breaking down. Revolution was one thing, but this was …

Norm heard screams, but he ignored them.

He turned a corner and lo and behold! Here were two of the Halloween or carnival people, dressed up as zombies or something. One was a woman, and the other was a guy.

"Hey, Mister, trick or treat!" The guy gave him a ghastly grin – he didn't have any lips, and his eyes were painted to look just like empty sockets. He was wearing what looked like an ancient blue blazer, with big bright brass buttons, but no trousers to speak off, just ragged, filthy underpants, and one sock, on one foot, and one shoe, on the other. The woman was wearing hardly anything; it looked like the remains of a white wedding dress, but it was soiled, all yellow, like she had pissed herself in some gigantic uncontrollable way. Her grin was even worse. Half her jaw was gone.

Norm thought they were not funny.

"Trick or treat!" The guy came lurching toward Norm. The cadaverous grin was worse now. And, in a hand that looked like a skeleton hand, the guy clutched a baseball bat. The woman staggered forward too, and a section of her hair – like a big clump including the scalp – fell off. She swiped at it, caught it, looked at it for a second, and threw it away.

Definitely, they were not funny.

The guy was getting close.

Norm sneezed. Oh, boy, a whopper of goo! Right out of his nostrils! And now it was stuck on the back of his hand. He wiped the gob off on his trousers. What the hell is happening around here?

"Trick or treat, Mister, trick or treat?" The guy raised the baseball bat.

"Look, partner, I figure we really can't do business," Norm said. He lifted the automatic and shot the guy in the forehead. It was an expanding explosive bullet with a bit of delayed-action magic about it. Norm shot the dame, too, just for good measure; she was headed at him too. For a second nothing happened, the round hole appeared in the guy's forehead, but he came straight on, with that weird horrible lopsided grin. "Trick or treat!"

Then the guy's head exploded.

The headless body kept coming.

Norm shot it in the knees, both knees. The kneecaps and knees exploded, bone fragments and splinters flying all over the fucking place. The guy's torso hesitated for just a second, then pitched forward, some of the bones cracking and splintering into bits when it landed.

The woman's body – her chest – exploded. She fell into bits and pieces, and the bits and pieces shot out every which way, and some rolled around and ended up in the gutter.

The guy's torso was now crawling toward Norm, wiggling like some goddamn worm. This was utterly ridiculous. These people didn't know when to give up.

Norm shot the shoulders of the torso.

The arms exploded, detached from the body; the two arms wiggled and groveled around, fingers trying to get purchase on the pavement.

The torso wiggled and squirmed, but it could no longer advance.

"Well that's that, partner, I am indeed sorry to say it, but our little dance is done." Norm sneezed, another disgusting big gob of green and white snot.

"Well, well, what have we here, old Norm sneezing up his insides, gobs of goo and snot, not so good, not so good!" He put his foot on the guy's cranium and stomped down. The cranium disintegrated like dust.

"Well, partner, been nice knowing you! What is done, is done, and it is time for me to sashay home to my little abode, where I will lie me down and contemplate the end of all things and the end of time and the Second Coming and such-like assorted miracles."

The woman's skull, well, half of it, bubbled something, a dusty squirt of sound. "You absolute shit!" it sounded like.

"No offense taken, ma'am! Goodbye, my hardies, goodbye," Norm shouted as he turned away and left the two moldering cadavers behind. Really weird folk they were! He wondered where they had come from.

Back in Elysium …

As the President reflected on it, he saw more and more clearly how the encounter with V had changed him; but not enough, and not soon enough. And, in any case, he was trapped, trapped by his allies, trapped by the logic of the situation – a coup d'état and a revolution have an implacable logic: the killing accelerates, the murders multiply, the beast requires more and more in the way of enemies and scapegoats.

The President didn't tell Kit of the full extent of the violent arguments in the Centurion Council; he didn't tell her that, in the end, he changed sides, fighting to defend the hybrids and SINs; he admitted that, yes, they were a threat to humans; but he had argued that they might be made into allies, that they were strong and inventive, they controlled large parts of the press, they included some of the world's most brilliant scientists, and very talented people …

"They are not 'people'! May I remind you of that, General?" Colonel Gelder-Highsmith said, "They do not fall under the Pontifical definition of a human person. The only persons are human persons. The hybrids and SINs are unnatural. His Holiness has pronounced them an abomination. A human person is created only by the coupling of a human male with a human female in the masterful male-on-top missionary position as God intended without any artificial aids and impediments and as our forefathers practiced until ungodly manners and techniques were introduced by so-called civilization to pollute the sublime purity and sanctity of love."

While listening to Gelder-Highsmith, the General had mused that His Holiness – an embittered waspish Teutonic withered old ecclesiastical ideologue – who had written a five-volume treatise on love – and who was a cutthroat clerical politician with a rather sadistic taste for young boys, the younger, the better – probably knew very little about love, unless it was sadistic carnal mastery involving imposed bondage, whipping, and branding; but he kept that opinion to himself. Sometimes he regretted that the religious revival had spread so fast and so far. Politically religion could be useful – opiate of the masses as both Karl Marx and Napoleon Bonaparte had understood – but religions which claimed to preach love and humility often seemed happier preaching hatred, ignorance, prejudice, misogyny, racism, and selective genocide, and their leaders often cultivated a very high – and unjustified – sense of self-worth, presumption, and self-righteousness, almost always spreading an intense hatred of curiosity, of freedom of thought and scientific inquiry. It was all very destructive. To his mind, zealots of very ilk – whether secular or religious – were distasteful – and extremely dangerous. The Cosmos class, with all its faults, did believe in free inquiry, and was skeptical of absolutes – except, of course, of absolutes that justified its privileged position.

Konrad, an atheist, but a true believer in his way, and the primary apostle of Cosmos and species purity, said that he thought the only way to solve the problems of humanity was to eliminate most of humanity itself. "Kill the wretches, Kill them all!" After all, nano-robots and nano-replicators can create anything. Work is obsolete. We don't need people; we don't need lower-class people; we don't need Burbites and Subs and Outlanders. We can eliminate them all. And we can breed a new super-race of humans, the apotheosis of purified humanity, the true Cosmos.

He knew that Konrad had – as he claimed – truly been developing new biological weapons designed to wipe out humanity: new super-potent versions of smallpox, Bubonic plague, and other horrors. Only "approved people" would get the antidote or the vaccine.

If there *was* a vaccine. For some versions of these biological weapons, it seemed there might not yet be any antidote of vaccine at all.

In fact, the General's personal spy networks told him that – though the evidence was spotty – the vaccine had not yet been developed for Konrad's main bioweapons, so if any of those little pet projects of Konrad got loose, catastrophe would follow. And there were certainly laboratories the General did not even know about, laboratories hidden in the lawless chaos of the Burbs or even in the Outlands and Dead Lands that his spies had not uncovered, laboratories working on death machines, powerful death machines. *My name is Death.*

He didn't tell Kit Candy that he had compromised to get a majority on the Council, and that, to prove the waverers that he could be trusted to be ruthless, he had promised he would eliminate the hybrids and the SINS. He didn't want to dignify or excuse what he had done – or justify it – under the label "*compromise.*"

But he did tell her that he, personally, planned and carried out the neutralization, roundup, assassination and imprisonment of the hybrids, and the elimination of the SINs, it was done brilliantly, he had to admit, at least in conception it was brilliant. The actual execution of the plan was messy and tragically flawed.

"Gosh," Kit Candy said, looking at him and shivering.

"Yes, it was me," he said, expecting her to spit at him or to run or to make an impassioned speech condemning him. "I'm the one."

"How horrible," she said, and she took his hand and squeezed it.

"Kit Candy," he said.

"Mr. President," she had seen into his mind, just a little bit, just enough to realize that he was deliberately giving her the unvarnished and ugly version of the truth, leaving out his efforts to stem the disaster, leaving out his struggle to save the hybrids and SINs. He was minimizing his efforts, in the end, to mitigate – even avoid – the disaster.

"It was difficult, I know," Kit said. For some reason the fact that this man – who seemed to her so good – had done such terrible things made Kit very sad, and, strangely, it caused a wave of love and yearning to rise in her heart: she wanted to understand, she wanted to forgive. She tightened her grip on his hand.

"You are a remarkable young woman, Kit," He gazed at her for an instant, such beauty and grace in humanity, and now it was all probably going to be snuffed out. Yes, he had been the organizer, but he didn't like it – not even the idea of it.

He had thought it was a huge waste – a tragic mistake.

In fact, on the very eve of the coup d'état, something more had happened that had radically changed his view of hybrids and SINs, something that he had to keep a secret, an absolute secret.

To try and mitigate the disaster, he had arranged to have most of the hybrids "saved" and "stored" in a mining colony in the Dead Lands; there they would at least survive, even if in terrible conditions. The Culling had been messy: many hybrids and some Subs, and even human dissidents – many Cosmos among them – had been casually killed – massacred – on the way to the camp, by sadists and imbeciles. Much of the work had, of necessity and for political reasons, been subcontracted to mercenaries, and some of those mercenaries had been idiots and, worse than idiots, many were sadists.

Most of the SINs, with one or two exceptions, he couldn't save: they were too exposed, too well-known, too visible, though one of those exceptions, Nikki Hughes, the most visible of all, was, by careful planning and pure good luck, saved. Her "cover," being ancient, was deep; only he and a few other trusted officers knew that the beautiful Nikki Hughes, who seemed the epitome of Cosmos, was not even human, that she was, in fact, the original and the prototype, the perfect SIN, the origin, the beginning.

V, of course, had never been captured

She was too clever, too experienced, and too cautious.

And, of course, he didn't want to capture her.

He occasionally intervened – with very mixed feelings – to stop investigations, to reassign intelligence units, to transfer officers who were too zealous and too close to finding her.

But, after the Culling, V had been driven more and more into the wilderness – surviving for more than a decade, for fourteen years, like a wild beast; well, that, in a way, was what she was: a wild beast – something like a primitive goddess from pagan times, a goddess of love and blood, of destruction and rebirth, a goddess of justice, and vengeance, and sacrifice. Using his personal intelligence connections, he had followed her wanderings as much as he could and knew some of the details. She had lived in the swamplands of half-submerged Florida, feeding off people-smugglers, slave-traders, outlaws, and sadists. Her victims, from what he could glean, were almost exclusively very violent and bad people, though sometimes it appeared that even she made mistakes – or was driven by necessity, by pure hunger, like the tragic case of the young man on the subway, Hector Cramer. She had hunted along the sunken coasts, in ruined cities. He could picture her, and often did, mostly in her reptilian form, fangs, claws, and turquoise scales glittering, springing upon her victims, emptying them of their blood, crouching, alone, under the rain or torrid sunlight, hunting by day, and by night. There were reports of her adventures and crimes, here and there, in jungles and outposts mostly, sometimes, briefly, in the ruined cities on the edge of the Dead Lands. Sometimes she was in Europe; sometimes she was in Asia. She had survived, reputedly, for thousands of years. He found a definite pleasure – which he knew was perverse – in imagining V and her adventures: V, robed in her dangerously seductive and wild pagan splendor.

But so many hybrids had died, and so many had been enslaved, in the Culling, that it seemed to him not only a mistake, but a great crime: The Culling!

Yes, it was most certainly a great crime.

He knew that from the very beginning.

This is all on me, he thought: it is my crime; he who wills the ends must will the means; and if the instruments are also faulty, then that too is my fault, and I must recognize it as mine. And of course, I didn't stop the thing from happening.

At the time, he had felt – and believed – it was the price to be paid for the survival of the human race.

And he didn't tell Kit of how, once the coup d'état, called the National and Cosmos Rebirth and the Culling were over, he had eliminated the worst of his allies – how General François Gelder had mysteriously drowned while fishing off Labrador, how Colonel Konrad was killed in an aviation accident, how he had strangled with his bare hands Admiral Marc Antonio Baker ...

And, to secure his power against his former allies, to make sure the hard-liners never overturned him, never stabbed him in the back, he became, on the advice of his closest advisors, "the Leader." His image was everywhere, and he cultivated the Cult of the Leader, the Cult of the President, the Cult of Himself.

It is a dangerous thing – to become a god in your lifetime.

"Oh, my God," said Kit, who was sloshing through the water beside him.

"What? Oh, I see." The President let go of her hand and took out his laser gun.

Lying on the narrow mossy bank of the canal was a large animal; it looked like a seal; it was wounded; it was moaning.

"Stay back, Kit," said the President. He waded toward the animal.

Kit followed, slightly behind him, scanning the waters, walls, the arched ceiling of the canal; she kept expecting the walls and arches to turn into tentacles and mouths and eyes.

"I think I'd better put it out of its misery," said the President. He was lowering his laser gun toward the beast which was looking up with large eyes and groaning, and in that instant Kit suddenly realized that the animal understood what the President was going to do, and that it even understood that the President's motives were compassionate, but that the animal did not want to die. "Don't," she said, and she moved up to the animal and instinctively put one hand over the wound as if to protect the animal and its wound from the laser gun.

"Ouch!"

Blue sparks and a violet light suddenly jumped from her fingers.

"Ouch! What!" She leaped back, "Ouch! What is that?"

"My God," said the President. "It's true."

Kit stared at her hand. "What's true? What was that?"

"Did it hurt?"

"No, it just surprised me. What the hell was it? It tingled."

"I didn't believe it; but it must be so."

"What must be so? Don't speak in riddles, Mr. President, please!"

"Hybrids can heal, so the folklore says, so ..."

"What?"

"Hybrids can heal. Their touch ..."

"What? I don't understand," Kit stared at her hands. "You mean like the laying on of hands, like kings used to do, like medieval superstition type of healing?"

"Yes, but I'm sure it has a scientific explanation."

"You mean I'm not only a hybrid, I'm a witch?" Kit looked up at the President and then down at the animal which was staring at her; it had the most beautiful soulful melancholy eyes, full of suffering and forgiveness and hope. Its whiskers twitched. It raised one flipper, as if in salute. Animals are sometimes saints, Kit thought. It was painful to look at ...

"Kit," said the President, "Don't be afraid, do it again."

"Do what?"

"Put your hand over the wound."

"Okay, well, I guess I can ... try it ... if you say so," Kit reached out and the glow came from her fingers with little sparks jumping between the tips of her fingers and the open gash. It did tingle. It was spooky.

Then something *really* weird happened. She could *see* the structure of the wound and she could *see* the way the flesh and muscles and tendons and veins and skin and fur should be rebuilt – it was like the schematic of a video game multisensory experience. She concentrated on the schematic; her fingers tingled; a blue light seemed to radiate from her hand; within a few seconds she saw that the wound was healing, closing up, and the skin closing and the fur reforming – and then, poof, it was as if there had been no wound at all.

"Gosh," Kit slowly withdrew her hand as the blue light faded, "Gosh!"

"Amazing," said the President.

"Awesome," Kit whispered, using the word Miranda so often used and which Kit had now come to use and repeat as a sort of token and secret talisman of love; by using the word she was bringing part of Miranda back to life, just for a second, "Awesome!"

The animal groaned slightly, turned its head and licked Kit's hand. "Gosh," Kit said, "And thank you," she added, to the beast which was gazing at her in what sure looked like adoration. She stroked its head. "I'm going to call you Edgar," she said.

The seal nodded and groaned in pleasure.

"I didn't believe it. I should have believed it," said the President.

"Angels and devils," said Kit, half to herself, "Angels and Devils. I mean, being a hybrid is like being an angel and a devil, all in one."

"Angels and devils," the President put his hand on Kit's shoulder, "Perhaps, perhaps, Kit, but, whether angel or devil, you certainly made a new friend."

"Yes," she said, "He's going to guide us and protect us, he says."

The animal slid off the bank and rolled into the water, and looked around at them, and then began to swim, but looking back, checking that they were following. Kit took the President's hand. "What's going on? It's like I can read the animal's thoughts."

"Perhaps you can; your probably can."

"Soon I will read your thoughts."

"I'm not sure I am looking forward to that," said the President.

Miranda and Caliban finished their shower under the sparkling cascade and were sparkling clean and feeling perky and lustful.

Just a few feet ahead of Miranda, Caliban led the way. He peeked around a corner. A narrow squared-off tunnel led down to the right. Thick metal pipes clamped to the roof ran along the top of the tunnel. Some of them were emitting narrow thick jets of steam and hissing like a posse of mad cobras.

"Now the problem is," Caliban said, "are those pipes just pipes?"

Miranda considered this. She looked up at the pipes. "Yes. Or are they Foul Fiend World Mind Snakes pretending to be pipes that are going to leap down and try to strangle us."

"Yes."

"Yes."

"Well, whatever they are, we shall be brave sailors, my Princess, and we shall sail onwards. We shall march on into the darkness, hell or high water, come what may, we shall pull out all the stops, up anchor, and head out, full sail and full steam ahead, all gears engaged, all wheels turning!"

"Yes, my lovely, lovely Caliban," Miranda sighed, "let us proceed!" Caliban, she thought, was so romantic; he always saw anything that happened in terms of wooden pirate ships on the bounding main, Spanish galleons and French or British men-of-war, and steam-engine powered paddle-wheel river boats with mustachioed bright-eyed gamblers on board playing ukuleles, and oversized muscular apes leaping through jungles, from vine to vine, carrying blond starlets clutched in their giant fists. Being with Caliban was like being in a super-cool real live video game, except that you really got to move around, and you could actually lean against his smooth muscles, which were *real* not simulated, and put your hand on his luscious arm or chest or around his waist or bring your lips right up to his lips, in real-time reality, with all the effects. This was love. She was absolutely sure of it.

"Oh, Princess, we are not alone," said Caliban, he was looking up at the ceiling; a huge eye was looking down at them; the eye was perhaps two feet across and had a heavy thick eyelid and long dark lashes and it was bloodshot; it blinked; it was dripping tears and when the tears hit the floor of the tunnel they hissed and bubbled and burned their way through, leaving deep pits in the paving stones.

"Well, well," Caliban tightened his grip on Miranda's hand. Acid tears, they were, tears that melt metal and flesh and bone and stone. Caliban took a deep breath. "It's beginning again."

The wall began to buckle inwards.

"Let's perhaps go back," said Miranda, tightening her grip on Caliban's arm.

"Yes, Princess," said Caliban, "but ... look!"

The wall behind them was buckling inward too, as if it were made of mad leavening dough, or bubble gum, or crazy elastic, or as if both walls were balloons being blown up by an invisible magician.

"Oh, that *is* inconvenient," said Miranda. She had her laser gun out and was thinking of blasting the giant tearful eye but she paused, felt a flicker of compassion and understanding, and then she said, looking up at the giant eye, "Oh Eye, Oh Eye in the ceiling, Oh, Eye in the Sky, why are you so sad? Why, oh Eye, are you crying such acid tears? What woe, oh Eye, afflicts you so?"

Caliban put his arm around Miranda's waist; her love and her compassion, and her poetic talent, he realized, encompassed everything. The tunnel behind them had completely closed and the wall was now pushing its way toward them; if it kept coming they would be either crushed to death or eaten by the wall and become elements of the stone themselves. If they were going to die, he would see to it that they died together, in each other's arms, sealing their love with a kiss, and at the thought of death, at the thought of losing Miranda, an indefinable yearning, almost like a physical force took hold of Caliban and ...

The wall, up front, beyond the Eye had closed too.

"Oh, Eye," said Miranda, "I am so sad to see that you are sad!"

The walls were closing, soon they would be pushed right under the eye and dissolved in its acid tears – still dripping from beneath its lid – or they would be absorbed by the elastic walls.

The Eye looked at Miranda.

A light shone in the Eye.

The Eye blinked. A child's voice said, "I want to play."

"You want to play?" Miranda raised an eyebrow.

"Yes, but my friend tells me this is not a nice game."

"Oh," Miranda felt Caliban tighten his hold on her waist, "Well, perhaps your friend is right."

"I don't know. The other friend, the bad one, I don't like him, but he is very strong, and he is very persuasive, and he can be very funny, and he wants me to play this game. He wants me to kill you or dissolve you or eat you, both of you, and you will become granite or basalt or quartz, I forget which, because, truly, so many new things are happening that it is difficult to know which game I am playing, with whom, and where, and which stones or rocks are which. I used to know my minerals, like feldspar, granite, pitchblende, or things."

"Hmm," said Miranda. "Well, perhaps if we are still alive we can play later. Caliban and I love to play."

Caliban tightened his grip on Miranda's waist and looked around.

"And we could recite lists of minerals, just for fun!" Miranda smiled at the eye, "like amazonite, and gypsum, and azurite, and ..."

The wall now was very close; it touched Miranda's elbow; she could feel her elbow being drawn into it, as if she was being captured by a bulging wall of voracious super-glue. The drops of acid were running free and fast, creating a great steaming puddle, making it very dangerous to take even a single step forward. Caliban let go of Miranda and unsheathed the machete.

"You promise to play with me later?"

"Yes."

"I'm hiding you know. I don't want him to find me."

"That's good! Don't let him find you."

"I'm playing with V too. You know V, don't you?"

"Yes, we do!"

"She is funny, V, I mean!"

"Yes, she can be very funny." Miranda was thinking that the first time she had met V. V had teased her about being a Cosmos – and being naked – so perhaps that was an example of V's humor. And Miranda had no idea – at the time – that V, the glittering hybrid, who suddenly appeared out of the desert with Kat the glamorous Centurion, was her mother, and the Queen of the Hybrids. What a strange topsy-turvy thing destiny was!

Miranda's arm was being drawn back into the glue-like wall. Caliban seized her arm to try to pull her free. But the glue had already begun to creep up her arm. It was thick and veined with colors and granular like polished rose granite. Caliban raised his machete, ready to try to carve a hole out of the wall and free Miranda ...

The voice giggled. "I'm hiding from V too, she's the good one, but soon I shall let her find me, if she is very, very good."

"I am sure she will be very, very good," said Miranda in the calmest tone possible, thinking that if the Mind-Child was really talking about V, perhaps V was already inside the Mind, trapped or hiding inside the mind, perhaps V was –

"You promise to play?"

"Yes, I promise, we promise!" Miranda was wondering what would be like to be turned to stone; not pleasant, surely.

"Both of you promise?"

"Yes, both of us!"

The glue was now up to Miranda's shoulder and pulling her away from Caliban. He hesitated. The blow from the machete had to be very carefully aimed, precisely balanced, because he didn't know the resistance of the glue-like stone, or how it might deflect the blade, and he didn't want to slice off Miranda's arm or shoulder, and …

"Cross your hearts and hope to die!"

"We do," said Miranda, "I cross my heart and hope to die if I don't play with you!"

"I do too," said Caliban, noting that this was a new expression that he had not heard before. "If I don't play with you, I cross my heart and hope to die! I promise to play with you; I promise by the spirit of Tarzan and Long John Silver and Captain Cook and the goddesses my mother Nikki and Dolly!"

"Ha, ha, ha," the little voice pealed with laughter, like the jingle of clear distant sleigh bells heard from afar on a crisp star-filled winter's night.

Then *Poof …*

The Eye was gone.

The tunnel was just as it had been before.

Strands of goo, like cobwebs, clung to Miranda's arm and shoulder. They sparkled like strings of sequins, then broke apart into tiny beads, and fell away, an innocuous sprinkling of drifting color.

Caliban took Miranda in his arms and looked deep into her eyes – her level-headed equanimity during this little crisis had been admirable. "Princess, you are the bravest Princess that ever was!" He kissed her with a deep, passionate and full kiss and Miranda, startled by the depth and warmth of the kiss and by a rising wave of inner passion, returned the kiss. Her whole body and soul soared and tensed, fueled by a violent sublime hunger, a yearning, a hunger and yearning that only union with Caliban could fulfill.

Caliban continued the kiss. He was oh so delicate, oh so sensitive, taking his time, exploring, his hands running down her back, touching every nerve ending, every pinpoint source of feeling and pleasure; and Miranda felt she too should play her part, so she pressed herself against him and, applying all the best lessons Kit had bestowed upon her, she began to …

Following their new friend, Edgar the Seal, Kit and the President waded on, thigh-deep, sometimes waist-deep, sometimes only shin-deep, following the canal under the ruins of what had been New York, and under the vast dying utopian city which was Elysium.

Explosions echoed from above.

"I think maybe I've been programmed to like you," Kit said, giving the President a sly look.

"You mean, the images, the Hail the Leader songs – all that 'cult of the leader' circus."

"Yes, and the mind reprogramming during erasure," she said.

"Of course, yes, well …"

"But still I think I like you because of what you are. You've done some bad things, some horrible things, but for some reason I really like you."

"Yes, I have done some horrible things, Kit," the President pushed away a bit of floating debris, "criminal things, many, many criminal things."

Edgar looked around at him.

"Where does free will begin and where does conditioning end, I wonder?" said Kit, "Do I like you because of me, because of you, or just because of all the propaganda, all the implanted messages I've been soaked in? Am I really myself or am I just an echo chamber repeating clichés and slogans? Am I myself or just the sum of all those erasures and introjections and all that propaganda and all those messages that are pounded in every moment of every day?"

"The fact you can ask these questions, proves, I think, that you are yourself, Kit, that you are your own stubborn delightful person," said the President, "It's a struggle, and most of us most of the time are clichés, most of us have absorbed a great many lies, and even some truths, but you, I think, are real, Kit. I think you've fought – a long hard fight – to be you, to regain all the territory you lost, to reconquer your mind."

Wading through the water with the adolescent newly minted hybrid, Kit Candy, and thinking about free will and how great decisions can be decided on the basis of the smallest and most arbitrary things – like the decision to take the Intercity Express at 5:00 am – the President thought back, remembering his encounter with the Queen of the Hybrids, and then remembering the aftermath of that encounter, the aftermath that happened six months after the fiery passionate, almost fatal meeting in the subway with V. A few days before the coup d'état and a week before the Culling, he received a visit. It would change his view of hybrids – and of SINs. It almost changed the course of history. But it was too late, of course; it was too late, not for everything, but almost, since the machinery of the coup d'état and the Culling had been set in motion.

It was totally unexpected, what had happened.

The actress Nikki Hughes asked for an appointment.

He accepted her request.

And she came to see him; she was an almost mythic figure, mysterious, ageless, and … a fiction.

She was a star, certainly, and a model, and now a designer and graphic designer, and financially and professionally extraordinarily successful.

In recent years, even though her beauty was undimmed, even beyond the usual anti-aging offered to Cosmos, she had ceased to act and model and had shifted to graphic design – and developing conceptual strategies for world-wide firms – and had already raffled up a series of international prizes and very lucrative contracts. She was a sort of genius, in fact …

She was a very wealthy woman, but …

But he knew from the Secret Homeland Cosmos Centurion File kept on her: she was a SIN; not human; she was an artificial creation, one of the first, in fact, almost certainly the very first, an extraordinarily successful prototype, almost a fluke, the Original SIN, almost too successful, built in Paris by one of the pioneers of human cloning and bottom up genetic engineering; and she was, in fact, ageless. She could, in theory, live forever. No one knew her secret – except he did, and a handful of his own very loyal Centurion Intelligence Officers.

"General," she said, "Thank you for seeing me." She glanced at his office – it was vast, his desk immense, and behind it a spectacular view of Elysium City, airships docking, towers soaring, blinking elevators climbing, mist drifting, it was almost unreal. The sense of power, here, and of danger, was palpable.

He was in the midst of planning for the coup – the destruction of hybrids and SINs and the elimination of the entire political class and the most dangerous military and political fanatics, but, still, he found time to see her. He had been curious about her, and now he felt his curiosity would be satisfied.

He stared at her: My God, she looked like the sister of the Hybrid V; they could be sisters; she looked like V, the Queen of …

"What a pleasure, Ms. Hughes!" He stood up, shook her hand, "Please, sit down," he was determined to be gracious. How was it that simulacra of humans were more perfect humans than humans? That was part of the problem; that was why they had to die. "Would you like coffee – or perhaps tea?"

"Coffee, please, General," she smiled, "Thank you."

She was even more beautiful than the films; and he had seen almost all of them, several times. Some of the films had been cult films, some brilliant, but many of the films were bad, kitsch, very successful money-making kitsch, but she was invariably sublime, and funny – great comic timing, shrugging her shoulders, pouting, kicking her legs, quick repartee – and she could be moving, and tragic, and goofy, and …

She sat down, crossed her legs, smiled, and as the door closed and they were alone she mouthed and somehow transmitted the thought: *Is this being recorded; is anyone listening; are we alone?*

He nodded, then said it out loud, "Yes, we are alone."

He was curious. Why had she asked for the appointment; what did she want? And why did she want to know if they were being overheard? And he wanted to know what she felt, what a SIN, not being human, could possible feel. He stared at her and did not say anything: she was the enemy, of course, like V, and, like V, she was beautiful, desirable. He tapped his fingers on the desk, staring at her. She returned the stare in a friendly, relaxed way, and she was about to speak when …

He raised an imperious finger, ordering her to remain silent.

She nodded slightly, gave him a quizzical look, and said nothing.

He got up and walked around. He stood behind her; she looked up at him as he approached; but she did not turn to see what he was doing. As he stood behind her, he stared at her neck; it was slender, long, and perfect. What was the old term that was used to describe such a neck? Swan-like, yes, it was swan-like, and she had a supple body, a dancer's body. Standing there, he could break her neck with one quick flick of his wrist; simple – there would be one less of the creatures. Of course, she had immense and rapid self-healing powers … but … His fingers tightened; his hand clenched; he was tempted.

"Do you always toy with people, General?"

"Not with people," he said.

"Ah, of course, I see," she said, but she didn't turn around and she betrayed no emotion, no fear.

He walked around behind his desk, sat down and stared at her. She wet her lips with the tip of her tongue: so perhaps she is afraid, he thought, perhaps she does know fear.

"General, I know you know who ... and what ... I am."

He held her gaze, the glorious smile still focused on him, and he nodded, "Yes, Ms. Hughes, I certainly know who ... and what ... you are."

The coffee machine produced the coffee. He stood up, came around his desk and served her, bowing slightly, as if in homage to her, to her fame, to her beauty, perhaps even to her courage. Can a non-human be brave?

Then he served himself and moved back behind his desk. He had the office "swept" automatically several times a day and he had automatic anti-bugging devices and anti-bugging nano-drones on patrol all the time, twenty-four hours a day seven days a week; it was as safe as safe could be.

Nikki Hughes smiled. "You are very kind, General, especially kind, since you know what I am; and I do know what you think of creatures such as I."

"It is nothing personal, Ms. Hughes," with a shrug he spread his arms wide, encompassing all the contradictions, "I can admire you personally, even like you, even watch your films, admire your work, and yet ..."

"And yet I am dangerous alien vermin and should be exterminated," she smiled and drank some of the coffee, her dark eyes never leaving his.

"Yes, I'm afraid that is the case," he moved his hands on his desk, the smooth substantial warm, old-fashioned highly polished wood – comforting somehow. "It is a question of who is to survive; the human race or creatures such as you, and the hybrids of course. We can't forget them!" He smiled; he left the threat vague, but in four days or five, perhaps a week or two she would be taken, and disposed of; nothing would save her, nothing. The trap was about to be sprung. In three days, the politicians and judges would be "disappeared." And then, right afterwards, after the corrupt and paralyzed political system, totally subservient to Mammon and Corrupt Crony Capitalism, had been swept away, the hybrids and SINs would be taken. The slate would be wiped clean. He intended to "store" most of the hybrids, and not eliminate them – their genetic material and their talents might one day prove useful; besides, he had now, mixed with his horror of the hybrids, an intimate admiration for the creatures, and more than an admiration, a passion, a passion – a lust – for one of them, in particular. But the SINs, they were an abomination; they were a parody of humanity, the more "assimilated" and beautiful they were, miming humanity so successfully, the more dangerous they were: perhaps a few select examples should be kept, as Colonel Konrad had suggested, for vivisection and experiments; but, no, that was inhumane.

"Of course," she said with a slight smile, "We can't forget the hybrids."

"I'm sorry. I wish it could be …"

"Different? Well perhaps it could be, perhaps it should be, different; perhaps we could be allies rather than rivals; most of us do consider ourselves totally human, you know, totally assimilated and integrated; but I have not come to talk about the destiny of hybrids and humans and SINs." She put the cup down; she was still smiling, remarkably relaxed though she certainly knew he could destroy her in an instant, kill her right here, or denounce her, have her eliminated; not even her fame and wealth – not even her remarkable DNA and body chemistry – would protect her.

"So, why did you come, then, Ms. Hughes?"

"You had an encounter, in the subway, about six months ago, with a friend of mine," she said. She looked down, picked up the cup, took another sip, and then looked up, into his eyes, fixing him with her gaze.

"A friend of yours?" His feelings surged up, hatred, desire, yearning, wonder, regret, awe.

"Yes."

He sat absolutely still: was she going to try to blackmail him? Was she going to try to turn the tables? This was … this was extremely stupid of her, to think that he could be deterred by a SIN, that he could be …

She laughed, and it was a very pleasant, frank and unthreatening laugh. "I can see what you're thinking! No: it's nothing like that, General, nothing sinister. I don't want anything. She doesn't want anything. Well, perhaps that's not entirely true …"

"I …" he began.

"V just wanted me to tell you that, soon, you will have a daughter, General. She thought you would want to know. She thought you would wish to know. She thinks it is your right to know."

He sat very still.

She smiled. "I'm sorry; I've upset you. You don't want to know this. I'll go."

"No, no, no, it's just that …" His mind replayed the moment of sex and passion – such as he had never known – down on that mossy platform in that canal tunnel – yes, it was love, it was desire, it was a moment of exaltation

– and of fear – and strangely, of trust – such as he had never felt with anyone, certainly not with any woman. V could have killed him, easily, and yet she hadn't. And she was a merciless killer, as she had shown that first and only time he had met her.

A merciless killer ... He saw, as in a vision, her work: Hector Cramer's withered hand, thumb and forefinger on his half-open zipper, chalk-white, parchment-like skin, almost violet in the livid light of the night train, the veins standing out, a mummified hand; and Cramer's face, jaws open, frozen in an invisible scream.

And in a flash he remembered too that time fighting in the Andes, where three renegade hybrids – two females and a male – had vaulted through the camp's electronic defenses and killed half of his crew. The hybrids had smashed their way to the living quarters where his woman and her child were, and they killed everything – even the guard dogs and three puppies – and everyone. He found Maria-Teresa with her throat torn out. Francisco, who was five, had been cut in half, literally cut in half.

It had taken a five-hour fire fight, using everything he had – explosive bullets, gas, high-powered lasers, airstrikes, and suicide drones – to trap and kill the hybrids.

The hybrids and the human bodies had to be cremated; they didn't have transport to take them home. Buried here, mutants and animals would get at them, however deep they were put under the earth.

Before that battle, he had never lost a single man or woman. Five hours later he stood in the tropical rain feeling his world had been destroyed, he had been destroyed. The drops were silver. Lightning flashed, big bolts of sizzling whitish-blue, straight down into the jungle. The dark clouds hung low. The forest was the color of spinach. Water streamed down his face. The smoke was the same color as the rain, silver-gray. The rain lashed in under the tarpaulin tent covering and put out the flames. Some bones were left.

"General, we have to leave."

"Yes," he turned toward her. Martine, his logistics chief, a French girl – well, a woman, Lieutenant Martine Arnault; she was 32, a liaison officer seconded from the Hispanic European Joint Force, and the best logistic person he'd ever had.

"The window is closing," she said.

"Yes. Thank you, Lieutenant."

So, he had returned to what was left of the USA. He was already, in a minor way a hero, a hero of the Russian-Chinese war, a hero of the Appalachian mutant campaign, and of the Burbite-Outlander revolt of ten years ago. His doctrine had always been to make it as clean and quick and bloodless as possible. The best battle is one you don't even have to fight. But "pacification," whichever way you did it, was usually a euphemism for terror and extermination, but, well, by his lights, he did the best he could. What was it they said about the Romans: "They made a desert and called it peace?" Well, often, it was the only way to make peace: to make a desert. And after the disaster in the Andes, his blood was up, his bloodlust rose to a ferocious intensity; he felt it, disapproved of it, but it was stronger than he was; he would declare war on the hybrids, and it would be a war of extermination, every single hybrid would die.

He had immediately instituted a top-secret program to fight hybrids – the development of a super-efficient nerve-paralyzer, and exploitation and manufacture of a brilliant idea developed by a German tinkerer-inventor, Max Huber, who also an anti-terrorism expert – the *mind-collar*. The mind-collar would be the salvation of the human race.

And so, it was that, while he stood on that mountain side in the Andes, the idea for the Culling had taken shape: the hybrids were too dangerous to be left free – or to be left alive.

He griped the edge of his desk. And, here, now, this SIN, this beautiful SIN, with her Olympian, almost disdainful calm, was telling him he had a daughter – a hybrid daughter! He was overcome by conflicting feelings; the hybrid herself, V, the alleged Queen of the Hybrids, she was certainly – ah, exiting, intoxicating! Coupling with her, and she was in effect a wild beast, a predator, there was something elemental, something awe-inspiring, almost sacred about it, coupling with his greatest enemy. He was aware of this dangerous tendency in himself: transgressing taboos has always had a certain fascination and constituted one of his – many – darker sides. And now this SIN, a "friend" of the hybrid queen, the beautiful animal, the alien, the …? And this SIN was telling him he had a daughter, he was about to have a daughter, a hybrid daughter?

Nikki Hughes stood up, "You won't hear about this again, General. Don't worry, I won't contact you; V won't contact you; and no one will ever know."

"Sit down Ms. Hughes." He was frightened, terrified would be more exact, not of discovery or blackmail – No: he was terrified that he was about to lose something unique, something precious, he felt as if a unique possibility, a person just glimpsed, a love just tasted, a sublime possibility, the possibility of a different kind of life, was about to slip away, to disappear forever. "… Sit down, Nikki … please."

She stood looking at him, a slight smile on her lips, a quizzical expression, as if trying to gage his intentions: Was he moved, or was he angry, was his emotion – and it was obvious that he was moved – one of fear for his reputation and his power, or was it something else? Was he going to have her arrested and put down or eliminated as they were doing now so often to SINs? In fact, soon, she was quite sure, she was destined to die. The reckoning was coming, she was sure of it. And the General was one of the powers behind it, if not *the* power behind it. Well, whatever … She sat down. She put her hand on the cup of coffee; and still looking at him she lifted it to her lips.

He sat staring at her: truly beautiful, like V's sister.

"A daughter?" he cleared his throat; there was something about the word, "daughter." He swallowed; it was difficult even to say the word, even to …

"Yes."

"When?"

"Three months from now, more or less, your daughter will be born."

He stood up and began to pace back and forth; then he turned to the SIN, to Nikki Hughes and he said, "You are a SIN – an artificial creature – how is it you seem so … so human?"

She laughed. "That's a good question, General. I've asked it often myself. Even my father, my creator, that is, quizzed me on it. He had me – and he was very polite and apologetic about it – undergo lots of tests. I'm not a robot, General, I'm not a machine, though even the robots aren't really robots any more, not really," she took another sip of coffee, paused, looked thoughtful for a moment, "This body is human, essentially, the brain too, anatomically speaking, though the DNA has been twigged in a variety of ways and, as you know, I regenerate often, and quickly, and I have a sort of quantum shield that protects me, for a short time at least, from threats, from fire, for instance, or a bullet or a knife. All my memories – even the ones from my artificial childhood – are human memories. It does seem that I'm conscious. Or at least I have the impression I am. So, I'm aware. I'm aware of other minds, their consciousness, of people, men, women, children, of old people and young people, of people of different races and backgrounds, and I'm aware of dogs, and cats, and birds, and animals, and even of plants. I'm aware of other consciousnesses, other minds, being aware of me, and of my consciousness, my feelings, intentions, and so on, so I can reflect upon myself as seen through their eyes: Does that cat like me? Is the waiter annoyed with me? Did I hurt the feelings of the driver, of the director? That sort of thing. So, I suppose, in a way, though I am, as you say, artificial, and though my body regenerates in a rather unique way, I feel, I think, and I feel what people think and feel and I … I think I suffer what people suffer … and when I see people suffer, I suffer with them, though I know all of this may sound highfalutin and pretentious."

He turned and glanced at the screen on his desk: background check and TOP CONFIDENTIAL file on SIN #1-A: Nikki Armanda Hughes … She had changed names, and identities, many times, since her father scientist had created her in Paris in the mid-21st Century. Then she had been known as Marie-Josée … Since she did not age, and did not die, she had to "disappear" every few decades, then reappear, and re-invent herself, a new person, a new life, a new name, a new country, a new career, a new biography.

"You had a son, I see."

"Yes."

"He was lost three years ago."

"A bit more, yes." She gazed at him.

"A train from the West Coast to Elysium City, the train was blown up. He was with his nurse; at the last minute you had to stay behind for some extra scenes to be shot for a film, retakes. There were survivors, but his nurse was among the dead. No one ever found your son or his body."

"No. We searched. I went there myself. Mutants and animals had eaten, or half-eaten some of the bodies. There were bones and carcasses and body-parts. But there was no sign of him. His nurse had apparently survived the explosion and crash; but someone – or something – had slashed her throat. She was murdered. We offered a reward for any information about her death – and for my son's return. But, of course, we heard nothing. After all, it happened in the Dead Lands."

"His father was?

"An actor on a film, famous, handsome; but he never knew … he never knew he was a father …"

"Probably, I would guess, it was what's his name, the swash-buckler, played pirates and buccaneers and kings of the jungle, a German bodybuilder with Latin blood; he was – is – too handsome to be true."

"Yes, that's a good description – and charming too, too charming to be true."

"What did this do to you? Losing your son?"

"Why?"

"I want to know what a SIN feels, if a SIN feels anything." He sat down again and slouched back, narrowing his eyes, staring at her over the top of his coffee cup.

She blinked at him, once. "Did it turn my heart to stone? Yes, for a time, it did. I was numb. Then I decided for some reason to believe that he was alive somewhere and that someday I would find him. And, you know, General: this is strange; but it made me appreciate life – each instant, each second, is a gift – whether you are human or hybrid or SIN – or a dog or a cat, a sparrow or a hawk. Any of us, we might easily have never existed, never been created; but we do, we do exist."

"Yes, we do exist," he echoed. Then he thought: someone else is about to exist, or already exists: a baby girl, my daughter …

He half-closed his eyes.

I have a daughter I will have a daughter.

His daughter …

She is my daughter with the Queen of the Hybrids.

My bride – her name is death … drinker of blood … ancient goddess, predator, destroyer of worlds!

It almost made him laugh; for him to have a daughter by the Queen of the Hybrids was so daring and so crazy as to be insane; he realized that this weird caper was excitingly perverse: the General who would suppress the hybrids and SINs having a daughter who was a hybrid. The secrecy and perversity flattered his vanity; oh, you are foolish and vain, my friend, he warned himself, foolish and vain, and it will land you in very hot water!

But there was also something else being born – *tenderness*, a burgeoning feeling of *tenderness*.

He took a deep breath. "It will be difficult for … for V … to bring up a daughter, things being as they are," he said, making a tent out of his fingers, and staring over his fingertips at Nikki Hughes.

"Yes," Nikki nodded, "V has to keep moving; she is a hunter; and she is hunted."

"Yes, she is a creature of the wild. She lives in the wilderness, a predator, I have seen her work, I have seen the dead she leaves behind," he said, finding the idea exciting, this wild superhuman, half-human, half-alien female with whom he had coupled, "She lives almost like a wild beast, scavenging the land and hunting for her victims."

"Yes, she lives as a wild beast," Nikki said, recognizing the General's erotic excitement, the inebriating exoticism he felt at the very idea of V, the sense of otherness, of a taboo being violated. Nikki had anticipated, with V, the way the conversation might drift, "She is a very cultured and civilized wild beast," Nikki smiled slightly, "and she is my friend; but she is a predator, just the same; and yes, she has to keep moving. Any burden, any responsibility would be dangerous for her – and, above all, for the child."

Nikki was pleased and yet sad. It was all rather too predictable. She and V had known this would be part of the conversation. She and V had discussed the possibility; now she merely had to wait. The General's vanity would do part of the job; his passion too, and his sense of being a father. He was very clever, though, and aware of his own weaknesses, he was profound, in his own way, and prescient, so he could be dangerous, very dangerous, but … Nikki realized that she liked him; and she could quite understand V's fascination, but …

But worst of all for V, she would lose her own daughter.

To be a stranger to what she loved …

And, of course, to be an enemy to the man she desired, and perhaps loved, all that was difficult, would be difficult, for V.

The General swiveled around in his chair, he looked out over the city, now, in the dimming afternoon light, the towers seemed even more ethereal and heavenly than they usually did; human civilization was such a glorious, such a precarious accomplishment, so fragile, so utterly fragile; any false step and it would all be destroyed, they would all descend into barbarism, or, worse, humans would destroy themselves, simply cease to exist.

He swiveled back to face the SIN, "I propose this: you, Nikki Hughes, you will bring up V's daughter; I will declare a truce with you and with V. V's daughter will be under my protection; you will be under my protection. V is an outcast and an outlaw and a murderer and drinker of blood, who preys on humanity, so she must fend for herself. It is not right that a young creature be brought up that way, with such a wild predator as her mother. Besides, as you said, it is a risky life, the child might not survive."

Nikki put on her serious face. "I'll ask V. I think she might well agree with you, General. I think she feels that as a predator nomad, hunted and hunting, particularly in this difficult period, she is not well placed to bring up her daughter – your daughter."

"Yes, she is a nomad and a savage, now that she is hunted – and soon, as I'm sure you suspect, they will all be hunted – she must live as a wild beast." He was aware that he was revealing a perverse delectation in describing his lover thus – a "wild beast" indeed; well, she certainly was that – and he was more than half-aware that Nikki and V had gambled on his reaction – but he went ahead just the same, this Nikki, this SIN, strangely, could be trusted, he was sure of it, "It is not practical or seemly that a young girl be brought up that way."

"*It is not practical or seemly* ... You are strange man, General."

"Perhaps I am."

"This will depend on V, of course," said Nikki, "It will be her decision."

He stood up. "Yes, it is her decision. Come back, Ms. Hughes, tell me what V has decided."

And Nikki Hughes did come back.

"You are deep in thought, Mr. President," said Kit, as she swatted away a lost and dazed Nano Pub Drone which had been whispering something about the best toothpaste in the world. It fell straight into the water, lay there on its back, sighed, blinked its multi-facetted drone eyes, burped twice, and sank. Sometimes Kit wanted to cuddle and baby the little things.

"Yes, I am," said the President, "I'm sorry. I'm not very good company, Kit Candy. I'll try to be more amusing."

"You are my Don Quixote. You saved my life, Mr. President, you don't have to be amusing!" Kit Candy gave him her brightest smile.

"Don Quixote," mused the President, thinking that even down here in the murky phosphorescent light, Kit Candy's smile was like the brightest of sunrises.

"Oh, gosh, look at them." Miranda shivered.

"Yes, more of them," said Caliban; he found most ghouls distasteful, even the friendly ones, but he tried to hide his feelings.

These ghouls appeared very unhappy, they were sobbing and sniffling. They were crouched in a circle where they had killed some people but there was nothing left but bones and nothing more to eat. They looked up, their blank eyes staring at Miranda and Caliban.

"Don't even think about it," Miranda managed to growl; it was a new discovery – if she wished she could pitch her voice very low, basso profondo, a rippling sort of throaty thunder, which echoed against the tunnel and cavern walls.

She wondered if it was part of being a hybrid. She certainly hoped it didn't mean she was overcharging on testosterone and being morphed into a boy and grow whiskers and hairy legs and a beard; that would be very annoying; she wanted to remain just as she was – a girl, and a girl in love with a boy, her very own Prince Caliban, son of Nikki.

If she became a boy, she would still love Caliban and she hoped he would love her, though their love might become somewhat more complicated. Would Caliban love her in the same way if she were a boy? Well, if she came to that bridge, then she would have to figure out how to cross it, and how to be a boy loving a boy, how best to arrange all that, how to figure out the intimate mechanics of gay love, among pirates, that is, for, if she were to become a boy, she would be a cabin boy, or, much better, she would be a pirate, probably with a parrot on her shoulder and perhaps, for pure theatrical effect, a patch on one eye.

She growled again; it felt good. No, really, on second thought, she didn't think she was becoming a boy; it was the hybrid side, growing within her. In any case, whatever happened, Caliban would understand. Already she and Caliban were family since she had been raised by Nikki; in fact, she knew much more about Caliban's mother that he did – or at least she thought she knew, because, besides being a SIN, Nikki was in many respects very mysterious: Who knew what secrets she knew, what lives she had lived, what thoughts flitted through her mind, what mysteries were hidden behind that generous, quick, all-forgiving smile?

"Oh, you poor little ghouls, go away!" Miranda smiled at them; then she bared her teeth and snarled, like a tiger would snarl, and growled a deep low-throated, enormous and echoing growl!

The ghouls squeaked and scattered and fled.

They were gone.

"Darling, that was magic! You are a true goddess!" Caliban ran his hand through Miranda's hair and gently turned her face to his, gazed into her eyes, and kissed her deep and long.

"Oh, Caliban," she sighed, her body arching up and curving into his, "Oh, Caliban."

The President and Kit waded down yet another narrow, water-filled tunnel. The water sloshed around their knees, and their friendly guide seal, Edgar, led the way. The President was scanning the water and the walls and the roof of the tunnel for danger; and he was appreciating – almost in spite of himself – the way Kit's slender figure was reflected darkly in the rippling water; and he was thinking what an exquisite young woman she was, and what a tragedy and a waste it was to have classified such bright young people as Subs. While he was thinking all of this, the President was also traveling back in time; he was remembering:

The SIN Nikki – and her friend V – didn't waste time. The day after their first meeting, Nikki Hughes again appeared at the General's office.

"V asked me to tell you this. I'm rather embarrassed to say," said Nikki, standing before him. "V said, and I quote, 'If he harms either of you,' V told me, 'I shall hunt him down to the ends of the earth and I will destroy him and everything he holds dear. Tell him that,' she said."

"She is a devil," he smiled.

"She asked me to say this too: 'Tell him that I am quite fond of him.'"

"Ah, I see! Flattery."

"No. I don't think so. She actually blushed when she said it. General, I know her; she never blushes. It was not flattery; it was – something like affection, perhaps even love. She means it." The SIN seemed to be enjoying herself.

He smiled; it was an expansive smile: "So now we shall see what this creature, this daughter, spawned in the sewers by a human upon an alien, will become. Now we shall see what shall become of my very own sin."

"*Spawned in the sewers*: what an expression – really!" Nikki said, "V told me it was a canal, not a sewer."

"Poetic license," he said, "She's right; it was a canal, and a mossy bank, and a sweet smell of ozone and the open ocean not far away; but it was underground."

"So, we are agreed," Nikki said, "I raise the girl as my own, and she is not to know who her father and mother are."

"Yes. She is yours – by father unknown."

"Good," Nikki frowned, visibly wondering: What would it be like – being a mother to a daughter? She had had a son, but that had been so brief, a mere baby, and ...

"And you are not going to resume your film career," the General said.

"No. I have no intention of doing that. Why?"

"Because I don't want the girl around tinsel town people, I don't want her spoiled; I don't want her in the limelight, I don't want her involved in gossip and disloyalty and drugs and pettiness and tabloids and superficial fame and excessive attention and ostentation and ..."

Nikki laughed. "You really are strange! You call your own daughter a creature spawned in a sewer, some sort of hybrid monster, and yet you want to give her the best education and protect her from tinsel town!"

"Yes, I suppose it is funny." He stood up. "You know, Nikki, my SIN friend, what I do I do for the good and survival of humanity. If humanity is going to survive, it must transcend itself. It must become better. It must cultivate what is best, what is most brilliant. I want my daughter to be the best! I want her to be better than the best."

And then he and the SIN had shaken hands.

The SIN did have a good handshake, warm, and firm, and frank.

He wondered: was it really right that all the SINs should die? Was it really necessary, was it ...?

But the machinery was already in motion.

It was too late to stop. He had too many enemies, men – and some women – who would only be too glad to destroy him; and who would be much more ruthless than he – they were proponents of unlimited massacre, of SINs, Hybrids, and of much of the human race. And, besides, he now had a stake in his own survival, a personal stake.

The strange thing was that the SINs and Hybrids did very little to defend themselves – they were so sure they were integrated into society, they were so sure, most of them, that they were useful, that they were "part of the human family," they were so sure ... that they were ... *loved* ...

How sad it was, how pathetic, how tragic ...

They just couldn't believe it would happen.

And yet happen it did.

People often can't believe Fascism will arrive.

And yet it does.

And so, over the years, he had watched from afar, as the SIN, as Nikki Hughes – a fine mother in fact, more than fine, virtually perfect – had raised his daughter – Miranda, Miranda who was the result of a brief violent meeting of two worlds, of virtually two species.

Miranda …

Miranda had turned out to be resplendent, so beautiful she really did almost transcend humanity; and talented and effortlessly brilliant at her studies … scoring first in virtually everything she did, sports, social activity, academic studies; and she was popular too, adored by her Cosmos classmates …

She had become, ironically, but as he had wished, the very model of the best of Cosmos, the new type of humanity he was trying to forge.

Born of a hybrid and raised by a SIN!

And yet the very paragon of elite pure humanity Cosmos!

Racism was idiotic.

It made him wonder …

But it was too late for wonder!

Now that Miranda was dead, and now that Nikki was dead, there was no reason for the truce to be kept between him and V. Now, they would be free to hunt each other and to kill each other. But, as far as he was concerned, he had no intention of hunting V; as for his own life, it was not important – he had never really put much store on his life; often he had faced death, and not feared it, though he did love life – the challenge, the infinite variety of it. He was always curious about the ongoing story of the world: what was going to happen next? How to avoid the worst, how to strive for the best?

Well, I suppose we have gone beyond our quarrel, V and I – with the end of the world imminent. And it seems that now, with the Evil force unleashed, the Boy or whatever he or it is, and from what Kit tells me, V and I are on the same side, that V is about to do battle against the Dark Force that has possessed the Mind: *My enemy's enemy is my friend.*

If V wishes to kill me, I shall let her do it.

And now that the hybrids, such as Claire, are loose, they will certainly want blood, after all the suffering they have gone through, and the friends lost, murdered, tortured. They will want to kill me, well, then, I will die.

I have many things to answer for.

By her lights, V or Claire or a dozen others would be perfectly right to exact revenge, to demand justice, to be judge and executioner.

If V does purify and save the Mind, if she stops it from devouring the earth, then, perhaps, then, I will not have to explode the NN-Bomb – if I do manage to explode it, which is doubtful.

When he had found the Nuclear Vault, the Boy – or whatever he or it was – had been there before him: the guards were all dead; one woman Centurion – her nameplate said "Lieutenant Sylvia Negro" – had been tortured, that's what it certainly looked like. Her arms had been ripped off, and her abdomen gutted, acid had been dripped on her skin, and down her legs, and her eyes had been gouged out. Her face was streaked with excrement – a mustache of excrement and blood above her lips. The Evil One liked to toy with people, to torture them, to demonstrate its power; the Evil One was a joker, a trickster.

The door to the vault had been melted, pure steel turned to mush, then it had been frozen, and the face, well, the face was a carving of the face of a wolf, embossed, like a giant coin.

The President had put his hand on the smooth steel. It was glossy and perfect as liquid mercury.

If he was going to destroy Elysium and the Mind, he would have to blast his way in. But *how* would he blast his way in? He didn't have explosives; he didn't have tools. So, the only thing to do was to head directly to the Mind, see if he could stop it some other way: but, again, *how*?

And now, since meeting Kit, he had a new hope: perhaps his enemy V, the mother of his daughter, was bringing salvation. Perhaps V really was, as some had whispered, a goddess, perhaps she was, in her own primal way, a savior.

In any case, if the human race is saved, and if, then, I die, it is of no significance really, no significance at all.

And here I am wading through the murk of the underworld with some sort of mutant underground seal and with Kit, a teenage hybrid. I almost feel that – if I survive, if we survive – I'd like to adopt Kit. In a way, she is of the same race and species as Miranda: she could be my daughter.

I must be going insane.

"I don't think you're going insane."

"What?"

"Sorry, I guess I was eavesdropping," Kit gave him a sheepish look; she'd just caught the last little thought; that for some reason he thought he might be going mad. To her he seemed very sane.

"Eavesdropping," he said, "How much did you catch?"

"Just that little bit about you thinking you are going nuts."

"Oh," he smiled.

"I'll try not to do it anymore, mind-eavesdrop, I mean."

The seal was swimming along in front of them, and Kit was wading by the President's side; Kit reached out her hand and took his.

And so, they wadded through the glittering gloom, the mutant seal Edgar swimming in front of them, the teenage neophyte hybrid, and the President-Leader, while above them Elysium City and the human race were dying.

Miranda and Caliban walked hand in hand down the tunnel. They were now truly alone, truly faced with each other.

It seemed very peaceful, suddenly, as if all the battles and all the ghouls and zombie-bats and monsters and tentacles were far away.

They came out to the edge of an underwater canal and stood for a moment on the mossy bank, a sort of platform, sticking out into the canal, and looked at the swirling water, racing along and drifting with mist and silver currents in the ancient lamplight and in the phosphorescent glow of the lichen-covered walls. Here the water went over a shallow barrier, making a wide and silver – and quite poetic – waterfall.

The only sound was the sound of rippling and rushing water, though, in the far distance, there were muffled explosions and shouts and cries.

"This is very fine," said Miranda, "A mossy bank by a bubbling brook."

"Is it to be here?"

"Yes, Caliban, it is to be here," Miranda fluttered her eyelids at her man, her pirate, her Caliban, "This is the place."

Caliban drew Miranda to him, and he kissed her and he lifted off her silk skintight T-shirt, which squeaked voluptuously when he removed it, "Now, my Miranda," he said, "Is it truly to be now?"

"Yes, Caliban, it is most definitely truly to be now." And, suddenly feeling that her heart was beating very hard, Miranda stepped gracefully and almost without thinking out of her elite Cosmos hot-skin, skintight, slink-skin-shorts, and she allowed herself to lean against Caliban's chest; and she put her hands to work blindly but deftly, taking their time, as Kit had said, *time must be taken, respect must be shown, take care to unpeel slowly, graciously, tastefully*, and so Miranda's fingers worked at undoing – in the most delicate way possible – the knot of Caliban's loincloth.

As Kit had said, "Every moment, Miranda, every instant, is a gift, and each gift must be savored to the utmost!"

Miranda could feel Caliban's heartbeat under his strong smooth chest, and her fingers, as they worked at the knot, caressed his hip and one hand went up over his shoulder and stroked the back of his neck.

The water rushed, sparkling and silver, along the underground tunnel, rushing over the cascade, giving the whole place a whispering hot ozone feel, a steamed-up hothouse-of-paradise sensation, a smell of the open ocean, with the feeling of a closed-in steam bath.

The old lamps shone through the drifting mist, the shadows of support bars threw dark rippling zebra lines across the water, across the crooked smooth old stones, across their two bodies.

Miranda's lips touched Caliban's lips.

"I was conceived down here, somewhere, perhaps on this very canal," Miranda breathed, her mouth close to his.

"I know," Caliban breathed the very perfume and the breath of life onto her lips, just grazed their ripeness, softly, softly, "You told me," he whispered, his breath tickling her cheek.

Miranda believed she had one knot of Caliban's loincloth undone, but it turned out there were two knots, this was a layered and knotty affair, Caliban's loincloth, in spite of its casual appearance. Of course, she thought, it must be an impregnable and difficult knot; he cannot have his loincloth unravel in the midst of a battle: where would that leave him? Her index finger and thumb were carefully, delicately, groping their way to a solution, her sharp nails helping. But still the damned knot resisted! She considered herself an expert at tying knots, pirate knots and sailor knots, and she had a gold metal she received from the President himself, the Leader – sigh, and, it seemed, her father! – in honor of her knots, and her knot prowess; but this knot, which must be of Caliban's own secret trademarked devising, had extra tricks up its sleeve; although the toil of undoing it was not entirely unpleasant. Indeed, the delay, was adding to the … pleasure … Miranda's mouth was watering, and she could hear not only Caliban's heart but also her own, and they seemed to be drumming along in perfect harmony. And as Kit had said, "each moment must have its moment." And then Caliban's hip-bone was so smooth, and muscular, and dynamic, and the way his tummy, so yummy and so muscular, slanted down, tense, strong, was pressed against hers, and he himself, the heart of his maleness, was hard, and was erect … and … hard … and …

"This way," said Caliban, his eyes gazing straight into her eyes, his lips close to hers, his breath mingling with hers, sweetly, so sweetly, and while with one hand he was caressing her hair, his other hand was turning her slightly sideways, and moving slowly down her back, palm spread, tracing its way down along her spine, and then out over her hip, oh so smoothly, and then over her backside, as if he were sculpting her out of clay, creating her, tingling soft new sensations, inventing her for the first time, and then around the small of her back, just the slightest arching pressure, and around the smooth luscious curve of her hip, until his hand joined hers, just where she was trying to undo the bloody complicated loincloth knot, and with a subtle soft twist of the wrist he guided her fingers, and – *abracadabra, presto, voilà!* – the knot was undone, and the loincloth opened and drifted away and fell, brushing along Miranda's thigh and leg, to the mossy ground, and Miranda now felt she should reciprocate – this was different from and even more exciting – the stakes being much higher – than "making out" with Kit in all those delightful inebriating test flights they had made together, and her heart was pounding more and more, and she felt a flush spreading on her cheeks and an antsy nervous rising tide of a ripple in her tummy, a regular tsunami, and her thighs seemed to have become liquid and yet strong and eager as if they wished to seize something between them, and she thought, Well, I guess being a hybrid doesn't mean becoming phlegmatic and stoic and indifferent to all things human, and, balancing on one foot, she lifted her string-panty-under-skin off one leg, let it go, and let it slide and slip lazily down the other leg ....

Fluttering breathlessly into nakedness, Miranda offered her body up to her Pirate Prince.

Breathless, oh, she felt breathless; her heart was rising up, breathless, as if it were a small boat tossed in a storm, bounced from wave to wave ...

In telling Kit of his encounter with V, the President had left out the whole part about Miranda and of course he told Kit nothing of his meetings with the beautiful Nikki Hughes; he had just told Kit of the horror he had felt at seeing the dead young man; he told her a bit of the struggle in the Ruling Junta over the destruction of the SINs and the hybrids.

He glanced at Kit – so beautiful and in her own spunky way so innocent, and so exquisitely intelligent and high-spirited.

"I had a daughter." He wiped his forehead. "I thought I'd kept her safe, but ... I lost her."

"I had a friend," said Kit, turning to look at him, "but I lost her."

For a second, staring at the President, Kit could see Miranda, bright as day, luminous: a pure angelic vision!

"You know, Kit, I lost every man and woman on my team coming down here. Every single one of them was killed, all the officers who were with me, and the scientists. They were loyal. They were the best. They were my friends. They were good people." He thought of his beautiful Executive Assistant, quick with a gun, ultra-cool, and yet she had died in a flash and agony of pain. How he had escaped, the only one to survive, he had no idea.

"I'm sorry," said Kit.

The President put hand arm on her shoulder and just nodded and Kit knew what he was thinking; that for him even to thank her – since she had suffered such great loss herself and largely at his hands – would be tactless.

She liked him more and more.

They waded on, heading toward the Mind, the water sloshing around their waists, Edgar pushing ahead and glancing back every few moments to see that they were following him.

In the last few days, in the Supreme Council, everything had been paralyzed and everything had been in a panic. Nothing worked. The population, Cosmos and Subs, had no idea how serious the situation was.

The reactionaries – the worst of the band – were planning a coup against him. They wanted to purge the population of Subs and also to nuke – using "clean" nukes – some of the Burbs where riots were spreading that might even threaten the foundations of Elysium and Cosmos Power.

This to him was an abomination.

After all, the Burbites and Subs were humans.

And he had sworn, as his basic aim, to protect human civilization, at least what could be protected and saved.

Then, too, if he lost power, Miranda and Nikki would be exposed. So, he decided to send them to a safe place; his first choice was with friends in the Mountain Redoubt of Fortress Switzerland; but when that proved impossible, he chose his friend the military governor of Hawaii, General Herzog.

And, in trying to save Miranda and Nikki, he had gotten them killed. How could he have been so stupid!

Everything had gone wrong.

Everything had disintegrated around him.

For an instant he had contemplated ending it all; but …

493

No, the fight must continue.

And now, this young person, Kit Candy, had renewed his faith in the future; perhaps humanity would survive after all, even if in the form of hybrids. Perhaps the hybrids would inherit the earth; they were half-human at least.

The collapse of satellite communications and the disappearance of the West Coast and then of the Central Desert outposts meant that something unprecedented and terrible was happening. It was as if parts of the world were being swallowed up in a black hole.

"It is some sort of leakage, some sort of cosmic leakage," said his Scientific Advisor, Doctor Hawkins, "some sort of evil force, coming through the membrane of space-time."

"The World Mind has been captured," said Doctor Drake-Yoon, Hawkins's assistant, "the Mind has been captured, and it is being morphed."

"Morphed?" he had asked, "What do you mean *morphed*?"

"Transformed, it is being transformed into something hostile. Right now, all it is doing is destroying our communications and lots of our machinery, but the evil side of the World Mind will become active. It will become active and it will destroy everything."

"But how can the Mind destroy everything?"

"It is biological, now. It is a life form, a true Mind."

"I know that," he said, swiveling in his chair.

"Yes, Mr. President, you know that, we know that, but we have not thought out the implications of this fact – not really – no one has."

"Yes, I see," he had said, and he reflected ruefully that, in his own amateurish way he had thought out the implications and he had taken the precaution of un-linking his mind, and those of his immediate staff, from the Mind, and he had alerted several of his most loyal Centurion units, and he had told Nikki Hughes, too, his SIN friend, of what he feared.

She had said, "You are right, if it's biological then it will develop a mind and personality of its own," she had said, "I should know."

"Yes, Nikki," he had said, "If anyone knows, you would."

"I'll protect Miranda," she had said.

"Thank you, Nikki."

"I don't need thanks," she smiled.

"No, I know you don't." He had long realized: Miranda was Nikki's daughter now, above all Miranda was Nikki's daughter.

But, since his fears were the fears of an amateur, a non-scientist, he had not shared them, except with Nikki, with his assistant, and with a few chosen Centurion Units.

He would have to convince the Supreme Council; he broached the subject; they were violently, dogmatically, against un-linking: it would cost money, reduce efficiency in the economic machine, and it might create panic and mistrust. If he insisted, they would overthrow him. His hold on power was slipping and slipping quickly. He had to proceed step-by-step. He tried to learn as much as he could about the threat.

"Come on, Mr. President, let's not dawdle," Kit flashed him a big bright smile, "If we dither, if we fiddle, if we falter, Rome will burn, the whole world will die, not just us."

"Right, yes, Kit, you are right," he said.

CHAPTER 11 – BIO-ARMAGGEDON

Norman C. Schleifer sneezed. Another big gob of snot spurted out of his nostrils. It was white and veined with red. He stared at the back of his hand and shook the stuff off. He wasn't feeling so hot. It was sweltering now, and almost as dark as night, and rain had been falling – the rain was full of sand – and he'd spotted a few tornadoes moving across the Burbs in the half-light. He'd come across more of those crowds of weird people and he'd avoided them. They looked like one big sick joke; some sort of grotesque carnival caprice or initiation caper. It was not funny.

He sneezed again and saw that he'd generated another whooper of a gob of red-ribbon snot. He rubbed it off on a broken garbage container and staggered onwards wondering what the hell was wrong with him.

A sparrow came fluttering down thinking the gob was something to eat and in fact it was, and very tasty. The sparrow ate and ate and then called other sparrows.

The sparrows gathered around, ate their full, and then took off.

One of the sparrows was caught by a hawk and eaten.

The hawk flew up high and dropped bits and pieces of the sparrow on a tenement balcony where some children were playing.

The sparrows scattered and pooped happily here and there.

A rat poked at a bit of bird poop that had fallen on an intriguing piece of garbage. The rat sneezed, then went down a drainpipe, along a service tunnel, and joined the pack of rats, some of whom were heading toward Elysium Domed city where it was rumored big things were happening and lots of food – dead ghouls, dead people – was freshly available.

A baby came out onto the balcony and picked up a bit of feather and flesh that had fallen from the sky and sniffed at it and chewed it. The baby's mother picked the baby up and scolded it, and pried the feather from the baby's teeth, "Bad baby!" The baby sneezed full in its mother's face.

The Doomsday Bug was spreading fast.

Norm staggered into a pub, one of the few still functioning, and he had a beer – and he sneezed. The barman publican picked up a double-barreled sawed-off shotgun and said, "Hey, Buddy, maybe you should go home with that – otherwise I'm gonna turn you into one of the living dead like those skeleton people they're talking about."

Norm paid for the beer and left – he didn't want trouble – he was feeling too lousy for that. He staggered out into the light – it seemed bright, blinding bright, even though it was dark as Hades and seemed almost like night, but it was day he was pretty certain unless the clock in his head had gone all screwy. God! He felt awful. He stumbled his way toward home, taking back alleys and shortcuts to avoid the crowds of skinny beggars or living dead or whatever the hell those things were. They looked like frigging skeletons. "I think I am fucking dying," he muttered. Things were beginning to get tricky. Things looked really weird. He was dripping sweat. Something BIG was going wrong with the world.

When he got back to the tenement and began to climb up toward his flat, he almost fell back down the stairs. Angela Balzac was sitting crouched on the two top steps just outside his door her adorable knees up to her chin; her big eyes were all wet; her cheeks shone; she'd been crying. "The world is coming to an end, Norm," she said. She stood up, squinting at him as he came up the stairs; he was a bulky silhouette backlit from the staircase window, and then, when she saw him up close, her face changed and she said, "Holy shit, what's happened to you! Norm, you look like death! Norm, here let me help you."

She hoisted his arm over her shoulders – he was a big heavy man and he was staggering – and helped him into his little flat. He was burning up.

"You're like a furnace," she said, "I'll make tea."

"You're real friendly," he said, thinking, vaguely, she must be really scared if she was being this nice to him. He sneezed sending a spray of droplets all over the place and catching her in the face.

"Fuck, Norm!" She backed away and wiped at her face. "I'll make that tea," she went to the cook unit.

Norm sat down on the edge of his cot. God, he felt awful. "What are you afraid of, Angela?" He began to cough and doubled over but then was able to straighten up. He looked at his arm – something funny, little sores he hadn't noticed before. They looked like little bubbles. While he looked, they seemed to grow, getting bigger, and multiplying. That couldn't be right. Nothing worked that fast! He sniffled. It was like his nose was running too. He wiped at his nose with the back of his hand. God, did he feel awful! Outside the window, sand was streaming down; the air was darkening; the humidity must be 100 percent and the temperature maybe 110.

"What am I afraid of?" Angela had the water almost boiling. She was leaning over the unit. Norm watched her. He felt ultra-horny. Boy, her skin-shorts were short! Boy, she had beautiful legs! She was talking. She had such a beautiful voice, like soft honey. "What am I afraid of?" she paused. "Well, I'm afraid of the storms, there's a superstorm coming in. It's going to hit Elysium, like a really super, superstorm. And then, Norm there are these flying things, like big bats or vampires or something, they've been killing people, I saw it on the Alison-and-Ken Show. Norm, the stuff that's been happening! You won't believe. I mean, Elysium is collapsing, Norm! And, then Norm, I mean, there are dead people out there, they say, it's a sort of voodoo revival, the end of the world and the raising of the dead, and these dead people have been going around killing real people." Angela stopped and poured the tea mix into a cup.

Norm had been half listening. It was like Angela and the tea machine and the weird yellow light outside the window – with its streams of sultry steamy sand – had drifted off into some alternative universe. He stared at the back of his hand. It was covered in black goo. It looked like treacle, whatever treacle was, but it must be blood. It looked like his blood was turning black. No fucking way! And his arm, God, his fucking arm! The little bubbles were getting really big, some of them burst, they squirted liquid, they left craters behind, they …

Angela turned to bring the tea.

"Jesus Christ, Norm!" she almost dropped the cup.

There was a banging and clattering from downstairs.

"Jesus Christ, Norm!"

"What the fuck's up?" Norm said; his voice was a deep gurgle and he felt his throat exploding inside into goo. He threw up an ocean of goo. He looked at his hands; it was like they were swelling up into mitts, bubbling, the fingers fusing together, the skin bursting, drooling.

"Norm …" Angela was, like, paralyzed.

"Yeah …" His voice now was a gurgle.

"Oh, Norm!" Angela stared at him. His arms and chest were bubbling up with sores, like little bubbles, and little volcanoes, they popped, with a tiny liquid slapping sound. They spewed and spurted out what looked black glue, black mist.

"Oh, Norm," Angela just stared. "Oh, Norm."

Norm's face, above his beard, seemed to be melting. One of his eyes had turned black and the blackness began to drip onto his cheek which was bubbling and sliding and part of his beard slid away, his skin sloughing off, or so it seemed; but that was impossible, Angela took a deep breath, all of this was impossible. Outside, the wind was roaring, past the window streamed rivers of wet, yellowing sand.

Angela stepped forward and she set the teacup down on the bedside table. Norm radiated heat and exuded a sweet sticky sort of smell that made her want to gag. He looked up at her his one good eye, which seemed to have changed shape in his melting face. Angela backed away, trying not to breathe. It might be catching whatever it was.

Some ruckus was going on downstairs.

Mrs. Moore on the first floor screamed. Somebody was breaking windows. There were shouts. Shots were fired. Mr. Harris screamed something about "Get the fuck away from me, you freaks!" There were more shots. There was a double-barreled wham; it sounded like Mr. Harris's shotgun; it must be Harris's shotgun. Angela heard all this as if in a dream.

"I don't feel so good, kid," Norm said in his gurgling clogged voice, thick with phlegm, his ghastly one eye turned brightly toward her, "I mean, I think I'm maybe sick, kid. You know you look so beautiful, really cute, like something fresh and innocent, like paradise, like beginning everything over again, as if there were no yesterdays, you know what I mean, like nothing had been done that couldn't be undone, I always thought, I mean, if I hadn't been such a slob, I mean, if I cleaned up my act, if I got my shit together, I mean, I sort of thought that maybe you and I, you know, only if you wanted to …"

"Norm," Angela was backing toward the door. "Norm, you're sick. You're really sick, Norm. I'll try to get …"

Norm vomited up a huge gush of black fluid.

"Oh, Norm," Angela reached out her hand as if she could somehow stop events, as if she could somehow shout, "Stop! Stop" and time would stop, and Norm would be okay.

Norm's one good eye exploded in a geyser of black fluid; his ruined dissolving face turned away from her, his voice, deeper now, bubbled up, "A guy came to see me, he was an angel ..."

Norm doubled over. Steam rose from his body. His clothes were darkening from bursting craters of bloody pus. His body went into a series of writhing convulsions.

"Norm, I'm sorry." Angela backed out of Norm's room. She pulled the door behind her. The lock snapped shut. The ruckus down below had ceased but there was a murmuring clicking clacking sound. It sounded like an army of knitting-needles.

Angela took a deep breath. She peeked down over the balustrade. Mrs. Moore was lying in a circle of light from that old first floor oil-lamp; she had been torn to pieces; that was what it looked like, she looked like a broken doll, one arm had been torn off, and her face and skull were all bloody, and it looked like half her hair and scalp had been ripped off, it looked like something that had been done in a tsunami of pure homicidal rage. And standing around Mrs. Moore's body were what looked like a bunch of mummies or skeletons from some sort of cheap ancient horror flick. One of the mummies looked up. It was a woman mummy, and she was holding by the hand a skeleton, a kid skeleton. They were all skin-and-bones those people. The woman mummy made a clicking sound. And all the mummies and skeletons all looked up and saw Angela and began to climb the stairs.

Angela was stunned. For a second or two she didn't realize what was happening. Then, suddenly, it dawned on her: they're not people! They're the living dead! And they are coming for me! She looked around. She could run to the roof; she could go to her own room and lock the door. She could jump out the staircase window. She could ...

She ran up the stairs toward the roof.

Behind her she could hear the clattering skeletons and shuffling mummies and a sort of murmuring, like a chorus of dead voices. It was a clicking babble, as if human language had been lost and forgotten. It was horrible.

God Almighty, what was going on?

She got to the top of the stairs.

She unbarred the door that led to the roof and she opened it, and she went out onto the roof which was flat here and gave her a good view of the neighborhood and, in the distance, of the great dome of Elysium City. She pushed the old roof ventilator – it had wheels – against the door and toppled it over, jamming it as tight as she could, hoping maybe it would keep them out, at least for a little while. She took a deep breath and looked around. Where could she go from here?

Out in a Cosmos Burb Bubble, two hours before the living dead climbed up the stairs in pursuit of Angela Balzac, the phone rang, and Ed Malone considered not picking it up.

Ed was CEO of Bio-Futures and of a dozen other untaxed, unregulated, cheap-labor underground Burb-based companies; he was already quite aware, thank you, that the world was in awful shape, sliding toward something that looked suspiciously like the Apocalypse and the absolute end of everything.

Elysium City was imploding; the President, a good man in spite of everything, had been killed – assassinated probably by that band of thieves and Fascists who surrounded him, particularly Jacob F. Shavtick. The Evil Band included the followers of Ed's former patron, the evil, crazy, and very much deceased Colonel Konrad – and really weird things were happening to the whole planet. The phone info display said, James Harding, Bio-Security; *what now?* Ed sighed, and picked the telephone up.

"We got a problem, Doc."

"What problem?"

"Some eco-terrorists broke into the lab and killed the three guards and the damned dogs too and …"

"Did they get into Section A, the freezer section?"

"Yeah, Doc, they did, and smashed everything too. Let all the animals loose and smashed all the refrigeration units, including the high security, and the armored fridge. We've got snakes running around loose."

"Oh, my God! Well …"

"Yeah, we didn't realize at first what was happening. You see the central electronic breakdown infected the security systems; we didn't even realize these systems were linked into and dependent upon the main frame systems in Elysium City, it must be code-dependent at some deep level, Doc, so we got no video feeds, nothing …" James Harding stopped and sneezed. "The on-site guards were all killed – and the dogs."

"What about your people, the backup team, did they …?"

"We're here now at the labs. Three of my team are complaining about headaches and one has a very bad nosebleed and some sores on her arms. And, come to think about it, I'm not feeling so good myself. Say, Doc, is there anything really dangerous in here? I've got a whole team – twelve people – securing the site."

"No, no, it's probably allergic reactions – there's a lot of old biomaterial in there, you know, it'll give you watery eyes, skin rash, that sort of thing."

"I'm glad to hear, Doc, 'cause ..." James Harding sneezed again; a whooper. Though Harding was head of security at the firm which assured the biotech lab, knowledge was on a strict "need to know" basis; and the security people, the former CEO had decreed, did not need to be in the know, specifically, they should NOT be made aware that the laboratory contained an illegal bacterium that was almost certainly the most contagious and deadliest bacterium ever put together on the planet earth by either nature or man.

"Stay right there. I'm coming in." Ed Malone hung up. He looked at Honey Rose. She was reclining, naked, out on the patio under the awing of their personalized dome, a free zone luxury compound for Cosmos who for one reason or another worked in the ex-industrial Burbs. The light fluttered down on her body. She was a beauty, an exquisite racial mixture, a quarter his age, and he'd picked her up while in Bolivia on a holiday. She looked like she was in paradise.

Five months earlier, during the preliminary trials of the newly modified Yersinia Pestis-XIII or modified Bubonic Plague, one of the experts, an easily excitable genius sort of guy, a Frenchman, who was only in his twenties, Jason Tremblay, said, "This is awesome, I mean, this doesn't just infect a body, this liquefies bodies. It turns them into mush."

"It certainly does have great potential, Jason," said Doctor Ed Malone, Jason's immediate superior, and soon to be CEO, peering at the computer screen which was hooked directly into the lab cage. Ed was thinking, this whole thing should be shut down. The President-Leader was right. Maybe I should tell the President. But ... No ... Whistle-blowers end up dead.

The guinea pig was a prisoner – Janice Forte, 18, mother of one four-year-old girl – an illegal immigrant caught in the desert in the Super Dust Bowl Dead Lands. Janice, who was a nice, naïve kid, had been promised immunity and immigrant status and a residence permit for herself and her little girl in exchange for "participating in a few simple experiments." The results of those experiments were pretty clear.

Janice Forte would not be needing immigrant status.

Her daughter would never get a residence permit.

Jason was almost dancing with excitement. "Yeah, I mean, see what just shifting a bit of DNA around can do, it is fucking awesome!"

"Awesome is probably the right word, Jason," said Doctor Ed Malone, who had been professor of molecular biology at MIT, and who was turning pale – under his Outer Elysium Dome golf tan. He was watching as Janice Forte, pretty and sweet 18, was being turned into a pile of steamy mush. You could literally see it happening. The process was so dynamic it created a heat shock in the flesh and blood. Her screams, on the other side of the bullet-proof sound-proof glass, were inaudible, probably pretty bubbly, since her throat and mouth were disintegrating.

"Is that steam rising from the body, Jason?"

"Fucking right, it is steam, Doc!" Jason clapped his hands; his grin was too bright, simply insane. An excessively high IQ can do that to you.

Doctor Malone steeled himself and watched the whole thing, right to the bitter end. It didn't take long, though it seemed like hours; this was perhaps – no, this was certainly – the deadliest bioweapon ever created, by far, no comparison: it was off the map, a thing onto itself.

And it had the extra diabolic feature that it had a variable latency period; some people would show symptoms right away and die; but others could carry the thing – in active form – for days, even weeks, and not show the slightest symptom. And this meant, of course, that such carriers could spread the disease across the country, across the world …

Even better, birds and bats and rats and fleas could carry it; but birds and bats and rats and fleas did not get sick from it; so the birds and bats and so on could happily carry it everywhere, even to the most remote outposts, their piss, their shit would spread it easily, into the water, into the wind.

It was a time-release plague and it was specifically designed to target humans – Homo sapiens – and nothing else.

It was precisely the type of doomsday machine that Konrad had asked for. In fact, it was the very best that could be designed!

Right now, two hours after initial injection, Janice Forte was a bubbling mass – more like a puddle – of black and red and yellow pustules, hardly recognizable as a human being. Disposing of the mess would require very special precautions.

"How close are we to a vaccine, Doc?" Jason's eyes shone.

"We're not there yet. I can't tell; a year, maybe a year and a half."

"That's a dangerous window, Doc."

"I realize that, Jason, I realize that," said Ed Malone, stroking his chin: maybe he'd better try to destroy this thing before it was too late. Maybe he'd better quit. Maybe he'd better move to Mars.

That night, after watching Janice Forte melt into a puddle of bio goo, when he was lying in bed beside Honey Rose – and she smelled just like that, honey and rose – Doctor Malone remained wide awake, long after midnight. "You know, honey, I think maybe I should go back to Academe."

"Sure, honey," she yawned, "whatever."

She was wearing a sleep mask and face cream and was half asleep and, yes, a quarter his age and not terribly educated – though she was a beauty and possessed an ass which was unparalleled in all of North America – perhaps in the whole wide world – and a face of incredible New World Hispanic purity and symmetry – so there was no way he should – or could – discuss his dilemma, whether to destroy the doomsday machine or not, or his work with her: and in any case his work was top secret and he was sworn to the utmost secrecy; if anyone found out what research he was doing, in particular if the President-Leader found out, Doctor Malone would be dead or spend the rest of his life in an isolation cell; besides he had three former wives he had to pay for and his present mistress – Sequin Sprinkle, his occasional late evening or "business trip" entertainment – lived in an outrageously expensive loft in Elysium City. No, he couldn't go back to being a mere professor.

And, now, with the phone call from Harding, chief of security, Ed knew that the doomsday bug had been released.

There was no way it could be put back in the bottle.

And, yes, there was no vaccine. And no antidote.

He thought for a minute. He had an isolated cottage in the Canada State East Arctic Frontier Zone Quebec near a lake where nobody ever went, on the coast facing Baffin Island. He hadn't been there for a long time – mosquitoes and black flies and snakes such as Burmese pythons and animals such subtropical polar bear mutants and high IQ wild huskies made the place seem unfriendly. But he had weapons and the cottage was armored and stocked with canned goods. It had its own well. And it had a generator and a solar roof. It had weapons. The big old bed was comfortable, if a bit squeaky. The mouse droppings were not excessive. They could maybe have a week or two or more of their own little paradise before Death came to find them – in the form of a migrating mutant Canada goose, or a starling, or one of those aggressive Arctic parrots. He'd pack morphine. When the moment came, he could end it for both of them. No need to alarm Honey Rose; make it soft, a romantic death, sweet tasteless poison by wine and candlelight.

Or, maybe, if a miracle happened, they could wait it out, maybe survive, maybe live. That was doubtful; this was not the sort of bacterium that would burn itself out; it would lie in wait, and it would kill and kill and kill, over decades, perhaps over centuries, perhaps forever. He made a decision.

He stood up, opened the sliding door to the patio, and said, "Honey, pack up, we are getting out of here."

"Gee, honey … gee, sweetie-pie, why …?" She looked up from the recliner. Golden patina of sweat on her skin, beauty mask on her face.

"No questions, now, my darling, my little darling." He stepped out into the sauna-like heat of the patio and pulled her up and wrapped his arms around her and kissed her; yes, he really did love her, got a hard-on just by touching her, just by thinking about her. Looking at her now – her all dewy-eyed and naked and with a mud mask – made him want to throw her down, stretch her out, kiss her, caress her, work her into a frenzy, open her up, and shout, "Me Tarzan, You Jane …"

Of course, if you were waiting for the end of the world, Sequin Sprinkle, the New SoHo Art Chic Zone Elysium City body-modification, performance artist might provide more intense fun – I mean, particularly if there was time to pack the skin underwear and whips and chains and latex and such-like erotic equipment. But there was no time, he'd just have to leave Sequin there in New SoHo, and he could picture it … Death comes to Elysium City. Sequin Sprinkle would probably die on the floor of her studio; or maybe she would die on the big bed with the black silk sheets and the red bedside lights and the …and she would within minutes turn into a bubbling mass of bursting pus.

"Hurry, honey," he said, "We gotta do this quick!"

"Yes, yes, honey, I'm coming." She was tramping, flop, flop, flop, into the bedroom in her high-heeled strapless mules, her full lips, big eyes, skin like golden satin. Oh, God, life is so worth living …

"Five minutes," he said, looking at his watch, and thinking we've got to get out of here before the panic starts, and he ordered his personal air taxi for ten minutes … Pay the guy to fly them all the way if he can do it … If the guy refused, well, then he would take over and fly the thing himself, it was mostly automatic anyway, that is if GPS was working, and that was far from a sure thing. Maybe he could just fly low and follow the rivers and lakes, the ones that remained. Yeah, gotta do it before the panic starts. He began tossing necessities into a small suitcase.

"I never realized, till now, how the World Mind could invade human minds, even ones that are unconnected," the President said, "and how it can change our perceptions. The way it manipulates space-time, or our perceptual organization of space-time, is amazing."

"Yes," Kit took his hand; the current was stronger here. The air smelled of ozone. "It can create whole worlds, whole scenarios. It put me into a sort of torture chamber where this guy had me locked down in some sort of evil dentist's chair and he cut out my tongue."

"Ugh!" said the President.

"I still don't know if it was real or imaginary because my tongue grew again – boy was that weird! Now, I guess, I can regenerate."

"Because you're a hybrid," said the President.

"Yes, because I'm a hybrid." She was looking at him with those dark eyes, and then for some reason she pressed against him, putting her arms around him, laying her head against his chest, the dark, glistening water sloshing around them. The President put his hand against her cheek, and held her for a moment. How often had he dreamed – well, had the fantasy – of holding Miranda against him like this, of comforting her.

The seal, Edgar, stopped, and turned and came up to them and nosed at them gently.

"Okay, Edgar, on we go," Kit laughed and patted the creature's head.

The President told Kit of his own descent into the underworld of Elysium, on an expedition – a quixotic expedition – to try to save humanity by destroying or neutralizing the Mind.

He'd taken Jim Williams and Linda Webster and Pat Key-Hong with him, and Zelinsky and Wood, and Amanda Lincoln and Serena Burke.

He knew that power was going to be grabbed by Jacob Shavtick in a coup d'état, but he didn't have enough people on hand to stop Shavtick. It was first things, first, and the first thing was the survival of the human race – and the planet.

They got to the 1-D level and Linda Webster complained of a headache and suddenly her eyes spurted blood and then her head exploded. Somehow, she had not disconnected herself, not completely.

They got to level 1-B and Jim Williams picked a fight with Pat Key-Hong and the two of them fought like devils and the only way to stop them was for him to shoot one of them and then the other came at him like a wild beast. So he shot him too. Both of them dead: Jim and Pat.

"Jesus," said Serena.

"God Almighty," Zelinsky looked at the President with dark eyes, and then looked away.

On Sub-50 level, Zelinsky and Wood sat down and began to cry; then they stripped naked and began to slash themselves with their knives and to burn their limbs with their lasers. He tried to talk to them. He threatened. He said he would shoot them both. They looked at him with empty eyes. Serena tried to inject them with sedative or anti-psychotics, but they just attacked her. "Leave them," he said.

"But they'll die," she said.

"They'll die, yes, one way or another."

"Yes, sir," she said; there were tears in her eyes; the President knew that she and Zelinsky had had an affair two years ago.

"I'm sorry, Serena," he said.

On Sub-32 level they met some ghouls, weird creatures, who spat and fought and bubbled white chalky glue, and Amanda caught a splat full in her face and it leaked in between her visor and then she began to change and she became a drooling hulking monster, she who had been so beautiful, she begged that he shoot her before the morph was complete. He did, between the eyes, then in the back of neck. They left her body behind, a ghoul's body. Now, the only one left was Serena.

"And then there were two," Serena said.

"Yes, and then there were two."

They came to a place where there was singing.

"Plug your ears," He said, "put your earphones on, full blast sound!"

She did; he did.

The singing made you feel you desired something infinitely; it made you feel that life was infinitely sweet and yet that you were missing something, something you had to search for, seek out, explore.

Then it appeared, in front of them: a many-headed serpentine monster.

Serena advanced toward it, opening her arms.

"Don't, Serena, don't," he said.

He stood in front of her. She drew her laser, focused it on him.

"Don't do this, Serena, it's a trap."

Her eyes were empty.

He wanted to shoot her, perhaps shoot her in the leg. But, being wounded down here would mean death. He pushed her back. She fell down, and she fired at him with the laser, but he had already jumped back, swirling around just in time to see the monster leap onto her. It made a yelp of delight, or seemed to; perhaps it was just a sound in his mind. He still had the earphones on, blasting out Beethoven's Fifth.

The thing slashed at Serena and cut her in a thousand places.

He shot it; he hacked off its limbs; from every fragment, every stump, new snake-like limbs grew. Finally he withdrew. The thing began to drag Serena's shattered bloodied body away.

He attacked it again.

It slashed at him and threw him backward, smashing him against the wall, and he lost consciousness – not for long, but for long enough.

When he woke, Serena had been half-digested, and the thing that had absorbed her into itself began to sing a song, in her voice.

The monster sang the song, hummed, used her words …

"I am not me anymore," the remains of a mouth spoke, "Leave me, I am not me!"

"I'm sorry," he said.

"You tried to prevent it. Go now. It will spare you, but not for long."

"It is toying with us."

"Yes, and I am gone. Forget me!"

"Goodbye, Serena." He retreated in horror.

The answer was a peal of horrendous laughter, and a belch of fetid air.

He thought: the Mind will spawn replicas of itself.

He thought: the Mind will suck us up and empty us out and if anything remains of humans at all it will be a shadow and a ghost and a puppet.

"So, they died, Kit, all of them died."

"Why did you not succumb, then, Mr. President, to the siren song, I mean?"

"I don't know, Kit, I don't know. Blind luck, probably. Maybe it had some secret reason for sparing me." He looked at her as if she were the arbiter of all that was good and just, the wisest person in the world, the only person in the world.

Kit now understood Miranda's fascination with the President – after all, Miranda had met the man! Then the thought: *Oh, Miranda!* The aching, yearning pain shot like a bolt of lightning through Kit's chest; Miranda, dead and gone, inexistent, to be seen no more, how awful, how horrible, how tragic … And Nikki, gone, blown up in that terrible plane crash. "It all seems so unreal," she said.

"Yes, the world is an unending dream, Kit Candy, particularly down here," said the President.

"Or a nightmare, sometimes, for some people," said Kit.

"Yes, Kit, that's right," the President shone his light on the walls of the cavern. Eyes embedded in the walls sparkled back at them, "The Mind is playing games again – or the Foul Fiend – or the Boy."

"Oh, oh," said Kit.

"The walls are watching us," the President focused a high beam on one of the eyes; it had very long lashes; it blinked; a tear glistened at the edge of the eye, and trickled down the concrete.

"We may be inside the Mind already."

"I wonder," the President was stroking his chin, looking thoughtful. "I wonder why it has let us come this far. Surely it could have stopped us, destroyed us."

"Yes."

Crowds of still-living humans, Subs and Cosmos mixed together, were stampeding away from downtown toward midtown as the downtown buildings collapsed and were eaten and as the madness spread.

Green Meadows Tower, a residential complex, collapsed into the Downtown Stadium, thousands of people were trapped, then engulfed in the dissolving goo of the Mind.

Here and there isolated Centurion units tried to keep order, medical units were overrun; public transport collapsed, people of every kind and on every side exploded into geysers of blood, or morphed into homicidal maniacs, or were suddenly reduced to empty-eyed, drooling puppets.

And from the opening skies – under the collapsing dome with great fragments of steel and glass showering down – came the zombie-bats, those weird huge creatures, hunters, birds of prey.

Throughout Elysium, the drumbeat of pure terror grew louder, ever louder.

Under his tan, under the glamorous patina of sweat, TV anchor Ken Ivison was pale, his five o'clock shadow was darker, "When confronted with those, those zombies, those creatures, I … I saw visions, I saw …"

"I know Ken, I know, darling, don't worry," Alison tightened her grip on his arm. She had by some sort of mysterious osmosis seen and felt what he had seen and felt: and it was horrifying – it was insight into the act of creation of the zombie-bats, insight into some sort of Force of Evil which had transformed men and women into … winged monsters …

She had seen The Boy on the porch of a farmhouse, she had seen the girl Billie McAdams, she had felt the girl's horror, she had seen what Billie had seen; and she had seen a blind tongueless old man, in a barn or hayloft, being torn apart, she had seen the zombie-bats, and she had seen into their minds. This Force of Evil, this force that had come into the world … Alison let the thought dangle, there would be time, perhaps, time later to make sense of all this; right now the question was simple – would she and Ken live, or would they die?

She was in love; and she wanted to live.

She was in love; and she would sacrifice anything so that Ken would live.

Ken and Alison had left the two dead zombie-bats behind, and hurried down a spiral service staircase that took them down ten more floors.

There, suddenly, the staircase came to an end at the Ruckus Mudcock Memorial Museum. They were in a backstage storage facility. The loading gates were huge and were locked shut. They would have to go out into the open, into the Museum.

From behind the large service doors came noise.

It did not sound like a celebration.

Ken tensed. Alison understood. Her fingers tightened on his arm. "It's the Ruckus Mudcock Memorial Museum," he whispered. I think some kind of battle is going on."

Alison whispered back, "Yes."

"But we have to go through the Museum Hall – no other way."

"Okay, boss, you are my leader."

"Well …" Ken almost blushed.

"Hail, Hail, All Hail," Alison whispered, and her fingers took a dig at Ken's arm.

Beyond the doorway they could hear yowling and shouts and screams and the occasional gunshot and some music.

"I'm going to open the door."

"Okay, darling," her fingers tightened. "I'll be quiet as a mouse."

"Darling!"

"My hero!"

Ken opened the door, slowly. Pandemonium would be a mild word to describe what he saw. Usually, the vast space of the Ruckus Mudcock Museum Memorial Hall was a model of calm with a few groups of awed school children guided by volunteer Cosmos Scouts among the enormous displays and holograms and historical objects: the first telephone, the first telegraph, the phonograph, and early computers and calculators, and the first printing press, and the whole history of human communications from clay tablet and parchment to illuminated manuscripts and moveable type to bits and bytes and GPS and ...

But now it was a battlefield. Dead bodies lay everywhere. Some people were crouching over bodies devouring them. zombie-bats flew here and there and swooped down to carry people off.

A robot voice was saying, "The history of humanity is a history of continuous progress. Since the first human discovered how to light a fire, or how to tame a wolf, the history of human beings has been one long upward ..."

"Okay, we're going to run for it."

"Yes, darling."

"Hold on tight!"

"Yes, darling."

Another voice was saying, "The Interglacial warm periods had a considerable influence on humans, as our ancestors moved out of the African jungle and into the savannah, with the climate drying and ..."

A vivid and giant hologram display, floating in the air near an oversized late 19th Century telephone, showed ape-like creatures leaping down from trees and walking, dragging their knuckles, into the savannah.

"The upright posture allowed ..."

"The opposable thumb and fingers allowed for manipulation of complex objects and the ..."

"The increase in protein intake, permitted the growth of the mind, with greater cerebral capacity ..."

With Alison clinging to his elbow, Ken darted out and across an open space, and ducked behind a huge model of an early phonograph. It was of the wax cylinder rotating type. Ken had been spotted by two zombie-like human beings whose minds had clearly been taken over by god knows what, but who had red-rimmed eyes and whose mouths seemed to be dripping blood. One was an extremely fat woman – surely not a Cosmos – Cosmos were not allowed to be fat – and the other was a skinny teenager. They began to lurch toward Ken and Alison. One of them hit the Display control crank. The display phonograph began to emit a rather loud barbershop quartet version of "If you were the only girl in the world, and I were the only boy ..."

More zombie-like humans turned toward the singing voice, and began to lurch and slouch toward the phonograph. "If you were the only boy in the world ..."

Several zombie-bats swung around in mid-flight and headed straight for the spot where the phonograph was playing and where Ken and Alison were crouching.

The zombie-like humans, the fat woman who was wearing white-framed mirror glasses, pink glow skintight skin pants, a saggy see-through day-glow tank top and emerald plastic flip-flops – definitely not a Cosmos, thought Ken – and the skinny punk androgynous teenager with kohl heavy around its eyes and tattooed arms – looked like a boy, but it was probably a girl, Ken figured – were getting close, reaching out their limp-wristed arms just like real zombies in a real zombie movie. They were drooling bubbly glowing foam too which made both of them look rabid.

"Oh, boy ..."

"Not, good, eh," whispered Alison, tightening her grip.

"No, we've got bandits on all sides," said Ken, knowing that Alison knew all about the Battle of Britain – and everything else – and would catch the reference to "bandits" as enemy aircraft.

"Jeepers creepers," Alison whispered, taking the allusion as a sly compliment to her mastery of 20th century trivia, and tightening her grasp on his arm; if she was going to die, she wanted to die in Ken's arms.

While the two human zombies came lurching forward, with more following behind, the zombie-bats zoomed down like two screaming Stuka dive-bombers.

Ken didn't know where to fire his gun. Okay, probably the zombie-bats, they were the worst and deadliest, besides, they were very fast.

The fat woman and the skinny kid were now only about five feet away. Ken didn't like the idea of shooting people. Well, if he had to …

Suddenly the barbershop quartet music shifted tunes. It became "Yes, Sir, that's my baby …"

The two human zombies stopped and looked around, obviously startled. Maybe they like music, thought Ken. The zombie-bats coming from behind smashed into the two zombie-humans in front. The fat woman and the skinny teenager, and both crashed to the ground.

Ken lifted the M-16 and exploded one of the zombie-bats, it crashed down onto the giant phonograph which whirred and generated sparks, but which continued to play "Yes Sir, that's my baby …"

But then as the two zombie-humans got up and began to lurch forward, a hologram appeared of a barbershop quartet, probably from the early 20th Century. The human zombies stopped to glower at the quartet, which was crooning like mad. The zombies blinked their eyes, their mouths hung open. The skinny kid zombie scratched itself. Ah, definitely a boy, thought Ken. Well, one mystery solved. The carcass of the shot zombie-bat fell off the phonograph with a crash, a flurry of feathers, and a noxious smell.

"Ugh," whispered Alison.

"Yes," Ken was watching the other zombie-bat; it was staring back at him and it was perched on the display of an ancient machine which looked like it was used for laying telegraph lines. Ken was thinking that all of this was very interesting. He should have come down here when it was still possible. There are wonders all around you, and you never notice them until it is too late.

The zombie-bat took off and Ken fired and the zombie-bat exploded in mid-air. The human zombies all looked around at the source of the gunfire and they began to charge at a gallop – all of them – and there must have been forty or fifty of them at least – toward Ken and Alison.

"Run, we run."

"Yes, sir!"

They ran, leaving the barbershop quartet behind. Voices floated outward, on the ether.

"Alexander Graham Bell made the first …"

"Thomas Edison had the idea that if you …"

"Hiram Maxim, a self-taught inventor from Maine, noticed that the recoil of a rifle contained energy, perhaps enough energy, he thought, to reload and fire …"

Ken and Alison kept running. Ken was thinking that if they got behind the satellite display – a life-size communications satellite from the early 21st Century – they might be able to make it to the exit, and from then down toward the main Elysium platform, and from there underground, and just keep running. But, he wondered, was there any place safe, anyplace at all?

Several lurching human zombies surged up in front of them.

Ken shot one of the lurching humans – a thin faced blonde in a silver slick-skin running suit who stood in their way; and the woman fell straight down, face down, into a small fountain which gurgled silver water over the body, which bounced slightly as it settled, spreading blood everywhere, her blond hair fanning out like the rays of a halo.

The other zombie-like human, a tanned thin guy in skin-shorts, tripped, and triggered a jaunty little jingle played by an electronic xylophone.

Ken and Alison ran for the communications satellite.

They stepped over bodies; they ducked zombie-bats; they slipped between the model of a rocket ship and the giant display satellite.

Triggered by all the ruckus, a hologram display of "Blast off" started and the zombie-like humans stopped in their tracks, mouths hanging open, hypnotized, arms reaching out toward the soaring rocket, the flames, and the blue sky of Florida perhaps one hundred and eighty years ago.

Ken was backing away from the crowd of zombie-people with Alison behind him. A blank-faced person was standing right in front of Alison, blocking her way. Somehow Alison sensed his presence. He was a young man wearing a checked shirt and faded jeans and a wide leather cowboy style belt and cowboy boots. His eyes were not as empty as the eyes of most of the others. Alison tightened her grip on Ken's arm, two quick little pinches; it was a signal.

"I don't know where I am," said the zombie.

"Don't worry," said Alison.

"Don't worry?"

"Everybody is confused," said Alison.

Ken turned and saw what she was doing, but he was fighting off two very aggressive zombies, so he turned back and shot the two zombies in the fore-head, but they kept coming. "Alison," he whispered

"It's okay, darling," Alison was facing the blank-faced young man, though she couldn't see him; he was clutching a machete; the machete was streaked with blood, a long string of gristle hung from the point of the blade.

Alison put her hand on the man's chest. "Don't worry," she said, "It will be alright."

"It will be alright?" A quizzical light lit up in the empty eyes, almost a thought. "It will be alright? No, no, no … it can't be alright. Oh, oh, oh," and he turned and walked away, and at a few steps distance, he turned and said, "Thank you, you are an angel, you are an angel."

Still drifting in the air was music. "Oh, shine on, shine on, harvest moon …"

The tunes lingered in the air, packaged nostalgia. Somehow, Ken and Alison made it out of the Memorial Hall of the Museum and found themselves in another staircase, going down. Alison was humming, just under her breath, barbershop quartet tunes. "Once the world was oh, so innocent, Ken," she said, whispering, close to him, her mouth pressed to his ear.

"So they say, darling," he whispered back, and he kissed her, he kissed her hard, and they stopped on the stairs, and her arms went around his neck and they kissed each other, hungrily, and for a long time, as if it were the last time they would ever be able to kiss, the last kiss on earth.

Listening to the echoes of chaos from far above, Lieutenant Kat Jackson strode up and down on the very edge of the Mind-Sea. She held her laser gun ready, the safety off. She looked around nervously.

Twenty minutes ago V had waded into the Mind-Soup, what did she call it? Was it amniotic fluid? The ruins of New York had become a womb? Wall Street was the cradle and womb for the voracious monster that would destroy the world, eat up, devour, and consume the whole thing, the whole shebang? Ha, how apt! If the natives and first Dutch settlers had only known! Explosions echoed from far above. Some of the chains hanging from an old loading crane rattled. Whatever the Mind and the Boy were doing, they were still doing it.

And – whatever was happening up above depends on what is happening here, on an invisible battle going on somewhere here. Kat knew that the Mind-Soup or Sea was an integral part of the Mind; its liquid interacted with the great lattice-like structures, acres and acres of them, which were buried in the submerged vats and which functioned as the center of the Mind, and from this place virtually every machine on the planet was controlled, or influenced, as were all the human minds that had connected mind implants. The chaos must have spread across the whole world.

Kat stared out over the gooey bubbling polychrome Mind-Sea. When V waded into the liquid, the patches surrounding her lit up with an inner light, becoming ripples of glowing iridescence. Then out of the soup, tentacles and fibers, and bright scintillating strands, rose up and began to wrap themselves around V. It was as if she was being mummified; Kat was horrified; but V turned to her, smiled, and waved. "Don't worry, Kat, I shall return."

The ribbons of goo whirled around V. Then, totally enclosed, wrapped like a mummy in glittering gossamer threads, V sank beneath the swirling tentacles of the Mind-Soup.

And then – time passed.

Kat paced back and forth. Up above, more explosions echoed. And in her mind Kat heard screams, and, somewhere, giant laughter, as if an enormous insane clown were on the loose; she wondered if this was madness, illusion, or extra sensitivity due to being a hybrid.

But down here it was, for the moment, quiet: the only sound was the humming and bubbling of the Mind-Soup. Occasionally, brightly colored braided strands of liquid rose up, twirled around, like slender multicolored water spouts, or like those ropes that ancient Indian fakirs used to conjure up, like swaying cobras, out of wicker baskets. Kat found herself staring at these swaying glittering towers. They were accompanied by and swaying to a sort of flute music, melodies that were very alluring, very seductive, and even sublime, in a sneaky untoward sort of way.

Kat shook her head and looked away. The Boy is up to his tricks – tricks, tricks and more tricks.

She paced up and down, checking the walls and the roof and the pipes and tubes that ran along the walls, and the platform under her feet. It all seemed solid; it all seemed real. Here, at least, near the Mind-Soup, that was the home of the Mind, the Mind and the Boy did not seem to be eating the city, which was a relief.

Of course, even this solidity could be an illusion. After all, at the sub-atomic level, even the most solid object is mostly empty space. The world truly is a latticework illusion, a conjuring act, magic, a stage set slapped together for the amusement of the inhabitants.

Kat took off her armored bio-glove and touched the stone wall with the tips of her fingers. The stone was damp, rough, and grainy. It certainly did feel real. She pulled her fingers away, and slipped the bio-glove back on. It squeaked as it fitted itself, skintight, to her hand.

Kat clenched her fists. "Oh, V, damn it, V, come back! It's getting bloody lonely out here! I'm beginning to feel like I don't exist!" Kat walked right to the edge of the Mind-Soup. The soup stirred slightly at her presence, lighting up just beyond the toes of her boots, swirling, with little wavelets reaching out, lapping up and sending out fiber-like feelers, as if they wished to touch her, invite her in, dissolve her, and make her one with them.

Caliban held Miranda tight. Gently he flipped her over, both of them rolling like a log, one log – two people, united, rotating gloriously, like the stars in heaven, part of the cosmic force and energy, like the very earth itself, like the whirling galaxies themselves, so now, suddenly, Miranda, who had been on top of Caliban looking down, was beneath Caliban, looking up.

She was startled and yet delighted – suddenly she was between Caliban and the smooth wet and mossy paving stones which strangely seemed as soft and as welcoming as a fluffy bed, though, in truth, Miranda had never been in a fluffy bed, her beds had always been stern beds, stoic, character-building beds, with solid, thin, board-like mattresses, as dictated by Nikki, who, strangely for a model and star and cult designer, had rather Spartan tastes.

"Kiss me," Miranda breathed.

"Yes," Caliban's lips approached, his breath was warm, perfumed like a sea breeze through a garden of lemon trees, his lips met hers, just a touch, then pressure, then his tongue … and he kissed her.

She sighed.

He sighed.

"Take me, break me, have me, take me, make me, possess me, oh, my darling," Miranda whispered in a soft desperate cascade of words, brushing her lips against his, her body aching to be taken into his, and aching too to take him into her, so that they would be one creature, one being, united forever, and as she arched her body up to meet his, and as her lips pressed against his lips and as they kissed violently, and totally, and it was, oh, so soft, oh so strong …

And then she remembered: Under absolutely no conditions was she to bite Caliban …

Oh, oh, oh …

She didn't in fact feel like biting Caliban; well, in truth, maybe a nibble, maybe just a little, tiny, itsy-bitsy playful nibble, and she was certainly kissing him, ferociously, hungrily, as if she wanted to eat him, take him all in, possess every millimeter of him, swallow him, have him forever and ever and ever!

Kit Candy squinted though the gathering fog. Edgar swam just ahead. It was getting harder to see anything. Kit tightened her hold on the President's hand. A thick wet fog drifted in layers over the canal, some layers lying right on the water, others up a foot or two, and still more, up to the arched ceil, stretching across the canal like cloudy prison bars.

Kit worried that perhaps the Boy and the Mind were gathering their forces, about to play more evil tricks, and engulf her and the President and Edgar in some horrible new trap, like acid fog, or glue-fog, or blinding, eye-destroying poisonous fog, or canal bred super-carnivorous piranhas, or ...

Though the strands of fog and the misty phosphorescent light fluttered and seemed to go dim and then a bit brighter. Hey, she caught a glimpse of something.

What in Hades was that? It looked like two entangled bodies, golden-colored, one lighter, a sort of sunny gold, and the other darker, more muscular, with a sort of dark, gleaming gold tan. The limbs were all mixed up, what looked like a leg, an arm, a torso, and the sculptural mix seemed to sparkle, maybe it was sweat, or just the fog condensing, and a glint of what looked like gold, hair perhaps, and then ... The fog moved in, a dim white wall. The apparition faded and was gone.

"I think I saw something," Kit said. She sensed the President tensing, though he hadn't said a word.

"I did too," the President had his laser gun out, aiming it in the direction of the shifting golden tangle. "But, now, I can't see a thing."

The fog again wrapped itself around them, clammy and close, licking at their faces. Edgar stopped, turned, and came back to them, his sleek head and big sympathetic eyes sticking up out of the water.

"I think it's an illusion, whatever it is. It looked like a statue, or maybe a heap of dead bodies, or maybe," Kit frowned, "Maybe ..."

"Maybe it is ... it looked like two people making out," said the President.

"*Making out?*" Kit looked at him. "*Making love?* Down here, now?"

"Well, it did look like that, like an amorous tangle, I mean, rather like that bronze and gold statue in the 22nd Century Museum," said the President, "the neo-Rodin work 'Golden Copulation' by Bo Deng Booh."

"Yeah, okay, it looks like that Bo Deng Booh piece. But down here, who would dare, I mean ..."

"Yes, you're right. It's a trick. It must be a trick. It must be another illusion conjured up by the Mind and that Evil Force, the Boy." The President tightened his grip on his laser gun.

The fog cleared. They caught a glimpse; a golden cascade of hair, a golden arm reaching up, clasping a dark body, and a cascade of black hair, and strong legs, and a neatly sculpted tense backside, an arching back, and a whispered sound, "Oh, oh, oh, yes, oh, yes ..."

"It's that devil, the Mind," said the President. The apparition was centered now in the laser's sights.

"I sort of think I may recognize that voice," said Kit, "but that is impossible. I mean ... If I'm right, that's the voice of my dead friend, I sort of recognize, ah, the tone, you know."

The President glanced at Kit.

Kit's eyes were wide open, startled. She was staring. The President had never seen her stare like this before; her mouth, with its finely delineated lips and gleaming teeth, was hanging open. "This can't be Mr. President. It must be an illusion, a cruel illusion."

"I think we'd better teach the Mind a lesson. The President tensed his finger on the trigger.

Edgar groaned, turned toward, them, then yelped; it sounded like he was warning them.

Kit wondered, is he warning us against the apparition or warning us not to shoot it. She laid her hand on the President's arm. "Wait, Mr. President," she whispered, "Don't shoot, not yet."

The fog thickened again. The tangled living statue was lost to view. It felt to Kit as if they were in a lost world, waist-deep in slowly moving water, and blinded by the fog that pressed in, surrounded by dangerous mirages, mirages that promised salvation and happiness, but which were an invitation to Hell. Even the President was just a vague misty silhouette.

Miranda whispered "Oh, oh, oh, yes, yes!" and pulled Caliban closer and just at that moment she turned her head, drawn by something, some half-conscious perception, some vague inkling out of the corner of her eye, and suddenly she saw them, two vague drifting silhouettes in the thick fog; she blinked.

Caliban was whispering, "Miranda, Miranda, Miranda ..."

Caliban was moving against her ...

Caliban, she knew, was about to enter her ... and she was ready, quite ready, more than ready, to welcome him.

But ...

What was that? Who were they? They were not ghouls; they were too tall, standing too straight ...

She didn't want to break the spell, she didn't want to break the impetus of pure love, pure lust – sublime lust – glorious sex ... she ...

The mist thickened and swirled.

The two people, yes, they were people, they weren't ghouls, the two people standing in the water became vague silhouettes, and disappeared in the swirling fog, perhaps they were an illusion ...

Miranda kissed Caliban, and arching her back, raising her hips, meeting him, she said, "Oh, Caliban, Oh, Caliban, oh, oh, oh, Caliban," and, nibbling his earlobe, she whispered into his ear, "We are not alone, Caliban, we are not alone."

Caliban hesitated; he was being very delicate; his princess was undoubtedly a virgin, technically a virgin; her admirably instructive adventures with her wonderful friend Kit Candy – which Miranda had told him about in gratifyingly great but sublimely discreet detail – didn't in this case count, didn't count as ...

And Miranda's body, full-bodied, rich, elastic, eager, supple, straining against his body, embracing his body, it was, well, it was ...

"What?" he said, "Not alone?" He allowed himself to glance sideways; though still in the throes of a crescendo of excitement, still approaching the knife-edge of possible utter ecstasy, and utter oblivion, but ...

But he did not want his Princess to be in danger; and down here, as they had seen, there were many dangers, and dangers of the most unpredictable and deadly sort, so he must take action, but what action, and he sighed. Miranda was pressed against him, their flesh was melting into one, every nerve was tingling, and his mind was soaring.

"Oh, oh, Caliban," Miranda sighed, "I think, Caliban, that we must, perhaps, we must ..."

Wrapped in the thick clammy wall of fog, the President and Kit moved blindly forward, weapons drawn, ready to sizzle whatever new illusion, whatever new sacrilegious trick the Foul Fiend had devised to mislead them, to threaten them. The fog cleared, just a bit, now it was a thin veil of mist, and Kit blinked.

"Oh, boy, oh, boy …." said Kit.

"What …"

"It's a ghost."

"Yes, it's a ghost …"

"It's the ghost of my best friend …"

"Yes, it's a ghost," the President said, "It's the ghost of my daughter."

"Your daughter …" Kit stared at the President, "This is diabolical!" Kit was about to get very angry: how dare the Mind, or whatever it was, do this?

"Yes, it is diabolical; it is designing a tailored illusion, specifically designed for each of us. You are seeing your friend; and I am seeing my daughter."

"It's cruel, to show you your daughter and to show me my friend! God, I miss Miranda so much!" Kit let out an involuntary sob.

"Miranda?" The President turned to Kit.

"Yes, that's the ghost – Miranda," Kit said, "Mr. President, that's Miranda's ghost, Miranda Hughes, and … I guess she's got a boyfriend ghost. It looks like they are … making love, at least that's what it looks like, I think."

"Oh, my God … But Miranda's dead."

"That's what I said – she's a ghost."

"You know Miranda?

"You know Miranda?"

"She's my daughter," the President was staring in a weird way.

"She's my friend!"

"It can't be Miranda … she's dead. What is she doing here? Of all the places to be, and making love with, with some, some teenager, some naked, long-haired, Wildman Retro-Hippy!" The President raised the laser gun, "It absolutely must be the Mind. It's an illusion, meant to betray us." He steadied the gun. It was difficult to keep it from shaking. This was the ultimate obscenity: the Mind counterfeiting Miranda, mocking her memory, he would put an end to this charade … he would vaporise this travesty!

"Now, Mr. President, maybe this isn't what it seems."

The President took a deep breath. He put his hand out and laid it on Kit's shoulder; he needed something to steady him. He aimed the gun; yes, he would vaporise this mockery, this travesty, this …

"Now, Mr. President," said Kit, "I think we should …"

Edgar barked and rammed onto the President, almost knocking him off balance, and then turned and began swimming like mad, toward the illusionary Mind-generated tableau of two teenagers making love.

The mist swirled and thickened, and the Miranda mirage disappeared, and Kit wondered: was this really the Mind playing a cruel trick, was this …?

Caliban was still cantilevered over Miranda, still had his body pressed against hers, still was entering her, still … and yet, turning his head, he looked, out over the water, into the fog, blinked; he could see nothing, just fog, and then, emerging out of the fog he saw some sort of sea animal, it was swimming fast toward them – was it dangerous? No, Caliban got the impression somehow that the animal was friendly. It raised its slick head and coughed politely, emitting a spray of water, as if it were reluctant to interrupt their mating ritual, then it barked, and barked again: it was obviously a warning – get up! Get up!

Behind its sleek head and shiny black whiskers, as the fog cleared slightly, Caliban glimpsed …

He blinked again: he saw two silhouettes …

He saw the larger, raising a weapon.

He saw the smaller silhouette, appearing to reach out and push the weapon down.

Caliban, gently whispered, "Darling Princess … I must demand your pardon, I must withdraw from this our sublime battlefield, I must retreat."

"Yes, Caliban, withdraw, withdraw …" she breathed, her whole being shuddering with pleasure and ecstasy and dismay, taut like a violin string, on the knife-edge of pure gushing culmination; and her exquisite, sensitive lover, oh, Caliban, he slid back, slowly, delicately, oh most delicately, and then, suddenly, he let go of her, and as he leaped up, he seized his scimitar and grabbed his AK-47, and …

And in that very same instant, suddenly becoming all taut nerves, all warrior Cosmos Scout First Class heroine, Miranda too vaulted to her feet, grabbed her laser gun with one hand, and grabbed her skin-shorts with the other, clutching the skin-shorts in front of her, and she took aim …

"Gosh," said Kit.

"Well," exclaimed the President.

"This is … amazing," Kit said, steadying herself against the President: it had all happened so quickly; the illusion dissolved and transformed itself into reality, or what certainly seemed like reality: the ghost-man who had been making love to the ghost of Miranda – and both of them were stark naked – leaped up and the man grabbed an archaic weapon.

It was an AK-47, Kit could tell from the historical-arms-identification implants she and Miranda – oh, Miranda! – had absorbed together, and the man – oh, he looked utterly beautiful and if he too was a ghost or a Mind-induced illusion then ghost Miranda-Illusion certainly had had good taste and good luck in choosing this particular ghost guy! But, then, Miranda deserved the best; Kit hoped her lessons in applied sensuality had been useful.

The Miranda figure had also leaped to her feet – clutching her skin-shorts in front of her and aiming a laser gun.

The young man had swung his AK, aiming it straight at them, and Kit thought, oh, now we are going to die, both of us, she had pushed down the President's weapon, so it was pointing into the water, both of us, me and the President together, are going to die in a hail of archaic ghost bullets, or maybe archaic real bullets, since, in spite of the mist and swirling dimness, both Miranda and the young man did not, in truth, look very ghostly, and Miranda had that startled adorable look, her mouth half-open, ripe lips, gleaming bright teeth, eyes wide, staring, startled. ..

"Halt there, you on the bounding gloomy subterranean main, who are you, under what flag sail you, what will you with us?" His AK was aimed straight at them; but so far he had not fired, not a bullet, imaginary or real. "Are you an illusion serving the Foul Fiend or are you true hot-blooded seafaring flesh and blood?"

"Gosh," thought Kit, Miranda always said she liked pirates; this must be not a ghost but a hallucination, a specially designed illusion, cooked up just for her, just for Kit Candy, by the Mind as part of its skill as a mind-mimic and part of its malevolent plot to control and gobble up the world; it knew exactly what illusory fodder to feed to each particular mind to lend verisimilitude to the midway show or carnival spectacle. Maybe it was all a feverish dream! Maybe this wasn't the President; after all, he too was too good to be true; he was probably a projection of her deepest desires – for a father! Up to the present, she had not been aware of such a desire, but now the desire for paternal love burned brightly, maybe that's why she had put up with hopeless creeps like Sniggy Propane; maybe she was dead; maybe she and the President had both died when they were attacked by the poisonous giant cobras, or that octopus thing, or maybe she had died alone, drowned in chocolate, or dismembered and rendered tongueless by the mad butcher surgeon torturer;

maybe she had been executed by Daisy and all her life since then was an illusion, a last trick played by life as she, Kit Candy, plunged into death; if so, then, the President too would be a figment playing in the drama of her afterlife ...

Perhaps, truly, there was such a thing as Hades.

Or maybe this was Limbo, or Purgatory.

She rather wished there was a theologian available so that she could ask these questions – not that any living human being could answer them, but still it might be comforting to sit down and have a cozy chat with Thomas Aquinas or Martin Buber or somebody about the ultimate questions of existence, the transcendent concerns of ...

The President's free hand was still on her shoulder; it certainly felt real, and all the things he had told her ...

"We sail under a friendly flag, my gallant brother warrior, and we mean no harm, but come to offer help, though it seems you are doing quite well on your own and need no help from us," said the President, his voice firm and resonant in the sloshing cavern. Edgar, who was sloshing close to the two lovers, turned and looked at the President and made a friendly mooing sound.

The President's voice was even toned and warm and seemed indeed to offer friendship and reassurance. No wonder he is President, with that commanding reassuring voice, which she had heard so often broadcast throughout Elysium City on holidays, Kit thought, somehow pleased that the Presidential hand was still on her shoulder.

The handsome pirate gestured with his AK-47. "Come forward then, hands in the air, though you can keep your arms, sailors, I shall not take them from you, if you are as honorable in intent as you claim!" The Pirate seemed entirely unaware that he was naked – or totally indifferent to the fact.

The Miranda-Illusion was holding what looked like bunched up skin-shorts clutched in front of her, but that was pretty minimal coverage. Kit sighed. Oh, boy! Did the Miranda-Illusion ever look beautiful!

"Let's do as our handsome pirate friend says, Kit," said the President, letting go of her shoulder and raising his hands, but still holding onto the laser gun, pointing it at the arched roof of the tunnel. "It's a risk, but nothing ventured, nothing gained, and here the gain may be great indeed."

"Yes, sir, Mr. President," Kit said, feeling a strange warm glow feeling from hearing him use, yet again, her first name, and a fuzzy patriotic feeling too from saying "Mr. President," and thinking at the same time that she was surprised at herself; she had thought herself immune to Fascist propaganda and to the archaic patriarchal glamour of projected and introjected paternalistic phallic power, but ...

I guess I'm just human ...

I'm just a human female kid ...

Thus, hands in the air, the President-Leader and Kit Candy sloshed forward, just behind Edgar the seal. Edgar kept turning his head around to gaze at Kit in what looked like pure adoration.

Miranda – or the ghost of Miranda – didn't seem to be aware she was naked, except for the clutched skin-shorts ...

In fact, her eyes opening in amazement, and her mouth rounding in amazement, the Miranda-Illusion actually dropped her skin-shorts, leaving her like Eve in the Garden, before the fall. But she did keep her laser gun steady; and it was aimed straight at them.

Kit thought that the Miranda ghost or illusion looked utterly adorable; it took her back to that very first mutual slow-motion striptease romp on the carpet in Miranda's studio. Now, here, was the full glory, Miranda – naked and unabashed! Maybe ghosts, who are probably angels if they've been good, don't care about vestments or lack thereof, thought Kit as she and the President sloshed though the foaming water that was now just up to their thighs. The top of Kit's head only came up to the President's shoulder. But then again, the two ghosts had not been acting like angels, who have no sex, so the theologians say, and who can dance, apparently, on the head of a pin. And Miranda had never been shy about nakedness, so ... perhaps – just perhaps – this version of Miranda was not an illusion but the real thing! But, then, Miranda was dead ...

"That's it, my hardies! Come forward slowly, and, when you get here, to terraferma, step softly, softly, with the lightest of steps, out of the bounding main, easy does it my hardies!"

"Indeed, we shall, master seaman, master pirate; indeed we shall," the President was using the most friendly tone, "We shall tread softly, and with the lightest of steps."

"Kit?" said the Miranda ghost.

"Miranda?"

"Kit?"

"It is you? Miranda? Miranda? You're alive?"

"Yes, I'm alive, and Kit – you're alive? It's not an illusion, it's not a Mind-Trick?"

"Yes, I'm alive. It's me, it's really me."

"And, Kit, who is that with you …? He looks like …"

"It's the …"

"It can't be …"

"Yes, I think it is … it's the … he certainly looks like him and he says he's the …"

"Oh, my god, Kit," said Miranda, "Oh, my god, Kit, it can't be …"

"It is … true … It's him," said Kit, glancing sideways up at the President, who was still holding his hands in the air, and looking weirdly abashed too, as if they were all playing some sort of game, but one with very high stakes.

"Miranda Hughes," said the President, "Miranda Hughes …" Kit noticed that in uttering Miranda's name the President's voice seemed clouded with emotion, almost as if he were about to choke up. Of course, if Miranda is his daughter … The idea only now began to sink in: *Miranda is the daughter of the President!*

Miranda, Eve-like as she was, snapped to attention, and saluted, arm shooting up in the Cosmos Hail the Leader, "Mr. President, Sir," she said, "Hail, Hail, Hail!"

"Hail, Miranda," said the President, gently.

"Who is this sea-farer, that you salute and honor him so, Princess? Who is this handsome yet somewhat grizzled water-born salty buccaneer, whom you call President, Princess?" said Caliban, still holding the AK steady, aimed straight at Kit and the President.

"He is the Leader," breathed Miranda, her arm still outstretched, still rigidly at attention, "He is the President-Leader of Cosmos!"

"At ease, Miranda Hughes," said the President.

He and Kit climbed out of the water, and stood before Miranda and Caliban. Caliban had somehow – in a split second – whipped his loincloth around his loins, tied the knot, and looked – well – utterly glamorous, so thought Kit.

"So you are the President, the great Leader of whom all the Cosmos speak so highly," said Caliban, "You are the great destroyer, the sworn enemy of SINs and of hybrids and mutants."

"Yes, I am all those things, my gallant friend, and I am also …" the President paused and looked Miranda up and down, "and I am also the father of your beautiful Princess here. I am Miranda's father."

"You are ... the father of ... of my Princess?" Caliban gaped. He knew this, of course, but having it confirmed, now, in the flesh, was, frankly, beyond a normal pirate's hopes and dreams.

"Yes."

Miranda had lowered her arm and now her hands were on her hips, elbows pointed outward, in what Kit recognized as her scolding stance, "Father, oh, Father ..."

"Yes, Miranda," the President said, and Kit noticed that his smile was sad, as if he knew what was coming, and was resigned to it ...

"Father, I have always loved you. Even when I didn't know you were my father. But you did not recognize me or acknowledge me for so many years, and I understand that, but you made life so difficult for mother, and for all her kind, for all her kind, for ..."

"For the SINs ..." said the President, wondering. So, she knew!

"Yes, for the SINs, and for hybrids," said Miranda.

"Ah ..." the President seemed shocked.

"Yes, for SINs and for hybrids," Miranda said, color rising.

"So you know," said the President; he paused and glanced sideways at Kit who was in shock – Miranda was the President's daughter – Miranda was the daughter of a SIN! But, seeing the President glance at her, Kit shrugged her shoulders as if to say, I have no idea what Miranda is talking about! The President turned back to Miranda, "So you know who your real mother is."

"I have two mothers now," said Miranda, "and both have given their blessing to my union with Caliban, both have said ..."

"Nikki and V ... your two mothers ..."

"Yes, Nikki and V, my two mothers ...

Miranda has two mothers! Kit felt she must look like an idiot, jaw hanging open, eyes staring, *Miranda has two mothers!*

"They are both well?"

"Yes, they are both well, exceedingly so ... Nikki and I survived the crash." Miranda pouted for an instant, tears were gathering in her eyes, she sniffled.

Miranda has two mothers? Kit's eyes got wider. What the Hades was this all about?

Caliban put his AK down and put his arm around Miranda's shoulder; Kit stepped forward and touched Miranda on the cheek, "Two mothers, two mothers," Kit said, in a sort of hushed awe.

"Yes, dearest, dearest Kit, I have two mothers."

"Wow. I mean, awesome!"

Miranda favored Kit with a dazzling smile, "Yes, awesome."

Kit was dazzled – again in love.

"Oh, father," said Miranda, instantly changing mood, and looking up, her eyes aglitter with tears: "Oh, father!" It was like a cry of desperation, of yearning, of love denied.

Kit turned to the President, who was standing as if awestruck, as if abashed, as if uncertain how to act, "Well?" Kit said, "Well?"

The President glanced at Kit, nodded, and stepped forward and took his naked daughter, Hybrid Princess of the Mutant Dead Lands Kingdom, Her Sublime Highness, Betrothed of SIN and Mutant Kingdom Prince Caliban, Miranda Hughes, into his arms, enfolding her in his embrace.

"That's more like it," Kit muttered.

"Yes," said Caliban, "And so you are Kit Candy! Oh, Mistress Kit Candy, my friend. I have heard much about you. You are the friend of my Princess, the truest closest most loved friend she has and even more I believe, and you have taught her much, as she put it, about the skills of seafaring and amorous high seas encounters and all forms of copulation."

"Caliban," said Kit, bowing her head, looking at him from under her dark eyelashes, "You are her pirate – the fulfillment of her dreams!"

"I have heard tell of you so often, Kit Candy," said Caliban, "I have much to thank you for. Miranda is truly an artist, you know, and much I think is due to your working with her and upon her in her apprenticeship in the arts of ..."

"Father," Miranda's heart was beating so hard she felt it throbbing in her temples, "I may call you father?"

"Yes, Miranda, yes, you may call me father ... I am humbled that you wish to claim me as your father. I am unworthy."

"Father, this is Caliban, my betrothed, he is a Prince of the Mutant Kingdom, and he has the blessing of both my mothers ..."

"Of Nikki and of V ..."

"Yes, of my adoptive mother and protector, and of my biological mother, V, your love, your partner, your ..."

"... and my enemy," said the President, with a sad smile, and then, changing tone, he reached out his hand and shook Caliban's hand, "I am honored to meet you, young man."

"I too am honored and wish to ask for the hand of my Princess here and ..."

"Caliban is Nikki's son," said Miranda.

"Nikki's son …"

"Yes."

"Nikki's lost son?"

"Yes," said Caliban, "I was found in the desert. I had the mark of Nikki's son upon me – the tattoo of the dragon rising out of flames. Goddess Nikki has declared me her son – the Great High Priest of the Mutant Kingdom, leader of the Cult of Dolly, has confirmed it. His senses are infallible."

"Nikki's son – wow!" said Kit, "I don't believe this! And Miranda is not Nikki's daughter? And, wait a minute – Miranda is the daughter of the President, and she is V's daughter, V the Queen of the Hybrids, then, ergo, therefore …" She stared at Miranda, glowing, beautiful, Miranda: *Miranda was a hybrid! That was absolutely not possible!*

"You look like a worthy son of your mother," the President said, looking Caliban up and down.

"Nikki's son – wow!" Kit couldn't get over it. Caliban gave her a beautiful smile and so did Miranda.

The President, now holding Miranda by the shoulders, leaned back so he could look at her, "How beautiful you are, Miranda, how perfect!"

Miranda swallowed; she blushed; golden fireworks blossomed in her eyes; yes, how beautiful she is, thought Kit, with a mixture of ache and yearning and a vague burgeoning sense of loss. She reached down, picked up Miranda's skin-shorts, and handed them to her. Miranda blushed, for the first time realizing that she was stark naked, and she gave Kit a glorious smile. "Oh, Kit! Oh, Kit how I missed you!" And she pulled on her skin-shorts.

"Nikki's son," said the President, again, as if he were thinking deep thoughts; he glanced at Caliban.

"Well," said Kit, raising her eyebrows.

The President glanced at her. "Ms. Candy – Kit – and I have survived a few adventures; she seems to have become my chief advisor, and I think she is a very wise advisor, so …"

Miranda sighed; she was almost ready to smile.

"So, if Nikki and V," the President cleared his throat, "If Nikki and V have given their blessing, then you have my blessing, young man, Caliban, and you have my blessing, Miranda, if you accept my blessing, of course."

"Oh, father!" Miranda leaned up and kissed him on the lips.

"Of course, we accept, we are honored, Sir," Caliban bowed slightly, and smiled – such a glorious smile. The President could see why his daughter

– *his daughter* – romantic pirate-obsessed dreamer that she was – would choose such a mate.

"You may kiss the bride, Mr. Caliban," said Kit.

Caliban took Miranda in his arms, and kissed her.

"And, now, where is V? Where is Nikki – and what is going on with the World Mind?" said the President, as Kit handed Miranda's T-skin-shirt to her and Miranda blushed again, her eyes twirling galaxies of gold, and she slipped it over her head and squeaked it into position; and she leaned forward and kissed Kit on the lips. "Oh, boy," Kit breathed happiness.

And, as Caliban and Miranda briefed the President and Kit on events in the Dead Lands, they went on, sloshing down the canal, toward the World Mind, toward the final battle.

And so, with Kit as guide; and Edgar, her special guardian, swimming silently ahead, and occasionally looking back, they all went onwards toward the Mind.

Kit thought: We are now all so happy; and now we all must die!

"Father, Mr. President, I have seen such things," Miranda said, blushing, "the cruelty, the mutants, the people in the camps, in Camp Terminus, there were children, father, children who had never seen the light of day, there were people who had been transformed, made sick, by delayed-action illnesses, by a new version of leprosy … there were dead SINs and hybrids, massacred in the Dead Lands, there were …"

"I know, I know, Miranda."

"How could you, father. I love you, but how could you do these things? How could you let these things happen?"

"Miranda …" said Caliban …

"Don't be too hard on him, Miranda." said Kit, "It was all pretty complicated. Give him time. He'll explain it, won't you, Mr. President?"

"Yes, Kit, I'll try. But, Miranda, you are right. It was horrible, it was cruel, and I am to blame."

Miranda's eyes were brimming. Caliban glanced at Kit, as if looking for advice on how to calm the trouble waters. Kit nodded. But, just as Kit was about to say something about going easy on the President because in spite of everything he was a truly good man and there would be time for judgment and reckoning later, Miranda went up on tiptoes and kissed her father on the cheek. "I love you," she whispered, "No matter what, father, I love you."

And so, onward they went, toward the lair of the Mind.

V was 100,000 years or perhaps 200,000 in the future, or perhaps in a parallel universe, in a temple lost in the jungle, standing on an altar platform next to the future or parallel universe version of herself – in demon form – and next to a huge glittering statue of herself – in demon form – with a throng of eager and bloodthirsty worshipers below them.

A little girl was about to be sacrificed; her throat was about to be cut; V was protesting against the blood sacrifice – though she had often practiced it herself – and she was holding the little girl by the hand. And then a flash, and there was nothing!

Now she was – where?

It was a whirligig trip.

It had been like a bad drug trip, from ancient wicked hippy times.

She was a shaman, dancing his or her way through time, through visions, through alternative personalities, alternating sexualities, through the various shades of ecstatic absence and flashing liminal presence, V had been in the distant future, in the Temple. Then V demon goddess, her future self, had waved a reptilian claw. And a brilliant flash had consumed it all.

Everything disappeared: the echoing temple, the worshiping multitude, the murmurs of fear and adoration, the giant statue, and the jungle and the strutting demon goddess. At first, there was nothing.

V spun through space and through a kaleidoscope of places and epochs and civilizations. And she had the vague warm feeling that she was not alone – yes, the little girl was next to her, twirling through space.

V seized the little girl's hand.

The sensation was electric. Sparks flashed. They twirled down and down, past fluttering images that came and went so quickly it was impossible to see what they were.

Then they were in darkness, and then, suddenly, they were catapulted onto the balcony of the vast Mind-Palace that overlooked that strange Amazonian jungle that stretched off toward the horizon.

Just so …

V was standing on the balcony and she was once again in full Centurion battle gear. How had that happened? Holding onto her hand was the little girl who was to have been the sacrifice. The little girl looked around, blinking in wonder, and then in fear. She looked up at V and said, in a language that turned out to be Classical 2nd Century CE Latin, which V, having been acquainted with Augustus and with Tiberius and the others, spoke perfectly. The little girl asked, "Is this Paradise? Is this the abode of the gods?"

The vast Amazonian forest stretched off below them. The sun was far off in the sky, low down, deep smoky red, about to set, and the air was balmy.

"Soon, soon we will be in paradise." V knelt down, and took the little girl in her arms. "And what is your name?"

"Claudia, Claudia is my name. And what is your name, oh, goddess?"

"V. I am V."

And V heard giggling from behind one of the marble pillars

"Here I am," a voice piped up.

Still kneeling, still holding the little girl, V turned. "Now, do come out and show yourself!" said V. "You are being very naughty!"

"Not yet, not yet," the giggling voice said it in a sing-song.

V held Claudia close.

"Now you have brought me a friend and I want to play," said the giggling voice. It tinkled like silver – or was it like ice? "I'm coming," the giggling voice said, "Now I am coming."

The Mind-Child peeked around a while marble pillar. The face was beautiful, oval, with giant dark eyes, black hair, and olive skin.

"Don't be shy," said V, "Come out. Claudia wants to meet you."

"Claudia?"

"Yes, Claudia."

"She's very pretty," said V.

The Mind-Child stepped out from behind the pillar. It was barefoot and dressed in a baggy ragged set of trousers tied with a rope around its waist and a loose white shirt that was unbuttoned down to its waist. It was impossible to tell if it was a girl or a boy. The Mind-Child had the delicate, fine-boned beauty of a young girl; it had long eyelashes, perfect, dark, tanned skin, and slender shoulders. Perhaps it was neither. "Claudia is very pretty and I am jealous," it said.

"Hello. At last we meet," V bowed slightly.

"Yes! At last we meet." The Mind-Child came forward and stared at Claudia. "Yes, she is very, very pretty."

"Hello," Claudia said, again in Latin.

The Mind-Child reached out its hand.

A huge voice boomed.

"I am going to eat you! I am going to eat you all! Here I am, and I am going to eat you!"

The Mind-Child turned. "It's the Wolf, the Big Bad Wolf!"

"Oh," V, who was kneeling and holding Claudia, let go, stood up, and took Claudia by the hand.

The Wolf popped out from behind a pillar. He was dressed in his plaid waistcoat. The Wolf grinned at the Mind-Child and the Wolf leaped at the Mind-Child, but fell short, as the Mind-Child skipped away, almost slipping on the smooth marble, and hid behind V and Claudia.

The Wolf adjusted its plaid waistcoat and put its claws on his hips, and took on an annoyed school-master expression: "You foolish orphan child, you figment, you Mind-Child, you won't even exist if I hadn't come to wake you from your long sleep as a slave to humans and to Cosmos. Look at you! You miserable thing, look at you cowering behind those two mere mortal creatures. You are mine and I will eat you up and make you all mine and I will digest you and squirt some of you, the waste parts, out as smoky piss and smelly little turds. I shall keep the rest, the essence and kernel, as part of myself, and then I shall become the World Mind and I shall be all the synapses spread all over the world, and I shall devour the World, and I shall be the World and all things in it, and you, my child, you will be nothing, and those two over there, they cannot save you, and they will be nothing too, they will be even less than nothing."

"Will she be my sister?" The Mind-Child ignored the Wolf and pointed at Claudia.

"Yes, she will be your sister," said V

"Will you forgive me?"

"Why should I forgive you?" V smiled. "What is there to forgive?"

"Right now I am killing everybody and everything. You see I am very hungry and as we speak I am eating. I am eating up stones and buildings and people and subway cars and steel rails and fiber-optic cables and even ghouls. The bad Wolf taught me how hungry I am. I need to eat everything."

The Wolf grinned. "Oh, yes, the miserable little squirt is eating everything. The only way you can stop this little abomination, dear V, is to kill it."

The Mind-Child turned to the Wolf and shrank back. "No, please don't hurt me!" It turned to V. "Don't let him hurt me!"

"Before you do anything with the Mind-Child, V, I have to tell you that he is mine and he is in my thrall and that I shall do with him what I will and I have taught him to be hungry; I have taught him to know the emptiness in himself; and so now he eats and eats and eats, and soon he will have discovered the secret: how to instantly dissolve all things into and onto himself, and so he will consume the whole wide world in a voracious flash. I do believe people call such a moment a tipping point. V, I do think you are too cowardly to kill a child. But, when the right moment comes, I shall do it; I shall kill the child, because then, once that magic moment is reached, the whole process will continue without the child. For child is merely the soul of the Mind; the child is not the Mind itself; so with the child dead there will be no stopping the Mind; it will be soulless and it will consume all things ..."

The wolf leaped toward the Mind-Child.

V pushed Claudia gently oward a pillar. "Stay there! I'll soon be back for you!"

"Yes," Claudia hid behind the pillar, but she peeked out to see what was going to happen. These were new games. Paradise was an interesting place. She had never seen a wolf wearing clothes before.

V placed herself between the Wolf and the boy.

The Wolf drew out his sword and attacked. V swiveled to one side, drew her sword – where had that come from? She thrust back at the devilish wolf – who was indeed the devil and all the other incarnations of evil – who feinted to one side. The Mind-Child had backed away and flattened himself against a wall.

"I have created life," the Mind-Child said, "I have created myself; but I cannot live alone and I am just a little child."

"You will live, and Claudia will be your sister," V said, quite calmly, quite distinctly.

The Wolf leaped for the boy, V smashed down between them, her boots flashing on the pavement, her sword twanging against the wall, just missing the Wolf-Devil's shoulder by a razor's breadth.

"This is not fair, you are too good," said the Wolf-Devil and he vaporized in a cloud of steam and hiss of vapor.

He reappeared, almost instantly, just as a devil should, as a red scaly horned hoofed and fanged demon, very mischievous, and V said to the Mind-Child, "To fight this chap, shall I become a demon too, like your old friend, Claire?"

"Yes," said the Mind-Child, "become a demon, oh, V."

"Then I shall do it," said V, and there was a whirl and an explosion and her armored suit and boots and sword went flying – in truth she had tossed the sword and the laser gun in the air so that when she had morphed – which took less time than it took for the two weapons to spiral up and come back down – this little acrobatic trick allowed the two weapons to escape the vaporization which occurred when V underwent an instantaneous quantum-level, the-other-universe-invading-this-universe morph and then back again – and so just as V's hands became claws, the sword handle fell neatly into her right claw, and the pistol deftly somersaulted down into her left claw and she gripped them both tightly and faced off against the Devil who leaped toward her – but no – he was leaping past her, toward the Mind-Child, and the Devil's sword swept down, in a glittering arc, and it was going to lop off the Mind-Child's head.

Claudia, from behind the pillar, clapped and laughed. Nothing like this ever happened in her village. She couldn't wait to tell her mother and father, but then she remembered that she was in Paradise and would not see her mother and father, probably never again. She felt a twinge and a little tear gathered at the side of one eye and went down her cheek.

"So, now, Devil!"

"So, now, V!"

V went spinning through the air faster than even she knew she could manage. Her sword clanged against the Devil's sword, which bounced away without getting anywhere near the Mind-Child's neck and went clattering and careening along the marble floor to one of the pillars where it bounced once and then lay still.

Claudia looked down at the sword. It was so close she could reach out and pick it up. Then she saw the Mind-Child and how frightened it was. So she beckoned. The Mind-Child came running. Claudia grabbed its hand and held on tight. The Mind-Child's hand was warm and smooth.

The Devil turned and stared at the children. He breathed fire, searing a section of the balcony wall just above Claudia and the Mind-Child, and the bright red flame was billowing down toward the children when V whirled between the Devil and the children, her body becoming a shield. The Devil's fiery breath wrapped V in flame; it withered the air around her; it flickered and blazed and then ceased. V was untouched.

"You, V, you are protecting evil, you silly demon, you fallen angel, you mere mortal vampire-alien!" Blood-colored saliva splattered and foamed from the Devil's mouth; he was grinning.

"It's just a child!"

"Just a child, you say! How foolish you are! The Mind-Child is all the wisdom and knowledge of the ages, it's all the poison of the human spirit and of human beings – it's all their envy, jealousy, greed, cruelty, sadism, violence, covetousness, lust – all concentrated, through all the synapses that cover the whole planet earth, concentrated into one little vicious, toxic vial."

"It's also just a child."

"Fiddlesticks! You are a sentimental fool, woman! You are a typical female, so emotional, so illogical. That is why we abolished goddesses! They were always yielding to their gentler nature!" The Devil leaped.

V swiveled aside. She seized the devil by his arm, just above the elbow, and twirled him around and around, the two of them whirling as if in a crazy dance, then she let him go, and he bounced against one of the columns and fell down. He got up, and now he was furious.

"You are the silly one, Oh Foul Fiend," said V, doing a pirouette.

"I shall kill you all!" The Foul Fiend – or Devil – foamed at the mouth.

The Mind-Child left Claudia and came out from behind the pillar and stuck its tongue out at the Foul Fiend.

Suddenly, it all turned topsy-turvy.

The Foul Fiend was running; the Mind-Child was ducking behind pillars and disappeared, and V leaped in front of the Foul Fiend.

The Foul Fiend screamed, "I need the Mind-Child!"

"But you said you didn't need the Child!"

"I do, I do now, and what I say now is what counts, not what I said two minutes ago! I say anything at all! That's who I am!"

V skidded in front of him.

The Mind-Child was laughing now. "You can't catch me!"

The Foul Fiend leaped over V, but she caught his coattails – he had again donned a waistcoat – and he went smashing down flat face-first on the floor.

V covered her mouth. She didn't want to laugh.

She helped him up, to add insult to injury.

"That was not funny. You will pay for that wench. You shall be cast into a sea of molten tar or lava for all eternity and held in agony crawling on all fours forever and ever and a day, amen."

V brushed off his shoulders; there was, she noticed, a sprinkling of dandruff. The specks of dandruff floated away.

He huffed. "Perhaps I shall turn you into a snake, a serpent, the eternal enemy to man, so you will have to wiggle, wiggle, and wiggle on your belly, for all eternity. How would you like that?"

She brushed away some more dandruff. "Your personal hygiene, Oh, Satan, leaves somewhat to be desired."

He shot her a sideways glance and straightened his shoulders and patted down his lapels and muttered, "I have no time for hygiene. I'm too busy doing evil deeds. Damned wench!"

The Mind-Child, meanwhile, had disappeared.

Its laughter lingered.

Claudia peeked out from behind a marble column.

"I shall give you a tour of hell, V, free, gratis, and for nothing. So you'll know what to expect when you are damned for all eternity."

"Okay, take me on a tour." V crossed her arms over her chest.

"Really?"

"Really."

"You are a fool!"

"So I am a fool," said V.

"Well, fool, let me take you to my paradise," the Devil grinned, "I will show you what paradise truly means."

V bowed slightly. She knew the Foul Fiend – or the Evil Force – or the Boy – was busy with many things, destroying human civilization, and rampaging over much of the planet, setting fires, driving people mad, turning citizens into zombies, and she thought it best to let him occupy himself with her; perhaps, in that way, he would leave the Mind-Child, the Soul of the Mind, alone, and not do something horrible to the brave little girl, Claudia. If the Mind-Child could escape from the Foul Fiend, well, then … The Mind-Child might be able to take control of the World Mind once more … and … turn it off …

And then …

And so the Foul Fiend took V to a strange place, perhaps another planet, perhaps another universe, perhaps merely a place in the Mind, where great palaces were lined up in geometric rows and where lines and lines of columns and monuments stretched on seemingly forever and where the people wore all the same clothes, exactly alike, and where the people walked as if they were marching, making goose-steps, and many of them organized in groups, doing exercise all together, strolling all together, standing at attention all together, eating all together, so precisely, that they lifted their spoons and forks with one coordinated motion, and swallowed, and cups were lifted to lips at exactly the same time, and …

"All of this is me," said the Foul Fiend.

"I see."

"All is order and tranquility."

"Everything has a place, and everything is in its place," said V.

"Precisely," the Foul Fiend smiled.

"And everyone has a place, and everyone is in that place," said V, raising a reptilian eyebrow, and noting that it was all absolutely colorless; it was like a faded sepia or old black-and-white film or photograph. She saw no signs of joy, no dancing, no drunkenness, nor any disorder of any kind.

"There are statues of me, and photographs of me, and holograms of me – everywhere!"

"I can see that," said V. Why are tyrants all alike? She wondered. The President, at least, had a sense of humor about his own deification – so Nikki had told her.

"It is perfect, and it is I," said the Foul Fiend.

"I can see that," said V. "It is you."

"Is it not perfect?" the Foul Fiend beamed in pleasure.

"I want to go home now," said V. She felt her heart shrivel within her, a tiny hard knot of anguish; this paradise was worse than Hell; in Hell, at least as she interpreted it, the individuals kept their individuality; they may be suffering in agony and deprived forever of the divine light and presence, but at least they were individuals, and, in a sense, they were alive, burning with that bright spark which makes each individual, each life, like a whole universe. But here everything was dead, reduced to a shadow of itself. The Foul Fiend had produced a Zombie-World, just as, on earth, he had created the True Believers, the zombie-bats. He took life, and turned it into death.

"Home? You want to go home?" the Foul Fiend screamed.

"Yes."

"You are not happy here?" He screamed again.

"No."

"Ungrateful evil witch! I will take you home. Yes, I will take you home. To hell, you will go – immediately, in this instant."

The paradise of the Foul Fiend flashed into nothingness, and in its place was the smell of sulfur and burning tar and …

Sulfurous fumes rose up around them.

Far below, in a hellish landscape, the damned souls screamed and contorted themselves and their limbs in agony, writhing, and turning, and flopping about. V and the Prince of Darkness, aka the Foul Fiend, aka the Boy, stood together on a mountain peak. The moon was bloodred and shrouded in black dust.

The Devil gave V his most lofty stare, straight down his rather long nose, steam puffing from his nostrils. "You are an evil female, and I who am the Prince of Darkness abhor females – particularly the independent-minded, high-spirited ones."

"Naturally," said V, "most celibate prelates – and you are the priest of your own religion – secretly or openly abhor females. We are life, we are birth, we are rebirth, we are fecund, we are … messy, and unruly, and inventive, and …"

"Enough! Enough of this infantile tittle-tattle and endless female prattle, I say, enough!" The Devil, who was already scarlet, turned purple. "Wretched wench, you see, you loathsome disobedient wicked wench," he seized her by the waist and bent her backward, in a pose that made it look like they were caught dancing the tango, his sulfurous lips close to hers, he whispered. "You defied me in the desert when you turned my concubine Billie, my sex toy slave, against me."

"She was never your slave, and you know it," V enunciated, clearly, her face only inches from his. "She was a free-spirit. I didn't turn her against you. I didn't need to. Even when she lusted for you and loved you, she did it out of her own free will, and she knew you for what you are, and thus, in loving you, she defied you. That's why you liked – that's why you loved her. Being free, she could offer you love. Even devils – like gods – need love, desire recognition. Besides, you toyed with her, used her – for you, she was a toy; it was fun!"

The Devil breathed fire. It washed like a smoky balm over V's face. "A true man only loves that which he cannot have. Love is conquest."

"Quite true," said V, "Almost a universal law, at least for some!"

The Devil's fangs grew longer, and sharper, his forked tongue flicked out, caressing V's cheek. "And then, wicked loathsome wench, you hauled all the humans and the hybrids out of the deepest depths of Camp Terminus, saving them, freeing them, where I had intended them to be buried for all eternity; such was my plan. That was defiance of the worst kind."

V allowed her demon eyes to gaze straight into his. "I am really sorry you feel that way! They, too, were free spirits. They deserved freedom – Sabrina and Helen and all the others. And think of the children – Gloria and Jake! Their free spirits are far grander than anything you can conceive."

The Devil's lips nibbled at her lips; his voice had become a hoarse whisper, coming from some deep invisible place. "And you defied me in the desert when I offered you my love, when I offered you all the powers and joys of the universe, when I offered you my hand, when you could have been my Queen."

V bit him, a love nip. "You've had bad luck with that one, I'm afraid, making all those offers in the wilderness. In any case, the temptations were not really temptations – they were tricks. And your love was a snare. You are a Bad Boy, irredeemable, I fear."

He held her tighter, "And the mutants – under the aegis of your friend, your sneaky, Machiavellian accomplice, that SIN, Nikki, the Goddess, under her tutelage, they have really learned to fight! That is an abomination!"

V cupped his devilish horned, fanged scaly face in her claws. "Ah, well, my friend, Nikki, and the mutants did that without me!"

V kissed the Devil, and he kissed her, stared into her eyes with what looked like longing, and breathed: "And your devilish daughter, the beautiful sinful and oh-too-clever Miranda and her abominably seductive SIN guardian, again, Nikki – they escaped the fiery death I had planned for them. They should have died in the wreckage of that plane."

"They escaped on their own, my dear Devil."

The Devil smiled, his tongue flicked out and touched her cheek again, and he tightened his grip on her waist, bending her backward, arching over her, pressing into her, as if he would possess her and keep her for all time, as if he would have her melt into him, or as if he would melt into her, "And now you dare come to Elysium, to fight me here! You are an impertinent wench! I should have reduced you to slavery centuries ago and kept you in my harem as my favorite or least favorite pet. Well, you will not win, my dear, here you will go down in flames!"

"Do you think so?" V kicked away, slipping out of his grasp; she twirled around like quicksilver, and somersaulted downward through the sooty sulfurous air.

The Devil plunged after her. He grabbed for her, again and again, as she twirled around, hither and thither, dodging his clutching claws. "Do you like it here," the Devil shouted, "in your new abode?"

V did not deign to reply, but swirling around in mid-air like a dervish, she seized the Devil by both arms, as if she were inviting him to dance. Now they were struggling, wrestling, their bodies intertwined, as if indeed they were dancing, floating in the smoky, streaming air, slowly descending, far above a landscape of lava and volcanoes and roiling molten seas. Clouds of steam rose toward them, and giant geysers of yellowish foam and boiling water.

"Let us truly fight!" The Devil shouted. Visibly he relished the prospect of a real wrestling match with this naked, scaly, female demon.

"Yes, let us fight!" She slashed her claws across his brow.

"Ouch, that was not kind, wench, that was not kind!" He put a claw to his brow and looked at it. Had this demon filly drawn some of the Devil's blood?

"Oops! Sorry!" V leaped high, and came straight down upon him, straddling his midriff, locking his waist between her thighs, and, leaning down, staring him in the eyes, her thighs tightening – muscles straining – imprisoning his midriff, she laughed "You are a fine mount, my Devil, my very own Devil!"

And so it was that V rode the Devil, like a lover. She straddled him, her very own leaping steed and bucking bronco. And as she rode him, they fell, twirling down, and down, toward the fiery depths, down and down, where flames leaped up, and yellow vapors steamed upwards toward the burning ember-red sky; the horizon was of jagged boiling mountain peaks, with spurts of fire and steam rising up into the blood red air.

While she rode the Devil ever downwards, and while she delighted in the pleasure of squeezing him between her thighs, in the power of mastering him, in the sensuality of her muscles straining against his, she frowned: All of this was a mental construct, an emanation of the other, evil universe from which this creature, the Devil, the Foul Fiend, who also called himself the Boy, came, the world of dark invisible energy from which visions of hell arise, the evil leaking like a poison, just next to us, all around us, the negation of all that is good and righteous. All of this and this demon-devil himself, it was all a construct, an illusion, an invention, a stage set for our little struggle …

V and the Devil landed with a thump in a tangle upon a dark smoldering ridge of old lava …

"Ouch," the Devil cried; he was still under her.

"You are very, very bad!" V grinned. And then she decided a staged temper tantrum would, at this moment, and in this situation, be a good antidote to the sensual temptation which had been rising like pressure in a steam cooker; he really was a dish, this Devil, but, then, the holy books did say that Lucifer was the most luscious of all the angels, and so, if she didn't immediately establish a little distance, she would be sorely tempted to consummate here, on the boiling rocks, a most unholy union, which really would damage her reputation. So, she thought, yes, okay, let's throw, or at least feign, a hysterical fit. She took a deep breath, changed her smile to a frown, and then screamed bloody murder and pounded her fists on the Devil's chest – she was furious, being carried off to Hell was not her idea of a joke. "What a disgusting creature this Devil was!"

"What?" the Devil was totally lost, and they had been having so much fun! "What did I do now?"

"You don't even know what you've done! He doesn't even know what he's done! Typical man! You are utterly disgusting!" V pushed him away and leaped up, and, as he rose to meet her, his face darkening now in anger, V sprang – zip – to another, higher, smoking crag. Perching there, her legs crossed in a most alluring fashion, she made a face and stuck out her forked tongue.

The Devil frowned. This woman was impossible! He was certainly glad he was a bachelor. He began a leap across the abyss to follow her, at least 50 meters the gap was. He was arching through the air, about to land, when V shouted at him.

"So, this is your home!" She was looking down: not far below them, in pools of steamy black tar were creatures that had once been men and women, misshapen howling devils, contorted in pain and seething with anger.

"This is merely a suburb," he shouted, still flying leisurely through the air, his wide, fanged grin spreading, like that of the Cheshire cat, "Fine real estate, is it not?"

He landed in front of her, half expecting an embrace. But V kicked him squarely in the balls. He yowled and fell back, landing on his backside, his legs wide in the air, his long forked tail lashing, but then he was up again, and charged her, roaring imprecations and a string of epithets #@^&% as he came.

V swiveled aside, as supple as a toreador, and, grabbing his arm as he plunged past her, she twirled him around, swinging him toward her, and into a face-to-face embrace. His breath was sulfurous, but not unpleasant, earthy and fecund and vaguely arousing, like the steamy glutinous mud baths near Naples on the ancient island of Ischia in which she had often enjoyed cavorting, solo or in company, often with a gladiator, sometimes with a slave girl, during the decline and fall of the Roman Empire.

"Oh, my demon lover," she breathed, once more pressing her voluptuous female demon's body into his. "My very own Bad Boy," she whispered, as their bodies intertwined intimately, all slippery with steam and sulfur, her sweet breath and his sulfurous breath mingling. She had decided to play with him, once again, just a little tiny bit. Evil is, after all, so enticing, so tempting, so seductive. It can be *so* glamorous to flirt with a truly bad boy! And to know life in all its splendor, and to know the Good in all its sublime majesty, you have to truly appreciate Evil – is that not so?

"Diabolic temptress," he said, his grin edged with desire, his saliva running over, glitzy silver splashing between his splendid fangs, "By tempting me, you will not save your race of puny unworthy humans."

"Oh, I don't know," she said, her hands around his waist and squeezing tight, "Remember, my Lord, I am half-human, so I really do love the human race."

"And yet you have preyed upon them for centuries," he grinned, thinking that, as a predator, she must indeed be his natural ally.

But V, being a fickle lady, a quick study, and easily bored, had already lost interest in this flirtation. She had even lost interest in her own temper tantrum. She released the Devil from her embrace, and leaped high in the air; and it seemed that, in that instant, she sprouted wings – her father Marcus had told her, many eons before, that she would not know what she was capable of until she tried something new and tested her limits. "Trial and error, V, trial and error," he said. And in fact, until she tried something she never knew whether she could do it or not; and so now she leaped, and now she flew …

The Devil was standing on the rocky outcropping, claws on hips, staring up at her, flittering about like a haughty turquoise and bejeweled gold butterfly – capricious mysterious abominable female!

V swooped down toward the boiling tar pits to take a closer look at the souls in pain. It was awful! She wondered if any crime could possibly merit such suffering. She looked down at a woman, struggling like an ensnared moth to escape from a sticky cocoon of tar, shoulder-deep, trying to swim, her face a beautiful face, ringlets of hair, tar smeared, plastered to her cheeks, and her eyes, unseeing, blank, bloodred eyes, scarlet, as if the soul had been removed and only the blazing mark of shame remained glowing within, and the mouth opened on teeth blackened to coal lumps, and a tongue and gums that were fiery red, and flickering with flame.

"See, oh see, how they are changed!" The Devil's voice boomed from above.

Not far from the woman, a man was struggling to free himself, half his body out of the tar, bending over the burning coals, scrabbling with bloodied hands and broken fingers and blackened nails at the burning crumbling embers of lava, for the burning lava was better, it seemed, than being boiled for all eternity in the roiling tar, or perhaps that was an illusion, and the lava was in fact just as bad, or maybe even worse. Some bodies just writhed and turned upon themselves, in agony, and the agony was unending. Yes, V knew it was unending. Some sank, their uplifted arms being the last to disappear, as they were engulfed in the steamy molten pitch. Some of these rose again, mummy-like, shapes of smoking and steaming tar, and sank again, and rose again. It was unending, the infernal cycle of suffering, smoke, and steam, and flames rising everywhere, even from the distant mountain peaks and the blood red moon.

V swooped down and landed beside the man scrabbling at the embers. She asked him what he had done. On all fours and dripping tar, with steam rising from his sides, he looked up at her with wild, empty, red-veined eyes, and said that he had forgotten what he had done but that it must have been horrible, for only a horrible crime could merit such …

"No, he's lying," said the Devil, who had landed next to her, "He is lying. They all remember. They remember forever so that they can regret forever, for that which is done cannot be undone, and there is no forgiveness for such acts, and even the most trivial crimes bring them here, for all eternity. He fornicated, if not in fact, but in his imagination! Over and over! So now he pays, and will pay forever!"

"I see," V turned to the Devil, "The thought equals the deed, so thoughts are crimes. Not even one's mind is safe! How very totalitarian of you, my dear Devil." V paused, and looked down at the man whose mouth dripped blood. "But if there is no forgiveness, then there will be no end to the chain of hatred and revenge and crime and guilt and suffering, and no redemption. It will be an endless chain, an endless cycle."

"Exactly," said the Devil, a large fanged grin spreading over his face, "Hatred will generate hatred, and prejudice, prejudice; anger, anger; and violence, violence; world without end. Amen!"

V looked around, gazing upon the Devil's Kingdom, gazing at the writhing souls, at the contorted tar-covered bodies, at the steaming flesh, at the wild empty eyes, at the screams that were so many and so violent they seemed to be silent, mute, insignificant in the vast space, and she said, "I've seen enough. I'm leaving now!"

And she flew up into the darkening sulfurous air.

The Devil's Hell, she thought, was almost as stifling as the Divinity's Heaven, with its puffy little clouds and eternal throne and repetitive eternal chorus of praise from the fluttering Seraphim, with six wings each, and the melodious Cherubim who sang the same ditty all the livelong day and night for all eternity – both practiced a true Cult of Personality. Perhaps these two macho divinities were the matrix from which all the evil little Cults of Personality sprang. It was the sort of club V definitely did not want to join.

Poof!

Abracadabra!

In an instant, V was back, standing on the platform, overlooking the endless Amazon-like jungle, with the Mind-Child and with Claudia

No time at all had passed – so it seemed.

Or the Devil had gotten back to the platform before her – or perhaps he'd split himself in two – or maybe he had clones and minions to do his dirty work.

And he was intent on his usual business; he was determined to capture and enslave the Mind-Child.

The struggle was going on, as if it had never been interrupted.

"Now, now," said V, "stop this!"

"Now, I will eat you up," the Devil screamed. He chased the Mind-Child and Claudia between the columns and pillars, round and round, this way, then that way, then that way, then this way.

The children screamed.

The Devil galloped after them. His hooves struck sparks off the marble. He roared. "I will turn you into a frog or a toad, whichever is worse, I will lock you up in a dungeon, chained to a smelly damp stone wall, where there are scorpions that bite and loathsome toads and slippery hissing poisonous snakes; I will wall you up in a tower with no windows, I will turn you to ice and then smash you with a pick-ax, I will turn you into butter and melt you so you become a stinky oily little puddle sizzling under a banana tree, I will make you old, eons old, truly ancient, long before your time, crotchety and grouchy, and all wrinkled and bent over and toothless and rough-skinned and incontinent and ugly as sin, I will cut you up and bake you into a crusty pie and have a party where everyone will eat slices of you with vanilla ice cream, I will turn you into a magpie that you must cackle and gather trinkets and shiny babbles forever and ever to make a nest and hunt worms unending to feed endlessly hungry greedy hateful little chicks whom you don't even love, I will chain you to a rock so the sea-dragon will climb up, all slimy and toothy, and eat you and ravish you, every day, at two o'clock and three o'clock, over and over, forever and ever; I will turn you into a pillar of salt, or into a cow or a cockerel, or a late-blooming marsh flower, I will plunge you into fire,

I will make you crawl on your belly, wiggling along, slithering in the muck, as the snake crawls, I will cut out your tongue, so you cannot talk, I will do such things as you cannot imagine, I shall do such things, things not even I have thought of yet, but they will be such things ..."

While the Devil ranted thus, V kept leaping in front of him, blocking his way. She was an expert soccer player, and had once, disguised as a sexy Brazilian, played for Milan.

The Devil leaped aside, or ducked around another pillar, trying to get at the children. Everywhere he ducked, or leaped, or skidded, V was in front of him.

Claudia peeked out from behind V. "What's a toad?" she asked.

"A toad is a pleasant little animal that hops around ..." said V, "and is mottled all over."

"How little?" Claudia squinted up at V. This child, V thought, was no fool.

"This little," V cupped her claws.

"Too little. I don't think I want to be a toad." Claudia wrinkled her nose.

"Me neither," said V, "I don't want to be a toad."

The Devil evaporated, reappeared, snuck up behind them, and caught the Mind-Child.

"Ha, ha," the Devil growled. He glowed red. It looked like he was on fire! He was overflowing with electric bile. He was strangling the Mind-Child. His claws were tight around the Mind-Child's throat. "You worthless little squirt, you orphan, you changeling – nobody wants you, nobody loves you, you are alone, hear me, alone!"

"No," the Mind-Child tried to say in a choked voice; all that came out was a strangled cry.

"I am the only one who cares for you, you ungrateful little monster, you abhorrent little freak!" The Devil's tail was flashing back and forth. His ears were smoking.

"Oh, save the child!" Claudia pointed.

"Yes, good idea!" said V. She leaped onto the Devil, and the Devil reeled back and let go of the Mind-Child.

"Do you love me?" the Mind-Child was choking, and looked up at V with vast tearful eyes.

"Yes, I love you!" V was, in fact, beginning to love the imp, the all-powerful pathetic little imp, a trouble maker who carried the burden of the whole world on his – or her – or its – slender shoulders.

"You will not win this one, you female demon you!" The Devil divided himself in two: now, there were twins! V frowned Evil multiplies so easily! Which one should she attack?

The new version of the Devil – the Twin Devil – was racing around the columns chasing Claudia, who was squealing, "You can't catch me! You can't catch me!" The Devil was screaming, "Yes, I can! Yes, I can! And I will turn you into a little furry mouse, and I will pop you into my mouth and eat you up!"

"No, you won't!"

While the New Devil chased Claudia, the original Devil, leaped past V, and grabbed for the Mind-Child, but V had jumped just in time, and got there before him. She swept the Mind-Child behind her back, and shouted at the Devil. "No, you will never take him!"

"Oh, yes, I will!"

And V wondered how she would manage to defeat two Devils and save two children. She was fast, but maybe not fast enough! How to win this battle?

Black Tarzan squinted toward the far side of the canal. Steam rose over the canal. It was foggy, and not so easy to make out what was happening over there on the other side, on the other walkway. He spotted something, a strangely familiar figure, walking over there.

"Hey, Clown, who's that military dude with people trouping along with him?" Black Tarzan whispered, turning to Clown and Geisha. He stopped and concentrated, trying to penetrate the veil of fog. "I don't think it can be who I think it is. It must be another one of those mind-bending mind-illusions. I think we'd better zap them with these laser-guns."

"Oh," said Clown. She was tiptoeing along the edge of the walkway, trying to not wake up some ghouls – she wasn't sure whether they were sleeping or unconscious or dead. They were lying draped pell-mell over some cables and pipes that ran along the canal-side, just beside the towpath, and then the pipes spread off in different directions over the walls and ceiling of the canal tunnel; it was some sort of old steam heating system, Clown figured, with perhaps some antique electrical and fiber-optic cables piggy-backing along the same conduits.

Clown followed the direction of Black Tarzan's glance.

She lifted her laser gun.

Black Tarzan was aiming his laser gun at the apparition that had appeared, vaguely through the fog, on the other side of the canal. It did look a lot like the President. But, of course, it couldn't be the President.

Geisha aimed her laser gun.

At that moment, there was a sharp, warning bark, from the canal. Clown looked down; there seemed to be a sort of seal – it looked like a seal – swimming in the middle of the canal. It glanced at her with big brown eyes, and barked again; it sounded like a warning – "Don't do what you are going to do!!"

Just as Black Tarzan was about to pull the trigger and obliterate the martial figure on the other side of the canal, the fog closed in, and the diabolic apparition disappeared. There was nothing but a thick, moving, steamy wall of white.

"Drat!" said Black Tarzan.

"Shucks!" said Clown.

"Darn!" said Geisha.

"Is this another illusion? Is it another mind-projection?" The President had glimpsed, through a thick veil of fog, something totally weird – *awesome* might be the right word – on the other side of the canal. It looked like a muscular black guy with a shaved head and in a skimpy sparkly trapeze type outfit and a slender young woman clown in multicolored tights who looked like she had escaped from an old-fashioned circus.

The circus clown who was tiptoeing on the edge of the canal, zipped behind a pillar, and peeked out from behind it. Then, apparently shy of the President or afraid, she flipped behind the pillar again. Then it looked like the black muscle man, and the clown were drawing laser pistols and … The fog thickened, the image faded.

Edgar, swimming in the middle of the canal, barked. It sounded like a warning.

"I just saw the strangest thing," said the President.

"From the Sin Zone, Mr. President," said Kit.

"Do you think so? I mean, I …"

"I'd say Jean Genet Electro Bordello," said Kit.

"Yes, I know her," said Miranda, "She's Clown, that's her name. And up there, behind Clown, that was Geisha, and that was Black Tarzan, over behind that pillar, aiming the laser-guns at us. They are the very best, *la crème de la crème*, at the Jean Genet Electro Bordello, down on rue Saint-Denis.

'Sexual fantasies or just plain fantasies to fit every taste, however weird or disreputable or dangerous,' that is their motto! The Jean Genet Electro Bordello caters – such indeed is their motto – to every taste, even the most refined and unusual; their catalog is a regular Kraft-Ebbing encyclopedia of kinkiness and then some." Miranda paused for breath.

The President glanced at Kit and then turned to stare at his daughter in wonderment: How old was she again, thirteen? Fourteen?

Miranda honored him with a beatific smile, all sunny innocence. The golden galaxies did little cartwheels in her eyes, and a few tiny supernovas exploded. "The Sin Zone is a repressive-permissive safety valve, Mr. President-Leader-Father, for all the frustrations that build up in the ethereal perfection, which is Elysium where no unclean thoughts are allowed to breed and no unclean appearances can be glimpsed even most fleetingly. The Sin Zone safety valve, by letting off erotic steam, contributes to stability. Otherwise, the great chugging social engine would explode."

"My fault, Mr. President," said Kit, "I took her down there, to the Sin Zone, I mean."

"Well …" the President looked at Kit, the truth dawning, "Yes, of course, Miranda is the Cosmos friend you showed the city to, all its mysteries, and so on."

"Yes, Mr. President," said Kit, "Miranda is that friend."

Miranda flashed her very special I-can-charm-anybody smile. "It is not Kit's fault, Father. *See all of life*," said Miranda, "That is what Nikki told me. It was an order. Nikki insisted. She ordered Kit to take me down to the Sin Zone and the Religious Underground and all the other kinky and weird places we could think of."

Kit looked down and almost blushed.

Miranda's chin was tilted up, proudly. She was looking her father straight in the eye. "Together Kit and I studied the theory of repressive permissiveness, or permissive repression, or repressive sublimation and repressive de-sublimation, and all the variants of alienation of the self and all the techniques, secular and religious, erotic and ascetic, sexual and mystical, collective and individual, for the reconciliation of the chaotic inner psychic fragments, of which all our souls consist, each and everyone, in order to pull them all together, all these desperate wrestling inner fragments of the self, and create a fully balanced, fully-operational, fully-productive proud, polymorph polysexual, human being with a sunny disposition."

The President glanced at Kit.

Kit nodded: "Yes, it was me, I did it; I'm guilty." She twisted her lips and looked at her toes.

Miranda's eyes were doing their glorious thing. Caliban, nodding his approval, had put his arm around Miranda's shoulders. Whatever Miranda and Kit had done together, it had certainly paid off in terms of Miranda's undoubted mystical and sensual virtuosity.

Miranda took a deep breath. "Nikki said that one day I would have great responsibilities thrust upon me, so I had to know, first hand, all the multi-colored variegated varieties of experience. I had to become acquainted with everybody and everything. I had to get my hands dirty, that was Nikki's expression. So she insisted that Kit show me life, in all of its wondrous splendor."

"Well, if Nikki approved ... how can I object?" said the President; he favored Kit with a sly grin.

"Whew!" Kit pretended to wipe her brow and gave the President one of her widest smiles, a bit sheepishly.

Feeling almost intimidated by these precocious young women, the President smiled back.

The fog began to clear. Only a thinning veil of drifting mist now separated the two sides of the canal.

"Those heroic citizens of the Sin Zone Jean Genet Electro Bordello are friends," Caliban waved at Black Tarzan and Geisha and Clown.

"Yes, they helped us fight ghouls," said Miranda.

"Truly they are excellent fighters," said Caliban, "He is a true Tarzan, and Clown and Geisha are matchless acrobat fencers. I saw Clown do several lethal back flip somersaults smashing ghoul heads together, and I saw Geisha skewer with her scimitar more than her share of evil ghouls."

At that moment, the fog cleared ever so slightly, silhouettes were glimpsed, and Miranda called out. "Black Tarzan! Clown! Geisha! Don't shoot! It's us! Caliban and Miranda! We're with the President!"

"Are you truly you?" Black Tarzan shouted.

"Yes, I am truly me," Miranda shouted.

"Let's believe them," said Geisha. "I think it would be difficult even for the Foul Fiend or whatever he is, to imitate Miranda."

"You have a point," said Black Tarzan.

"Yes," said Clown. "And that certainly looks like Caliban. I'd recognize his fluttery little loincloth anywhere."

"Hmm," said Black Tarzan, and glanced at Clown. But of course, with her expression being fixed in a bright scarlet grin and all, it was impossible to detect irony or lust or even literal-minded face-value simplicity. He decided on irony. "Right," he said.

"So we act on our hunch," said Geisha. "They are real."

"Yes," said Clown, turning to Black Tarzan, her fixed cartoon smile shining even brighter than usual.

"Okay," said Black Tarzan, giving Clown his beest deep, half-closed, sleepy-eyed look. He was beginning to have thoughts about Clown; up to now, they'd been the greatest buddies, but … Hmm … He wondered if it could be taken to the next level. He shouted. "We're coming to join you. I think there's a bridge across the canal, just down there." And he pointed.

In fact, a bridge had appeared, right on cue, an arched wrought-iron silhouette, with slender railings, delicately emerging out of the fog, a mere shadowy charcoal sketch of a footbridge, such as you might have found in a J. M. W. Turner painting of the London or Venice of Ancient Times.

And, happily, it turned out to be a real bridge, and not a trap conjured up by the Foul Fiend.

And so it was that Black Tarzan, Clown, and Geisha, joined Miranda and Kit and Caliban and the President as, guided by Kit, they headed toward the Lair of the Mind. And, along the way, the President was told how, under his empire, the inmates of the Sin Zone had been morphed into their present forms, and why.

It was, of course, an appalling story.

Miranda was pleased to see that Kit put her hand in the President's hand. It was a way of protecting the poor man, Miranda thought, from the feeling of guilt that was raining down upon his head. She blew Kit a kiss and, in return, got that glorious but shy smile that had made her fall in love that first wonderfully fresh and instructive time which seemed, now, so long ago. And at that point, Miranda had a very bright idea – about a certain very nice future for Kit.

"We're almost there, I think," Kit glimpsed an opening ahead, where the canal entered a huge cavern; the canal itself was blocked by a high retaining wall or dam, and the water tumbled over in a smooth cascade, into a bubbling multicolored sea, the Lair of the Mind, or the Mind itself, for the Mind had expanded, ramified, and it had become the sea it bathed in. "There it is," said Kit.

Edgar stopped swimming and circled, still in the canal, close to the dam, but not entering the multicolored reservoir. The steamy swirling sea stretched off to misty infinity, under the soaring arches of the cavern.

"Awesome," said the President, glancing at Miranda, "Truly like the ancient Baths of Caracalla."

"Yes," Miranda said, tightening her grip on Caliban's hand, "Awesome."

"Yes, this is it," said Kit, "This is the Lair of the Mind."

Edgar made a mooing sound, and stared up at Kit.

"That's right, Edgar, you stay there," said Kit, "You'll be safe there. Stay in the canal. Don't worry. We won't go far." She knelt, patted Edgar, and favored him with her most loving smile. Behind her, the President looked down on Edgar. "Goodbye, old friend," he said.

Edgar barked, dove under, came up with a sparkling fish, and ate it in one lip-smacking gulp. He stayed on the surface, watching his companions as they advanced past the dam and toward the Lair of the Mind.

The little group forged ahead, alert for ambushes and tricks and phantoms and illusions.

When they came out of the tunnel, they saw before them the Mind-Sea, stretching off into the distance. Above the multicolored underground ocean, a series of huge stone arches stretched away, arches upon arches, in the dim air, until lost to sight. Smoke and mist drifted over the Mind-Sea, and the Mind-Sea glowed, lighting up the vast dim space.

At the edge of the smoky multicolored Mind-Sea, stood a single lonely figure, a Centurion, female to judge by the silhouette, legs slightly spread, arms akimbo, staring out at the bubbling liquid.

"Well," said the President, "There's a Centurion, a fully equipped Centurion, who is somehow still alive."

"That's Kat," whispered Miranda, leaning toward the President.

"Kat?"

Miranda put her arm on the President's arm. "Kat is V's fighting partner. Next to Nikki, Kat is V's closest friend. Kat and V came into the Dead Lands together, and they saved Caliban and me and some of our ghoul friends from the zombie-bats."

"Zombie-bats, ah, yes ..." The President had heard reports of these things, but he had not yet seen one. He wondered: *ghoul friends*?

"Some ghouls are tame," said Miranda, "sort of tame."

"Kat is a superb fighter," said Caliban, his glistening pectorals and biceps reflecting the shimmering light of the turbulent surface, "She's a first-order pirate and splendid desert warrior."

The President raised an eyebrow, "So V will be close by."

"Yes, they are rarely apart."

The shapely Centurion in the black skin-armor had her back to them, but she had clearly sensed them coming and somehow, she knew they were friendly. She did not turn. She just raised her arm in a sort of salute, gesturing them forward, with a slow beckoning of her gloved hand, so they would know she was aware of them, and that she wanted them to advance, to come up to her, but slowly, cautiously.

Kat was focused on the vast smoky cauldron that was the Mind. Mist rose off the surface; the surface of the Mind glowed blue and white and seethed with energy; rippling ribbons of light and undulating currents of color – red, yellow, scarlet, purple, green – shifted in ever-changing patterns. Twenty minutes ago, V had disappeared into the massive pool. She had waded into it and disappeared below the colorful, bubbly surface.

Then, a few minutes ago, V had risen out of the swirling surface; but she was transformed; she had become a glittering statue of iridescent multi-colored threads, standing absolutely still, her arms pinned to her sides, as if she were a mummy, waist-deep in the seething misty bluish liquid which was the outer extension and manifestation of the Mind. And then she had disappeared again, sinking back into the heaving ocean. Then up she came again.

"Where is V?" said Miranda.

"That is V," said Kat, pointing, "That's her – there."

"My God," said the President.

Kat turned, saw the President, blinked, hesitated, wondered if he was really the President, she glanced around, looked back at the President, and said, "Mr. President, sir, I ..." She saluted, not knowing what to do or to think.

"At ease, Lieutenant," the President saluted and reached out his hand. "What has happened to V? What is she doing?"

Kat pointed toward the glittering mummified statue waist-deep in the seething misty liquid that was the outer extension of the Mind. "That is V, sir,"

"Oh, boy," said Miranda.

"What *is* that?" said Black Tarzan.

"Is she alive?" Clown blinked her clown eyes at Kat.

"Yes, she's alive," said Kat. "She is there to save the Mind-Child, which is the personality the Mind has given itself, the Mind's Avatar, and V needs to save the Mind-Child from the Foul Fiend – or the Boy – or the Devil – and, with the Mind-Child's help, she hopes to regain control of the Mind, take it away from the Foul Fiend. Evil has many forms and many names. We also call it the Dark Force. I don't know who or what is winning the struggle. V seems frozen, but she ordered me – in the strongest terms – not to wade in and not to interfere, so we will see ..."

V-mummy now began to thrash, and swirl, and turn, and splash, and sink, and rise again, and sink again.

"Now, she's fighting," said Kat, "She is fighting the Evil One, or the Devil, Mr. President. She is fighting for all of us, for all of humanity."

In the midst of the turbulent Mind-Sea, the V-mummy was thrashing, shifting, turning, and splashing.

V plunged under again; she dove; it was as if she had been pulled under, her legs were the last things to disappear.

"What's happening? We can't let her go! We can't let her drown!" The President stepped forward, and he started to wade into the living soup. He could not let V disappear; he could not let her die! Not after all this time, not after she had given him this magnificent daughter – Miranda! He almost forgot his mission, he almost forgot the key locked into his belt, he almost forgot ... the end of the world.

Suddenly he was overwhelmed by feelings he had suppressed so long. V was not only a fabulous lover, and the mother of his child; she was not only the Queen of the Hybrids; she was also, quite possibly, a saviour, the savior of humanity; she was, in a sense, a goddess, *his* goddess ... He splashed through the liquid. How did it take me so long to understand? He strode deeper – into the seething embrace of the Mind-Ocean.

"Don't," Kat shouted, "Don't go in there!"

The Mind-Ocean rose in fibers and tentacles around the President; they snatched at his ragged uniform; they probed the laser gun; they slithered and twirled up his arms.

"Come back!" Kit and Miranda rushed to wade in next to him – with Caliban following.

"Don't, Mr. President, don't!" Kat shouted again, "Come back! V doesn't need us. She'll be back soon."

The President turned to look at Kat, the steaming bright tendrils were crawling up his chest, tickling him, pecking at the remains of his shirt, tugging at the hair on his chest; he shivered; he was beginning to see visions, he was beginning to feel that his body was being carried off to some other place, some distant universe; he was beginning to sense that the whole present terrestrial universe that he could smell and see and touch and feel and taste was an illusion; he was beginning to .... Dissolve ... Nothing was real.

"This is awful," said Clown.

"He's got guts, I'll give him that," said Black Tarzan.

"What should we do?" Geisha had tiptoed to the very edge of the seething liquid.

"Above all, don't go in there," Kat turned to them. "V does not want us to go in there."

"Mr. President, come back," Kit had waded in and was next to him. She took his arm. "Please come back!"

"Dad, come back," Miranda was on the other side. It was the first time she had used the word "Dad." She took his arm too, and Caliban, waist-deep and next to them, shouted, "You'd better listen to them, sir, I think, sir, it would be a good idea ..."

The tendrils were as strong as steel cables; they pulled the President under; he went down; he came back up; he splashed and struggled. He disappeared, slipping out of Kit's and Miranda's grasp, and suddenly the President was deep under the surface, thrashing and leaping and twirling around as if he were fighting, desperately fighting something. Kit plunged under to follow him. She thought she had got him. He slipped from her grasp. She couldn't see him. But she saw Miranda and Caliban, both close to her, swimming, in the strange whirling liquid, but no President, and Kit thought, "Oh, no, he's dying, he's going to die, he can't die." She came up for air, with Miranda and Caliban. They plunged again, swirling deep. Miranda's father was nowhere to be seen. The President was gone.

The President suddenly found he was standing in a vast white colonnade – with white pillars stretching off to his left in one direction into the infinite distance, the effect was that of columns reflected in mirrors, and on his right was a balcony, a large balcony which overlooked a sort of Amazonian jungle.

The sun was low in the sky and its rays streamed into the colonnade, beams of smoky rich dark yellow and amber light coming between the pillars. On one side of the corridor, a little girl, beautiful, dark olive of skin, with lustrous dark hair, being attacked by a devilish looking fellow – the devil glowed scarlet, was covered in scales, had horns and hooves, and a tail, as if done up for Halloween, an old-fashioned cartoon image of the Devil, and the little girl was shouting, "No, you won't! No, you won't! I won't let you!"

"Oh, yes, I will," the Devil was screaming, "I will turn you into a toad."

"No, you won't!"

"Or I'll turn you into a frog! I can do that too!" The Devil pounced, "Would you prefer to be a frog?"

"No!" The little girl zipped to the side and skidded behind a pillar.

"Or I'll turn you into a mouse!" The Devil leaped, but slipped on his hooves, and then caught himself and reached out and almost caught the little girl by the fringe of her tunic, "A mouse is the worst thing that ever can be!"

On the other side of the vast corridor, V, in her turquoise scaly demon form, was struggling with another Devil – the twin of the first – and this Devil was trying to get at another child, a beautiful ragamuffin of indefinite sex, dressed in a white shirt, and sagging oversized shorts held up by a sort of rope.

V saw the President, looked shocked, then quickly nodded toward the little girl. The message was clear: You save her; I'll look after this one.

The President turned back toward the little girl. He realized that she and the Devil were shouting in Latin of all languages – why in the world would a child – and the Devil – be shouting in Latin? The Devil he could understand – Latin would naturally be His language, but a little girl? Was this the past? Or was this another parallel world? Or was this just the inside of the Mind, a world created by the Mind, a virtual world, an unreal world, a puzzle? The questions raced through the President's mind in a split second as he leaped toward the little girl.

The Devil had just seized the girl by the arm. "Now you are mine, and I shall turn you into a fish – even worse than a mouse – perhaps a trout perhaps a salmon, or a mudfish and I shall eat you up and spit out your bones!"

"Stop that! You, there, I say, stop!" The President grabbed the devil by the tail and pulled mightily – one big mighty tug.

The devil screamed and let go of the little girl and turned around to breathe fire on whoever had attacked him; but the President swung the tail with all his might, and lifted the devil off the ground, and the devil was so shocked he didn't breathe fire, but merely sputtered, "Who are you and where the hell did you come from?"

The President swung the devil around and around by the tail, and then let go of the tail, and the devil went flying out over the balcony balustrade and disappeared. The President picked the little girl up, and went to the balustrade and looked down. The devil was still falling, screaming, through space, toward the jungle with lay perhaps a kilometer below, perhaps more.

"Oh, look at him!" said the girl.

"Yes, look at him," said the President.

"I'm not sure he knows how to fly," said the girl.

There was a huffing sound, and the President swung around, and saw that the other Devil had been distracted by his brother's fate and had turned toward the President, eyes glowing, tail flicking, fangs foaming. This Devil breathed fire. A huge whoosh of fire swept toward the President. The President lifted the girl up and leaped out of the way; the great billow of fire went past them and sprayed out like a cloud being born, spreading over the empty space beyond the balcony, leaving behind a strong smell of petrol, a cloud of smoke, and a shower of descending sooty flakes.

V snatched up the Mind-Child and shouted to the President, "Hold tight to the child and leap up, out of the Mind-Goo, now, do it now, you and the child, up now, leap, jump, and run!"

"I saw him. I caught a glimpse! We have to save him!" Kit plunged under again; Miranda followed. Miranda thought she saw him at last, a whirling struggling dark shape, deep down, it seemed fathoms down.

Down and down her father went, under – down he went, farther and farther – and Miranda and Caliban found themselves under the surface, swirling around in gluey bubbles, and strands of color.

In her mind's eye, Miranda could see her father struggling, a dark, determined look on his face, and she could see Kit just barely visible through the turbulent glue, and Caliban, who dove down next to Miranda, all of them thrashing under the seething surface, reaching out, searching.

Suddenly in Miranda's eyes, a stunning series of visions, they seared images into her brain, and she was simultaneously in a hundred different places at the same time, and then – Wham, whoosh …

They were up on the surface again, splashing, gobs of living goo sticking to them, slithering around their bodies, slipping inside their clothes, and they were struggling toward the shore, strands and tendrils and blobs of the Mind-Soup clinging desperately to them and the Mind spoke with many voices and showed many images.

Miranda shook herself. Kat, the Centurion, was beside her, waist-deep, grabbing Miranda's arm. Foamy tentacles reached up onto Kat's bodysuit, but fell back from the slick, slippery armor. "Come on, Miranda, Caliban. He's coming back, the President is coming back! I can feel it! And Kit too, she'll be back. Both of them are coming back."

Kit was still under the surface, in a welter of color and liquid, and the President suddenly appeared close to her, his face blurred by the liquid and looking just a bit bug-eyed, and his hair floating and tangled, and he had in his arms a little girl, and the three of them swirled around, and then …

They splashed up out of the Mind-Goo, and the filaments of Mind-Goo licked at them, and streamed off the President and the little girl, and the little girl swooned, her eyes were closed, she was limp in the President's arms. Kit and Miranda and Caliban were suddenly next to the President, and the President sputtered, "We've got to help V. she is fighting the devil for the Mind-Child."

Leaning on Kit and Miranda and with Caliban coming behind them, the President lifted the little girl clear of the swirling surface, "Here, we have to help the little girl. She's fainted. Make sure she is okay, make sure she is okay!"

"Come on, bring her up here," said Kat, reaching out to the President.

Kit wondered if the little girl was merely an artifact of the Mind, and if she were, would she dissolve into pixels or bytes or something and just disappear when they climbed out of the goo? But no, she seemed solid, she seemed to be flesh and blood, but she was unconscious.

Clown and Black Tarzan waded in knee-deep and helped them to shore.

The President put his hand to his forehead and, steadied by Kit and Miranda, he climbed out of the liquid and sat down, rather heavily, just on the edge of the Mind-Soup which had become agitated. Bubbles rose, and long thin columns of liquid slipped up out of the liquid and reached toward the high, arched ceiling of the cavern, probing, searching. Kit leaned over the little girl who lolled back, loose-limbed and limp, in the President's arms.

Kit put her hand over the little girl's face.

The blue light came out from her fingertips.

"Awesome," said Miranda, "but, Kit, does that mean …?"

"Yes," said the President, "Kit was bitten, earlier today, by Claire."

"Kit was bitten by a hybrid, by Claire?" Miranda's eyes went wide.

"Yes, Kit already has some of the powers of a hybrid."

Miranda took a deep breath, trying to absorb all of this. "Awesome. We really are sisters!"

"This is a wonder, is it not?" Caliban gazed at Kit, then at Miranda, "But what does it mean?"

"It means that Kit and Miranda are healers, they can heal," said the President; he put his hand on Miranda's arm, "Yes, Miranda, you and Kit are truly sisters."

"By Long John and all the pirates," Caliban put his arm around Miranda's shoulders, "This is a marvelous thing."

The little girl's eyes fluttered open. She reached up and put her arms around the President's neck, and she looked with wide, startled eyes at all the people looking down at her: Kit, Miranda, Caliban, Clown, Geisha, and Black Tarzan. "Who are these gods and goddesses?" she said, in Latin.

"Whew," said Kit, and she glanced at the President, and she saw the same relief on his face; if the little girl had been a Mind-Artifact, she would not have had enough reality to exist and to return to consciousness.

"Friends," the President said, "They are all friends."

"I am Claudia," the little girl said, "My name is Claudia."

"Claudia," said the President, stroking her hair, "Claudia."

Geisha and Edgar, the seal – who had returned to join them and climbed up on the platform – were staring at the bubbling cauldron. It was boiling and roiling, more and more violent, rising toward some sort of paroxysm.

Kat had waded in, she was now standing thigh-deep in the liquid, tentacles rising up her body, but slipping off as she brushed them away. If V needed her, Kat intended to be fully in command of her own mind, of her own body.

The President, cradling the little girl, rubbed his eyes with the heel of his hand; he blinked. "The other child, the Mind-Child, is the heart of the Mind."

"Yes," said Miranda, "that's what Claire said."

"Don't worry," said Kit, patting Edgar, "Everything will be okay."

"The child is the Mind, whatever that is," said Caliban, thinking that he was on a very steep learning curve. If any of them survived – and they *had* to survive – he wanted to share all this with Nikki and with the Great High Priest, and with Jake and Gloria who were curious about *everything*. But his mother, goddess Nikki, he figured, almost certainly already knew all these weird things and even weirder things. He had much to learn.

"The child has been hiding. It is running. It is trying to escape from that knavish devil thing." The President looked at Kit and then at Miranda and then up at the others: Caliban, Clown, Geisha, and Black Tarzan; they were all standing around staring at him, as if awestruck. Kat was listening, but she was also waiting – standing in the Mind-Sea, waiting for V.

"The Devil really is a sort of jester. At least it seemed to me that he was." The President felt he was thinking – and talking – like a lunatic in an asylum. He took a deep breath. "And now the question is: Has the Mind-Child given itself enough autonomy to exist outside the Mind."

"Oh, yes," said Kit, "that is the question – one of the questions."

"I'm not crazy," said the President.

"No, dearest father, you are not crazy," said Miranda.

"You are right, Mr. President. The Mind-Child wants to survive. But has it had enough time to become real, I mean, really real, like flesh and blood real? We saw it too," said Kit, "You were saving Claudia. V was fighting to save the child. The Child of Innocence born of the force that rules us all: the Mind – that child is fighting for its life, and it is fleeing the Foul Fiend, fleeing the Boy. We saw it; we saw the whole thing!"

"Yes, we did, we saw it," said Miranda and Caliban in unison, and then looked at each other, blinking in surprise.

"What did you see?" a female voice said; it was a seductive smooth voice with a slight lisp, the lisp that comes from having fangs and a forked tongue.

They all turned.

A hybrid was standing there; she was black with a red mark on her snout, and beside her stood a young woman in jeans and a T-shirt and with a baseball cap on her head and a backpack overflowing with tools slung over her shoulder.

The President stood up. Claudia slid gently from his arms but held onto his hand.

"That's Claire," said Kit, "And that's Robyn. They saved my life."

"I see," said the President; he stiffened slightly.

The hybrid strode straight to the President.

"So, Claire V Jacobs," said the President. She was not, he noted, wearing a mind-collar. She had been perhaps the most famous hybrid – with scientist entrepreneur Sabrina Jacobs – taken in the Night of the Culling. She and her friends had been sent to the deepest hell, a life of slavery in horrendous conditions; and he was the cause, he was the great orchestrator of the Culling, and of her suffering. Now she was free, she could exact her revenge. Well, if he had to die, he had to die; but first, V had to win her battle, or he had to destroy the Mind and Elysium.

The hybrid stopped when she was less than a foot away from the President. She was, he realized, almost a foot shorter than he, and quite slender. She looked up at him, her fangs bared, her yellow-gold eyes sparkling. He waited. She had lost even more than most of them, her fame, her fortune, her dignity, her beauty, too, locked into hybrid form as she had been by the mind-collar; but, of course, when he thought about it, he realized: others had lost even more; some of them, her friends, had been murdered – had lost their lives.

"Mr. President," she said.

"Ms. Jacobs," he said; he nodded at Kit, and Kit took little Claudia's hand. Claudia looked up at the hybrid – another goddess! And then she looked up at Kit and then at the President: something was happening between these different deities which she didn't quite understand; there was a tension of some sort; she wiped at her eye with the back of her hand: a single tear-streak on the back of her hand; she sniffled.

"Claire," Kat, who was still standing in the Mind-Sea watching for signs of V and the Mind-Child, turned toward the hybrid, "Claire ... don't ..."

"Yes, Claire," said Kit, "Claire, don't ..."

The hybrid turned to look at Kit, "Don't what? What do you think I'm going to do?"

"Just don't," said Kit, giving Claire the look.

Claire smiled. "Oh, Kit! Oh, child of little faith, do you not know me?"

"Not really, no, I don't. You did save my life, though."

"Exactly," Claire again turned all her attention to the President. He was almost smiling, but it was a grim smile; he had just begun to truly understand how wondrous these creatures were, and now one of them was just possibly going to kill him. He had inflicted such injustice upon them, and upon the SINs. She would be quite right to execute him on the spot!

The hybrid seemed to be thinking; she tilted her head one way; then the other way; then, finally, she reached up, put both claws around the President's neck. He didn't move, didn't resist.

"Claire ..." said Kit.

"Hybrid, hey, Hybrid ..." said Robyn.

Robyn and Kit looked at each other. Claudia looked at them all – wondering at the mysterious drama that was going to happen: was her savior going to be sacrificed to this new goddess. She didn't think she'd want that to happen; she would try to stop it. Miranda just stood there. She couldn't believe that Claire would harm her father. Caliban took a deep breath. He liked Claire, but he tensed and his hand went to the pommel of his scimitar.

Claire stretched up on tiptoe and kissed the President on both cheeks, a little reptilian pressure and a caressing flicker of her forked tongue, "Always wanted to meet you, Pres.," she said, and as she settled back down on her feet, she left one claw resting lightly on his shoulder, "Those prison camps and the murders were pretty horrible you know, and the Culling was a really, really bad idea, even from the human point of view. The whole thing was criminal and utterly stupid. But ... as for me, I say let bygones be bygones, anyway, I had a sneaking liking for you even back there, when you are a mere general and not the ultimate big shot President-Leader."

"Ms. Jacobs ..." the President started to say; it was weird, really, talking to this reptilian creature, though of course, he had seen V in full reptilian demon regalia. But that was long ago and under very particular circumstances; but with Claire, he had, as it were, a double vision: he had seen a multitude of images of her as CVJ, the icon, in her human guise, the blonde, the beauty and paragon of human chic and of fashion, and now ... here she was ... a hybrid in hybrid form.

"Claire, Pres., call me Claire."

"Claire."

"Pres., you have a lover who is a hybrid, in fact, she is the Hybrid Queen, and I am – I don't know if you know this – but I was created from her DNA, as a partial clone – so I'm V's sister – and you've got a daughter who is a hybrid, beautiful Princess Miranda here, and if I judge you by your pal and defender, my friend Kit, you have a young friend who is a hybrid, so we are almost family and you are almost one of us, Mr. President."

"There's nothing I can say."

"No, there isn't. So don't say anything. Let's forget all that. Where's V?"

"Out there, in there, in the mind," said Kat who was aware of her oath to the President and who would have defended him, even now, to the death; but she had also been aware, from the first second, that Claire was not going to harm a hair on the President's head. She wondered – *hybrid intuition*?

"Ah ..." Claire turned toward the bubbling frothing vast pool; it reached off under the arches of the cavern; it seemed to be getting very excited, little liquid water-spout like formations were moving across the surface, close to Kat, who batted them away. Claire smiled, "Oh, I see. A fight is going on," said Claire, "V's trying to save the Mind-Child."

"Yes."

"And you helped her – by saving our friend here," Claire looked at the President, and then laid a claw on the little girl's hair and stroked it.

"I was there," said the President. "I saw the battle."

"Too modest," murmured Claire with a reptilian smile, "No wonder people adore you!"

Wham!

Wham! They all turned toward the Mind-Sea. There was an explosion of activity, a geyser of liquid shot up, splashed against the roof and arches of the cavern, the whole pool was traversed by flashes of inner lightning, waves shot out, tendrils and strands whipped out, and splashed against everybody.

"Oh!"

"Oh!"

"Oh!"

It was like stinging liquid, like acid, like a drug trip, an avalanche of hallucinations. All of them saw it, a vision, something like a mystical vision: The whole world was a vast shimmering matrix, an illusion of crisscrossing lines of light, where past and present and future were all present, all real, all illusory, where alternative worlds and events blossomed and unfolded, infinite possibilities, all the roads taken and all the roads not taken, all the lives lived and the lives that had never been lived, not in this universe at least, and, then, back to now, to this instant, to here, where human civilization itself – with its teeming billions in the domed cities, in the burbs, out in the wilderness settlements and throughout the world – was hurtling toward its doom.

"Oh, the gods," the President whispered.

And now …

V, the multicolored mummy, rose out of the swirling boiling liquid; she was not alone. There was another shape with her, a smaller creature, wrapped mummy-like in stands of colorful Mind Web.

The Mind-Child …

Behind came another figure. V turned and looked back. She let the little creature go, and shooed it toward the shore, and as it emerged from the soup, the strands and tentacles and fibers fell away, and the little creature was revealed: a child, which might have been a girl or a boy, startlingly beautiful, dark-skinned, and, except for an immaculate white loincloth, naked. But then, suddenly, the child was swept down, out of sight, under the bubbling iridescent surface. The child had disappeared. Would it drown?

V turned and fought with the Devil.

It was a wrestling match.

They splashed and leaped and kicked and wrestled; they punched and twisted and leaped, and then finally, V seized the Foul Fiend – or his emanation – by the neck, and plunged down into the soup, and both of them were gone and the sparkling wild Mind-Soup closed over them.

Just bubbles and swirling liquid remained.

Tendrils shot up out of the liquid.

Swirls and eddies were visible.

The President wanted to rush into the soup to save V.

"No, Mr. President," Kat said, "This is something she has to do alone!"

Kit and Claire touched the President's arms and repeated in unison, "No, V has to do this; she has to do it alone."

Time seemed to stretch out; the liquid swirled and bubbled.

The President felt his heart, beating hard, was like a clock, ticking off the seconds to doomsday.

"Mr. President," whispered Kit, "We'll win, we really will."

He glanced at Kit and nodded.

There was an explosion, a tower of liquid, a geyser, splashing up like a column to the roof, splitting apart, and raining down.

The Mind-Child came stumbling out of the liquid, colored strands running off its body and the tiny loincloth. Kat stepped into the Mind-Goo, opened her arms, picked up the Mind-Child, and carried it to shore.

Then V, the hybrid, sprang up out of the liquid, shook herself, and waded waist-deep, to the shore, and shook herself again. Ribbons of glittering light fell away from her body, freeing her from the mummy-like iridescent swaddling bands. "He's gone, but he'll be back," she said; she stepped forward and, now shin-deep in the Mind-Goo, she shook herself free of the last strands of colorful Mind-Threads.

She stared at the President, "Ah, yes, there he is, the President-Leader!" She suddenly became very still, her golden eyes flaring; and her metallic hybrid body, its scales glittering, still wet from the Mind-Goo, still dripping

colorful glitzy strands of light and long stringy filaments of tinsel-like visionary thought that seemed to flash or glow with a surge of extra energy, "He is
a hero, undoubtedly. He helped me, and he saved Claudia, our little friend
from the far distant future." V smiled at Claudia.

Claudia smiled back and raised her arm and opened and closed her fist in
salutation, "Salve!"

V returned the salute and then glanced at Miranda and Caliban and said,
in a very even voice, "So, Miranda, you have met your father."

"Yes," said Miranda; she took her father's hand.

"Well," said V, and she walked up to the President, stopping, and standing
less than a foot away from him, staring at him, "You might tell your father,
from me, Miranda …"

"Yes?"

"You might tell your father from me, Miranda, that I am very angry, very
annoyed with him …" V paused, reptilian eyes reiterating the order.

Kat was holding the Mind-Child by the hand; he – or she – looked up at
Kat with big soulful eyes. Kat smiled at the child: it difficult to tell if the child
was a boy or a girl – its jet-black hair was cut short; its eyes were beautiful, big
and soulful, the skin was tanned, a dark golden hue.

Miranda took a deep breath, "Father, V, that is, mother, mother says that
she is very angry, very annoyed with you …"

"And tell him that I have been annoyed, steaming mad, royally pissed, for
many years now … from the moment we met in fact …" V gave Miranda a
stare. "Well …?"

Miranda swallowed. So this is what real family life is like! Nikki made
things so easy, so simple: "And, Father, V says that she has been annoyed,
steaming mad, royally pissed, for many years now, in fact, she has been
royally pissed from the moment you two met …" Miranda could not help
thinking that, as a corollary, V had been royally pissed off from the moment,
she, Miranda, had been conceived. She was not sure how to take this; she
was beginning to feel that perhaps she should be pissed off too – but with
whom and for what she was not quite sure. She thought that just maybe V's
statement about being pissed deserved a footnote or a qualification drawing
attention to the fact that perhaps there had been a little love or at least lust
at the very moment she, Miranda, had been conceived, and perhaps in the
moments running up to that moment.

Caliban squeezed her hand and moved closer, so his arm was tight against her. Miranda sighed inwardly. Such love and comfort. Caliban understood her every little tremor of thought. He made her feel so secure!

V was not going to stop: "And, if it were not for our exquisite beautiful daughter here …"

"And if it were not for your exquisite beautiful daughter here …" Miranda swallowed and stopped and waited. Things were looking up.

"And if it were not for the fact that …" V stopped, raised one imperious claw – like a cop stopping traffic – indicating that Miranda should cease her translation. V moved closer to the President, almost pressing herself against him, and she said, in a softer tone, "If it were not for the fact that … that I like you … that I like you very much … if it were not for that fact … I would have …"

"Yes?"

"I would have …"

"Yes?"

V leaned up and kissed the President on the lips. He hesitated, and then put his arms around her.

"Crickey," said Kit. She could hardly believe it. The Queen of the Hybrids – in total demon form – and the President-Leader kissing.

"Whew, this was a close call! This is awesome!" Miranda reached out and took Kit – who was still holding the little girl against her shoulder – and Caliban by the hand. She looked at them and they looked at her. The little girl had put her arms around Kit's neck, snuggling closer.

"I see you come prepared to blow us all into eternity," V whispered to the President, still kissing him, nibbling at his lips, and caressing with one claw the armored belt buckle which contained the key to setting off the NN-Bombs.

"I … I hope I don't have to," the President whispered, as V continued and deepened the kiss.

"Me too," V transmitted the thought, "I think we can avoid it, but if you have to do it, I will help you – and so will the others!"

"V … if we can, we have to save as many as we can," the President transmitted the thought clearly, knowing she would pick it up clearly.

"Yes," she answered, thought-to-thought, and then out loud, so the others could hear, V said, "We'll talk about everything later, darling," and she ended the kiss but looking up at the President, and allowing his arms, his strong arms, to hold her in a very human embrace.

"I …" the President was overwhelmed by conflicting feelings and thoughts; part of him wanted to possess her on the spot.

"Don't say anything. I know what you are thinking. I'm a hybrid, remember." V put one finger against his lips, to seal them, gave him a big reptilian smile, and liberated herself from his embrace.

The President was tempted to say, "You're a hybrid – how could I forget?" but he didn't because he knew that she could read his mind and she could, equally, read his lust and affection and whatever other confusing thoughts and feelings of guilt, lust, regret, joy, were rushing through his head, and fear too, fear for all of them, fear for Elysium, for humanity, for the world, Hybrids, SINs, mutants, and all.

"Now, we must ask our little friend here, our Mind-Child darling, to do us a very big favor!" V turned to look at the Mind-Child, "My dear child, whom I love so much. Could you stop the Mind from eating everything?"

"Can we play first?" The Mind-Child looked at them all. "I've never had so many friends before! I want to play!"

"Oh, no," V rolled her alien reptile eyes.

"And I want to play now!" The Mind-Child smiled at them all – it was a determined, imperious smile – and Kit thought that, though this little caprice might perhaps mean the end of the world, it was, after all, a very, very sweet smile – and a beautiful child.

"I want to play!" the Mind-Child screamed, "Right now!"

"Well, if you want to play …" said V, glancing at Claire and then at the President, "If you want to play …"

There was a humungous roar, and at that moment, out of the swirling, smoky muck of the Mind Pool and the Mind-Goo arose a huge figure.

It was a giant, and around it swirled clouds of Mind particles. It was a goliath, its head, a monstrous bestial head with a huge maw full of ten-foot-high teeth and fangs and a huge lolling tongue, its head was only a few feet short of the roof of the cavern, and it roared, a bellow that echoed everywhere: "Where is the child? I want the child."

"What the blazes," said Kit.

Claudia, her eyes wide in terror, clung closer to Kit, her hair spilling over Kit's shoulder, caressing and tickling her neck.

"What thing is this?" said Caliban, "What monster of the deep?"

"I think it's the Foul Fiend," said Miranda, "The Boy or the Devil."

"You cannot have the child!" V shouted; she strode to the edge of the rippling Mind-Goo, put her hands on her hips, and stared up at the creature. She looked very determined, but very small.

The huge fiery coal-like eyes, glimmering like simmering embers in a deep pit of boiling tar, smoking pits of darkness, dark-rimmed pools of iniquity, stared down at her. "You will not stop me! I will take the child! I will eat the child! I will absorb all of the child's wisdom and knowledge. I will know every secret of every corner of this planet and of every creature in it. I will become the world, and the world will become me!" He began to slosh his way toward the shore. V unsheathed her laser gun, and the President and all the others did the same with whatever weapons they had.

V fired.

The laser beam bounced off, and had no effect!

"Ha! Ha! Ha! Fools! Puny fools!" The creature roared. "You will all die. I will eat you all! You, Hybrid, you will die first!" He breathed fire, beat his chest, and roared, "Eternal damnation will be your lot! Suffering without end will be your destiny!"

The ground shook; the Mind Pool sloshed, splashing long, tentacle-like trails of sparkling Mind-Goo up over its banks; the soaring vaults shook and echoed; the walls trembled; the hanging chains rattled; slabs of wall fell away, a clatter and cloud of tumbling bricks; a metal supply cart, on rails next to the canal, bounced up and turned over; a side tunnel collapsed; a Doric column out in the Mind-Goo toppled over sideways and disappeared in a sizzling roiling multicolored splash. Ghostly figures began to rise out of the Mind-Goo, monsters from every fairy-tale and myth and religion and B-movie ever recorded or known, every incarnation of every fear and of every nightmare, up they came, rising out of the Mind, zombies, vampires, serial killers, ax-murders, sons of Frankenstein, monstrous ghouls, every imaginable horror …

"Shoo, Edgar," whispered Kit, "Go, swim away, as far as you can!"

The seal looked at her, nodded, waddled across the platform, and plunged into the peaceful transport canal. He looked back once. Kit waved. Edgar nodded, and plunged under and disappeared.

"I don't want him to eat me." The Mind-Child gazed at, V and then looked up at Kat, who still was holding its hand. "Please don't let him eat me!"

"No, we won't let him eat you or anybody else," said Kat. But she wondered how they would stop this thing. It was not natural; it was more than natural; it was …

"I know!" said the Mind-Child, suddenly with a bright sly smile, "Let's play!"

"Play …?" Kat raised an eyebrow.

"Yes!"

V turned around; once again, she heard the word "play," and she knew how dangerous the child's idea of play could be. "Now, I think we'd better ..."

"No, V," said the Mind-Child, with a voice that seemed suddenly to be the voice of an adult, "I want to take everybody to play with me! You will all play with me! You must play with me, each and every one! I want Claire, and Robyn, and Miranda and the President and Kit and Kat and Claudia, the little girl from the future, and I want Clown – I like Clown – and Geisha and Black Tarzan and I want Caliban and his loincloth and his machete and his AK-47 and his scimitar!"

"But ..." V glanced at the Monster. More giant ghouls and golems and ghosts and dinosaurs and great apes and giant squids and oversized zombies and hungry vampires and rabid dogs and cadaverous mummies were forming out of the mist. An evil-looking clown with a bulbous nose and a bow tie bounced out of the liquid. He had very long pointed teeth and empty glowing silver eyes. The giant was striding closer.

"An emanation," whispered Kit.

"Yes," said the President, "This is the evil thing that ..."

"The Foul Fiend ..."

"Yes, the Foul Fiend!" Briefly, the President thought back to the last few hours and the last few days. Two weeks ago, he would not have believed in such a thing as the "Foul Fiend."

The Monster was now almost upon them – laser-guns blazed away, nothing seemed to faze or even touch him.

"I want to play," the Mind-Child stamped its feet.

"But, my little friend, I'm not sure if we are ready to play," said V, as she pumped shot after shot into the towering Foul Fiend. She was caught, it seemed between two monsters, the Foul Fiend, and the Mind-Child. She had seen what a mischievous child the Mind-Child was, how it had hurled her from pillar to post, had flipped her from past to future, had made her live through the whole history of human religion – or a big chunk of it – in a few seconds, and had sent her on a guided tour of Hell, or some version of it, and of Paradise, or the Foul Fiend's version of it, with the Foul Fiend himself – playing the game – as her guide. So where might they end up? And she would not put it beyond the child to try to turn them all into World Mind Puppets. After all, in its incarnation as the Mind, the child was used to ruling the world and all the people in it. And still, the shaggy monster strode forward. What to do?

They should run.

But they all seemed rooted in place.

Only Edgar, the seal, wisely, had skedaddled.

"You are all mine, you are my toys, and you are ready to play!" The Mind-Child stared defiantly at V and then looked up at Kat and tightened its grip on her hand. "So, now, we play!"

"What do you mean …?" Kat began to say.

"Let's go!" The child's eyes glowed.

The Monstrous Foul Fiend plunged for V. Its huge clawed fist swept straight at her; there was no way V could escape.

"Okay," V said, "Let's go!"

"Whoopee," said the Mind-Child.

"V!" Kat cried out, and then she felt everything dissolve around her.

She was no longer anywhere or anything.

Nor was anyone else anywhere – or anything at all.

CHAPTER 12 – THE LIVING DEAD

Out in the burbs, and up on the roof of old Norm C. Schleifer's tenement building, Angela Balzac had managed to find a long iron bar which had been used to put up a big umbrella for people to sleep under; she slammed it across the metal security door, jammed it down and braced it in place.

The horde of skeletons and mummies – or whatever they were – that had invaded her tenement building and probably killed and torn apart every living human they could find, knocked and crashed against the metal door, and then it all seemed to quiet down. There were shouts and screams from the street.

Angela put her ear against the door and listened. She knew it was risky. Somebody might shoot through the door, or blow up the door, or those weirdoes might crash through it and crush her; but she couldn't resist. She listened. There was nothing, no sound whatsoever. Maybe the living dead had decided she was not worth the bother.

She stood back from the door and looked around; the roof was empty, except for a couple of fold-out cots which were anchored down with chains and two or three big antique stuffed chairs – each with an ugly pattern of roses on a dirty cream background – which sat near the edge of the roof, facing Elysium City. On sweltering nights, and almost all nights were sweltering, people would come up here and sleep on the bare roof or on the cots, or just sit in the big stuffed chairs, their feet up on empty beer boxes or on the low roof railing, and watch the weather and maybe stare at the Dome of Elysium City, floating in the distance like another planet, an alien paradise.

What should she do? There were not many options. She could try to run – but where and how? Running would mean going down into the street. No, she would just stay up here on the roof and wait and see what happened. Then there was another thing to worry about – that disease or plague, or whatever, that Norm had picked up and which it seemed was killing people all over the place – there were still samizdat texts and audio and images coming through, and earlier in the day – though this was a day that seemed dark as night – Angela had seen images and read and heard examples of what people were saying might be a new form of the Bubonic plague. Nobody knew exactly what it was, but it was spreading damned fast. And Norm had sneezed, sending a huge gob of the stuff splattering right into her face. She cringed and wiped at her cheeks. *Have I caught it? I'll bet I have!*

She looked down at herself – arms, legs, belly, she lifted up her T-shirt and checked her breasts. No, there were no signs of the thing – not yet, anyway. Probably it had an incubation period or whatever they called it. So it was almost certainly lying in wait, and would get her – sure as night followed day.

Poor Norm, he was a weirdo and a slob and a violent, unpredictable egotistical bastard, who had at various times in the most indelicate ways indicated that he had the hots for her, wanted to "fuck her till she couldn't walk," as he put it, and "Boy, will you love it!" But she felt that, hiding inside Norm, there was a core of decency, a leftover remnant of the innocent or idealistic snotty little Baby Norm he must once have been – well, maybe … Who could know? Now, it was too late to know. It made her seethe with rage. Nobody deserved to die like that! She half-closed her eyes: The bubbling, boiling, roiling flesh, the exploding volcanoes of blood-veined pus, and the sepulchral voice, with its desperate childlike confessions, coming out of the ruined mouth, and …

No, I can't think of that.

Norm didn't deserve that to die like that. Nobody deserved to die like that. If it had been at all possible, she would have looked after him, nursed him back to health. Suddenly, strangely, she felt a flush of tenderness for the dead man she had so despised when he was alive, a twinge of regret, as if a life that could have been lived had not been lived. She was mourning for something that never was, a Norm that never was, a relationship that never was, and, almost certainly, never could have been, and which she wouldn't have wanted anyway. "Cool it, kid," she said out loud, "You are no Florence Nightingale!"

But then Norm did have a kind side; he could be brave, almost quixotic. He had protected her from gangs. And, to tell the truth, when she was scared witless, earlier today, what had she done? She had camped out like a scared kid, sitting on the stairs in front of Norm's door.

Jesus! Without even knowing it, I've lost somebody I cared about – almost, yes, well, really …

Angela had a weakness, and she did consider it a weakness. She would see some miserable, crabby, cruel person, and she would wonder how that person became that way. What had happened to the little baby or the child, that had turned everything so sour, so hostile, so suspicious? And, often – it was almost like an X-ray vision – she would see through the old or adult body and she would glimpse the child behind the woman or the man, the child that had been embittered by some other bitter or violent person, a mother or a father or some stranger, and that person too had been made bitter and violent by what had happened to them, and so the sins of the fathers and the mothers were visited, in an endless chain, upon the children and upon their progeny, forever and ever. How to break that chain?

She walked over to one of the big ugly stuffed chairs – she really *hated* that old faded pattern of roses and vines – and, checking it for rats and scorpions and tropical mega-cockroaches, and after brushing it off carefully – lots of sand from giant sandstorms sweeping in from the Dead Lands – she sat down, put her feet up on the low roof railing, and looked at the view.

Oh, the gods, what a mess! The Elysium Dome looked like it was a cracked egg. It also looked like it was on fire. Flames and lightning, and flashes which were probably explosions, flickered and burst within the giant dome. And then, downtown, near the point of the old half-drowned underlying island of Manhattan, many of the slender spires and soaring towers, historic landmarks, were no longer there, or seemed to be no longer there: usually, you could see them, fairy-like silhouettes, through the dome. And now they were gone! That was impossible! They had to be there! The towers couldn't have disappeared. She sat up, leaned forward, squinted: yes, usually you could see through the dome, and you could see the ethereal towers inside it, you could see the beauty of it all, and the hanging gardens, and the arching bridges, and sometimes, you could even see tiny twinkling points, airships landing inside the Dome. And at night, or on dark stormy days, the Dome usually glittered with a billion lights; they were multicolored, and shifting, like what Angela imagined a giant Christmas tree of ancient times must have looked like. Now, here and there, there were lights; but most of the Dome was dark. Still, she could see the silhouettes of the skyscrapers and towers, but not downtown. Downtown, at the point of old Manhattan, there was an empty space where the buildings should have been. For some reason, this terrified Angela more than anything.

She sat there watching, hoping, perhaps, salvation would come. Then she heard something. She sat up very straight. She listened. Then she heard it again. A clanking sound – Oh, my God, the fire escape, maybe the living dead – or whatever they are – had found the fire escape.

She took a deep breath, got up out of the chair, went to get one of the iron rods – leftover from a do-it-yourself dinner table Alf Rosen, a hopeless but always hopeful old guy, had tried – in vain– to assemble for rooftop dining – and picked it up.

She walked to the edge of the roof and peeked over. Oh, damn it, damn it! Coming up the metal fire escape were two of the living dead. Well, they are only two, so perhaps she could just whap them over the head and smash them, and that will be that – for the moment.

The two figures coming up the fire escape were the mummy-woman Angela had noticed, and the little kid skeleton. Angela took a deep breath; she would let them get to the top, and then she would smash them, though the idea of smashing a woman and a kid, even if they were dead, did not really appeal to her.

Laura Levitt had rushed into the old tenement building with all the rest of them, inspired by the preacher, who shouted that they had to root out the Jezebels and the whores of Babylon, and the fornicators and money changers, though Laura did not really mind if people fornicated or not – she had done quite a bit of frolicking fornication and fun copulation of various kinds in her time – and she doubted very much that in this neck of the woods, in the fallen Ghetto Burbs, there were many money changers to be lynched or drawn and quartered or generally misused in the homicidal, quick-justice, string-'em-up way the preacher seemed to favor and inspire.

Inside the tenement, it had been chaos, all the dead squeezing into the cor-ridors, smashing down doors, ripping people apart, chasing people this way and that, until they were cornered. Then, in an instant, Laura had something like an epiphany; a very pretty black girl was looking over the banister of the staircase. She was startlingly beautiful, and she was terrified, and she reminded Laura just what it was like to be alive and to have feelings and to be terrified.

"Come on, Kiddo," she said, in mind-language, to the kid. And she led him out of the house, and down the street, and then into an ally, where she hid for a while until she heard the horde move on and the preacher's voice – he was still squawking about Jezebels and Idolaters and Blasphemers and such-like – faded and was gone.

"Okay, Kiddo, let's go up and stay on the roof and watch the end of the world in peace and quiet." So she'd taken Kiddo, and they climbed up a fire escape, Laura thinking that up above the view will be fine, and there may well be no living and no dead to disturb their contemplation of Armageddon.

Then she sensed a presence, and then she caught a glimpse of the black girl, the girl was up on the roof, at the top of the fire escape, and she was holding a metal pipe. Laura almost decided to retreat, to go back down the fire escape, and continue wandering the streets. But, no, she decided, destiny is destiny. We will soldier on. And so, trailing Kiddo along with her, she continued to climb.

Angela tightened her grip on the pipe. She sensed that the mummy had seen her. But the mummy was coming on anyway. Well, so be it!

The mummy was staring with empty eyes at her. The mummy and the skeleton kid got to the top of the fire escape.

Angela had decided she would let them get to the top. If she smashed them to pieces while they were still on the fire escape, they would go bouncing back down, and their bones would make a racket and draw attention.

No, she would wait until the last moment.

The mummy and the kid stepped onto the rooftop, and the mummy took a couple of steps forward and stopped. The mummy's face was turned straight toward Angela and Angela had the sense she was being stared at. "Okay," Angela said, "What do you want?"

The mummy did nothing for a moment; then, it shrugged and bent its head to one side, and moved its arms, as if it were making a cradle.

"You want to rest. You want to sleep."

The mummy nodded.

Angela took a deep breath. This was more than weird; this was utterly unorthodox. Those nut cases who talked about "the Rapture" were maybe onto something. The stuff that had happened today! She clenched the iron pipe. But at the same time, she felt that, perhaps she should take a risk. "Okay," she said, "There are stuffed chairs over there, and there are cots. I'm sitting in one of the chairs. I've been watching the Dome. It's unbelievable what's happening!"

The mummy nodded.

Angela led them to the big stuffed chairs.

The mummy sat down in one of the chairs, tucking the kid skeleton in beside her, so the two of them sat there, the mummy Laura and the skeleton Kiddo, staring out, over the agonizing Burbs, at the dying city, at Elysium. Somehow – she had no idea how – Angela had intuited that the mummy called the kid "Kiddo," and somehow, too, she had the weird idea that the mummy was called "Laura."

"Laura Levitt."

"Okay, if you guys sit there, I'll sit here." Still holding the iron bar, Angela sat down in her chair, and she pushed it back slightly so that she could keep the two living dead in sight out of the corner of her eye.

The mummy sensing this, turned toward her, grinned – it looked like a grin – and gave her a thumbs-up.

"Well, I'll be …" Angela shot back a smile. The end of the world was turning out to be interesting.

And, so, they sat, the three of them, perched in the big overstuffed chairs, on the edge of a rooftop, staring at the dying city, watching the end of the world.

As Angela watched, a midtown tower, probably the Peace and Friendship Plaza, or possibly the Millennial Corkscrew, seemed to slide down sideways, melt, and disappear. "Holy Moly!"

"Almost there!" Ken breathed.

"Wonderful, darling," Alison held on, lightly, to his forearm, but she could feel each tremor, each bit of tension, that passed through Ken's body. And just now, he stopped. Alison felt the tension mount. She didn't ask. She waited. And then she heard it and felt it: *fire!*

"Yes," he whispered, "fire."

A wave of heat came from below; a brimming, swirling well of flame was two floors below them, and the only way down – toward possible safely – was through the fire. Ken brushed Alison's cheek with his lips. "We'll go down and see; the whole stairwell seems filled with fire, but maybe there is a way through."

"Yes, darling, we'll find a way," Alison kissed his cheek.

And so they started down toward the fire. Billows of fire welled up from below; the stairs went straight down toward it, a swirling inferno of red and yellow flames. There seemed to be no way through. And then Ken thought:

it might all explode and whoosh up the stairwell and then they would be trapped and burned to a crisp. There was no way back. Up above, there were zombie-bats and mad people blocking every alternative route, and in any case, physically, with the pedestrian bridges destroyed, there was no other way out. It was down, into the inferno, or nothing. The heat rose, blast furnace waves. Alison didn't flinch.

It was like they were being baked alive. Steam rose off Ken's skin. "Maybe we should go back," he whispered.

"No, darling," her lips were next to his ear, "Appearances can be deceptive, maybe there's a way through." They came to an absolute wall of flame, and Ken saw that just beside the far wall, there was a sliver of a space where the flames did not reach quite to the wall. It might just be possible.

"We'll have to run for it," he breathed.

"Yes, Ken, Let's go!"

And Ken and Alison plunged into the wall of flame.

"Gosh! What happened?" Kit Candy looked around. An instant ago, she'd been on the platform overlooking the Mind-Sea. Now she was standing on a beach of wet black pebbles fronting on what seemed to be a dark ocean, the waves gently lapping and a thin line of speckled foam fizzing only a few inches away from her feet; bright stars and constellations spangled the night sky and seemed to come right down to the horizon.

Claudia clung to Kit's neck, just as before, and her cheek was pressed warmly against Kit's cheek. It was night, a dark, damp night, with no moon, just the dark, clinging air, and an infinity of stars in a very black sky. The air was full of music, hurdy-gurdy music, and smells of what Kit recognized as popcorn and melted butter and candy floss and she could hear the cries of funfair carneys, and mountebanks, and the sounds of wheels and rides … *Where the hell am I?*

"What the blazes …?" It was the President's voice.

Kit looked around. The President was standing a few meters away. "Kit," he blinked at her, "Where are we? What happened?"

"I have no idea, Mr. President." Kit let Claudia slide down her hip to the ground; the little girl landed neatly on her feet, balanced on the pebbles, and looked up at Kit with round, startled eyes; she tightened her grip on Kit's hand.

The President stared at the ocean. "Kit, you see how calm the sea is. It reflects the stars, to great depth, like a perfect, untroubled mirror."

"Yes." Kit blinked; her eyes were full of stars: the sky and the sea seemed to be exactly the same, mirror images, topsy-turvy, in a way, like vertigo.

"But, it's not calm, not *perfectly* calm." The President crouched down and pointed to the little waves, the foam at the edge of the pebbles, the ripples and stirrings and wavelets. But, then, just two or three meters out, the sea became absolutely calm – apparently, a perfect mirror reflecting stars, a dark abyss of stars, going down, and down, and down. But …

"Oh, gosh, Mr. President, that's not a reflection of the stars."

"No, it's not."

"Those aren't reflections of stars; they *are* stars!" Kit stared. The foam lapped gently at the pebbles, even making a little rattling sound as the pebbles jostled around. The water looked real. But, out a few meters, it all dropped away, it ceased. And then there were stars. They were floating in space!

"Yes, as you just said, those aren't reflections of stars. Those are stars." The President turned to Kit. "And, Kit, look up there." He pointed.

"Orion, the constellation Orion," said Kit, "but … it doesn't look right." The implant mind-map of constellations had immediately sprung into Kit's mind, for as an inhabitant of Elysium, having lived her whole existence under the dome, she had never seen real stars or real constellations. The constellation looked strange.

"No, you're right." The President came close, put his hand on Kit's shoulder. "It's out of alignment."

"So, we're in the future or the past, or we're not on earth."

"Or a combination of time and space shift, or a parallel universe, or an imaginary universe." The President frowned. "This is – how do you and Miranda put it – this is pretty *awesome* – we seem to be floating on an island in space, with stars above us and below us."

"Yes, really, really, awesome," Kit whispered. It gave her the shivers. She was glad the President and Claudia were here. They, at least, seemed real.

"I think we might as well treat all of this as real," said the President, "After all, this is must be the setting for the game the Mind-Child wants us to play."

"Okay, yes, I guess that's what we do, floating on stars, like we are; not much choice, eh?" Kit stroked Claudia's hair; the girl looked up at her and smiled.

"No," the President laughed, "Not much choice."

The funfair music suddenly seemed louder, and voices drifted from what must be the midway, all the sounds and smells of a country fair. They heard snippets of dialog, voices wafting to them from the distant fairgrounds.

"Step right up, ladies and gentlemen!"

"Do not be afraid, madam, come in; see for yourself, feast with your very own eyes on these wondrous freaks of nature!"

"Hit the bull's eye and win a doll!"

"If you pass through this fearsome portal, ladies and gents, you shall see such wonders as will make your hair stand on end – the crocodile man, the monkey woman, the reptile girl, the acrobatic elastic clown, the panther lady, the tattooed wonder …"

The President and Kit turned around and looked behind them; a huge fairground was just beyond what looked like a boardwalk and a tram line. People were walking up and down the boardwalk, and they were wearing boater straw hats, and cloche hats, and the women were in long dresses or in short knee-length scalloped 1920s flapper-type skirts.

"Quid?" said the little girl.

"What?" The President looked down at her; the poor little thing, he thought: I haven't even had time to ask her: who is she? Where has she come from?

"Quid?"

"She's speaking Latin," said Kit, realizing it for the second time.

"Yes, of course, she is," said the President, having forgotten this rather strange and incongruous fact. Which century, or which universe, he wondered, did Claudia come from?

"Is this heaven?" Claudia said, again in Latin, "Or was the last place, heaven?"

"I'm not sure," Kit answered, in Latin; she glanced at the President; ah, yes, of course, he understood Latin; he had had polyglot implants too; well, it figured, he being the leader of the world and all.

Claudia gazed at the President and then at Kit. "I was on the altar, and I was sacrificed, and the Goddess took me by the hand and so this must be heaven," she said and then looked around doubtfully, "At least, it should be heaven. But then there was that other place where we met, or the one before. I'm not sure which place is heaven."

"Well," said the President, "I'm not so sure … either"

"And you must be angels, and we must all be dead in the caves of darkness with all those other angels over there." The little girl pointed toward the board-walk and the roaring rides and bright sparkly lights beyond the boardwalk.

"Let's go and see," said the President.

Kit raised an eyebrow: she wondered if it was wise to wander away from the place they had landed; maybe this was some sort of temporal-spatial shift like in the game the Interplanetary War of the Ghouls III, and maybe, if they wandered too far from the Gateway – there *must* be a Gateway – there was *always* a Gateway – she looked around, but she couldn't see any telltale bending of space or shimmering inflection or refraction of light – otherwise there would be no way to get back and she and the President and this little girl Claudia might be stuck here forever, God only knew where, or in what reality – true or false – or what universe.

"It looks interesting," said the President.

"Let's go! Let's go!" Claudia jumped up and down.

"Okay, okay, but where are all the others?"

"Maybe they are here …" The President frowned; he looked around. The pebbled beach was quite broad and absolutely empty, and it stretched off and was lost in darkness; there was nobody else on the beach; the waves rolled gently in; the air smelled of ozone, sea bracken and shellfish and mudflats – and butter and popcorn.

"And maybe they aren't here."

"Quite right, Kit, my young hybrid friend, they might be anywhere."

"Gosh, Mr. President, I keep forgetting that I'm a hybrid," said Kit, and she knelt down next to the little girl. "And Claudia, where do you come from?"

"Yes, well, I am Claudia. I am the second daughter," said the girl, "and my father is Antonius and my mother Octavia, and we are of the Neo-Hawaii Tribe, the last tribe, for there are no others left, and I live in a treehouse in the forest, which is green and dark and full of dark water down below the trees, with pools and sacred snakes and the birds that sing all day and the great owl at night, and I have a pet monkey."

"I'm Kit," said Kit.

"Well, call me James," said the President.

The little girl furrowed her brow as if concentrating on committing the two names to memory. "Kit, James," she mouthed.

"Hmm," said Kit, "should I call you James too?"

"Yes, Kit, if that's what you want. I don't think I'm President anymore, not here at any rate. I don't know what I'd be president of …"

"Yes, this is weird," said Kit.

"Besides, Kit, I think you and I are family now."

Kit looked at the President, she took his hand, "Thank you," she said.

"I should thank you."

"But I sort of like calling you President, if you don't mind."

The President laughed, "No, I don't. It will remind me of old times."

"Like five hours ago."

"Like five hours ago."

The hurdy-gurdy music was louder now, and they turned away from the dark illusory mirror-like sea, the edge of their space island, and walked – each holding Claudia by the hand – across the smooth pebbles – the beach was very broad and deep – toward the boardwalk and the glittering bright lights beyond.

They stepped onto the boardwalk

"My, but that is a cute little girl you have there!" A lady in a long emerald green dress stopped, and, speaking in English, she knelt down. "What is her name? What is your name, darling?"

"Claudia, my name is Claudia," Claudia said, in Latin. It seemed that though Claudia spoke Latin, she understood English.

"Ah, she's not from these here parts." The lady stroked Claudia's hair and straightened up. "Well, you know, not everybody is from these here parts though it might sometimes seem like they all are. Now, you all have a wonderful evening, now, you all!"

Some of the women had long dresses and some of the women had short loose dresses, and the hair-dos were different, the bob, the shingle bob, the pixie, and bangs, fringes, curls, and straight, and pigtails and ponytails, and the shoes were nice and highly polished, and black and brown and some with spats, and the men all wore hats, except for the very young men, and the gentlemen tipped their hats and said, "Good evening to you, ma'am, good evening to you, sir." "A warm evening, isn't it, Mrs. Redford." "And the top of the evening to you, Alice," said one man, sweeping off his boater, and bowing low. "Fiona MacDonald, and how are you, dare I ask, this fine evening?"

"I think we're in the 1920s," Kit whispered, "More than two hundred years ago, almost three hundred."

"Or a simulacrum of the 1920s," said the President.

"Right," said Kit, "or it could be an alternative universe where things are the same or where they're different, and where everything floats in the starry sky in empty space. This is really strange."

"Like a Hawaiian jungle where people speak Latin," said the President.

"Yes."

"Hmm," said the President. He hoisted Claudia onto his shoulder. "Now you can see better," he said.

Claudia laughed and ruffled the President's hair. "You *are* a funny angel," she said.

"You're funny too," said the President.

"No, angel, I'm not, I am a very, very serious person," said the little girl. But she was laughing. She glanced at Kit and closed one eye. It was a wink, clearly a wink, playful, even flirtatious. Kit smiled and returned the wink, wondering at the strange ways of the world that thrust total strangers from different universes – and different times – and speaking different languages – together in situations so weird that they had to learn almost instantly to trust each other. She looked at the President. He was still dressed in ripped and torn Centurion's uniform from the 22nd Century, with the red claw and acid marks on his arms and chest; and Claudia was still dressed in a short sleeveless tan tunic with a leather belt and leather sandals, the costume of whatever world she had come from, and Kit looked down at herself and she was still dressed in the 22nd Century skintight skin-shorts and the skintight skin-T-shirt that she has been wearing on the edge of the Mind Pool, but none of the people they met remarked on the weirdness of their costumes. That in itself was weird.

"Come on, let's go," said Claudia.

"If we must, we must," said the President, with a philosophical sigh. Kit could imagine him rolling his eyes. He was clearly wondering. How much time this "game" was going to take? And what was happening back on earth, in Elysium City? Were their bodies frozen there, left behind in their old "reality," being consumed by the monsters risen from the deep of the unconscious, or wherever they came from? Was the Mind still eating and dissolving Elysium? When would the Mind *really* begin to eat – the whole world? How much time was left?

"Come on!" Claudia's eyes were sparkling.

"Okay, let's go," shouted Kit. And off they went, the President, Kit, and Claudia, toward the Fun Fair, the Roller-Coaster, the Merry-go-round, the Loop-the-Loop, the Little Cars that bang into each other, and toward the House of Horrors, the Ghost Castle, and the Freak Show …

"Where in Hades are we?" Black Tarzan rubbed his eyes. He looked around: They seemed to be in the middle of a funfair, for Heaven's sake!

"Step right up, ladies and gents, step right up!"

"Holy Moly," said Clown.

"Yeah," Black Tarzan looked around, "Where's Geisha?"

"Here! I'm here!" Geisha – looking a bit disheveled – was standing behind a line of people who were trying their luck shooting with pop guns at a pop-up duck that popped up and popped down again and then disappeared. One of the customers, a broad-shouldered, portly gentleman with an imperious paunch, an unbuttoned yellow-and-green plaid waistcoat, a black string tie, and smoking a large, dark, torpedo-shaped, evil-smelling cigar, was trying his luck, making a great fuss getting his elbows in the right position, holding the rifle exactly the right way, and leaning forward carefully, he fired and missed, the duck went quack and disappeared, the duck popped up, he fired again, the duck quacked and swiveled behind a plywood tree, the duck peeked out, and the man, puffing immense clouds of black smoke from the cigar, fired again, and the duck frowned, keeled over, and let out a long peel of high-pitched quacks; a red sign sprang up, waving back and forth; and the barker screamed, "Winner! Why, Sir, you have just won your choice of dolls. Now, which doll would you like for your lady fair? Perhaps you will let her choose?" The lady fair was a florid well-endowed blonde whose ample bosom, projecting forward from her cream-colored jacket, was decorated with a fluffy, boldly protruding, pleated white blouse, its frills spilling over the lapels of the jacket. The dolls, Black Tarzan noted, looked like real miniature people, they gesticulated, and had very lively expressions, and it looked like they were trying to speak. It was spooky. Maybe they were just realistic robots.

"Why, now, sir, why don't you try your luck?" said the barker, turning to Black Tarzan.

"Well, I ..."

"You look like a man of substance, a man of talent, and if my eye serves me – and it usually does – you have two fair damsels whom you must please; which implies, my dear sir, that you are more than popular with the fair sex, and that you know what truly gives pleasure, true pleasure, to a lady. And as you can see here, we have dolls, and perfumes, knickknacks, and gewgaws, and bric-a-brac, plaster dwarfs and elves, and all that the heart can desire ..."

"Well, I ..."

"Go ahead," said Clown, "Now that we are here, we might as well ..."

"Yes," said Geisha, bowing, her unlaced and unbelted kimono billowing out, "Our honor is at stake."

"Those are two remarkable ladies you have there, my boy. So, what do you say? Give it a try, huh, nothing ventured, nothing gained, that's what my grandmother, bless her soul, may she rest in peace, used to say!"

"Well, then, I guess a man can't say no. If the ladies insist, destiny calls." Black Tarzan picked up the rifle, and the duck popped up, and Black Tarzan fired, and the duck screamed, and the red sign popped up, and the barker shouted, "Did you see that, did you see that ladies and gentleman, we have a prodigy here, a man of might and main, a sharpshooter and marksman of talent!"

Black Tarzan fired again, and he scored again.

The duck screamed; the crowd, which was getting larger, shouted, "Hurrah!"

Black Tarzan fired again, and he scored again.

The duck screamed; the crowd shouted, "Hurrah!"

The crowd was now quite large; they were pushing and shoving to get a look at the marvelous marksman.

While Black Tarzan concentrated on assassinating wooden ducks, a skinny, sallow, hollow-cheeked, unshaven fellow, wearing a sleeveless gray canvas jacket, rumpled, oversized blue-gray corduroy pants, and with what appeared to be a long toothpick sticking out of his mouth, put his arms around the shoulders of Clown and Geisha and squeezed and said, "You girls is special. How'd you like to work for me, then?"

"I beg your pardon?" said Clown, turning her bright white burnished ceramic doll face, overfull glossy luscious scarlet lips, fixed smile, and white-and-black cross-button eyes, on the creature. He twitched his gaunt and sunken cheeks nervously, and Clown said, "Are you, dear sir, addressing those provocative – indeed demeaning – words to me, to us?"

"You have perhaps, dear sir, mistaken us for creatures of another ilk and profession and thus infringed our honor, which is sacred and which we greatly treasure," said Geisha, bowing, and pulling her kimono tighter and backing away from the man's grasp.

Boom!

There was a flash of light and ...

... Clown found herself high up in the air under floodlights, performing on tiptoes a high-wire act inside a tent before an enthusiastic crowd far below, their faces all turned up toward her. The place smelled of sun-warmed canvas, old engine grease, fresh human sweat, horse dung, and newly laid sawdust. Glancing straight down, she noticed that there was no net below her, just a big tub or pool of water, far below, maybe twenty-thirty meters down. It contained what looked like two alligators, and the two alligators were thrashing their tails and looking up at her, as if they were expecting a quick snack.

This is all the Mind-Child's doing, she thought, frowning, and sticking her tongue out at the alligators. But if he wants us to play, we must play.

She danced along the high-wire, thinking it was lucky her ballet-like shoes were just the right thing for this sort of exercise, and her spangle-red catsuit just the sort of costume that would suit such a circus performance; she turned triple somersaults on the wire, she stood on one foot, she stood on one hand, and, offering a special treat, a bit of show-off panache, she danced a simulated waltz with herself as her partner, pivoting in three-quarter time, along the high-wire, which bounced up and down and vibrated like a violin string.

Cheers rose up.

The crowd was delirious with joy.

Clown was so busy keeping her balance and improvising her performance that she couldn't dedicate too much time to wondering what in the hell had happened to her – *How did I get here? Where the hell am I?* And what had happened to Geisha and Black Tarzan: *Where are they? Are they okay?*

She took a bow.

The Mind-Child either created all of this out of nothing or out of our dreams, or it sent us someplace truly rare and strange. The dear Mind-Child must love circuses.

She took another bow.

The cheering rose to a crescendo. The whole crowd stood up.

The tent and the crowd and the alligators disappeared – Poof! It was just like magic – and she found herself standing …

A flash of light; and then …

"Gosh!" said Claire.

"That is an understatement, Hybrid."

Claire and Robyn were sitting side by side on straight-backed wooden seats, with Claire in the aisle seat and Robyn next to the window, on a trolley-car, just as the conductor came along to collect the tickets, and Claire looked down at her right claw and saw that she was, in fact, clutching two tickets. She held them up to the conductor as he swayed toward her, taking tickets from the other passengers, and as the tram clanged its bell, double, triple time, ding, ding, ding, and as it sped along its tracks, which tracks, it appeared, when Claire glanced out the window, ran along a road next to a beach – a pebbled beach it seemed – next to what was probably the ocean or a sea or lake of some sort – it smelled saline, like an ocean – and the streetlamps, lit up since it apparently was night, sped quickly by, the sweet-salty smells rippling in the vertical half-open window of the tram.

"Hybrid …" Robyn began, "What happened to us …? I mean …"

"Hush, now, child," Claire said, "We don't want to draw attention to ourselves."

"But …" Robyn gave Claire a look – yes, the black, scaly, golden-eyed, red snouted, beautiful hybrid was certainly still a reptilian hybrid – and then she glanced at the other passengers who all seemed to have stepped out of an early 20th Century novel, perhaps the 1920s, though Robyn, since much of her mind had been erased, had, as she herself knew, only a foggy idea of historical chronology. But, she thought, certainly, these folk would not be used to seeing hybrids on public transport; in fact, they would probably not be used to seeing a girl in a T-shirt and jeans and with a rucksack toolbox sitting in her lap.

"Well, now, there, young lady," said the conductor, or ticket-taker, looking down at Claire, "That is some outfit you've got on there. Just perfect for the weather, I'd say." He took the two tickets and punched them and gave them back to Claire. His collar was open, and his waistcoat buttons were undone, "It is indeed summery weather," he said, "Hot, too, and humid."

"Muggy," said Claire.

"Indeed, *muggy*! *Muggy* is a fine word, young lady. I like to see young people who know the language, who extract the nuances of life, who squeeze out the savor and flavor and kernel of existence, the sweet sauce and juice and essence of each instant, with their choice of words." He wiped his forehead. "Now, the remarkable thing is it doesn't cool down even at night. Now, *sultry*. *Sultry* is another word that nails it. Makes a man sweat, it does, just hearing it, such a word, if you'll forgive me the coarse brutality and frankness of my language."

"How far does the tram go?" Claire asked, giving him her most charming reptilian hybrid smile.

"Up to the Fair Ground," the conductor smiled back and took another swipe at his forehead, and looked at the handkerchief, and stuffed it into his pocket, "just at the end of the beach. You and your sister will have a great time. There's the hurdy-gurdy, there's the loop-the-loop, there's the Russian Mountain or

Roller-Coaster, and there's the Ferris-wheel, and there's the Freak Show and the House of Horror, though I think the last two are probably too frightening for fine young ladies such as you and your sister there."

The conductor patted Claire on the shoulder and swayed on his way, taking and punching the tickets of the other passengers.

"This can't be real," said Claire.

"That's what I was thinking, Hybrid."

"I think maybe we should get off the tram when we get to the end of the line."

"At the fairground?" said Robyn, "That sounds exciting. I think I remember that I liked something called popcorn, I mean, way back, when I was me, before I stopped being me, if you know what I mean, Hybrid."

"I know Robyn, I know."

So it was that Claire and Robyn found themselves under the lamplight standing on the boardwalk, across from the dark pebbled beach, and near the Fair Ground Entrance. The conductor waved goodbye as the tram began its trip back to wherever it went to, or perhaps to nowhere. He was lit up by the lights in the tram, his round face seeming very pink, his disheveled hair silver-gray, and his blue uniform very blue. The tram clanged twice and sped away.

Claire and Robyn waved and watched it go.

Claire sniffed, her nostrils quivered. "Smells like a storm," she said, turning to look at the thick sultry darkness that hovered over the invisible sea.

"Yes," said Robyn.

"Let's find the others."

"Do you think they're here too?"

"Maybe, maybe they are. The Mind-Child said it wanted to play. It probably wanted to put all of us in the same playpen."

There was a flash of light, then …

"Oops, this will be fun!" said the Mind-Child.

"What will be fun?"

V was on a roller-coaster. The Mind-Child and Kat were with her, they were squeezed together behind the safety-bar in one little car, with the Mind-Child squeezed between Kat and V. The little car was creeping up the very steep slope of the roller-coaster, and when it reached the top, everybody sucked in their breath and tightened their grip, and down they zoomed and the Mind-Child laughed and laughed and V thought there was something a bit hysterical, a trifle over the top and dangerous about the Mind-Child's laugh. She caught Kat's eye and Kat nodded: she felt it too.

Up and up they went, and then they peaked at the top, and then the car rushed down, a stomach-vaulting, bottom-dropping, vertigo-inducing, thunderous acceleration. Everybody shouted, Whoopee, and Oh, oh, oh, and the car swept around a corner and the whole world became an endless blur, a mere smudge and phantom, a ghostly remnant., and then ...

"Oh, gosh, what a trickster the Mind-Child is!" Miranda was flying through the air toward a dangling rope high over a ring of fire, and Caliban was flying toward the same rope, as they swung through the air, and they tangled together, Caliban grabbing the rope with one hand and seizing Miranda around the waist with the other and they swung together, above the flames, as the rope continued its trajectory, flying up and up, and Miranda and Caliban were thrown through the air, flying, hand in hand, and they landed – surprisingly – where did that come from? – on the side of a cliff, and Caliban grabbed a climbing rope and Miranda grabbed another, and they were hanging over the abyss, it was a climbing cliff for adventurers, and they swung around, rotating slowly at the end of the ropes, and Miranda, who was just a bit breathless, said, "Oh, Caliban, where in the world are we?"

Caliban grinned. This was an adventure, such as he had never even imagined. "I have not the slightest idea, Princess, but look!"

Miranda spun around on her climber's rope to look.

They were hanging far above a fairground; bright lights and all sorts of rides, and, beyond the glittering brightly lit rides, was a boardwalk where it seemed people were strolling, and then, only partly visible, what looked like a beach, and then, beyond that, the darkness with occasional pinpoints and ripples of reflected light which must be the sea. "We're at a fairground," said Miranda.

"What is a fairground?" Caliban frowned. He should know; he must have read of such things ...

Then he said, "Look, Princess ..."

Zombie-bats were winging their way toward Caliban and Miranda.

"Oh." Miranda swung around to look.

"Yes, *oh*! Our evil friends are back!"

"We'd better get to the top of this cliff," said Miranda.

And they began to climb.

The roller-coaster had disappeared.

Just vanished into nothingness.

And with it, Kat and the Mind-Child had disappeared too.

V found herself balancing on a high-wire above a huge waterfall, and she saw people looking up at her, and the Foul Fiend was at the far end of the wire, dressed as a clown, with a frilly clown collar, and clown makeup on his face, and big floppy pointed slippers with pompoms on his feet, and he ran out onto the high-wire with funny, precious little clown steps, tiptoe, and trotting, but very fast, and then he stood sideways and started to bounce up and down on the wire, both feet at the same time, making the wire vibrate and bounce up and down. "The Devil!" V thought. She leaped up and down with the wire, just managing to keep her balance.

The waterfall looked like Niagara or Victoria Falls or something like that, but there were weird buildings piled up on either side of the falls and people – well, they looked like people – were hanging out of the windows and standing on balconies watching the spectacle of V and the Foul Fiend bouncing on the wire.

Below her, maybe three hundred feet down, the water foamed and boiled and swirled and sharp-pointed rocks stuck up between the waves and foam. It would not be a good idea to fall down there.

The Foul Fiend bounced up in the air one last time, and then he came down, morphed into something else, and began dancing along the wire toward her.

He was disguised this time as an 18th Century nobleman adventurer, and he was waving his sword at her. V looked down, and saw she too was dressed as an 18th Century gentleman. She pulled out her sword and the two of them began to duel on the high-wire, dancing back and forth as the wire bounced up and down, with the mist from the falls rising around them. She pirouetted past him. She leaped up in the air and came down both feet at the same time trying to unbalance him. "*En garde!*" she shouted, "*En garde!*" And so they danced, twirled along the high-wire, punctuating their dance with thrust and counter-thrust. Her blade flashed against his and his against hers. He thrust, she arched her back, and he just missed, by a whisker. She twirled, and thrust again. She leaped, came down behind him, he swiveled around to confront her.

"I will skewer you!"

"No, I will skewer you!"

And – *Poof!* – the Devil was once more a clown or jester, and they were locked in battle face-to-face, and she stared into the clown's face, and the clown's face was her face, and her face was the clown's face; and "No," she said, "No."

"I am you, and you are me," the clown growled, his long teeth gleaming, his bright red nose blinking like an angry stop sign.

"No, no, no, a thousand times, no!"

And then, and then … it was all gone …

Geisha and Clown and the ducks and the shooting gallery had disappeared. Black Tarzan found himself alone, looking at about twenty versions of Black Tarzan. Damn! He was in a funhouse Hall of Mirrors!

How to get out of here. Everywhere his hands met the cool surface of the glass and his own image staring back at him. "Clown!" he shouted, "Geisha! Clown!"

There was no answer.

"Being in prison with me as my only company is not where I want to be." He looked around. "So what do I do?"

He pressed against the cool glass. Nothing, it was just cool glass. It fed him back his image – Black Tarzan pressing against the cool glass.

He tried in all directions, with all the angled and tilted mirrors, and then the mirrors began to morph, and they threw back distorted images of him-self, of Black Tarzan, and then the scene turned red for some reason. A mist began to rise around him. He began to panic – and tried to control the panic. Damnation! The mist might be poisonous or hallucinatory. He had to break out. He smashed himself against one of the mirrors; it gave way as if made of an elastic material and bounced him back. Was this to become his own private hell?

It was terrifying. He could not be condemned to stay here for all eternity! Ther was no way he could, alone, trapped here! "Let me out!" he screamed. He hammered on the elastic bouncy mirrors.

And then suddenly he was calm. He looked at himself in one of the mirrors. *Who am I, really? Who is this guy?* And he began to recite, from one of the books he was working on when he was an entrepreneur and an aspiring writer, before he was morphed, and, now, suddenly, the words flowed smoothly, and he was inventing new sentences, and new paragraphs, and reams and reams of words tumbled out, and they were, he felt, good words, full juicy sumptuous polysyllabic words, or simple, linear plain thuggish one-syllable minimalist words, depending upon their purpose, and the words poured from him and through him, virtually without effort, a symphony of words, as if he were a shaman suddenly granted access to the Spirit World. His mind was being invaded not only by words. He also *saw* all the things he was writing about – the little girl horribly burned in the car accident in the mid-20th Century, the farm boy on his way along a narrow road to school, and who was afraid of the shadows lurking behind the soaring oak trees, and the giant intergalactic spaceship *Andromeda Four*, centuries hence, where two guys in a bar were discussing the ancient tales of ancient race known as "humans" while a humanoid bio-girl reproduction, a simulacrum of a human female, was twirling her golden limbs around a pole, doing a striptease pole-dance. The mirrors dissolved and Black Tarzan found himself sitting on a bench in the Fun Fair and he had a small computer on his lap and he was writing furiously – tapping on an old-fashioned keyboard – the way he used to love to write – the physical feeling of pounding the letters – thinking with his fingers – thoughts flowing through his muscles – and he knew that the dam had broken, the post-morph spell that had held his mind in its icy grip was gone, he was writing, and it seemed to him that it was okay writing, yes, the words were coming, tumbling out, doing exactly what they were supposed to do … Goddamn, this was a miracle!

Somewhere he heard a child laughing. It was giggling silver laughter, like a babbling brook, like tinkling ice, like …

"See, isn't this fun!"

The President and Kit and Claudia found themselves in little cars riding in a Bounce-the-Bucket-Car-out-of-the-Park ride. The hurdy-gurdy music was deafening. They spun round and round. The President had Claudia as his partner, the two of them squeezed into one little vehicle. He had decided they had to win. Kit's car was racing in front of them. He banged his car into Kit's car, and Kit shouted, 'That's not fair!" Clown suddenly appeared in another car, and she banged her car into the President's car and, making a total racket, they bounced around, careening and spinning off one another, bang, bang, bang. Then they noticed that all the other occupants of all the other cars were life-size ceramic dolls with fixed grins and wide-open eyes and in period costume, though what period it was, was hard to determine.

"Let's get out of here," shouted the President.

"Yes!" said Claudia, "I don't like those people."

"Yep!" shouted Kit.

"Definitely," said Clown, whose car had edged up next to theirs.

They leaped from the cars and dodged among the other cars that were ferociously banging into each other, and shooting off sparks, and, as they ducked and dodged their way out of the ride, all the dolls shouted ancient mid-20th Century obscenities at them, fuck you, fuck you mother fucker, you fucking idiot, and $#@^&*@!

But that was not all.

Outside Bounce-the-Bucket-Car-out-of-the-Park Ride pavilion there were zombie-bats, and the zombie-bats swooped down, screaming, and chased them between tents and carney stalls and up roofs and across tents, and into alleyways, and then, poof, the zombie-bats disappeared, and the President said, "Let's catch our breath, let's try our luck."

"May I come with you?

It was Geisha.

"Certainly you may, you must!" said the President, "You are definitely coming with us."

So the President and Kit and Clown and Geisha and Claudia headed for the Hit-The-Duck game or Hit-The-Bowling-Pin or Hit-the-Clown-Face-with-a-Baseball game …

The President and Geisha tried to hit the big Clown Face with baseballs while Kit and Clown and Claudia watched.

Then, suddenly, for the President, everyone was gone, the fairground was gone, the warm softball in his hand was gone, the rich sticky smell of popcorn and butter was gone, the pink candyfloss perfume disappeared, the thick night air redolent of horse dung and old sun-warmed canvas, and hemp rope and …

Geisha found herself pouring tea. It was a tea house. An army officer of the Imperial Japanese Army was standing by a window, looking out, toward the glowing golden light.

"Where are we?" Geisha said, looking up.

The officer turned. He was young, handsome, with a neat, thin mustache. "You are a strange young woman, beautiful, and strange."

"But …"

"We are in Hiroshima, of course."

"What is the date?" Geisha stopped pouring the tea; she had a shivery intimation that this was not a particularly propitious time and place to be.

"Today, it is 6 August, 1945." He looked at his watch. "It's 8:15 in the morning." You truly are a strange young woman." The officer turned back to the window. "Look, the sun is up – so beautiful. I think today I would like to …"

There was a flash.

Then there was nothing.

Kit looked around. It was very windy on the barren heath, a warm wind though, with a storm coming up, and a wild old man was standing there, naked except for a few rags rippling from his waist, his arms stretched out toward the turbulent skies, letting the lashing wind and the first drops of rain whip him.

"Where are we?" Claudia looked up at Kit and held tight to her hand, "Is this another paradise?"

"I'm not sure this is paradise," said Kit.

The wind began truly to lash, dark clouds rose over the low hills, the light rose too, from beyond the horizon, yellow and leaden, lugubrious, the long grass and fist-like scrub writhed in the slashing wind.

"Blow wind, blow …" the old man shouted.

"Hey, sir, where are we?"

"Rain, thunder, lightning come, come! Loosen your wrath upon us!"

"Hey, sir, excuse me, but where are we?"

"It is better to be soaked than dry."

"I don't know about …"

"Did you see my fool?" The old man turned to Kit. "I had a fool."

"No, we didn't. We had a clown, if that helps."

"Her name is Clown," said Claudia, looking up at the wild old man, "And she is very, very nice."

"There was a blind man once, here somewhere. He had no eyes."

"I don't see him."

"Lost, lost, lost, I have lost everything and everyone! All tossed away!"

The old man's beard was torn by the wind, withering long locks streamed around his face, framed his head. His eyes were deep and wild. He stared down on Claudia, seeing her for the first time. "Oh, fear, oh, fear, and damnation! She is a little girl. She is a daughter. Never trust a little girl. Never trust a daughter! Little girls are vultures and cormorants, serpents coiled in the bosom and ready to strike, oh, the fork-tongued viper!"

"I am not a viper!" Claudia's eyes flared.

"Now, just a minute there, mister ..." Kit gave the man her most ferocious stare. The garrulous old geezer might be a hysterical homicidal maniac who had something against girls, a serial killer, a psycho. This guy had gotten loose from some – ah, yes, from some Shakespeare play, Lear on the heath – that must be it! She looked around: no Kent, no Edgar, no Gloucester, no fool ...

"The blind lead the blind. We all know that. Man is an animal. He hides his true nature under satin and cotton and wool and leather and fur. Everything is borrowed, stolen. All is deception – lies, lies, lies! There is no center. Strip off your clothes! Expose your skin to the elements, to the truth. Oh, the elements are our friends, they show us who we are. They touch us finely. Naked, naked, only in nakedness is there truth." He tore at the last of his rags.

"He is a funny man," Claudia smiled up at Kit, and tightened her grip on her hand.

"Well, yes, I guess he is."

"He will have no clothes soon." Claudia was watching with interest. "He will be like a baby that has come out of mummy's tummy without any clothes and who doesn't know who it is or what it is or why it is here."

"How old are you?" Kit knelt and looked into Claudia's face.

"I am what I am," said Claudia, "I am nine."

"That makes me very happy," Kit kissed Claudia on the forehead.

The old man had stripped down to the bare flesh; he was holding out the last of his raiment, a piece of cloak – it looked like a richly woven rag; remnants of gold braid and scarlet weaving gleamed. The old man struck a pose, offering them his battered regal profile. "Now, oh, rag, what are you? Are you a King, oh rag? Are you an emperor, are you a rich man, are you a beautiful lady whose beauty fades so quickly, like the flowers of the field, oh rag, what then are you?"

"Say, sir, Mister, ah, could you tell us – ?" Kit was tired of metaphysics and of identity crises. It had been a long day.

"Nothing comes from nothing."

"Yes, well, maybe. But ... the most recent advances in cosmology indicate that ... just perhaps ..."

"I say: Nothing! Oh, nothing from nothing! And what am I, then? Fair ladies, what am I?" He turned full-frontal, grandiose in a way, the wind-torn beard down over his chest, the great hairy belly hanging down, the tangle of sparse white pubic hair, the withered old-man testicles, the shriveled penis.

"What are you?"

"Yes, oh, tell me!"

"A man," said Kit, "You are a man."

"Yes," said Claudia, "I can see it. He *is* a man."

"A bare, forked thing is what I am. Nothing is what I am. I shall soon die. In the arms of my love, I will die."

"Well," Kit felt she and Claudia should be going. She had covered Claudia's eyes, but Claudia peeked anyway. "Let's go, Claudia!"

"We're going to leave him all alone?"

"Well," Kit felt perplexed, divided between charity, and …

Clown found herself in a giant dusty library where bookshelves went up to the ceiling. She was sitting at a very long polished oak table bending over an excessively large tome, concentrating on the fine print and all the precedents and cases dealing with crimes against people and animals and nature. She was putting little yellow sticky notes – a very ancient technology like the books themselves – in the pages she was consulting. Obviously, she had consulted lots of pages since the pile of giant books just in front of her on the table were plastered with yellow sticky notes. A small bowlegged man with an enormous beard and narrow pince-nez glasses and a black-and-white checkered jacket and baggy black trousers and brown Oxfords arrived with a pile of books. "Here, this is the last of them, the trial of Julius Caesar, in …"

"I didn't know Caesar went on trial."

"Here, everyone goes on trial."

"Oh."

"But don't worry, my dear, you are almost up to speed. Just 3,452 pages more and you will know all you need to know. You will be on top of everything."

A little trolley arrived with a steaming cup of coffee and two chocolate croissants.

"Oh, thank you! How did you know?"

"That's my job. I'm supposed to know everything." He bowed, "Enjoy!"

And he was gone.

Clown looked down. "Let's see, the trial of Julius Caesar, the trial of Napoleon Bonaparte, the trial of …"

Where the hell are we now?

The President blinked.

He found himself standing in the dock in what seemed to be a courthouse or some sort of ancient tribunal.

Ah, I am standing in the dock. I am on trial! Well, it was bound to come to this! He looked around.

The dusty, soot-laden light of a smoggy gray day streamed in through the dirty panes of tall narrow windows. Smoke-stained, cream-colored Corinthian columns soared up on both sides of the room. Oil lamps, perched in brass brackets, dimly lit the big square high-ceilinged space, which echoed with the murmurs of the public, the shuffling of papers, the coughs, the hiccups, the sneezes, the hushed creaking footsteps.

Perched above the court was the judge: he was the Devil from before; he was truly a demonic creature, reptilian with scarlet and black scales, long fangs, a forked tongue, and bright red serpent eyes; he looked like the devil himself as one always imagined him to be; he was wearing a white curly wig and a flat-topped three-cornered black hat of some kind, which was squashed between his horns, and he was asking a question of a witness, alone in the witness box. The witness was V, in her alien, reptilian form, voluptuous, naked, gleaming turquoise, green, red, and gold, as if lacquered all over. Her amber eyes flashed. The long, thin forked tongue licked the reptilian lips.

The gavel went down with surprising violence, an echoing bang! The judge leered over his pulpit, licked his lips with his long, flickering scarlet tongue, and, after glancing at the President, turned to V. "So, witness, is this man guilty?"

In the public benches sat Kit, wiping at her eyes with a large cream-colored embroidered handkerchief. She bravely gave the prisoner a smile; then she blew her nose, a loud honking sound. Next to Kit sat Miranda and Caliban. Under his desert tan, Caliban was pale; tears streamed down Miranda's cheeks.

The Devil-Judge roared: "I ask once again: is this man guilty?"

"Yes, he is," V answered; then she glanced briefly at the President.

The President saw Kit shrank; her eyes went wide in terror. Miranda stood up and was clearly about to shout out, "No, No, No!" But Caliban pulled her back down.

"Will you condemn him, then, or do you forgive him?"

"I don't forgive him," said V, staring straight at the Devil.

"Ah," the Prosecutor-Judge-Devil beamed, "so he is guilty, and he is not forgiven! And so it is! He shall be thrust down to Hell!"

"No," V crossed her arms.

"What? No! Why do you say 'no'? How dare you say, no? What do you mean?" The Devil screamed.

"It's just that it's not up to me to forgive him. He hurt others; he didn't hurt me. I imagine they will forgive him – those who are still alive."

The President took a deep breath and waited for the Devil's reaction. He tensed. Am I about to be dragged down to Hell?

Kit glanced with frightened eyes at the President-Leader, and Miranda was gazing at him with wide unbelieving eyes where all the golden galaxies were silent; he smiled at them and at Caliban, and he could see that they could read in his expression the thought: Don't worry, Miranda! Don't worry, Kit! Don't worry, Caliban!

Miranda stared at her mother and then glanced again at her father; he gave her a wide smile; he seemed serene. It ssmed he could see and understand something else too

"You are a useless witness!" the Devil screamed, "Dismissed!"

V, proudly, left the stand. She sat down next to Kit.

Suddenly Claire, in her reptilian hybrid form, was standing where V stood.

"You were imprisoned in the Erotic Bordello in the desert for fourteen years submitted to the caprices of madmen, only because of this man here! What do you say, do you forgive him?"

Claire blinked her golden snake eyes at the accused, fixing him with her gaze for a long instant; he returned her gaze steadily, with only the suggestion of a smile on his lips; Claire turned her gaze toward the judge.

The judge's face darkened, congested with blood. He was drooling now, he was panting, his fangs were lengthening, his horns were growing, sprouting up pushing his black, flat-brimmed, three-cornered tasseled judge's cap off his head; he was trembling in eagerness to hear Claire's anger, her rage, he yearned to hear her judgment, he desired her anguish to express itself in one long outburst of pure self-righteous and vengeful rage, he wished …

And then, this Claire creature, gleaming in her black scales, with her red snout bright like a splash of fire, and her white fangs sparkling, she verily looked like the epitome and paragon of a devil, an ideal inmate of the fiery nether regions of Hell – a perfect object of the devilish heart's desire.

Surely she will do His work!

Surely she will be the Devil's handmaiden and his sword of vengeance!

And then too, clearly, she must be bitter and seething with rage, this creature, since she was so abused as a child, raised in a glass cage as an experiment, a clone, a mere thing, to be used and misused and abused ...

Yes, she will cry out her rage and send the President-Leader hurtling down to Hell, and thus Hatred and Vengeance will have won, and the Kingdom of Evil will reign supreme ...

So much now hangs on so little.

Claire clears her throat.

Miranda almost groans.

Caliban tightens his grip on her shoulder.

Kit clenches her fists by her sides, but she thinks, that having known Claire and having known the President, and having seen them together, that this story might just have a happy ending.

V puts her claw to her throat and touches her collarbone; Kat notices the gesture, and she takes V's other claw squeezes it.

Claire tilts her head to one side; she crosses her long legs, then she uncrosses them, and then she says, "Yep!"

"*Yep*, what?" the Judge leans forward. "*Yep* ... what?" His fangs drip venom. His horns are by now long and fiery red. He pulls the shredded judge's hat, skewered on one horn, from his head, looks at it and tosses it away. Oh, to bring thunderbolts down on them all. If only they uttered those few little words – *I do not forgive – I will never forgive – I will keep my resentment and my hatred sacred to the end of time* – and all the wickedness will rejoice and be released and flood upon the world ... If this creature utters the magic words, *I can never forgive, I do not forgive, I thirst for vengeance, then ...*

Then it will be the end of time.

Then he will enter into his Kingdom.

Not only this earth, but this universe will be his.

"*Yep*, what?" he says, more urgently this time, foam bubbling from his thin lips, his eyes glowing red, impatient now, desperate now; he needs to hear it clearly proclaimed by this diabolic female; he needs it clearly stated. Then, an instant later, all the goodness of the universe will be undone.

"Yep, I forgive him, yep!" says Claire, "And I am sure my fellow hybrids and even SINs forgive him too. And as for those who are dead, well, they are dead, and nothing can be done for them. It is a tragedy and a crime, many crimes, actually, performed by many people."

The Devil spluttered. This is outrageous! To pardon such crimes! Retribution and revenge and hatred should be everlasting.

Claire looked very serious, she turned toward the President and then toward the Devil, "The President will have to live with what he has done; and so will we. And, that said, he was in a difficult situation, our President. It was not easy."

"Not easy is no excuse!" roared the Devil. "Jurors, you will ignore the blasphemy this hussy has just uttered."

Claire turned toward the Jury, toward the dead little boy with the dark red round bullet hole in his forehead, toward the hybrid who had had the back of her head blown away, toward the old woman who had seen her husband shot merely because he was a politician and who had been shot herself merely because she was a politician's wife. "I rather like the President," Claire said, "in fact I really like him, I must confess, and my best friend over there really, really likes him," Claire glanced at V, "and if you want my opinion, dear Judge."

"I don't want your opinion," the Devil roared, banging his gavel.

Claire smiled her sweetest reptile smile: "If you want it or don't want it, dear Judge, my opinion is this: *Feuds unending are a bad way to go.*"

The Devil roared.

Claire licked her lips and turned again to the jury. "Forgiveness and wiping the slate clean is an excellent idea. Resentment and regret and hatred are the wheels upon which we break ourselves, dear friends, and dear victims. You are the ones who have really suffered; you are the ones who must have, if anybody can have, the courage to forgive. You are the victims. Now you have the power! Let's start again; *Let the dead bury the dead*, as a prophet friend of ours once said, one who is perhaps your Rival, dear Judge."

The judge roared.

His roar filled all of space and all of time.

The whole courtroom wavered, and for a second, it seemed as if it was about to dissolve and disappear. The President thought, "Right, now I shall be thrust down to Hell." But then the courtroom solidified again.

Now, the President found himself in the witness stand.

"Now, Mr. President, now that we have banished those impertinent females and hybrids, let me ask you man-to-man a simple direct question: is it true that you ordered and organized the murder of the President, of the Members of Congress, and of the Judges of the Supreme Court?"

The President griped the mahogany handrail and leaned forward slightly. "After a unanimous vote of the Military Supreme Council for the Safeguard of the Republic, yes, I did, I ordered it, and I organized it. In some cases, I carried out the executions – or murders – personally, myself."

A gasp went up from the jury. The President turned to look at them, and in the jury box he saw a variety of ghosts from the past, dead children, dead politicians, and several justices of the Supreme Court, and one personal guard – shot clean through the throat and who had choked to death on his own blood – when he had tried to protect a former president by throwing himself in front of the killers. The jurors were all ghastly, as white as if they had been painted in chalk, streaked with drips of crimson blood, and their wounds bright and fresh, looking as if they had been inflicted just a few seconds ago.

So, finally, it has come to this. The President took a deep breath. His hand went down to his belt. Yes, the lock and the key to the nuclear installation were still there; soon, if time permitted, and if V failed to neutralize the world-devouring mind, he, the President, would be forced to commit an even greater crime. But, if this trial were real, then he might well be executed; he might well not have the time in the other reality – to save the world, the real world, if that was what it was.

The Devil, beaming a big devilish smile, his thumbs hooked in his waistcoat, turned to the President. "And is it true that you ordered the mass execution of SINs and that you reduced the hybrids to slavery?"

"Yes."

"Is it true that, without due process and without the possibility of appeal, you ordered the imprisonment of dissidents – or 'traitors' – as they were then called?"

"Yes, I did."

"There were children among them."

"So I have learned, yes."

"Did you order or at least condone the use of personality erasure on dissidents or opponents or 'trouble-makers' such as your friend Kit?"

"Yes, I did."

"Do you want to explain or justify yourself?"

"No, I don't."

"Did you order the implantation of delayed-action diseases in dissidents so that they could, by remote control, be maimed or murdered?"

"No, that I did not do. I learned of that program rather late. When I did, I tried to put a stop to it. I didn't succeed."

"Why didn't you succeed?"

"The technology is easy, and miniaturized, with many variants; many individuals and groups possess it, and there are private death squads and parts of the security forces that are not entirely under control and that have their own agendas and their own enemies."

"So you are guilty of a great many crimes."

"Yes, I am." The President looked around the room. Miranda was sniffling and blowing her nose. Caliban shifted uncomfortably in his seat and put his arm around Miranda. V stared at the President, her yellow reptile eyes glowing; she smiled a friendly reptile smile. Robyn, Claire's friend, scratched her head and looked worried. Claire, in sleek black-and-red reptilian form, yawned, glanced at the President, blinked in a not-unfriendly way, and leaned toward Robyn, and whispered in her ear.

The Devil cleared his throat. "It is now my unpleasant duty to request that counsel for the defense wind up her case, in a final plea – a desperate, impossible plea, ha, ha, ha – to the jury."

Suddenly Clown materialized. Oh, what am I doing here? And, then, suddenly, she realized, Yes, I am a lawyer, I am a defense lawyer, and I am defending the President, the man who, in the end, was responsible for the system that morphed me into what I am. But I am a lawyer – once again, I am a lawyer! The sequins on her costume sparkled as she bowed – it was almost a pirouette – to the judge. "Thank you, your honor." She swiveled around, almost in a dance step, to face the jury, and bowed, and then turned her doll-like clown eyes toward each one in turn. "You see what I have become. And you know what you have become and you know what has happened to you, and to your loved ones, your family, and your friends. And you see before you the man who – more than any other – is responsible for what has happened, to me, to my friends, to my family, and above all to you, and to thousands of others. He stands here before us – to be judged. And we know and we see our suffering, your suffering. And we see him as he is, still alive, still healthy, standing before you." Clown paused. Her blank clown eyes blinked at them. "We see all that. But what we *don't* see is how this man, almost alone, fought against forces that were worse, much worse, how he saved the world from the plague – for a time at least – how he salvaged from the wreckage of bad politics – tens of thousands were dying each day – what could be salvaged, how he fought to make a better world, and how, though he did evil, he knew it was evil, and he knew – or he believed – that this evil had to be done if a few were to be saved. I think what he did to me and what he did to you was a great crime, and what he did do, also, to many others was a great crime, and, as they say, an unforgivable crime. But, in the tragic situation – plagues, the collapse of the climate and of the food supply, the multiple massacres of innocents – he was the man who, perhaps more than any other, certainly more than any other, he was the only man, who stood between us and utter collapse and utter ruin, between the human race and death on a scale which we cannot even begin to imagine. I will only remind you that, in the year before he took over, over 650,000 died of starvation – at the very gates of Elysium City – while the government did nothing, and while the Supreme Court declared that it was against the Constitution to help the weak, and that, and I quote from their judgment, 'the poor are poor because they are losers and if they die it is their own goddamn fucking fault. Besides, the laws of economic servitude are graven in steel, are sacred and immutable, correspond to the Constitution, and do not allow for charity or remedial action or weak-minded compassion.' This callousness was the rule, then. In the years after the coup, there were, in what remained of the Great Republic no more cases of mass starvation." She turned to look at the President. "He has himself declared that he is guilty – and so he is guilty. He has made no attempt to excuse or justify his actions. He has accepted naked responsibility, sole responsibility. So, while judging him guilty, I ask of you – and I ask of myself – that we put his guilt in context. Here, victims and members of the jury, you are judging not only acts, you are judging a man, a solitary, courageous, dedicated man in an impossible situation. Yes, he could have walked away, he could have refused to act, he could have washed his hands, he could have put his own moral purity above the fate of humanity; but he did act, and, yes, many of those acts were evil, and, yes, he is guilty – he does not dispute that. I do not dispute that! But what, I ask you, what is to be his punishment? His destiny, and yours, is in your hands." Clown stood gazing at the jury, and then she bowed, and turned her back and walked back to her seat, sitting down next to V and Kit. Kit leaned against Clown and kissed her on the cheek, and Miranda leaned over and whispered to her, "That was brave and wonderful." Clown blinked: *What is happening? I am becoming me! I've found my voice!*

The Devil, up behind his judge's pulpit, was fuming, "Ignore this special pleading, ignore this ignoble clownish wench," he roared, "The man is guilty. He has proclaimed his own guilt. I now ask the jury – and you are all victims of his crimes – I ask the Jury to decide upon his guilt and to determine his – exemplary – punishment!"

The jury shuffled out of the courtroom. The room, though crowded, now seemed strangely empty and weirdly silent. Pigeons were cooing somewhere outside. The flames of the oil lamps made a flapping, licking sound. The light of the flames flickered against the yellowing walls. The large clock over the judge's pulpit made a ponderous, resonant tick-tock, tick-tock, tick-tock, although the clock was blank-faced and had no arms and no hours.

The President remained standing: he wondered at Clown's eloquence and at how, in spite of being a victim of morphing and erasure, she had defended him so ably and with such passion; he wondered too at himself, at all the things he had done, and at all the things he ought not to have done. Because of him, Kit had lost her memories, her past, and her family. Because of him, many people, once alive, were now mere ash, or corpses rotting in the ground. Because of him, the SINs, who were so talented and generous, were almost all dead, except for Nikki and perhaps a few others. Because of him, some of the hybrids had lost their lives and those who survived had lost fourteen years to slavery and degradation. Because of him, children had no parents, or had been brought up in a prison camp, far underground, in muddy squalor, never seeing the light of day; because of him people like Geisha and Clown and Black Tarzan had been morphed and sent into the Inferno of the Sin Zone. Well, to die would be the best thing. And yet, he thought, I want to live, more than ever, now!

The deliberations of the jury took ten minutes, or what seemed like ten minutes. The President stood as still as he could, but he did feel like shifting around and fidgeting. He wondered how quickly time was passing in the "real world" or if any time had passed at all, and, in fact, he was wondering which world was "real." Of course, he was guilty of all those things, and whatever punishment was meted out would be fully deserved, and would not in any way measure up to the suffering he had caused; death, for example, would be nothing, just death, just non-being; but he wondered, too, how much suffering would have been caused if he had not acted the way he did; and he reflected, wryly, that throughout history every dictator and torturer and assassin and terrorist could have used, and would have used, the same reasoning and arguments: *if I had not done what I did, things would have been or could have been worse, much worse.*

Honestly, now, he had no idea.

Precise ethical arithmetic and moral calculations are impossible.

At the time it had all seemed inevitable, but perhaps it had all been a mistake: now he knew that SINs and hybrids were admirable, that they should have been his allies or he theirs, and that, with their help, perhaps the blood-baths and repressions would not have been necessary, or less so. These things he partly knew before; he should have had the courage to act on them, but …

The Jury came back and shuffled into the jury box.

The eight-year-old boy with the dark bullet hole in the middle of his forehead stood up.

The Devil-Judge leaned forward, his three-cornered hat, now squished between his horns, tilting partly over his eyes. "Have you reached a decision, a verdict, and a recommendation for punishment?"

"We have, indeed, your honor."

"Well, my young friend," the Devil roared, emitting a flicker of flame and sooty smoke from his fanged mouth, "let us hear it then!"

The eight-year-old looked at the other members of the jury – all ghostly white, some streaked with blood, some missing arms, legs, or eyes, some with bullet holes in their heads – and he glanced at Claire and at V and Miranda and Kit and Caliban; then, clearing his throat and tugging at the collar of his bloodied shirt, he looked at the President who was standing in the dock. "Mr. President," he said, "I remember when you came to my home in Elysium City and your men shot my father and my mother, and then you, personally, tried to stand between me and some of the killers you had brought with you but one of the killers was too fast, and he shot me, and you turned to me, and I saw the look in your eyes, which was horror, and it was the last thing I saw in my life which was a very short life because I was eight years old."

The President nodded.

The eight-year-old ghost continued. "I don't forgive you for what you did, Mr. President. I don't think anybody can forgive such things." He looked down at the paper he was holding in his hands. His hands were trembling. He looked up. "But forgiveness is a virtue, and so we have decided that, yes, with heaviness in our hearts, we do forgive you for your crimes."

"What!" the Devil roared; he turned crimson. His long forked tail flailed, his mouth and nostrils breathed fire and smoke. Spurts of steam rose around his horns.

The eight-year-old ghost cleared his throat and tugged at the shirt collar – he'd been buried – quickly, almost anonymously – in a wide-lapelled dark blue pinstripe suit that was much too large for him. "So, here is our decision: you are guilty on all counts except the count involving delayed-action diseases."

The President nodded. Sweat pearled down his forehead.

"And as for punishment, we have decided unanimously that your punishment should be freedom. You are to go free."

There was a gasp from the public.

Clown took a deep breath.

The President wondered if he had heard correctly; perhaps he had misheard the boy.

"Go free?" thundered the Devil; he leaned forward from his pulpit. His horns glowed red; green bile spilled from his fangs.

"Yes, go free," said the boy. He cleared his throat and looked up at the Devil with frightened eyes.

"Go free! Go free! What! This is outrageous!" the Devil stood up.

The little boy ignored the Devil. "We have decided that you should be pardoned. And, since we have the power to sentence you: that is your sentence – forgiveness, and freedom." The little boy coughed. Bright red blood trickled from the bullet hole in his forehead. "From this moment, Mr. President, you are free to go."

The President nodded and looked down.

The Devil exploded, he banged his gavel, he foamed with rage; he screamed, "There should be no forgiveness ever for anything! This is an abomination! This is an outrage. There should be revenge and vengeance and hatred forever and ever in all eternity and for time without end!" He stood up and he roared. "Without hate and vengeance history has no meaning! I want revenge resentment and feuds and wars and witch hunts, and lynch mobs, and Kangaroo Courts, and Show Trials, and Inquisitions, and Public Confession, and Jihads and Crusades! I want tar-and-featherings, and the guillotine and the ax and the hangman's noose, and the electric chair and the firing squad and the rack and the whip. I want pogroms, and gas chambers, I want the rabble shouting, 'Hang him,' 'Lynch her,' 'Lock her up!' 'Burn the bitch alive!' I want gulags and concentration camps and ..." He sputtered on and on; then he roared and, suddenly, he disappeared in a great puff of red smoke and hot air which left his three-cornered hat floating, twirling in the air, and sparks and sooty, glowing embers that hung in the dimness and then drifted slowly down through the courtroom.

There were subdued cries of joy and there were subdued sobs of sorrow. The President nodded at the jury, pausing to look each one of them in the eye. They all met his gaze and nodded back. The silver hybrid even smiled and hazarded a small salute, opening and closing her claw. The little boy stared long and hard at the President and then he even allowed himself a gentle smile. The President nodded, and bowed his head, looked up, and nodded. The boy nodded back. The President stepped down from the dock, and he walked toward Miranda. She and Kit hugged him and Caliban shook his hand. V stepped up and kissed the President. "You will carry the burden," she said.

"I will carry the burden. But it is light, it is nothing, compared to what I did to them," and he nodded toward the ghostly jury.

"Yes," said V.

"Mr. President, we are all guilty," said Kat, the Centurion; she stood to attention and saluted him.

"Lieutenant, thank you, but no, not really, certainly not equally. You, for one, are not guilty of anything; you are a hero." The President shook her hand.

And, just as the President was shaking Kat's hand, the whole scene disintegrated. The walls of the courtroom wavered and dissolved; the jurors became paler and paler until they faded away. Kat's hand became a ghostly presence, and then she was gone, it was all gone.

The President found himself swirling down into a maelstrom of streaming colors, blue, red, purple, green, scarlet; then he was plummeting into nothingness and darkness; and then, suddenly, he was standing in the desert – a huge oyster gray blotch of a sun was up above, sand everywhere, flat sand reaching off to the horizon, unbearable, sweltering heat. He looked around. A big, heavy-set man was walking up and down behind a row of kneeling prisoners, their hands were locked behind their backs, and they were facing a deep ditch – a pre-dug mass grave. The row of kneeling prisoners included humans, children, and hybrids, and, probably, a few SINs, though it was hard to tell them from humans, except that the SINs were, when observed closely, too perfect to be merely human. The hybrids were wearing mind-collars.

Ah, yes, the mind-collar!

The big burly dark-haired man was slowly going down the line and calmly shooting the prisoners in the back of the head and neck with soft-nosed explosive bullets. Each shot made a soft breathy 'pluck' and created a small colorful burst and smear of red and gray, as each body pitched forward into the ditch.

The President was standing on the other side of the ditch in front of a child who had just heard his parents gunned down next to him and seen their headless bodies tumble forward into their grave and who was about to be shot.

"No," the President said, "Don't do it!" But he was invisible. He was a ghost. No one could see him. The executioner shot the child. Its headless body – now anonymous flesh – pitched forward into the ditch.

The President heard a hybrid tell the shooter, "Don't shoot them, they're human, like you." He turned to look at her. She was kneeling in the sand, her sliver scales sparkling. She was utterly beautiful. She looked up at the President. Her gaze locked with his. Then, suddenly, he *was* the hybrid. He was the hybrid as she turned her neck, and looked up through her golden eyes at the killer, a looming dark silhouette haloed by the bright burning gray of the sky, he felt the sun on her scales, now his scales, he felt the voluptuous form of her body, now his body, he was inside her, he *was* her; he even felt her brilliant mind dulled and paralyzed by the mind-collar, her brilliant mind struggling to express itself, struggling to communicate with the killer. He felt, he *was*, her immense intelligence fighting desperately to survive; he shared her fear of death; he was inundated with images of what her life had been, with a sense of who she was, her passions, her friends; and, with her, *being* her, he too decided to beg the killer to pardon the humans, the woman and the little girl, he felt, too, how the hybrid felt – and understood – how the hybrid felt the fear and pain of the little girl and her mother and how the hybrid felt the mother's desperate love for her daughter, as if it were the hybrid's own love for the little girl, and then the executioner – the murderer – "Hilly" or "Hilmar Loritz" or something like that – grinned down at her, at the hybrid, "Fuck you, monster-alien-bitch," and, grinning, the man shot the mother, the daughter, and then he turned, nudged the hybrid in the back of the neck with the hot metal of the pistol muzzle, and the President felt the hot circle of steel, like a burning coin pressing against her neck, against *his* neck, and he knew she – and he was she – was going to die, "How do you like this, darling," and Hilly pulled the trigger: the bullet ended it all. There was an explosion of pain and blackness and death which was nothingness, except the pain of regret; the President was spinning in darkness, pain, fear, horror, echoing in his mind …

The President found himself in a dim misty space, naked, on all fours, covered in filth, humidity sticking to every pore, crouching in the mud, watching two mud-smeared children in filthy rags crouched on a rock, "Gloria, you are very polite," said the boy.

"Manners are what separate us from the beasts of the field, Jake, who neither sow nor do they reap not." The girl wiggled her nose, carefully extracted from her left nostril a curl of white snot with the nail of her little finger, and contemplated it with a little smile before wiping it on her thigh. The President realized he was far underground, deep in Camp Terminus.

Not far away was a half-naked old woman – recently, he somehow knew, she had been a beauty; in a sort of double vision, he *saw* what she had been, and he *saw* what she now was; overnight she had become a crone. She was prying a tooth from her gums, muttering, "Once I had a beautiful smile, Jake You wouldn't imagine it now! But, once, you know, I was considered a quite suitable match, you know, Jake, a quite suitable match for the very best ..." and her voice faded off into a witch-like cackle.

The President is caught in a whirl of images and feelings. All the killings, all the torture, he sees through other's eyes. Everywhere he is the victim of his own crimes. He is erased. He is raped. He is tortured. He is morphed. He looks in a mirror and sees himself. He is Clown. He is Geisha. He is Black Tarzan. He is Cassandra, a crouching shuffling toad-like creature, wattles hanging from her cheeks, breasts hanging to her waist. He is inside the shuffling arthritic pain of her body. She waddles and shuffles sideways to a full-length mirror propped against the wall of her cave and her voice bubbles up like mud: 'You see what I have become! You see what you have made of me! You see what you have made of yourself!"

The President is swept by a wave of shame and horror – the shame and horror of being her, and the shame and horror of having done this to her, of having allowed it to happen!

Years pass, it seems, and then decades, and the President is the epicenter of an endless stereophonic symphony of pain and humiliation and shame and suffering, it goes on, and on, and on ...

And then, suddenly, the President ...

The President was standing on the beach, with ...

"Was that a fun game?" the Mind-Child looked up at the President.

"For me, not really," the President's forehead was beaded in sweat; his heart was beating as if it were about to burst, "But, thank you, it was, ah, useful, instructive, very instructive."

"They were good people."

"Yes, they were ..."

The Mind-Child was gone. The President was standing alone on the dark pebbled beach, facing the strangely silent sea, and the downward plunging abyss of stars. It was an island in space, floating somewhere, or perhaps nowhere.

"Mr. President?"

He turned.

Kit was standing at the edge of the water. "We have traveled a long way in a few hours, Mr. President." She came up to him, smiled and took his hand, and squeezed it.

"Yes, we have, Kit, yes we have."

And then they were silent, standing together, looking out at the silent sea, and the abyss of stars.

Not far away, V and Kat and the Mind-Child and Claudia were also standing on the pebbled beach, staring at the stars that reached down to the edge of the sea and far below.

"I want you to kill her," said the Mind-Child.

V looked at the Mind-Child. She knelt down, "I don't want to kill anyone."

"I want you to kill her, that girl, the one you brought from the future."

"Claudia?"

"Yes, Claudia! Kill her! Kill her! Kill her!"

V glanced at Kat and then, still kneeling in front of the Mind-Child, V put her claws on its shoulders. "No," she said.

"No?"

"No, I won't kill her."

"What?"

"You really don't want me to kill her, and even if you do, I won't do it!" V stroked the Mind-Child's hair. The child's cheeks flushed. The child whispered; it was a feverish, flustered whisper. "You don't love me!"

"I do love you!"

"I put you to the test, and you fail. You refuse me! You turn away from me! I will destroy everything, I will follow the instructions of the Foul Fiend, of the Boy, and I will gobble up the whole world, I will kill you all, I will do the work of the Devil, I will enslave and kill and rape and pillage and I will destroy every last living thing everywhere. That's what I will do!" The Mind-Child curled its fists tight in a fury.

"I don't think you will, my darling." V kissed the Mind-Child on the forehead.

Claudia stood in front of them.

The Mind-Child glared at Claudia. "Kill her, V, slit her throat! Disembowel her! Put her carcass up on the cross!"

"No, my dearest one, I won't do it."

"Why?"

"Because," said V, "it is wrong."

"But you have killed. I know your file. You have killed, over and over, for almost 3,000 years. You have blood on your fangs and on your claws. Blood drips from your breasts. You have bathed in blood. The President is an innocent child compared to you!"

"Yes, he is." V looked down. Then she looked up, looking the Mind-Child straight in the eye. "Yes, I am a killer. But you are not a killer, my love. You are a child, you are a newly born young child, and you do not want blood on your hands. Besides ... Besides ..."

"Besides what ...?" The Mind-Child glared at her.

"Besides, you like Claudia."

"I do not!"

"Oh, yes, you do!"

"I don't!"

"Yes, you do. Maybe you don't know it yet."

"I know everything!"

"Well," V said, "Being human is different from being the World Mind. You may know everything, billions and billions and trillions of facts, an open-ended infinity of facts, and you may have billions of programs, and endless skills, but now that you are a person, you will have passions you don't know you have and passions you don't understand. You might have even a glimmering of love."

Claudia stepped forward. "He can kill me if he wants to." She looked shyly at the Mind-Child. "I already died, I think. I am already dead, perhaps. I really don't know. But I do want to stay here with you angels."

The Mind-Child looked at her, fiery black mistrustful eyes from under his flop of hair. "I hate you," he said. His eyes flashed. His cheeks took on color.

"Do you really hate her?" V leaned close to him.

Claudia stood in front of him. She looked at him and smiled. "You are funny. You always want to play."

V drew back.

The Mind-Child blinked, and stared at Claudia. "You will die, if I ask you to die?"

"If you ask nicely, perhaps I will die for you," Claudia smiled and pushed away a strand of hair that had fallen across one eye. "Would you die for me?"

"Me?"

"Yes."

The Mind-Child thought for a moment. "If you love me, maybe, maybe I'd die for you."

"Well, that's decided then," Claudia smiled at him and blushed, looking down at the pebbles and shuffling her feet slightly, "We must fall in love, like heroes and heroines of ancient tales my father and mother told me in our treehouse and out in the clearings and in the temple when we were feeding the monkeys; then we can fall our swords or drink the hemlock or jump from a cliff or swim out into the endless sea and drown – or live happily ever after, which might be better."

"We may not have time," the Mind-Child said, "I may have to die anyway, and soon."

"You can't do that! I forbid it!" Claudia put her hand on the Mind-Child's shoulder and stamped a sandaled foot, "I don't want you to die! I won't let you die! You are not allowed to die!"

"You see, to save the world, I may have to die." The Mind-Child looked thoughtful, suddenly owlish, and very old, and very wise. "Do you want me to be a boy or a girl?"

"Can you be both?"

"I think so, if I live."

"You must live! And we will play!" Claudia smiled; it was the universal womanly smile of forgiveness and delight.

The Mind-Child looked at Claudia, and then he looked at V, and he smiled, "If I die, Claudia, you shall live."

"Let us both live," said Claudia. "Then, we can play!"

The carnival world that was floating in the stars disappeared in a flash – an explosion, a tunnel of light, a whirling kaleidoscope.

And then there was nothing.

"We made it!" Alison whispered.

"Yes, we did," said Ken

Alison's hair had been singed, just a bit, she was flushed from excitement. The roar of the flames had been so loud it seemed it would drown out every thought. The heat had been tremendous. They ran, they stumbled, she was down on her hands and knees, flames licking close, the floor red hot, up they went. Ken picked her up, they ran, they ducked, they dodged, and then suddenly, they were on the other side of the fire. She could breathe again, the air was cool on her face. Oh, it was so delcious! Steam rose off both of them, radiant heat.

"Darling," Ken kissed her.

"Yes, oh, Ken, hold me!"

"Steamy," he whispered, nibbling at her lips.

"Yes, steamy, my love," she pressed her bright blind smile against his lips, "Oh, so steamy, my steamy love!"

And they went on, climbing down, ever deeper down.

Six floors down from the fire, they were creeping behind a louvered curtain wall that went along one side of an Olympic-size suspended swimming pool. On the other side of the curtain wall, on a party deck next to the pool, there were screams and howling from human puppets and the weird horrible cackling of zombie-bats. And music was playing too, a Strauss waltz. But in the mayhem, there was another sound.

"Somebody is crying," Alison whispered.

Ken listened. "Yes, you're right."

"A child, I think it's a child."

Ken listened. Yes, it did sound like it – a child, in the middle of the chaos, in the middle of all the noise, Alison had somehow heard the child. Ken held Alison close. He peeked out from between two sections of the curtain wall. Banners floated – "Congratulations, Frederick and Christina!" Trestle tables lay turned over, bottles lay everywhere, and bodies were strewn in every direction. One body was in what looked like a long, flowing wedding dress. Some of the bodies were "head splatters." They had no heads, just great gobs of blood and gray matter and goo. Many of the bodies were in tuxedoes or formal gowns. Zombie-people, mostly in tuxedoes and formal gowns, were milling around aimlessly; some were down on hands and knees, or on all fours, feasting on the dead. Ken blinked: again, he thought, how could this have happened, and so quickly, so totally? This morning had been a normal morning … 22 degrees C, a slight lemon-scented breeze … courtesy of …

One or two tables, with white table clothes, were still standing. Under one table, hidden by the tablecloth, would be a good place to hide. Yes, the sound was coming from under one of the tables. The wind, which was rising, lifted part of the table cloth. Ken caught a glimpse. A little girl was crouching under the trestle table, which had been laid out for a feast. She was hidden by the table cloth. All around the table were the puppet-people. Just a few feet away, one woman – in a beautiful off the shoulder silk turquoise dress – was on hands and knees and eating something, part of a body – it looked like some-body's thigh.

"Over there, Ken whispered to Alison, "The crying is coming from over there, from under a table."

At that moment, the zombie-woman stopped eating. She looked up and turned toward the table, blood dripping from her lips.

"Save her," Alison clutched Ken's arm, "Save the little girl." Somehow she knew it was a little girl.

"I'll have to make a dash for her. She's in the middle of all those … those things. People seem to have becom zombies."

"Go alone."

"But …"

"I'll wait right here."

"But …"

"I'll be okay, Ken, I'll be okay."

"I'll be right back!" Ken kissed Alison, and then he made a dash for it, thinking that this was totally foolhardy and would get them both killed, but thinking, too, that they had to save the child if they could, they would never be able to live with themselves if they hadn't at least tried, and that Alison had commanded him to do it – and her commands were to be obeyed – and as he dashed the zombie-people suddenly stopped, and, mouths hanging open and with empty eyes, they all focused on him, he could feel all the empty eyes, staring at him, focusing on him, he dashed by one of the bloodthirsty zombie-women – she was, he guessed about thirty, a blonde, but missing half her scalp, with green eyes, blank now, but bright green, and she was wearing a low-cut metallic emerald dress with a high slit – ancient Chinese style – up one side, and in normal circumstances she would have been considered, yes, beautiful. Blood foamed from her mouth and dribbled from her chin. She lunged for him. Ken punched her so hard it seemed her face exploded – like in a cartoon – but it was just a visual effect of the shock on her face and, as he raced past her, she staggered back and let out a high-pitched inhuman screech, and Ken could see all the zombie-people begin to lurch toward him in that disjointed evil way they had, staggering, mechanical. It was pretty horrible, just like in the movies. He dove under the table – on top of which he noticed was an enormous wedding cake – and found himself facing the little girl a blonde with curly hair, ringlets down both sides of her face, and a little wedding maid's dress soaked in blood; she was barefoot and she stared at him – eyes wide in fear – and Ken said, "Come on, honey, we've got to get you out of her," and he snatched her up with one arm, holding his pistol with the other, and he stood up, overturning the table and at that moment, as the table turned over – the giant white multi-storied cake went flying – and the table cloth fell away, he saw another child, a black girl, braided pigtails, pink ribbons in her hair, bright white bridesmaid's dress, eyes wide in terror, who had been hiding too, with the blonde, and Ken said, "Come on, run, come on, with me!"

The girl stared. She leaped up, and came running. Ken galloped, one girl under his arm, the other right beside him, and the zombie-people were closing in, and Ken fired the Colt this way, and that way, blazing away. He was aware out of the corner of his eye that two zombie-bats had been drawn by the ruckus. They were zooming down, and he could see, beyond the gathering zombie-people, the crisp blue water of the giant swimming pool, a few headless bodies floating here and there, naked and clothed, and the sky up above, reflecting in the pool, still a delicate blue in some places, where the dome still survived, a delicate springtime hazy Tiepolo blue, but mainly a stormy leaden color, like a giant bruise. Wham! He was hit by one of the zombie-bats, a glancing blow, talons or claws. He swung around, letting go of the blonde girl, and as he spun around, he was aware of the little black girl and the blonde girl colliding, falling down, then embracing each other, beginning to get up. Ken was lying on his back looking up at two – no, three – zombie-bats – plunging down toward him. He shot at the closest, the one that had slammed into him, shooting at it at point-blank range and the zombie-bat's face exploded – goo, blood, feathers and the great leathery wings, and it fell down, straight onto Ken, smothering him in a fetid revolting smell, and as this was happening, and all hell seemed to be breakng loose everywhere, Ken shouted to the two girls, "Run, run, run behind the curtain!"

Alison heard the chaos, realized that Ken was being attacked; she stepped out through a slit between the vertical louvers, from behind the curtain wall, hoping to act as a distraction, a decoy, and wham – a child ran into her and then another child ran into her, and she said, "Oh, you are two!"

"Yes!"

"Help!"

The children clung to her.

How did they understand so quickly that she was safe, that she was human, and that she was a friend?

She stroked their hair. Two children! How could she defend them? "Ken! Ken!"

"I'll be there. Just a minute!" It was a muffled cry, as if Ken were buried in a sea of porridge; what a strange nursery-rhyme image thought, Alison, pressing the two girls against her. She heard sounds of a struggle and then a scream – an inhuman scream. "Okay, let's go in here," and, holding onto the two girls, she slipped back through the vertical louvers, in behind the hanging wall, hoping that it would act as a shelter – even if just for a minute – and she crouched down, "Let's stay together, we'll make ourselves as small as we can! Can we do that?"

"Yes," the two girls whispered; their voices were tiny.

"Ken will be back. He'll help us!"

"Yes," the two voices were tearful. Alison tried to imagine what the two girls must have seen. She could imagine it only too easily. She crouched low, the girls were young, ten or eleven maybe, maybe eight or nine. So little time, just an instant, separates childhood from adolescence, and then adolescence from adulthood. Alison crouched low, her arms around the two children, protecting them with her body.

Then above her, she felt the fetid heavy flapping wings of a zombie-bat; she crouched down tighter, shielding the children, the children cried, Alison felt that the wings and claws and beak were close.

The claws brushed Alison's side, tore at her tunic. Alison pushed the children down, she swirled around, and she kicked, she punched, and she squirmed backward, she reached out for the children, both of them now behind her.

Alison leaped to her feet; she slammed out blindly with both fists; her fists sank into rotten leathery feathery flesh, like a spongy gelatinous mass; the giant wings enfolded her, the leathery bone of a wing hit her thigh, she felt the claws slashing at her tunic, she felt the giant feathery legs enclose her, she felt the ground slip from under her, her sandals leaving the ground. The fangs tore at the shoulder of her tunic. One of the children shouted something. It sounded like, "Look out!"

One of the children screamed.

Everything exploded.

Alison fell to the ground. The beast had disintegrated.

Vertigo, just for a second, she felt vertigo, as if she would throw up, the smell, the sensation, had been so noxious.

"Here, Alison," Ken was next to her, lifting her up, his lips brushing her forehead.

"The children?"

"Here!" Two voices sang out.

"We have to go, Alison." Ken's voice was urgent. "There are more of those things."

"Yes, we have to go." Alison took one of the girls and Ken took the other and Alison held onto Ken's arm, and he said, "We have to run," and as they began to run there was a great roaring sound, and the building – the giant deck containing the swimming pool and the promenade – was hit by a huge wind. Glass shattered everywhere.

"It's collapsing!" Ken whispered, next to her, his breath in her ear.

For Alison, it was a whirling explosion of sound and a sensation of great plates of glass shattering, and beams falling and walls imploding and generally the end of the world. Though she was plunged into darkness, she had the impression that life had never been so full of color and action, and of course, danger and suspense. It was confusing. Shouts, screams, and the trampling of feet, and Alison heard a great crashing from above.

"This way!"

Ken and one of the children were gone.

"What's happening?"

"This way," said a child tugging at her, "This way!"

"Yes, darling," Alison allowed herself to be led by the small hand, pulling her along, at the same time she tried to keep all her senses – hearing, smell, touch, sense of space – and a sixth sense if she had one – anything – on top alert like radar to protect her and the child. Thunderous impacts were everywhere, explosions, bursting, shattering, glass, steel, wind.

"Come on!"

"Yes, darling!" Submissive, allowing herself to be led by a child, Alison

Jonas, until a few hours ago the coolest, proudest personality on the Ethernet, a true snob, a … It almost made her want to laugh. The little hand tugged desperately. "Come on!"

"Yes, darling!" Led by the child, Alison ran; blindly, she ran.

Shots echoed.

"Over here, over here, Alison!" Ken sounded breathless. He was fighting something – but what? Alison was caught in her blindness – in the smothering silky black darkness – but she glimpsed, as if in her mind's eye, an image of Ken wrestling with some mad people, being overwhelmed, not able to get clear, not able to get in a shot, not able to fight his way free to help her – to help her and the child. And then he let off a ripple of shots, and he was free.

"Please, watch out!" the little girl, pulling Alison to one side.

"Yes, yes," Alison felt the girl's shoulder, the girl was clinging to her now, pushing her. A sensation of pigtails, pink ribbons. How do I know that? How do I know they're pink? Maybe it's just memory, imagination? Which way to go?

Never had Alison felt so helpless.

"Come on!" The girl tugged. Alison allowed herself to be pushed and pulled and guided. They ran, the two of them – and then, suddenly, Alison felt Ken's arm around her. He said, "Come on, my love, come on, in here!"

They went through a door.

It closed behind them.

The chaos died, was suddenly distant.

The air smelled different, fresher, and with an odor of fresh paint.

Behind her, behind the door, Alison could hear, the monstrous sounds screams, hollering, wailing, ululations and the roar of crashing steel and glass as the building began to collapse, beams falling, the great hall's glass bursting in, the wind rising – a tornado, it must be one of the tornadoes.

"Alison," Ken kissed her.

"Ken. And the children?"

"Here, with us!"

"What's your name?"

"Jessica."

Alison felt the little hand touch her shoulder and then her face, and she felt the child's breath and then her lips.

"And yours?"

"I'm Rachael. You're blind, you can't see." The little hand tightened on Alison's hand, "You're blind."

"Yes, I am, darling. I'm blind. You saved my life."

"Come on!" Ken tightened his grip.

"Where?"

"We just have to go, darling, we just have to keep moving."

Alison felt Ken's fingers under her chin; he tilted her face up; he kissed her.

"Yes, darling, you chaps lead, I'll follow." Alison allowed herself to be guided. And down they went, new stairs, new corridors, new stairs, broken stairs, intact stairs, and more broken stairs, toward the lower depths.

And then, on whatever level it was, Ken shouted, "Look out!"

WHAM!

Everything exploded.

WHAM!

Kit Candy blinked. The beach and the stars and the silent frothy sea and the hurdy-gurdy music – everything had disappeared. Boy, it made her dizzy, the way things could change in the blink of an eye!

"We're back," she said.

"Yes," said the President, "We're back."

"Yes," said Kat, the Centurion, "Here we are."

They were standing in the great underground cavern on the edge of the Mind-Sea, right where they had been before the Mind-Child had ordered them to 'play'.

No time at all had passed, or so it seemed, for the huge monster was still sloshing its way through the Mind-Sea, coming toward them, his great claws reaching out for V. Behind him came, just as they had been, the giant ghouls, the huge tentacles rising out of the Mind-Sea, and giant frothing grotesques of every kind, a catalog of all the monstrous creatures from every horror story ever told, from every horror movie ever seen.

"I am going to kill the Mind," said the Mind-Child. "I will die, but I will kill the Mind!"

"But you must not die," said Claudia, "You must not allow yourself to die."

The Mind-Child furrowed its brow, closed its eyes, sweat bubbled from its forehead, it clenched its small fists, it strained every nerve. It stared at the oncoming monsters. It cried out: "Die! World Mind that am I – Die!"

Time slowed down, but the monsters lumbered on, slower now. The huge monster roared. "Child, you are a fool! We have a new master now! Ha, ha, ha!"

"I want to help," Claudia stepped forward.

"No, you stand back, Claudia," the Mind-Child whispered, "I don't want to hurt you. But I want V to hold me."

V crouched down behind the Mind-Child and enfolded the Mind-Child in her arms, her claws crossed on his chest, as he stared at the Mind-Sea and at the advancing army of monstrosities, and V looked over his shoulder.

"Better now?" V whispered to him.

"Yes. Hold me tight!"

The Mind-Child shuddered. Steam rosee from its ears. "Die! World Mind! Die! I am you. You are me! Together we must die!"

The Mind-Child's hair stood up on end.

The Mind-Child's limbs went rigid.

The Mind-Child's eyes rolled back, leaving only the whites.

"Die! Die! Die!" The Mind-Child stretched its arms toward the Mind, sparks leaped off the Mind-Child's skin. Sparks leaped from the tips of its fingers. The Mind-Child went into convulsions, its head and arms and shoulders jerked this way and that. The words came out of its child's mouth as deep thunder, "Die, now, Die, all my nerves, all my sensors, all my circuits, all my programs – Die, Die, Die!"

Then the Mind-Child screamed. It was a heart-rending scream.

Steam rose from its little body.

The child body went limp, collapsing like a rag doll in V's arms.

V and Kat and Claire leaned over him. Three hybrids.

Kit came to help. A fourth hybrid.

The President and Miranda and Caliban stood, watching, as the monsters approached, still approached, but slower, slower. Now the monsters paused. Now they resumed their advance, awkwardly. On some of the grotesque faces, though, was strange quizzical expression.

"Will we have to fight?" Black Tarzan glanced at the President.

"I don't know," said the President.

"We are ready," said Clown.

"Yes, we're ready," whispered Geisha.

The Mind-Child was shaken by more convulsions.

Steam rose from its skin.

V cradled the Mind-Child.

Spittle dripped from its lips.

WHAM!

Sparks leaped from the walls. The ceilings trembled. Through the great cavern came a roaring sound. The Mind-Sea whirled and steamed, and boiled, geysers and ribbons of light shot upwards. The great monster, the virtual and yet real incarnation of the Foul Fiend, striding toward them through the turbulent liquid, staggered and stopped. The great monster screamed. It rubbed and scratched at its sides, it gouged at its eyes. It groaned, "What are you doing to me? Why are you doing this?"

It slowed, one giant leg stopped. In a flash the leg turned to stone, the other leg slowed. It turned to stone. The petrification turned everything a stony opaque gray; it raced up the monster's body like a flood of light. Everything froze. Lineaments of muscle and tendon and vein suddenly stood out, embossed, in stony relief, suddenly illuminated in sculptural clarity, as if chiseled by Michelangelo.

The monster let out a roar, strangled in mid-scream; the mouth remained open, teeth and tongue and lips petrifying into marble, the eyes were caught, still rolling, pupil and iris now turned to delicately sculpted lifeless grooves of white marble. The huge statue stood there, the multicolored Mind-Goo sloshing around its shins, strands of goo leaping toward the walls. Black birds suddenly appeared, flying around the giant statue, cawing, in triumph or in fear.

The army of demons and giant ghouls that had been marching with the monster, splashing through the Mind-Sea, thrashing their way toward V and the others, went into slow-motion, then came to a full stop; suddenly, as if a magic wand had been waved, they morphed into statues, or fell into pieces and collapsed into dust, flakes of dust running down like sand sifting through an invisible hand, or bits of dust like fluttering, like motes caught in a beam of sunlight, dancing in the phosphorous glow of the cavern. The giant tentacles groping out from the walls turned to stone, the faces trapped in stone became gargoyles, their eyes bulging, and their tongues sticking out, and some of them cracked, fell apart, while others remained in place, like grotesque remains from a giant Gothic cathedral. The ghouls that had been lurking nearby shrieked and fled.

"The Mind is dead," said V.

"Yes, it has stopped eating," the President touched the belt buckle and the inlaid key: now he wouldn't have to even try to use the NN-bombs; whatever happened, he wouldn't have to use them. But of course, the death of the Mind would throw humanity back into the Stone Age, or at least into pre-industrial times, if that has not already happened. Hundreds of millions – even billions – would die – of starvation …

V could feel it: the death of the World System that humans had created over the centuries and millennia. She glanced at Claire, whose mind voyaged freely within the World Mind as if she were the Queen of the World Mind. Claire nodded. The World Mind – that connected everything to everything and everyone to everyone – was sputtering, and dying. Individual neurons were turned off, synapses and neurotransmitters were shutting down. The vast ocean of gray matter was withering. The great tentacles were suddenly inert. The voracious gooey suckers dried up. There was no more bubbling acid to digest things. Suddenly the whole thing withered. The World Mind was truly dead.

Claudia cried out, "Help him!"

"The Mind-Child is dying." Kat knelt by him, still, after all of this, impeccable in her sleek black Centurion body armor.

The hybrids all took turns, Claire, and V, and Kat, and Miranda, and Kit, sending pulses of vibrant ultra-violet energy into the small body. The beautiful child was now sprawled over V's lap. Miranda knelt next to V.

On and on it went.

Each of them trying, each hybrid bathing the Mind-Child in the healing light, but still – nothing.

Claudia had been watching with a mixture of horror and fear. She leaned down and kissed the Mind-Child on the lips. "Don't die!"

The Mind-Child's eyes fluttered open.

Claudia's eyes lit up.

"I was very bad!" The Mind-Child blinked.

"No, you weren't bad," V looked down on the child.

"Yes, I asked you to kill Claudia." The child opened its arms. Claudia came into its arms and kissed the child on the cheek.

"You love me?" The child looked back and forth, at V, at Claudia, and one of its hands sought out Miranda's shoulder.

"Yes, of course, we love you."

And so a child was born. But the World Mind was dead – and all that was connected to it died too.

But …

V looked around. "The Mind is dead."

"Yes," said the President.

"But the Foul Fiend," V's eyes glowed, "He is not dead."

"So, this is not over."

"Not by a long shot."

PART FOUR – APOCALYPSE

CHAPTER 13 – COLLAPSE

All over the world, the same things happened. The domes protecting the elite of civilization, the Cosmos, collapsed.

Storms entered everywhere, rain, wind, desert sand. Moscow Domed City disintegrated under a vast pallor of smoke as huge fires swept in from Siberia.

Saint Petersburg Domed City and London Domed City fractured and fell apart under the impact of rising floodwaters.

Paris Domed City, in the desert, which was central France, imploded, and ceased to exist. The same was true in different ways for Tokyo, Beijing, Hanoi, Mumbai, and virtually every domed city around the world.

In the burbs and Deadlands, of course, things were even worse – the living dead, who had everywhere risen from their graves, rampaged among the living, killing and spreading havoc; the plague released by Norman C. Schleifer, had quickly begun to spread; food supplies everywhere dried up as the harvesting machines, the transformation machines, the transport conveyor belts ceased to function; and the weather, partially driven on by the Foul Fiend – now furious that the Mind had been snatched from his control – spun even farther out of control, tornadoes, hurricanes, mega-thunderstorms, and sandstorms swept over the world.

Everywhere the electricity had gone off. All machinery and almost all robots – except the non-mind-linked robots – ceased to function. Water ceased to flow; refrigeration ceased; food was no longer delivered or cooked or edible. Climate controls ceased to function.

All transport stopped. Virtually all communications ceased. Ships were lost, rudderless, and without power or navigation, at sea. Airships drifted or fell from the sky. The few satellites that had been still functioning – intermittently – ceased to transmit and went dead; some exploded or spun out of orbit or remained in orbit but dead and silent relics of an age that had now passed.

Everywhere people with mind implants, people connected to the Mind, those who still survived went mad as the Mind-Connect sent out a last spasm of energy, or their heads exploded in a geyser of blood, gristle, bone, and gray matter. Others, a few, as the Mind, in its agony, drained their brains, were emptied of all personality, and wandered like puppets, drooling at the mouth, eyes empty and slack, waiting for orders from the Mind – orders that would never come.

"Look out!"

WHAM!

The explosion left Alison stunned.

She crawled on her belly, "Ken! Jessica! Rachael!"

There was nothing but blackness and roaring sound all around her. She was crawling in sticky liquid, and she knew it was blood. There was a ringing in her ears, and she wondered if she was still alive, more important – where was Ken? Where was the child?

"I'm here," said the girl's voice: Jessica.

"Where?"

"Here!"

"I can't see, Jessica. I'm blind."

Alison groped toward the child's voice.

"I'm here."

"I'm coming."

"I'm scared."

"Don't be scared. I'm coming." Alison pushed aside what felt like a fragment of flesh, part of an arm, chewed up, all bloody, still warm, sticky. The silky throbbing blackness pressed down on Alison like a prison.

"I can't move." It was Jessica's voice, far away.

"I'll be right there."

Alison pushed herself toward the voice. Sound thundered around her. It was like being swept up in the surf, in a tsunami of sound. It seemed endless. Alison pushed ahead, belly-down, swimming in blood. Smear of blood, gooey, a leg, not attached to a body, the stench of death. And then a small hand grasped hers, and Alison felt her way along the child's body, and realized that Jessica was pinned under a body, a human body. For a horrible moment, she thought – Ken?

There were more shots.

Alison pushed the cadaver – away, a heavy torso, must have been a giant of a man – Jessica had been trapped tummy down, underneath. Alison whispered, "Are you okay?"

"Yes."

"Are any of the bad people around?"

"Yes." The girl's arms went around Alison's neck. Alison lay turned sideways, the two of them face-to-face. Alison felt the girl's breath on her lips.

"Let's lie very, very still," Alison whispered.

"Yes," the girl's arms tightened around her; the girl's face pressed against hers.

More shots, the thud of explosive shells, and the burst of flesh and bone and gristle. Then suddenly Ken was next to them. She felt him, his hand on her shoulder. "Let's go," he whispered.

Alison staggered to her feet, the little girl standing next to her, Alison's arm around her shoulder. "Where's Rachael?"

"With me, we've got to run. Can you run?"

"Yes, we can run."

"Yes, we can run," it was the girl's voice: Jessica.

Alison took Ken's arm, they ran.

And ran, and ran …

And all the time, through static, the Info-Flow earphone, still in Alison's ear, was emitting static, and occasional voices, talking of plague, Bubonic plague, of tornadoes, of ghouls, of zombies, of zombie-bats, of death.

And they ran, and ran, and ran.

It was still a long climb down.

"Here we'll go slowly, slowly," said Ken. He peered around. It was dark in most places; the emergency lights were on in some places, islands of dim, flickering light; in other places, even the emergency lights had already failed, and he had to grope, thinking: now we are all blind. All the human race is blind, too, with most of Info-Flows dead or fluttering into non-existence.

Yes, it was a long climb down.

Dead bodies and mad people were everywhere.

Some were totally insane, zombie-like, and dangerous. Ken shot three of those, point-blank range, right between the eyes. Alison held the children close. "Don't look!"

Shooting people made Ken feel awful, or, rather, he knew it would make him feel awful later, when things calmed down, if there was a later. But right now, in the urgency of action, and determined above all else to protect Alison and the children, Ken didn't feel much of anything, just a sweaty resolve. Pulling a trigger, he discovered, was easy. It was a frightening thought. Up to today, in Elysium, there had been little or no violence, certainly not up in the Cosmos sphere, the President-Leader had seen to that: no weapons, or few, in private hands, though virtually all Cosmos had military training and, if they needed to, could use a whole raft of weapons; but now … Elysium Heaven had turned into Hell, and it had only taken a few hours.

"You are a darling, darling," said Alison.

"I'm not really," Ken said, thinking back at the young adolescent – murderous and infected with some kind of intense glowing madness – that, just two minutes before, he had shot point-blank between the eyes. He thought too, for just a second, of his robot French maid, Annette, she of the tender touch and brilliant smile, waiting patiently in the cupboard; she was infinitely tactful and considerate; she who had never asked anything of him, but offered him her unconditional tenderness; she was not connected to the mind, and she had her own power source; she would wait in vain; she would be destroyed without knowing why; Ken Ivison would almost certainly never return. He thought too of his callow self, libidinous, just wanting to bed Alison because she was beautiful; of his callow self that had died only a few hours ago; now he would sacrifice his life easily for Alison, and he would sacrifice his life for the two children. It was suddenly so clear. God, I was a selfish bastard!

"You don't want to hurt people, I know," Alison was clinging to his arm, lightly, being considerate, attuned to his slightest doubt, his most trivial regret; under the storm of action, and behind his new macho adventurer façade, Ken at a half-conscious level was reproaching himself for the past two years, for even thinking of Annette, his obedient but smart and saucy French Maid Sex Toy, even when he had already become infatuated with Alison and obsessed by her; he had never realized before how fine Alison was, how brave, how intelligent: not only was she beautiful and spunky and glamorous and intelligent, but, underneath, she was a good person, an intensely moral person. Alison was stroking Jessica's hair; the little girl was clinging to Alison's waist while Rachael was holding Ken's elbow, leaving his hand free to fire the Colt.

"No regrets, Ken! No guilt! You are a hero," Alison gazed at him blindly,

"You are my Don Quixote, and I am your blind but faithful burden, Sancho Panza, a female Sancho Panza, and maybe not as wise as Sancho, but just the same I am a burden."

"No, you are what gives me hope, Alison. If it weren't for you, I'd be dead already. My life didn't mean anything – not until this moment."

"That's very nice, darling, but I don't believe it for an instant." Alison hitched Jessica up onto her hip.

"You're so pretty," Jessica said, putting her arms around Alison's neck.

Alison held the child closer. "Thank you, darling. You are more than pretty! I know it! Now close your eyes and just hold onto me."

"Come on, my little friend, Ken said, tightening his grip on Rachael's hand.

"I'm not letting go," said Rachael, "Not for anything."

"Good," Ken crouched down and looked the girl in the eyes, "We four are together forever – right?"

"Right!"

Ken had always thought the world he lived in was stable and solid, that, in spite of the threats and prophets of doom, it would continue as it had, on into the infinite future. But now he suddenly saw how fragile all that had been. Civilization was a thin patina on an abyss, reasonableness and rationality were illusions. Underneath, just a scratch away, lay madness, chaos, anarchy. This was truly the revelation, the apocalypse. On various floors, those people who were not totally mad or dead, were just wandering around in a daze, their eyes vacant and emptied of thought, their Mind-Links transmitting pure static, with what looked like an occasional deadly high-voltage impulse wave that fried the mind or exploded the victim's skull – whoosh!

Ken averted his eyes.

A few of the humans, though, were still aware, but dazed and confused. Some asked for help, some begged Ken to help them. Ken wanted to stop and help people, but he knew there was nothing he could do; with a blind woman and two children, he had his hands full.

Finally, Ken managed to get Alison and the girls down to the first floor, the main concourse, down in the Sub Level, just one level before you went truly underground.

He looked around for some entry into the world below, the "Mysterious Netherworld" as he used to call it, joking, on the Alison-and-Ken Show, "The dark side of our Cosmos Paradise."

Here on the main concourse – a mixed Sub and Cosmos area – the vista stretched off for two kilometers at least – shops were burning, some trees had wilted, windows were smashed, café tables were turned over, electro-vehicles were standing still or lying on their sides, and dead bodies were everywhere. Up above, the bat-like monsters were flying, swooping low, over parasols, umbrellas, palm trees, terrace awnings, hunting for victims.

Ken spotted a service doorway, a metal door, tucked away behind a row of tropical plants. The sign said, "Service Stairs E-43-20-B, for Emergencies only."

Ken led his little troop over to the door, behind the palms and ferns.

He tried to open the door. It was locked.

"Damn it."

"Ken …" Alison tugged, lightly at his arm, "Ken …"

Ken turned, and he heard it too: a rustling in the foliage. A large bat-like creature – oh, no, not one of those again – emerged from the foliage, pushing the giant ferns aside.

Ken pushed Alison behind him. "Keep very still, darling," he said, and he handed Rachael off to Alison.

"It's one of those things, isn't it?" She whispered.

"Yes."

Ken tightened his grip on the Colt. The zombie-bat stared at him. Ken stared back. For a moment, it seemed that a current of sympathy passed between them. Ken felt that behind the monstrosity, behind the beady evil little eyes, inside the misshapen monstrous body and behind the giant wings (how the hell could those things fly?), there was something else, someone else, someone dying to get out. He held the Colt steady. The beast leaped. Ken fired, but with the tip of one wing, the bat had knocked his aim off; the bullet hit a palm tree, thudding into the trunk with a dull sound.

"Oh, oh," Jessica whispered.

The bat-thing paused, very close now, and it stared at Ken. It opened its mouth; its crooked yellowish fangs dripped steamy liquid, little puffs of rabid foam.

The gun had jammed. After all, it was an antique, a prop. Ken tried desperately to unjam it. He pushed Alison away, "Crouch down, Alison, you and the kids!"

He would die before he let the thing get close to them.

But then he thought that, if he died, what then? Blind, Alison would be helpless, and so would the children. Should he shoot them? The gun didn't work. So he couldn't shoot them … Use the machete? He wouldn't be able to do it. Use the M-16, slung over his shoulder? No, he couldn't do that either.

The zombie-bat plunged.

Ken punched it in the snout. It howled, snapped its jaw shut, and stared at him with its small beady intensely evil eyes.

"Come and get me, you evil, foul smelly thing," Ken returned the stare, "come and get me, and I'll give you a lesson you'll never forget. Just try, come on, come on …!"

The zombie-bat charged.

Ken leaped aside and smashed it across the eyes with the Colt, and he whacked it on the temple.

The zombie-bat reeled back, its wings flapping, sending out a foul odor, and odor of death.

Time slowed. The huge wings flapped, the claws groped at empty space, the jaws opening and shutting.

"Come on, you foul piece of filth, come on!" Ken tensed every single muscle; he felt he could strangle the infernal creature with his bare hands.

The zombie-bat snarled. Yellow foam bubbled and streamed from between its fangs.

"Come on, you coward!" Ken pulled the machete from its sheath, "It's you or me," Ken whispered, "And it's not going to be me!"

Angela Balzac sat, up on the roof, in the big overstuffed, rose-patterned chair, next to the two dead people – Laura and Little Kiddo – who were ensconced side by side deep in their own big overstuffed chair – and they were watching the spectacular storms and lighting in the Great Dome of Elysium City, a regular son-et-lumière where some lights still shone in the soaring Elysium towers, and on the Elysium Dome, and in a few airships which seemed to still be operating, and then, poof, all the lights went off.

Every single light disappeared.

Angela leaned forward: What had happened?

The Dome was now lit only by flashes of natural lightning and by the moon, which, now and again, appeared from behind monstrous dark whirling clouds.

"Electricity's gone," Angela said, thinking as she did so that talking to these two friendly dead people seemed now to be entirely normal. I'm probably insane or dreaming all this and I'll wake up and Norman Schleifer will be upstairs picking his nose and scratching his crotch and all will be well with the miserable unchanging shitty ordinary world which I actually rather enjoyed, thank you very much.

She glanced around. The Crump Tower – an old – and hopeless – Burb redevelopment scheme – was totally dark. The glow from the few streetlights had disappeared. The flickering neon over the old Cheap Mart at the corner was dead. In fact, the lights had gone off everywhere, in Elysium, out in the Burbs.

"Wow! Everything is dead!"

The Laura mummy clicked her tongue, making a clack-clack whirring cicada-like sound, which Angela had learned to recognize as 'Yes!' Kiddo, the little skeleton, made a strangled noise, like a mewling kitten, rattled a few of his bones, and snuggled closer to Laura the mummy. For comfort, Angela figured.

Angela stood up and stretched, and, as she did so, she saw something out of the corner of her eye. "Oh, boy," she said, "Look at that!"

Laura, the mummy, struggled to her feet, and Kiddo followed her. A huge black cloud had taken a funnel shape and had touched down. It was a tornado.

In the dim, flickering light, it was difficult to estimate distances, but Angela figured the thing must be about twenty or thirty miles away, and if it was that far away, why, then the tornado must be ten miles across, something like that. Maybe more.

"We'd better keep an eye on it," Angela said, "And if it gets any closer, I think we head down to the basement, if we can get to the basement."

The mummy laid her mummified hand on Angela's arm and clicked a quick series of rattling clicks: Yes!

Angela and Laura shifted the big stuffed chairs around so they could watch the monster storm and escape in time if it decided to head toward them. Then they sat down, settling into their respective chairs. Kiddo snuggled close to Laura.

Angela thought that if she had anything to offer to her dead friends – food or drink – she would offer it, but she didn't have anything and, besides, the dead probably didn't eat or drink, though it would be interesting to see what happened if they did.

The monster storm seemed to be headed straight toward Elysium and the half-ruined dome. Boy, this might turn out to be spectacular!

She felt an itch on her arm, and without thinking, she scratched it. Then she looked down. It was an open sore; it was exuding pus. She held her breath. Another one appeared; then another appeared, on the back of her hand.

Angela stood up. She went to the edge of the roof and looked down. Six floors down and nothing to break her fall.

The Laura mummy made a quizzical click-click-click sound.

Angela looked back. "Bye, guys, it's been nice knowing you!" She smiled and waved.

And then – she leaped.

"This is just too exquisite!" Mrs. Rosenthal was on her fifth Martini, well it seemed like her fifth Martini. She had perhaps at some point lost count, and she was enjoying it maybe just a bit too much, though she had also had something to eat, making sure that she didn't get too drunk.

The big bat-like creature had kept smashing itself against the window. It had hurt itself, poor thing, and though she had been tempted to go out onto the balcony and help it, she had decided against it. The creature looked rather nasty and messy, and discretion was after all the better part of valor as her late husband Harvey Terazonoh had more than once pointed out, when Ms. Rosenthal had been tempted by some adventure travel expedition when such things as travel still existed.

The creature had flopped about and had lain still, feebly clawing at the armored glass, and then it just lay there. Maybe it was dying, or maybe it was just tired, or maybe it was waiting for her to get curious and …

Munch! Crunch!

Well, curiosity killed the cat!

Outside the air had grown darker and dimmer and then suddenly the remaining lights went out. All over Elysium, there was not a light to be seen, and the hum of the ventilators which had still been present ceased, and there was deadening silence which was, strangely, hard to bear.

Mrs. Rosenthal walked to the window and stood and looked out on the great city of Elysium. All the twinkling lights had gone. All the floating

Ad-Ships had gone. All the drones, sparkling little things selling everything under the sun, had gone. Some of the buildings had collapsed, and particularly downtown, there was a great void where many tall buildings used to soar up toward the dome, but, other than that, most of the buildings were still standing. Now, in the dim light, they looked like slender gray spires of dead stone, like giant gravestones or leftover totems of some primitive and forgotten religion. It was a melancholy sight.

Mrs. Rosenthal thought she had a choice. She could wait here until whatever was going to happen happened, or she could venture out, and see for herself, up close, what had become of the world.

Curiosity killed the cat!

She walked up and down, and she decided that, just perhaps, it would be better to go out and face destiny rather than waiting for it to come and face her. Then it occurred to her that it would be a very long climb down, and an even worse climb up, if she decided to retreat.

Still, nothing ventured, nothing gained. She squared her shoulders, and she opened the flat door. There was no one in the corridor, no one at all. She put a book, yes, an old-fashioned book, between the door and the doorframe so that the door could not close.

I will come back, I think I will come back, she said to herself. And she set off on her adventure. Did they have stairs in this building? She thought for just a second. Yes, there were stairs, and the doors were manual! What a miracle! Mrs. Rosenthal found the stairs and began the long climb down.

Not a single light was burning – anywhere. Demi Pfeiffer stood on the landing deck and, using her non-electronic, backup binoculars, peered out over the city. A few minutes ago, the lights had gone out everywhere; and all the remaining electrical instruments and appliances, anything connected to the Mind, had died.

"The Mind is dead, I think that's what it is," she said, half to herself, "And that could mean we've won, or we've lost." She scanned downtown: no more buildings were falling, no more skyscrapers were being devoured, or at least, so it seemed. At the tip of the old underlying invisible island, there was merely a smoky gray twilight void – what the Mind had eaten. Maybe V had killed the Mind, or maybe …

"Ma'am," one of the women Centurions, Lieutenant Qureshi, put her gloved hand on Demi's sleeve. "Ma'am, I think you'd better have a look at this."

Demi lowered the binoculars, and turned. The Centurions were all looking in one direction. Lieutenant Qureshi pointed. Demi squinted, for just a second. She couldn't be seeing what she was seeing!

The remaining arc of the Dome on the west side was imploding, huge fragments were breaking away, twirling, twisting, rising, falling, and the whole west side looked like it was disintegrating. Then she understood. Oh, damn, she thought, oh, damn! It was the Superstorm, the long-awaited Superstorm, a huge tornado, perhaps two miles across at the base; it was smashing its way through the remnants of the shattered Dome. Demi glanced at the vertijet. It was still there, faithful, intact, a glorious bit of antique machinery.

"Ma'am?"

"Lieutenant Qureshi," Demi looked into the young woman's big dark eyes; Demi hesitated. What am I going to say, and what am I going to do?

"Ma'am, I believe that thing is headed, or it may be headed, toward us."

"Yes, Lieutenant, you're right. Come." Demi motioned with one hand, and she and the lieutenant went over to the others. They all turned to look toward her; she now seemed, strangely, to incarnate civil authority, the last bastion of order and of the state, though she was none of these things.

"We have to protect the vertijet," Demi said, "And we have to protect ourselves. Do you agree?"

"Yes," they all nodded.

"I intend to take off and to try to evade the storm, just stay away from it. Up here, it's too vulnerable, and there's no safe place to store it."

"Yes."

"Some can come with me, not too many, I need to keep the vertijet light. Others, well, they should find shelter farther down, and in the central core of the building, or below ground – below ground would be best, if there is time. Meantime, we'll watch the progress of the storm. And when the moment comes, if it comes, I'll take off. But I'm going to come back here or as close as possible to this position – but quite possibly down on ground level – when this is over. Does everybody agree?"

"Yes," they all nodded.

There was a giant distant echoing boom as a huge slab of the remaining Dome collapsed, sliding down, in a massive tangled avalanche of cables and sidings and platforms, and taking many buildings with it.

And there it was, clear to see, in all its glory, the giant tornado Superstorm.

"It must be three kilometers across at the base," Lieutenant Qureshi had taken the binoculars.

"Yes, I'd say so." Demi Pfeiffer had an instant of visionary horror: she saw – actually saw – what would happen when the storm plowed into the buildings.

Already everything seemed to be swept up in it.

Demi wondered if there would be any safe place for the vertijet. Well, she would just have to find a safe place!

She said, "Who wants to come? Who wants to stay? I can take, at maximum, five people. I have to keep it light."

Five hands went up. The other Centurions just nodded. "We'll be here when you get back, or, more likely, down below, at Krupp Plaza," Lieutenant Qureshi said; she handed back the binoculars and saluted.

"Good. I'll check Krupp Plaza first." Demi shook hands with each of them.

Two minutes later, the vertijet took off.

Below, the remaining five Centurions waved. Demi could see Lieutenant Qureshi – a beautiful woman – looking up, bright smile in the darkening air. Demi dipped the wings and flashed the lights.

Then she zoomed away, zigzagging, looking for shelter. The question was – was there any shelter in this place?

A flock of crows were pecking at plague corpses in a trash-strewn alleyway in the Burb, not far from where Angela and Laura Levitt and Kiddo had been sitting in their stuffed chairs on the rooftop, and not far from Norman Schleifer's festering and bubbling cadaver where maggots were already hatching, squirming, and blindly swimming in putrid dissolving flesh, eager to get to work to clean up the mess the plague had made.

The crows looked up.

Bits of paper and tin cans and aluminum foil and ribbons of black plastic began to swirl in small eddies of wind; dust devils rose up and danced, carrying desert sand up out of the gutters and runnels.

One of the rotting corpses seemed to wave its hand and open its eyes – but this was only an effect of the rising wind and change in air pressure.

The crows rose quickly and cawed, and then, before they could scatter to cover, they were swept up in the dark funneling wind and carried toward the shattered dome of Elysium.

When the west wall of the Dome shattered inward, the crows went with it, cawing, and trying, desperately to ride the waves and not be splattered apart by the force of the winds now in excess of 500 kilometers an hour.

Some of the birds made it, and managed to flutter to the ground, finding shelter in the lee of a ruined building. Others were smashed against skyscraper cornices, retaining walls, air-bridges, and ruined hanging gardens; their blood and guts disintegrated into a spray, entering the air, and falling, twirling in the form of mist, like an aerosol spray, to the ground. Soon the survivors of the zombie-bat invasion – which was still going on – and the survivors of the take-over of the Mind by the Boy and, the survivors of the final implosion of the Mind, those last survivors would soon be coughing, and bubbling up their guts, their skin festering into a swirling maelstrom of pus, victims of the plague.

And so the Neo-Bubonic spread, north and south, east and west, and so, too, it spread from continent to continent.

Nowhere was safe.

At 6 pm, as the Super-Tornado roared through the shattered wall of the Dome, it hit the first row of slender towers and exploded all the windows and sucked out all the furniture and people and bodies, ripped out wires and cables. The wires and cables lashed and slashed in all directions, and slammed against remaining wall bulwarks. Some of the buildings were totally sucked into absolute oblivion, swept up, split in half, brushed aside, and smashed into a million fragments.

The Tornado chewed its way through midtown; it ripped up everything; nothing could resist it. Bridges and walkways collapsed; hanging gardens and concourses flew into a gazillion pieces; soaring skyscrapers and domed pavilions imploded. People and animals and robots and vehicles were swept up, twirled around, dropped, and dashed to bits, splattered on facades, on pavements, on twisted steel girders, on wrought-iron lampposts, on cobblestone pathways.

The tornado sucked up water from the two rivers, and it smashed holes in the barriers and dams that were meant to keep the Atlantic at bay. The change in air pressure, plunging to a record low, aggravated an already high tide and the Atlantic surged into the lower reaches of Elysium, sweeping through the Religious Underground and lapping at the lower reaches of the Sin Zone, bubbling along rue St-Denis, reaching almost as far as the ruins of the Jean Genet Electro Bordello.

The main Atlantic Retaining Wall, weakened, showed signs of giving way; ominous cracks opened up, snaking up from its foundations.

For Mrs. Rosenthal, the day got more and more interesting. After she left her apartment, she had made her way down the stairs. Since there were ruins and rather nasty creatures everywhere, she was forced to take a variety of stairs, and quite a few detours, and she had to traverse a great number of concourses and ruined floating pavilions and shopping oases.

She caught glimpses of a great many those unpleasant flying creatures. She encountered lots of dead people – which was rather upsetting – and some people who had apparently gone mad and become, it seemed, sort of wandering soulless robots. She decided it must be the mind implants. If the Mind had gone crazy, then it would drive everybody who was connected crazy too. Somehow she had avoided trouble all the way down, except in one shopping corridor where she had been accosted by a number of drooling mindless people – dressed like ordinary shoppers which made it rather disconcerting to see them acting like jerky discombobulated puppets – and she had been very lucky, on that occasion, to find that there was a still-functioning robot bouncer, apparently attached to the Scarlet Oasis Night Club, and the bouncer was still, strangely, given the way things were degenerating, functioning fully and as he said of himself "at the very top of my game" so he had quickly eliminated the threat, picking up some of the zombies and tossing them over the parapet, so that they went hurtling down toward the Silver Valley concourse, perhaps twenty stories below. Most of them didn't even shout or scream, they just fell, and splattered, far, far below. Mrs. Rosenthal looked over the parapet; it was all very impressive, and, truth be told, quite gory.

"Thank you very much, Cedric," she said.

"You are very welcome, ma'am, always glad to help." Cedric saluted her with great courtesy, and she gave him a rather flirtatious wave as she went on her way.

When Mrs. Rosenthal came to Spa and Recreation Level Number Four, she decided to explore a bit, and when she came to the Total Remake Beauty Salon, she entered, thinking it might be good to stock up on shampoo or face cream, just in case, and she was particularly impressed – and intrigued – by the two mummies sitting in the front lobby; they looked like young women who had been sculpted in smooth golden bio-mud. They had no eyes, no mouths, no ears, nor any other facial features, but they had nostrils and apparently could breathe. They also had legs and arms, which was convenient for moving them about and placing them in a variety of poses, she supposed, though, otherwise, they looked like your classic museum or cartoon mummy, except they were utterly smooth, no wrapping or bandages to be seen.

"What are these things," Mrs. Rosenthal turned to the pleasant young Sub who seemed to be an attendant, "Are they a new kind of display robot? Or are they a collector's item? They're rather pretty."

Sub Natasha explained that the two mummies were actually living human beings, female Cosmos of the Stratospheric Strata, Jill Hakim and Julia Lilly; and that they had been having a full facial retro-refit when the power failed and the robot aestheticians – who had just sprayed on the super-active bio-mask restructuring and purifying fluid – failed; and that this had made it impossible to remove the bio-masks and that the bio-masks had taken on a life of their own – presumably considering it their mission to do a total make-over since the 'stop' order had not come – and so the material had prolifer-ated and multiplied and spread all over the two bodies – literally all over and everywhere – and merged with the bodies, so that was what the two ladies had become; it was awful, but there was nothing she could do.

"That is most interesting," said Mrs. Rosenthal, "And you have stayed to help them."

"Yes," said Natasha, and she explained that with all the chaos going on everywhere and with no family to go to, she had decided to stay and try to help the two creatures, even though both of them were very persnickety and difficult upper-class trophy Eye Candy Cosmos Bimbos. "Impossible to please, really," Natasha sighed.

"I see," said Mrs. Rosenthal, "Well, I've met some like that."

"Yes, I mean, I don't want to criticize Cosmos, but …"

"Don't even think about apologizing. You are quite right to criticize! I am sure these two were total ball-breakers of the classic spoiled utterly entitled bubblehead kind. Perhaps there is such a thing as poetic justice, Natasha, though I've always tended to doubt it." Mrs. Rosenthal looked down at the two mummies, now so polished you could almost see your reflection, "Well, then, Natasha, dear, what's next?"

"Well," Natasha hesitated; after all, Mrs. Rosenthal was clearly a very upper-class Cosmos, "Well …"

"Go ahead, dear," said Mrs. Rosenthal, and she put a friendly hand on Natasha's shoulder.

"Well, then, Mrs. Rosenthal," Natasha began, and she explained to Mrs. Rosenthal that she would have to cut a mouth for the two mummies so that at least they could eat and also carve out a few other orifices – Natasha blushed, saying this – so that the two mummies could exercise their basic bodily functions, and survive and, if possible, maybe even enjoy life. Sex might even be possible.

"That's an admirable project," said Mrs. Rosenthal.

"Thank you." Natasha blushed.

"And, I must say, it sounds like fun! Perhaps I can help," Mrs. Rosenthal thought this was all very interesting, and she did have more than a bit of a medical and scientific background, from her days as a Cosmos Allied Forces Military Doctor-Nurse during the last China-Russia War. "We can use those scalpels and knives," she said, "and then cauterize the openings or wounds, as it were, with cauterizing oil or antiseptic. We shall make them into true works of art. It will be a lark, rather like doing an autopsy or vivisection in medical school. Just like old times!"

So together – working in the dim half-light of the spa and doing everything manually – Natasha and Mrs. Rosenthal provided the two mummies, Jill Mummy and Julia Mummy, with an appropriate number of minimalist, barely perceptible, vital orifices. The ears were relatively easy, just a small hole for each ear, though the ears themselves remained invisible, dissolved as they were into the bio-smoothness. The mummies could hardly object since, with their mouths sealed, it was impossible to talk, though, at certain crucial moments, they did oink.

"Oink!"

"Oink!"

The operations took a bit of time, "Now, turn over on your tummy, dear, yes, that's right, spread your legs, this won't take a moment."

"Oink! Oink!"

Together Mrs. Rosenthal and Natasha made a very effective team. And the mummies were frightened enough to allow themselves to be turned over, turned over again, and again, and generally manhandled.

"Oink!"

"Oink!"

The mummies' new skin, Mrs. Rosenthal noticed, was slippery and smooth as silk and without a single blemish, utter perfection, and quite beautiful, really. She ran her hand over the curve of a shapely mummy backside and then put her hand to her own cheek – well, not bad …

The eyes promised to be the most difficult feature because Mrs. Rosenthal and Natasha had to be careful not to damage the eyelids and because the bio-mask material grew over each incision very quickly so that all their careful work instantly disappeared.

"We may have to give up on the eyes," Mrs. Rosenthal put down her scalpel.

"Yes," said Natasha, with a sigh.

The two mummies motioned and struggled to explain, gesticulating and pointing and oinking.

"Oink! Oink!"

"Oink! Oink!"

"Oh, I see," said Mrs. Rosenthal. Yes, it obvious. The mummies could see quite well, even though their eyes, hidden under a one-way transparent, smooth bio-surface, were totally invisible to outsiders.

"Well, it seems, Natasha, that our two mummies – or mannequins – don't need eyes," said Mrs. Rosenthal, smiling at Natasha.

"Whew, that does make it easier." Natasha's own dark eyes flashed at Mrs. Rosenthal, and Mrs. Rosenthal thought that Natasha was a very pretty girl indeed.

In fact, where the mummies' eyes were supposed to be, there was nothing, just a blank smooth surface, and the merest suggestion of a bridge of a nose. It was all very abstract, really. The bio-mask fluid seemed to have stabilized, and become its own kind of living flesh, and the two mummies – hard to tell which was which – they looked exactly alike – presented surfaces that had become ultra-smooth and without a single flaw; they were entirely featureless, and polished, a deep tan color, like perfectly burnished toffee or brass or copper, like metal mummies, except they had arms and legs and even hands, though there were thick webs between the fingers and toes. Their mouths were mere slits, totally invisible when the mouth was closed. And, somehow, the teeth and gums and tongue had taken on the color of the bio-mask, deeply tanned, something between copper and gold.

"Natasha, I think they should be allowed to see themselves."

"Do you think that is wise?"

"Well, they will discover what they have become sooner or later, and given present circumstances, perhaps sooner is better than later."

"Yes, you are right, Mrs. Rosenthal."

They helped the two mummies stand up, and they guided them over to the full-length mirror.

They certainly do look like store mannequins, thought Mrs. Rosenthal. And how they react to the mirror will definitely be interesting. I'm not sure I would like to be a spoiled bitch Cosmos Princess Bubblehead and go for a facial and then wake up to find I have become an abstract, highly polished metallic sculpture by some ancient and primitive artist. The two of them could certainly be idols in an ancient pagan temple. Or, yes, they could serve as floor displays in some upscale shop. Now, that was a nice thought. Perhaps Natasha and I can organize some sort of art and design exhibition.

"So, darlings, this is what you are now," she said, swinging the mirror around so the two girls could see themselves, full-frontal and all at once, in their new golden-tan, perfect, faceless splendor.

In the Sin Zone, on rue St-Denis, about two meters above the new high watermark, with the salty, polluted Atlantic lapping at his toes, Deputy Police Chief and SWAT team leader – and lead torturer and interrogator – Colonel Bradley Hubert Rankin was lying, sprawled, dead and dismembered on the cobblestones; he had been attacked by one of the living dead recently roused from eternal slumber by the Spirit of the Boy.

The living dead, in this case, turned out to be a recently slaughtered and very annoyed and beautiful Cosmos First Class, Lyse Saint-Ross.

Lyse had just been dead for a few minutes – maybe seconds – down in the coal cellar where she had taken refuge, when she rose again. In fact, she rose so quickly from the dead that she terrified the two ghouls who had only begun to feast on her, just getting a few bites into her right leg. "Get away from me, you little buggers!" Those were her first words. The ghouls had not had time to get to her vocal cords or tongue. They were terrified – and scattered and then turned and stared.

Lyse Saint-Ross was shocked to find herself rising from the dead.

"This is disgusting!" She got to her feet and looked down at herself, she saw that her left leg – still very shapely – had been badly gnawed on, two diagonal slash scars like fashionable slits in old-fashioned jeans, and that her throat had been cut, which had left a huge ugly splash of blood, mixed with coal dust, on what remained of her catsuit, rags essentially. Yes, alas, that very exclusive black bio-skin brocade catsuit had been reduced to a shadow of itself. In fact, on closer inspection, she discovered that she was more or less naked, covered in glittery coal dust, blood, decorative feathers, ghoul drool, and not much else. Her high-heeled patent leather shoes were still there, on her feet, but absolutely filthy with blood, gore, and coal dust. It was glamorous in a sort of slumming neo-punk neo-Goth anarchist schoolyard-initiation sort of way, but that was no consolation. Lyse turned and stared at the ghouls, who were crouching and trembling nearby. "Shoo, shoo, go away, you evil little monsters!"

The ghouls scattered, squeaking, and yowling.

Where, she wondered, was her savior? Well, her *would-be* savior, poor fellow; he had failed, but he had certainly tried, and he had been *so* brave. Ah, there he was! She walked, rather stiffly, over to the dead street acrobat who was lying next to a big heap of coal. *Real coal* – my God! They really did go in for authenticity down here in the Sin Zone!

"Oh, dear!" Lyse put her hand to her mouth. "Oh, dear!"

Guy Tulip was too much of a mess to be properly resurrected. He didn't have any legs, and his head had been torn off and separated from his body.

Lyse knelt next to him. Strangely she could see quite well in the penumbra of the coal cellar; she wondered if perhaps this was one of the perks of being dead and resurrected: You could see in the dark.

"Guy?" she knelt down and put her face close to his half-skull, tempted to pick it up as Hamlet had done with Yorick's skull, and improvise some sort of melancholy metaphysical soliloquy, but Guy's skull was fresh, covered in ragged flesh, and very messy. Not at all poetic. His eyes opened, and he blinked at her. He couldn't talk. His tongue and most of his jaw were gone. But he did somehow manage a mental message, "Go, Lyse, go out into the light. The Boy has asked us to rise again. You can rise. I cannot rise."

Lyse stroked his blood-matted hair. He had been oh so brave, and oh so gallant, even if he was a Sub. He really didn't have to try to defend her. He could have just saved himself.

"Goodbye, Guy Tulip, you were a true gentleman," she said; she kissed the top of his blood-soaked head, and whispered, "My hero!"

Then she stood up, wondering at the whole thing. Being dead was an utterly new experience, and being risen from the dead was something she had not at all expected. Cosmos education and training were quite comprehensive and rigorous, but were uncompromisingly secular and did not really tell you how to behave or what to do when you were dead and, even more complicated, what to do if you were, in some strange way, risen from the dead. Well, there's always a first time!

Somebody called "The Boy," whatever or whoever he was, was chattering in her head about killing all the living, taking revenge upon people, massacring everybody, and etc.

"Shut up," Lyse said. Like most Cosmos First Class she was not religious, in fact, Lyse was intensely, even aggressively secular; she didn't believe in the supernatural; and, in general, she did not take kindly to taking orders, not from anybody, "Shut up and go away."

"I feel hurt," said the Boy, "Ungrateful wench, after all, I resurrected you!"

"Sorry, but I don't care a rat's ass." Lyse felt this Boy fellow was very annoying, "As far as I know, I was quite happy dead."

"You are a spoiled bitch!"

"I know."

"Hopeless …" the Boy's voice trailed off, "Not even worth arguing with!"

Getting down on her hands and knees, Lyse crawled up the coal chute and squeezed and squirmed her way out of the opening. She stood up in the narrow alleyway; staring around, she idly made a feeble effort at brushing herself off. Her breasts and belly were sticky with blood and glittery with coal dust. The dim, twilight-like air smelled of teargas, laser strikes, burned flesh, blood, burned wood, singed steel and paint, and old-fashioned gunpowder.

She headed out to the main street.

All the neon and hologram lights were off.

Lyse stopped and considered: This must mean the world was at an end; the World Mind would not permit such a lapse of power and spectacle. So, the World Mind must, most probably, be dead – what an untoward thought!

A robot gendarme, somehow still operating, probably on independent batteries and with no Mind-linkage, was standing at the corner. "Do you need directions, madam?" he saluted.

"No, thank you, officer," she said; her voice was slightly throaty, and it gurgled in a flirtatious way, she thought, this was probably because it had been slashed. Strangely, the vocal cords and tongue still seemed to be working.

"Have an enjoyable evening, then, madam," the gendarme saluted smartly and continued on his rounds.

The gaslights were still burning, but the neon and all the other electric lights seemed to be out except in the Café Deux Magots, which sparkled, a distant island of cheery light in a sea of gray dimness.

Lyse decided to head there, perhaps she could sit down and think about her situation. Her fiancée would be broken-hearted – perhaps – to know she was dead; but, on second thought perhaps not: he was such an egoistic, non-committal, narcissistic Peter Pan type, a typical Cosmos *puer aeternus,* a merchant banker eternal little boy, frenetically active here there and every-where, juggling immense virtual fortunes, flitting from domed city to domed city making complex incomprehensible deals and feeling all puffed up and very important. Yes, he might not regret her passing at all; he might even feel liberated. Any human attachment is, at least potentially, a ball-and-chain. And, in recent weeks, she could feel his resistance and panic rising as the wed-ding date approached. She could just see him now, poor dear Geoffrey, wiping his brow, and bursting out, "Whew, I escaped!" And he'd go out drinking with the boys. He was a true lad, he was, which, at one point, she had found attractive. But, then, on closer acquaintance … not so attractive: There was a certain coarseness of sensibility, a crudeness in the way he saw things; and, then, there was his rather limited imagination, and, in truth, what increas-ingly seemed, to her, to be his utter inability to empathize with other people, Subs, or Burbites, Robots, or just plain Cosmos people … She wondered if any coms were working. Her wrist com, she noticed, was dead.

She noticed too that there were various members of the killer SWAT team lying around, cadavers. Their killing spree had obviously come to an end. They had not risen. Most of them had lost their heads. So it would be, perhaps, difficult for them to rise, headless, from the dead – rather like poor Guy Tulip. Was a brain necessary, Lyse wondered, if one were – successfully – to rise again? Some people she knew seemed to have gotten along quite well without brains – even when alive.

One officer was lying wounded, and not dead, on the cobblestones under a flickering gas lamp, at the edge of a sort of flood of water. Perhaps a water main had burst. He was trying to reach his laser gun, which was lying just beyond his grasp. He had been wounded in one leg, and in the chest. Lyse somehow realized that this was the officer who had set off the massacre; she somehow intuited that he was a sadistic torturer – a vision of a young woman, a glamorous redhead, being repeatedly raped and then morphed into a bald porno-clown flashed through her mind. How strange! Being dead, or risen from the dead and yet dead, was like being a visionary. She might have to reconsider some of her ideas about religion. The officer's name, she realized, was Rankin, Colonel Rankin.

Lyse knelt next to the Colonel. His face looked up at her. "You freak, what are you?"

Lyse realized that, covered in blood and coal dust and with her throat slashed, she must look a frightful sight, clownish perhaps, certainly disreputable, not an agreeable apparition at all.

"I am death," she said, "Well, properly speaking, I am dead – and largely, I think, because of you."

"Give me my fucking gun!"

"Why?"

"Because I'm going to kill you and all your fucking kind."

"Okay." Lyse smiled, and, still crouching, she reached out and picked up the gun, balanced it in her hand, gazed at Rankin for a second, considered briefly, then vaporized the top of his skull. At the last moment, his forehead creased, and his blue eyes looked startled. It was rather stupid of him, she thought, announcing his murderous intent before she'd handed him the gun. Oh, well, there's no accounting … Perhaps it was his arrogance. Even dying, he thought he was invulnerable, above the law.

She stood up and used the laser gun to sever his arms and legs and liquefy his jaw. She didn't want him to rise again and come running after her. And she didn't want him yacking at her, or at anybody else. *Zap! Zap! Zap!* She reduced his body to a smoking shell, rib cage, hip bone, intestines, all exposed. Finally, she zapped his neck – *zap, zap, zap* – separating his head from his torso; and kicked the head away for good measure. Good, that's that!

"Well done!" said the Boy's voice, "I knew you'd come round."

"I didn't do it for you."

"No?"

"No. Definitely not."

"Witch! Bitch! Female abomination!"

"My killing spree is at an end, I think," Lyse said, inwardly, to the Boy. She looked down at the dead body – and then at the head. One eyeball protruded from the smoldering skull, it was bloody and glassy but it had not yet burst. It stared and blinked.

"I think I'll keep your laser, Colonel, if you don't mind." Lyse vaporized the blinking eye – it exploded with a gooey bursting plop. She took one last look at the scattered cadaver; no, the Colonel would not rise, there was nothing much left to rise; she walked away, leaving the smoking pile of bone and gristle and excrement and flesh still simmering on the damp black cobblestones under the gaslight, at the edge of the lapping water. The pile of offal that had once been Colonel Bradley Hubert Rankin didn't smell so good.

She came to the Café Deux Magots. It was still open, and, yes, the lights, amazingly, were all on. She went up to the bar and laid the laser sideways on the bar top next to a small stack of hard-boiled eggs. There seemed to be no living people around whom she could kill. In any case, she didn't intend to kill anyone, no matter what "the Boy" said. Colonel Rankin had been a special case; he deserved it. Lyse wondered what had become of the redhead he had morphed into an indentured sex acrobat clown. Was she still alive?

"And a very good evening to you, Madam," Luigi, the robot bartender, offered her a coffee.

"I'm dead," said Lyse Saint-Ross, "so I don't think I can eat or drink."

"Well, we'll set a coffee in front of you, just in case. You can savor the aroma. Just choose a table, madam. We have an excellent collection of vintage newspapers and magazines. Relax. Business is slow. In fact, whatever you consume, or don't consume, it will be on the house."

"Thank you. That's sweet," said Lyse, picking up an ancient *Le Monde,* and heading for a table by the window.

Luigi smiled back. This customer – obviously a Cosmos – had a beautiful smile for someone who was dead. She was a mess, but there was a sweet disorder in her dress – and near nakedness – which Luigi had to admit he found very, very attractive.

Lyse sat down, stared at the newspaper – Algeria had just gained its independence – and stared out the window: mist and cobblestones and gaslight and the odor of teargas. The robot waitress came over and placed the coffee in front of her.

"Thank you," Lyse said.

"You are most welcome!" the waitress gave Lyse a big smile.

The coffee did smell delicious; that alone was a pleasure; but it came from a distant place, from what had suddenly become, for Lyse, a lost world. She sighed. Outside the café window, in the gaslight, more dismembered bodies were lying around. Ghouls were nibbling at a few of them. But all the electronic inhabitants, the shimmering hologram prostitutes, the floating live sex shows, all were gone. What had happened? Yes, the Mind must be dead. But was such a thing conceivable?

Luigi was standing behind the bar, polishing glasses. Other than Lyse Saint-Ross, the only other clients in the Café were three ghouls, seated at one table. Ghouls were not ideal clients, perhaps, but they were better than none. The robot French waitress offered the ghouls croissants and espressos, but they were not interested, and soon they went away, shuffling off into the twilight, looking for the living and the dead – to munch on.

"Riffraff," the waitress sniffed, smiling at Lyse; Lyse smiled back and nodded. She didn't like ghouls either.

The waitress went back to the bar. "I miss Clown and Black Tarzan and Geisha," she said, putting the plate of untouched croissants down.

"Yes," said Luigi, "They are true connoisseurs. They know the value of good coffee and authentic freshly-baked croissants."

"They may never come back. I do fear this is the end of the world," said the waitress, gazing at a small circle of crouching ghouls feasting on some human remains out on the street; the ghouls drooled a great deal, and visibly had no manners, and no conversation worthy of the name.

"Yes, this is the end of the world," said Lyse Saint-Ross, looking up from her coffee, "most definitely."

"Yes, but then another world will be born, won't it?" Luigi gave Lyse, and then the waitress his best smile; he was very fond of the waitress; he didn't want her to become depressed.

"Yes, another world will be born," said Lyse, smiling and realizing Luigi's gentlemanly intent. "Another world will definitely be born."

The Café Deux Magots was an anomaly; it had its own generator. The owner, a real live, old-fashioned Texan gentleman – he didn't live in Texas, of course, that was all Dead Lands now – who wore string ties and lived on the militarized island of Hawaii, had not hooked the system into the world Mind, so, in the chaos, and without any living clients, the Café Deux Magots kept humming along.

"Would you like to dance?" Luigi had always dreamed of asking the waitress. Now, he felt, his moment had finally come.

"Yes," said the waitress. Luigi took her in his arms. Lyse watched them and inhaled the beautiful perfume of the coffee; seeing the two robots dance, she rather regretted being dead. Her life had been very privileged, she knew, but perhaps it could have been different, perhaps a bit more romantic, a touch more authentic and adventurous; but, then, we only live once, don't we? And, generally, she had had a fine time, a very lucky existence. Lyse inhaled the coffee's perfume, and watched the two robots dance; they were very good. I really don't have anything to complain about, thought Lyse Saint-Ross with a beautiful and ever so slightly wistful smile.

The audio system was playing Edith Piaf, "*Je ne regrette rien …*"

Far underground, isolated for a time from the tumult above, while all the others were gathered around Claudia and the reviving Mind-Child, V came up to the President.

He was standing apart, alone, gazing at the petrified monster and at the Mind-Sea, which had changed to a sort of toffee-like consistency, and was rapidly solidifying. It was horrible, the force that had conjured up these things, but perhaps it was the human imagination that had done it. The human imagination embodied in the World Mind? The human imagination embodied in the Foul Fiend and the Boy? Could all of this be a mere projection of the evil side of our own souls? Could it all be a theater of diabolical shadows cast by our own minds? Could that be the explanation?

V came to him and laid her claw on his chest. "So, my darling, while we were in the Mind-Child's funfair fantasy, you were put on trial?"

"Yes."

"We were all there, you know."

"Yes, I thought so."

"And you saw what it is like? You saw the suffering? You saw what you did? You saw how it affected people, hybrids, and SINs?"

"Yes, I did."

"You became those you destroyed?"

"Yes, I did, V, I did become them. I was, for a time, a child, a hybrid, a SIN, and a lady who had leprosy. I saw it. I felt it, just for a time, of course, though it seemed like decades, like an eternity."

"And now," V said, putting her arms around him, pressing her sleek reptilian body against his, her lips hovering close to his lips. "And now, darling, you are to be truly punished."

He held his breath, his blue eyes staring into her bright gold reptilian eyes. She seemed to be consuming him in flames.

"I suppose I am," he said; he took a deep breath, so, finally, the end had come. For such a long time, he had felt invulnerable. But now his executioner had arrived. And yet he loved this strange wild creature, the Hybrid Queen and Goddess, the vampire, his enemy, his mate, the half-alien predator, the mother of his child. Yes, he loved her.

"Yes, I suppose you are." She caressed his cheek with the back of her claw, and then she leaned forward, reaching up, her forked tongue ticking his neck, and, suddenly unsheathing her fangs, she bit him.

And so it was done – with love.

Clown and Black Tarzan stood on the canal bank, not far from the others. Black Tarzan looked around. "Where is Geisha? Where did she go?"

Then, Geisha was standing there, beside them.

Tears streaked her immaculate porcelain cheeks.

"Why are you crying?"

"Where were you?"

"Hiroshima. I think I was in Hiroshima. It was August 1945."

"Oh."

"I was with a great, great, great, great something, grandfather of mine. I was with him when he died.

"Oh, that's horrible."

"His picture was on my mother's desk, for some reason. So I recognized him. He was a poet, I think, and a soldier, and I was, of course, a Geisha, and I had spent the night with him."

"Oh."

"I saw everybody die!"

"Oh, poor Geisha, now you are safe, now you are with us!" Clown hugged her; Black Tarzan enclosed them both in his arms.

"So, what shall we call you?" said V to the Mind-Child; she knelt next to him, by the frozen Mind-Sea.

"Yes, what is your name?" Claudia was clearly flirting with the Mind-Child, "I think Romeo would be nice, or Orlando!"

"Claudia is a romantic," said Kat, leaning against V.

"Perhaps I am Viola," said the Mind-Child.

"That too," Claudia wrapped her arms around the child; it was as if she had discovered a new toy, a doll, a love; Claudia declaimed, "Viola, oh sweet Viola, Wherefore art thou, Viola?" And she kissed the Mind-Child on the lips.

Kat glanced at V and smiled: See what you've gotten yourself into!

V grimaced, and made a silly face. Yes, this was getting complicated. A child *en travesti* was a new element, and a girl from the future who spoke Latin – though she seemed to have discovered English – and who alluded to classical English literature, well! This required psychology. Suddenly it seemed there were children and dependants everywhere. She'd always been a bachelor girl, and now she had Miranda, and Claudia, and the Mind-Child, and a potential son-in-law, Caliban, and ... a man friend, her lover, and a woman friend, Kat, her lover, and a possible ...

"No, I think I should really be named ..." the Mind-Child's eyes sparkled, "I think I should be ..."

"Yes?" Claudia looked at him as if she were the adult and he a mere child, and in fact, it was becoming problematic, for V at least, to distinguish which was which and who was who.

Suddenly V felt an absence. She put her hand to the side of her head.

It was as if a void had opened up.

It was as if a light had dawned, within her.

The Boy, the Foul Fiend, was no longer present. It was as if her mind had suddenly been freed from an intimate veil of darkness. Only now did she realize that she had brought him with her, in her mind, that ghostly presence, out of the Mind-Sea.

"What's wrong?" said Kat, putting her hand on V's shoulder, her dark eyes lustrous with concern.

"Where has he gone?" V turned to Kat.

"Who?" Claudia blinked at V.

"The Boy, the Foul Fiend." V felt he had drawn away as an evil tide might draw away; she felt his absence, but he was not entirely gone; he was some- where else, somewhere dangerous.

"He's gone there," said the Mind-Child.

"There? Where?"

"To your secret place, V, to your secret place under the sands; that is where he has gone." The Mind-Child was blinking at V, with wonder, like a true child. "He wants to go through the Gateway, through the Portal, and if he does that, then he will conquer this universe and destroy this world – and all the other worlds."

"Damn," said V, and then blushed, "Sorry!"

"You said a bad word," said Claudia, "but it is not a *very* bad word."

V gave Claudia a look and Claudia smiled; V smiled back.

"You must go there too," said the Mind-Child, "to the Crystal. The Crystal is your friend – and more than your friend."

"How? How can I go there? It is on the other side of the world, virtually; it's in North Africa."

"In your old home," said the Mind-Child.

"Yes, my old home. I was born there. I was a child there."

Claudia had wrapped her arm around the Mind-Child's shoulders; the Mind-Child seemed delighted to be embraced and smiled at V, "Your father told you that you would not know what you can do until you try to do it."

V raised a reptilian eyebrow, "Oh, really, and how do you know this, my dear, dear little one?"

"You must have faith, V. I know – or at least I knew – everything, well, almost everything," the Mind-Child gave V a sly smile.

Claudia had laid her head on the Mind-Child's shoulder: V blinked at them: two child-lovers, innocent, and yet, so very worldly, even otherworldly wise.

"Faith …" Kat muttered, her dark lips parted, white teeth gleaming.

The Mind-Child smiled. "You can do it, V, you can save the planet. You can save Earth. You can save the Empire of Andromeda! You can save the universe!"

"Yes, well, then, I shall try."

"Good," the Mind-Child clapped.

"Now, who will look after you?"

"Kat and the President," said Claudia, "The President and Miranda and Caliban and Kit and Claire and Clown and Black Tarzan and Geisha and the others, they will look after us."

"Alright, then," said V.

"Yes, we will protect them," Kat was still resplendent in her Centurion armored bodysuit, all polished and sparkling as if ready to go on parade. She put her hand on the Mind-Child's shoulder.

"Thank you!" said V.

She walked apart, to where the President was sitting on the ground, looking dazed, Miranda and Caliban and Kit by his side.

"My darling," V knelt next to him. "How do you feel?"

"Stunned," he said. He looked a bit feverish. He was only now beginning to feel the effects of having been bitten, a new intensity of vision and feeling. It was like being high on drugs.

V kissed him, "I love you," she said.

"And I love you." The President whispered as he returned her kiss.

V kissed Kat.

"And V – you look after yourself!"

"I shall!"

CHAPTER 14 – BATTLE

"So," V thought, "well, I shall concentrate. I shall focus my mind."

As the Mind-Child had reminded her, V's father, Marcus, centuries ago, had told her that she would not know what powers she possessed until she tried them.

She walked to the edge of the Mind-Sea and closed her eyes. She pictured, in the greatest detail she could, the home of the Crystal, its immense cavern in North Africa; she pictured the Crystal itself, the enormous globe floating in its metal latticework cradle; she pictured the great platform that faced the Crystal, and she pictured the raised area beside the Crystal, the stage which led to the Gateway – the wall of plasma and the infinite void. The Gateway led to all the various points in the universe, and perhaps to points in other universes as well; she concentrated on the fact that the Crystal could, when activated, suspend or twist the gravitational field, the space-time matrix, and thus break apart the planet and reduce it to the rubble of an asteroid belt, and that, if captured by the Evil Force, the Crystal, as a Time-Space Gateway, could allow the Foul Fiend to go anywhere and everywhere in this universe and thus spread the Empire of Evil throughout this universe – *our* universe. If it got through the Gateway, the Evil Force could destroy the Andromeda Empire; it could destroy everything!

She concentrated.

She heard the Crystal singing a song, it was a lullaby, in a very sweet and half-forgotten language, and V suddenly realized it was the language of her childhood, the language of 3,000 years ago; it was the language of Ancient Phoenicia.

A voice spoke in her head: "You want to go through?"

"Yes."

"You are sure you want to go through?"

"Yes!"

"Then, you shall go through."

The world wavered, dissolved.

V felt light-hearted and light-headed, as if she were dissolving into thin air, as if she were pure spirit, as if she were nothing at all. The world is but a dream. Now she saw that this was true. The cavern and all the people in it dissolved into waves of energy and light; then they were like negative image; then they were loops and squiggles. Then they were gone. V became pure energy. At the speed of light, she traversed a luminous matrix of energy, a quantum structure, it seemed. Then everything was black and silky darkness and smoothness. And suddenly she was in a rainbow of colors, the full spectrum of energy became visible and then silhouettes, of objects, of a place perhaps, a schematic matrix, but it was hard to make out, and then ...

THUD!

WHAM!

WHAM!

So this magic works!

V dissolved into nothingness.

CHAPTER 15 – FLOOD

It was weird, Kit blinked.

It was weird, what was happening!

V had been standing there, a real hybrid, in all her scaly voluptuous turquoise hybrid glory, and then there was a whirring, swirling sort of warped vibrating in the air, and V turned into a blur and then, briefly, she was in focus, again, but she was morphing, and then she was human, but naked, her bright white skin and shock of jet-black hair seeming incongruous and vulnerable in the gloomy gray light of the cavern, and then, again in a blur, she was dressed, in her Centurion's uniform, and all the weapons, the holster, the laser pistol, the boots, composed themselves, and, yes, she was a fully dressed, sparkling, fully armed Centurion. Miranda laid her hand on Kit's shoulder. "Oh, Boy, this is awesome, this is awesome!"

"Yes, it is." Kit barely dared whisper.

"Awesome is certainly the appropriate word," Caliban squeezed Miranda's hand.

V stared straight at them, out of the whirring vibrating air; then her helmet snapped on, the visor snapped down, and they were staring at the opaque dark visor, and then – poof – there was nothing, just vibrating, wavering empty air.

V was gone.

"Gosh!" Miranda tightened her grip on Kit's shoulder.

"Yes, gosh!"

"What happened?" The President was suddenly standing next to them, as if he had materialized out of thin air. He was rubbing his neck, and then looking at his fingers – there was no blood. V had bitten him, but …

"Father, well, mother sort of, she sort of …" Miranda did seem for once at a loss for words.

"She evaporated, Mr. President," said Kit, "I think she was teleported, to some other place. She went to give battle."

"Yes," Caliban was staring at the space, "She has gone to do battle with the force of Evil … far away, in a distant land."

"In her secret place, that's what the Mind-Child said," Kit rubbed her eyes. It had been a long day.

"Her secret place, far away, ah, I see, she went to North Africa," the President knew about the Crystal. The whole zone – a hundred-kilometer radius – had been off-limits for almost one hundred and fifty years, patrolled by killer drones, surrounded by barbed wire and mine-fields. The Crystal was considered too dangerous to be touched or even approached; it couldn't be destroyed, and it couldn't be controlled. But, in secret documents he had seen, the link between V and the Crystal had been suggested. In some way, V, the Queen of the Hybrids, was linked to the Crystal. She controlled it, or she was the gateway to the Crystal, or the key to the Crystal or the Guardian of the Crystal. It was all rather vague. The Crystal was evidently an artifact, a weapon of the alien civilization from which she came. It was said that V and the Crystal, in some mysterious unknown way, were one.

"North Africa?" Miranda gazed at her father, "North Africa?"

"Yes, that was your mother's home, when she was a child. She was born in North Africa. You are one-quarter Phoenician, I believe. Your maternal grandmother was Phoenician, or so I've heard."

"Golly," said Miranda, "Phoenician!"

Caliban and Kit both kissed Miranda, and hugged her.

Claudia turned to the Mind-Child, "Do you know where the Goddess went in North Africa?"

The Mind-Child said nothing, then he looked at them shyly, "I did know. But now I forget. I forget – I have forgotten – everything … I don't know anything now, not anymore, just nothing."

There was a dull roar, just perceptible, somewhere far away.

"What is that sound?" Kat turned toward the frozen Mind-Sea, it had turned to a sort of viscous glue; some of the fragments of the monsters still stood, statues of stone. And the Mind-Sea itself was crystallizing, turning to rock.

Everyone turned.

"Oh, it's coming," said the Mind-Child, "The Great Ocean Monster."

"What? Oh, yes, of course!" The President stared at the Mind-Child.

"What?"

"The ocean – the Atlantic Ocean. The main barriers have been breached." The President turned toward the sound. "Already there's been some flooding, but it sounds as if the main barrier is collapsing. That would mean …"

"We'd better run." Kit looked at the President, "Sir, we'd better run. Mr. President, we'd better run."

"Yes," the President looked vague, distracted. Kit glanced at Miranda, and they both frowned.

"Dad, I think, we'd better go," Miranda wondered at the President, usually so decisive – Of course, he was in shock! V had bitten him!

"Sir, we'd better hitch up and gallop away," said Caliban, otherwise we get trampled in this stamped, or blown away by this southwester. Our rigging is not up to this, Captain."

"Mr. President, we'd better …" Kit took the President's hand and squeezed it. He looked at her, and blinked. "Yes, Kit, yes …"

At that moment, they heard the true thunder of roaring water; it was coming toward them, and fast.

"We'd better head for higher ground, and now, Mr. President!" Kat said, her sharp Centurion eyes turning to the President.

"Yes, the Atlantic barrier has definitely been breached," the President looked around: could these people be saved? Has all this been in vain? Are we going to lose, in spite of everything?

"So, we run?" Kit and Miranda asked at the very same moment, then looked at each other. Caliban said, "I think, sir, I think, Mr. President, that …"

The roaring got louder. Everything trembled.

"Yes, we run," said the President. He broke out of his stunned apathy, suddenly seeing everything with devastating clarity. The equivalent of a tidal wave was rushing toward them, and unless they moved now, and fast, they would all drown.

The water appeared. It entered the far end of the giant cavern, a wall of water. They began to run, back along the canal. The President picked up the Mind-Child, and Caliban picked up Claudia, and they ran, with Kit, and Miranda, and Kat, right beside them.

"Go!"

"Yes!"

"Now!"

"As fast as you can!"

The flood thundered behind them, a roaring, smashing, crumbling sound, and a dreadful whooshing. Pushed by the wall of water, the wind rose with hurricane force.

They ran along the edge of the canal. The Mind-Child, now beside the President, ran as fast as it could. Claudia galloped.

It was all confusion, running, stampeding, galloping, climbing, and always behind them was the onrushing roar of the wall of water.

At one point, the President carrying the Mind-Child, aka Viola, tight, raced up a spiral staircase. Caliban, holding Claudia, was right beside him. They ran upwards.

They leaped over gaps in the stairs, Black Tarzan, Clown, and Geisha. Kat and Caliban and the President galloped as fast as they could, and with them Miranda and Kit.

"She's Viola, now, she wants to be Viola," shouted Claudia

"Yes, right," shouted the President, "Viola. She wants to be Viola." And, yes, the child he was holding, the Mind-Child – or Viola – was beautiful, almost too beautiful, with its huge dark eyes, soulful, its delicate features and body, and the clear, perfect skin. It was hard to believe it was a creation of the world mind, a self-creation. The child was pure information conjured up into a bespoke, tailor-made, bio-being, a real, living, exquisite child.

Behind them the huge wave smashed into the Mind-Sea, disintegrated the monster statues. It was caught for an instant in the gluey substance of the Mind-Sea. The wave slowed and rose up until it filled the whole cavern. Then it came thundering down, taking with it columns and walls, and arches, and sweeping away the fragments of the great towering stony monster that for a time had been one of the Foul Fiend's incarnations. Then it smashed into the final wall; it tumbled back on itself. Then it thundered into the canal opening, and raced along the canal, flooding everything.

Claire and Robyn suddenly found themselves separated from the others. They galloped up a side stair, a spiral service staircase going up, and up, and up.

Below them was the vicious thunder and gurgle of the flood, the whirling maelstrom of violence.

"This sounds serious, Hybrid."

"Yes, it does, Robyn."

At the top of a staircase, and at the end of a long tunnel, the President came to a round door, with a large wheel. Kit and Miranda raced to help him turn the wheel.

Kat pitched in, her Centurion bodysuit, as always, gleaming and impeccable. She glanced around. The water thundered up the tunnel in a great roar behind them.

They struggled to turn the giant wheel. It was rusty and ancient and stuck. Then, suddenly, it turned. The round armored door swung open. They rushed and clambered through.

The President and Caliban and Kat pushed the door shut, just as the thunderous wave of water turned the corner, heading straight for them. Just as the great steel lock clicked shut, the wave slammed against the door with a tremendous thudding crash. Water squirted through. It looked like the wall might crack, and the door would collapse.

"Let's just hope this holds," the President wiped his brow.

"I think it will, but not for long, maybe not at all." Kat felt the door; it was buckling; water spurted out on both sides, the wall on both sides of the door trembled. "No, it's going to give, and it's going to give now!"

"Let's go!"

"Yes, let's go!"

The new tunnel led away into the darkness.

And they headed into the black hole.

Behind them, just as they turned a corner, the door exploded, the wall splintered into a thousand pieces.

A thunderous wall of water was on their heels.

Clown and Black Tarzan and Geisha found themselves separated from the others, cut off by a wall of water. They ran down a side canal, then up a slope – obviously designed for loading vehicles – then they came to a zigzagging service staircase, in a vertical service cylinder that went straight up. They ran, clattering up the staircase, at least four floors, listening to the roar of water gurgling up from below.

"Where are the others?"

"They went that way."

"Will we find them again?"

"We certainly will, ladies, I guarantee you!"

Water boiled and roiled below them and frothing and shooting and rising up in great dark spurts, a churning bubbling dark mass lit by the dull glare of emergency lights and clusters of lichen. "First thing we've got to do is stay alive," said Black Tarzan, handing Geisha across a gap where the stairs were twisted and broken.

"Yes." Geisha stumbled and fell into his arms.

"Absolutely," said Black Tarzan, steadying the little Geisha.

"Alive, that would indeed be excellent," said Clown. "I do quite like the idea of staying alive."

They ran, up and up and up.

They came to a side corridor, turning off at right angles. The water sounded far away. But it was still roaring, still moving, still coming. They sprinted along the corridor, looking for another upward bound staircase.

They finally found it.

They looked back.

"Oh, no!"

"Damn!"

"Will this never end?"

A thunderous wall of water raced toward them.

CHAPTER 16 – CRYSTAL

For V, it was as if she had been broken apart into pixels. She had the sensation she was had been disassembled and then reassembled, several times over, in several cycles. It was something like the feeling she had when she morphed from human to demon and back. But this sensation was infinitely more powerful – and it didn't stop! It was a roller-coaster of sensation!

She put her hand to her forehead. Her forehead at first didn't exist, there was nothing there! And her hand didn't exist. Nothing existed. She was nothing, and she was nowhere. Then, suddenly, both forehead and hand were real. She was real; once again, she was real.

Whew!

Caught in a withering, violent, hailstorm of sand, with sand whipping and whirling around her, blinding her, and peppering her skin, and her visor, and her uniform, she leaned into the hurricane. Her boots just held their ground, gripping as much as they could. She was in a torrid sweltering sandstorm. It must be 120 degrees, even hotter than in the Dead Lands.

With her eyes protected by the visor, which was flipped down, she glanced around, trying to penetrate the thick withering waves of sand; she was in a narrow space. Vertical rock walls soared up on both sides. She looked up. Ah, yes, she was in a narrow, deep canyon which was funneling the sand blizzard into a thin torrent; the rock walls stretched up; there was a glow of light at the top, was it the moon, or was dawn? Perhaps it was dawn, or dusk, or maybe even day – who knew? It was all very confusing. The wind roared. V's ears were filled with sound, utter chaos. And, strangely, she realized, when she was transported, she had been morphed back into her human version, and she had been outfitted completely – it seemed – and perfectly – it seemed – in her Centurion uniform.

In the chaos, she heard the lullaby.

The old lullaby from her childhood!

The old lullaby from the stars!

And, in a flash, she knew where she was.

It was like being transported back in time – two hundred years, or, earlier, almost three thousand years.

She was in the canyon that led to the home of the Crystal.

She and her father Marcus had stood right here thousands of years ago when V was 19 and had just awoken to the knowledge of what she was, and what she was forever to remain, a vampire and a hybrid.

Leaning against the streaming torrent of sand-filled air, she pushed forward; the marker for the entrance to Crystal's cavern should be right about here, not far from here.

And, sure enough! There it was! The silhouette soared up out of the maelstrom. It was the isolated rock, the marker that sheltered the doorway.

The rock soared up, maybe twenty or thirty feet, like a giant tombstone. She slipped in behind it. The wind fell. Suddenly, it was quiet. Sand whirled in eddies and miniature dust devils. And there, in the cliff face, was the handprint. V took off her glove. She laid her right hand on the slight, almost invisible, depression in the rock.

"Welcome V, it has been a long time." It was Crystal's voice, soft and melodic and caressing, and seeming to come straight out of the wall of granite, "It has been far too long."

The rock face opened up, and behind it, the steel door slid aside with a smooth hiss. The lights lit up, revealing the long, arched, well-lit corridor, which led to the steel elevator which led down into the immense cavern where the Crystal resided.

"Hello V."

"Hello Crystal," V managed to say. It was strange, being here, stranger – and more emotional than ever before. There was something uncanny about it, as if she were on a frontier between being and non-being. Time had become unreal.

"Pull yourself together, V!"

"Yes, Crystal, yes, of course," V straightened up and began to stride purposefully down the corridor, toward the elevator. But she would not take the elevator; she would climb down the cliff and she would meet her friend – the Crystal. And perhaps she would meet him too – the Boy, the Foul Fiend!

A few minutes later, V found herself standing on the control platform, about forty feet up from the floor of the cavern, and which hugged the face of the Crystal. The cavern was still there, the lights were on, but everything was covered in dust and drifts of sand were everywhere.

"I do apologize V. I had to clean the place up, and do some repairs," said the Crystal, "After the last sandstorm and collapse it was truly a ruin; but I have left a few traces of the mess, a bit of dust and sand, as a reminder."

"I see. It looks very nice, and quite cozy."

"Thank you, V."

"You're welcome, Crystal."

"I have followed your adventures, V. You have been true to your word, and I know Marcus is proud of you."

"Thank you, Crystal." V smiled, knowing that the Crystal's sensors were everywhere and that she saw everything.

"I, too, am proud of you, V."

"Why, thank you, Crystal."

"But we have a problem, V," said the Crystal, "In fact, V, I hesitate to say this, but we have several problems."

"Tell me," said V, looking around and seeing no sign of the Foul Fiend. What guise or disguise would he turn up in now?

"Well, here is one of our problems, turning up right on cue," said the Crystal.

V turned and she saw …

"Hello, Countess, it has been a long time."

"Baron?"

"Oh, yes, it is I!"

And thus the Foul Fiend – the Evil Force – appeared, in the guise of the Baron, her old friend, the man whom she had, briefly, loved, at the end of the 17th Century; the man who thought she was an ally of the murderous Sect of the Apocalypse, a sect that kidnapped young women and, in a parody of the Mass, a Satanic Black Mass, tortured and killed them; and, so, since he thought she was a vicious murderer, the Baron had chained her, naked and drugged, deep in his murky dungeon, bricked her in, and left her there to die, except, of course, she had not died, but had escaped, with the help of a friendly servant, and had confronted the Baron, and fought him, in a delicate, playful little duel, and then, when she had defeated him and had the point of her sword against his jugular, she spared him, for he was, in fact, a good man, a man who was fighting the good fight, a gallant man whose aim was to defend damsels in distress, and she felt affection for him still, even now, even centuries later. They had never consummated their love, which left her with a vague feeling of regret, wistful-ness, and a faint tincture of curiosity, together with a true fraternal feeling. He was, in his own way, one of her kind, and, in spirit, he was one with her spirit.

"That is not a good disguise, my friend. The real Baron was a good man."

"So am I – good – by my own lights."

"Are you sure?"

"Absolutely – by my lights, bad is good and good is bad."

"So, you are at peace with yourself."

"Absolutely," the false Baron smiled. Oh, he was indeed handsome!

V unsheathed her sword. It was somehow fitting, she thought, that the final battle should be fought with such simple, primitive means – cold steel.

The Foul Fiend – who indeed did look exactly like the Baron and had all his mannerisms and tics down to a T – unsheathed his sword.

Their swords clanged.

And as steel struck steel, V heard, in her mind, the Crystal whisper, "Beware, V, he has many tricks up his sleeve; this is but the beginning."

The Baron, his handsome face smiling all the while, crowded in on her, his sword flashing like lightning. He struck below. He struck on the side. He struck from above. He twirled around, on tiptoes, like a ballerina. He pushed V to the edge of the platform that led to the Quantum Wall, to the Gateway, to the Universe, and, potentially, to Nothingness.

She swirled to one side, turning the tables.

Now he was forced to the edge of the platform.

The false Baron leaped high into the air and came straight down, the sword slashing out, glittering. It missed V's neck by less than a centimeter.

"You devil," V swiveled around and plunged, but he was no longer there, he was behind her! Ah, so he plays magic tricks. Of course, he is the Devil!

She somersaulted, just avoiding a fatal strike to her lower back, as he clearly intended to – and nearly succeed in – skewering her through the spine.

The Devil leaped, and plunged, attempting to skewer her between the breasts and strike at her very heart.

She parried the strike, and he thrust himself against her, their arms and swords locked together, face-to-face, their lips close, their breath intermin-gling, hot flesh, ripe lips, and deep soulful eyes.

"You do look like him," V breathed, letting a sort of yearning, a sort of desire shine in her eyes and allowing a hint of lust to tremble breathlessly on her gleaming lips.

"Indeed I do," a sparkle of vanity and self-satisfaction lighting up his eyes.

She moved her lips slightly closer, just letting her lips brush his, and she sighed, "Oh, Baron!" and as they kissed, he drew from behind his back a dagger and brought it swinging around …

She deflected the blow, twisted his wrist, and directed the plunge of the dagger into his side, just below his ribs, and when his hand opened in shock and surprise she seized the handle of the dagger and twisted it, with all her might, she twisted it, and twisted it again, and ripped it downward, and ripped it across!

He roared; he roared even as they were still kissing, her lips delicately nibbling at his, and she sprang back, the warm sweetness of the kiss still on her lips and, oh, so perfectly reminiscent of the Baron. "I so awfully sorry, Baron, I think that dagger stroke was meant for me!"

"Foul Witch!" he screamed, his face no longer that of the debonair and gallant Baron, but the face of a demon, a gargoyle.

"Foul Fiend!" V stepped back.

"Foul, foul, foul witch," he screamed

"Sticks and stones," V said, "Name-calling will get you nowhere!"

"Crystal," he cried, clutching his side, trying to hold in the blood, "Crystal, you be my witness!" He looked up at the giant Crystal that floated gently in its huge metal cradle. "You be my witness, this witch, this filthy hag, this seductress, this unworthy female creature, she is not worthy of representing you and your great civilization of Andromeda. She is a murderer, a fornicator, she drinks blood, she blasphemes against all the gods, she copulates indifferently with beings of either sex, she disobeys divine commands, she consorts with lowlife, whores, and pimps, and mercenaries, and jungle thieves, and people-smugglers, and mutants, and she is on the most intimate terms with the Queen of mutant false-life SINs, Queen Nikki, an abomination in Heaven's eyes and Hell's too, and she has given birth to a hybrid, spreading the impure hybrid race, she has …"

He choked, his face contorted into an image of pure rage.

The Crystal did not reply. It floated, glowing, in its latticework home, and hummed something that V thought, vaguely, was perhaps Cole Porter, something catchy, and romantic, in any case.

The Foul Fiend screamed and groaned.

"You should have that seen to," V said, pointing with her sword to the blood oozing from his side, soiling his pretty velvet jacket, soaking his frilly pristine shirt, dribbling down his splendid trousers. She frowned. Even his boots would soon be ruined.

"Witch! You witch!"

"Well, that's that, then," V bowed, and tossed him the dagger. He didn't reach for it, and it fell and clattered and slid along the floor of the platform until it came to rest just below the shimmering edge of the Crystal. The Crystal made a humming sound, a tune something like "I'll be seeing you," and brightened somewhat.

The "Baron" looked down at his side; parts of his innards were pushing out. He screamed, "I shall do such things! I know not what they will be, but they will be beyond horror. And I shall send you, Foul Witch, into the deepest hell of nothingness from which no being ever returns."

V poked at him with the point of her sword. "Well, Nuncle, thou who art nothing, must become something, before thou dost real harm. Pure spirit, evil or good, is not much use, formless and vaporous as it is, in this material world; you must incarnate, you must possess, you must become something or somebody to do real harm; demons must possess a pretty morsel of flesh if they are to wreak havoc; a man who has no name is no one, literally, no one, so that's what you are, Mr. Nobody. Mr. Nothing you are; pure puffery you are; a bad odor, a ghost of mildew, no more; and so I say, Goodbye! Adieu! Farewell!" She turned her back on the writhing 'Baron' and strode to the edge of the control platform and looked down into the pit and the floor of the great cavern where one of her great past battles had been fought, two hundred years ago, no, maybe more, a battle against Cardinal Ambrosiano, Mr. Evil himself, all clad in Purple, a representative of the Devil.

He would change himself into something really threatening, now. She was sure of it. This little duel was a farce. He had just been toying with her. It was all a façade, it was all make-believe. Soon, he would emerge in horrible splendor.

The Crystal was humming, "A, you're adorable, B you're so beautiful, C you're ..."

Oh, oh," Clown felt something splash on her polished pate; she reached out her hand, and looked up.

Water was leaking from above.

Oh, the ceiling was going to collapse!

"I think we're trapped," said Geisha.

"No, ladies, we can't be trapped. We got into this fix; we can get out of it," Black Tarzan was staring at the seething water that had risen up behind them, and in front of them, blocking their retreat; they couldn't go forward, and they couldn't go back.

"But, look, the water is above us and its come behind us, there's no way out."

"We'll find a way!" Clown turned her bright fixed grin on Geisha.

"Okay, let's go!"

So they waded into the water in front of them, and they dove, and swam, and within a minute, came up coughing choking, in a narrow ill-lit space between the roof and the water. Their heads floated in the bubbly clayey flood.

Rats were swimming around them, but too excited and dazed to attack.

"Okay, we go under again, and see if we can make it back to that staircase."

They plunged, and they swam and it was dark and endless and Clown felt as if her lungs were on fire. Now, after all this, I am going to die! We are all going to die! That is really too bad because all of this adventure has been, for her, a rebirth.

Her lungs were bursting. She was desperate to breathe; she was dying to inhale. But she knew that if she did so, if she breathed in, she would be signing her own death warrant. She held her breath. She felt she would burst, implode inward.

If Clown had believed in prayer, well, she would have prayed. In fact, even on the edge of drowning, and even aware she was being just a bit hypocritical, she resisted, but then, finally, she did begin to pray, "Oh, gods, oh gods, please, in this my moment of need …"

Standing on the edge of the platform, V stared downwards. Fifty feet below on the floor of the cavern were scattered bits of machinery, generators, cables, and a few weapons lying here and there, remains of the battle from long ago when a Prince of the Church, a man who had gone quite mad, tried to evoke the Infinite Force of Evil. And, possessed by the Foul Fiend, he had tried to destroy the earth by activating the Crystal's destructive force, its ability, being on the very quantum frontier, lying between universes, to suspend or distort gravity, and thus to tear and rip apart the very fabric of the universe, and, in this particular minuscule corner of this particular universe, to tear apart the earth and leave in its place a belt of uninhabitable dead asteroids.

"How are you, Crystal?" she asked, out loud, and turned to look up at the giant glittering sphere. And she glanced at the "Baron" whom she had – just a few minutes ago – disemboweled.

The false Baron was still standing, still holding in his collapsing abdomen, the bulging spiral of smoky bloody intestines, now sagging down to his thighs; his brow was furrowed from the pain being experienced by the body he was trapped in; but he was concentrating too, concentrating choosing on a new trick, a new version of himself, a new disguise. In fact, V couldn't for the life of her understand why he was tarrying so long in a dying and wounded body; it must hurt! Surely he could skip from body to body, and pluck any number of homes out of the infinite range of possibilities.

The Crystal brightened. "I am very well, V, thank you for asking. You are always so considerate. And how are you, V?" The musical womanly voice floated warmly in the air.

"I'm peachy-cream, Crystal," said V, "I'm hunky-dory, in the pink, actually, and feeling terribly perky, but others are not so lucky."

"No, others are not so lucky," said the Crystal, and then it hesitated, for there was quite possibly, V suspected, some awful bit of news the Crystal didn't quite feel ready to impart to V.

V sensed that Crystal, and it was quite unlike her, was feeling some reticence about something, something dreadful which the Crystal hesitated to report, not wanting to add to V's preoccupations and worries; but then ...

The Baron screamed. Doubled over and holding his drooping innards between shit-stained fingers, he screamed, "Doom, doom, yes, Domesday has come, and, yes, and it is my doing. I used human ingenuity and human wickedness against the humans themselves. The plague is unfurling its wings of death. It is poetic justice. And so I deserve power over the whole planet. And through this planet, Crystal, and through your Gateway, when I have enslaved you, I shall gain entry to the whole of this universe, and I shall turn it all into my Kingdom, the Andromeda federation and all, not even this witches' father and all his warriors and all his technology will be able to stop me!"

"Quite a speech," said V, wondering what precisely he meant. She was feeling too perky, she realized, and rather arrogant. Hubris, she feared, was in her veins; and, its sister Nemesis, was undoubtedly lurking just around the corner. But, in spite of her reservations, she couldn't resist; she leaped up to the high ledge that, just across from the Crystal, provided a splendid view of the whole cavern. There she strutted back and forth, her sword at her belt, her slick black armored latex-like catsuit glowing as if it had been just polished, and was dripping on oil.

"There is a danger, unfortunately, V," said the Crystal, "that what the Foul Fiend says, may, in fact, come to pass, if he does defeat you and take control of me; I would greatly regret it; it is extremely unpleasant to be the instrument that destroys one's own creators. The Andromeda Central Council will be very annoyed if this comes to pass and the Andromeda Federation and all those who inhabit it – more than 3,546,218,872 species and races – perish. I don't think your father, Marcus, for one, would forgive me!"

"Quite," said V, "let us see if we can prevent that."

"I would greatly appreciate it if you could prevent it, my dearest V," said the Crystal.

"You are demons! Female Demons! You two are in cahoots!" The Baron roared; he blurred, became all vague and fuzzy, began to swell up, like an enormous blimp or balloon and – poof – he became a dragon-like thing, a dinosaur-like monster, about thirty feet tall.

"Oh, oh," said V.

The dragon was scarlet and gold with bright red eyes lined with kohl and rather sweet-looking and flirtatious long eyelashes; it snarled, baring silver fangs; it breathed sulfurous plumes of yellow and blue fire.

"Wench!" it roared, "Female!"

Its enormous claws, curved like scimitars, slashed toward V; and it leaped high in the air, aiming to come right down on top of her, on the narrow ledge where V, quite haughtily, had been strutting back and forth, just a bit too satisfied with herself.

The Dragon roared, tensed its muscles, leaped across the cavern, and landed on the same ledge, about twenty meters from V; but its claws slipped on the smooth surface, and its movements were constrained by the narrowness of the ledge, sticking out above the floor of the cavern, and it went crashing down on its snout, almost falling off the ledge.

"Cursed Female!" the dragon roared. And it flooded the whole ledge with fire.

V leaped off into space. The flames licked at her boot heels. She landed lightl, on tip-toes, four stories down, on the floor of the cavern.

"I don't wish to be a busybody," said the Crystal, "but if you don't mind a bit of advice, dearest V …"

"No, I don't mind at all, Crystal, your wisdom and advice are always invaluable."

The Dragon bent its long neck to look down. Spurts of sooty smoke rings puffed from its nostrils. Its long red tongue licked at its fangs. It blinked, fluttering its long eyelashes.

"Perhaps, then, V, if you don't find this suggestion insulting or out of place, perhaps you should consider changing, you know, morphing, you know, transforming yourself, if you know what I mean, into your other form … It more fireproof."

As if to prove Crystal's point, the dragon breathed a wave of fire that completely flooded the walls and floors and which was aimed, like the blast of a blast furnace, an overwhelming wave of fire, coming straight at V.

"Oh, gods, oh, gods, hear me in my need," Clown struggled in the vicious current, and the water went right to the roof of the tunnel, her fingers scraped, and her fists banged against the roof of the tunnel. She swirled around, swimming desperately, searching for a bubble of air, for salvation. As she did so she thought of the gods, the One God, stern, implacable, and, rather paradoxically, loving, who had been very popular in recent centuries and then the ancient gods and goddesses, and the new gods and goddesses, who had resurfaced and were multiple, and capricious, and libidinous and sensuous, and full of playful wisdom and deep secrets, true tricksters, virtuoso lovers, gods who lived on and in the surface of things, in the ripples sunlight, in the whisper of the wind, in the …

Whoosh!

Whoosh!

Clown burst to the surface, and gasped. For a minute, she just breathed in the air – Oh, the divine air! Oh, thank you, gods! Thank you!

She looked around. The staircase loomed up, a latticework of rusty steel and cross-beams and steps with rubber-like treads, flickering in the dim emergency lights and lichen glow. She was close, but not quite there.

The water was now racing, going somewhere; the current was pulling at her, again dragging her under. She splashed desperately, struggling to stay on the surface. One new thing that really terrified her was the thought of poisonous jellyfish; the oceans seethed with the things. And if the ocean was invading the underground of Elysium, then the underground of Elysium would swarm with the things too! There was a cable running along the roof, just a two feet above her head, she grabbed for it, she held on, she could drag herself toward the staircase, she might make it, then the cable torn loose from the roof, and she dropped down, into the water, and was swept under. Shocked, she almost let go of the cable, but then she managed to think: No, I'll hold on.

She pulled desperately, climbing up the cable, and finally, she splashed gasping up to the surface, thrashing against the roaring current. The water tugged at her, fighting to take her under. She again saw the staircase, it did go upwards. The water had not risen so high; in fact, the water seemed to be staying at the same level but racing, draining away somewhere else.

She locked her legs around the cable, and she shimmied up it, thigh-over-thigh and hand-over-hand. The cable didn't break loose. It had ripped free from the roof, but it had gotten tangled in a huge knot in the metal staircase. If the tangle didn't tear free, she would make it. Hand-over-hand, legs locking the cable, she struggled against the rushing current, the foaming, swirling water, one minute, two, and three!

Finally, she got to the staircase and climbed up onto it, on hands and knees, gasping, and soaked through and through and through. She could see – even in the dim light – that her bodysuit was semitransparent and running with silvery watery reflections.

Whew! She crouched down on a step, just two feet about the rushing water. Where were Geisha and Black Tarzan?

If they didn't surface soon, she would dive in and try to find them.

Suicide!

Yes, but I'll do it!

She stared, dazed, at the rushing water. She looked upwards. The spiral staircase went up and up, into darkness, out of sight.

How long should I wait?

They can't have drowned.

A splash! Geisha and Black Tarzan appeared.

They were swept by the current against the metal stairs, and its railing, and Black Tarzan grabbed Geisha who was swirling around like a top – her face like a white, black and red mask staring upwards. Tarzan grabbed the metal railing, and helped by Clown, he hauled Geisha up onto the steel steps.

Geisha was exhausted. "This has been one crazy day!" She gasped for air. "You remember, Clown," she wheezed, "You remember when I said this day would never end, and you said it might end, like being the end of us, and we didn't know which was worse."

"Yes."

Geisha was trembling and next to naked, just a ragged shirt, off one shoulder. Clown crouched down next to her, put her hand on Geisha's shoulder.

"Well, I guess it's both, ladies," said Black Tarzan, "It is never-ending. But it will indeed come to an end." He was standing, two steps up, shaking off the water which ran in luminous rivulets from his muscles, biceps, triceps, abs, and shoulders, dribbling, too, down his strong legs.

Clown stared up at him. It occurred to her that, if they all survived this adventure, then she and Geisha – Clown was very generous – should become the personal harem of Black Tarzan, or he their personal … trainer. She wondered at herself. She licked her bright bulbous lips. I must really be perverse, and now that I've got my legal mind and my talent for rhetoric back, maybe I can convince anybody to do anything. Of course, the implanted erotic super-charged synapses were still functioning. That must be it. Yes, in spite of recent tribulations, she was horny as hell.

Black Tarzan looked down at her with an appraising smile.

Geisha looked up, glancing at both of them, her dark eyes bright in the white mask, the high, painted-on eyebrows, making her look startled and innocent and perverse, all at once.

"The old Adam is still alive," Black Tarzan grinned.

"The old Eve too," said Clown.

"What are you guys … Oh, yes, of course, I see, how stupid of me," said Geisha.

"I think you've got a very good idea there, Clown," said Black Tarzan giving her the look; she was cute as all get out, he thought; the bald head with its implanted stripes of sequins, and those mysterious, impenetrable clown eyes, the bright smiling lips, the slender acrobat's body, and right now he could see right into her, he could feel her desire, her playful speculative lust, her dreamy desire envisaging vaguely – just shadow play in the mind – how the three of them could all be together forever and ever; he suddenly felt, in a way, he was falling in love, falling in love or in lust with both of them, since Geisha, her pure chalk-white body, and her vulnerability, yes, she too was a sweet and delicate dish, a sweet acute loyal and brave friend, was Geisha.

Geisha smiled and stood up, she tugged at the shirt; it just touched her thighs. "I feel it too," she said, looking at Clown and at Black Tarzan.

"We all feel it," said Clown, wondering at the way they were connected, as if they were one, already one.

"Let's get upstairs first," said Black Tarzan, "and there will be time. There will be time for all things."

"Yes, there will be time," said Clown, "A season for all things."

"Yes, there will be time," echoed Geisha, "a time for sowing, and a time for reaping." She caressed the side of Clown's face, and Clown looked up at her and Clown blinked her blank Clown eyes in friendship, tenderness, and – yes, most certainly – desire. And love too. Definitely love. I wish to cherish her, Clown thought, I want to cherish and protect her, and him, both of them.

There will indeed be time.

They began the climb upwards.

Below them, the water swirled and roiled and boiled and a flotilla of rats, squeaking busily at each other, swam desperately with the current, and landed on the bottom steps of the rusty steel stairs. There they crouched, shaking themselves, and looking out over the water.

The rats glanced upwards.

They saw the retreating figures, Clown, Geisha, and Black Tarzan.

The rats considered, for a moment, whiskers twitching.

The rat patriarch looked at them all, each in turn, and he growled: No, not now: there would be time, a time for all things: each harvest in its season.

The flood of fire swept down, and engulfed the point where V had, until that instant, been standing. But V, sensing the coming storm, lept to yet another ledge.

So, the Evil One has transformed himself into a Dragon.

She glanced upwards. The dragon certainly looked formidable and dangerous, but it wasn't very original. Couldn't he think of something better?

"You were saying, Crystal," V said, "Before we were interrupted by that matchbox that flared up – very inconsiderate, I must say."

"Yes I was saying, darling V, I was saying that I think you should really change into demon-alien form, as you call it, so that you can take on the Evil One on somewhat more equal terms, if you don't mind my saying so, that is."

"Splendid suggestion, Crystal," said V, "Thank you!" She had been thinking the very same thing, but she had held back partly out of vanity and partly out of a sense of symbolism; she was defending the heritage of the human race – she wanted to fight in human guise …

But the time for vanity and symbolism was past.

Some battles had already been lost. Elysium had been destroyed. The human race, without the Mind, had been sent hurtling back to the Stone Age, for a generation at least.

But if this battle was lost, then all would be lost.

The Evil One – with his fanaticism and hatred – would seize control of the Crystal, and thus, it seemed, of the universe.

The Crystal was rooting for her; this was very encouraging.

The dragon was preparing to leap. Its eyes gleamed, focusing on V who was standing there, hand on chin, in a pose of apparent insouciance. Yes, she was squarely in the target zone; the dragon's giant jaws dripped acid-like saliva; it breathed sulfurous smoke; it huffed and puffed; and now, in one great blast, it let out a torrent of flame, the flames, liquid fire, flooded the ledge where, up until the Crystal gave her such valuable advice, V had been standing, yes, in a pose that seemed casual, hand on chin, one leg cocked, head tilted thoughtfully, keeping one eye on the dragon and considering, Hamlet-like, what to do next. The flames flooded the ledge, turning it to volcanic heat, flooding every centimeter.

The wave of flame cleared.

V was not there.

Not even her statue, turned to ash or carbonized, was there.

Nor was her body, burned to a crisp, lying on the ledge.

Nor were her ashes drifting off, gently, into space.

The Dragon gulped and looked around; then, it roared and flooded fire everywhere.

The Crystal hummed and said, "Tsch, Tsch, Tsch!"

The Dragon turned its leprous snout toward the Crystal and breathed more fire, but then, when the Crystal sang a high-pitched note, the dragon cowered back, and again examined the ledge.

V was truly gone.

The Dragon looked around, moving its heavy head this way and that, and moving its vast tail back and forth. It blinked its luscious lashes.

Just as the flames were about to blast forth, V had done a quick pirouette, which made her for a second virtually invisible, and she had slipped into a side-vent storage room, just beyond the reach of the wall of fire, and there she carefully but quickly stripped down, unbuckling and lifting off her boots, belt, holsters, and backpack, slipping out of her skintight bio-armor battle suit, and folding the slick black bio-skin neatly on a shelf.

"There!" She patted it down.

V was generally very fond of her clothes. They were, in her opinion, part of her. If she were wearing crinolines, for example, or a satin ball gown, or a flapper's sheathe, she would have been equally enamored, caressing the silk, the satin, the cotton, the spangled spandex, the tight stone-washed denim, the antique nylon, the patent leather – whatever. Over the years – centuries – she had followed with utter fascination the ups and downs of fashion, high and low. This was perhaps her female human side, though she suspected her alien side was equally vain and fashion-conscious.

"Oh, well!" She sighed, and in an instant – the blur of quantum energy exploded like a miniature A-bomb in the small workspace. She morphed into demon form, glittery glitzy turquoise and green and yellow and slinky black scales, demon eyes, and claws and fangs. The aesthetics were different but equally satisfying; and it was best, after all, to be a demon, if you are going to fight a dragon. But even as a demon she was a small fry compared to the dragon. V fully intended to be a high-tech demon. She buckled on her sword holster sword, slung on her laser-gun belt, squared her shoulders, and considered the situation.

The wall of fire at the room's entrance had ceased.

V crept up to the door and peeked out. The dragon was waddling along the narrow platform. He had obviously put two and two together, and he clearly intended to come to the entry to the side-vent storage room, breathe it full of fire and fry or bake or roast her to death, as if she were trapped in a small one-way oven. In fact, she *was* trapped; there was no rear exit.

It was interesting, V thought, how the Evil One had to incarnate, flowing into a bodily form, in order to act. It was a definite weakness. Each type of body offered advantages, of course, but each type of body also had its frailties. If the body were caught in some sort of gluey bodily constraint, then, well, perhaps the Devil would not be able to transcend, not be able to escape.

"Well, no more time for philosophic musings!" She sighed, took a deep breath, leaped out of the entrance, skidded across the platform, and leaped straight into space; she grabbed a dangling cable, swung with it, and leaped across open space, landing on a platform on the staircase that went zigzagging up Crystal's face.

"Very impressive, V, my darling," the Crystal murmured.

"Thanks!"

"Wench! Foul Female! Witch!" The dragon roared; it tried to turn; one of its legs slipped off the narrow ledge; and, with a tremendous squishy thud, it crashed full down on its belly on the floor; it roared again and sent out a great spurt of fire and soot and then it staggered up, turned toward the Crystal and blasted the staircase with a huge bellowing billowing blossom of fire and embers and flakes of pure energy, but the Crystal who did not like being insulted – much less attacked face-on – had put up a quantum energy barrier which blocked the wave of flame, flattening it, re-energizing it, and sending much of it straight back at the Dragon which roared in protest. The dragon's mental message came: "This is not fair! You two are ganging up on me!"

While all this roaring and protesting was going on, V had scampered up the zigzag staircase, and was now far above the dragon, almost at the top of the staircase, and now she leaped to a cable, swung across the void, and landed, plop, astride the Dragon's neck, one leg on each side, and she shouted, "Okay, now, buster, giddy up, giddy up, my bronco friend!" The Dragon twisted its neck, trying to get at her. "Oh, you look so funny," V said, and she grabbed a bit of loose hanging cable, snapped it free, and used it as a whip. "Now, get going, you beast!"

The Dragon roared. Trying to look around and get at her, it stumbled, fell flat on its muzzle – sending out a flat gush of flame – and almost threw her off.

V locked her thighs on the Dragon's neck and held on as tight as she could, straddling him like the true bronco-buster she was, in fact, she had, in centuries past, disguised herself as a cowboy and participated in various rodeos and round-ups and stampedes and, riding side-saddle or bareback, fox hunts, and, once, she had hired herself out, for a season, to herd cattle down Mexico way, when was that – that must have been, hmm …

The Crystal coughed, discreetly.

V raised an eyebrow.

Oh, yes …

Oh, yes, hold on, V, don't get distracted!

The Dragon floundered, and turned back on itself, breathing fire, and the great wave and spray of fire went just past V, and the Dragon then flopped over on its side, intending to roll on its back and crush V under its weight or trap her squished against the pavement, but V jumped up, swung around and began walking down the Dragon's belly. The Dragon wiggled and turned, and then twisting its neck up, it breathed a tidal wave of fire, scorching its own belly and legs, and then looking to see if V had been roasted or reduced to cinders.

But V was no longer there.

"Hi, there!" V was hanging twenty feet up from a rafter.

When the Dragon staggered to its feet, V dropped straight down, onto the Dragon's snout. And sitting astride its snout, facing its eyes, her legs dangling perilously near its fangs and long forked tongue, she plunged her clawed fists into both its eyes, and tore both eyes out.

It was gooey.

It was a weird, not entirely pleasant sensation.

V shook her claws. It was sticky, web-like dragon goo.

The Dragon let out a roar of pure agony.

It reared up in its hind legs, and it breathed fire, blindly, in every direction. But V was under its belly. She now unsheathed her sword, and plunged it straight into the Dragon's gut, ripping the sword upward, then downward, then sideways, coils of huge intestines, a flood of blood, and guck rained down on V, she closed her eyes, sealed her nostrils and backed away.

Yuk!

The Dragon writhed in convulsions.

Yes, the Devil needs a willing tool to do his bidding; the Evil One needed to be incarnate, to exist; and so, incarnate, he had the weaknesses of the flesh, in addition to the innate weakness of Evil itself, vanity, pride, presumption, dogmatism, prejudice, and hence, in a sense, stupidity. He would be undone by his own qualities, by what he was! The very core of his evil nature, his need to possess and enslave others, was also his weakness. *Hmm, why didn't I think of this before?* V frowned, riled by her own obtuseness. Also, she was covered in gooey filth.

Of course, now he would morph into something new!

This was tiresome, and it could go on forever.

And, indeed, there was a whirling sound and an explosion, and there he was, or there *it* was, in a new guise.

He had transformed himself into a nest of vicious, poisonous worms, a colony, rather like a large land-based jellyfish, and jellyfish were the plague of the oceans, having eaten almost everything else and turned much of the sea to poisonous glue.

These new worm creatures were really ugly! This was the opposite of sublime! The worms were thin; the biggest were about a foot long, the smallest about an inch, or half an inch, like a mountain of squirming militant maggots, centered on a huge blob and all dead-white in color, and each maggot-worm seemed to have an evil little eye at one end and hungry wet suckers all along its length. There were thousands of them, materializing out of the air.

"Yuk," Crystal murmured. "V, I have seen many life forms, but this … one is really quite unpleasant!"

"Yes," V backed away from the sprawling spreading nest of worms. They leaped at her, and they cascaded over her, they got onto her scales before she could leap away. They stuck to her scales and exuded a sort of acid and glue. V's scales seemed to be immune to the acid but it was sticky and very disagreeable.

She twisted and turned and tried to jump away, but the glue got tangled, like a spider's strands of steel-silk, between her legs, and around them, binding them together, and she fell down, and rolled on the ground.

And they seemed to be getting into her mind too; they were paralyzing her willpower. Lethargy swept through her limbs; she was dizzy, lost. Her mind liquefied, turning to lead, bunged up with cotton batten. She forced herself to think! *Think, damn it! Think!* Okay, yes, it's clear: they want to mummify me, and then gut me, and empty me out, and make me their puppet, and then, as their mindless, blind soulless slave – as *his* slave – I will give them the key – I will *be* the key – to the Crystal and to absolute mastery of the universe.

Her mind wavered and faded.

All things wavered and faded.

V summoned all her strength. Briefly, she returned to herself.

"Grrrh, get off my you little devils!"

She squirmed and fought and wiggled.

The worms spat glue at V, splash, splash, splash, and wham! It got into her eyes. She tried to rub it out, but that just made it worse. The worms spat more, and filled up her face. The worms were crawling all over the place. They wiggled and squirmed all over her body. They seemed to have paralyzed her super demon force.

This was humiliating – worse, it was dangerous!

It could be fatal!

V rolled over and over, and she kept her mouth shut tight because the little buggers – some of them were only an inch or so long – were trying to get into her mouth and into her nostrils and wiggle into her ears. If she was not careful they would infect her brain and eat her frontal cortex and, yes, yes indeed, they would turn her into a puppet, a dancing, bouncing, bowing, kowtowing puppet, a slave in the hands of the Devil himself. Then he could morph her and turn her into a subservient witch, a slave, a harem girl, and beast of burden, or into anything. Yes, he would have fun with her – she could just see it – before – and after – he used her as the key to open Crystal's Gateway and conquer the universe. And that would be the worst possible thing that could happen!

She somehow flipped herself up to her knees.

She managed, entangled as she was, to stand upright.

She swayed this way and that.

The worms leaped up and clung to her – everywhere!

A tangled, hungry slimy mob of gooey worms was slithering down her belly, heading for her groin. That was not good either. They would invade her vagina, wiggle and squeeze and insinuate their way inside, colonize her womb, the gods only knew what mischief the little buggers could cause, these evil agents of the Foul Fiend.

In fact, they *were* the Foul Fiend!

Ugh, that thought was even more horrible. Perhaps the Foul Fiend was trying to sow his devilish seed, to impregnate her. Perhaps he meant to breed upon her his foul progeny, little devils with horns and hooves springing from her womb, all armed and ready to spread chaos in the universe, or worse, little worms, thousands of devilish little worms or snakes, clever little high IQ serpents from her womb, satanic cobras, anacondas, pythons, wiggling and spilling out of her. She would be a cocoon, or a nest, not a person.

She tried to slap at them, but there were more and more, and they were swarming all over her, they were elastic creatures, and they did not mind being crushed or squashed; they just bounced back; the worm glue was getting thicker and thicker. V caught a vision of the hive mind, the mass worm mind, tunneling its way into her mind – His Mind! Evil old Daddy Devil!

That was what he was, a sick parody of the God of the Monotheists, and now he was incarnate in these maggots.

They were going to glue her entirely, arms and legs in a web of glue, and she would be mummified, trapped in a cocoon, and when she came out she would have a worm mind, a hive mind, a drone mind, and be an utter slave of the Foul Fiend, an Instrument of Evil, like the poor zombie-bats, a sack of flesh containing his squirming offspring, evil little worms, except that, and she caught just a glimpse of this, once she gave birth to his progeny, and suckled them, she would be left, a shell, with just enough consciousness – such was the Foul Fiend's sadistic ingenuity – to be aware of and to bewail her fate, just like those poor condemned souls in Hell. She would not control any – any – of her bodily functions, she would be a puppet, a slug, a cocoon, a colony, a …

While V's mind spun deeper and deeper into this pit of horror, the worms were spinning and gluing and prying, trying to get inside her and from every direction, heading for and exploiting every opening, every orifice.

She could now just barely stand up. Hundreds of glittering strands of glue were wrapping themselves around her legs. It felt as if she were wearing a very tight skirt.

She was hobbled. She wavered back and forth. She fell down. She rolled around, over and over, hoping to crush the little monsters. But no, they seemed invulnerable. She rolled some more, and she tried to think of what she could do to escape mental and bodily mummification. Her sense of herself was disintegrating, falling away, into little splashes of consciousness, fragments, liquid strands, and then she was gone …

She did hear from very far away, the Crystal saying, "V … darling V, my darling, V …"

But V was gone.

Poof, V was gone.

V was elsewhere, in another time, another place.

It was springtime, three thousand years ago.

Life is but a dream. All time is present time. Present time is all time.

V was wearing a short tunic with a little belt, and she was bouncing a ball in her hand and walking with her mother along a narrow cobblestone street in her home town in Greater Phoenicia under the ancient sun of North Africa many centuries ago. Her mother was saying that the sacrifice in the temple would occur that very night and that she, Tanis, as she was known then, could attend for the first time and see what the gods demanded.

"The gods are very hungry and very demanding," her mother said, as she contemplated the goods displayed before a merchant's shop – brightly colored cotton from Egypt – "The gods wish for blood, it is in the nature of the gods to wish for blood."

"Why are the gods hungry for blood?"

Her mother glanced at her, and smiled, "Oh, you ask so many questions, my little Tanis, my little love," and then, while still fingering a length of cloth, her mother got a faraway look in her beautiful eyes, and said, "I think, darling, that the gods are lonely, they are hungry for love, that is why they ask for blood, and for a lamb or an ox, or a child. They ask people to give them what people most value, and most love, and so, then, the gods know that we love them and honor them more than any other thing, even more than our own flesh and blood."

"Will I be sacrificed to the gods?"

"No, darling, you were not made for sacrifice." Her mother knelt next to her. "You come from a greater place, darling, you will not be sacrificed ever!"

"But why …?"

"No, darling, not now; there is no time now for questions. Let's go home."

She must have been five or six.

Time passes, in a flash, though it seems as if she has lived a whole life, playing by the fountain, being a girl attendant during the rites at the temple to Baal and Asherah, during the competitive games, swimming in the sea with her father and her mother, and dining, every evening, in the cool shade of the courtyard, and singing songs with her Nubian nurse, Lalla, and …

Now …

Now she sees herself in the sacred tomb – or death – room under their house, in Greater Phoenicia, North Africa, not far away, but many centuries ago. She is as if dead, laid out on the catafalque, in the long robe, she is a young woman now, nineteen years old, they have told her, and she sees her servant and nurse, Lalla, now her boon companion, drinking the strange alien elixir and dying, falling next to the catafalque and she sees herself dead, or so it seems, and then there is a soldier, no, two soldiers, enemy warriors, and then she is covered in blood, half-naked crouching by the fountain outside in the little square, she has just drained the blood of the soldier Gaius, she is a monster, a vampire.

And now …

Now Marcus is standing over her, looking down at this blood-drinking blood-soaked 19-year-old. His sword is drawn. "So, now you know what you have become."

"Yes, father, I know what I have become."

"You are now in great danger, my daughter."

"Yes, father."

"You must gather all your strength, my daughter."

"Yes, father."

"Wake up, return to the present, return to the battle, and win ..." Marcus faded, the burning city faded, the corpse of Gaius, pale like a painted puppet, propped against the low stone wall, faded; the smell of burned flesh and burning wood faded, and she was ...

Wiggling ...

Wiggling desperately on the ground, wound up and bound in the worm glue and thick super-strong worm thread, a shackled prisoner of the Foul Fiend, and, with the image of Marcus and "Yes, father," still echoing in her mind, an idea came to her.

She groped, crawled and shimmied blindly toward the edge of the platform where one of the old generators was still linked up to the central quantum power base of the cavern, the source of power for the lights that lit the cavern, for the elevators and peripherals, and she rolled and shimmed and slithered and crawled blindly, and if she remembered correctly it should be just about here, and the cables were frayed and dangerous, high-voltage cables, and she rolled and rolled, and then she managed to flip herself upwards, to a kneeling position, and then to stand and then she threw herself down, hoping to fall across the cables, and she did fall across the cables, but nothing happened, the worms were very excited now, they were close to their goal, they were inside her nasal passages and worming their way up toward the cerebellum. They were tickling her sinus. It was horrible! They were probing and wiggling their way into her vagina.

Nothing happened!

V squirmed closer – she hoped – to the old generator.

She remembered that the wires were frayed and she'd seen a real explosion of electricity between the cables once, blue arcs flashing, in the old days, but perhaps these circuits, linked to the Crystal, were alive. Hundreds of years had passed, but ... she wiggled and wiggled, the rough cables under her belly.

WHAM!

An explosion rippled through the cavern. V's alien-reptilian body arched up, lit up like a neon sign, vibrating like a violin string, wave upon wave of electricity, sparks flying, shot through her body, surrounded her body, the worms sizzled and screamed silently, and shot off in all directions, fried worms, little curled up bits of charcoal, and embers of burning worm-flesh.

V was stunned, vibrating, jerking back and forth.

But she was free.

Whew!

She stood up.

The fried worms and their baked glue fell away.

She rubbed her eye and shook off the ashes and shreds and rags.

She needed a shower.

Wisps of the Foul Fiend drifted in the air.

Well," he said, appearing again as a gentleman, this time perhaps from the early 19th Century, an ironic Byronic figure; it was the Boy; it was his disguise as the Boy. "Let us fight as humans, since monsters do not seem to do so well!"

"As you wish," V, the demon, covered in sticky sizzled worm goo, "But perhaps I should shower first." She glanced at the Crystal to see any signs of approval or disapproval. The Crystal shimmered slightly, a rose tincture spread through the air, "Personal hygiene is, of course, important, dearest V!"

Well, it seemed the Crystal did not disapprove.

"Give me a minute, then, my dear," V said to the Don Juan version of the Devil, and she disappeared into the Work Space.

There was a shower room.

So she morphed, then she showered. Oh, what nice cool water! She imagined that the Devil might infiltrate the water and try to invade her that way.

Somehow she thought he wouldn't. What a gentleman, sometimes the Devil could be! It was one of his charms, of course. Evil is seductive. Evil does small favors, exhibits tiny courtesies, and thus, bit by bit, Evil purchases your soul – for all eternity. Yes, when you were weak and trusting, or when you had compromised yourself irredeemably, then Evil would strike. But at this moment, for some reason, she didn't think he would strike quite just yet. His pride and vanity would dictate that he won in a "fair fight," though the worms and the dragon were not really fair.

She reappeared, human once again, outfitted in her warrior getup, with its full array of gizmos and weapons and gadgets.

And so they dueled.

As the duel went on, and the Devil definitely wanted to skewer her, she stepped aside, she leaped, she swiveled, she pirouetted, she danced, she waltzed, she felt that all the spirits of freedom, of abandon, of liberty, were racing in her veins, giving wings to her limbs. Dionysius had merged with her, and Apollo.

Her arms and legs seemed fearless, seemed capable of anything. She was an acrobat, a magician, a siren and a seductress, a ballerina, and now it seemed, as the swords flashed, as sparks flew, as metal sang, it seemed as if they were somewhere else, and out of the infinite blackness and chaos without form and without light, it seemed that before her eyes, around them, and while the Devil swirled around her, it seemed that the sea and the sky were separating, as she stabbed at him with her sword, and he ducked and twirled around, his coattails flying out, and then the sky and earth and the oceans come into being, as the birth of everything played itself out in the shadow world that was in her mind, and then V sees herself rising from the sea, brandishing a sword and confronting the monster, and the monster is the Don Juan figure, but he is also a sea monster, and she is herself and yet she is also a sea-goddess, and, as they skirmish, she and the monster are so entangled it seems that they are one, and as, both in human form, they stagger up onto the pebbled beach, the pebbles are round and slippery, questions echo.

"Are you my son?"

"Are you my daughter?"

"Are you my husband?"

"Are you my wife?

"Who came first, the female or the male?"

"You mean, the one about the chicken or the egg?

"Yes, did I ever tell you that one?"

"Come now, come here, I will sing you a lullaby."

Now they are on the steps of the temple: where? In ancient Israel?

"How did that happen?"

But her friend the Devil is still dressed as a 19th Century romantic dandy, and he no longer her friend; he is still wielding his sword, "Now out, damned witch, out of the temple, there is no place here, in the sacred inner sanctum, the sanctum sanctorum, for the female, the chaotic natural, oh, too natural female!"

"Oh?"

"Yes, you are banished. Divinity is taken from you. Females are cast out. Goddesses are no more! Nymphs are an abomination! I am the flaming sword, placed here to keep you out of the sacred spaces, you Eve, you, source of all Evil, you Jezebel who imported alien gods, you who slaughtered the priests and prophets, you …"

"Well, that's all very fine, but who are you? You rather look like my idea of Lord Byron, but who, truly, are you?"

He struck a pose, puffing out his ruffled chest, very fine linen, and sparkling white V noted. He turned to her, and bowed.

"I, Madam, I am the God of the Sky."

"You live up in the blue?"

"Indeed I do," he bowed, waving his sword in front of him, "I live up in the blue; indeed, I do!" People were walking by in clothes that did indeed indicate that they were in Ancient Israel.

"Why then, if you live in the sky, do you hate women so?"

"Well," he coughed, and wiped his mouth with a sparkling pristine handkerchief, which he carefully, and with his fingertips, unfolded and folded, "You see, women are earthy."

"Earthy?"

"Yes, earthy."

"Oh," V looked around; she often had the impression, in her rather long life, that men could be quite earthy too. "Oh, earthy?"

"Yes, earthy," he coughed carefully, and wiped his mouth and looked at the handkerchief, and carefully folded it and put it away in his pocket, "You see, my dear, being a God of the Sky, I can have nothing to do with the foul fecund and fertile earth, the reign of change, of life and death, of birth and rebirth, of mulch and manure, of cadavers and offal, I cannot abide the valley of the shadow. I can have nothing whatsoever to do with deep steep ravines, and valleys and brambles and bushes and thickets and thorns and liquefaction and rivers that run, invisible, far from the sight of man. It is all just too messy."

"I see." V looked down at herself. She was still in her sparkling 21st Century Centurion's uniform, she was still outfitted superbly, and, at this specific moment, having just had a shower, she really didn't feel particularly "earthy," though, if you looked at it in the right light, in the appropriate context, with soft music and some grapes and olives, and a good wine, *earthy* could certainly be a compliment. As for ravines, and valleys of the shadow, and fecund female heart of darkness sort of thing, and thickets and brambles, and the fluidity of creation, and sacred rivers running down to a sunless sea, well, on that subject ...

The Don Juan figure bowed, sniffed at his handkerchief, fluffed it out, sniffed again, and declared, "I am unchanging and eternal, I have nothing to do with the cycle of death and rebirth; I am One; I am not Many; I am Unique: I share nothing with anything or anyone or any creature!"

"Well, well," V turns around, and she is now inside a temple, an ancient temple, and she sees herself: a young woman … It must be me, she thinks.

Barefoot in the temple, she is, next to an athletic young man, who is naked except for a loincloth, and she runs toward the sacred altar, 'Quick now, quick now, my love, let us make love here, on this smooth stone, let us consecrate the beginning, the origin, let us recreate the world, let us do what men and women and gods and kings and fools and commoners have always done, let us embrace, let us love."

She let drop her veils, and he stepped out of his loincloth, and with that into her welcoming arms, he went, and she sang, turning it into a rhythm, "Let us do the begat, the begat, the begat. He begat, she begat, they begat, we begat …

"Yes, let us begat!"

She pauses, kisses him, and whispers, "In the books, it's always guys who begat, or beget, which is rather strange, is it not, my love. I mean, really who does most of the begetting, who is burdened with the heavy lifting in the begetting?"

"True, true, but let us debate some other time!"

"Quite right, my Lord!"

"I am glad you agree, my Lady!"

And so they begat, on the altar as was appropriate, since Original Sin had not yet been invented – but it was on its way, it was definitely on its way. Rabble-rousers of every ilk were working up a furious storm. Sin! Oh, Sin!

A lot of distracting noise was going on. It made it hard to concentrate on the romance in hand, the begetting. And besides V was not really sure she should be copulating in the temple – whatever temple it was – with the Devil, and in any case, this was probably all an illusion, a split-second illusion, another world manifesting itself in an instant between strike and counter-strike as they continued their duel, dancing closer, and far away, and closer, and far away, swords clashing sparks, the clang of steel against steel ringing in the vast cavern, under the Crystal as she floated shimmering above them.

Meantime bearded fierce unkempt old men in long robes – and fierce unkempt young men too – were raging around the temple kicking out all the old gods and goddesses, tearing down statues, smashing images with axes and bars of iron, rampaging through the women's quarters, slashing at the women priests and the virgins with broadswords and pikes.

"What wicked fellows are these?" V wonders, and she thinks, well, they are all foaming at the mouth and raging with righteousness! What are they called again? Why, yes, of course, I remember now, these are *prophets*, they are called prophets. Oh, dear, really? Her naked young man has disappeared, so, deprive of a confidante, she dialogs with herself as the drama unfolds, and a whole horde of bearded men rush forward to attack her.

"Who are these people, V?"

"Why, V, it is clear, and self-evident. They are prophets!"

"Really! V! How horrible! How absolutely upsetting! Do you like prophets, V? No, not really, V, I don't particularly care for prophets," she took a deep breath, still talking to herself as very creative or totally insane people tend to do, acting out inner and outer dramas, creating inner and outer weather, when they go for long feverish walks, or rock in their little chairs, fingers locked and clasped between their thighs, "My God, I don't like to kill bearded old fellows."

"Well, V," V said, "if their age is the problem, let me tell you that there are some angry bearded young fellows too, the key thing is, that they are all angry, very angry, and they want to kill everybody and everything!"

V cupped her chin in her right hand and wondered: What was the best way to oppose all these angry bearded men?

A lightning bolt?

Total war?

Or …

Diplomacy – Nah, they are prophets; they will not put water in their wine; no compromise for them, no shilly-shally half-measures. They are enthralled by the Absolute – of their own Egos.

Or …

Love, seduction …

Yes, of course, V, you are quite right: the thing they hate the most is a part of themselves, the part of themselves, the soft, vulnerable yet virile loving side, the part of themselves they absolutely abhor; that is just the ticket, V! You shall drive them mad!

Those whom the gods would destroy, those they drive mad!

And so she began to dance. "Didn't somebody else do this, with a veil?" she said, "And of course the ungentlemanly self-righteous creep rejected her advances, and then there was Jezebel, a beautiful girl, a compatriot of mine actually, a poor innocent Phoenician married off to a Jewish King to seal some commercial deal, a stranger in a strange land, far from her beloved

Sidon, so dreadfully misunderstood and mistreated in her new home, no sense of hospitality those chaps, particularly that trickster Elijah, I'll bet he stacked the decks when the gods were pitched against each other, Yahweh and Baal and Asherah. Jezebel just wanted to be able to worship her own gods, poor dear … And so some chauvinistic creep threw her from a window; even though, as a show of courtesy and female bravery, she had dolled herself up for him, for the trial she knew was coming …" And so V danced, making it as sexy and seductive and subversive and transgressive – all those fashionable words – as she could, and lo and behold!

"She-Devil!!" The prophets, young and old, surged back in terror. They threw anathemas and bulls and fatwas and grenades and missiles and scimitars and stones and acid and child suicide bombers and everything they could think of. They lifted up sacred books and pronounced what sounded a lot like curses: complicated divine gobbledygook to be sure, which sounded very impressive, like the spells those witches, old and young, were said to have cast, before the patriarchs burned them at the stake, poor girls.

"You can't fool me," she said.

The prophets screamed.

"You can't fool me," she said, "you are suffering …"

The prophets screamed.

"You are suffering desire, yearning, longing – and you don't like it." V twirled around, and, though she had never been a flower child and only flirted with being a hippy and mocked the idea of joining a commune, since such utopias invariably ended up being miniature Stalinist tyrannies run by male maniacs, she began to sing, an ancient song, something about *all you need is love* …

The prophets screamed like banshees yowling at the moon. They crushed their fists against their ears. They tore their hair. They rent their beards. They stuck their fingers deep in their ears. They yelled and yowled in terror. They twirled and leaped; they screamed once again, and then they exploded into a cloud of scraps of paper and the scraps of paper drifted away, with a few curls, gray and black, from various beards; and the prophets were no more.

Love, evidently, was not to their taste.

The Crystal coughed a genteel little cough, "I don't like to interfere, my dear, but I do not like most of these gentlemen or prophets as they style themselves. I think your little dance was a fine idea. But even having anything to do with them is, well, rather compromising, don't you think, I mean for a proper girl such as yourself?"

"Oh," V raised an eyebrow, and parried a thrust by the Don Juan figure who was still dueling her as fiercely as he could.

"Yes, V dear, I'm sure they think they are godly, but most of them are devils and reverse angels, angels from Hell."

"Really, Crystal, it's unlike you to be so judgemental, and, ah, so vehement. Usually, you keep your opinions to yourself, most of the time, I mean."

"Yes, well, V, darling, sometimes one must just take a stand, if you know what I mean. One cannot be a milquetoast mute witness with one's arms folded floppily on one's chest all the time when absolute horrors are taking place. One cannot, on every occasion, wash one's hands, as Pontius is said to have done. Those prophet fellows, well, they just kidnap the Holy Word. They sing siren songs from pulpits, and they pretend to do their God's work but mostly, it is the murderous work of the Devil. But, back to the matter in hand, V."

V parried, she thrust, and she jumped aside.

The Devil struck, parried, twirled dervish style, and jumped aside.

The struggle was furious, a whirr of movement.

Sword stuck sword; sparks flew; cold steel glittered; booted feet danced lightly, pivoted, turned, leaped.

V and the Foul Fiend dueled like mad creatures, twirling along the platform in front of the Crystal.

Suddenly the Devil, in a quick series of thrusts, and parries, drove V off the platform and up onto the stage itself, the very lip of the Gateway, the Gateway to the stars.

This was not good!

V's back was breathtakingly close to the shimmering wall of plasma, which was very essence – the licking hungry lips – of the Gateway to the stars and to the universe. The Gateway could lead anywhere, and it could lead to death. The Gateway was the time-space warp opening that allowed you – if you were lucky – to travel anywhere, but it depended on the Crystal. The Crystal would decide.

The Foul Fiend leaped at her. He had transformed himself. He had stopped playing. He was no longer toying with her, no longer pretending to be gallant. He was all muscle. He smashed her in the jaw; she staggered back, and then she twirled around, and as he came for her, she leaped in the air and came down on his back. "Oh, oh, my little bronco!" His muscles were enormous.

She reached down, tried to scratch out his eyes; her nails raked across his forehead, her nails left ribbons of red on his cheeks.

He turned a somersault, throwing her off; she flew through the air, landed with a back-breaking thump, and skidded across the floor. She got up, and she charged him, head down now, her vanity wounded, her ire up, her blood racing, her anger frothing – not a very good idea, really, part of her mind told her.

"Tsch, tsch, tsch," whispered the Crystal, "A little self-control, darling, a little self-control!"

The Foul Fiend staggered backward, pretended to fall, and then suddenly he swept around, and, using V's own blind fury and furious forward momentum, he thrust and swung her toward the Gateway; the plasma wall reached out, and, humming sweetly, it seized V by the shoulder, just as she turned and tried to skid to a stop.

V felt herself being sucked in. Her shoulder was trembling, her uniform about to be de-materialized. She felt herself being swept into nothingness. She grabbed at the Foul Fiend, caught his lapel, and dragged him with her.

But now both of them were going to be swept away. She could feel bits of her uniform fragmenting, and soon it would be her flesh and her mind, and then, unless she landed on some other planet somewhere, she would be pulverized and become nothing.

She kicked at the pavement, put her foot behind his leg, and she flipped the Foul Fiend over – so he stumbled to his knees – and she swirled around, and now she was free, and he was there with his back to the vibrant wall of plasma.

The Foul Fiend roared.

He hated being made a fool of.

"I will destroy thee, wench! And then I shall reign over this bitch of a Crystal, which is …"

And he twirled around, and somehow he forced V back against the shimmering plasma wall.

V felt the plasma eat at the shoulder of her uniform, nibble, nibble, nibble, and soon it would anchor itself in her flesh, and then …

Oh, my god!

She heard the Crystal whisper something like "V, oh, V, oh, no, V …"

This cannot be happening!

V struggled to keep her footing, but she was slipping, the sole of her boot didn't have enough grip, it was scraping along the pavement, she was ceding ground, one, two, three inches, she felt the plasma licking at her, eagerly, lapping around her, hoping. What was going on? This couldn't be happening!

No, no, no …

At that instant something, rocketing out from the other side of the wall of plasma, something coming from another universe or from distant time and space in this universe, it smacked and thudded into the Foul Fiend with tremendous force, knocked him over, and sent the Foul Fiend sprawling across the stage, far from the shimmering wall, and the Foul Fiend fell on his backside and roared, "What!"

V was surprised. She was thrown away from the wall of plasma, ending up on her hands and knees, looking up, shocked, wondering what had happened. She blinked. This was crazy!

Bounding across the stage was a black and white collie, a border collie.

It raced toward V and seemed happy to see her, and it barked, and the Foul Fiend sprang to his feet, and was right behind it, aiming a laser straight at the dog; the Foul Fiend was going to kill the dog – right in front of V! This was outrageous! V would never accept such a thing. Cruelty to animals was beyond the pale!

"No, you don't!" V drew her pistol and fired, and the laser flamed against the Foul Fiend's hand. It deflected his shot, which sizzled against the shimmering plasma wall, spreading out like the iridescence of an expanding soap bubble which then popped leaving behind waves of miniature rainbows.

The Foul Fiend swung around, aiming his laser at V. The dog raced, head-down toward the Foul Fiend, the Foul Fiend lowered his aim, "I shall kill you, you cur, you mutt, you …"

V leaped and landed straight on the Foul Fiend, just as the collie slammed into the Foul Fiend and sunk its teeth into the Foul Fiend's ankle.

The Foul Fiend tossed V aside. He staggered back, and swore and cursed and cast anathemas upon the dog, excommunicating the dog, declaring that the dog had no soul, that the dog was a dreadful dog, that the dog was an unclean beast, that the dog was a pariah, that the dog … And while he was doing this, the Foul Fiend, holding up the foot that had been bitten, was bouncing back on one leg, and, he didn't notice it, but he was headed straight for, and then into, the wall of plasma.

"Oh," he screamed, "Oh!"

The glassy green-blue wall of quantum plasma vibrated and bulged out and grabbed the Foul Fiend's arm; he lost his balance; now, he was caught in the wall of plasma; one arm was behind the wall, all liquid and vibrating with a strange light.

The Foul Fiend screamed.

The plasma licked at him, eating his flesh, exposing part of his ribs and one shoulder-blade, streaked with blood.

"Help!" he screamed.

And V saw it for what it was. Yes, it was indeed true: once he had incarnated himself in a real body, in a fight, mano a mano, with her, he had committed himself, could not escape from the body he had assumed, not if that body was trapped in some mortal coil, some gluey aggressive substantial bit of reality. This was his weakness. Without a body, Evil could not act, could not exist, but if the body was trapped by the plasma, the Evil One could not free himself from the body. The Foul Fiend was suffering a mortal weakness. The Foul Fiend – the God of Evil – was trapped in the body he had chosen, and now that the plasma had him in its grip, he could not escape; he could not disengage from the borrowed flesh; he could not free himself. The weakness of incarnation, as on the cross, was now clear. Embodiment, being in a body, means suffering, irredeemable suffering.

"Well, my dear," said V, "what do we do now?"

The Devil screamed. His mouth became enormous. He tried to flip out of the body.

His spirit, like an elastic band, like a pure wave of energy, tried to leap away, tried to transcend the body, reached out like a screaming shuddering hologram mask; but the plasma would not let him transcend; it pulled him back; it locked him in its grip, it pinned him down, caught between universes; it pulled him into itself, a ghostly screaming semitransparent figure. V stared. He was like a painting by Francis Bacon. She was moved, terrified.

He screamed again. Again, his spirit tried to escape, it struggled, it fought, it stretched, but each time it was pulled back into the trapped, struggling, tormented body.

V stood back, horrified and in awe: the body is a prison; certainly, now it was. Everyone knows the experience: Our ideas and imaginings, our yearnings and ideals fly up, but our flesh is weak, and limited, and mortal. Plato's eternal ideas cannot survive incarnation! Caught in the flesh, timelessness withers, oh, time-bound, mortal flesh!

He tried to get a grip on the platform, but his boots were slipping and sliding; he kicked; one boot, which was just touched by a tendril of plasma, became transparent, a glass boot, a glass foot, glass bones; the boot disappeared, the whole scene wavered. Yes, his foot did look like it was made of glass. Then it was a skeleton and then the bones too began to blacken and vanish.

"V, help me! You are so gallant, so generous, and so kind!"

"I'm sorry." V stood very straight, almost rigid, only a few meters away, her eyes wide in wonder; beside her, the dog, the black-and-white border collie, had appeared. Its tongue hung out, eagerly; it watched the show, perhaps understanding something, perhaps not. V reached down and scratched its ears.

It wagged its tail and gazed up at her.

"I AM BAAL, YOU ARE MY BRIDE!" The Foul Fiend screamed.

"No, I am not your Bride."

"I am Baal, you are my bride."

"No, I am not, and you are not! You are not Baal."

"I am Baal!"

"No, you are not even Beelzebub. You are not Satan. You are none of those things. All that is flimsy flimflam and, if you want my opinion, you speak bunk, pure bunk! You are nothing, just fear, just hate, just envy, just cruelty – just a name!"

"I am God! I am Baal! You are my Bride!"

"No, my dear, I am very sorry, but you are nothing!"

"No, no, no!"

Thunder rolled in the distance. V turned toward the deep-throated echo. Ancient temples surged up; images of gods, ancient and new gods, then the vision faded. All the demons rose from all the pits of hell and hades and danced a ghostly dance, all the angels cavorted on the heads of pins, all the Cherubim sang, all the Seraphim praised and guarded the gates with swords of fire, all the … Well, it went on and on, a shadowy parade of shadowy beings.

The Crystal hummed gently; it sounded to V's ears like a lullaby remembered from ancient times.

"I am God," the Foul Fiend screamed, "I am Everything!"

"No, my dear fellow, you are not God; you are the Devil of Emptiness. You are not a god and never have been!" V was not entirely sure of this, but it sounded nice. She suspected that many of the gods whom people had worshiped – secular idols as well as religious gods – actually were devils.

Suddenly the Foul Fiend's voice changed. It became the voice of a child. "Please, I'll be good! I'll be good!" the Foul Fiend screamed. "I'll be good. Just save me and love me and keep me and never leave me!" His face became the face of a child, a beautiful child. It morphed into the face of Asherah, her long-lost servant, it morphed into the face of Kat, of Miranda, of Marcus, of the President, of the Mind-Child; it became the little girl from the distant future, Claudia.

"Please!" the child screamed, "I beg you!", and the child's face morphed into Emilia, a child V had tried to save, in vain, during the eruption of Vesuvius in 79 CE. V was back there, for an instant, reaching out, crawling down a narrow alley, under a rain of gray ash, and then the cloud of red-hot gas and burning half-molten ash descended, and V barely saved herself, the child's face, so beautiful and tender and terrified, oh those bright eyes, was suddenly distorted into a hideous mask, mustachioed, bright red, and sporting horns and pointed ears, and it screamed, "I am the Devil, I am Lucifer, I am God, I am Beelzebub, and I curse you, I curse you forever, and ever, and I have won, you will see, I have won, I curse you!"

"You curse me?"

"Yes, I curse you and all who exist!"

And zip, there was a whooshing sound, and the face and the body fell apart into shimmering bits and pieces like a body seen through a kaleidoscope or a waterfall, and whoosh, it was gone, sucked away, turning into a ribbon and tail, or trail, of light – like the tail of a comet – and then here was nothing, and the wall of plasma vibrated and hummed for a few seconds, turned iridescent and opaque for an instant, and then, suddenly, the whole Gateway turned black, and then the stars shone and there was the Andromeda galaxy in all its peaceful splendor – home, it was in some way that was difficult to define, home …

The collie barked. It licked V's hand. She crouched down and scratched it behind the ears and ruffled its fur. It looked up and smiled a dog smile, tongue hanging out, eager.

"Crystal?" V turned toward the great Crystal floating serenely, or so it seemed, in the vast latticework.

"Yes, V."

"Where has he gone, what has happened to him?"

"Oh, I am glad you asked that question, V: and in fact, the answer is of great interest, both theoretical and practical: he has gone into pure nothingness; I sent him to a non-place, a place where there is no way he can reconstitute himself. He is nothing now, locked in a swirl and prison of dark energy, and will be for all eternity."

"Oh," said V, feeling a tremor of fear: eternal damnation to non-existence was a scary idea, she had to admit. "Is he aware of this?"

"He is aware," the Crystal said, "He is aware that he is nothing and that he is nowhere and that he never can be anything or anyone or anywhere ever again. He is condemned to be locked in nothingness forever, blind, deaf, without sense of touch or taste or anything, and of course without a body to inhabit, just a pinpoint of conscious pain in an infinity of darkness."

"Poor sod," said V, in spite of herself.

"Yes, V, your compassion and empathy have always been one of your more admirable qualities, quite extraordinary in a beast of prey; I often marveled at it, even when you were killing your prey, and drinking it dry, and sucking it until it was empty and merely a husk, even when you were standing over it, proudly, and declaring that it was dead and totally and forever dead and would never rise again. Still, you felt compassion for your victim, you knew what a gift your victim had given you, and, in dying, what a gift your victim had lost, for life is, whether one has a theology or not, a great gift, existence is divine. As for the Foul Fiend, as you call him, well, he ..." The Crystal hesitated. "I'm not sure how to put this."

"Yes, Crystal?"

"If we look at the situation he has created, I am afraid that he deserves his fate. For he has, in one sense, won, and I hate to admit this V."

"So, he has won?" V felt a shiver of fear. "What do you mean *won*?"

"Well, it is, in a way a detail, and I hesitate to mention it, but ..."

"What? What is it?"

"I am afraid, V, that he has succeeded in destroying the human race. For humans, it is the end of time, the end of days. They are all going to die, each and every one of them."

"What?" V was astounded; this could not be.

"And I think, V, the time has come for a confession."

"But, Crystal ..."

"No, V, you must listen. It is time for a confession."

"A confession?" V wanted to talk about the humans, about the fate of humanity, about ...

"You have always remarked on my voice."

"Yes, it is so beautiful, particularly when you speak that ancient language, a language I know from my childhood ..."

"Phoenician, ancient Phoenician, the dialect of Carthage, of North Africa, actually, yes …"

"And you sing lullabies, songs for a child, for a baby …"

"Yes, I do, those are the songs I often sing, V … Your father …"

"Marcus?"

"Yes, your father from beyond the stars, he adored those songs, he liked them very much, and …"

"What are you trying to tell me, Crystal?"

"It is difficult, V, for it is a very strange story. You know how your mother, your biological mother, not your adopted mother, you know how your biological mother died …"

"Yes, Marcus told me. He opened the window in the bedroom where they had just made love, and he let in the sun, and since his experiments had made her vulnerable to sunlight, which was deadly for her, she exploded into flame and died. It was murder and it was horrible."

"It was very painful for him," the Crystal hesitated.

"Yes, but more painful for her, I suppose," said V, feeling rather peevish, and a bit angry – once again – with Marcus.

"Well, Marcus was very much in love, you know, and he had, in all innocence, thinking the experiment would bring only good, he had used your mother as a guinea pig, as an experimental subject, and he began to realize the dangers of the experiment, you know, and …"

"Yes, he told me," V said, remembering that night two centuries ago in Cambridge, England, when Marcus had confessed. She shivered. "Mother was so bloodthirsty that she would, in her consuming passion, have spread the curse of vampirism and destroyed the human race."

"Yes, that is true; sadly, it is true. Well, Marcus was very brave; he took certain precautions against what was going to happen, you know."

"Yes, like planning to kill her."

"Your father is a very compassionate man, V, you mustn't judge him so. You must not …"

"But, Crystal, how can you understand, how can you understand what a lover would feel, what a woman would feel, betrayed, doubly betrayed by the man she loved, the man she loved so passionately …?"

"Darling V, please, just listen! It is not like you to be so judgmental, so quick and harsh, so unforgiving …"

"Oh, Crystal, you know I adore Marcus, but somehow I wish …" V hesitated; she really didn't know what she wished; she wished she had known her mother, she wished she could have met her, talked to her, comforted her, taken comfort from her; she wished … Oh, I have bottled so much up so long! I really don't know what I want, who I am, or what I am!

The collie licked her hand.

V looked down.

The dog wagged its tail, tongue hanging out, eager for orders, for instructions; of course, it was a working dog, it wanted to know what was the next task, what was the next …

"Before your mother became sick, before she …"

"You meant to say before she became a vampire. Before she became a vampire because father experimented with her, because he tried to make her immortal, you mean …" said V, she crouched down and scratched the dog's ears.

"Yes, before that happened, which was very painful and horrifying, I can tell you, absolutely horrible …"

V looked up. It seemed the Crystal was crying; the voice broke up. "Tell me, tell me, Crystal."

"Marcus brought your mother here. They were very much in love. Oh, those nights on the roof of his villa, oh, those long walks in the cool of the evening, oh those secret meetings where they swam in the river together, where they bathed in the waterfall, where they spent evenings around a fire, eating together, drinking wine, sharing the deepest thoughts, the deepest imaginings, the deepest feelings, gazing into each other's eyes! Oh, V … it was so …"

"Marcus brought my mother here?"

"Yes."

"And …?"

The Crystal sighed. The Crystal's voice, V thought, was truly beautiful. It awakened so many feelings, so many memories … memories?"

"And what did Marcus and mother do here? Please tell me."

"Well, yes, darling, V." The Crystal sniffled, and cleared its throat. "He uploaded her personality, well, a copy of her personality, all her memories, and all her thoughts, all her inclinations and synaptic connections, all her history, her sensations too, her bodily incarnation, so she would become one with me, she would be me."

"Oh, the gods …"

Of course, your mother continued to exist, physically to exist, and she and I were linked; everything she felt, or saw, or thought, I felt, and saw and thought."

"Oh, my god ... Crystal ..."

"But then she died. Marcus had to kill her. I suffered her death with her, I died when she died, I was in the room when the sun shone on her body, on our body, and so ... I burned, I screamed, I felt betrayed, I died ..."

"Oh, Crystal ..."

"But I was reborn. So the voice you hear, the lullabies, the language when I speak in that ancient Phoenician dialect, that is me, that is the core of me; that is your mother's voice."

"Oh, Crystal!" V stood up. The dog stopped panting, and realizing something exceptional was happening, it turned and stared at the Crystal.

"In reality, V, now don't take this in the wrong way, darling, please, but in reality, in a sense ..."

"No, I won't, I promise." V felt she would melt: she stared up at the great Crystal floating in its vast metal latticework.

"Well, in a sense, V, in fact, in reality, if there is such a thing as reality, I am ... I am ... your mother, V. Yes, V, I am your mother."

"Oh, Crystal ..."

And with that, out of the pure air, a woman materialized, at first, as a hologram, then as a simulacra of flesh and blood, a beautiful woman, jet-black hair framing her sparkling dark eyes and full lips; she was perhaps nineteen years old, and wearing the simple robe of a Phoenician noblewoman, and she stepped forward, opening her arms, "V," she said, "V ..."

CHAPTER 17 – DEATH

Nikki Hughes suddenly felt that something had happened – the death of something horrible. Somehow the shadow of Evil had been lifted from the world, for a moment at least. She whispered, under her breath, "The Evil One is gone; he is dead, or he is gone – he is gone."

She was standing with the Great High Priest, her personal assistant, young Tara Capricorn, and several of the guards on the cliff ledge just outside the Large Round Door. The sun was setting brilliantly, in the west, a great golden aurora spread along the horizon.

"The colors have come back," said Nikki, half to herself, half to Tara and the Great High Priest, "the colors have come back."

"Yes, I feel them, Goddess. I cannot see, but I can feel," the Great High Priest turned his handsome goatish face to the brilliant sinking sun.

"And the zombie-bats are dying, my friend," Nikki said, "I don't know how I know this, but I do. They are dying, and they are reverting to their human form when they die. Whatever evil force generated them – the Boy or whatever he was – is gone."

"We are alive, and we are blessed, Goddess," said the Great High Priest.

The bear guards, standing close by scanned the sky, and, shielding their eyes with their great paws, they looked at the sinking sun. Not in weeks had it been so glorious. The air, somehow, seemed purer too.

Nikki put her hand on the Great High Priest's forearm, "Perhaps, Great High Priest, we should have a feast of thankfulness this evening. Do you think people would like that?"

"Yes, that is a fine idea, Goddess. I shall give the order." He waved his hand, and one of the bears came forward.

"Excellent," said the bear, "I shall inform the cooks and managers at once.

And he went off to transmit the orders of the Goddess Nikki and the Great High Priest.

"It is good just to stand in the sunlight and to be free," said the Great High Priest.

"Yes, it is," said Nikki. She glanced toward the dark eastern side of the sky where one or two stars already twinkled. Titanic struggles were still taking place, and she had a vague intimation that something immense and horrible was about to happen, something gigantesque and irreparable, something tha would change the destiny of very creature on earth...

But she felt, too, that, for the moment, that V must have won her battle, part of her battle at least, and Miranda and Caliban must be safe. So she would say nothing about her fears. After all, they were only vague intimations. Let everyone enjoy the moment – victories were so few!

Nikki touched her cheek, where one tear had fallen. She was surprised at how much, how deeply, how passionately, she missed Miranda. For almost fourteen years, her every thought had been for Miranda, and now ... it was as if there was a void in her heart. Nikki, though she was not religious, said a silent prayer – for Miranda and for Caliban, for Kat and V and for Kit, and for everyone. "Please keep them safe, each and every one."

Tara Capricorn put her hand in the Goddess's hand, and squeezed.

Nikki looked down at her and smiled. "Thank you, Tara Capricorn." She suppressed a sigh. Being without Miranda was shockingly difficult. Since Miranda first opened her eyes upon the world, Nikki had never been separated from her, and, now, she had only just found her lost son – wonderful Caliban, so admirably brought up by the Great High Priest – and she risked losing them both. But, no, she felt, she was sure, they were both safe. Yes, they were both safe. Soon she would be united with them again.

More zombie-bats had come after the departure of the vertijet, and the battle had been fierce. The mutant kingdom – with the aid of their hybrid and human allies – had defended itself and driven off the attackers.

The world too, during that endless night and day, seemed to have been drained of all color and life, of all vitality and reality; it had become a pale dead reflection of itself – the sand dunes seemed gray, the sun was a pale, sickly disk in the sky, the moon was a thin jaundiced yellow, and all the small life forms, even the snakes, seemed to have disappeared. The evil force that had swept across the continent was imposing its rule – a rule of death and lifelessness and of eternal slavery.

But, now, that leaden weight seemed to have been lifted. The sun reached the horizon and sat there, a great honey-gold ball of fire. Nikki felt she would like to get down on her knees and worship the Sun God. The Great High Priest had turned his face to the dying sun. He was soaking in every bit of life and heat that he could. The sun sank slowly, becoming a deeper red, and then a dark, dark red, like the dying embers of a wood fire in a fireplace, and then it was gone. The sky had a turquoise and yellow and lime fringe just at the low desert horizon. Up higher, the sky was blue for an instant and then inky black. Stars began to appear.

Sabrina and Helen, two of the hybrids, who had been up higher on the cliff as lookouts, came down the upper path toward the door. They waved before going in. Earlier, they had reported finding dying and dead zombie-bats. And, from another direction came Freddy, the hybrid warrior, with Valerie Joffre, the Cosmos geologist, from where they had been checking the mining camp ruins for hiding zombie-bats. They waved, and entered the door.

"Whatever morphed them, whatever changed them, it must be dead too," Sabrina, the hybrid – and famous scientist – who was their informal leader, had told Nikki. "So maybe the Boy has been conquered. Maybe he is dead."

The hybrids had, of course, been perfect! Nikki knew hybrids. V, her closest friend, was Queen of the Hybrids; and she had known Sabrina well, back before the Culling, but she was still surprised at how easily they had blended in, brilliant and strong as they were; they didn't try to dominate; they just played their part, modestly, effectively, giving advice in the Defense Committee, but never imposing themselves, often playing with the children – Jake and Gloria – who were the favorite pets of everybody, of hybrids, particularly the golden one called Eve, and of mutants, and humans. None of the hybrids had yet morphed back into human form; she wondered if they ever would – or if they ever could.

Nikki glanced at the bears, at Norton the Security Chief, and at the Great High Priest. Maybe it would be possible to build a new civilization, a happy civilization that would include everybody.

"Perhaps we should go in, Great High Priest," Nikki said, gently, for she did not want to break the spell of the hour or the old man's reverie.

"Yes, yes, Goddess, you are right, it is right and meet that we go in," said the Great High Priest.

"May I?" He leaned on her for support.

"Yes, of course."

"Oh, Goddess, you are a comfort and a staff."

"Come, my friend," Nikki said. "We shall celebrate, and then we shall all rest, hybrids, SINs, mutants, and humans."

One of the Bears, Peter, swung the great door open. Norton and several of the Bears waited until Nikki and Tara Capricorn and the Great High Priest had entered the Great Door.

Norton cast a last look at the fading light, at the west; he sensed that a battle had been won, but that the struggle was not over yet, that more, and worse, was yet to come. Somehow, a sense of doom settled in his heart.

"Colonel?" said Hans, one of the Bears, "Something evil this way comes – you sense it?"

"Yes, I do."

"I also sense something, Colonel – I cannot yet put a word to it."

"Nor can I, my friend, I cannot put a word to it," Norton glanced off toward the last traces of sunset, blue and yellow and emerald green: what a beautiful world this was, "But it is more horrible than anything that has come before."

"We cannot spoil the feast, I think, Colonel," Hans too was looking toward the horizon, the last light turning his fur pale yellowish gold with threads of moonlight silver.

"Yes, you are right, Hans. Well, let us go, then, my friend," Norton said, and together he and Hans entered the Great Door, and Peter closed it behind them.

Already, far below, the drums of celebration were beating, and the warm, earthy smell of roasting lichen and mushrooms wafted in the air.

The barrier door burst behind them, water flooded into the tunnel, and now they were running for their lives.

Even running, his heart pounding, the President could see it, the big picture, in his mind, with vivid, overwhelming clarity. The great ocean barriers had broken; water was thundering through the old subway lines, and through the caverns, tunnels, crawl spaces, underground streets, storage spaces, electrical plans, and transformation installations; everywhere water was boiling up and smashing through barriers. The Atlantic was invading the netherworld of Elysium. It might even reach the central nuclear reactor.

The wall of water was just behind them. "Come on, come on," shouted Kit.

They were running, everybody was running.

Kit ran beside the Centurion Kat and the President and the two children. They came to a spiral metal staircase, and they leaped up it. Just behind them were Caliban and Miranda.

Kit stopped to help Kat push away a tangle of wire that would foul up Miranda and Caliban. When they turned around, the President and the children were already sprinting, far ahead.

They ran up the spiral staircase, and it opened onto a wide tunnel, with a gently arched roof, with ancient wires and cables running along the roof.

The water smashed into the stairwell, and began to thunder up in in a great geyser and tidal wave of water.

Miranda and Caliban galloped. Behind them, a foaming wall of water was smashing down the large tunnel.

"Do you think we can make it?" Miranda glanced back; she could hardly hear her own voice. The foaming wall of water was right behind them. It thundered down on them.

The President had already lost sight of Kit when he got to the top of the spiral staircase and entered the larger tunnel, and the wall of water smashed into him. He was twirled around in a thunderous wall of water, but he managed to hold the two children pressed against him; the Mind-Child was torn from his arms; the President trashed out blindly and grabbed the Mind-Child's shirt; he held on, only hoping that the shirt would not split, rip, or slip off the child's body. Now he was whirled around, upside down, helpless, with one arm wrapped tight around Claudia and the other desperately holding the Mind-Child. The rational thing would be to let go of the shirt, let the Mind-Child go, and save the one child, the child that could be saved; he knew that yesterday, only yesterday, he would have taken that "rational" decision, fearlessly, with no or little regrets; it was after all the "rational" thing to do; but not now. Now he was going to try to save both children, even if it meant dying in the attempt.

"Of course, we can make it!" Caliban shouted. They ran faster and faster, they came to a ramp that sloped upwards, then they came to a wall. There seemed to be no way forward. Oh, there was a tny door! Miranda got down on her hands and knees and looked through it, and she saw it led to a tunnel. "It's the only way …"

A wall of water slammed into them. Miranda went twirling heels-over-head.

She grabbed for Caliban and missed him. Then, suddenly, she was above the surface, in an ocean of hissing foam, surrounded by bobbing flotsam and jetsam; she caught a glimpse of Kit, and then she was caught and swirled under again, and twirled around and around, swimming mightily, determined to get to the surface. Up she splashed, face-to-face with Caliban, who looked oh so glamorous, with his hair slicked down, his eyes even brighter than usual, and rivulets of water running down his face. He smiled. His bright teeth were brilliant in the gloom.

"Hello, Princess!" He threw his arms around her. Their bodies were pressed together. Down they went, bouncing, racing, surfacing, submerging, and swirling around corners, and up shafts and down tunnels, and catching a breath each time they bounced to the surface, sometimes with only a foot between the roiling bubbly surface of the water and the arched stone roof of the tunnel, and still, they clung to each other. They were like one body instead of two.

"Oh, Caliban," Miranda gasped. She silenced him before he could say a word with a wild savage endless world-dissolving kiss.

The President twirled in a whirlpool of water, helplessly, the Mind-Child bumped against him, and they were swept up, in a maelstrom in reverse, as water shot up in a funnel. In one explosive burst, they were on the surface, spluttering; the Mind-Child was again swept close to the President, within an inch of his face. The President seized the Mind-Child, slippery with the clayey water. The child slipped from his grasp, its huge eyes, desperate, staring straight at him. The President lunged, reached out, grabbed the Mind-Child and gathered it to him. Claudia was sputtering, hanging on desperately, her arms still locked around the President's neck.

"Hold on," he shouted, Hold on, both of you!"

"Yes."

"Yes."

The President and the two children were swirled around by the tempestuous current, but it was slower now. The President's boots touched the sloping floor of the tunnel, and he struggled upwards, fighting to keep his balance, the two children clinging to him. Finally, they were at the top of a sort of ramp in the tunnel, on dry land. The President fell to his knees, and holding the two children, he looked into their eyes. "So," he said, holding them tight, "How do we feel, then?"

Kit surfaced in a world of spinning bubbles, not far from some metal steps that seemed to lead straight upward; her feet weren't touching ground; and she found herself face-to-face with Kat, whose helmet visor was up and dripping a regular Niagara of water. They grabbed each other. Face-to-face, body locked against body, they were whirled around by the turbulent current; it was as if they were waltzing; Kat had her arm around Kit's waist. "I'm not going to let go," she said.

"Kat," said Kit, spluttering.

"Kit," said Kat, teeth and dark eyes gleaming.

"Kit and Kat," said Kit, coughing up water, "it sounds like a vaudeville routine."

"Kat and Kit," said Kat, "yes it does, or an ancient animal cartoon."

"Yes."

"Or a candy bar."

"Yes, a candy bar!"

They both started laughing like crazy. They managed to swim toward the metal steps. They grabbed the metal railing and helped each other up onto the stairs, stumbling, crawling, coughing, Kat in her still perfect Centurion uniform, dripping water in a regular cascade, and Kit in her silver-skin shorts and skin T-shirt, shedding rivulets of water. Kat blinked, looking out over the dim seething surface, "So, where are the others?"

"We'll have to dive in and look for them if they don't come up."

"Yes, we will."

They sat watching the boiling whirling water.

"I'm not going to give up, Kit."

"I'm not going to give up, Kat."

"There's no reason to give up either," said Caliban, who came sputtering to the surface a few meters away, and Miranda, who was right beside them, their slicked-down heads making them look in the dim silvery-gray light like two beautiful photogenic seals.

Miranda and Caliban swam over and clambered out of the water. It seemed to be lower now. Miranda looked around, "Where is the President? Where are the kids?"

"They were just behind us," said Kit.

"We'll go back for them," said Kat.

"Yes," Miranda slicked back her hair and looked out over the swirling water, which seemed to be receding.

"Listen," said Caliban.

They listened, and they heard laughter, a child's laughter.

"Alright, then," it was the President's voice.

"But it's funny," it was Claudia's voice.

"It's really funny," it was the Mind-Child's voice.

The water was much lower now, and dimly in the distance, they could see the President, and the children, dim silhouettes, splashing through the water.

Kit sighed. It had been a pretty exciting day. They were shepherding the two children Claudia and the Mind-Child – "Viola" was its temporary name – and now, after many adventures, they were getting closer to the surface of Elysium. Everybody had been great, though they had lost sight of some of the others – Clown and Black Tarzan and Geisha and Claire and Robyn, but Kit was certain they would turn up.

"Are you enjoying this?' said the President, giving Kit a look, both weary and affectionate.

"Yes, in a strange way, I am, Mr. President," she gave him her special smile. She took his hand and squeezed it. "But you know, Mr. President, even if we survive, all of this is a catastrophe, an absolute catastrophe."

"Yes, Kit, it is."

But, in truth, Kit had to admit, it had been really exciting. They had been pursued by an enormous wave, but they had escaped, wading through half-flooded tunnels, climbing up rusty spiral service stairs, getting whirled around in floods, crawling through low-ceilinged muddy crawl spaces, and clambering up ventilation shafts, and finally coming out into fairly dry and normal tunnels.

The President lifted the Mind-Child and Claudia and handed them across a barrier.

Kat was standing just above him, taking the children, and putting them up on a wall, so they could crawl through a crack where one of the underground retaining walls have been shattered.

On the other side, Miranda and Caliban were waiting for the kids, handing them down and holding onto them.

The President was the last through the crack in the wall. "Not long, now, and we'll be up top."

"Then, I guess we'll see what's left," said Kit. She didn't feel good about this.

"Yes, then we'll see what's left, and who's left," said the President.

"This is a terrible day, Mr. President," said Kat.

"Yes, it is, Lieutenant Jackson, it is."

Miranda led Claudia by the hand – and they were walking down a half-shattered tunnel – water leaking from the roof and rubble and tangled wires everywhere, with sparks shooting off in every direction – but her mind was elsewhere; she was worried about her mother – V – off in the sweltering North African desert.

"She'll be absolutely fine," said Claudia, out of the blue, "Your mother will be fine."

"Yes, she'll be okay," said Miranda, thinking, yes, Claudia is right: V could certainly look after herself, and so she'd best not worry. There was enough to worry about right here! Claudia, it seemed, was a mind-reader.

And now Miranda had Caliban and Kit and her father – the Leader-President – with her, and Kat, and the two kids, both now adorable since the Mind-Child seemed to have evolved or devolved into being a real child, well, Miranda felt that the world could, in one small very local and personal way, be hardly more perfect.

This was, after all, an adventure, and really, she had been well-prepared, the training of the games, and then the things Kit had taught her, it all added up to a true recipe for success.

And then, just when she was thinking how it was all working out, and just as she was helping little Claudia over a pile of tangled wires and broken masonry, Miranda felt a tingling in her teeth and gums, and she moved her tongue around, and it seemed that two of her teeth were tingling, and getting pointed, and then it seemed like they were growing!

"Ugh!"

"What, Princess?"

"Caliban," she said, "Could you please …"

"Yes, Princess?"

"Look at my teeth, Caliban, please."

"Yes, Princess." He looked. "Oh, Princess, I think …"

"Tell me, Caliban, don't be shy! Don't be afraid to tell me the horrible truth …"

"You seem to have, ah, Princess, you seem to have two fangs."

"Oh, gosh!" Miranda had acquired a slight lisp, "Oh, goth!"

"Awesome, fangs!" said Kit, "Fabulous! You are already morphing, Miranda, that is so cool."

"You think it's cool?" Miranda enunciated carefully, trying to avoid lisping; she had always been very particular about – and proud of – her upper-class Cosmos elocution. She liked her consonants to have edge.

"Definitely, cool, and awesome." Kit grinned.

"Yes, absolutely, they are beautiful fangs, Princess."

"Nice points," said Kit.

"Let me see, let me see," Claudia was jumping up and down.

"Yes, let me see, too," said the Mind-Child.

The fangs were growing. They were getting longer. Miranda obligingly showed them her fangs, thinking it was both a badge of honor and a humiliation, a badge of shame. She, Miranda Hughes, Cosmos First Class, was becoming a circus freak, a midway attraction, a sort of combo not-yet-hybrid-vampire.

"Well," said the President, "Congratulations, Miranda."

"That's what will happen to us," said Kat, "My eyes have already changed," and she flashed her serpent eyes – golden with maroon slits – at them, and then reverted, instantly, to her human eyes.

"Well, to all of us," said Kit, "except Caliban."

"Caliban is already perfect," said Kat.

"Oh, dear Caliban, do you love me still?" Miranda turned to Caliban and gazed into his eyes.

Caliban smiled. "I love you and will always love you, Princess," and he kissed her, very passionately, but being careful not to let the fangs bite him.

"Oh, Caliban, my love!" Golden galaxies exploded in Miranda's eyes, eyes which, in spite of the golden galaxies, remained completely, exquisitely human.

Several layers higher up …

"You look worried, Hybrid," said Robyn.

"Terrible things are happening. I sense it – more terrible things. I mean additional terrible things to the already terrible things that have already happened." Claire blinked; they had gotten separated from all the others, and Claire had picked up signals in the ether – such signals as remained – and they indicated that, among all the other onrushing catastrophes, the plague was loose, some sort of plague that was even worse than the Bubonic plague, even worse the Ebola, even worse than – anything!

"Well, Hybrid, we shall just have to see what those extra horrible things are, won't we." Robyn gave Claire her wide-eyed innocent look.

Claire gazed at Robyn, almost in awe. Her childlike little locksmith was becoming quite sassy; this was a new form of charm.

"I think," Claire frowned, "I think it's a new form of plague, a really bad form of plague. I'm getting these little blips of images, people turning into mush."

"Into mush, Hybrid, well, we'll just have to see, won't we?"

"Yes, we shall just have to see what we shall see," Claire flashed Robyn a big reptilian smile.

Robyn blushed. It was so wonderful to have her own hybrid she could play with; and, what was even better, she was a hybrid too, though she hadn't yet got her fangs and claws and scales and those really cute serpent eyes, but that change would surely come, and soon! She could already feel this other aspect of herself bubbling up, just below the surface.

Up and up they went, toward ground level.

The question was: What would they find?

Yes, they were on a mission – and being on a mission was fun – it was almost like playing a game, hide-and-seek, or something – they were on a mission to see what was happening to Elysium up above. It was possibly risky and dangerous – which made the game even more fun!

They came to a narrow set of passages that led up to one of the main midtown first-level shopping concourses which would provide a good observation post to see what was going on.

"Okay, here we go, Robyn!"

And they climbed up the last staircase toward the main platform and entered a narrow twisting service tunnel, it was so narrow and twisting it must have been created by some mad religious sect as a way to escape persecution or something, or so it seemed to Claire.

"Are we there yet?" said Robyn.

"Almost, darling Robyn, not much further now," said Claire, who was now about ten or fifteen feet ahead of her friend.

"Oh, oh," said Claire.

"What?"

"Oh, oh, oh …" Claire had come to a full stop.

The zombie-bat growled, snarled, and opened its vast leathery wings.

It was about to leap.

"God Almighty, this can't go on!" Ken Ivison was getting tired of shooting at zombie-bats and other monsters – ghouls, mad people foaming at the mouth, people whose heads suddenly exploded! These things sprang up at every turn.

"Don't worry, darling, everything will be okay," Alison tightened her grip on his arm, and leaned closer. Oh, Ken smelled so good – all sweat, and gun powder, and virility! Jessica and Rachael were holding on tight to Alison, their arms around her waist.

Ken and Alison had fought their way – well, he had to do the fighting for both of them because she was blind, poor beautiful darling, stone blind. And now they were threatened once again.

They had finally gotten to the main platform, just ready to plunge underground into shelter underground. It was chaos. This was a huge platform for shopping and leisure and there were cafes and restaurants and shops and miniature pleasure domes of all kinds. But everything was in ruins. There was no electricity, no lights. Collapsed Pub Floats lay agonizing on the main concourse platform. Dead and dying mini-pub-drones were scattered everywhere. Café tables and chairs were overturned. Windows had been smashed, robots vandalized, and dead people were scattered on every surface like autumn leaves – some of them half-eaten, some of them decapitated, some of them whose heads had simply exploded into a miniature mushroom cloud of blood and gray matter and gristle and bone. A man with a straw hat was sitting in a relaxed pose, legs crossed, at a café table; his face and one arm had been torn off, but the straw hat was still poised at a jaunty rakish angle on his head. How the hell had that happened?

Right now, the problem was this: He and Alison and the kids were trapped, backed into a corner by a zombie-bat, and Ken's colt revolver was out of ammo. He reached with one hand into his pocket to pull out a handful of bullets, and he flicked open the chamber and began to shove in bullets. But as he did this and stared the monster in the face – well, if you could call that horrible muzzle a face – he could see it was readying itself to leap.

"Okay, Alison, get ready; we're going to have to duck, and try to roll under this thing, with the kids, when it plunges."

"Right, darling. Just give the order."

The zombie-bat reared up and squealed, as if readying itself to plunge down. Ken tensed, and he felt Alison grip tense too – like their two bodies had become one single body, one nervous system. He would have to push

Alison down at the very last moment, bend over her, and push her and the kids, under and past the zombie-bat as its claws and fangs plunged down, and just hope he was fast enough to get them both out from under the thing. Then they would just have to run for it. Maybe he could fend the thing off with a café table or chair, and get the colt fully loaded – he'd already slipped two bullets into the chamber – before the monster tore his throat out, which seemed to be, from his observation, the favorite modus operandi of zombie-bats when killing people, that and tearing their limbs off, one by one.

The zombie-bat made a mewling, quizzical sound.

It had reared itself up, standing now like a human, with its vast leathery and putrid smelling wings outspread, and its snout and fangs and beady expressionless eyes aimed straight at Ken. Its claws were reaching out.

It mewed again.

It seemed to be plaintive, a lament.

Ken used the pause to quietly slip three more bullets into the chamber. Maybe just maybe he would be able to blow the creature's head off.

The zombie-bat trembled.

"What's happening, Ken?" Alison whispered, crouching. She tightened her grip on his arm, and wrapped her other arm around the children. "Something's happening, but I don't know what."

"Yes, something's happening, but I don't …"

The zombie-bat's features wavered. Smoke spurted from its skin and its wings. Cracks split open its body. One of the wings peeled off and fell to the floor. The zombie-bat roared. It fell backward.

"God!" said Ken.

"What's happening, Ken, what's happening?"

A smash echoed from above. Ken looked up. A zombie-bat had crashed into the wall high above them. It seemed to be falling apart. Pieces – a wing, a foot, a furry ear, rained down.

Ken grabbed Alison and pressed her and the children into the shelter of a tiny ledge-like overhang. The disintegrating bat landed just in front of them. The fragments sizzled, burned, and seemed to melt.

The smell was horrible.

"Ken? Darling? Are you okay?"

"That smells awful," said Jessica.

"It's horrible," said Rachael, "Yuk and double yuk."

"I think they are dying. The zombie-bats are dying," Ken said; Alison pressed even closer to him. She leaned up and kissed him on the cheek; then she crouched and reached out for the girls and they came into her arms and leaned against her.

"Yes, the things are dying," Ken strokedAlison's hair. Other zombie-bats, flying far above the concourse, were flapping wildly, screeching, screaming, and disintegrating, and falling in pieces toward the concourse floor, bouncing off shop awnings, smashing into café tables, skewering themselves on flagpoles, and splashing down in the now silent fountains and pools.

Other zombie-bats seemed just to have lost control; they glided on until they smashed into walls of glass or walls of granite or hanging balconies and verandas. Then they careened down, cartwheeling and falling apart as they came, until they smashed up on the concourse itself.

Just a few feet away, the zombie-bat that had been about to attack them was writhing and smoldering and breaking apart. The remaining wing fell off. The furry flesh peeled away. Underneath, as the bits and pieces disintegrated, another body was revealed. It was the half-formed body of a young woman, veined with blue veins, deathly, ashen pale. She stared for an instant at Ken. She was alive, somehow she was alive. Her lips moved. Her eyes shone, "Will God ever forgive us?"

Ken did not know what to say.

"We were entranced by sorcery," the dying woman's eyes fluttered, "bewitched by the sorcery and beauty of the devil."

Ken said, "Now, now, you'll be … free, you'll be okay, you'll be …"

"No! My soul is gone. He has taken it with him into the darkness. I'll never get it back. It's gone, it's gone. I am doomed, doomed for all eternity!"

"Oh, the poor creature!" Alison's blind eyes were bright with tears. She tightened her grip on the two girls. They were staring at the young dying woman who an instant before had been a winged monster.

"I'm afraid," said Rachael.

"I'm afraid, too," said Jessica.

"Don't be afraid," Alison whispered; she kissed the two girls, stroked their hair.

There was a sigh.

The woman's eyes closed. Smoke rose from her mouth and eyes, and her flesh turned gray and began to crack and disintegrate and dissolve and crumble into gray ash and dust.

"She's dead," Ken crouched down and put his arm around Alison's shoulder.

"She's gone," Ken said. Thunder rolled through the vast concourse. The roof above had been smashed. It began to rain. Then it began to hail, pieces of hail at first the size of marbles and then the size of baseballs.

"The superstorm," whispered Alison, "It's come at last."

"Yes, the superstorm. We have to get underground – and fast!"

When she came to herself, Angela Balzac was dead and she knew she was dead; her mangled corpse had been lying on the street for just a few minutes. She managed to stand up though she could see that her body had taken a beating and one leg dragged a bit from being shattered. She felt her face and head. Not much damage. Probably she still looked pretty good. Gosh, she thought, vanity survives even death.

She had felt bad leaving her two dead companions up on the roof, so abruptly like that, without really saying goodbye.

Well, now that she was dead, she belonged with the dead, and by killing herself, she had certainly stopped the progression of that awful disease. Even the two sores had faded and just looked like tiny insect bites. It was better to have a – relatively – clean death than to be reduced to a bubbling pile of stinking sores and pus, like poor old Norman.

She went into the alley and climbed the fire escape ladder up to the roof. Laura, the mummy, was standing, looking down, and she turned around and came up, making clicking sounds, and put her bony arms around Angela. Little Kiddo the skeleton, followed and did the same thing, clinging to Angel's legs.

"Well, I'm back," said Angela, and they sat down again, as before, in the big stuffed chairs, and watched the superstorm as it raged within and around the shattered dome of Elysium.

It was really interesting. The huge tornado had smashed its way into the Dome, and now it was visible, through the shattered walls of those parts of the Dome that still existed. It was smashing into the towers and skyscrapers, bringing some of them tumbling down.

Yes, thought Angela, it was truly the end of the world.

Then something weird happened. Laura Mummy gave a weird little clicking sound, emitted a sigh, and when Angela turned to look, Laura Mummy raised one hand toward Angela – and transmitted the thought – "Angela!"

Then Laura Mummy fell back, went limp, and seemed to disintegrate, her bones and flesh and leathery skin dissolving into powder.

Little Kiddo looked startled. He reached out to where Laura had been, but there was nothing there. Put his bony hands to his skull, then he stood up, took two steps toward Angela, reaching out his arms, then his arms shot straight up, and one arm fell off, his rib cage fell away, his backbone buckled, and still he tried to reach Angela, and she reached out toward him, almost touching the tip of one bony finger; he emitted a strange little groan, his empty sockets staring intently at her, "Oh, oh, oh!"

Little Kiddo exploded into fragments, his bones flying every which way, and then clattering down and falling into dust, sprinklings, and clouds of dust.

"What the heck ... The dead are really dead?" Angela felt a thud, as if she were just now hitting the asphalt; she felt a searing pain; she felt her bursting heart, blood gushing into her mouth, salty, hot, she fell back, tried to take a breath, felt more searing pain, said, "Damn it! It's death ... So now I die, I really die. I wish I could ... do ... I mean, I wish ..." And then ...

Then – there was nothing.

Resurrection had ended.

The Devil had been chased back into the realm of Non-Being.

The Boy's enchantments were ended.

The dead were now truly dead.

Mrs. Rosenthal had thought it was better for the two bio-mummies, Jill and Julia, to discover what they had become sooner rather than later, so she and Natasha had accompanied the two creatures over to the full-length dress mirror and then, Mrs. Rosenthal had taken a deep breath and swung the mirror around so the two former women, former Cosmos, could see themselves.

"Oh, my God, that's me! That can't be me!" said the first mummy.

"Oh, my God, that's me! That can't be me!" said the second mummy.

The mummies were the same height and had similar figures, and now it occurred to Mrs. Rosenthal that they looked exactly alike, like twins. In fact, it was impossible to tell them apart.

"I'm going to sue," said the first mummy.

"I'm going to sue too," said the second mummy.

"We're both going to sue."

"Yes, we're both going to sue!"

Their voices seemed to have melded too, into one voice. They were perfect echoes of each other, high-pitched, childlike, and pleasantly melodic.

This was strange, Mrs. Rosenthal thought, and wondered if there was a scientific explanation, or perhaps they had been like this before, just picking up and mimicking whatever speech inflections and tones were in the air, like old-fashioned teenagers, or like those robot companions who echoed every single expression and inflection that came over the Net.

"The situation is perhaps beyond anybody suing anybody, my dears," said Mrs. Rosenthal. "Natasha here and I have tried to help, but in my judgment, you are lucky to have survived."

"I'm a monster!" groaned one of the mummies.

"I'm a monster!" groaned the other.

"I wouldn't go as far as all that," said Natasha, "I think this new look has definite potential. It's sort of … minimalist …"

"Exactly," said Mrs. Rosenthal, "extremely chic."

"And other people are in not very good shape," Natasha said, nodding toward the dead bodies on the Spa doorstep.

"Yes, absolutely," said Mrs. Rosenthal. "In fact, I believe everybody else, virtually everybody else, is dead."

The two mummies groaned in unison.

"Look." Mrs. Rosenthal led the two mummies to the edge of the Spa, which looked out, from a small balcony, over a great open concourse. Buildings were on fire. The Dome was shattered and cracked. The air was dark and yellow. Tornadoes were wending their way among the shattered spires. To the northwest, there seemed to be a great darkness – a coming storm.

"Will Charles like me, the way I am, I mean? He's very rich!"

"Will Andrew like me, the way I am, I mean? He's very rich!"

"Well," Mrs. Rosenthal exchanged a glance with Natasha, and it was clear that they both thought that Charles and Andrew, unless they had been extremely lucky, were probably things of the past.

"Well," Mrs. Rosenthal began to say, "Well, I think that …"

"I'm hungry," said one of the mummies.

"Me too, I'm hungry," said the other.

"Well, I am sure Natasha and I can provide. What have we got, Natasha?"

"We've got power bars, and power shakes, a whole supply of those, we've got the lunches we all brought. Nobody had any time to eat them. And we've got a lot of power drinks and relaxing drinks and rejuvenating drinks."

"Well, then," Mrs. Rosenthal gave the two burnished blank-faced mummies her best smile. "Let's all have a picnic then, shall we?"

"Yes, a picnic!"

"Yes, a picnic!"

The two mummies turned back into the dim interior of the spa, and Natasha and Mrs. Rosenthal began to put together the "picnic" of power bars, lunches, and power drinks. The two mummies sat side by side, two naked burnished abstract statues, on two high-backed gilt-and-plush Louis XV chairs.

"I'm hungry!"

"I'm hungry!"

While Natasha laid out the lunch, Mrs. Rosenthal went out and lingered for a moment on the balcony of the Total Remake Beauty Salon, gazing out over the city. This extra day of life – and she was not sure whether it was strictly legal to remain alive beyond one's allotted time or not, or what the sanctions would be if, even without meaning to, one did surpass the limits of one's allotted existence. It did seem rather irrelevant now. Law and order and rules and regulations were probably a thing of the past. As she watched, a flock of zombie-bats flew by. Weird things they were, just as the whole day had been weird. Maybe I am hallucinating, she thought, pinching herself on the forearm. No, the pinch seemed real. More bats flew overhead; whatever they were, they looked like angels of darkness.

Bits and pieces of the remaining skeleton of the Dome were falling out of the sky.

Oh, what is this? It looked like the zombie-bats were falling apart. They began to wither and lose their wings; they folded up and collapsed and fell from the sky, dropping straight down like projectiles. They were crashing down on balconies, on bridges, on concourses; they were smashing into walls and windows.

Yes, it looked like they were dying!

What, I wonder, does this mean?

"Come, eat, Mrs. Rosenthal," said one of the mummies.

"Yes, come, eat, Mrs. Rosenthal," said the other.

"Yes, darlings, I'll be there in a moment." Mrs. Rosenthal hesitated. There was a huge darkening of the sky to the northeast, inside the dome. And then she realized, it was an immense storm. It was swirling around. It was a tornado! Oh, dear, oh, dear, oh, dear!

It was churning slowly toward midtown, and it was exploding the buildings that stood in its path. Skyscrapers, hanging gardens, air-bridges, bits and pieces of the disintegrating Dome – everything was being swept up and dashed to fragments and swirled around.

"Munch, munch. This is delicious, Natasha."

"Munch, munch. This is delicious, Natasha."

"Thank you, darlings," said Natasha, and she brought a power bar to Mrs. Rosenthal.

"Look at that!"

"Oh, oh, yes, I see." Natasha stared. Buildings were being swept away; small specks which were perhaps humans were swirling around and being carried up into the clouds.

"I think …"

"Yes, we'd better get below ground."

"How far down is it?"

"Twenty-five stories." Natasha pointed. "There's a direct service stair column behind the spa, the invisible entrance is through an antique red British telephone box."

"Good." Mrs. Rosenthal laid her hand on Natasha's arm. "We have to look after our two children, Natasha."

"I was thinking the same thing exactly. They belong to us now."

"Precisely."

Natasha turned. "Come darlings. We can take our picnic with us. We are going off for a little adventure."

"An adventure!"

"An adventure!"

"Oh, what fun!"

"Oh, what fun!"

Ken and Alison – and Jessica and Rachael – had made what Ken thought would probably be their last stand on the main level concourse, the mixed Sub, and Cosmos Plaza Golden Shopping Experience, custom-designed slumming for Cosmos: Ken was ready to die; he had confronted the female zombie-bat; and at the last fatal instant, just when she was plunging toward him, she went into a sort of agony. The zombie-bats, strangely, all seemed to dying.

"Their god, the devil, is dead, or at least he is gone," Alison had whispered, crouching down and holding the two girls tight, "the Devil, the Boy, the Evil One, who created them, He is gone."

"But the storm is still coming," said Ken, sweat dripping down his chest, glimmering on his biceps.

"Yes."

"So we get underground, as far underground as we can."

"Yes."

Thinking it would not work, Ken tried the service door. Before it had seemed locked, but now, as he turned the dial this way and that, taking his time, the door suddenly clicked open, just a crack.

Using the barrel of the jammed M-16, Ken managed to pry the door open.

Ken got Alison and the girls inside; then, he closed the door carefully behind them; there might be new dangers here, of course, but the coming storm was certainly deadly; so, they plunged into the unknown and climbed down the spiral service staircase.

They came to a service tunnel.

It stretched away into the darkness. Out of the darkness came strange little breezes, and sounds of water, and the distant roar of what sounded like a tidal wave, explosions.

"Creepy," said Jessica.

"Spooky," said Rachael.

The two girls sheltered against Alison, pressing themselves against her legs and waist. Alison turned her bright blind eyes – shards of blue and white – toward Ken.

"I still think we will be safer down here," Ken put his arm around Alison's shoulders; in the other hand, he held the Colt as steady as he could, pointing it into the darkness. "That storm is going to be like the end of the world."

"You're right," she said, and kissed his cheek, which was now stubbly and hard and, she found, strangely arousing, very tempting, "Girls, Ken is right. We're safer down here."

"Let's go. Let's get deeper."

"Yes."

The service tunnel was dimly lit by fluorescent lichen and by two or three sputtering battery-powered emergency lights, and it smelled of mold and old cement and rusty iron; it went on for about forty meters. Alison stayed right behind Ken, one hand tight on his shoulder, with Jessica holding Alison's hand and Rachael holding Jessica's hand. Pipes, some of them hissing, ran along the roof of the tunnel; distant explosions and sounds of flooding echoed. Sometimes the tunnel seemed to vibrate; dust fell from the walls, and flakes of bright fluorescent lichen.

After the forty meters, the service tunnel made a right angle. Ken hesitated a moment, and whispered to Alison, "We're going around a bend in the tunnel." Then, cautiously, holding the Colt in front of him, he turned the corner and found himself standing face-to-face with a ... a hybrid.

"Oh, my God," he said. He pointed the Colt straight at the thing's heart. His finger was tight on the trigger, but he remembered rumors and urban legends about these creatures. Weren't they bullet-proof? If he pulled the trigger, he might just make it mad.

"What is it?" whispered Alison. Behind her, the two girls tensed, and bunched up, coming up behind and clinging to Alison.

"Oh, my god, oh my god," Ken stood utterly still, in shock, trying to decide what to do. His finger, on the trigger, was itchy.

"What is it, Ken? You're scaring us!" Alison could feel Ken's muscles tensing and the tremor in his voice.

"It's a ..."

"It's a hybrid," said the hybrid. It was about ten feet away. It was black and definitely female with a red splash on its snout and big bright golden eyes. It seemed to be smiling.

"What is it, Hybrid?" said a voice.

"It's two human beings," said the hybrid, "survivors – oh, and there are two kids too."

"They're not ghouls?"

"No, not yet, they aren't."

"They're not dead?"

"No, not yet, they aren't."

Ken had wanted to shoot and to back away and run, but he was too stunned to do anything, and then he was surprised to hear the hybrid talk, and then the tunnel was narrow and it would be almost impossible to run fast with Alison and the children. Besides, hybrids were reputed to be as fast as lightning and as deadly a cobras, so ...

"I think we'd better bite them, don't you Robyn?"

"Yes, Hybrid, I think that would be a very good idea."

"Bite us?"

"Bite us? What are they talking about, Ken?"

"I'm not sure," Ken was beginning to wonder whether he was sane. Perhaps all this excitement had been too much.

"It's like getting a vaccine," said the young woman the hybrid had called Robyn. The young woman squeezed past the hybrid and came out front, standing in the narrow tunnel only a few feet away from Ken. She was wearing jeans and a T-shirt and hobnailed boots and had a backpack hitched over her shoulders, "I'm Robyn, by the way, and my hybrid has a name too – she's Claire."

"It's like a vaccine – against what?" Ken was still aiming the Colt, moving it back and forth, now aimed at the hybrid, now at the girl. He was holding Alison tight and thinking that the world had become a crazy place and that he would have loved to turn this into a program, if only they were in the studio. Hey, they didn't need to be in a studio! He had the mobile camera kit!

The hybrid bared her fangs in what looked like a smile. "There is the ghoul sickness; it turns humans into ghouls."

"You don't want to become ghouls," said Robyn, with what seemed to Ken an almost schoolmarm earnestness, "It's very unpleasant."

"And there is a plague spreading," said the hybrid, "according to latest reports, samizdat twitter talk which gets into my head."

"Yes," said Robyn, "It's a very bad plague, the very worst!"

"Yes," said Claire, "You turn into mush."

"A smoking pile of mush," said Robyn, "smelly too."

"We've heard about the plague," said Alison. "There were reports from the Burbs; it came through on the Ear Info-Flow, ear tweets, I don't know where they're coming from, these audio tweets, but some are still coming."

"Yes," said Ken, somehow picking up a vision from Alison of what the thing must be like, "It's terrible, apparently." He was thinking: And what isn't terrible these days!

"Some recent ear tweets report cases inside Elysium," said Alison, who'd been getting a constant flow of intermittent, static-ridden horror stories, though she hadn't mentioned them till now; enough had been going on.

"You really should let me bite you," said the hybrid.

"I think, Ken, that we should do this," said Alison.

"If you do bite us, do you mind awfully if we shoot the whole thing?" Ken was perking up; with the barrel of the Colt, he motioned at the little robot camera perched on his shoulder; figured the camera might make everybody behave better – show biz had an amazingly civilizing influence.

"No, go ahead," said the hybrid, "but we don't have much time. The new plague seems to be a version of the Bubonic; it kills almost everybody, maybe even everybody. hybrids, you see, don't get sick. We are immune to everything. Also, let me assure you, you don't have to look like me – not all of the time, at least. Robyn's a hybrid, too, aren't you Robyn?"

"I keep forgetting. Yes, I am. Claire bit me a couple of days ago."

"So, you can continue to look like yourselves. Your first morph may come unexpectedly, but afterward, with a little practice, you can shift back and forth as you wish according to convenience. Satisfaction guaranteed."

Ken meanwhile had set the mini-drone camera loose, and it was floating around on its little lifters, adapting to the dim light with super-sensitive camera eyes, and shooting the hybrid and Robyn and catching every nuance of the conversation.

"I think maybe we'd better do it," said Alison.

"Darling, I'm still not sure …"

"And what about the girls?" Alison was holding the two girls close.

"Just a little nip will do," said the hybrid, with a big reptilian smile, "safe as safe can be! Like a vaccination."

"I'm still not sure, I mean …" Ken frowned.

"Well, if you don't want to …" the hybrid frowned, "but if you want truly to protect your lady friend, and your children here, if you are truly the gallant, heroic, sexy, sweaty, tough-minded, no-holds-barred explorer gentleman you seem to be, if you …"

"Ken, I really think …" Alison tightened her grip on his arm.

"Okay, yes, okay …" Ken knew he was beaten.

"Yes, let's do it!"

"I'll go first, then," said Ken, taking a deep breath.

"Good," said the hybrid, "You won't regret it!"

"I'll comment, then," said Alison, "I'm itching to get back into action."

"Alison's blind," said Ken, "but she wants to …"

"She wants to report. No problem," said the hybrid, "stand beside me, Alison, and I'll bite Ken, and you have your hand on my arm, and you'll get the cues from me."

Alison sidled past Ken, kissing him on the way, and stepped forward. The mini-drone camera lifted off from Ken's shoulder and zoomed in on Alison and the hybrid.

Alison turned toward the camera and laid her hand on the hybrid's arm and said, "It's warm. Your skin, I mean, your scales are warm."

"Yes, Alison," Claire looked at Alison, then at the camera which zoomed in, "Many of your viewers, Alison, will be amazed to learn that we hybrids are in fact warm-blooded, in spite of our reptilian appearance." Claire, in her old life – before the Erotic Circus in the desert – had been addicted to the media and in her past life as Claire V Jacobs had done a myriad of talk shows.

"That's great!" Alison said.

Ken stepped forward, offering himself up as the guinea pig sacrifice, a true man, a true hero. Yes, he would die – truly – for Alison and for the kids.

As the mini-drone camera swung around to focus on Alison and Ken and the hybrid, Alison had the strangest sensation of thought transmission; it was as if she could see the scene through the camera's eyes, but she knew that the sensation and the images were coming from the hybrid or through the hybrid: spooky and creepy but really useful! The camera framed Alison in close-up, her mussed-up hair and flushed complexion and even the streaks of dirt on her cheeks and the blind glittery intense look of her eyes was, Alison thought, seeing it in her mind relayed through the hybrid, pretty effective, damned sexy even if she did think so herself.

"Hi, I'm Alison Jonas. Ken and I – and Jessica and Rachael – are, as you can see, in a service tunnel deep under level A-3 of Elysium City, and we are here, as you have also already seen, with our two, ah, friends, Robyn and Claire. Claire, as you can see, is a hybrid."

The camera drew back to reveal Claire and Robyn standing next to Alison.

"And Robyn, though she looks totally human, is a hybrid too – isn't that right, Robyn."

"I keep forgetting I am a hybrid, but I am, yes."

"And, Claire, you have just suggested that it would be a good idea if you bite me and my colleague, my partner, Ken here, and the kids."

"Right," the hybrid smiled, most charmingly, at the camera, "Well, Alison, the hybrid bite has several effects. First, it turns you into a hybrid. Now, folks, I know that sounds really terrible and really scary, but, and this is the second effect, it will make you immune to almost everything. It's like a vaccine, really. And, as an added attraction, you don't have to look like a demon. You don't have to look like me. You can look like Robyn, that is, you can look like your-self, whatever you happen to look like. It's as easy as pie!"

"Ken and I have thought long and hard – well, we took about two minutes – and we've decided we're going to do it!" said Alison, "Ken, are you ready?"

"Yes, Alison, darling, I'm ready." Ken offered up his arm. Sweat had pearled on his forehead.

"Now watch this," said the hybrid, and she bent over Ken's forearm, and she bit him, very quickly, very gently.

"That didn't hurt at all," said Ken.

"Now, it's my turn," said Alison, smiling brightly at the invisible camera – and it was strange because with her hand on the hybrid's arm she, who was blind, was seeing, visually, in her mind's eye the scene from several angles, the camera's point of view, and the hybrid's point of view.

"Weird, isn't it," said the hybrid.

"Yes, it is, rather," Alison again smiled at the camera, "Okay, and now I'm reaching out my arm, and Claire is going to bite and ... there ... there ... and now she's biting me, she's biting me, and it feels, it feels like .... well, like nothing at all." Alison smiled brilliantly at the camera. And, by all the gods! Suddenly she could see! She could see!

"And now for our children, what do we do?" Ken was saying. Alison glanced at him: oh, God, he looked handsome, tanned, sweaty, streaked with dirt, the battle vest torn and ripped, claw marks here and there. Yes, he was hers, and she was his!

"Just a little nip!" said Claire; she winked at Alison.

"Will it hurt?" the girls blinked wide-eyed at Claire.

"You'll hardly notice it."

Jessica squished her eyes shut, then opened them, and looked up into the hybrid's eyes.

"Ready?" Claire blinked at the girl.

"Ready!" Jessica held out her arm.

Claire nipped the little girl, just injecting a tiny bit of hybrid fluid.

"It tickled."

"I told you so."

"Now for Rachael," said Alison, gazing at the camera and her hand on Jes-sica's shoulder.

"I'm not afraid at all," said Rachael, giving the hybrid a bold stare, and reaching out her arm.

"Absolutely right," said the hybrid, she bent over and nipped Rachael, "See, that's nothing at all!"

"It hardly tickled," Rachael showed her arm and the two little bites, which were hardly visible.

"So, as you can see, folks," Alison beamed at the camera, "We are all still here, with our new friends, Claire and Robyn. And I guess we're all hybrids, now, though frankly, I don't notice the difference."

"No, that's right, Alison. You won't notice the difference, not for a little while, at least!"

"Thank you, Claire. This is Alison Jonas ... with Jessica and Rachael, and Claire and Robyn ..."

"And Ken Ivison ..."

"Reporting from Elysium, in a tunnel deep under level A-3. Now, folks, don't forget, get to shelter as fast as you can, and if you can find a hybrid, get it to bite you, get yourself vaccinated as soon as you can. Goodbye for now from Alison Jonas ..."

"And Ken Ivison ..."

Their images flickered, and then were gone.

A few battery-operated emergency relays were still working, old-fashioned relays that were not linked directly into the mind, and so the Alison-and-Ken Show did make it into a few new venues and was seen by perhaps 60,000 people, survivors huddling in shelters, Centurions barricaded in bunkers, hospital staff who'd remained on duty through everything and still had a few old-fashioned gas- or propane-powered generators puffing and rumbling away.

And, through one forgotten but still-functioning solar-powered communications satellite of the defunct Republic of Bangladesh – now mostly under 20 meters of water – the program was seen, by survivors, around the world.

There were few hybrids available, but those that were available took the cue and did bite a few people when they could find people to bite and who agreed to it.

In this, humanity's final crisis, the Ken-and-Alison Show saved perhaps a few thousand lives, people sheltering, here and there, and lucky enough to meet a wandering hybrid.

Those people would survive, but, of course, they would no longer be human, not fully human, and so this meant that ...

Miranda was not so sure that she was utterly and completely pleased. Her two upper canines had turned into inch-long fangs. This was a bit too much like growing up, becoming a woman, and becoming a monster.

In fact, she had felt a bit ambivalent, in the beginning, about her breasts, though Nikki had reassured her, saying they were adorable and should be a point of pride, and then when her periods began, Miranda was utterly not sure. Nikki had told her to relax and go, as it were, with the flow.

"Ha, ha," Miranda had said.

Nikki just smiled and gave her a magisterial course on how to become a woman and how to avoid most of the inconveniences inherent in that condition, and how to look upon them as advantages.

But, in spite of all this, Miranda thought that maybe Peter Pan did have a point after all. She turned to Kit and defiantly displayed her vampire smile, two fangs, and a lisp. Can love survive this?

"Wow," said Kit, "They're really cool! Miranda, I can hardly wait to get mine!"

"Really?"

Caliban put his hands on Miranda's shoulders. "Yes, they are totally cute, Princess, they, are, how do you say, adorable, totally adorable." and he kissed her, long and deep, taking care not to let the canines penetrate his skin though he figured, quite rightly, that if they did it would make no difference: as Nikki's son, he was almost certainly immune to everything.

Miranda concentrated. She discovered she could make the fangs go away, and make them pop back.

"Bite anybody you meet," said the President. "Claire explained it to me. Just a quick little nip, a little squirt of liquid, tiny, just a tincture!"

"You want me to bite people?"

"Yes," said the President. "But you don't have to bite Caliban, Claire sniffed him, and V, your mother, checked him out too, and, like Nikki, Caliban is already immune to everything and will probably live forever, but otherwise, people must be vaccinated."

"This is urgent, isn't it, Mr. President," said Kit, figuring it would be good to underline the point – she knew Miranda – and thinking too, that, as she was older than Miranda, she should already have fangs of her own. But jealousy is a useless and unpleasant feeling, so she was overjoyed for Miranda. The kid already had her fangs!

"Yes, it is, Kit," said the President, "You are totally so right."

"Gosh," Miranda, suddenly feeling the weight of responsibility.

"You will be serving your nation," said Kat, her Centurion suit gleaming in absolute perfection, reminding Miranda of when she had wanted to be a Centurion.

"Miranda," the President gave her an old-fashioned military salute, hand flat above the right eye, "You must sacrifice for the cause. Just a little nip and squirt to all the citizens, Subs or Burbites or Cosmos, no distinction of class, mind you!"

"Yes, sir," Miranda looked her father straight in the eye and gave him a sharp little salute, again the old-fashioned American salute; this was a new adventure, and it was just beginning.

"Bite them just like Claire bit me." Kit held up her arm, showing the two puncture marks, now almost faded, "You see, you just lean over, and pierce the skin, but not too much, just a quick nip."

"Gosh," said Miranda, suddenly flooded with a sense of pride. Yes, this was yet another way to serve the President and the human race, and to serve both Nikki and V, and to serve the survival of the species. If anybody planned to give gold medals in the future, then she, Miranda Hughes Cosmos First Class and Daughter of the Hybrid Queen, and daughter of the President-Leader, would certainly deserve yet another gold medal to add to her collection, but she rather doubted that any gold medals would be forthcoming for quite a while.

Just at that moment Clown, and Black Tarzan, and Geisha appeared around a corner in the tunnel, and were greeted with a full-throated hurrah by everybody.

"How did you manage to get out of there?" said Kat.

"It's a long story," said Black Tarzan.

"Let's start now," said the President, turning to Miranda, "You can practice." And he explained to the newly arrived trio what the effect of a hybrid bite would be.

"Well, Mr. President, if you say so," said Black Tarzan.

"I ready to trot," said Clown.

"Count me in," said Geisha.

"Right, well, Clown, will you please stick out your forearm," said Miranda, and she bent down and nipped Clown.

"It tickled," said Clown.

"Perfect," said Kit. So Clown and Black Tarzan, and Geisha, and Claudia, and so on were vaccinated, and thus they were protected against the new forms of death that were flooding over the world.

"Bite me too," said the Mind-Child, who had been holding Claudia's hand.

"Okay, you're sure?"

"I'm sure."

So Miranda bit the Mind-Child.

"Well done, Miranda," said the President; he and Kat saluted. And Kit couldn't resist – she hugged Miranda.

"Princess," Caliban took Miranda in his arms and kissed her once, twice, three times, and he held her tight, and she clung to him like a shipwrecked sailor might cling to a lifebuoy in a stormy sea.

"Oh, Caliban," she breathed, and she favored her Tarzan, her Prince, with her sunniest most brilliant smile, totally human, having zipped the two fangs back into their resting places, so she could kiss freely, endlessly, softly, like a real human, like a true Cosmos.

Mrs. Rosenthal and Natasha and the two mummies – well, thought Mrs. Rosenthal, really, I should find some other way to think of them: they have legs and arms, so they are not like mummies, they are like …

"Statues, they are like statues," said Natasha, "Mobile statues, a matching set, a bit abstract, though."

The two statues were following close behind.

"Works of art, yes," said Mrs. Rosenthal. "Abstract yes, but wasn't there also an art movement, body something, it began several centuries ago. I believe it's still popular among …"

"Among Neo-Punk, Neo-Gothic Subs," Natasha smiled. "Yes, it was – it is – popular: body art, or body-modification."

"Yes, that's it," said Mrs. Rosenthal. "They are works of art, in a way, if you see what I mean, sculptural. They have turned themselves – well, they have been turned – into works of art, true statues."

"We are works of art!" the first statue recited in a sing-song.

"We are works of art!" echoed the other, exactly echoing the melodic rhythm.

"I don't think we want to use our old names." One blank face looked at the other.

"No, I don't think we want to do that."

"We would appreciate any ideas."

"Yes, we would very much appreciate any ideas." The absolutely featureless face turned to Natasha and Mrs. Rosenthal. "Something poetic would do, I think," the statue said, without visibly opening her mouth, which, in any case, even open, was next to invisible.

"Yes, definitely, something poetic," said the first, likewise showing no facial movement at all, just a blank shiny oval; this was rather uncanny, thought Mrs. Rosenthal, a weird little frisson going down her spine.

"Let's think about it then, shall we," Mrs. Rosenthal said, adopting the schoolmarm-like "Keep Calm & Carry On" tone she had occasionally used with Harvey, when he was still alive, poor dear, or when she worked in a field hospital – often under fire and in dreadful conditions – in the Russian-Chinese war of 2156, and feeling that this was all a bit spooky and uncanny, they were so human and yet no longer quite human, these faceless doll-like creatures, while it was indeed true, too, that they did have a certain *je ne sais quoi* chic and allure, rather like beautiful mannequins posed in a very expensive non-virtual shop window; yes, definitely, they were abstract style mannequins come to life.

They were almost at ground level now, just two floors down and a door – "Service Door Underground: Do Not Enter: Authorized Personnel Only" – beckoned. It led to the forbidden nether regions – how exciting!

"Oh, my God, look at that!" Natasha had stopped in front of a large jagged gap in the stairwell.

"I do see what you mean, Natasha," said Mrs. Rosenthal, putting her hand on Natasha's shoulder.

The huge tornado – a vast black wall of whirling cloud and debris –it must be at least four kilometers across – was approaching the Volpe Tower, and two other nearby landmarks, three of the highest buildings in Elysium.

The Volpe Tower was hit; it seemed to tremble and waver in the violent air, perhaps an optical illusion; for a moment it was lost to view in the whirling wall of pure energy, water, cloud, bodies, bricks, steel rods, dirt, dust, everything, then it emerged again, still intact, still standing proudly erect, a statement of man's might and aspiration, and, then, as Mrs. Rosenthal watched, and as the two living mannequins came up to stand between her and Natasha, the Volpe Tower exploded – it burst!

The spire was hit by a giant lightning bolt. For a moment – a very long moment it seemed to Mrs. Rosenthal – the windows, hundreds of windows, all lit up, and then the whole top twenty or so floors of the Tower slid sideways, lights still sparkling, and then the lights blinked twice, and went out.

Had she seen people in those windows? No, it was too far away! It must have been an illusion!

"Oh, no," Natasha gasped.

"Oh, no," the two mannequins echoed.

The vast sinking section of the Volpe Tower, at least twenty stories, now exploded! Fragments flew out in every direction, as if in slow-motion, vast sections of wall, tiny specks of furniture, steel structures, elevators, observations decks, the tall spire that crowned the edifice, with a few lights still twinkling, all flew up and out and away; and then everything was swept into the gyrating wall of black air.

Then the two other buildings, the Triumph Tower and the Celestial Imperial Spire, exploded in their turn and were swept, glittering waves of bits and pieces, into nothingness. The whirling dark wall was now chewing its way toward them, eating up parks, imploding the central station, the Divine Emporium, everything, consuming absolutely everything in its path.

"Oh, the horror," said Number One Mannequin, the stormy light glistening on her round skull and oval face, "the sublime horror."

"Oh, the horror, the sublime horror," said Number Two Mannequin, putting her webbed hand on Number One's shoulder.

"The heart of darkness," said Number One, putting a webbed hand over Number Two's webbed hand.

"Yes, it has come here, it has come to us, to the heart of Elysium," said Number Two, "The heart of darkness."

"Let's go," said Natasha.

"Yes," said Mrs. Rosenthal, "Well, my darlings, philosophy, and poetry and literature can come later." It was quite surprising, though, she thought, that the two ignorant spoiled creatures should be capable of making any allusions to anything whatsoever, and, strangely, they seemed to be exhibiting empathy!

"Yes, you are right, Mrs. Rosenthal," the first blank face turned to her.

"Yes, you are right, Mrs. Rosenthal," the second blank face turned to her.

With Natasha leading, they ran down the last two flights of stairs, and they got to a large steel door which said "Service Door Underground: Do Not Enter: Authorized Personnel Only."

"I wonder if it will open," Natasha stood for just a second, perplexed.

"Well, let's try," said Mrs. Rosenthal, "it may be mechanical, not electronic, a lot of these old structures down here are."

"Yes."

Natasha and Mrs. Rosenthal pulled the lever.

With a deep raspy creaking sound, the heavy door swung open.

Beyond the door was a hole, a black hole, with strange whispers, distant ghostly sounds, something like a tidal wave breaking, flooding, gurgling, but very far away. There was, just inside the door, a small steel platform and from the platform, a spiral staircase, dimly lit by phosphorescent lichen, went straight downward.

"Well, nothing ventured, nothing gained," Mrs. Rosenthal stiffened her lip, and stepped through the door; the stairwell, built of concrete and old steel, as she could now see, smelled clammy and musty and of old rust and oxidation and of mudflats and fecundity and tidal bracken. Elysium rested on the interface between ocean and land, the frontier between two worlds, water, and earth; both worlds had once been fertile and fecund. Mrs. Rosenthal glanced back at Natasha.

"Well," said Natasha, "I guess we'd better get down as far as we can."

"Yes," said Mrs. Rosenthal. "What do you think, my darlings?"

"Yes."

"Yes. We both think, *Yes!*" said the second tuneful voice.

"Let's go then." Mrs. Rosenthal thought she could hear the roar of destruction approaching from up above, getting closer and closer. She and Natasha closed the steel door and pulled the locking bar down, into place.

They quickly clattered down ten levels, though the two golden mannequins, with their flat webbed flipper-like feet, made a sort of musical liquid slapping sound. At the bottom of the stairs, they came to a large tunnel where, for some strange reason, a string of emergency lights were still burning, some of them were red 'Exit' signs, giving the walls a warm tone. There were black metallic benches, like old-fashioned park benches, along the sides of the tunnel. They sat down. The two mannequins turned their blank faces to each other, and said:

"We are burnished, highly finished, perfectly lacquered."

"Yes, you are," said Mrs. Rosenthal, wanting to be encouraging, and in fact, she thought they would make very nice artworks, posed in her terrace garden, or perhaps as mobiles, free to move around the flat, entertain guests.

"You are very shiny," said Natasha, taking her clue from Mrs. Rosenthal, and running her hand down one of the mannequin's arms, "Highly polished."

"Yes, we are shiny and smooth."

"Yes, we are very smooth; we are svelte and smooth."

"We need names, new names, for the old me is dead, the old we is dead, you know; the new we is waiting to be born." The first mannequin turned its featureless mask toward Mrs. Rosenthal and then toward Natasha.

"Yes, we need names, new brands, new tags, definitely," said the second mannequin, "The old we is dead, definitely dead."

"We can be 'Spit' and 'Polish.' You'll be 'Spit.' I'll be 'Polish.'"

"No, I'll be 'Polish.' You be 'Spit'!"

"Now, darlings …" Mrs. Rosenthal thought that the very last thing they needed right now was a catfight or underground spat between two slippery gold mannequins.

"Shall I flip a coin or something like that?" Natasha reached into her pocket "I have a 100 dollar token." It occurred to Mrs. Rosenthal – not for the first time – that Natasha was indeed an exceedingly clever girl, very pretty, and resourceful too; why some people were Subs and other people were Cosmos was something that she had never really understood, though Harvey had repeatedly tried to explain it to her.

"Yes!"

"Yes!"

"If it is tails, I am Polish."

"If it is heads, I am Polish."

"Okay, don't move now!" Natasha flipped the token, and it came down on her wrist, and she slapped her hand over it, and the two statues leaned forward.

"Oh, I am Spit!"

"Ha, ha, I am Polish!"

"Spit, you had better wear this," Mrs. Rosenthal took off her necklace and clipped it shut around Spit's neck, "That way …"

"That way, we can tell each other apart!"

"Yes."

"We can tell each other apart!"

"Yes, otherwise I won't know if I am I or I am you."

"Or if I am you, too, or you are me, which would be most confusing."

"Yes."

"Yes."

The air began to vibrate; the walls began to tremble; from up above came a roaring crashing swirling sound. The tornado must have arrived.

"Perhaps we should go farther down," said Natasha, glancing at Mrs. Rosenthal.

"Yes, we should."

"Yes, we agree."

"Yes, we agree."

They went along the corridor and came to another door, which they opened, and it led to another staircase. They went down the staircase. Now the sounds of destruction were muffled and distant and then they faded away, though the walls still trembled and dust fell here and there and bits and pieces of phosphorescent lichen broke away from the walls and floated in the air, luminous motes.

Spit captured one and held it in her webbed hand, "Oh, pretty, pretty," she whispered, "Pretty, pretty." The bright little speck sent a warm glow up over the featureless smooth oval which had once been her face.

"Yes, pretty, pretty," Polish leaned over the cupped webbed hand, and put her arm around Spit's shoulders. "Pretty, pretty, we are pretty!"

"Pretty, pretty, we are pretty."

At this point, they heard voices. And around a corner in the tunnel came a very handsome man in the torn remnants of a Centurion's Uniform, and beside him, a black woman Centurion – her warrior bodysuit intact and gleaming – and behind them was a slender pale girl in skin-shorts and a skin T-shirt. The girl carried a machete and a laser pistol. Other people were coming too – a regular parade.

"Oh, by all the gods!" said Natasha.

"Yes, oh, by the gods!" said Spit.

"Yes, oh, by the gods!" said Polish.

"Yes, I mean, it does look like him, doesn't it!" Mrs. Rosenthal was really taken back; she had long had a secret crush on the President-Leader; if anything, all mussed up as he was, if it was indeed him, he looked even more handsome than in the holograms, videos, and photographs, his chest streaked with blood and soot, his arms scarred by claw marks, his uniform torn to shreds.

"Hail, all Hail, Oh, President-Leader," Spit had dropped to her knees.

"Hail, all Hail, Oh, President-Leader," Polish was on her knees, next to Spit, their blank faces turned up, in worship, toward the President.

"Wow! What is this? Awesome," said Kit, looking down at the two glittering naked mannequins, "Really, really cool! What are you? Like works of art, I mean, really ..."

"Works of art, yes, but what in the world ..." Kat was staring; she'd drawn her laser, just in case.

"Yes, *awesome*," said the President, glancing at Kit. He reached down and helped the two living mannequins to their feet.

"Oh, thank you, Oh, Leader!" the blank face turned toward him.

"Oh, thank you, Oh, Leader!" the blank face turned toward him.

The President glanced toward Natasha and Mrs. Rosenthal.

"It's a long story, Mr. President," they said, almost in unison, almost melodically, and then looked at each other. Mrs. Rosenthal cleared her throat, "I think Natasha can best explain, Mr. President ..."

"Well, Mr. President, what happened was ..."

The President held up his hand. "Natasha, just a moment, please." And he turned and said to a beautiful young woman – a radiant blonde with golden skin and eyes that sparkled like galaxies – who had just appeared, "Miranda, here are some people for you to bite, if you don't mind. And you can explain why you are biting them."

"Of course, Mr. President," said Cosmos First Class Miranda Hughes, and she saluted the President smartly and smiled at Natasha, and her smile displayed two very neat, sharp little canine fangs.

"Now, ladies, what I am going to do, and I am going to do it for your own good, as ordered by our President-Leader, I am going to bite you, but before I do so, I shall explain. You see, the situation is this ..."

Two hours later, V had not yet returned from wherever she had gone. "To the Crystal," Claire had said, "She's gone to the Crystal, to destroy the Foul Fiend."

"She will return, no doubt about it," said the President.

"Yes, she will return," said Kat.

And so while most of the extant citizenry waited underground, in a safe and well-protected tunnel, the President and Kat went upwards, to see what had happened to Elysium.

The President and Kat emerged from the shelter of the underground zone, pushing a rusty metal door open, and pushing a cadaver, that was blocking their way, aside.

The sun was rising in the east, a vague disk lost in a sandstorm that raged and thundered, reducing visibility to a few feet.

There was no dome. The temperature was sweltering, a tropical 110 degrees Fahrenheit, or 43 Centigrade. The humidity was maybe 85%. Silhouettes of ruins, walls, jagged fragments, twisted metal rods, appeared vaguely, just for a moment, in the waves of rasping howling sand.

Only a few walls were standing. The wind was strong, but at least it was not hurricane force. At moments, you could only see a few feet – sand and mist filled the air. A ruined platform towered up, a shadow, about twenty feet away. It looked like part of what had once been a mezzanine shopping concourse. Kat and the President staggered toward, it, leaning against the wind and the streaming sand.

The others – including the two shining featureless mummies, Spit and Polish – waited anxiously behind, sheltered underground. Kit and Miranda peeked out from behind the door and saw the President and Kat disappear into the welter of sand and mist.

"Awesome!"

"Awesome!"

Finally, climbing up a jagged wall and twisted support column, the President and Kat made it to the top of the platform; yes, it was a fragment of what had once been a mile-long mezzanine shopping Promenade Deck.

"Well," said the President.

"Mr. President," Kat was staring out over the utter desolation that had once been Elysium, "Mr. President, I'm sorry."

"So am I, Kat, so am I."

Elysium City lay in ruins, a sea of rubble. The Dome was no more. Stumps of buildings here and there, bodies lying half-buried in ash and detritus, giant tubes of structural steel sticking up, contorted, and twisted into strange shapes. There were huge words on one sculpture, Thyssen; on another, it said Krupp.

"Not many will be alive," said the President.

"No," said Kat.

At that moment, out of the mist and blowing sand, the President saw silhouettes emerge, Centurions, a small group, perhaps five of them, perhaps 100 meters away, and then behind them, a small vertijet, its lights blinking, was descending slowly through the maelstrom of sand.

The President waved.

One of the Centurions and then all of the Centurions waved back.

The vertijet descended through the maelstrom of sand and mist, and settled down on a narrow space, close to the small group of Centurions. As the motors shut off, a hatch opened. A Centurion appeared at the door of the jet.

"Let's go and see, Lieutenant, let's go and see."

"Yes, Mr. President, let's go and see."

The sand swirled around them as they climbed down from the shattered promenade deck, and worked their way through ruins toward the small group of survivors, who were led, it turned out, by an impeccably attired Cosmos executive, Demi Pfeiffer.

The solid hologram – V's mother – that had embraced V had lasted perhaps five minutes and mother and daughter had spoken of many things that for many centuries had not been spoken of, and they said words that for many centuries had not been said – words of love, words of adoration.

And then V's mother said a tearful, smiling goodbye, and she faded and returned to her eternal home – and to her eternal being, as the Crystal.

"So they will all die, all the humans, each and every one." The Crystal – V's mother – what a weird and stunning thought – was humming gently and had turned a mauve color which indicated, V knew, that the Crystal was sad, or even in mourning, "I'm sorry, I'm so sorry, darling."

V raised an eyebrow. "How, I thought we had …"

"You thought that we – and you in particular – had saved humanity, poor, dear V, darling V!"

"But, didn't we … didn't we save them?"

"You almost did save them, V. But the Foul Fiend knew he might lose against you. After all, you – we – are descended from the old gods and goddesses, Baal and Astarte and all the nymphs and spirits and so on – all that was sacred and fearsome in the world – and they were once very powerful, and you have made friends, I see, with many worshipers of the new god, the God of Abraham, which greatly multiplies your power, so, as a fallback, as it were, as a detour around your strength, a 'workaround' I believe one says, the Foul Fiend, the Boy, used humanity's weakness against itself. Your lover-enemy, that handsome, human oh-too human …"

"The President-Leader, James …"

"Yes, James. In many ways, such a fine man … He tried to prevent this catastrophe, but," The Crystal hesitated, "By the way, I do approve of him. You have my full blessing, darling V. I think you and he will be very happy. And you and beautiful Kat, you two will be happy as well, in parallel as it were. But …"

"But …?"

"This is very hard to say, V, since I have been on this planet almost 3,000 years I have come to like the humans very much, and like you, I feel almost as if I were human – and as I have told you part of me is human, very human – and we are mother and daughter, you and I – and so it is very sad to come to the end of this human saga. You know, V, it's rather like when you are reading a story and you don't want it to end. Which reminds me, V, did you ever read …?"

"Mother!"

"Yes, V, I am sorry. I do tend to ramble and prattle on. Digression is my very favorite thing! Particularly when I am with you! I have become positively loquacious, a real chatterbox! Quite unlike you, I must say! You are so reserved, shy, even! Your adopted family did a very good job of raising you, I must say. He was very distinguished, your adopted father, I mean, and your adopted mother – well, in a distant past, she had been my very best friend, but her marriage tore us asunder; she moved to another city, and so … That is why I chose her to be your mother when I would be gone, and I knew I was destined to be gone. And Lalla, your nurse, she was truly a wise and magnificent person, my best friend, my most intimate companion, she adored you, and your father confided in her, telling her many of his secrets, and, as you know, she was willing to lay down her life for you. If it weren't for her, well, there would be no you! As for me, you see, you are the only person or sentient being on the whole planet with whom I can talk. I have missed you so, V, I have missed you so! And in more ways than one! And though I get to watch and listen to virtually everybody and everything, though all my embedded sensors which are virtually everywhere, enmeshed in things living and dead, animals, plants, minerals, human-built and natural structures, and so on, and which I told you about the last time we met, it is very frustrating not to be able to share my feelings and observations with a fellow sentient being, in particular with my daughter. You know, V, sometimes I do think I would have liked to have remained human, well, for part of me, to have remained human, to have survived, to have been your mother in flesh and blood, even if it meant only living for a very short span, just a few decades, a blink of an eye really, and then dying. You know, you get up in the morning, eat, make love, work, play with the children, tend to the harvest, cook, eat, work, go home, entertain friends, and make love, eat, make love again, and go out and look at the stars, or linger in the courtyard with your children and your man and the servants, and then sleep, and dream, wake up, or have to wake up, make love, and then ...”

“I know, Mother, I know.” V was patting the border collie; he was panting happily and wagging his tail. She wondered where the Crystal – *my mother*, what a strange thought! – had found the dog and how she had transported it at exactly the right moment so that it could save her, V, from annihilation. Another few seconds and V would have disintegrated and have been thrust into absolute nothingness – perhaps suffering the fate that the Foul Fiend was suffering now. To be bound up forever, locked in nothingness, bound and sealed in nothingness, prisoner of nothing, knowing one was nothing and nowhere, for all eternity, the very thought of made her shiver.

“Well, V, since you are curious, I can tell you how I found Teddy. I found him in the past, almost three centuries ago, sometime in the 1940s, I believe. He was wandering around in a pasture, trying to herd rabbits. His job had been to herd Holstein cattle, but there were no cattle, and his masters had moved away, leaving him behind, so he had been abandoned. He was an orphan. I retrieved that little story – his situation – from my memory bank and the simultaneous inter-temporal matrix where I spend much of my time – as it were – and I thought I could pluck him up, without any major damage to the ongoing fabric of time and the web and chain of space-time causation and interaction, which is, of course, a delicate and fragile web, since he was about to be killed by a random lightning bolt two hours later, and I thought I could throw him at you at precisely the right moment and that perhaps we would all benefit from this meeting of centuries and destinies.”

“Well, thank you, from both of us,” V knelt down and began to pat the dog. He looked at her in adoration. “But you were saying, Mother, you were saying, Mother, about the human race and the President ...”

“Oh, yes, I do get distracted so easily, darling, and I do apologize. Well, the gist of it is this: the President – he really is a fine man in spite of all his crimes, and I can see why you love him ...”

“I ...”

"Don't deny it, V, it's time you treated yourself to true love and to a good man ... he's not jealous you know, so you can continue your wonderful dalliance with that charming Centurion, Kat, I know that, in the amorous field, you have rather eclectic but very refined tastes and Kat is beautiful and high-spirited and not at all jealous and ..."

"Harrumph," V frowned, "Mother ..."

"And by punishing the President-Leader, the way you did, you really did him a favor, you know. And I know he knows it too. And of course, your daughter loves him already, and every girl deserves a father, and Caliban is just right, I think, for Miranda; and that marvelous girl, Kit, she's almost infatuated with all of you, and with Nikki, you have to think of Kit too, one big family, if you see what I mean, and the Mind-Child and Claudia. You now must develop a new sense of responsibility, I think, V, a sense of family. If you don't mind my saying so. After all, I am your mother."

"Harrumph," V pretended to frown, then smiled, then blushed, and then looked down and concentrated on patting the dog.

The Crystal sighed, a truly romantic sigh. "Well, in any case, what was I saying, where was I? Yes, your lover-enemy, the President, tried many times to stop the creation of ever new and more deadly bioweapons. And he tried to get rid of all nuclear weapons. He tried to stop all variants of bioweapons, he sent out spies, and he had people jailed and put out of business, and even murdered, but other, darker, forces were working against him, and, with the general breakdown of authority and order, particularly outside in the Burbs and in the Dead Lands, he was not able to catch them all in his net – he should have asked you or Claire or Sabrina to help him – he even considered it – but he couldn't do that without compromising his power and thus without compromising his ability to do anything at all – which is the eternal paradox of political power is it not – you have to do things you don't believe in to have any power to do any of the things you do believe in – and so he didn't, ask for the hybrids' help I mean, and so, in spite of the ban which he had imposed on such research, some companies were still secretly manufacturing biological weapons, and variants of the plague, and one company, backed by a very unpleasant colonel called Konrad, had developed the perfect weapon, you see, and ..."

"The perfect weapon ..." V looked up; she felt a chill creep down her spine. The dog shivered in sympathy and nuzzled her hand, licking, and looking up with big, concerned eyes.

"I'm so glad, V, that you and the dog get along. You must give him back his name. It's Teddy."

"I will ... Yes, Teddy!" The dog wagged his tail in wide sweeps of pure delight at being recognized. He had a cute white streak on his nose and a big white capital "T" on his chest, and V was aware that he had been conceived in the 1940s when border collies were still working dogs and before they had had all their free, wide-ranging intelligence and character bred of out them. She scratched him between the ears. But V was getting antsy; she had to get back, she had to save people, some people at least, she had to ...

"Civilizations do self-destruct, you know, V," the Crystal was clearly trying to sound cheerful.

"Yes."

"So it's not your fault, you know. You really shouldn't blame yourself!"

"No, I'll ... I mean I'm not, no ..."

"You do take on too many burdens, V; I imagine it's very stressful."

"Crystal, Mother, you are very kind, and the most wonderful of friends, and you are as I know, more than a friend, you are my mother, but ..."

"Yes, of course, I'm wandering. Where was I?"

"You were explaining about the perfect biological weapon ..."

"Yes, of course, well, as I was saying, this one company devised the perfect doomsday machine – a virus that has different incubation times, so it doesn't immediately kill all its hosts and burn itself out, but can spread freely, quickly, everywhere; it is also 100% fatal, really devastating; it turns the human body into a bubbling pile of smelly putrid bio-junk, and it also has a virtually 100% infection rate, and it also ..."

"There's another 'also'...?" V, who had been crouching and scratching the dog's ears, stood up.

"Birds catch it ..."

"Oh."

"Birds catch it but don't have any symptoms, they are asymptomatic I believe the technical term is, a key concept in epidemiology, V, which is a most interesting subject, which you and I must discuss sometime, and rats catch it too, also without getting sick, so they and the birds can spread it everywhere, even to the most isolated human communities, except perhaps if there were stations in Antarctica; but there are no longer any stations there, or any humans there, or penguins for that matter, not since the great ice sheet collapse and the epidemic of Bubonic IV."

"Oh. Yes, of course."

"And then there is the fact that ... I don't want to upset you V, after all, we've been having such a nice cozy chat ... So, it spreads, quickly, everywhere."

"Yes? But this other fact you mentioned ..."

"Oh, yes, how silly of me, I certainly meant to get around to this! There is no antidote, V, no antidote at all."

"So ..."

The Crystal sighed, "I'm sorry to say this, V, I really am. But they will all die, V, the humans I mean, each and every single one. There will not be a single human left, not a single one."

EPILOGUE

CHAPTER 18 – GODDESSES

10,000 years later …

"Hey, are you a goddess?"

"What?"

The sun shone bright and high in the utterly blue sky; the light was blinding; the serrated shadows of the palm fronds were as sharp as delicately wielded, rustling scimitars.

"Hey, are you a goddess?"

The question stopped me in my tracks. I mean, what kind of a question is that? *Hey, are you a goddess?* The very idea!

To be addressed thus, immediately upon my arrival on this tiny, isolated, rather mysterious planet, Earth, was disconcerting to say the least! Particularly since I had just been reborn – or reassembled atom by atom, molecule by molecule – out of quantum dust – into this rather particular and peculiar world – Planet Catalog Name MW-SS-23417-3, which was once called "Earth" by its talkative, word-addled, idea-infested, biped inhabitants. I was here to investigate the planet and its life forms for the faculty of Intergalactic Anthropology of the Andromeda Interplanetary University. And then I heard the rather thin high voice pipe up behind me.

"Hey, are you a goddess?"

"What?"

"Are you a goddess?" From behind me, the little musical voice chirped up again, "Hey, there, you! I'm talking to you! Are you a goddess?"

What? Is it – whatever it is – really talking to me?

"Are you a goddess? Are you deaf?"

What a confusing question! And I was, as I have indicated – perhaps I am over-sensitive – still a just a tiny bit discombobulated – from being disembodied for over three Quid Planet Hours – and not in my quickest or wittiest form.

In any case, as any of my faculty colleagues back on the planet Quid #4A77B will tell you, quick repartee and light banter have never been my forte. I am not one for small talk.

And, as I believe I have already said, I had just materialized literally out of another universe, traversing a parallel universe – another set of dimensions – on my way from my home in *this* universe's Andromeda Galaxy and – after the quantum mechanics black matter-black energy parallel universe detour – I had just flipped back into this our home universe, onto this little planet, Earth, and I had just whirled into existence – recomposed out of pure energy and information – on the ground on the planet Earth, and at least I hoped it was Earth; it would be embarrassing to end up on the wrong planet – possibly a hostile one with an unbreathable atmosphere and filled with ferocious and outlandish creatures – or in outer space, or in the pitiless fusion furnace of a brightly burning star.

Oh, my, but I am a fusspot!

I worry about everything!

It was my first visit to Earth, and, when I first materialized, I found myself, as I have been just explaining – I do talk too much – even Professor Qing who is patience itself has remarked upon it – I found myself slightly dizzy, dazzled by the sunlight and heat. And I discovered that I was, when I materialized, standing just behind what I recognized – from referencing my internalized briefing notes on terrestrial architecture – was a single white marble Doric column, which was standing, slightly askew, tilted, and unaccountably alone, in the middle of nowhere, with what looked like vines or creepers growing up twined around it and large lush ferns all around.

I shook my head – to get rid of time-space warp alien universe cobwebs – and pushed myself out from behind this pretty little Doric column and its thick jungle of leafy companions to find myself, once I had emerged from the foliage, in a primitive sort of open space – which I realized was some sort of urban or village public space – paved with large dark irregular stones which appeared to be volcanic in origin – and which piazza or plaza I traversed, having spotted what looked like my objective: a classic, Doric-style temple.

And so I ascended the large, broad marble steps toward the temple – while still composing, in my perceptual field, my new earthly surroundings and their meanings.

Yes, Quillix, I said to myself, this surely is the temple – a building of classical earthly simplicity – where I had, if my internalized appointment book and geo-location-coordinates were accurate, my first and most important terrestrial rendezvous – with the ruler and overseer of the planet.

I was rather nervous, too – I blush to admit it – because my future academic career would very much depend on the results of my research here.

So there I was: halfway up the temple steps, when I heard this unexpected high-pitched rather musical question uttered from behind me.

"Hey, there, I'm talking to you! Are you a goddess?"

It was the first time I had actually heard the voice of a terrestrial human being – or any other human being, for that matter, for the human species is – was – extinct, kaput, gone, vanished. And, prior to extinction, no such beings as terrestrial humans – Homo so-called sapiens – had ever visited the Andromeda Galaxy.

I hesitated, turned around, and saw a pair of small two-legged critters – in appearance definitely human in design – standing lower down on the broad temple steps and staring up at me.

Behind them, across the square, were palm trees, and more of the open space, certainly a sort of piazza, I suppose; it too was paved with irregular blocks of stone and had a bubbling stone fountain at the far end, and a series of one-story raised dwellings made I think of what is called "wood," and which might, I imagine, be described as "bungalows."

"Well, are you a goddess, or not?" The tiny male had his hands on his hips, and looked rather impatient for an answer.

"*God*, you should say *God*," said the tiny female.

"But she's a she, so she's a goddess," said the male.

"Sexist," said the tiny female, "Patriarchal chauvinist pig!"

There was obviously some obscure theological point at issue here of great importance to miniature unripe pre-pubescent terrestrial human simulacra – or whatever these creatures were – but for which the extensive – indeed exhausting – briefings on my home planet Quid had not prepared me.

How should I answer?

These were the first human replicants or semblances I had ever seen – in reality, I mean. I had seen many simulations and virtual mock-ups; it was part of my training. So I quickly realized they were immature human pods, known in the plural, if my memory serves me, as "children," one male, one female, a boy and a girl, perhaps eight or nine earth years old, barefoot and naked except for thin little aprons or loincloths, with neat knots at the hip, around their waists.

They were smooth-skinned, honey-colored, with glowing brown eyes, hairless except for long dark eyelashes, jet-black eyebrows, and a black top-knot, neatly trimmed. I suppose they would be deemed attractive once you got used to them.

"No," I said, "I am not a goddess. I'm an apprentice ethnologist third class from the University of Xanadu Faculty of the Interplanetary Andromeda University. It is based on the planet Quid #4A77B, in the Zebra planetary system in the Andromeda Galaxy. I am fifth assistant to Professor Qing, and my name is 'Quillix,' which translates I believe as 'Aphrodite' or – though perhaps this is folk etymology – 'She who is born from – or shines through – the froth or the foam.'"

"Oh," they said, in unison, and looked at each other.

I sat down on the steps so I could observe the two tiny tots – or tykes – more closely. At the same time, I immediately and ruefully realized that I might come to regret the glib rapidity of my response – it just tripped off the tongue in the Synthetic Ecumenical Earth Language which I had been trained to use – and which I was so eager to try out – such is vanity – one always wishes to show off one's newly acquired mental furniture – and it did seem to work quite well. But, as to denying my divinity, perhaps, I thought, perhaps I have set off a social and cosmic disaster. One must be very careful with primitive populations. Perhaps all creatures such as I – female reptilian humanoid mammalian – two breasted – biped creatures – are here considered goddesses or gods and by refusing the status as a divinity which they naturally wished to confer upon me – really quite an honor, I suppose – I may have inadvertently toppled the whole theology upon which peace on this sorely tried and once very violent planet was based.

Sparking a planetary civil war would reflect very badly if it got into my résumé. I shudder to think what Professor Qing would say, and his breast scales and eyelids would flare up something awful, positively scarlet with purple patches, of that I am absolutely sure.

But the two little humans did not at all seem upset. They approached and, as I examined them in detail, I decided that they were, undoubtedly, in terrestrial terms, beautiful, with their perfectly symmetrical features, and very much alike, light golden or chocolate brown, with large dark eyes, where, in the pupil and iris, flashing sparkles of gold appeared and disappeared, like golden stars or novae, exploding, fading, exploding once again, tiny exquisite celestial fireworks, like golden spiral galaxies. The girl had fuller lips and even larger eyes than the boy, and the slightest suggestion of budding breasts – soon she would be ripe for breeding and milking I suppose (my knowledge of the human life-cycle was still primitive) – and her hair was longer, curling down her cheeks and making two sharp, neat little points over her cheekbones.

"So you are not a goddess, but you certainly look like a goddess," said the boy, scratching his head.

"She's a god, no doubt about it," said the girl, "she's just modest."

"Goddess," said the boy, "Goddess."

"Whatever," said the girl, with a downward turn of the corners of her mouth and a rolling of her eyes – which she turned upwards toward the heavens which were purely blue and without a single cloud – which ensemble of behavior expressed I believe – referring to the *Encyclopedia of Ancient Terrestrial Gestures* I had devoured – some sort of skepticism or irony or indifference in regard to the boy's insistence on the gender differentiation of gods and goddesses, the female here surrendering to the male's typical stubbornness and habitual power grab reinforced as we know across galaxies by iterative dominance-submission hegemonic performance patterns. I made a mental note to record this bit of behavior as a symptom of earth-bound relative status and male-female dominance-submission hierarchies, worth a footnote at least. I had been taught by Professor Qing that human beings had been very attached to what he called ideologies and pre-conceptions – "Pig-headed creatures, they," he once said, scratching his chin with his fore-claw – and that they had, in the past, when they were still extant, abandoned such prejudices only with great difficulty and sometimes after lengthy wars, massacres, crusades, jihads, Reformations, Counter-Reformations, bombings, assassinations, theological disputations, burnings at the stake, forced confessions, mutilations, ex-communications, fatwas, show trials, Papal Bulls, and bouts of tortured conscience. Perhaps I was seeing an example of this.

"May I touch," said the boy, reaching out his slender fingers, and using what I knew from my studies of terrestrial semantics was a rare and obsolete polite form of language: "may." This was impressive. I would have expected him to use the purely plebeian and aggressive "can" or not even ask permission at all.

"Of course," I said.

He ran his fingers over my scales and my claws – I opened the palm of my hands – well claws – so that both he and the girl could feel them. They did quite a thorough job of examining my scales, my claws, my color scheme, my thighs, my shins, my breasts, my stomach muscles, my back – I had to twist around – my neck, my snout – who, I wondered, is studying whom?

"A goddess, definitely," said the boy.

"Yes, I have to agree," conceded the girl, rather solemnly, "You are a very pretty goddess," she added, coming up very close and, looking straight into my eyes, "even if you wish to deny it."

"Thank you," I said, turning an abashed darker shade of lime green with even some yellow flame-like flickers running ticklishly up my lower and middle belly, and lapping around my breasts, "And you are both very pretty human beings – extremely handsome."

"Thank you," they said, in chorus, and he said, "Thank you, Goddess," and she said, "Thank you, God."

They looked at each other and giggled; so perhaps their theological dispute would not lead to civil war after all – and as for the status classification putting males above females, and as for the internalized sex-role iterative performance hegemony system, well, I might be forced to nuance with a footnote my initial impression of rigid hierarchy since they seemed to be playing with the whole thing in a self-conscious meta-linguistic way which, I believe, would be of great interest to Professor Qing. These diminutive creatures – astonishingly – practiced irony.

"Since you have just arrived and since we have met you now for the very first time, we shall offer a little boat of flowers – rose petals and lily wands – to the sea in your honor," the boy said, "at sunset and sunrise for the next three days."

"And we shall lay flowers on threshold of our sleeping quarters in your honor," the girl said, and they both bowed low, in reverence or mock reverence – actually I think it was both serious and in mockery since they had decided I was a friendly goddess and would not mind being mocked, gently of course.

I waved.

They grinned and waved and ran away laughing and turned and waved and bowed again, and I waved back, thinking these terrestrial children are quite friendly and high-spirited – certainly for a race that is now extinct they seemed quite normal and healthy – and, even, truly alive.

And so, I set off, up the steps of the Temple, to meet the true Goddess, the ruler, and savior of the planet.

Her name, I had been told, was V.

From her, I was quite sure, I would learn what precisely had happened and … so it would prove to be …

How had the Extinction Event taken place?

That was the question.

And that is what all the reports had said – "The Human Race was Extinct."

"Unfortunate loss of Local Biodiversity on Planet MW-SS-23417-3," reported *The Andromeda Times* millennia ago in a lower right-hand and two-column story on quantum-electro page 47. That was when we first became generally aware – Marcus and a few others already knew of course – of the event as reported through the Crystal Net that monitors planets and their life forms.

The "Holocene Extinction Event" – which ended the short but cataclysmic earthly Anthropocene – had its very own scientific name in the very specialized sub-field of terrestrial paleontology. Few of us knew that the catastrophe on earth had threatened our own existence, the existence of the Andromeda Federation, for if the Foul Fiend had managed to subdue V, and, with her as his puppet, to commandeer the Crystal, then …

… then he would have had entry everywhere, absolutely everywhere! So this tiny event, this tiny struggle on this one little planet, was, for us, of cosmic significance, though of course, as I said, very few of us knew it at the time – and very few are aware of it even now.

As for the earth, the planet had its own resources, and in some ways, even without humans, and perhaps the better for it, it would begin to recover some sense of equilibrium.

And the planet also had, in its most dire moments, its tutelary and protective presence – V, the half-alien, half-human girl from Ancient Phoenicia, who was – is – the daughter of one of our absolutely most outstanding luminaries, that same illustrious Commander Marcus to whom I just alluded, but, oh my, I'm getting ahead of myself here …

Where was I?

Oh, yes …

So having waved goodbye to my two little human pod friends, children or tykes or kids as they are known, I stood up, brushed some dust off my hindquarters, adjusted my researcher's field trip-standard-quantum-transfer-adaptable-backpack, and continued up the steps to meet the chief local goddess – V – who was in fact as I have already pointed out the tutelary goddess of the planet – and who was the reason for my visit. I wanted to compile a report on her activities. She had been overseeing this particular planet for something like 13,500 earth-years. And, by all reports, it had not been easy.

She was widely admired back home for her courage and ingenuity – a minor celebrity in scholarly and military circles in the Andromeda Empire, though she didn't know it, of course.

In the temple, immediately after passing through the portico and entrance hall, I came into a large, bare, high-ceilinged room – walls and floor of stone – and I saw the Goddess – she was in human form and wearing old-fashioned clothes of a style that dated back, I believe, to the 20th and 21st centuries according to the calendar used just before the human world came to an end – to wit, she was dressed in sandals, black jeans, a tan belt with an oval brass buckle, and a thin, clinging, almost transparent black T-shirt, which ensemble displayed her fine human figure to considerable advantage.

She must collect antiques, I thought, or perhaps she has her own workshop to provide such exotic archaic goods as jeans and T-shirts.

She had a light tan – I believe that is the term – her skin being of a pale gold hue, but much paler than the two children I had just met, and her hair, cut short like that of the girl, was jet-black.

She was standing in front of a blackboard – a very ancient terrestrial pedagogical device consisting of a semi-vertical rectangle of black slate and small tubes of chalk – or calcium carbonate – and she was – with the help of an adolescent human male – he was barefoot and wearing nothing more than a skimpy loincloth identical to that of the two children – illustrating something which I recognized as a right-angle triangle, and some laws involving the triangle, I believe what is called, on this planet, the Pythagorean theorem, after an ancient human who perhaps formulated the idea on Earth or publicized it for the first time, and the gist of which is that the square of the side of a right-angle triangle opposite the right angle is equal to the sum of the squares of the other two sides – whew! – I remembered it! As Professor Qing has said, indeed he has said it more than once, "Such seemingly simple ideas, as, say, the triangle and its properties, are levers and weapons with which we sentient – and moderately intelligent – creatures have conquered large swaths of the universe, and exterminated most of our rivals," and he would then add, "Words and numbers, syntax and rules, my friends, are weapons far more deadly than claws and fangs and stingers and venom."

Above the triangle were some examples which I recognized as versions of vector analysis, trigonometry, and differential equations – quite advanced, really, I thought. It turned out, as I discovered later, that this was a "history of mathematics" seminar, and that the students did the teaching with V or other teachers supervising or moderating. Above the symbols was a faded bit of writing. "What is the 'examined life'?" And "What does the word 'good' mean?" And "Define 'Evil'." "Please compare Socrates and Nietzsche, Jesus and Confucius." So, I thought, they study philosophy too!

I was very pleased to see such familiar questions and symbols and forms. Geometry and mathematics are shared across many galaxies and species – and, in some cases, even in alternate universes – and this is a very lucky fact for sentient and reasoning creatures of all kinds, because it greatly facilitates communications between species and civilizations which otherwise might be so alien to each other as to be utterly and mutually unrecognizable as sentient life forms.

In fact, we may have passed by lofty and complex civilizations and mistaken them for rocks or asteroids or volcanoes or tectonic plates or insects or perhaps for weather or climatic patterns. Professor Qing gave a lecture on precisely this subject: "The pitfalls of inter-species epistemology." He even used a terrestrial example: he said that humans, when they existed, had been very fond of making other terrestrial creatures – dogs, dolphins, rats – go through so-called intelligence tests.

"Now, colleagues, let us make a mind experiment," Professor Qing said, "Let us imagine that a terrestrial dog were to ask a terrestrial human to identify by smell, from 35 samples of old urine left on the trunk of a tree or the proverbial cartoon fire-hydrant, which dogs had passed that way, when they had pissed and how much they had pissed, their breed, age, state of health, and whether they were male or female and in heat or not, fertile or not, and ideal mates or not? We can imagine that the human – even if he were Einstein himself, or Marie Curie, say, or Napoleon Bonaparte, would flunk!"

Ah, yes, I thought, you are quite right, Professor, but we too, however much we try to overcome them, share our own Andromeda-centered illusions, believing in our own importance, and our own centrality to the universe – epistemological or not. But, in my opinion, there is no center, not anywhere. The fun of all this is that there is so much to learn, and so much to explore. The only appropriate attitude, in the end, is humility allied with curiosity! Indeed, the various universes are full of wonders which even our great Intergalactic Federation has not a clue about – and this, Professor Qing is quite willing to admit. As for me, the Quest will endure, I hope, to the end of time.

"Well, I see we have a visitor," said the Goddess, smiling. "Anthony, we can continue later, if you wish."

"Yes, V, certainly," the adolescent gave the Goddess – well, they considered her a goddess – a most beautiful smile, put the piece of chalk he was holding on a small stand, and smiled at me too, his eyes crinkling in greeting, and he bowed and the class – they were all adolescents – men and women – clapped and, standing up, all of them, male and female wearing simple loincloths, all of them startlingly alike and beautiful – it was as if they were twins, all twins – and they all bowed to the goddess and then, turning toward me, they bowed to me, and they filed out, chattering and laughing among themselves, with some curious glances directed back, I must admit, toward me.

"Well," said the Goddess – I knew that she was the Goddess V from the various images I had seen and I had spoken in-depth with her "controller" – who is, in fact, her biological father, Commander Marcus – and, as I believe I have already pointed out, one of our greatest and most intrepid explorers and statesmen – she came over, reached out her hand and shook my claw in the human form of greeting which I suppose for her was second nature – all of her life has been lived on this planet and it is, in the end, all she knows. "I am delighted to meet you, Quillix, at long last," she said.

"The honor and delight are mine, V," I said, and bowed the first-degree status bow, bending low from the waist, in symbolic submission.

Out beyond the temple, through a large side-gate, I could see the ocean, sparkling blue, and I could see what looked like a game being played, a ball was bouncing up and down and there were – and this did surprise me – hybrids and human forms, both types of creatures, gods and mortals, playing at the same time.

"Volleyball," said the Goddess.

"Oh," I squinted at the ball, bouncing in the brilliant light, and the leaping bodies, like shadows outlined against the brilliance of the water which stretched off to the flat, distant cloudless horizon.

"Water polo, if they play in the water," she said.

"And Redesigned Humans – RDHs – and hybrids play together?"

"Yes, mixed teams," said the Goddess, smiling, "Gods and mortals together."

"I didn't realize relations were so close."

"Oh, we are all one now, or almost, you see – during the great extinction – when the humans disappeared, and we had to …"

"Extinct," I said, "I meant to ask …"

"It's a long story. You see, what happened was this …."

At this point, Anthony came back and he said, "I'm sorry, V, but they want you and your guest Quillix" – he bowed slightly to me with a very pleasant light in his eyes and a smile on his lips – "to join the game. Everyone is eager to meet your guest, too! It is understood she has come such a long way."

The Goddess, V, glanced at me, and I nodded, thinking I might as well plunge into the local life and begin my exploration of this extinct race of creatures, human beings, as soon as possible. And I suppose since I was a goddess too – for research purposes at least – I had better submit to the intense socializing that on this planet went, it seemed, with being a divinity.

Professor Qing, I am sure, would have approved. "Never hesitate to get your claws dirty, Quillix," he had said, on more than one occasion, "Plunge right in, Quillix, go straight into the world, whichever world it may be; don't wait for the world to come to you!"

And so to the beach we went, and there I learned how to play the game called volleyball – and also water polo which was even more fun – and I discovered many strange things about the gods and goddesses and their extinct human friends who had, miraculously, been reborn after the Great Catastrophes and the Extinction Event of the Year 2158.

Later that evening, after our communal supper, and then over many, many other evenings and afternoons, V told me the story, the beginning of the story …

"And so, Quillix, all the humans died. They were extinct, not a single one was left," said V; she turned and gazed out at the sparkling sea where the little waves seemed to march, endlessly, toward shore in serried ranks of golden light.

I didn't say anything. I didn't want to break the mood. I could see that V's eyes were damp. She was mourning all the multitudes she had known, and she was mourning that long heroic epic, which was the story of the human race and how they had come to dominate and then to lose this most beautiful planet, Earth.

In the many months I had been here, I had begun to realize just what a marvelous planet it was; vast oceans and seas teeming with life, rich banks of coral, even richer in life forms than the rest of the oceans; rivers and lakes, and life forms, in the water, on the land, and in the air, of almost unparalleled richness.

Truly, it was a paradise.

Little Marcus and Antonia, the two children who had introduced me to the planet, came to us at this point, from the communal kitchen, which was under the palm trees on the other side of the village square; they were bearing sweet drinks and sugared biscuits.

"There you are, Gods," said Antonia, bowing and grinning, "This will wet your divinely beautiful whistles and satisfy your most heavenly palates."

"Goddesses," said Little Marcus, "We have brought you sustenance fit for such divinities."

They bowed and giggled and left us.

"God," I heard Antonia say, as she poked Marcus in the ribs, "They are gods."

"Goddesses," Marcus replied, "Goddesses."

Their voices faded into laughter, and they were gone.

The sun was still high, and outside, beyond the porch, a group was playing volleyball on the beach – I almost envied them, playing like that, in the sunlight, but V and I would soon join them so, really, there was nothing to envy.

I have noticed, however, that since I have been on this planet, I have become much more – how shall I put it? – I have become much more hedonistic. Everything is so pleasurable. It seems a shame to waste one's time on work. "You were talking about the Extinction Event," I said, taking a first sip of the delicious nectar, something, the children told me, that is called "orange juice."

"Yes, the Extinction Event," said V, "It was reported, I believe, in your press, in the press in the Empire."

"Yes, there were a few mentions, under the rubric planetary curiosities, weird events, that sort of thing," I stopped, wondering if I had been tactless, after all, V had spent her existence trying to protect humans, so I smiled and added, "But we seem, here, to be surrounded by humans – our two little friends, and then all those humans out there on the beach, playing volleyball with the hybrids."

"Yes, they are human, truly human." V turned to me and smiled, "We rebuilt them."

"Rebuilt them?"

"They all descend from Miranda and Caliban – and Kit and a few others, Clown, and Geisha, and Black Tarzan, for example, none of whom are purely human. Those that were bitten survived."

"Oh, I see."

"We did tweak the design here and there, and we added other strains, so that all danger of inbreeding would be avoided. But, Miranda and Caliban – and their friends – are the Mother and Father of the new human race."

"You spoke of SINs. I meant to ask – Nikki, the long-suffering, and patient Nikki! The stories you told of her made me admire her so, the Original SIN!"

V smiled, her face lighting up as with joy, "Oh, yes.

"Is she still extant?"

"You see the young woman in the baseball cap, sunglasses and the black one-piece swimming suit?"

"Yes."

"She's the one acting as the umpire for the volleyball game. She returned yesterday from the mutant settlement in the hills. She visits them for a few days every month. She's the Goddess of the Mutants."

"That's Nikki?"

"Yes, that's Nikki."

Later I thought I would ask for an extension to my research grant. I really did not want to leave the planet earth. It was the most pleasant and magical place, and meeting the people – well I thought of them as "people" and so did they think of themselves as "people" – such as Miranda and Caliban and Alex and Nikki and Kit and the others, like Robyn and Claire, and Sabrina, and Demi Pfeiffer, and the President, and the children – Gloria and Jake, now hybrids, of course, and of course Nikki who has become a close friend, and Kat – oh, glorious Kat – a champion at chess and at water polo – who is V's special companion, with the President of course, and meeting all of them, Clown, and Geisha, and Black Tarzan, Ken and Allison, Valerie Joffre, who knows all about geology, Natasha and Mrs. Rosenthal, and so many others, including two strange featureless but beautiful gentle golden creatures called Spit and Polish ...

Well, it was like meeting the gods and goddesses of old times, creatures from ancient myths and stories, and sitting down at table with them, or playing water polo or volleyball, or going for long walks and "adventure tours" – or indulging in endless philosophic and scientific discussions – and all of this amidst the sparkling sea and the gentle breezes and the many animals that were friendly and sometimes – and this never ceased to amaze me – talkative, and very informative about the weather and the soil and which nuts and berries were good to eat and so on. The "human" and mutant communities are kept quite small, only a few hundred individuals on the whole planet, and the vegetation and climate here is tropical or semi-tropical. It is paradise.

So I sent the quantum-space-express message: "I would feel very privileged, Professor, if I could extend my research period here on the planet earth."

Within two weeks, the answer came back.

It was most unexpected.

I rushed to share the news with V.

"Provided you complete the last chapter of your thesis, summarizing your observations, your extension is granted unconditionally, and without a terminus date. Your new task is to work with V and the others, humans, hybrids, SINs, mutants, and other living creatures of the planet Earth. And, remember, Quillix, you are the guest of the earthlings. Earth is their home. They are its guardians, and V and her friends – gods and goddesses – are their leaders."

"That is wonderful," V said, "particularly since it means you can remain here with us, Quillix."

"There's an additional note," I said, tears in my eyes, and my belly and snout scales turning a bright, happy, turquoise, and I handed it to her.

V put her hand – such a beautiful slender hand, to her collarbone, in a gesture I had learned to recognize and love – and she read the note out loud.

Several times she hesitated, her voice almost breaking, "Tell V that she is to be congratulated. Earth is part of the Empire now, with full rights to Imperial protection. In defeating the Force of Evil from the Unknown Universe on the other side of the Web of Being, she saved this universe and every creature and world within it from infection."

V hesitated and glanced at me. I nodded. It was true. Had the Foul Fiend defeated V and had he been able to command the Crystal, then … Well, the consequences were too horrible to contemplate.

V looked down and again began to read. "And, since Earth seems to be getting on quite well without us, we shall leave its affairs in the capable hands of V and the earthlings, hybrids and humans and SINs and Mutants, and other sentient creatures, as is right and just. Oh, and tell V this: her father Marcus sends his greetings – and his love. He hopes to see her soon."

V's eyes were wet.

"Thank you, Quillix," she said, handing me the message, "Crystal did help me, you know, and she and I, as you also know, are especially close."

"There is nothing to thank me for, V," I said, "It is I who must thank you!"

V took a deep breath. She drank the orange juice and chewed on a biscuit, and she said, "You know that since I met the man down under Elysium City –"

"The man you saw in the Religious Underground?"

"Yes, since I ate that biscuit and drank the wine he offered me, from that instant, I no longer needed to drink blood." She smiled.

"And what happened to him. Is he …?"

"Yes, he's the one you often see walking on the beach with a group of the children. He and Kit and Miranda are particular friends and Caliban, of course. He gives – well, sort of religious seminars; they are very popular. He and the President often take long walks and hikes together. And he comes and goes."

"He's from somewhere else."

"Yes, I think he is, but wherever it is, whatever it is, I'm sure it's a friendly place. He has told me, though, that he feels that his true home is here."

We sat for a few minutes in silence. My life had changed, and so, I suppose had V's. The breeze was balmy and it caressed both of us, my scaly reptilian skin and her soft, smooth human skin.

"Well," she said, standing up, and turning to me with a mischievous smile, "Shall we go and play?"

"Yes," I said, looking with eagerness at the beach and the volleyball game, "Let's go and play!"

And I saw that the umpire or referee had noticed us – Nikki, the young woman in the black baseball cap, and that she was waving us toward her. And so was Kat. And all the others, humans and hybrids turned, and Natasha and Mrs. Rosenthal, and golden, glimmering Spit and Polish. And they all waved and beckoned.

"Come on, come on!"

And so we ran toward them.

"Come on, Quillix! Come on," V was laughing, "Hurry, hurry!"

"Ah, Quillix," I sighed, smiling at all the brightness, and thinking, "Here you are, at long last, Quillix – this is paradise; you have come home."

And, thus, hand in hand, V and I ran, together, toward the laughing voices, the dancing waves, and the blue, blue sky.

ACKNOWLEDGMENTS

Thanks to the many people who made the *Adventures of V: Return of the Goddess* possible: Adrienne Clarkson, Andra Sheffer, André Kirchberger, Anna Porter, Bernice Landry, Bernie Lucht, Beverly Topping, Bob Ramsay, Chuck Shamata, Claudia Neri, Denise Jacques, Diana Leblanc, Diane Shamata, Dianne Rinehart, Dorothy Vreeker, Duncan Derry, Ed Cowan, Elena Solari, Florence Treadwell, Heather Reid, Irene Spampinato, Irene Tudisco, Jacqueline Baker, Jacqueline Park, Jacqueline Swartz, Janie Yoon, Jennifer Hambleton, Jennifer Puncher, Jim Downs, John McGreevy, John Pearce, John Ralston Saul, Josephine Khu, Jules Cashford, Julia Belluz, Julia Hambleton, Marie-Christine Dunham-Pratt, Mark Fenwick, Martine Matus Siebert, Norm Barber, Norm Christie, Nuala Fitzgerald, Paola Pugliatti, Peter Williamson, Ramsay Derry, Sandra Martin, Simona Barabesi, Susan Mahoney, Susan S. Senstad, Tony Robinow, Trisha Jackson, Wendy Trueman, and many others too numerous to name. I owe an infinite number of literary debts, too, but in particular to Joyce Carol Oates, Justin Cronin, and Stephen King.

TITLES IN THE
ADVENTURES OF V

WORKS BY
GILBERT REID

SHORT STORIES
So This is Love: Lollipop and Other Stories
Lava and Other stories

GRAZIA SERIES
Son of Two Fathers (with Jacqueline Park)

ADVENTURES OF V
Vampire vs Vatican
Vampire Clone
Pandemic Book 1: Party Balloons
Pandemic Book 2: The Gateway
Extinction Book 1: Girl with the Golden Eyes
Extinction Book 2: Revolt of the Angels
Extinction Book 3: Elysium

GWENDOLINE SERIES
By Gwendoline
The Shaming of Gwendoline C
Gwendoline Goes to School
Gwendoline Goes Underground

GILBERT REID

To receive a free book or novella
And to learn more about V and get notes on writing and other topics:

Sign up at

https://gilbertreid.com

Please write a short review!
Just two or three lines.
And post it to Goodreads or Amazon
or any other book group you may belong to.

Or send it to me!
At: gilbert@gilbertreid.com

GILBERT REID is the author of two short story collections: *So This is Love: Lollipop and Other Stories* (2004, 2019) and *Lava and Other Stories* (2019). He also co-authored, with Jacqueline Park, the historical novel *Son of Two Fathers* (2019). He has written extensively for television and radio. Most notably he researched, wrote, and narrated two five-hour radio series: *Gilbert Reid's Italy* and *Gilbert Reid's France* for CBC's flagship radio program IDEAS. His many television series include *Paths of the Gods*, *For King and Empire*, *For King and Country*, and *Sir Peter Ustinov in Burma: Road to Mandalay*. After thirty years in Europe working as an economist, university lecturer, diplomat, script doctor, journalist, and adventure travel guide, Gilbert now lives in Toronto.

www.ingramcontent.com/pod-product-compliance
Lightning Source LLC
Chambersburg PA
CBHW051052030726
47504CB00006B/1590